ED KIGHTLINGER

AVA NOELLE
AND THE
UNVEILING OF WENDIGORIUM

A NOVEL

Tales That Last Forever

Lynnville, Tennessee
United States of America

For information about special discounts or bulk purchases, please contact Tales that Last Forever at www.evaroblins.com or email evaroblins@gmail.com.

Cover Design by EbookLaunch

ISBN 978-1-7337962-2-4

Printed in the United States of America
Publisher - Lynnville, Tennessee 38472

SPRINGTIME

by Mary (Polly) Hall, circa 1950

Strolling down a Country Lane
Watching nature's glory
Trees all budding once again
Speaking out their story

Violets with their heads of blue
Daffodil bills of yellow
Tulips with their pretty hue
Soft scents sweet and mellow

Birds now are on the wing
Filling the air with song
Heralding a bright new spring
Helping nature's work along

Lambs are playing in the sun
Tis a very pretty sight
They don't stray but romp and run
Their mother watching day and night

The bright blue sky, the birds that sing
The beasts and pretty flowers
The budding trees, the gentle breeze
We thank you, God for everything.

DEDICATION

With love to my great niece
Ava Noelle McClure

"The moment you doubt whether you can fly, you cease forever
to be able to do it."—J. M. Barrie, Peter Pan

ACKNOWLEDGEMENTS

———————————

———————————

My beloved children (Rick, Angie, Tony, Shelly, Eddie, Josh, Jay, and Liz (Alex));their spouses, loved ones, and my precious grandchildren; Rose (mother of five and stepson) and her husband, Eric

~ ~ ~

My brother, James O Kightlinger and his wife, Kathy; my nieces, Debbie, Sandy, Pam, and Racheal; their spouses, loved ones; and my great nieces and nephews

~ ~ ~

Stephanie A Esmonde whose fictional character likeness is the primary deuteragonist, Stephanie JoAnne Galanos – Steph's likeness by the same name is the central character of my novel *The Spirit Within, Tale of a Fearless Heart: A story of a Teen's Love and Compassion*

~ ~ ~

My dear friends Rose M Davenport and Lindsey M Powers

~ ~ ~

My dearest, sweet cousin Kimberly M Meisenburg

~ ~ ~

~ always ~

LIST OF CHARACTERS

(includes those mentioned with no speaking parts)

Protagonist

Ava Noelle – Recognized by Earthly World and Inner World mystical beings as "Avaïnoάel, O Poica Katharos – the Purest of Elves." (Less commonly referred to as the "Protector of the World.") Reawakened Greek Goddess, Athena. Earthly World best friend of Stephanie (Steph) JoAnne Galanos. Companion of Galadriel, Nessa, and Voronwe.

Deuteragonists (In order of importance)

Steph (Stephanie JoAnne Galanos) – Ava Noelle's closest companion and confidant. Companion of Galadriel, Nessa, and Voronwe. (Stephanie's character is the protagonist of the novel *The Spirit Within, Tale of a Fearless Heart: A Story of a Teen's Love and Compassion*.)

Fluescere (Flame) – Faithful dragon of Avaïnoάel, O Poica Katharos.

Godroh of Mystic Mountains (official name: Blade Gruqiohr WyrmBlood) – Twin son of DragonCloud WyrmBlood of Hellas (ancient Greece of the Earthly World) and Athamia Oakheart the Enchantress. Archrival of Haldir of Mountains Cross. Twin brother of Ineuvious. Brother of sisters Emal and Eitthe.

Galadriel – Bkotn elf warrior. Second in command of the Bkotn Etanpioa following Morwen's banishment. Assumes command of the Etanpioa after Elbereth's death. Companion of Ava Noelle, Steph, and Voronwe. Best friend of Nessa.

Nessa – Bkotn elf warrior. Companion of Ava Noelle, Steph, and Voronwe. Best friend of Galadriel.

Voronwe – Royal Timbre messenger, spy, and warrior. Companion of Ava Noelle, Steph, Galadriel, and Nessa.

Confidant (Protagonist's sidekick) – Stephanie (Steph) JoAnne Galanos.

Antagonists (In alphabetical order)

Bralead (Bralead Bonefursome, son of Thralotum) – Leader of the Dwarven Federation of Mountains Cross. In charge of small group of archers: Dammuth, Jotog, Tuzumri, and three others during a skirmish with the combined Etanpioa. Assassin of Bkotn leader, Elbereth.

Haldir of Mountains Cross (official name: Magnus Nightmancer, son of Caster NightMancer of Hellas (ancient Greece of the Earthly World.) Archival of Godroh of Mystic Mountains.

Siofra – Third in command of the Bkotn Etanpioa until she is exiled.

Wendigorium (Caedes) – Also known by scholars as "Occisor de Orbis" (Slayer of the World). Reincarnated Greek god, Ares.

Tertiary characters (In alphabetical order)

Aredhel – Inconsequential Bkotn elf (no speaking part).

Arun – Timbre warrior that assumed second in command of the combined Etanpioa under Galadriel after his predecessor was slain in battle.

Athamia Oakheart the Enchantress – Godroh's mother and wife of DragonCloud WyrmBlood of Hellas, Godroh's twin brother, Ineuvious, and daughters, Eitthe and Emal. (no speaking part-deceased).

Ava (Princess) – Newborn daughter (named after Ava Noelle) of King Poldo and Queen Estel. Sister of Prince Earendil (no speaking part).

Avaiä (Lady Avaiä) – River Goddess of the Solenom (no speaking part).

Blissia (Lady Blissia) – Leader of the Mystic Mountains unicorns.

Caster NightMancer of Hellas – Father of Haldir of Mountains Cross (no speaking part – deceased).

Cassandra – Jason's dog (no speaking part).

Ckiotn – Timbre architect that reportedly taught Earthly World humans how to build treehouses (no speaking part – deceased).

Dad (Ktli) – Winged Fairy. The "Dad" in DooDad. Doo's father.

Dammuth – Archer under the leadership of Bralead Bonefursome, Leader of the Dwarven Federation of Mountains Cross.

Deroinde – Vice mayor of the human domiciles of the Mégedale katállilosly (no speaking part).

Doo – Winged Fairy. The "Doo" in DooDad. Dad's daughter.

DragonCloud WyrmBlood of Hellas – Godroh's father and wife of Athamia Oakheart the Enchantress. Father of twin son, Ineuvious, and daughters Emal and Eitthe. (No speaking part - deceased).

Earendil (Prince) – Leader of the Timbre Elves and Governor of Mégedale. Son of King Poldo and Queen Estel. Brother of his newborn sister, Princess Ava.

Eitthe – Youngest sister of Godroh of Mystic Mountains, sister Emal, and Godroh's twin brother, Ineuvious. Daughter of DragonCloud WyrmBlood of Hella and Athamia Oakheart the Enchantress (no speaking part – deceased).

Elanor – Inconsequential Bkotn elf (no speaking part).

Elbereth (Our Lady, Heroic Leader) – Leader of the Bkotn Etanpioa.

Elva – Inconsequential Bkotn elf (no speaking part).

Emal – Oldest sister of Godroh of Mystic Mountains, sister Eitthe, and Godroh's twin brother, Ineuvious. Daughter of DragonCloud WyrmBlood of Hellas and Athamia Oakheart the Enchantress (no speaking part – deceased).

Estel (Queen) – Wife of King Poldo of the Timbre elves. Mother of Prince Earendil and newborn daughter, Princess Ava.

Fedelium – Bird friend (Klıni species) of Ava Noelle (no speaking part).

Gklimbopa (Gklim) – Chamber goblin of Gnαèfa tower.

Grandpa Jim – Grandfather of Ava Noelle of the Earthly World.

Haleth (Exalted One) – Inconsequential Bkotn elf (no speaking part).

Ineuvious – Twin brother of Godroh of Mystic Mountains and sisters Emal and Eitthe. Twin son of DragonCloud WyrmBlood of Hellas (ancient Greece of the Earthly World) and Athamia Oakheart the Enchantress (no speaking part – presumed to be deceased).

James Hall – Great-great-grandfather of Ava Noelle (no speaking part).

Jami – Middle sister of Ava Noelle of the Earthly World.

Jason – Name of human child imposter unknowingly masquerading as Godroh.

Jordyn – Mentor of Ava Noelle and Stephanie JoAnne Galanos.

Jotog – Archer under the leadership of Bralead Bonefursome, Leader of the Dwarven Federation of Mountains Cross.

Kathy – Grandmother of Ava Noelle of the Earthly World (no speaking part).

Lexi – Oldest sister of Ava Noelle of the Earthly World.

Lia – Bkotn elf punished by Siofra that is appointed third in command of the Bkotn Etanpioa under Elbereth and later by Galadriel of the combined Etanpioa.

Lindsial (Queen) – Queen of the ancient realm of Spardom beneath the sea (no speaking part).

Maida – Ava Noelle and her sisters' dog (no speaking part).

Mary – Great-grandmother of Ava Noelle. Mother of Grandpa Jim and his brother (no speaking part).

Mary (Polly) Hall – Great-great-grandmother of Ava Noelle (no speaking part).

Melian – First assistant to King Poldo.

Mérino (Lord) – Ruler of the Konoanlia, the freshwater lake in the center of Antiquom where the Solenom River empties (no speaking part).

Metamorhirío – Fearful creature of the Inner World (no speaking part).

Morwen – Second in command of the Bkotn Etanpioa until she is banished from the Bkotn Tribe and relieved by Galadriel.

Noble – Mayor of the human domiciles of the Mégedale katállilosly (no speaking part).

Pam (Mom) – Mother of Ava Noelle of the Earthly World.

Poldo (King) – Ruler of the Timere Elves. Husband of Queen Estel. Father of Prince Earendil and newborn daughter, Princess Ava.

Siofra – Third in command of the Bkotn Etanpioa until she is exiled.

Strum (Madame) – Leader of the belugas (no speaking part).

Tuzumri – Archer under the leadership of Bralead Bonefursome, Leader of the Dwarven Federation of Mountains Cross.

Vena – Bkotn warrior. Close friend of Siofra.

Wade – Stepbrother of King Poldo.

Wlknoo (Lord Wlknoo) – Leader of the centaurs of Mystic Mountains.

Yavanna – Inconsequential Bkotn elf (no speaking part).

Yavanna (Lady Yavanna) – Village elder (no speaking part).

Foil (Protagonist's opposite) – Siofra

PART ONE

_____

_____

MY GRANDPA & GREAT UNCLE'S TOWER

"Do not go where the path may lead, go instead where there is no path and leave a trail."—Ralph Waldo Emerson

~~~

CHAPTER 1

A GLIMPSE OF THE UPCOMING

"Like madness is the glory of this life."—*William Shakespeare,
Timon of Athens*

4 Októvriosom (October), 2021

The peacefulness of the sunshiny, mid-afternoon had evaporated in a blink of an eye. In its place roared the bleakest, most terrifying, chaotic blackness imaginable. Muddy, somersaulting clouds were colliding viciously; their howling, tormented moans boding unspeakable evil. Their savagery a terrifying prediction of what was to come.

Uninterrupted streaks of blinding, bloody red lightning flashed cruelly within the swimming, murky gloom. The ruthlessly exploding, forked lightning stretched out in all directions. Like the gruesome, skeletal fingers of a vicious, evil murderer possessed by Satan himself. A brutal killer at the ready to pounce on its unsuspecting victim. Mercilessly. Ruthlessly. With no sense of right or wrong. No feelings of good or bad. A heartless assassin lacking a soul.

She slammed her eyes shut in a feeble attempt to escape the shocking horror. But there was no escaping the sinister scene. The gory flashes of lightning continued to flame cruelly beneath her tightly sealed eyelids.

She wanted to cover her ears. To oust the deafening, thunderous groans of the ferociously roaring clouds. But as frantically as she tried, she could not move her hands. Her arms were brutally stretched behind her back encircling a thin sapling. And her hands were attached at the

3

wrists. She wiggled her fingers to feel what had bound her wrists, but she could not feel anything.

She also could not move her legs at the ankles. They too were bound to the sapling. She opened her eyes and looked at her feet. Nothing was binding them. Just like her wrists. She rightly thought it must be magic, evil magic, the evilest magic imaginable! Not surprising given everything that had happened to her since her friend was murdered.

But why is this happening to me! What could I have done that is so horribly wrong to deserve this terrifying nightmare!

She crouched slightly at the knees to stretch her legs. Bending over just a little and leaning forward against the flexible sapling. As she bent over, her arms simply slid up and down on either side of the sapling. But her wrists remained tightly bound. Her ankles remained firmly locked in place as well. Mercifully, she was able to wriggle her toes and stretch her calves. If she were unable to stretch her lower body, even a little, she knew that her legs would have fallen asleep. Then she would have been nothing more than a calcified, breathing corpse of an immovable statue.

She screamed angrily at the chaos swirling above her. Her tone was alarmingly desperate yet enraged.

"Why are you wicked clouds, thunder, and lightning directly above me and only me?" Her eyes darted back and forth warily, to her left and right. "Why are you not at the outside edges of this clearing or above the forest? Why only here, above me!" She inhaled a long breath then exhaled sharply.

"I feel so vulnerable. So alone—"

She started to shiver. Her lips trembled. She lowered her head and asked for forgiveness.

Tears began to well up in her eyes. She tried to blink them away. But they continued even so. Straight away her tears began to cascade down her cheeks. Like panic-stricken, flooding waters exploding from the shores of a swollen river.

Then she stared, utterly confused as a soft, greenish light slowly enveloped her trembling body.

She began to feel drowsy but not in a normal way. It was an odd sensation. Almost like she was being forced to somnolence. She tried to open her eyes—

CHAPTER 2

CREATION OF THE INNER WORLD

"I belong to two worlds – yours and mine."—Avaĭnoᴕel

Roughly 66 million years ago. Long before the age of humans and contemporary beasts. The Chicxulub impactor (also known as the Chicxulub asteroid) crashed on the Earth. The asteroid was roughly seven to fifty miles in diameter. It struck the Earth at a speed of roughly twelve and one-half miles per second. Its powerful impact formed the massive Chicxulub Crater.

The crater is estimated to be ninety-four miles in diameter and twelve miles deep. Its center is buried offshore below the Yucatán Peninsula of Mexico. A few miles from the present-day town of Chicxulub, Mexico, for which it is named.

The Discovery of Chicxulub Crater, as recently as 1978 CE, is attributed to geophysicists Antonio Camargo and Glen Penfield. The geophysicists were looking for petroleum in the Yucatán Peninsula. Subsequent scientific studies and explorations of the area confirmed the existence of the crater. As well as the asteroid's spectacular effect on the planet's ecology after it struck the Earth.

The event quickly acidified the Earth's oceans causing immediate ecological collapse. The cataclysmic incident foreshadowed the Cretaceous–Paleogene extinction event. The mass extinction of three-quarters of all living animals and vegetation on Earth. To include the death of non-avian dinosaurs. It also signaled the end of the Mesozoic Era and the beginning of the Cenozoic Era, the age of climatic cooling and humankind.

The geological devastation to the Earth's outer layer stretched far and wide, hundreds of miles from the impact site. Cracks, or fissures, in the Earth's crust spread outward from the impact area in every direction. The numerous fissures were like spidery webs that result when a rock smashes a glass window without shattering it.

Over the millennium, many of the fissures gradually closed because of natural erosion and earthquakes. Nonetheless, vestiges of some of the more extensive, larger fissures remain to this day. Because of the dense vegetation and inhospitable terrain, they are largely hidden from view. To include detection by manned spacecraft and satellites orbiting the Earth.

One of the more impressive, deep fissures was discovered in 1521 CE by the Spanish conquistador Hernán Cortés (c. 1485-1547 CE). Because he had set off to explore a wide area, what is now Mexico, Cortés did not concern himself with the fissure's natural features. Despite this, he recounted the discovery of the fissure in his memoirs, even if in a few words. Consequently, Cortés' discovery of the fissure is essentially buried in the annals of forgotten history. Largely overlooked by all except the most questioning of historians and geologists.

The impressive fissure that Cortés discovered is known as *Thávma*.

When the Thávma fissure was created 66 million years ago, prehistoric living organisms steadily crawled inside its deep cavities. At the time, the fissure's innermost ambiance, unlike the inhospitable ecosystem taking place on Earth's surface, was more temperate. The air cleaner. The temperature more obliging to sustain life. Also, water was plentiful.

Nevertheless, just like the prehistoric species on the Earth's surface, many organisms could not adapt deep below the Earth's crust. They too succumbed and ceased to be. Yet more resilient organisms did survive. They adapted over time. They flourished, inherited new genes, and evolved.

Creating the Inner World.

CHAPTER 3

WIZARDS, WITCHES, ELVES, AND FAIRIES

"Ava Noelle, the world knows not of your power and of what you are capable. It merely knows your name."—the author

1

The amazing world of truly spectacular wonders you are about to enter has to do with the perilous adventures of a legendary heroine known the world over as Ava Noelle.

Ordinary humans would assume that Noelle is our heroine's middle name. They would be incorrect with their assumptions. Ava does not have a middle name; her surname is Noelle. Hence, our heroine's full name is Ava Noelle.

In the everyday world of ordinary humans, Ava Noelle seems the same as any other average human being, just like you and your friends. She goes about her life like the billions of ordinary humans throughout the world. She attends classes and is a member of the school basketball team. Owing to her competitiveness and athleticism, she is a member of a traveling volleyball team as well. She plays the French horn in her school band. She has a cellphone like most teenagers her age, a bedroom to herself, a loving family, and great friends. She seems as normal as the next ordinary human being. Nevertheless, something about Ava Noelle makes her different than the rest of us. A fact that ordinary humans do not realize. At least not yet.

Owing to her distinctive birthright, Ava Noelle is known by another name. It is a name of unequaled, celebrated prominence. Known only to the mystical beings that inhabit the magical realms of Earth's two worlds: The Earthly World and the Inner World.

Millions of mystical beings live amongst ordinary humans in the Earthly World – the world of you and your friends. The mystical beings of the Earthly World include thousands of wizarding humans (witches and wizards), pointy-eared elves, and magical, winged fairies. Along with a handful (perhaps hundreds – no one knows for certain) mystical beasts (primarily mermaids of the sea and the occasional dragon dwelling in the highest peaks and the most isolated of islands).

Nearly all the mystical beings living in the Earthly World of ordinary humans are descendants of the Inner World. Over the millennium, their ancestors climbed out of the Thávma fissure that was discovered by Cortés. Some come and go to this day just like you and your friends walk from one neighborhood to another.

Which leads us to the Inner World.

The Inner World is a preternatural, magical world comprised entirely of mystical beings. Like in the Earthly World, there are wizarding humans, pointy-eared elves, and magical winged fairies in the Inner World. There are also ghosts, goblins, dwarves, dragons, and many more mystical creatures. There are giants as well. Most of the creatures are ordinary while others are unusually bizarre. Also, the overwhelming majority of the creatures are generally kind-hearted and friendly. While some of the creatures are evil and ill-disposed.

In both the Earthly World and the Inner World of mystical beings, Ava Noelle is well-recognized by her legendary and rightful name. That name is Avaïnoάel.

In the Elvish language known as Fortunomy, Avaïnoάel means *O Poica Katharos* – the Purest of Elves. Naturally, Ava Noelle does not know her rightful name that is recognized by mystical beings of both the Earthly and Inner Worlds. At least not at the onset of her journey.

(Author's note: Avaïnoάel is pronounced *ə-vä-ī-nō'-ĕlō*.)

2

Anthropology and genealogy studies of the origins of ordinary humans have proven there is no such thing as 'pure' or 'impure.' Humans naturally come from mixed ancestry. According to the geneticist David Reich of America's Harvard Medical School of the Earthly World, "No human population is, or ever could be, pure. Ancient DNA reveals that the mixing of groups extremely different from each other is a common feature of human nature."

All the same, this pure/impure reasoning does not apply to mystical beings (elves, wizarding humans, and winged fairies) of the Earthly and Inner Worlds.

There are two categories of purity as it relates to mystical wizarding humans and elves: *Katharos* (Pure) and *Akáthartos* (Impure). The difference between the two is simple enough and does not suggest that one is better or of inferior quality than the other. The distinction purely is a matter of wizarding human and elven ancestry . . . and (as it applies to elves exclusively) immortality.

Because of their complex, genetic makeup, winged fairies of both worlds cannot have offspring with elves and humans. Thus, fairies are Katharos. They are Pure.

Returning to elves, both Katharos and Akáthartos elves have a chromosomal, genetic makeup that is comparable to humans (including magical witches and wizards). Therefore, elves and humans can marry/produce offspring. Elves have wed and produced offspring with humans over the millennium, and many do today.

However, descendants of elves whose ancestors have married/produced offspring with humans are no longer immortal. They are subject to death just like any other natural, non-magical human being. They are Akáthartos (Impure) as well.

In contrast, descendants of Katharos (Pure) elves are immortal. They will live forever.

Likewise, the descendants of wizarding humans that marry/have offspring with ordinary humans also are Akáthartos. They too have no magical powers. Katharos wizarding humans do. (Of note, the immortality of wizarding humans is a nonissue. Unlike Katharos elves,

Katharos wizarding humans are not immortal, and they will eventually die; although they can live tens of generations longer than ordinary humans.)

Katharos elves age naturally from childbirth to adulthood. It is when they reach parenthood age (19 years of age), that the elves' internal maturing ceases. Although they continue to age physically albeit gradually.

Even though they are immortal, Katharos elves can die by two methods: one – if they are slain in battle by an elf or by way of a weapon of war manufactured by elves; and two – if they are imperiled by a deadly magical spell cast by an evil witch or wizard.

So, one may ask, how does all the preceding affect Ava Noelle? What makes her so special? Why is she, Ava Noelle, ostensibly Avaïnoάel, O Poica Katharos – the Purest of Elves? After all, Ava Noelle, like her two older sisters, is the offspring of ordinary humans who are descendants of the same.

We will soon learn the answers to these powerful, compelling questions as we journey with Ava Noelle and her companions in the ancient realm of Antiquom of Earth's Inner World.

We now turn back in time to another realm – to the ordinary human Earthly World of you and your friends.

And that of Ava Noelle.

CHAPTER 4

HOW ALL OF IT BEGAN

*"Give me a bag crammed with mushy gummy bears,
and I'll pay you a smile."—Ava Noelle*

Every exciting fairytale must have a beginning.
As does Ava's. Her tale begins innocently enough.

31 Ioúliosom (July), 2020

Cars were whizzing by on the left as the eight-passenger van in which Ava was riding crept agonizingly slow in the outside lane. The sun was fiercely harsh in the sky. Its blazing sunbeams playing eyeball tricks. Giving rise to shimmering heat vapors and mirages flowing in waves from the boiling blacktop. The mid-morning temperature was equally harsh. An unpleasant, suffocating, eighty-one degrees Fahrenheit.

The temperature itself was not so bad considering it was the last day of July. It was the high humidity that was causing the discomfort. It was stuck at ninety-nine percent. The unusual humidity so early in the day caused the pedestrians to feel miserable as they ambled along the steamy sidewalks. Their foreheads beaded with perspiration. Their shirts and blouses already sticky untidiness. Their gait slow, sluggish, and sweated.

Ava was sitting in the middle back seat of her grandfather's van. She was unmindful of what was happening on the other side of the passenger seat window. Because she was hard at it, mentally, physically, and expressively. Grunting, moaning, and groaning. Muttering unintelligible words of frustration. Struggling with a plastic bag crammed with multicolored, mushy stuff that resembled minuscule bears: gummy bears to be precise. Her favorite candy.

Grandpa Jim, as Ava preferred to call him, was at the wheel. He seemed to be looking everywhere as he drove – to the right and left and back again – but rarely straight ahead. Where he probably should have been looking, concentrating on the road. At least it appeared so to Ava. Yet she felt safe in his hands, nonetheless. Grandpa Jim seemed to know what he was doing, even if he did drive at a snail's pace. Besides, he looked as if he knew the area better than the back of his hand.

Ava's mother, her name is Pam, Grandpa Jim's second to youngest of four daughters, was in the front passenger seat. She too was looking here and there as Grandpa Jim prattled on and on as he pointed out buildings and other sites to her.

The threesome had completed their grocery shopping at a local Walmart about ten minutes earlier. They were returning to the sleepy Campgrounds of the World recreational vehicle (RV) camping area. They had been staying at the campground for the past five days. Campgrounds of the World (repeat campers jokingly refer to them as COWs) are popular the world over. The first COW was founded in Vladivostok, Russia, of all places. There are now over two thousand COWs throughout Europe's sprawling countryside.

Like in Europe, COWs are becoming the latest RV camping craze in America. Especially among tech-savvy millennials. That is because the COW website (user friendly in all the Earthly World's human languages) pledges an *easy-come-and-go* camping experience for RV travelers. With an extra bonus: *or-your-money-back, no questions asked instant refund guarantee*. The easy-come-and-go experience is exactly that. You come camping. Then you go. Whereas the or-your-money-back, no questions asked instant refund guarantee is still open for debate.

The site where Ava's grandparents' four-year-old RV was situated was in a choice, secluded, shady spot. It was relatively quiet. That is saying a lot – about the site's relative quietness.

Like many campgrounds throughout America, COWs are conveniently located along America's busy interstates, state highways, and close to popular tourist attractions. Therefore, they tend to be awfully noisy. Especially at night when campers would like some shuteye after a long day on the road or exploring the environs' money-entrapping tourist sites. Cars and 18-wheelers zipping by noisily on the thoroughfare's. Their raucous motors and honking horns echoing like cries in a valley. All are part of the so-called, exciting *let us go camping* "adventure."

Also, notwithstanding obnoxious, external noises, most COWs are anything but quiet within their confines. Especially on the weekends, starting around four o'clock every Friday evening. Without fail. Like clockwork. Rain or shine. Sleet or hail. Or imminent doom.

That is because Friday evening is when the boisterous, partying, whooping it up two-legged animals come out of hiding. Loaded down with six-packs, sometimes twelves. Open bottles in paper bags hiding from the cops. And above all, empty heads filled with ridiculous conspiracy theories along with foul mouths. Hooting and howling day and night all weekend long. Until Monday morning when they head off to work with pounding heads.

Then again, to be fair, not all COWs are like the preceding horror show. Some are nice getaways for family and friends. Happily, the camping site Ava and her family members were staying was such a getaway. It was about a half-hour drive from their present location. A dozen or so miles outside of the city limits.

Grandpa Jim and Ava's grandmother, Grandma Kathy, as Ava refers to her, along with Ava's mother, slept in the comfortable, air-conditioned RV. The grownups shared the RV with three dogs. One of the dogs, Maida, belonged to Ava and her immediate family. The lovable pooch was about to be one year old in people's years.

At the time Ava strongly asserted – she does even now – that sleeping in an RV while camping is not real camping. She considers real camping to be roughing it in a leaky, mildewed, stinky tent. Dribbles of morning dew falling on your head, snapping your eyes open wide awake with each successive drop. Rocks assaulting your back as you toss and turn in your sleeping bag on the hard, unforgiving ground. Ants crawling all over the tent floor and invading your opened bag of potato chips and nachos, and God forbid! Crawling inside your improperly sealed bag of gummy bears! Best of all, roasting marshmallows gooily ensnared on a stick, flaming burnt black but tasting heavenly sweet just the same.

None of those memorable things seemed likely to Ava if one opted to sleep in an RV.

She was fond of saying to anyone who would listen – most everyone did not because she was the youngest of the lot – "Sleeping in an RV while on a camping trip is like being home and sleeping on a mattress beneath a sheet draped over the dining room table. Totally boring, unexciting, and uninteresting!"

Ava and her sisters were sharing a three-person tent. Naturally, Ava, the youngest of the three siblings, would have liked a tent all to herself. Her sisters would have liked their own tents as well. For as many different reasons as their differing personalities. But Ava stated the main reason she wanted her own tent was because of her older sisters' snoring. She insisted they snored much too much and much too loud and kept her awake much too often.

Ava and one of her sisters had a lighthearted argument the night before. Ava was complaining about her sisters' dueling, symphonic snoring routines. Their snoring overtures usually occurred after a difficult, day-long hike in the woods. Like the hike they had earlier in the day.

"Oh, get over it," Jami said in a jesting manner. Jami is Ava's middle sister. "You snore occasionally as well, Ava. I have heard you." She glanced at their older sister. Her name is Lexi. Lexi was playing a game on her phone. Her fingers slipping and sliding on the phone's surface like the slick stick of a hockey player skidding on ice. Her expression total concentration. Her brow furrowed. Her eyes riveted on the screen like it was about to burst if she did not prevail.

"Am I right, Lexi?" Jami stated. Lexi nodded her head without looking up. It was obvious she was not paying attention. Older sisters are good at that – even pretending from time to time that their younger siblings do not exist. That is until they want their younger sisters to do some of their chores or else, "I'll tell Mom what you did!"

"Snoring is a natural element of sleep," Jami explained to Ava. "Everyone snores now and then. It is part of life; you of all people should know that." The sides of her nose wrinkled as she frowned. She grinned. It was a particularly cheeky grin. Meant to annoy rather than to reveal frivolity. Siblings the world over smirk such grins at one another. Especially at younger sisters. She said in a sarcastic, but slightly joking manner, "As the presumed, scientific genius in our family!"

Ava wanted to say something uncouth to counter her sister's affront. But, surprisingly, she decided to stay on topic. She appreciated that her sister had her strong points. Just like their older sister and herself. One of Jami's many strong points was her exceptional musical ability. Ava could only wish she could play the French horn as well as her sister played the drums.

"I do not snore," Ava countered sarcastically. She folded her arms over her chest. Then she glared with a defiant pout of which only a younger sibling can do. "But if I did snore. Which I most certainly do not. I would never make as much racket as the two of you. You sound like two out of breath, snoring and snotting freight trains racing each other down the tracks in the middle of the night. Trying to outdo each other as you noisily snot like grunting pigs. It is disgusting. One grunts a snore—"

She inhaled a long, drawn-out, booger-filled *Zzzz!* It was followed by a horrible-sounding (once again) booger-filled *Srnnk!*

"Then the other has to grunt even louder. All night long, back, and forth, endless *Zzzz's!* and subsequent *Srnnk's!* You sound like a discordant, symphonic calamity, like the end of the world is coming! Or even better. Invasion of the *Zzzz'ing* and *Srnnk'ing* older sister snorting piglets!"

Jami was about to refute what Ava had said. But she noticed that Lexi had looked up from her phone.

Lexi's fingers were poised on the phone's screen suspending whatever it was in virtuality. She cleared her throat with two noticeably sardonic *ahem's.* She said in her usual, calm, older sister's voice, "Excuse me for a second you two if you please." She tilted her head to one side. Like she was pondering an earthshattering thought that just popped into her head. She did not say anything for at least a half-minute. Probably for added effect to add to the drama of the situation rather than to think of what she was going to say.

Lexi turned eighteen years old a while back. Her two younger siblings had always looked up to her. They admired her very much. Lexi was super smart, a terrific basketball player, and now she was on her way to college. They had no doubt she would be a basketball star. But their respect for her had increased ten-fold. Now she was their *adult* sister! How could anything be cooler than that!

Lexi looked at Ava, and then she looked at Jami. Her eyes were twinkling as she grinned good-naturedly. Her siblings stared at her eagerly, their faces awash with impatience. They were anticipating that she would say something critical. They knew from previous sibling arguments that whatever Lexi had to say would put an end to their disagreement.

Lexi smiled and said in a teasing manner, "Ava, what exactly do two out of breath, snoring and snotting freight trains racing each other down the tracks in the middle of the night sound like?" She laughed and returned her attention to the game she was playing on her phone. She murmured, "Because that . . . that I would like to hear."

Ava and Jami stared at her for a few moments. Finally, unable to contain themselves any longer despite their disagreement, they burst out laughing. As they had anticipated their oldest sibling had, no pun intended, laid their snoring squabble to rest once and for all.

*****

After a while, Ava got pretty much fed up with messing with the bag of minuscule bears. So, she stared out the passenger window in a meaningless way. She was thinking about how she happened to be where she was at that very moment. She leaned back in the seat. She placed her hands behind her head and interlaced her fingers. Her lips formed a faraway, contented smile as she closed her eyes.

Finally, she thought, I am going somewhere by myself. Without my obnoxious, yet endearing sisters tagging along. Bugging me about one thing or another. Ah, but this is so peaceful and pleasant. No bickering and no pains in my tush. And the backseat all to myself.

Ava's sisters had opted to remain at the campground with their grandmother rather than going to the store. They were looking forward to a fun, sit around the campfire breakfast. Pan-fried bacon and scrambled eggs with steaming cups of cowgirl coffee on the side. Their campfire fun involved breakfasting with two good-looking boys they had met the night before. The younger one was Bill. The older one was Chad. Like Ava's middle sister, Jami, the brothers were redheaded gingers.

Pam had presented Ava with two choices before she turned in for the night. Go shopping with her and her grandfather. Or remain behind with her grandmother and sisters. Ava's first reaction (naturally, she did not say this to her mother) was, "No way am I going to go shopping with two uninteresting adults. I will be bored out of my mind! Also, talk about embarrassing!"

Yet the longer she considered what staying behind would entail, the ghastlier that choice seemed to be. Staying at the campground would place her in an awkward and theoretically mortifying position. She could picture it in her mind.

Two guys and two gals – her sisters and their friends – happily rolling along with guy-girl conversations. All the while they would be flashing love-struck glances at one another. Hopelessly smitten, one step short of being in love, or so they would think. While she, the youngest of the lot and the fifth wheel, would be snubbed entirely. Depressed, irrelevant, and ignored. Cast off each time she opened her mouth. Consequently, she realized that pretending to be a part of what was going on between the foursome would not work. She knew from her experience as a third wheel on more than one, dreadfully awful occasion.

That would stink royally, she thought. Sure, I could hide out in the tent. Pretend I did not exist. But that would be just as bad, perhaps far worse. I would have no way of escaping their insufferable chatter as the four of them told stories, laughed, and whispered, mushy boy-girl stuff as they ate. Then again, I could always wear my earbuds.

She also considered a third option – hanging out with her grandmother in the RV. That would be fun. They certainly would do arts and crafts together. Her grandmother, like her Aunt Sandy, is one of the family experts when it comes to arts and crafts and creativity. But Ava was certain that would be just as bad as the two other options. She would be able to hear the four teenagers whooping it up around the breakfast campfire through the RV's thin walls.

So, after careful deliberation that involved a restless night's sleep as she mulled over her few choices, Ava decided. She would choose the lesser of the three crummy options. She would accompany Grandpa Jim and her mother to the store. Much to her surprise (and happy relief), everything had turned out okay.

They stopped at a McDonald's fast-food joint for breakfast on their way to the store. McDonald's was, and is to this day, her grandfather's favorite breakfast restaurant. He usually has the Egg McMuffin combo with orange juice to drink.

Due to the ongoing global pandemic, COVID-19, the fast-food dining area was closed. Therefore, they ordered breakfast via drive-thru and ate in the car. Ava thought eating in the car was simply fine. She never did like the idea of eating in front of strangers in fast food joints. Even now she does not like it.

She had two doughy pancakes that she smothered in syrup. A crisp sausage patty (she took one bite and spit it out in the napkin). And a practically rock-hard, overcooked biscuit. The hash brown was good. She downed it in three bites. The scrambled eggs she smothered in ketchup. They too were good.

She managed to soften up the gritty biscuit with enough butter and grape jelly to make it swallowable. A plastic bottle of orange juice helped drown the otherwise tasty food. She did not bother to see what the adults had ordered.

Grandpa Jim bought Ava and her sisters a ton of snacks at the store. The snacks were for the next leg of their vacation, which was like a godsend to Ava. Chips, nachos, candy, pretzels, and gummy bears, lots of gummy bears. She knew that having a ton of snacks for their return trip to Tennessee was a stroke of good fortune. Her previous family car trips were quite boring. Playing license plate alphabet games with her mom and sisters was barely tolerable at best. She always had trouble with the *Q*s and *Z*s. And staring at YouTube videos on her iPhone really got old after a couple of hours.

Ava's grandparents reside in Middle Tennessee, fifty or so miles south of Nashville. Ava and her mother and sisters were going to stay overnight at their house. Her immediate family planned to start on the long drive up to Illinois early the next morning. Illinois is where Ava lives.

Ava opened her eyes and stared out the window. She began to think about her grandfather's ten-year-old van. She suspected there was nothing wrong with the van from a mechanical standpoint. Grandpa liked saying that the thing ran like a top. She reluctantly had to agree with him. It started each time it had to start, and it never stopped running whenever it was supposed to run. The old vehicle's engine did not clickity clank. Nor did it thump and bump appreciably when it was idling at streetlights. It did not bounce up and down; nor did it sway back and forth on its springs every time it struggled with potholes or turned at corners. It did not stall at busy intersections – thankfully. And it had new, shiny tires with excellent treads.

Her grandfather had said, "Minus the whitewalls, naturally." He added with a snicker, "Went out with the seventies."

Ava was unfamiliar with the term whitewalls. So, in her usual inquisitive manner, she entered "white walls" on the Safari browser of her phone. When she read the meaning of white walls, "… is a song by the U.S. hip hop duo Macklemore & Ryan Lewis" she felt sort of miserable. She was sure that her grandfather was losing it – or perhaps he already had. She was going to ask him what in the world white walls had to do with tires, as he had said, "Went out with the seventies." Especially considering the hip hop duo did not publish the song "White Walls" until 2012 when they released their album *The Heist.*

She thought to herself; I probably should not question him even though he is wrong about white walls. I learned my lesson long ago to not correct adults. What she did not know is that her grandfather had been correct. Had she Googled the term "whitewalls," one word instead of two, she would have discovered that tires with whitewalls have a stripe or entire sidewall of white rubber. Also, as her grandfather had said, they were largely phased out in the mid-1970s.

As you can tell, Ava was inquisitive back then, exceedingly so. She is today, perhaps even more so. Her curious, answer-seeking mind seemed to be going at full throttle. As we will soon discover, it still does. She constantly was trying to understand new things. She would make an extra effort to investigate the whole lot. Things others might consider unexplorable. Things not worthy of others' time and effort.

As an example, curiosity took hold when her grandfather had mentioned that the van's tires had good treads. She inserted a penny in one of the treads like she had seen in a Firestone commercial. She needed to check for herself if the treads were, in fact, as good as her grandfather had said. She did not know what she was supposed to see with three-quarters of a penny sticking out of the tire tread. But she did it, nonetheless. Her curiosity had gotten the best of her once more. She did not notice anything particularly noteworthy or interesting. So, she stuffed the penny in her pocket, and off she went in pursuit of something more fascinating.

Ava's grandparents on her mother's side have a huge family, spread out all over the country – Texas, Illinois, Tennessee. Probably a bunch of other places in between that Ava does not know about. Therefore, the van had nearly triple the number of miles than its one hundred-thousand-mile warranty had ever anticipated. But, as her grandfather had said, mechanically it seemed simply fine. Happily, the van's air conditioning unit was belching frosty air. Which was a wonderful thing, especially on that day. Like Ava's hometown in Illinois that time of year, Buffalo, New York, where her family was vacationing, was blisteringly hot and spitefully humid.

They were on the final day of their vacation to Upstate New York. Buffalo is where Grandpa Jim and his younger brother were born and raised nearly three-quarters of a century earlier. While vacationing, they took in the breathtaking grandeur of Niagara Falls. They walked the shores of Lake Erie and listened to her grandfather tell stories of long ago. Expectedly, they did a little fishing. Casting worms in Lake Erie made her grandfather's day. Even though the only thing he caught was a flattened Coca-Cola can. They planned to visit Canada. Ava really wanted to see the Horseshoe Falls up close. But the ongoing, worldwide pandemic thwarted their plans. The border was closed.

Grandpa Jim was chatting away with Pam as he drove. She was obligingly turning her head this way and that, trying, without much success, to keep up with her father's finger-pointing. He was directing her attention to interesting neighborhood places. Fun places where he and his brother hung around when they were kids.

Ava was not paying the slightest bit of attention to their conversation. She believed nothing he could say or point out in the rural area of Buffalo could ever surpass the exciting, spectacular sight of the grandest spectacle of all during her vacation – Niagara Falls. Consequently, as the adults chatted away, she once again was grunting and groaning and whispering silent, non-swearing curses as she toiled in the backseat. Her face was contorted in disgruntled-looking, albeit just as entertaining-looking death stares. There were accompanied by entertaining pouts of annoyed suffering along with grimaces and furrowed-brow pouts. But she could have cared less how ridiculous she must have looked. She had been battling earnestly to open the see-through bag of super gooey and gummy minuscule bears. Without success. For at least five minutes.

She could have sunk her teeth in the plastic bag and ripped it open easily enough long ago. Except she knew what would happen from her previous, foolishly impatient exploits. The vacuum-packed bag of gummy delights would explode like a rocket. Then it would splay its sugary contents everywhere. Inevitably, some of the precious gummy treats would tumble out of the bag onto the floor of the car.

Ava also knew, again from experience, if she ripped the bag open with her teeth, it would be impossible to reseal along its so-called *easy to open and reseal* line. Then, within a day, the gummy bears would no longer be gummy. They would be hard, tasteless, stale bears. One step shy of being walked to the trashcan. As she toiled, her mind seemed to be screaming, so much for ridiculous technology! Gummy bears are for teenagers and kids. They are not for adults with nonsensical here is how to open and close Ziplock bags engineering degrees! She muttered under her breath, "I sure would like to give the morons who invented these so-called easy to open and reseal bags a piece of my mind!"

"What was that?" her mother asked as she turned in her seat. She promptly set out laughing because Ava was gnawing away on the plastic bag with a look that could have slain a giant.

Ava mumbled between her clenched teeth as she stopped gnawing, "What's so funny, Mom?"

Trying not to smile given Ava's ugly frown, her mother replied, "Did you say something to your grandfather or me?"

Ava shook her head with obvious irritation. She freed the hopelessly tattered bag from her clenched teeth. She mumbled in a grumpy manner, "No, Mom, I was not talking to either of you." She held the bag out and showed it to her mother. It was a disgusting sight, sort of gross. Teeth marks and drool, loads and loads of slimy drool. "As you can see, I am trying to open this stupid bag of gummy bears. I have been at it for quite some time now. Almost ever since we left Wallymart. It refuses to open above the easy to open and close line. The zip open, dotted line thingy doesn't seem to be working."

With too much of a patronizing tone for Ava's liking, her mother said in jest, "Oh, my poor sweet, struggling, baby girl, Ava. Do you need your mommy's help?"

"No, but thanks anyway," Ava replied. "I'll get it eventually." As her mother turned away, she removed the cloth face mask from the pocket of her jeans. Like the others in her family, she had to use the protective face mask whenever she could not socially distance in public. To avoid catching the dreaded COVID-19 virus. She positioned the spread open mask directly beneath the bag. So, as she thought, if the bag explodes open, which I am positive it will, the mask will catch the bulk of the gummy bears.

Unexpectedly, her struggles with the pliable bag of gummy goodies were brought to an abrupt halt. She slid sideways in her seat as Grandpa Jim violently veered off the road to the right shoulder's bicycle lane. Thankfully, she was buckled in. Cars and trucks continued to speed by on the left gently rocking the van as they passed.

She laid the unopened bag of gummy bears and the protective mask on her lap. She stared at her grandfather's light blue eyes that were reflected in the rearview mirror. His eyes seemed to be dancing with excitement as he gawked to his right. Ava followed his gaze. Her curiosity was piqued at once. So much so that her life would be changed forever – along with the lives of countless others the world over.

CHAPTER 5

THE FAMOUS, THE NEARLY UNCONQUERABLE

"When we climbed the tower, we were in a new province. Like our very own innermost world."—Grandpa Jim

Her grandfather bellowed at the top of his voice eagerly, shocking Ava back to reality, "There she is, Ava!" He was pointing to a towering, eight-story octagonal structure in the southwest corner of an expansive, recently mowed meadow. He instantly set out to snap photos with his cellphone.

Ava looked away from his reflection in the rearview mirror. She followed his gaze once more and stared in awe at the behemoth, octagonal structure.

The structure was well-known to Ava's grandfather, as well as to hundreds of thousands of Buffalonians, merely as the tower. A historic, eleven-decade-old landmark in the formerly upscale area of the Kensington community of Buffalo, New York.

Unbeknownst to Ava at the time, as well as everyone else in the everyday Earthly World of ordinary humans, there is a similar structure on the planet. It is referred to by another name, a legendary name that has endured the test of time. A great name that symbolizes a protected place where the powerful provide refuge to the weak. More significantly, it is located near the Thávma, the passageway between Earth's two worlds described earlier.

Mystical beings of both the Earthly World and the Inner World call the tower *Gnæèfa* – the Spire of Time. More on this later.

Ava continued to stare at the tower as her grandfather snapped pictures. She was vaguely familiar with the structure. She had noticed its unusual, octagonal pattern on the satellite map displayed on her phone a few days ago. She had been Googling the environs of her grandfather's childhood neighborhood at the time. Back then she paid little attention to the structure. Except for its unusual octangular shape, it looked like all the other structures on the satellite map. Like the other structures, it was too city-like, commercialized, and wholly uninteresting for her liking.

Ava is not fond of being in the city and thus besieged by its crowded, busy, and noisy ways. She prefers a bucolic, less sophisticated, old-fashioned, and laid-back way of life. Sort of like her small town back home in Illinois. Or better yet, like when American pioneers were roaming the prairies or even centuries before. Perhaps even as far back as the Renaissance, the Age of Discovery. Better yet much further back, possibly to the Fifth Century. When the collapse of the Roman Empire occurred, which paved the way for the Dark Ages.

Now that she was looking at the octagonal structure up close, she instantly recalled its surroundings from memory. Despite not giving it much more than a second glance while Googling.

Ava can recollect immediately the most seemingly inconsequential trivialities, such as images at which she merely glanced. Her ability to do so is unsurprising given her exceptional mental acuity. She has a photographic memory, the ability to recall an image with precision even after only seeing it briefly. Moreover, she is uncannily curious, quickly intrigued, and she readily embraces all things technical, complex, exciting, and new.

She closed her eyes and thought hard about what she had seen on the satellite map three days earlier. She distinctly recalled she had been indifferent to the structure and the immense meadow at the southwest corner on which it sat. Despite her lack of interest at the time, she recollected vividly that the structure and the meadow were bordered on three sides by two-lane highways. Thanks to her instant recall ability, she remembered that Kensington Avenue was to the north. Grider Street, where the van was idling in the bicycle lane, was to the west of the structure and the grassy meadow. A highway called Colfax Avenue bounded the structure and the meadow to the south.

She opened her eyes and stared at the structure. She pondered if Colfax Avenue was named after Schuyler Colfax. Colfax was the United States Vice President under Ulysses Grant. She recalled reading about him a few years ago in history class. Colfax also had served as Speaker of the House of Representatives, in addition to other political positions.

Makes sense to me, she considered to herself wordlessly. Colfax was born in New York City in the 1820s. But I could be way off base. Perhaps Colfax Avenue, like so many cities, towns, and highways, could be named after someone unheard of, essentially a nobody. Sort of like the city of Buffalo itself. Most residents of Buffalo assume it was so named because herds of buffalo roamed the prairies centuries before. However, from what I have read, the city probably received its name from a nearby creek called Buffalo Creek. British Captain John Montresor mentioned the creek in his 1764 journal. The journal almost certainly was the first official record of Buffalo and its environs. But it does not matter really, does it? Goodness, I must stop thinking about unimportant things too seriously and learn to go with the flow!

Ava guessed the octagonal structure was at least one hundred feet high. Even its base was huge, perhaps as tall as two adults standing end to end. The base was fashioned with large, quadrilateral, solid-looking concrete blocks. The blocks were weather-stained a dark gray. While the upper part of the structure was made of lightly sun-bleached bricks spaced horizontally from end to end and stacked on top of each other.

The tower was cordoned off by a sturdy, ten-foot-high chain link fence. Two spotlights were mounted on tall poles at either side of the tower's entranceway. She accurately supposed there must be other spotlights along the fence line behind the structure. A concrete sidewalk encircled the tower at its base. Another paved sidewalk led from the perimeter of the meadow to the structure's staircase. The staircase had nine concrete steps that ended at a dark blue metal, double-hung door. The door was padlocked.

From where she was sitting, Ava could see an opening on one of the walls. The roughly eight-foot in diameter opening was covered with a copper louver and glass blocks. She correctly assumed it used to contain an exceptionally large clock. She also saw bordered up openings on each of the three walls within her sight. She considered, once again correctly, they were once windowpanes. She thought to herself; I bet this used to be a watchtower. And I bet it used to have eight lookout windows in addition to four clocks! Nowhere as large as the four clocks of Elizabeth Tower in London, England. They are almost twenty-four feet in diameter—

Suddenly, before she could complete her train of thought, it was shattered by her grandfather's loud shouts. He had finished snapping photos of the structure.

"Ava! I give you the famous, the nearly unconquerable, Kensington Water Tower, as it is now named! Way back when, long before my time, it had three functions, triple duty if you will. It was a waterworks structure. It was a clock tower. And it was an observation platform. There used to be four clocks. As you can see by that opening with the copper louvered glass blocks, they are gone. Happened in 1947. As you can probably fathom by the boarded-up voids, they used to contain windowpanes.

"When I was a kid, my father told me there used to be a belvedere or observation deck at the top of the tower. Belvedere in Italian means great view. Considering the height of the tower, I bet the view from the top was spectacular!" He chuckled and signaled his excitement with a solid thumbs up. "Thank goodness, it isn't what it used to be as well. It no longer is unconquerable. At least as far as our family's legacy is concerned."

Ava and her grandfather's eyes met up in the rearview mirror. If eyes could smile, her Grandpa Jim's eyes were doing just that. They were also twinkling with delight. She had never seen him so happy.

"Ava, the tower is where your great uncle and my dreams sort of came true. It is here where your dreams can come true as well. I honestly believe that." He winked at her in the mirror. "This is where adventures untold and unseen by others can be achieved. Yes indeed."

Ava pondered; he has got to be kidding. Untold adventures unseen by others? Dreams coming true? A family legacy? What in the world is he talking about? Yes, I love make-believe stuff just as much as other people who have vivid imaginations. But all that? C'mon—

But what her grandfather said next refocused her attention. A lot. As a result, her imagination began to roll along quicker than a flash of lightning bursting from the clouds.

"Your great uncle and I actually climbed that behemoth, Ava! If I had to venture a guess, I would say we climbed it a dozen times, perhaps more. Vanquishing the famous tower without falling to the ground was part of being a real guy, at least we thought so in the day." He frowned and looked at Ava's mother. "Goodness gracious, Pam! To think that was over fifty years ago. How time flies!" His eyes returned to the rearview mirror. They were sparkling with rekindled excitement as he addressed Ava once again.

"Yes, Ava, he and I climbed the beast." He shrugged his shoulders. "Well, to be more accurate, we didn't climb the tower actually. We traveled around it, circumnavigated its entire perimeter." He waved his hand from left to right. "In our day there was not a dagburned, nasty-looking chain link fence around it either. Like someone is going to steal the tower and haul it off in the back of his truck. Anyway, we would get on the staircase, and then we would hop on the ledge. And off we would go, to another world, another dimension. But let me tell you, climbing the tower was downright difficult.

"That is why you had to wear sneakers. Doing it barefoot or with leather-soled shoes would not cut it. Because the ledge was slippery even if it was bone dry. You had to press your body as tightly as possible against the wall and place your arms in a spread-eagle manner with your palms facing inward. All the while trying to ignore your screaming toes and calves – all your upper and lower body muscles – as you navigated the slippery slope of the ledge."

Ava's thoughts seemed to be screaming as she pondered everything her grandfather had said. To another dimension? Really, to another dimension, another world? Cool! She undid her seatbelt and slid to the other side. She re-buckled herself in and stared out the window. An odd warmth was overwhelming her body, and her heart was racing excitedly.

"Can you see the ledge, Ava?" Her grandfather pointed to the tower. "It's the slightly curved outcropping, about five feet from the ground."

Ava nodded her head. "I see it, Grandpa."

The slightly sloping ledge appeared less than two inches wide and looked smooth as silk. She thought to herself; how in the world did they hang on? The ledge is barely wide enough to plant one's toe on it! I wonder if they moved to the left, or right?

As if he had read her mind, her grandfather stated, "Come to think of it, and as best as I can recall, we never moved to the right. I do not know why. But we did not. We always moved to the left. Anyway, we pressed our bodies against the wall firmly and slithered along the ledge taking it steady and slow like a snail inches on the ground. If we leaned back too much or even coughed or sneezed, we were goners. Down we went to the ground, and we would have to start all over again.

"In our day there were heaps of shattered glass from soda and whatnot bottles scattered at the base of the tower. Probably why there is a fence now. To keep kids from smashing glass bottles on the walls. If you slipped and did not pay attention to where you were going to end up, you could land on the shards of glass. That would be the end of your climbing, at least for a few days." He sighed deeply and cringed.

"Not to mention the explaining we would have to do to your great-grandmother, Grandma Mary. If she saw the cuts on our hands and knees, we would be in a world of hurt. Anyway, climbing the tower took us over an hour, sometimes longer. Yes, Ava, there is a piece of history on those towering walls. And your great uncle and I are part of it!" His ecstatic expression unexpectedly turned sad. His tone was somber when he finally spoke a few moments later.

"Yep, those were the good old days. I wish we could repeat them; I truly do. Those were the days before the Internet, smartphones, videogames, Netflix, and YouTube. Reading books, watching a bit of black and white tv before bedtime, and doing your homework – they were but a few of the outlets for youngsters back then. The big one, the most important pastime, was going outside and playing. But, naturally, only after we had finished our chores. Including Saturday and Sunday chores.

"For my brother and me, our grand times included going to the playground." He gestured over his shoulder with his thumb. "And to the swimming pool during the summer. The pool is that fenced-in area behind us to our left." He gestured to the tower once more with a slight nod of his head.

"Or playing baseball in the tower's huge, grassy meadow. There was no baseball diamond in the day. We simply tossed pieces of cardboard on the grass for bases and pretended it was Yankee Stadium. Naturally, I was Mickie Mantle, probably the best baseball player of all time." He turned in his seat and looked at Ava. She appeared spellbound with what he had said. She was smiling a huge grin. What her grandfather said next was like he once again had read her mind.

"You would have liked it during the day, Ava. I know you would have. You have spunk. I admire you for that. Especially considering you are gung-ho on the basketball court despite not being six-feet-six like the competition. You also are a skilled volleyball player. And I know you better than any of my descendants. You have always said you would like to go back in time – to experience the good ole days. In some ways I wish you and I could go back in time, Ava. Bring your sisters along – all my grandchildren, great-grandchildren, even my four kids – so you could experience everything of what I am speaking."

He playfully jabbed Ava's mother on her shoulder with his forefinger. She was typing away on her phone. He said in a joking tone, "And there wouldn't be any phones allowed either. At least not the kind that you tuck in the back of your pocket or in your purse." He shook his head disapprovingly. Yet he was smiling. "And here we are, discussing one of the grandest of adventures known to man, and you're busily texting somebody! How could you, Pam?"

Ava's mother replied, "Oh, stop it, Dad. I have been listening to everything you have been saying. I just snapped a picture of the tower and emailed it to your brother." She laughed. "So there!"

"Was it scary, Grandpa?" Ava asked hesitantly. "You know, to climb the tower at such a young age?"

"Not really, hon. Well, maybe it was a bit scary. When we were kids, about your age, and even when we were much older, climbing the tower without our parents' permission, worrying about getting caught, was a whole lot scarier than doing it. Your great uncle was just a little snot back then, a short guy for his age. I imagine his staring up at the ledge looked scary at the time. He was a weakling sort of kid, skinny, freckled face, uncombed red hair that all but covered his eyes. Never combed his hair unless forced to. He had a knack for getting in trouble as well. He had a big mouth that was too large for his size if you know what I am saying. I was always bailing him out of trouble, finishing his fights.

"But he was an alright kid, just a royal pain in the caboose sometimes. Anyway, it took years before he could navigate the gate in the back of the tower successfully. Tried like a dozen times and never could do it. Happily, one day he did." Grandpa Jim smiled and nodded. "I was very happy for him; indeed, I was."

"The gate?" Ava stammered with genuine surprise. She looked at the tower and craned her neck. "What kind of gate? I cannot see it. Where is it?"

"It is on the other side of the tower. It was a padlocked, four-foot-wide band of vertical wrought iron bars and a dozen or so horizontal crossbars spaced a half-foot or so apart. There was a hinge on the left side, so the gate could swing outward. The gate was padlocked. It protected a similarly locked, wooden door that led to the inside of the tower. I guess it is still there and serves as an emergency exit.

"Traversing the wrought iron gate without hopping to the ground looked, to those who lacked gumption, completely out of the question. It seemed insurmountable. But my brother and I did it. We did it on many occasions. You could not boast that you had successfully climbed the tower unless you were able to cross the forbidding gate without hopping to the ground. At least that is what my brother and I believed. Makes sense if you think about it.

"It was quite difficult actually. You had to inch along the crossbars of the gate. They were like horizontal rungs of a ladder. You had to lean back with your arms outstretched before you as you held on for dear life onto the uppermost part of the gate. To do otherwise would mean hitting your head on the ledge above the door opening. To do otherwise spelled failure. Then you had to hop to the ground and start over. Or give up and try again another day. It was grueling, challenging, tedious work. It seemed to take at least a half-hour to get across the gate. It required stamina along with patience, not to mention all the upper arm strength you could muster. It was the hardest part of the climb, I must admit.

"A couple of our male cousins, they would later brag that they had climbed the tower, actually hopped down on the right side of the iron gate. Then they climbed onto the left side of the gate and continued skirting along the sloping ledge. Of course, my brother and I would applaud their efforts, which was the respectful thing to do at the time. He and I would openly agree, just to be nice, that our cousins had climbed the tower. However, we knew better. We would exchange

Machiavellian glances when our cousins were not looking. In our eyes, no one could savor the glory of successfully climbing the tower unless he or she navigated the four-foot-wide wrought iron gate without hopping to the ground. Or worse, falling to the ground, arms flailing to avoid the shards of broken bottles below.

"Yes, Ava, to climb the tower meant to suffer the agony of your outstretched arms, the agony of your screaming calf muscles, and the excruciating pain in your spread wide fingers as you precariously slid along the wall. All the while your aching toes were screaming bloody murder. Your toes sometimes went numb!"

Ava slid back to the left side of the seat and buckled herself in.

"Yes, Ava, to have claimed the bragging rights – that you climbed the tower – meant going all the way around without hopping or falling to the ground. That included crossing the gate without hopping to the ground and then climbing on its left side back onto the ledge."

"Wow, Grandpa!" Ava cried earnestly. "I am impressed. I wish I could have lived way back when you were a kid. I also would have conquered the tower like you and my great uncle! It must have been a wonderful feeling. I wish I could do it right now!"

"Not only that," her grandfather said, "climbing the tower was sort of calming if that makes any sense. While you were climbing the tower, it was like you were in a different world. A diametrically opposed dimension. Certainly, there were the usual sounds of moving traffic along Grider Street, people talking as they walked on the sidewalk or waited at the bus stop. You could hear the sirens from the hospital down the highway. Nevertheless, those sounds were distant, way off, seemingly far beyond your everyday consciousness." He glanced at Ava's reflection in the rearview mirror. She was staring at the tower. He nodded his head appreciatively.

"Yes, Ava, it may sound weird, even magical. When we climbed the tower, we were in a new province, like our very own innermost world. Of all my grandchildren, you would have been the one to have conquered it. There is no doubt in my mind. You have the tenacity, courage, and physical endurance to do it. I am confident that you do."

Ava smiled at her grandfather. He could tell she was excited. He smiled in return. "Thank you, Grandpa. That means the world to me. I wish I could climb the tower someday because I know it would make you and your brother proud of me. That I was able to renew the family tradition, to keep its legacy alive." As her grandfather steered the van to reenter the highway traffic, Ava turned about in her seat and watched the tower as it slowly disappeared in the rear window.

The tower. Forbidden yet inviting. Imposing but conquerable. Alluring yet repulsive. An out-of-place octagonal structure within a formerly upscale, middle class neighborhood. But surprisingly majestic! – beckoning. Challenging Ava to hop the chain link fence. To climb the tower!

CHAPTER 6

AVA CLIMBS THE TOWER

"It is one thing to mortify curiosity, another to conquer it."
—*Robert Louis Stevenson*

1

9 Ávgoustom (August), 2021

A little more than twelve months later, Ava found herself standing alongside the fence that surrounded the tower. To say she was scared out of her wits does not even begin to describe how she was feeling. She was petrified! Because she was thinking about the good and the bad – the whole shebang that could stem from whatever decision she soon would have to make.

What if Mom and Dad find out I either attempted or succeeded in climbing the tower? They will ground me for at least six months. Gosh! Maybe longer, a whole year. Yet if I am successful and climb it, I will have well-deserved bragging rights. Grandpa and my great uncle will be so proud of me! Their adulations will be well worth whatever punishment Mom and Dad can dole out. Yep, I can see it now. Screaming excitedly at the top of my lungs.

"I climbed the tower! I did it. I conquered the sucker, Grandpa! I bet you're proud of me, huh?"

Okay, mom will be angry. No question there. Dad will be even angrier. However, Grandpa will be delighted, and I bet he will tell me so in private, out of earshot of my parents. My great uncle, when he learns what I have done, I suppose he will publish a book about my adventure and tell the world! That would be totally cool!

Suddenly, more terrifying thoughts than being punished by her parents invaded Ava's mind.

But what if the police catch me scaling the fence? They surely will arrest me for trespassing. Can they do that even if there are no signs posted that say *no trespassing*? I guess they can if they want to. I mean, what is the point of a fence if not to keep people from infringing on another's property? Grandpa had mentioned something about the fence being installed to stop people from smashing glass bottles on the tower's walls.

One element of Ava's conscience, her senses of right and wrong, decided to speak up first. Ava jokingly refers to this part of her conscience as Miss Pragmatic, Peg for short. Peg's reflective views are the stiff and prissy, overly cautious philosophies of Ava's moral values. She equates Peg's opinions to those of a goody-two-shoes. Being labeled as a goody-two-shoes is another way of saying you are too nice and being politically correct, disgustingly so!

Peg's thoughts started off by saying the following. Nowadays, unlike when Grandpa was a kid, just about everything drinkable comes in plastic or aluminum cans. Some, like fruit juices, are in cardboard cartons. So, having a fence to keep people from smashing glass bottles on the tower wall does not make a lick of sense. The fence was erected to keep trespassers out. Pure and simple. Moreover, just because there are no signs posted does not mean you can hop the fence.

Peg's twin interrupted rudely, but there are exceptions you silly moron!

Ava calls this thought process of her senses of right and wrong Miss Idealistic, Ida for short. Ida's reflections – most are angry, argumentative, and directly to the point – are Ava's happy-go-lucky, carefree, and reckless, just go for it sentiments of her moral values. Ava tends to follow Ida's viewpoints more than she does Peg's. Perhaps it might be a sixty-forty split.

Ida said forcefully, a lot of iced tea beverages come in glass bottles! So do mayonnaise, spaghetti sauce, alcoholic brews, iced coffee, and loads of other stuff. The list goes on forever. Therefore, as Grandpa Jim had said, the fence probably is to keep people from smashing glass bottles on the tower. Makes perfect sense! Hence, the fence is nothing more than a superficial, temporary obstacle. It will be okay to climb over it.

Ava murmured aloud, "Neither one of you is making a lick of sense. Be quiet! I have to think." She purposely ignored her dueling senses of right and wrong, at least for a few moments. They never could find common ground, were forever arguing, and they seldom came to a point of agreement that proved useful. Nevertheless, every so often one of them came up with something worthwhile. She resumed pondering her predicament in real-time and on her own terms.

After I am caught, and I just know I will be caught, the police will handcuff me – would they do that? I guess they would if they wanted to. That will really suck! I can picture it now. She bit her lower lip and shuddered.

The policeman or policewoman – I guess I should call them law enforcement officers – will impolitely stuff me inside their squad car. One of them will place the palm of his or her hand on top of my head like they do in the movies. So, I will not bump it against the door frame. Soon they will be nibbling on chocolate-covered donuts with little sprinkles on top. Sipping their tepid, black coffee. And telling off-color cop jokes. Then off we will go – siren blaring for the whole world to hear. Lights blazing blue and red so everyone can peek inside. At the horrible criminal in the back seat on the other side of the fencing.

Me. Ava Noelle. Slouched as low as I can possibly go. Struggling to hide my face. Hands handcuffed behind my back. Crying my eyes out.

On my way to juvey!

The police will fingerprint me. Take my photo – a mug shot. Hopefully, they will allow me to comb my hair before snapping the picture. She unconsciously ran her fingers through her hair. It felt messy which caused her to grimace.

Given the topic of a mug shot and her appearance, Ava's two senses began to argue over the extremely trivial issue – what could or could not be a good mugshot photo.

Smile or frown? Does not really matter. No biggie, honestly. But no crying. No tears. No looking sad. Could be beneficial to cry, look sad. Proves remorse, caring. Naw, too feminine, too weak if tears flow. Even so, crying could help. Make things easier in the end. No. Indifference and calmness are the way to go. Shows resolve and guiltlessness. Tears are out of the question. Why? Because they are!

As usual, Peg and Ida could not agree, and all they did while arguing was waste Ava's brain cells.

After they book me, take my mug shot and fingerprints, I will be placed in a cell with hardcore, underage criminals. Perhaps I will have to use the bathroom. In public! In full view of the others. Nooooo! Maybe I will have to go number two. The others will be watching me out of the corners of their eyes. Waiting to hear the telltale passing of stinky gas. They will pinch their noses and laugh at me! There probably will not be any toilet paper either. Yuck! That would be like totally disgusting. No food. No drink. Just a hard bench to lie on. Maybe nothing more than the floor.

If all that is not enough to make me sick to my stomach, it will be nothing compared to what happens next. The police will call Mom and Dad! After they bail me out of jail, I will not see daylight or my friends or have phone privileges like forever. I probably will be forced to forfeit my allowance too! They will make me move back in with my sister. And after all the pleading, beseeching, and even writing my parents a note begging to have a bedroom all to myself. Not having my own bedroom will be horrible. I will have zero privacy and will be forced to listen to my sister's snores all night long. Yuck!

Despite the unknowns, and Ava knew there were many, there was one thing she knew for certain. Everything of which she had wished, dreamed, and hoped, all her scheming and planning about conquering the tower – everything would have been for nothing. A total waste of time! But only if she were caught!

But I have been planning this for a year. And now I am here. So, it is now or never! I need to act. Because I probably will not have an opportunity for the rest of my life!

You could always keep what you are about to do a secret, Ida contemplated curtly. Just tell Grandpa, maybe even his brother, but not via text message to your great uncle. Too risky. Or keep it a secret for a half-dozen years until you are an adult.

But you have no secrets from your parents! Peg contradicted irritably. Why start keeping them now? Once you start along that path there is no going back.

Ida stated vehemently, nothing is going to happen fussbudget!

Peg seemed to sigh as she said, but what if they find out? I cannot even begin to imagine what will happen.

Ida countered, so what if they find out. Who cares really? Life goes on.

Perhaps I should wait until I am an adult before I try to climb the tower Ava pondered, ignoring her twins' conflicting thoughts one more time. Maybe contact the fire department and ask for their permission to climb it. They will probably say yes. It will be good for the tower's publicity. After all, there is talk about making the tower a national landmark. They might take pictures, perhaps a video. I could be featured on the Buffalo nighttime newscasts or in the newspaper! I would have concrete proof that I had climbed the tower like my Grandpa and great uncle. I would be a family heroine!

She considered what if the officials say no? What if I never have another opportunity outside of today? Being a grownup means responsibility, having a job, making money, raising a family, not to mention maintaining one's dignity! Climbing a tower does not portray dignity for certain.

You should just wait a half-dozen years or more. Hop the fence as an adult and climb the sucker on your own terms, Ida exclaimed with her predictable, risk-taking attitude.

No, Peg seemed to scream inside Ava's head. That will never work! Hopping the fence and climbing the tower as an adult would be a misdemeanor. They would probably take a mug shot, and goodness no – it could result in a lock-up overnight in a full-sized jail for adults! If you think juvey was going to be bad, imagine a real jail full of hard-core adult prisoners! There definitely will be no toilet paper there!

Suddenly, peculiar words seemed to bark inside Ava's head. "Face the facts, Ava Noelle. Today has to be the day!"

Ava's eyes widened as she did a double take and looked around. There was no one in sight. Yet she had heard the words, at least she felt she had. Moreover, the voice-thoughts she was experiencing were brand-new, something she had never come across before that day. They appeared to allay Peg and Ida's arguing thoughts instantaneously, shutting them up completely. Which was a miracle in and of itself.

"Be sensible, Ava Noelle," the mysterious voice-thoughts declared. "What are the authorities going to do to a kid who hopped a fence and climbed onto the ledge of a concrete, locked up tower? Lock her up and throw away the key? Put her in solitary confinement? Fingerprint her? Book her? Take her mug shot?

"No, I seriously doubt any of that will happen. There is no harm in hopping a fence. Kids and adults, they do it all the time. Sometimes for the good like helping someone or rescuing something in danger, and yes, sometimes for the not so good. It is the intent that concerns authorities. The intent, Ava Noelle. Also, stepping onto a ledge of a virtually indestructible tower is not going to result in damage or harm to the structure. Authorities will know that. Your intent is innocent enough. The authorities will understand, especially after you tell them your grandfather and great uncle's story. That is if you are noticed hopping the fence and climbing the tower in the first place!

"Yes, if you are noticed by the authorities you may – and I emphasize *may* – have a problem with your parents. You *may* have to suffer negative consequences if there are any to suffer. But either way, it will be what it will be, and you can live with whatever comes your way, both good and the not so good.

"Because the result will far outweigh whatever consequences you may suffer. That is if you are caught in the first place. Hence, Ava Noelle, stop your pondering, procrastinating, and attending to the pandering foolishness of your innermost senses of right and wrong. The ones you lovingly refer to as Peg and Ida. Do what you intend to do, Ava Noelle." The strange voice-thoughts paused briefly. "Or go home and forget about the whole thing and your destiny, your family's legacy – as a washed-out, I wanted to do it, but I did not have the courage, miserable failure. A failure that will never look at herself in the mirror in the same manner from now until forever."

Ava could sense the warmth that was gradually radiating throughout her body. She suddenly felt strong, powerfully resilient as adrenaline coursed through her veins. She repeated over and over in a whisper, "This is going to be amazing!" She squared her shoulders and faced the chain link fence that surrounded the tower. Then she looked through the links and spoke to the tower like the massive stone column was an actual person.

"Okay, tower, this is it. Over fifty years ago you were conquered by two teenagers, my grandfather, and great uncle. So, get ready to be conquered once more. Because yours truly, Ava Noelle, is going to climb you no matter what. To revitalize my family's tradition!"

2

Having made her decision, Ava tried to muster enough nerve to scale the fence. She was trembling, so severely her legs refused to move. Despite her unease, she felt refreshingly resolute. She took one last, quick look around to make certain no one was in the vicinity. There was no one in sight. The last thing that she wanted was an audience as she broke a half-dozen rules, most of them in her mind.

That there is no one in sight should come as no surprise, she thought. It is pouring rain! I am soaked to the bone. Thankfully, it is a scorching day. The rain plastering my face and drenching my clothes feels good, refreshing.

Yet, despite her resolve, Ava remained motionless. Frozen in place. Worse, she was on the wrong side of the fence, her back to Grider Street. She was facing the row of houses across the vast, lush, green meadow. The meadow was where her grandfather and great uncle used to play baseball over a half-century ago. The row of houses was bordered by tall hedges on the side that were fronting the tower. From old photographs she had seen online, she had noticed the houses looked almost the same as they did over fifty years ago.

No one was in the meadow or walking on the sidewalks. However, the houses were several hundred yards away, so she could not be certain if people were standing outside in the pouring rain. Even so, there was nothing to prevent a person from looking across the meadow from one of the upstairs windows. If they spotted her hopping the fence and climbing the tower, they could call the police. But that was a risk she knew she must take.

Then again, the more she considered it, the more obvious reality became. Observers probably could care less what they were seeing. So, she felt there was no harm in climbing a wall. It was not like she was going to break in the front door to steal stuff. The real threat was getting caught while scaling the fence.

Unexpectedly, the mysterious voice-thoughts seemed to echo in her mind as their words replicated what they had declared moments earlier. "Do what you intend to do, Ava Noelle. Or go home and forget about the whole thing and your destiny. Afterward, live with the knowledge that you have failed. That you botched your grandfather and great uncle's legacy and were not good enough to live up to their courageous values."

Ava tried to ignore the voice-thought's foreshadowing warning as she turned around in a complete circle. She was checking once more to make certain no one was watching her. If only she could muster up enough courage to move!

When Grandpa told me that he and his brother climbed the tower, I meant to ask him if they ever climbed it while it was raining. Grandpa had said the sloping ledge surrounding the tower was plenty slippery and tough to navigate on your tippy-toes, even in the driest of conditions. What did he mean by that? Was he warning me that I should not attempt to climb the tower in the rain? Could he have known I was going to try and climb it today, in the pouring rain? If so, how could he foresee what I was going to do a year later? She recalled his exact words the last time she saw him.

"That is why you had to wear sneakers. Doing it barefoot or with leather-soled shoes would not cut it. Because the ledge was slippery even if it was bone dry. You had to press your body as tightly as possible against the wall and place your arms in a spread-eagle manner with your palms facing inward. All the while trying to ignore your screaming toes and calves — all your upper and lower body muscles — as you navigated the slippery, slope of the ledge."

Ava could only imagine what it would be like on the tower's precarious, sloping ledge during a rainstorm. Water pouring down the tall concrete walls onto the ledge like a powerful waterfall cascading off a mountain. Relentless and unstoppable. She considered that was the purpose of the ledge, its design. It was designed that way to deflect the pouring water away from the base of the tower. She wordlessly pondered her dilemma.

If I slip and fall, so be it. I will pick myself up, race around to the front steps of the tower, and begin all over again. Grandpa said he and his brother had to jump off the ledge many times. Whenever they did, they just started at the beginning. Therefore, so will I. Besides, there is no way to hop back on the ledge – it is too high – without starting at either the staircase or the wrought iron gate at the back of the tower. And restarting at the gate is not going to happen.

Things did not start out well as she began to climb the chain link fence. In fact, what happened was quite comical. She had placed the toe of her tennis shoe in one of the diamond-shaped openings of the fence. It was slippery as ice from the rain. She lost her footing and promptly fell on her backside.

"Okay, Ava, get a grip on yourself," she whispered. "Offset the wet conditions. This is nothing compared to what lies ahead. If you think the fence is slippery, imagine what the sloping, two-inch, sopping wet ledge is going to be like!"

She got to her feet and massaged her sore butt for a few seconds. With a serious look of determination, she stuck the toe of her right tennis shoe in one of the diamond-shaped openings. Then she climbed the fence slowly. Soon, she was straddling the top of the fence with her feet planted on either side. She lingered a few moments to stare with wonder at the tower from her ten-foot-high vantage point. She started to descend by swinging her right foot over the uppermost links. What happened next caused her to freeze in place just as a look of absolute horror showed on her face.

The shoelaces of her right tennis shoe had snagged on the uppermost links of the fence!

She yanked her foot with all her strength, but she could not extricate the shoelace from the links. Along with loud grumbles and groans, she repeatedly tried, unsuccessfully, to reach the shoe with her outstretched hand. Soon the hamstring of her right leg began to scream in pain. She had stretched the muscle to its limits.

"So much for all those touching my toes and deep knee bend exercises I did this past year! I feel like an old lady. I must look totally stupid!" She glanced around to make certain no one was watching. She was relieved no one was around. "Here I stand, in full sight of anyone who cares to walk by and observe my clumsiness. Dangling from the top of a fence by a shoelace. One leg stretched out as far as humanly possible. While one foot is trying to stand on a two-inch-wide opening. Getting nowhere fast. What is worse, I am held captive by a fence that I am not supposed to be climbing in the first place! What a way to start! What in the (bleep) did you get yourself into, Ava Noelle? What in the (bleep) were you thinking!"

At that moment she knew that things probably would not get any easier or better going forward. Frankly, she imagined things would only get worse. She closed her eyes and said a quick prayer. After uttering a few more offensive words, words she will never admit to having said, she yanked her foot out of its imprisoned shoe.

Now she was standing on a fence rung with her shoed foot, while the other dangled helplessly in the air beside it. She had two choices. She could climb down using both her shoed and shoeless feet – knowing that the metal rungs would tear her unshod toes to pieces. Or she could jump the six or so feet to the ground and hope for the best. She chose the latter and leaped to the ground. When she landed, she distributed her weight so most of it was on her shoed left foot. All at once she teetered, lost her balance then fell onto her butt in a three-inch-deep pool of muddy water.

"Well," she exclaimed miserably, "at least I managed to do that properly – not!" She turned around on the seat of her sopping wet pants and gawked at the tower. The daunting enormity of its gigantic, century-old size was overwhelming, unforgiving, seemingly unconquerable. She got to her feet and contemplated her quandary.

Here I stand, this time on solid ground. Sopping wet in the pouring rain, but with two extra bonuses. One, I am on the correct side of the fence. Which is good. Bonus number two, one shoe is on one foot, the other shoe is dangling by its laces at the top of the fence. Which is not good! Talk about karma!

Ava did not even consider jumping up to grab the shoe. She was but five feet, two inches tall at the time, a good three or four feet short of being able to grab the shoe, even with her arms outstretched. Instead, she shoved the big toe of her left, shoed foot in one of the diamond-shaped chain link openings. She stretched as high up the fence as she could. Still, her outstretched hand was more than two feet from the ensnared shoe.

Despite the pain she knew was coming, she shoved the big toe of her shoeless right foot into one of the openings. The swift, excruciating pain as the metal cut in her squished toes was too much for her to bear. She was forced to leap to the ground. Fortunately, she remained steady and did not fall on her rear end.

I have got to reach my imprisoned shoe. If not, my goal of climbing the tower will be over. Worse, I will be stranded on the wrong side of the fence. Unable to either climb the tower or get back to the other side. I will be a sitting duck, in full view of everyone! She ran her fingers through her sopping wet, tangled hair. Think, Ava Noelle, think. There must be a way to get your rebellious shoe from the top of this stupid fence! Then something occurred to her.

She almost yelled, but caught herself and said in a whisper, "My backpack!" She had tossed the backpack over the fence before she set out to climb. It was a few feet away. She crawled over to it, zipped it open hurriedly, and peered inside. There was a half-eaten PB&J sandwich, squished beyond recognition, apparently smashed when she tossed the backpack over the fence. She continued rummaging in her backpack. There was a book she had almost finished entitled *Puppet*. A half roll of orange-flavored Life Savers. A pack of gum – Big Red. Best chewing gum in the business. A wad of tissues, most unused, some streaked with yucky stuff. Nail clippers, a comb, a brush, some cosmetics, a folding mirror, and then she saw it – an unopened bag of spongy, gel-filled, gummy bear candies!

"Ah, just the thing I need to protect my shoeless toes! Spongy, soft, and cushioning." She added with a sad face, "But what a waste of delicious candy!"

She untied the shoelace of her left shoe and wrapped the sole and toes of her right foot with the bag of gummy bears. Then she meticulously secured the whole lot with the shoelace. That took about five minutes. All the while she was in full view of anyone who cared to observe her shenanigans. And sopping wet in her now shivering, petite frame.

She slowly climbed the fence. Indeed, it was an inelegant way to climb, but she managed to ascend the fence without torturing the toes on her right foot. She reached up and grabbed her captive shoe and tossed it to the ground. She quickly descended after it.

3

After she attended to her shoes and eyed the bag of ruined, watery gummy bears with a hopeless look – the bag had ripped open – she grabbed her backpack and walked to the steps of the tower. She sat down on the landing and contemplated what awaited her. As she had anticipated, Peg set out to lecture in her polite way.

You do not need to do this. You must not feel obliged to prove your gumption and courage by climbing the tower. Let your ancestors' legacies be theirs. They own the true entitlement to conquering rights. Face the facts. Look at all the trouble you had climbing the fence in this soaking rain! That was supposed to be the easy part of your climb. How do you expect to climb the tower when you cannot even negotiate a stinking chain link fence?

As if on cue, Ida admonished by saying, Grandpa Jim almost begged you to attempt the climb. If you accomplish your goal, and I expect that you will, you too will have indisputable bragging rights. You will be your grandfather and great uncle's heroine. Think of the tales you can tell your children's children, children!

Do not listen to her, Peg's thoughts admonished. Think about the consequences. Being grounded for Lord knows how long. Losing your phone privileges, your allowance too. Not hanging out with Chloe and your other friends. Losing your parents' respect and most of all their trust. Not to mention if the police see you and discover that you are trespassing right now— goodness! Turn back before it is too late.

She is not going to get caught, Ida argued coldly. Look how it is raining! The cops are snug as bugs in their squad cars munching on donuts and drinking coffee. They want no part of snooping around to see if someone is on the wrong side of the tower's fence.

Peg was about to reenter the conversation when she was interrupted by the exceptionally strange voice-thoughts. The ladylike, third voice in Ava's head had returned.

"Ava Noelle, my dear, this is your destiny. It is an important quest that has summoned you for the longest time. You must do everything in your power to obey what you feel in your heart, what you know is righteous. You must succeed. Not only shall you join the ranks of your ancestors as one of only a few who have conquered the tower's outwardly insuperable power, you just may save—"

Ava interrupted the voice-thoughts with a shout. "Be quiet, the three of you! I am going to do this. Okay?"

She jumped to her feet and hesitantly placed her left toe of her tennis shoe on the two-inch sloping ledge. She breathed in deeply and began to inch along the slippery footpath. Her heart was thumping loudly, and she was out of breath with excited eagerness. Before she realized what was happening, she lost her footing and had to jump to the ground.

4

Ava looked down at her tennis shoes and laughed. They were caked in mud and barely recognizable.

No wonder I could not take more than one step. I am lucky I jumped from the ledge and did not slip, fall backward, and slam my head on the concrete. From five feet high, that would have smarted royally! It would have been the end of my quest as well.

She sat down and began to scrape the slippery mush from her shoes with her fingertips. Almost immediately, her fingers were a gooey, muddy mess. She pressed her hands against the wet wall. Soon, her hands were clean. She got to her feet and raced to the staircase to give it another go. As she inched along the ledge, she was starting to become more confident. Just as it looked like she was getting the hang of slip-sliding along the ledge but managing to stay on, she was forced to hop to the ground once more.

What in the world am I doing wrong? My toes were planted firmly on the ledge. My arms were spread out wide with my palms flat against the wall. What in the world was I doing incorrectly? Why had I slipped a second time?

Ava mulled over how she must have looked as she slithered along the ledge. Something her grandfather had said suddenly came to mind. He had said that one had to face one's head to the left and press it closely against the wall. Otherwise, one would have to hop from the ledge and start all over.

That must be it! I was staring straight ahead instead of resting my cheek on the wall. So, my equipoise was all messed up because my weight was distributed unequally.

She jumped up and sprinted to the staircase for a third try. That time she managed to stay on the ledge for what seemed longer than an hour but probably was fifteen minutes, twenty tops. She had completed three and one-half sides of the octagon before she hopped to the ground.

I had to stop! My toes are killing me. My calves are screaming bloody murder. Even though I paused every so often to stretch my legs, toes, and arms, I am sore. But I refuse to give up. I must try again.

Just as she turned in the direction of the staircase for another go, she noticed something odd. She could not believe what she was seeing! The tower wall, the ledge, and even the ground below, where she had already traveled, was bone dry! It was like it had not rained in that area, but she knew that it had. She had felt the raindrops as they fell on her head and shoulders as she inched along the slippery ledge. She had felt the clammy, wet, cold wall on her cheek and the palms of her splayed hands! She turned around. What she saw shocked her even more. The area where she had yet to move along the wall was soaking wet. Rainwater was cascading down the steep, concrete walls of the tower onto the ledge. She wordlessly pondered what she was seeing.

It is like Divine Providence has protected, consecrated, and renewed every inch of the ledge, wall, and ground where I have already traveled! Like it recognizes I must repeat what I have already done. So, it has dried everything, thereby making my repetitive attempts less difficult, more tolerable.

She also noticed something else that was even more incomprehensible. She was soaking wet and as grimy as an excited puppy frolicking in a mudhole. Nevertheless, above her and along the entire area to her right where she had already traveled was devoid of rain. The sun was shining brilliantly. However, to her left where she had yet to travel, stormy clouds were pouring down buckets of rain.

Naturally, the inquisitive, curious part of her mind wanted to stop, so she could consider the miraculous phenomena further. However, the strange, third voice in her mind was summoning her to move on. She complied and raced back to the staircase. She carefully stepped onto the ledge and began to inch along a fourth time. Because it was no longer raining where she had traveled previously, and the ledge was dried out, her progress was speedier and more promising. The warm sunshine on her back felt good as well. Its warmth slowly started to dry out her clothes.

Ava knew she was on the verge of exhaustion. She purposely paused on the ledge more frequently than before. She stretched her aching toes, calf muscles, and thighs by performing carefully balanced, slight knee bends. She gently shook her tired arms and hands and wiggled her fingers. She wanted to move her head from left to right to stretch the neck muscles. But she was afraid she would lose her balance once more. Instead, she frowned, puckered her brow, and pulled loads of ridiculous-looking faces to stretch the tendons of her neck and cheekbones.

Just as she supposed she could not endure the pain wracking her body for much longer, Ava saw the daunting hurdle she would have to tackle next. It was the wrought iron, nearly unpassable gate! The halfway point of her climb. She halfheartedly inched toward it.

She recalled her grandfather had said, "You had to inch along the crossbars of the gate. They were like horizontal rungs of a ladder. You had to lean back with your arms outstretched before you as you held on for dear life onto the uppermost part of the gate. To do otherwise would mean hitting your head on the ledge above the door opening. To do otherwise spelled failure." He also stated that navigating the gate was the hardest part of the climb. Every slithered step before and after the gate was nothing compared to crossing the gate successfully without hopping to the ground.

"Gosh!" Ava whispered in an anguished tone. "My toes, calves, arms, everything – my entire body from end to end, is aching! The palms of my hands are sore, scraped from inching along the tower's wall. Even the right side of my face is sore from sliding along the wall. I cannot even begin to imagine how tough the hardest part of the climb, crossing the gate, is going to be!"

Despite her exhaustion and the pain tormenting her body and mind, Ava pressed on. Her progress was owing to her tenacity and her strongmindedness. She continued to inch along the ledge slowly. Unexpectedly, her heart began to race, and she started to feel strangely dizzy, shaky, uncertain.

She was at the right side of the gate. She stared at it with a dazed, skeptical expression. The gate seemed impossible to traverse without hopping to the ground. However, her grandfather had said it could be done. He and his brother had crossed the gate many times. Something inside her brain, the very something responding to the pain wracking her limbs, was telling her to quit, to abandon her conquest. She shook her head vigorously as she tried to ignore the resigning feelings.

I am not going to quit! Not after going this far and being nearly halfway around the tower. Perhaps I should place my left foot onto one of the rungs. So, I can stretch a bit and give the left side of my body a chance to rest, especially my toes. It should give the right side of my body a break as well.

Despite the thoughts burning inside her brain, oddly, she did not move. Her aching toes that were precariously perched on the ledge started to lose all feeling. If she did not do something to move about, soon they would be fast asleep. Then she would be forced to hop from the ledge to start all over again – or worse, abandon her pursuit.

Suddenly, a sense of refreshing, rejuvenating, intense resolve seemed to engulf her entire body. The feeling in her toes sprang back to life. Her muscles no longer ached. Her head cleared the doubt that had held it captive for nearly ten minutes as she stood, seemingly frozen in place.

Gosh! I do not know what is happening, but I feel great! Is it possible that my lengthy breather has rekindled my strength?

She unexpectedly set out imagining events of her past. Fleeting scenes exploded before her mind's eye like bursting firework spectacles on the Fourth of July. She was racing across the basketball court. Her team had won! Next, she was in a concert. She and her fellow musicians were playing "Tchaikovsky's 1812 Overture." The scenes vanished.

She yelled at the top of her voice, "What's going on?"

When suddenly, she was watching the Holocaust movie *Shindler's List* with her mother and sisters. She was swimming in the lake. Sitting in history class. Reading a book about a daring warrior of a world beyond and a pixie named I Dunno. In front of her class narrating a book report about the book. Standing in line at McDonald's. Visiting her cousin's farm in Tennessee. Bouncing a huge, red ball. This time as a little girl. Swinging high in the air as her mother pushed her ever higher and higher. Laughing girlishly. Sitting in a highchair stealing food from her sister's plate. Staring up at a baby mobile hanging over her crib, its cute honey bears going round and round tirelessly as music played on.

She unexpectedly yelled as loudly as her voice could go, "Oh my gosh, now I am a baby! What is happening to me!"

As quickly as the scenes showed, they stopped abruptly. A strange silence seemed to saturate her surroundings. She wanted to jump from the ledge, to escape the madness she had witnessed in her mind's eye. Yet she was powerless to move a muscle. Her eyes widened as she stared panic-stricken with disbelief. The century-old padlock on the tower's wooden door had snapped open all by itself! It set out swinging back and forth slowly on its shackle! A moment later it freed itself from the staple of the hasp and fell to the ground with a deafening *Clang!* The door promptly swung wide-open, its corroded hinges squealing a high-pitched, shrill shriek of what was to come. A blast of musty, stale air rushed from the door's opening causing Ava to feel sick to her stomach.

A split-second later, the rusted padlock on the century-old wrought iron gate snapped open! It too swung back and forth on its shackle until it freed itself from the staple. It fell to the concrete with a disgusting *Clank!* A second later the gate started to open gradually. All the while, its rusted hinges were squealing with a stridently loud, torturous, *Screeeeeeech!* The screeching reminded Ava of disgusting-looking alien monsters in a Sci-fi movie she had seen. She very much wanted to cover her ears, but she could not move! When suddenly, she was forcibly yanked from the tower's ledge by some unseen, powerful force. Whatever it was that had grabbed her swiftly carried her inside the tower. The wind was knocked out of her when she landed on her back. Fortunately, she was not injured.

As she sat shell-shocked on the cold floor, she heard the wrought iron gate slam shut. Then the wooden door slammed shut. A few seconds later the clanking of the padlocks as they closed told her she was locked inside.

Everything was pitch-black.

CHAPTER 7

GNAÈFA – THE SPIRE OF TIME

"Never listen to your fears. They know nothing of your incredible power."
—Stephanie JoAnne Galanos

1

One would think that Ava's initial reaction would be to start pounding on the walls in a desperate attempt to escape the tower. That tears of hysterical horror would be gushing from her panic-stricken eyes. That she would be screaming, "Help! Somebody! I want to get out of here! Help me please!" Astonishingly, she did nothing of the sort. She merely sat cross-legged in the dark patiently waiting for something, anything to happen. She was behaving in a relaxed and composed, contemplative, inquisitive way. Yes, she was a little scared. Who wouldn't be given what just happened to her? Imagining things of her past back to when she was a baby. Being whisked forcefully inside the tower by some unseen force. Predictably, she was more curious than anything. Her inquisitiveness was going all-out. Wondering how and why and what caused her to be whisked inside the tower.

The walls are too thick, she pondered without a word. The day is too stormy. No one in her or his right mind is going to take a stroll by the tower on a day like this. No one is going to play ball in the open meadow. Also, it is rush hour on Grider Street. That is why I chose this time of day to climb the tower. Therefore, hoping someone from outside is going to hear my calls for help is plain, foolish idiocy. Whatever is going to happen will happen soon enough, and there is not a thing I can do about it. She

51

rubbed the back of her neck to ease the tension that seemed to be inching up from her spine. But I swear, if whatever is going to happen is too shockingly frightening when it occurs, I will scream. Yes, I will scream until something stops me, someone outside hears me, or I pass out.

She shouted to the darkness angrily, "As much good as it is going to be to call out for help from inside a tower with thick, century-old concrete walls!"

She suddenly realized that she was shivering, not because she was overly scared but because her sweater was damp. She removed her sweater and began to feel warmer almost immediately. She called out once more. "Hello, hello? Is anyone in here?"

There must be someone in here. If there is not, how did I get in here? What caused the padlocks to unlock and the doors to open and close on their own? No human being could have made all those things happen as quickly as they did. Likewise, if someone had physically pulled me inside the tower, which I seriously doubt, I would have seen him or her.

She yelled in a furious tone, "Hey, you, whoever you are, the joke is over! Please turn on the lights. Or at least say something. Even better show yourself. I am really starting to get annoyed here!" She lowered her voice and said to herself in a soft tone, "Not to mention I am getting more worried, and yeah, more scared as the second's tick by. Moreover, I wonder if there is enough air inside to keep me alive until someone finds me?" Suddenly, goose pimples hastily raced across her shoulders causing her to shiver yet again.

She thought to herself, I never told anyone I was going to climb the tower! No one knows I am in here! But even if I did tell someone, they would never suspect that I am trapped inside, would they? The doors are locked. I saw that the tower's front door was locked, and I heard the back doors lock as well. What is worse, I bet the fire department almost certainly will not be coming in here like forever. After all, this is an unused, ancient, derelict tower. It long ago outlived its purpose. Does this mean I am trapped in here for life? Gosh, I hope not! She was shaking her head as a miserable look appeared on her face. Whispering to herself once more she said, "Smart Ava, smart! You have really outdone yourself this time, haven't you!"

At one point she thought about crawling around in the dark to try and find the doors. But she had no idea where exactly the doors were. Besides, there was no light inside the tower and no way of knowing which way to crawl. She could be crawling around in circles and never get back to where she started. She also knew, even if she were to find either of the doors, she could not open them. They were padlocked from the outside. Thus, there was no point in crawling around, so she remained in her spot.

After a while, she noticed that her leg muscles were starting to stiffen because she had been sitting cross-legged for so long. She stretched out her legs and massaged her upper thighs and calves. She removed her sopping wet tennis shoes and socks and rubbed her aching toes.

Ah, this feels so good. I have no idea how long I was on the ledge. How many attempts did it take for me to reach the gate finally? Three, four, maybe more? I also wonder how long it took me to get as far as I got. Oh well, I guess it does not matter anymore. I did not complete my climb. She shook her head and whispered to herself, "I failed."

Suddenly, a dismal feeling of loneliness and slowly building fright began to overwhelm her. Her chin began to tremble. She started to weep. Even in the dark, where no one could see that she was crying, she was ashamed of her tears. She considered that crying was a sign of weakness and still does to this day. She wiped the tears away and swallowed hard. Then she slumped forward and drew her knees to her chest. A few moments later she fell asleep sitting up.

2

Ava did not know how long she had been asleep when she was roused by the soft glow of light. The milky-white glow was coming through an opening in the tower's floor. The opening was quite large. It was a little over six feet from where she was sitting. She considered that it was a good thing she did not crawl around in the dark. She could have fallen head over heels into the hole!

She slipped on her socks and tennis shoes – they were dry – and tied the sleeves of her sweater around her neck. She slowly crawled toward the opening in the floor from where the light was coming. When she reached the edge of the opening, she let out a loud gasp. She was looking down at what appeared to be a bottomless chasm. A rickety looking, corroded wrought iron staircase ambled from where she was crouching down to somewhere far below. The light's soft glow seemed to radiate from the base of the chasm.

Oh, my goodness! It is a long spiral staircase that leads – she narrowed her eyes – to where I cannot see, but the bottom sure is way down there!

She backed up a couple of feet and looked around the inside of the tower. The tower's innards were nothing but hazy, dark shadows. Since she could not see anything recognizable or even meaningful, she crawled back to the hole. She was shocked to see that the staircase did not appear to be attached to the hole's opening. She scratched her head in thought.

It is like the staircase is suspended in the air! I bet its only support is at its base. And the treads, the stair treads are of the floating variety. Ah yes, now I remember. What I am looking at are called cantilever stairs because there are no supports between the treads. Thus, the stairs have the illusion of floating in midair. And my goodness! There are no handrails or balusters, at least as far down as I can see. So, the staircase must be super unstable and dangerous. But how in the world did I get from ground level to the top of this staircase? Then again, does the staircase lead to something deep beneath the tower's base? I wonder if I should descend the staircase. Maybe it is down there, from where the light is coming, that I will find a way to escape this insanity.

She suddenly remembered she had deposited her backpack at the tower's entranceway landing. She knew there was no way she could have climbed the tower with the backpack strapped to her back. She would have been way off balance. She figured she would retrieve it after completing the climb or failing to do so.

Oh no! I left my cellphone back home along with my ID. Mom will be calling or texting me before long if she has not already done so. She will discover that I left my phone and wallet on my dresser. She will be frantic. She will probably call the police because she will be thinking I have vanished. Which I have! Then they will find all that remains of me – my backpack! Since I forgot my phone and wallet, there will be no way for authorities to know who I am!

Without warning, the strange voice-thoughts Ava had perceived when she was outside the tower revisited her. As they had earlier, the voice-thoughts were not entering through her ears. They seemed to be speaking in her head although, oddly, they were crystal clear, unlike anything she had ever experienced. Also, unlike her normal thoughts, to include those of her dueling twin consciences, Peg and Ida, the thoughts did not belong to her. They were the voice-thoughts of someone or something else. As before, they seemed to belong to a female.

"Ava, do not be afraid," the voice-thoughts said. "You are safe here. I assure you. After all, this is your tower, the place of safety. "Also, do not worry about your parents and sisters, your friends, everyone else. They do not know you are here."

"Do not know I am here?" Ava said aloud as she squinted at the tower's shadowy walls. She shouted sarcastically in a booming voice, "Of course, they do not know I am here! How could they actually? I am lost, locked inside this tower! Soon, they will be frantic with worry, that is, if they are not going crazy with worry even now. I bet they have already called the police!" Her eyes began to mist over as she imagined how frantic and worried her parents and sisters were. She added in a screaming voice, "But they will never find me, never see me again. Unless I figure out a way to get out of here!" Her voice abruptly became softer, pleading. "Can you help me?"

She sat up and shook her head dolefully. She repeated back what she had just said as a question. "*Can you help me?* How stupid of a question is that?" She ran her hands through her hair. She noticed it was a tangled mess. Clumps of dried mud were clinging to the strands. She unconsciously began to straighten the strands and remove the clumps of mud with her fingers. "What in the world am I doing – thinking? I am talking to myself! Asking myself if I can help myself! Am I going crazy? What if—"

"You are not going crazy, Ava," the strange voice-thoughts interrupted. "And you are not talking to yourself."

"To whom am I talking?" Ava shouted testily. She scrambled to her feet, wisely stepping away from the hole in the floor. She folded her arms over her chest and looked around the darkness. Her eyes were probing, on the lookout for any sign of movement. She noticed that she had been

55

biting the inside of her cheek nervously. The taste of blood seemed especially nasty. She swallowed hard and said, "If I am indeed talking to someone and not going crazy, obviously she, assuming you are a female, should respect my wishes. As a matter of simple civility. She, that would be you, whoever you are, should give me the courtesy of revealing herself to me!" She cringed once again with the thought that she could be talking to herself, that she was going completely insane.

The voice-thoughts said, "You are not going insane, Ava. And you are not talking to yourself. You are talking to *me*. My name is Jordyn." Jordyn's voice-thoughts paused for a few moments, so Ava could register in her mind what she had said. "Unfortunately, I cannot be seen. But about your parents—"

Cutting Jordyn off mid-sentence, Ava snapped, "What *about* my parents? What do they have to do with you not showing yourself to me? And what in the world do you mean when you say you cannot be seen? Everybody is capable of being seen unless he or she is invisible." She rolled her eyes and snickered. In a dreadfully nasty tone that was brimming with sarcasm, she said, "And I seriously doubt you are invisible. Being invisible is the stuff of fairy tales. Do not think I am stupid or something because, for your information, I am a teenager. I turned thirteen in December, so I know stuff. Lots of stuff. Probably more than you can imagine." She turned up her nose and hissed, "Like being invisible is just plain dumb, at least in real life."

Jordyn's voice-thoughts asserted, "As I just said, your parents and everyone else that you love and know will not miss you. And yes, Ava, I am invisible. Utterly invisible, at least to you. You must have trust in my words."

"And why won't my parents miss me?" Ava said indignantly in a trailing voice that was very nearly inaudible. She was pouting and almost on the brink of tears. "Tell me the reason why my parents will not miss me!" She pointed her finger at the ceiling. "Just so you know, they love me! And I am missing, having vanished without a trace, at least in their minds." She turned around slowly, her eyes once more scrutinizing the darkness. "Also, how about answering my question why it is you cannot be seen." She clenched her fists tightly. "Can you at least do that for me? Like right now! Because once I see you, I am going to punch you right in the nose for scaring me like this and making me think I am going insane!" She whirled around in a circle and said angrily, "For telling me that my parents are not going to miss me too!" She quickly realized she was being too curt with the owner of the unseen voice. She added a polite, inquiring, "If you please. Can you show yourself?"

"You may find what I am about to tell you as untruths, Ava," Jordyn's voice-thoughts said. "Things that are hard to believe. But hear me out. Also, please sit back down. I am afraid you may plunge head over heels down the staircase, and that is the last thing I want to happen to you."

"How in the heck do you know I am standing up?" Ava shouted. She slowly moved in a complete circle, her eyes continuing to seek out something, anything in the murky darkness. "Where are you, Jordyn? If that truly is your name."

"I am here, Ava," Jordyn's voice-thoughts said. "Also, Jordyn is my true name. Once I explain myself, you undoubtedly will recall who and of what I am capable."

Ava thought wordlessly, I do recognize the name, Jordyn. Maybe from something I read? She shouted, "If you are here, why is it I cannot see you?"

Jordyn's voice-thoughts said, "I must ask you again to sit down on the floor. Please. I will tell you everything once I know you are safely sitting on the floor." Jordyn's voice-thoughts seemed to chuckle inside Ava's mind. "Also, yes, you have seen my name before today, in a book given to you by your great uncle. It is a book about the tales of a teenager much like yourself. But you have yet to finish the book. Now, please sit down and try to relax."

Although she was reluctant to obey commands from someone or something she could not see or hear, Ava sat on the floor in a huff. She drew her knees to her chest and pouted. The tower's chill had returned, probably a draft from the hole in the floor. She put on her sweater. She was happy that it had dried out completely while she slept.

"Jordyn," Ava said softly, "I think, and I know this may sound weird, I think I heard you laugh a few seconds ago. It was when your voice-thoughts said I had, in fact, seen your name in a book I started to read but I haven't finished."

"Indeed, Ava, I can read your mind, and what you thought you heard *was* my laughter."

"That is incredible, truly incredible," Ava said. "Does that mean if I want to address you, all I have to do is think of something, and you will know what I am thinking?"

"Exactly. It is okay to either think a thought or to say what you are thinking out loud. You can converse with me either way, verbally or in your mind. Moreover, I usually know what you are going to say before you even open your mouth and say it. Due to the fact that the human brain processes our thoughts a split-second before the organs of speech form the words."

"That is incredible!" Ava shouted excitedly. "All the organs of speech – the voice box, the lungs, the oral and nasal cavities, the tongue, the lips, all of it – need to unite before words are formed. It is a complex process. So, before any of that can even occur, you already have read my thoughts? That is so cool!" She added lightheartedly with a pleased grin, "I learned all that stuff in my science class. Science is my favorite subject because it tends to quench my curiosity. So, why bother talking in the first place, huh?"

"Impressive," Jordyn's voice-thoughts inferred. "You truly are a scientific genius as your middle sister is fond of saying, usually in jest I must add. By the way Ava, it is now tomorrow. You slept over twelve hours. Probably why you are so hungry now. I can sense that your stomach is growling."

"Oh, so you know my sister, Jami?" Ava asked in a skeptical tone, completely ignoring that Jordyn had said she had slept twelve hours and her stomach was growling. "What else do you know about me, my family, my friends?"

"I know everything about you, Ava. Everything possible there is to know."

Ava's overpowering curiosity was now in play completely. Having ignored the fact that Jordyn said she could read her mind, she thought to herself; so, Jordyn thinks she knows everything about me, huh? I seriously doubt it. I am going to test her.

"Oh, really Jordyn? If you know so much about me, when was the last time Jami said I was a scientific genius? What were we discussing at the time?"

Jordyn said, "It was a friendly argument. You were complaining about your sisters' snoring. You had said, and I repeat what you said word for word, 'You sound like two out of breath, snoring and snotting freight trains racing each other down the tracks in the middle of the night.' She had said it when you were camping.'"

Ava was slightly embarrassed for testing Jordyn's mind-reading ability and doubting her word. Nonetheless, she felt wonderful. Because she was acknowledging the facts that were staring at her in the face. Magic, miracles, invisibility, strange phenomena, telepathy, all those things that resist scientific realism and physics; they were real. And she was experiencing some of it right then and there!

"Jordyn," Ava began cautiously, "as you almost certainly know, sometimes I tend to speak before I engage my mind properly. It is one of my bad habits, I must admit. When I do, it may come across that I am rude, even if I do not mean to be. Perhaps I should abide by the wise words of that Indian Mahatma I read about in English class. If I recollect his words accurately, he had said, 'Speak only if it improves the silence.'" She cleared her throat. "I apologize if I have offended you, Jordyn. It is just that everything that has happened to me is nothing short of a miracle."

Jordyn replied, "One of Mahatma's other quotes relates to you quite nicely, Ava. It is worth repeating."

Be the change you want to see in the world.

"Now, Ava, about your parents, loved ones, and friends. You need not worry about them. Please trust me when I say this. They do not know you have vanished. You are with them doing the things you normally do. That is because you are now two beings. One is here conversing with me. The other is home at this very moment helping your mother bake a cake. It will be the first cake you have ever baked."

Ava was very relieved knowing she would not be missed, triggering her family to be concerned. "That is good. I would not want them to worry about me. I love them too much." She rubbed her forehead. "But how, Jordyn; how is it I am there at home with them but here with you at the same time? How is that possible? Has time stopped for them, for me?"

"Time has not stopped," Jordyn said. "Can you recall what your grandfather said? What he said about climbing the tower and feeling like he was in another world, another dimension?"

Ava replied as she closed her eyes, "Yes, I remember. Grandpa Jim also said, and I think I can quote his words precisely, 'When we climbed the tower, we were in a new province, like our very own innermost world.' Am I correct, Jordyn? Were those his exact words?'"

"Yes, Ava, you are correct, impressively so given that your unique recall ability allows you to remember word for word what your grandfather said over a year ago."

"So, I am in another dimension, my own innermost world?"

"Yes, Ava, you are."

3

Ava said, "Once again I must apologize, this time for interrupting you a while ago. You had said something about one of Gandhi's quotes that pertained to me." Before she could say anything further, she stared straight ahead in shock and began to shiver. Someone or something had tapped her on the shoulder! Dreadful thoughts began to flash through her mind.

Suddenly, a light turned on illuminating her surroundings with its bright glow. She remained in place and kept silent, all the while gawking at the dancing shadows that were splayed on the wall. They were a double act. She knew that one of the shadows belonged to her. As far as the other shadow that was holding the light was concerned, she had no clue. She quickly balled her hands to tight fists and placed them in front of her face. She was prepared to go down fighting if that is what she had to do. She turned around slowly and quickly dropped her hands to her sides.

Standing before her was a beautiful, female teenager. She looked like she was seventeen or eighteen years old. She was the one that was holding the source of the light. It was a battery-operated Coleman lantern. The teenager was a couple of inches taller than Ava. She had long brown hair and dark brown eyes. She was grinning. Her charming grin highlighted a pretty dimple in the heart of her right cheek.

"Gosh! You are gorgeous," Ava exclaimed, "even though you scared the wits out of me!" Promptly realizing what she had just said to a stranger, she sputtered, "Oh, I truly am sorry. I tend to say what is on my mind. Nevertheless, you sure are pretty." She tilted her head to one side as a questionable look appeared on her face. "Are you Jordyn? If you are, you had said that I would not be able to see you."

"No, I am not Jordyn," the teenager said in a gentle tone. She glanced around the tower. "But Jordyn is here, well, as much as she can taking into consideration her manner." She extended her hand. "My name is Stephanie, Stephanie JoAnne Galanos. My parents, sister, and friends call me Steph."

"It is a pleasure to meet you, Steph. My name is Ava Noelle. Most people call me Ava."

"That is a pretty name," Steph said. "Christmassy too. If you do not mind me asking, Ava, what is your last name?"

"Noelle," Ava said bluntly. "Most people think Noelle is my middle name. It is my surname. I do not have a middle name." She gave Steph a playful grin. "I am just me, plain ole, Christmassy Ava Noelle." She bowed at the waist and said with a sweeping wave of her hand, "At your service."

Steph held out her hand for Ava to shake it. She said, "Well, it is a pleasure to meet you." After they shook hands, she began to spin slowly in a small circle. She was illuminating their surroundings with the light of the lantern. "Seems like nothing is in here but a circular wall and a bunch of rusty pipes." She peered down the large opening in the floor. "And that lengthy spiral staircase with the soft glow of light at the bottom. It looks pretty dangerous if you were to ask me."

Ava opened her mouth to say something, but nothing came out. Instead, she just stood staring at Steph. Her mind was racing, and she had a bewildered expression on her face. When, after a few uncomfortable seconds she finally was able to speak, she said in a cautious manner, "Okay, Steph, first things first. What are you doing here? And how in the world did you get in here? Is there another way out?" She glanced around. "I certainly hope so."

Steph replied, "I honestly do not know why I am here, where *here* is actually. But it is good to be here. How I got here, I assumed you knew." She had a quizzical expression on her face. "Naturally, Jordyn brought me here."

Ava said, "Have you been with me the entire time? I mean, how did you manage to get through the gate and doors? I heard the backdoor and gate lock behind me when I was whisked in here. Yesterday. I supposedly have been in here since yesterday. At least that is what Jordyn said."

Steph replied with a shrug of her shoulders, "I did not arrive through the gate or doors. I did not even know this place has doors. I was in my barn back home in Tennessee. That is where my horse Spirit is. When Jordyn asked me to grab the lantern off the shelf and make sure the battery was good." She hunched her shoulders and frowned. "The next thing I knew I was standing beside you. Where are we anyway? Do you know?"

"We are inside a tower in the city of Buffalo, New York. At least I believe that we are. I was climbing the tower wall – well, frankly, I was climbing along an edge on the tower wall. Then poof! I was whisked inside before I could react. Jordyn told me that I fell asleep. She said I had slept for twelve hours. She and I struck up a conversation when poof again!" She waved her hand down her sides and smiled self-consciously. "And here I stand, plain ole me, Christmassy Ava Noelle. All of this is truly astonishing if you want to know the truth."

Steph stared at Ava with apparent, renewed interest. "Sounds pretty exciting. Why were you climbing the tower wall? Do you rappel? If so, that is pretty cool."

Ava said, "No, I do not rappel, and rappelling was not involved. I set out to climb the tower so I could further my family's legacy. My grandfather and great uncle climbed the wall when they were teenagers nearly three-quarters of a century ago. Climbing the tower wall involves traveling around it on a sloping, two-inch ledge without hopping to the ground. The ledge is about five feet from the base of the tower. I thought it was a rather good idea at the time." She did a half shrug and gestured with her hand at the dancing shadows on the wall. "Now, I am not so sure given that we seem to be stuck in here." She gave Steph a suspicious, glancing look. "So, you do not know how you got in here or why you are here? Yet you said Jordyn brought you here. Do you know why she did that?"

Steph was shaking her head. "As I stated earlier, I do not know why I am here. But one thing I know for certain. And I suspect you do as well. Jordyn's telepathic powers and ability to move people from one place to another are amazing. Do you agree?"

"Yep, I must agree. Although, no offense, I do not like being stuck in here."

Steph said, "To be perfectly honest with you, I never expected to hear from Jordyn again. Especially considering she had previously sent me on a few exciting adventures. I am thrilled that she has called on me yet again. Even if I am only here for a short time. And I must say this, Ava. Jordyn is the sweetest, most adorable person I know. I have never met her, but I understand much about her past. I also have had the pleasure of observing her from a distance."

Ava appeared perplexed. She shoved her hands in her pockets and walked off. After a few seconds, she turned around and said in a doubtful tone, "Hold on a second. You have never met Jordyn in person? Yet she spoke to you. I mean, communicated with you telepathically – as she did with me?"

Steph said, "Yes, she did. She spoke to me telepathically across many miles, even across three centuries. She transported me back in time too. I was in Nazi, Germany, during World War Two, way across the Atlantic. All the while she was in touch with me telepathically. I was in the mid-eighteen hundreds on a Southern plantation. It was a year before the Civil War. And she was with me, perhaps not physically but in my mind and heart. She saved my life on both occasions. Maybe not directly. But if it were not for her, I would have been a goner for sure.

"Afterward, she relocated me across time and space to the mid-1960s. It was there I befriended a handful of unforgettable people like I had in Germany and on the plantation. Finally, she moved me back in time to an orphanage that dated back to the early 1900s. Just about the whole time, except for a brief period when I was in the 1960s and at the orphanage, she and I communicated telepathically."

Ava said with a dismissive wave of her hand, "I am sorry, Steph. But I simply cannot believe what you said is true! Please understand that I *want* to believe you. I truly do. After all, I figure why would you lie to me, especially considering we are standing inside a tower illuminated by your lantern only." She pointed to the opening on the floor. "And yes, along with that weird light down at the bottom of the nasty-looking staircase. Frankly, I cannot even begin to imagine how incredibly exciting it would have been to go back in time. I have always dreamed of going back in time. I obsess about it more than I should. Then again—" She abruptly stopped talking and began to eye Steph up and down suspiciously.

As much as she wanted to, Ava could not bring herself to believe everything Steph had said was true. She had to look the other way to avoid Steph's imploring eyes. She placed one hand on her hip and whispered, "But what am I saying? How is it possible you traveled back in time, across centuries, across the ocean of all things? Also, as you say, while traveling across time and space Jordyn was linking with you telepathically. Yes, Steph, I too enjoy reading about fantasy tales and adventure stories. I enjoy reading about dragons and other fantastic creatures too. However, what you said sounds like something straight out of a fairytale. I simply cannot believe all that happened, everything you said was real." She moved back a few steps and looked at Steph straight in the eyes. "Perhaps you are lying to me, trying to make me feel good given our predicament? You would not do that to me, would you?"

Steph had stood silent the entire time Ava had been talking. When Ava implied that she had been lying to her, a pained look showed on her face. She lowered her head and stared at the floor through teary eyes.

In reaction, Ava spread her hands out wide and mumbled, "Oh, I am deeply sorry if I insulted you. I did not intend to do it. Sometimes I speak before I think. The more you get to know me the more you will understand. And I certainly was not implying that what you said is untrue. But honestly, Steph, it sounds too exciting, too unreal, too fairytale-like, and way too adventuresome to be true. However, to be honest with you I truly wish it were. Lord knows I wish everything you said was authentic. For one simple reason. Everything that has happened to me up until now with this blasted tower also seems just as unreal. So maybe, just maybe anything is possible to include everything that you said." She stared at Steph, her eyes pleading. "Does any of what I just said make sense to you?"

Steph looked up. As she wiped at her tears she said in a soft tone, "It does make sense, Ava. Nevertheless, what I said, what I experienced – all of it happened. Honestly, it did." She crossed her heart. "I swear to it. And if my suspicions are correct, you too will live through some if not more of what I experienced."

Ava smiled at her for a few moments. She muttered glumly, "Honestly, Steph, I am sorry if I insulted you. Please forgive me."

"No problem, Ava. And yes, of course, I forgive you even though there is no forgiving to be had. Just so you know, you and one other are the only persons I have ever talked to about my dealings with Jordyn and my exciting adventures across time and space. I did not tell my parents or sister either. For the simple reason that no one even knew I had disappeared. I guess it is the same with you. Your psyche may be in two places at once. Frankly, I cannot blame you for being skeptical. I would feel the same way if I were in your shoes." She rolled her eyes and said with a chuckle, "The main reason I never told anyone until now, well, no one would have believed me. But seeing that you and I are standing here," she gestured to the hole in the floor, "next to a gaping hole that contains a worn-out spiral staircase, now is a good time to tell my story."

"Who was the other person that you talked to about your story?" Ava asked.

"It was the man that wrote the book about my adventures. The book is called *The Spirit Within, Tale of a Fearless Heart: A Story of a Teen's Love and Compassion.* It is a book of fiction, obviously unattributable to me." She chuckled once more and rolled her eyes sillily as she twirled her forefinger at the side of her forehead. "I did not want anyone to think I was crazy, one step away from the looney bin!"

"So, what was it like?" Ava asked excitedly. "Were you in real danger? Did you get to fight and all that?" She clenched her fists in tight balls and pretended to land a punch with her right fist. "Did you get to kick butt? I bet you did because you look really strong."

Steph replied in a casual tone, "Yes, I faced a bit of danger. I was in Nazi Germany when soldiers shot at Spirit and me. They also had attacked me physically, tried to wrestle me to the ground. The shooting started outside a cathedral as Spirit and I hid behind a bullet-pocked wall. There was a war going on, and we were in the middle of it. Thanks to Jordyn's coaching, I managed to race safely to the cathedral.

"There, inside the cathedral, is where I saw an emaciated young boy, a Jew. He was being hunted by the soldiers. I was attacked physically by the soldiers inside the cathedral. One even shot at me. But I managed to escape, along with Spirit and the boy. His name was Adalard. Without Jordyn's guidance and support, I would have been, like I said, a goner. There also was the time, back here in America, that an evil Southern plantation owner pointed his rifle at me." Steph seemed to tremble ever so slightly as she recollected the incident. "I have to admit that was much scarier. I thought for sure he was going to shoot me! He hated me that much. It was on his plantation where I liberated three of his slaves. They were siblings, two girls, and a handsome teenager. When the plantation owner discovered I had freed his slaves, well, you can imagine his furor."

What Ava said next had nothing whatsoever to do with what Steph had been saying. Once again, as is her way, she had said something completely out of the blue. "Where is Jordyn, Steph? Is she here with us?" She pointed down the spiraling staircase. It seemed to go on forever. "From where that eerie light seems to be coming?"

Steph shrugged her shoulders. "Beats me. But this much I do know. Jordyn has a special mission for you – probably to help or to save others. She may not always communicate with you telepathically. I know that for a fact. I often worried about her not staying in touch. Looking back now I know why she, to put it in my own words, wanted me to be on my own.

"Being on my own without direct guidance or contact with her allowed me to be myself. I had to do things that I normally would not have done because I was young and inexperienced. As the saying goes, I had to think on my feet. I had to respond to situations that were both scary and foreign to me. However, by doing what I needed to do, I discovered who I truly was, who I truly am. I spoke to everyone I encountered from my heart. And my actions were from my heart as well. I suspect Jordyn will have you do similar things. I am not certain. Your experience could be completely different than mine. I have no way of knowing."

Ava said, "Why is it Jordyn speaks to you and me in our minds, Steph? Why does she not appear before us in person?"

With another shrug, Steph replied, "I do not know. Maybe she will appear before you in person at some time. You will have to wait and see. All I know is that I only had a glimpse of her as she sat across the street from my house. Looking back, perhaps what I think I saw was nothing more than a figment of my imagination. The light was extremely poor. Also, I was exhausted, mentally, emotionally, and physically from my many adventures. As to why Jordyn does not speak to us in the normal way, you know, through our sense of hearing, once again I am not certain. However, this much I do know. Jordyn is deaf. She has been deaf since birth." She kicked at the floor with the toe of her shoe. Her smile had vanished, and she looked distraught. Like Ava, she was thinking that she could not even begin to imagine what it would be like to be deaf.

"Also, Ava, there is something you need to know. Jordyn was in an orphanage most of her life – until she became of age. She was picked on unmercifully as a child and as a teenager. Physically and emotionally. Despite the horrific pain, suffering, and mental anguish she endured, she moved on. She wanted to help others. Thus, having me help those in need was her way to display her true love and compassion for others, her method of showing forgiveness. Through me.

"As I said earlier, Jordyn once whisked me to a more modern time – to the 1960s. It was there I befriended a teenager and his wonderful family. His name is Christopher. He has spastic cerebral palsy. Just like others with disabilities back in the 1960s, Christopher endured hateful bullying. People silently ridiculed him with insulting stares and tauntingly pointing fingers. Of course, they did not know better. People with disabilities were hidden from public view during that era. Nevertheless, the cruelty Christopher suffered did not stop him from pursuing his goals. He graduated early from Yale and went on to help others afflicted with deadly and debilitating diseases, to include cerebral palsy. As far as I know, he is still actively involved in helping others.

"Finally, as I said, Jordyn sent me back in time to the early twentieth century, to her orphanage where she was raised. I met her bullying tormentor, Roger Clyde. At the time Roger was just a child himself. I also met the woman in charge of the orphanage. Perhaps she did not know any better, but she too was a horrendous bully. Yes, things were different in the old days than they are now. But even back then she should have known better that what she was doing was wrong. She evilly used a leather belt as a disciplinary tool. She taunted and scolded Roger unmercifully. I could tell.

"Jordyn had not yet become a resident at the orphanage when I was there. She would not enter the children's home until much later. Although I understood why Roger, the boy who bullied Jordyn later in her life, acted out his bullying at her. He too was bullied as a little boy. And, like Jordyn, he suffered a disability." She crossed her arms over her chest and heaved a sigh.

"Well, that is my story about how Jordyn and I interacted as friends. Thanks to her challenging me, guiding me, and allowing me to help children in need, today I am a much better person. I really owe my love and compassion for others to her."

4

Ava stood rooted to the spot and seemed to be genuinely impressed with what Steph had said. After a few moments, she exclaimed, "Wow. I am totally amazed, Steph. You did all that?" Steph was blushing when she replied that she had.

In the brief period Ava had known Steph, she had come to admire the older girl immensely. Steph looked exceptionally powerful, and Ava thought her athleticism must be superb. Steph would later go on to tell her that she was recently chosen as her undefeated rugby team's MVP (most valuable player). When Ava considered Steph's condensed, but genuinely exciting, almost unbelievable story, she was convinced that Steph was incredibly brave and loyal as well. That was unquestionable because she had been confronted by evildoers and equally trying circumstances. Likewise, Ava could tell that Steph was super smart. She had to be to think on her feet the way that she had.

Ava was also a little envious of Steph's thrilling adventures that Jordyn had put her through. How incredibly exciting it must have been to travel back and forth over the Atlantic and across centuries. As she mulled over everything that Steph had said, Steph was standing motionless before her. Her eyes were closed. She appeared to be deep in thought. She nodded her head every now and then, and she mumbled a few words every so often. Ava correctly assumed she was conversing with Jordyn telepathically. After a few moments, Steph's eyes snapped open, and she looked Ava straight in the eyes. Ava managed to hold her gaze even though she was feeling incredibly nervous. She was certain that whatever Steph and Jordyn had been discussing had everything to do with her. And when others said things about her of which she was ignorant, she got nervous, even a bit upset. Understandably so.

At last, Steph said out loud, "Okay, Jordyn, I understand. And yes, I hope and pray you will be in touch with me before long. I have missed you these past two years!" She grabbed Ava's hand and began to guide her to the edge of the jagged hole. After a brief but strong hug, she gripped Ava's shoulders tightly.

"First, Ava, I must tell you this. You have to trust your instincts. You must have faith in yourself, your intellect, your abilities. Also, you have to follow your heart no matter what. Second, trust in Jordyn. When she contacts you telepathically, do exactly as she says. If you do exactly as she says you will be okay, and no harm will come to you. She placed the lantern on the floor next to the hole. "Can you trust me? Will you trust that what I just said is the truth, that Jordyn will keep you out of harm's way?"

Ava nodded her head halfheartedly and flashed a grim smile. She was shaking from head to toe because she finally understood the whys and wherefores, the reasons, and purposes of her nearly obsessive, year-long thirst to climb the tower.

It is because I must enter that forbidding, scary hole! To descend that scarier, rickety staircase. But why? Can it be that this is the only way out? Or is there another explanation?

Steph said in a calming tone, "I understand you are scared. And that is okay. Feeling scared is natural." She squeezed Ava's hand. "Lord knows I was scared on more than one occasion during my adventures. But I trusted Jordyn. Also, and perhaps more crucial, I had absolute confidence in myself, in my own abilities."

Ava tried, unsuccessfully, to ignore the tightness that seemed to be gripping her chest. She also attempted to dismiss the negative thoughts zooming like exploding rockets in her head; as well as the crushing misgivings blanketing her entire psyche. Even so, she managed to smile and said in a strong voice, "Yes, I am a bit scared, I must admit. Perhaps feeling overly anxious is a better way to describe how I am feeling. Yet for some strange reason, I also feel super positive, like I am a superwoman or something." She pressed her lips together as a slight quiver vibrated in her stomach. "But I know that is impossible. I am just little 'ole me, Ava Noelle," she flashed a forced grin, "your new Christmassy friend."

She looked into Steph's eyes. What she saw was honesty, love, compassion, but most of all, understanding. Steph had once been in her shoes, perhaps not exactly, but close enough to grasp what she was thinking and feeling. Steph gave her hand one last, firm squeeze. As tears welled up in her eyes, she said something that will remain in Ava's heart and mind until the end of time.

"Never listen to your fears. They know nothing of your incredible power."

CHAPTER 8

THE SPIRAL STAIRCASE

"History does not repeat itself. But it does rhyme."—*Mark Twain*

1

"My power?" Ava asked in a skeptical tone. "What power? To what kind of power are you referring?" Steph did not reply to her question. What she said instead caused Ava's skin to crawl.

"I am sorry, Ava. But Jordyn told me to remain up here at the opening in the floor while you step down the staircase. That way you will have adequate light from above, you know, so you do not stumble. She also said once you get far enough on the staircase, the lighting from below will be sufficient to guide you just properly."

Ava was giving Steph a disbelieving look. Her mouth opened wide. Beads of sweat began to develop above her upper lip. She said in a shaky, depressed tone, "Are you not coming with me?"

Steph slumped forward and crossed her arms over her chest. She was staring at the floor and shaking her head. Her lips were pinched together in a heartbreaking grimace. When she looked up, Ava saw that her eyes were bloodshot as if she were about to cry.

Ava could tell that Steph was disappointed just like her. That she would not be accompanying her inside the godforsaken hole in the floor. More so, she was relieved that Steph did not cry. If she had, Ava knew she would not be able to help herself. She too would have burst out in tears. But unlike Steph, who would be crying because she would not be descending the staircase; *Ava would be crying because she was!* Mercifully, she held back her tears even though it was extremely difficult to do so.

"No, Ava, I am not going with you," Steph said. Her tone was miserable. "If I were going with you, Jordyn would have told me by now. I guess she will send me home, to where I was before I arrived here — inside my barn hanging out with Spirit." She exhaled a long, put-upon sigh. "Even though I wish she would permit me to accompany you." Despite her disappointment, she somehow managed a sincere smile. "I feel as if I am long overdue for another exciting adventure. But I guess it is what it is. I must face the facts. I am not going anywhere." She added cheerily, "However, I just know you will have a wonderful adventure. To tell you the truth, I am envious. Because something tells me you are going to have a blast! I just wish I were going with you, to keep you company, and to keep you safe."

"But where is Jordyn?" Ava asked nervously. She glanced down the seemingly mile-long staircase. Despite her trust in Steph and marginal trust in Jordyn, butterflies were fluttering crazily in the pit of her stomach. She felt as though she was on the brink of all-out panic. But by inhaling deeply and slowly exhaling, she was able to keep her anxious feelings in check. She managed to speak in a faint whisper, "Is Jordyn or someone else going to meet me down there?"

"I have no idea," Steph replied in a frank tone. "But I can tell you this much. Jordyn will connect with you when the time is right. In the interim, you have to trust her — trust in yourself."

Ava said in an uneasy voice that bordered on being accusatory, "Trust her, Steph? How can I trust her when I do not even know her? Unlike you, I have not even seen her, or at least thought that I had! Jordyn and I just met an hour or so ago, crazily in our thoughts of all things!" She peered down at the staircase once more. "What is down there, Steph? Do you know?"

With a slight shrug of her shoulders, Steph said, "I do not know. If I knew I would tell you."

Jordyn's voice-thoughts suddenly entered Ava and Steph's minds. "It is called the Inner World, Ava. Your very own Inner World. Now, off you go one stair tread at a time. I promise you will be fine. Trust me."

Ava and Steph locked eyes. Ava could tell that Steph was happy to know she was about to travel to a place that was called the Inner World. However, she was disappointed that Steph was not going to accompany her. She had come to like Steph immensely, and she dreaded the thought of not seeing her again. Still, she knew that occasionally life tosses you a surprise. You get to see a good friend once more when it is least expected.

After a few moments, she looked away and gawked at the spiral staircase. She knew that it was even more dangerous than it looked. Goose pimples raced up from the small of her back and across her shoulders causing her to shiver once more. The staircase did not have safety handrails and balusters. Thus, there was nothing that she could hang on to for support, to keep her balance in case she was to trip. What was worse, she guessed that the rusty treads were only about two feet in length and ten inches in width if that. She was already imagining stepping carefully with her arms held out wide to keep from stumbling. If she made even one clumsy misstep, she would slip and cascade headlong to the abyss. Never to be seen again.

Steph got to her knees, and then she stretched out on her stomach at the edge of the hole. Ava knelt beside her. Steph grasped her beneath the armpit and said, "I will support you until you are out of my reach, okay?"

Ava nodded. She tried to reply but she was too afraid to say anything. She had the feeling that everything was moving too quickly. If she knew of a way out, she would have already fled.

With a thin smile, Steph said, "You got this, Ava. Have faith in yourself. Stay strong too. I will remain up here until you are safely at the bottom or Jordyn whisks me off to my home. I promise."

Ava was still unable to speak, so she mouthed a silent, "Thank you." She stared at Steph wide-eyed, her face pale, devoid of color. She was shivering. When suddenly, now that the moment of the unavoidable had arrived at last, her customarily stubborn self-confidence seemed to evaporate into thin air. Her extraordinary quest for knowledge and adventure vanished as well. In their places, along with dread and apprehension, were immense self-doubt and distrust. But most of all, there was unbelievable fear that was close to panic.

Her thoughts seemed to scream. I must be crazy! I do not want to go down there! Why am I trustful of someone I have never met? Goodness, it could be a nonhuman *something* instead of a someone! Why in the world am I trusting this invisible thing, this maker of voice-thoughts in my head that calls herself Jordyn? Could it be she is trying to deceive me? Is she even real? Or is she a ghost, perhaps an evil spirit?

But Steph is real. I felt her human touch, both in my hands and within my heart. I saw her tearful eyes, and I felt her disappointment because she will not be coming with me. And her understanding eyes! I could tell by her eyes that she would never deceive me, lie to me. Even though she said I must descend the staircase which I do not want to do. Because Jordyn had told her that I must.

She glared at the abyss of the staircase's underbelly from where the soft glow originated. What she saw caused her to cringe. She was imagining a bewitched evil eye was staring up at her contemptuously. The longer she stared the brighter and more ominous the wicked eye seemed to be. She started to tremble uncontrollably. Her mouth became desert dry. Nevertheless, she struggled gallantly to compose herself despite her nervousness. She laid her body flat alongside Steph. Without hesitating, she cautiously scooted her legs over the jagged rim of the hole one after the other. She placed her left foot firmly on the first stair tread followed closely by her right.

Steph was clasping her forearm firmly as she gingerly stood on the first tread. Predictably, the staircase was unstable. Even the smallest shifting of her feet caused the entire staircase to tremble to some extent. As she slowly but steadily stepped onto each successive tread, Steph gradually slid her gripping hand up Ava's arm to keep her steady. Just as she stepped onto the sixth tread, Steph moved her grasp onto Ava's left hand. She squeezed it firmly to give her one final smidgen of hope, that all was going to be okay. Two steps later, as she moved onto the eighth tread, Steph could no longer hold her hand and released it. She was on her own.

"Steady as she goes, Ava," Steph whispered from above. "You can do this. I have faith in you."

"Thank you, Steph," Ava replied as she looked up at her brand-new friend. "Thank you for helping me." With a forced smile, she added, "And for being my friend too. I hope to see you again someday. Soon."

Ava was pleasantly surprised that she no longer felt overly scared, nothing even comparable to how she had felt a few minutes earlier. She still was trembling, but nowhere as violently as before. She licked her lips. They were moist, and the nasty, dry taste in her mouth had practically disappeared. Finally, thankfully, her loudly pounding, previously racing heartbeats were beating at their normal, silently rhythmic tempo.

She instinctively understood why she was feeling better and more assured as she gradually returned to her intensely tenacious self. She had felt that way countless times before. She realized that her renewed vigor and self-confidence were owing to one factor, a special quirk of her character. Her incredible thirst for knowledge had taken control of her psyche. It was driving her forward eagerly, passionately in the direction of her objective. Toward another of life's fascinating adventures. This time, as Jordyn had said, to the Inner World, a world she hoped would be exciting.

She descended four more stair treads and paused. She turned about and glanced over her shoulder to the top of the staircase. The lantern was sitting on the edge of the hole. Its soft glow was illuminating the uppermost treads of the spiral staircase just as Steph had said it would.

But Steph was not there!

She cried out anxiously, "Steph? Steph, are you up there?" There was no reply. She heard nothing but the terrifying silence and the loud thumping of her heart that had begun to race. Panic slowly crept up her spine. "Please Steph, answer me. Are you okay? I know you could not have gone far. The tower isn't that large in circumference. Also, there is no way out because the doors are locked from the outside." There was no answer. "C'mon Steph, no kidding around okay? You promised me you would stay at the edge of the hole until I reached the bottom. I am getting scared, Steph. Hello?"

She gradually slid her right foot to the left until it was parallel to the tread. She carefully removed her left foot from the tread and placed it next to her right foot. Now her feet were side by side parallel to the tread. She slowly turned completely around being extra careful she did not trip. She knew if she tripped in that awkward position, she would fall. There would be nothing to slow her tumble short of her body brutally slamming onto one or more of the stair treads on the way down.

You know there is no way you could survive that; Peg worriedly whispered in her mind. Yep, Ida chimed in excitedly. One slip and poof! Say goodbye to your boyfriend!

"Oh, shut up you two!" Ava said aloud, her focus once again on her newfound friend, Steph. She yelled, "Okay, Steph, now I am more worried about you than I am worried about myself. I managed to turn around and am on my way back up to you. I am on the twelfth step, so hold on. I will be right there even if I must climb hand over hand. Should only take a minute or two." She gingerly placed her right foot onto the eleventh stair tread. Just as she did, the tread and the ten treads above it evaporated!

"What the heck!"

Now that the stair tread on which she had placed her foot had disappeared, Ava's arms were flailing in the air crazily. She was trying to stay upright, balanced. Her right foot was poised in midair like it was unsure what it should do next. She wanted to slam the foot onto the twelfth tread, but she was too much out of balance. All the while her left foot was slipping and sliding on the thin twelfth thread as the staircase gently swayed from side to side.

I wish there were banisters to hold on to! But no, this staircase must test the limits of my patience!

She was scared beyond recognition. Her lips and chin were trembling. Her whole body, from head to toe, was laboring to keep from plunging below. She closed her eyes to avoid watching what she thought was the unavoidable, the unthinkable. Finally tumbling from the stair tread on which she was balancing on one foot clumsily. In a last-ditch, frantic attempt to keep her balance, she smashed her right foot on the tread. Her action was so intense, the ends of her toes seemed to cry out in agony. Fortunately, now that both feet were on the tread, she regained her balance. She repeated the difficult process of turning around on the slender stair tread. Once she had done so successfully, she sat down and let out a long sigh of relief. A watery smile appeared on her face when the realization of what almost happened hit her.

She looked up at the jagged hole in the floor and thought to herself, thank you, God, for not allowing me to fall! She jammed her hands deep inside her armpits and gave herself a self-hug. Droplets of salty sweat were dripping from her forehead, stinging her watery eyes. She wanted to wipe them away. But she did not dare to move, so her eyes kept on stinging. She was afraid if she moved, the entire column of stair treads would collapse taking her with it.

Ida said in a sarcastic manner, well, it looks like you must descend the staircase to the depths below after all. No one said it would be easy. Besides, Steph probably is not up there, and there are no treads to climb to the top anyway. You have two choices – continue descending or jump and hope for the best.

"But why is this happening to me?" Ava cried out. "Can you answer that? Can anyone answer that! Why am I here, sitting on a step of a staircase that is not supported by anything above it? And how did eleven steps simply vanish? It does not make a lick of sense. Their vanishing defies reality, defies common-sense physics! It is like this blasted staircase does not want me to return to the real world. To reality!"

Ida did not know how to respond, so, thankfully, and surprisingly, she kept her thoughts to herself.

"Steph? Are you up there?" Ava whispered as she glanced over her shoulder. "If you are, please tell me that something, anything is keeping the upper stairs in place, something not apparent to me. I dread to think that the entire column is being supported by its base." She glanced down the length of the meandering staircase. "Then again, as I thought earlier the staircase might be like cantilevered stairs or floating stairs. But floating stairs are anchored at one end to something at its side. In this case, I would expect the stairs to be anchored to the inner walls of the chasm. However, nothing is holding the stairs up except its base! In any case, Steph, I am afraid if I move too much or start to go down again, the staircase won't be able to handle my weight."

The staircase seemed to corroborate her suspicions. It began to tremble ever so slightly, swaying a little – first to the left and back again to the right. She held her breath, not wanting to breathe. After a few moments, the staircase's swaying ceased.

She thought to herself, I think my shouting may have upset its stability. I need to get lower and as soon as possible. The lower I am on the staircase the less stress there will be on the middle and upper portions. It is a simple matter of physics. So, no more shouting out to Steph. That could cause the staircase to wobble all over again. But I wonder why she left after she said she would remain until I reached the bottom. Maybe Jordyn decided it was time for her to go home? She frowned. Thanks for nothing, Jordyn. Great timing too. I knew I should not have trusted you!

Ava gave her last thought a dismissive shrug and carefully got to her feet. With her arms held out wide to keep her balance, she began to move down the staircase slowly and ever so cautiously. She had no clue how long she was on the staircase up to that point. From the first tread when she first began descending, the staircase seemed to go on forever. She thought it could be a hundred miles long. It looked that far from its top to the barely visible light at its bottom. She pondered if maybe the light was only halfway down or even a quarter of the way down the stairs. She considered that to be completely unthinkable.

For the first ten minutes or so as she cautiously descended the staircase, she was oblivious to time. She thought of nothing but trying to keep her balance. Striving to go as slowly and steadily as she could so the trembling stairs did not sway too much. After a few more minutes, her mind began to race with inexplicable, thorny questions. She seriously doubted they ever would be answered, at least to her satisfaction. But she thought them just the same.

Where am I going? what am I supposed to do when I get there? who or what am I going to see when I arrive? anybody at all? when will Jordyn contact me? will she contact me? why in the heck am I here on this wobbly staircase in the first place? where is Steph? why did she leave? is she okay? What in God's name is the Inner World?

Like before, when she was standing on the ledge at the wrought iron gate, she started imagining things. She wondered if they were something less than true visions. Perhaps her mind was simply remembering things she had seen, heard, or personally experienced. Things to help her forget the dangerous predicament in which she found herself.

As the images flashed before her eyes, she believed the makeup of the visions was not as important as her unusual reactions. The fleeting scenes moved her heart greatly. Her emotions swung from one extreme to the other. She shed tears. She passionately yelled out loud, "No, no, no!" every so often. All in the span of a few minutes. She also reacted with ferocious anger; her heart filled with crushing disgust. Again, all in the span of a few minutes. She also cheered jubilantly as feelings of overpowering happiness shrouded her mind.

Then the unthinkable happened.

2

Ava's grasp of sanity seemed to have left her completely. She realized that she was in another world, another dimension. Just like her grandfather had said. But what her grandfather had imagined while climbing the tower was nowhere close to what she was envisioning on the tower's staircase.

She was standing near the edge of an expansive pasture on the crest of a mountain. The air was thin, and her breathing was slightly labored. The early morning sun seemed blistering hot, much warmer than usual. She was looking down, across a grassy landscape of lush green. The entire terrain was covered with enormous ferns, horsetails, and green plants that resembled club mosses. The scene appeared strikingly familiar to her. Like something she had read about in a science book.

Like the Jurassic Period when dinosaurs roamed the earth!

She sensed the unmistakable tinges of salt and fishy aromas in the air, like the smells of a nearby ocean. She narrowed her eyes. There *was* an ocean! It was to her left as well as to her right. She figured she was standing on a peninsula. Hundreds of strange-looking animals with long beaks soared above both bodies of water. Many were diving headlong to the water, probably searching for fish. They looked vaguely familiar to her.

Oh my God, they are pterosaurs! Flying reptiles that thrived on Earth millions of years ago, before they became extinct!

A beautiful, cascading waterfall to her right was sending plumes of mist high in the air. The rays of the searing sun were partially obscured by the vapor mists, creating a half dozen multicolored rainbows. The dazzlingly beautiful, kaleidoscopic arches stretched across the sky from one side of the body of water to the other. She was mesmerized totally as she stared in awe at the unbelievable scenes that had unfolded before her.

Suddenly, an immensely thunderous, howling sound thrust her back to realism. She froze in place unmoving as if her feet were glued to the spot. The veins in her head began to beat in step with the slamming sound. She covered her ears with the palms of her hands to ward off the thunderous reverberations. The mountaintop began to shake violently. After a few moments of unbelievable terror, the thundering sound abruptly ceased. Mercifully, the ferocious quaking ended a few moments later.

She reasoned it was an earthquake. Just an earthquake. Nothing to worry about. A minute or so later another vision began to appear in her mind. She was standing in the middle of a meadow, on a plateau. The air was heavier here, unlike when she was on the mountaintop. Her breathing was less labored as well. She was staring, utterly flabbergasted, hardly believing with what she was seeing! A plant-eating brontosaurus and its offspring, a juvenile, were grazing quietly about a mile away. They were feasting on conifer leaves and melon-sized fruit high in the trees. The surprisingly nimble adult dinosaur was teetering on its gigantic hind legs. It was craning its immensely long neck to feast at the uppermost parts of a giant tree. The tree must have been at least forty feet tall. The juvenile was nibbling on the fruity blossoms of a smaller tree that was at least three times taller than herself.

Suddenly, a huge fireball appeared far off in the sky to Ava's left. Its glow was so bright, for a moment she thought there were two suns on the horizon. She screamed, "Oh my God, no! I bet it is the asteroid that impacted Mexico's Yucatán Peninsula millions of years ago. The asteroid that resulted in the extinction of land dinosaurs. It all makes sense now. I am witnessing the end of a remarkable era and the extinction of the dinosaurs!"

A few seconds later a gigantic column of water shot high in the sky. It quickly intensified in breadth and height. As the water vapor and steam from the column spread, it formed numerous, stunning rainbows of every color imaginable. The huge column of water blocked out the morning sun, obscuring the sunshiny rays, turning the daytime to dusk.

The plume kept going up and up and up, seemingly never-ending until it began to spread far and wide in all directions. Then it formed huge, hundreds of miles-wide, irregular-shaped globules. The moment the plume formed in the shape of a mushroom cloud, like that of a nuclear explosion, Ava knew she was in trouble. A shockwave of roaring wind slammed her body punitively. It nearly knocked her off her feet and covered the front of her body with a shroud of powered ash. The ash was the color and texture of expresso coffee grounds.

The intense blast of punishing air was immediately followed by a powerful earth tremor that came from deep within the ground. What the wind had not managed to do, the tremor did. The pounding shockwave slammed Ava onto her rear end. A few moments later she managed to struggle to her feet after a few pathetic attempts. But the relentless shaking of the ground was dreadful. It was like trying to maintain one's equilibrium on a ship in the eye of an angry sea. Standing upright was nearly impossible.

Ava was swaying back and forth, her arms held out wide as she desperately tried to keep her balance. She was witnessing the aftereffects of the explosion. A gigantic, thousands of feet tall wall of brown water was headed straight at her! The wall of water was packed with colossal boulders the size of cars and houses! The boulders were cartwheeling madly as they soared through the air like angry shots of a cannon.

Understandably, she was freaking out with what she was seeing. But oddly enough, her attention was directed toward the momma and baby brontosaurs. They were looking listlessly at the massive column of water rushing at them as they munched on the leaves, completely unaware of their fate. The gracefully beautiful, prehistoric creatures were about to be obliterated along with everything else on the plateau, including Ava!

A tremendously powerful, shuddering earthquake shook the ground, throwing her flat out on her stomach and causing her to cry out in disbelief. A split-second later a thunderous rumbling overwhelmed the plateau. She looked up and saw that the portion of the plateau where the dinosaurs had been eating had vanished! Soon, she was tumbling headfirst as the entire world whirled around her. The centrifugal force of her fast-moving plunge shoved her back and forth and up and down cruelly. She felt like she was on a roller coaster ride gone totally out of control. The insides of her stomach were lurching nauseatingly until she could no longer resist the urge to vomit. Rocks, trees, grass, and dark clouds of dirt were shrouding her vision. Shadowy silhouettes of enormous boulders were whirling all around her – threatening to crush her to smithereens.

She closed her eyes and said a silent prayer.

3

Just as Ava said amen, the tremendous shuddering ceased. She cautiously opened her eyes one by one. She was shrouded in absolute, unnerving stillness. Her heartbeats had stopped. She no longer was breathing. Or so she thought. Everything seemed mystifying. Empty. Hollow. Meaningless. Yet strangely, she was conscious. Mindful. Aware.

She considered that she probably was in heaven.

But reality was staring at her in the face. She was back on the tower's staircase. She was lying on her side on one of the countless treads, clutching frantically to a stair tread above her. The knuckles of her hands were white from her frantic grip. She let go of the tread and sat up.

Out of the blue, a dazzling, golden light slowly encircled her entire body. She watched spellbound as particles of silvery flakes fell onto her head. They seemed to twinkle like fine granules of fairy dust one sees in storybook movies. Her first notion was that she had died peacefully and painlessly. That she had entered heaven's embrace. That her living life had vanished.

Perhaps this is how I died. My last breath. Clutching at a stair tread as I lay – dead. The tower's curse. Retribution for Grandpa Jim and my great uncle having conquered it so many years ago. The tower's last hurrah. Its morbid way of proving to me that I did not stand a chance of conquering it. Showing me who is the boss. All the while conspiring with Jordyn.

My soul's way of passing from the real world to heaven.

Were Jordyn's voice-thoughts about the Inner World implying something other than what I assumed? Was I to pay a price for something terrible I did earlier in my life? Someone I had insulted, hurt? If so, I have no idea what it could have been. I like people, well most, and I go out of my way to help others in need. Nonetheless, could it be that the Inner World is opposite of what I have come to believe.

Or, as I hope, is the Inner World my everlasting wonderland of dreams?

4

The staircase unexpectedly lurched violently to the left, taking Ava completely by surprise. Once again, she was in a state of utter panic and had to lie on her side and grab onto a stair tread above her.

The staircase was trying to balance itself out as it viciously wobbled to the right. Unable to correct itself, it lurched to the left violently once more. Now its tortured, rusty seams were screeching ferociously like a horde of angry howler monkeys. Its juddering as it rocked back and forth had become much more brutal than it had been earlier. Yet Ava was hopeful that it would correct itself as it had before. But the staircase was not going to abide by her hopeful optimism. At least not yet. It started to zigzag and weave, slowly snaking its way inside the chasm, totally out of control. Like a poisonous snake crawling out of a dingy hole, ready to take one's life. Its ravaged, terribly strained, and weakened seams and joints could no longer endure the vicious, undulating spirals. Critical rivets, bolts, and steel welds that kept the structure intact and held it upright started to fail one by one. She winced repeatedly as terrifyingly loud explosions resonated all around her.

Bang! Pop! And *Snap!*

The blasts were immediately accompanied by the distinctive reverberations of echoing whizzes and twangs as countless fragments of metal ricocheted off the walls of the chasm. The shattering blasts of failing and rebounding projectiles quickly increased. Soon the explosions were like a huge Fourth of July fireworks spectacle gone horribly wrong.

She buried her face in the crook of her arms to protect her head from the bursting objects. But she knew it was of little use. All it would take was one bolt to hit her in the chest or stomach or pierce her hands, and she would be a goner.

This is the same dreadful feeling I had when the mountaintop on which I was standing started to collapse! Except this time, I am lying prone on the tower's dreadful staircase hanging on for dear life! And soon the staircase will break apart in to a million pieces and give way. Then it will chuck its former, rickety, rusting self along with me to its grave! Nothing will remain but twisted wrought iron and what is even recognizable of my body's squished flesh and shattered bones!

The explosions of shattered metal seams steadily increased, forcing the staircase to thrash even more. It began to corkscrew savagely like a child's errant kite caught in the wind. Like it was gearing up to flip-flop madly before it made a beeline plunge straight to the ground.

When abruptly, just as it had in the past, the staircase gradually slowed its brutal corkscrewing. The explosive *Bangs! Pops!* And *Snaps!* decreased as well until they were no more. The staircase was still rocking back and forth. But now it was more like a backyard swing moving in the kindest breeze than an enraged staircase impatient to cave in.

Ava noticed that the sharp, metal rungs of the staircase were no longer digging in her backside. Once more, the staircase had disappeared. It had been replaced by solid ground. The ground was covered with a grainy substance. It was straw. She reached below the straw and felt pebbles, stones, dirt, and sand. Suddenly, the scene surrounding her began to appear fully. She was sitting in the middle of a yawning cave. She looked around. What she first noticed caused her heart to race with excitement.

Oh my gosh! It is the cave's entryway. I can finally escape the tower and leave that stupid staircase behind!

She carefully crept toward the cave's opening, feeling her way cautiously with her hands as she crawled. When she reached the opening, what she saw caused her to shuffle back a bit. A fluttery feeling was spreading in the pit of her stomach. She crawled back to the opening and did a doubletake.

The shimmering, golden, full moon was on the horizon. She thought it looked like a magnificent spectacle of unreal beauty. Especially after what she experienced on the staircase. The orb was enormous, seemingly larger than any moon rising on the horizon she had ever seen.

I know from a science class that it is an optical illusion for the moon on the horizon to look like this. To appear much larger than it is. However, the moon seems many times larger than it should be, even under normal circumstances. This is very strange. But so is everything else that has happened to me since I set out to climb the tower. But where are the moon's dark areas and its seas, its lunar maria's? She narrowed her eyes. I cannot see the Sea of Tranquility! Also, there is no Copernicus, the moon's most noticeable crater to the human eye. I should be able to see Copernicus if nothing else! She sat back and studied the moon thoughtfully. Fuzzy feelings were racing through her mind. This is not the Earth's moon! It is a moon from somewhere else or, who knows? Maybe, given everything that has happened to me, what I am looking at is a planet!

She looked away from the celestial globe that was baffling her. Her curiosity had been drawn to the silvery specks of countless stars sparkling in the clear, nighttime sky.

Goodness gracious, no. Where the heck is Orion? It is the most well-known constellation. I should be able to see it since it is visible throughout the world! Am I in heaven? Or am I in the other place? Because wherever I am, this is not Earth, at least not the Earth that I know!

Suddenly, voices that sounded like they came from humans started to filter through the cave's darkness. She was about to crawl toward the voices but hesitated for a moment. She considered that maybe the voices were not those of humans.

After all, she thought, the moon surely is not Earth's moon, at least as far as I can tell. The stars look totally out of whack too. Maybe I should stay right here, or better yet see if I can escape. She peered outside the cave's entrance. A frown appeared on her forehead. But it is too spooky out there right now. I should wait for daybreak, or I could find myself tumbling down the mountainside. That would be just as bad as tumbling from the staircase. At least I am safe inside the cave. Well, I hope so anyway.

Predictably, Ava's curiosity slowly took charge of her mind and body. She gingerly crawled toward the voices. She cautiously peered around the corner once she reached the place from where the voices were coming. A man and a woman were sitting around a firepit. A half dozen skewered sticks of raw meat were on the ground next to the man. Her empty stomach growled hungrily at the sight of the meat, even though it was uncooked.

She guessed that the fine-looking man was in his early thirties. He had a rugged, square face, and bushy eyebrows. His unkempt, light brown hair had golden highlights and fell far below his collarbone. His shaggy beard matched his hair. He was very muscular with a golden tan. His powerful muscles strained against the fabric of his long-sleeved tunic at the forearms, biceps, and chest.

The female, sitting on the other side of the firepit, was cradling a small child in her arms. She was nursing the child and softly humming as she gently stroked its cheek. The child looked to be about six months old. Ava could not tell for certain because the baby's face was hidden. The child had a tuff of his mother's hair clutched in its tiny fist. The woman's yellow hair had a tint of ginger. Her hair cascaded in beautiful, untangled waves well beyond her waist. She had a pretty smile, and Ava thought her to be incredibly attractive. Her face and upper arms were covered with freckles. She looked much younger than the man, perhaps in her early twenties.

Ava considered that the trio did not look dangerous. She was anxious to crawl from her hiding spot to approach them. Just as she was about to move, the woman spoke to the man. Ava immediately froze in place and stared. She wondered; what language are they speaking? It certainly is not English, nor is it anything like I have ever heard before. It sounds oddly exotic like it is unearthly and not human speech. Yet they look like humans, not aliens from Mars or someplace else. But then again, the weird moon and the strange stars—

The man laughed and clutched at his belly. His sputtering, joyful laugh seemed to put Ava more at ease. That was until he picked up a whittled stick that was on the ground beside him. He had laughed again and pointed the stick at the firepit. A soft white glow like a low wattage light bulb emerged at the end of the stick. He uttered a few unrecognizable words, and then the firepit immediately burst into flames!

Ava quickly slipped back within her hiding spot. Her eyes were blinking rapidly with alarm because she could not believe what she had witnessed. She replayed in her mind what she had just seen. It must be magic! There is no other explanation. And the whittled stick must be a wand. Is the man a magical wizard? Or are he and the woman something else entirely?

After a few moments, she crawled from her hiding spot in the shadows and peeked. She watched the man once more. He was pointing his whittled stick at the wall. Her astonished thoughts seemed to shout; he is painting by using magic! The stick is not even touching the wall, although lines are miraculously being drawn!

As the man painted on the wall without touching it with the stick, the woman was holding what looked like a similar-looking stick high in the air. A glow was shining from its end. She pointed the stick at the meat-skewered twigs and muttered unrecognizable words. The twigs began to rise one by one in the air to hover a few inches above the fire. They set out turning in little circles as if they were impaled on invisible skewers in a rotisserie!

Unable to control her excitement and wonder any longer, Ava gasped. She had covered her mouth with her hand; however, she did not muffle the sound sufficiently. The woman, having heard her gasp pointed the stick in her direction. As the light from the stick shone on Ava's face, the woman seemed to look directly into her eyes. She scurried backward in the shadows. Her heartbeats were racing as her stomach began to roil. She heard me; her inner thoughts seemed to shriek. She nearly fainted because of what happened next. The woman was speaking to her!

"Will you not join us, dearest Avaïnoάel? I presume you are ravenous. There is enough for three."

All at once, Ava was back on the stair tread. She turned around and grabbed the upper treads and held on as the staircase resumed its stomach-churning, wobbling gyrations all over again. Rivets, bolts, and strained metal started to explode like a backyard firecracker show having gone totally berserk.

She closed her eyes and screamed, "This cannot be happening to me!"

CHAPTER 9

FLYING THROUGH TIME
TO THE BEGINNING

"Knowing what must be done does away with fear."—*Rosa Parks*

1

Ava cried out in pain as her backside awkwardly thwacked down nine metal stair treads one after the other. As soon as she stopped thumping along the bone-jarring treads, she turned around and grabbed onto the stair treads above her. Before she could even start to grasp what was happening, the base of the staircase surrendered to the strain of its severely damaged middle and upper seams.

Clang! Twang! Screech! Squeal!
CRASH!

The screeching sounds of the metal finally admitting defeat were horrendous! Ava wanted to cover her ears, but she could not. Or else, she would have fallen off the stair tread on which she was sitting!

Like in a creepy, slow-motion science fiction horror movie, the upper portion of the staircase abruptly drifted to the right at a slower than snail's pace. It slammed with tremendous force to the concrete wall of the chasm. A microsecond later the entire staircase sluggishly set out to crumple by degrees.

Then it exploded with a thunderous *BOOM!*

Thousands of braces, rivets, bolts, and strained metal stair treads had detonated at the same time. The thundering sound was so strong it would echo over and over within the chasm for a least a minute.

The sudden displacement of air caused by the explosion created a huge blast wind. Ava at once was flung high above the collapsing staircase. She was thrown so high; her seemingly weightless body soared in a vertical position well beyond the entryway hole in the tower's floor where the staircase formerly began. As she skyrocketed high in the air, she watched dully as Steph's lantern fell over onto its side and slipped into the chasm. Everything turned pitch-black.

Luckily, although it did not occur to Ava until much later, the explosion's blast wind had hurled her well out of harm's way. She had been propelled far above the hazardous metal bits and pieces of the exploding staircase. Because she was thrust so high in the air, her pressure-sensitive organs – eyes, ears, and lungs – were spared the sudden increase in pressure that had occurred. The thick concrete flooring of the tower had absorbed the energy of the forceful blast wave. In the end, her grandfather and great uncle's conquered tower had not abandoned her. It had saved her from being blown to bits.

A split-second later gravity took over. Her body started to freefall as it followed Steph's lantern in the chasm. The lantern, oddly it was still lit, cast gloomy shadows as it shed light on the end of their fates.

What seemed like a female's voice-thoughts suddenly bellowed, "Et no moriatur!"

Initially, Ava was unable to speak. She was grinding her teeth, her jaw clenched tightly with sheer panic. After a few moments, she managed to squeak out a scarcely perceptible whisper. "Whoever you are please help me if you can! Please!"

"Et ego salvum te! Et no moriatur!" the voice-thoughts bellowed. Like before, its words were utterly undecipherable, strange, and unfamiliar.

"I cannot understand you!" Ava screamed in a desperate tone. "I speak English only. Please help me." She could see the bottom of the chasm as it rushed up to her at lightning speed. Ironically, the soft light at the bottom of the chasm seemed to be guiding her fall. She thought she had but a few seconds to live. "Please help me and stop talking that gibberish. I cannot understand what you are saying!"

The voice-thoughts commanded, "Manibus tenere. Sicut avis volat!"

Ava was feverishly saying a silent prayer when Jordyn's voice-thoughts abruptly entered her tormented mind, thus interrupting her prayer. "Speak to Avaïnoᴆel in her Earthy World language, Fluescere. She does not yet know Fortunomy! Hurry now."

"Avaïnoᴆel, et ego salvum te. You will not die," the voice-thoughts promptly said in a mixture of English and its odd language. "Close your eyes and hold out your arms to your sides. Like a flying bird. Et no moriatur. I will save you."

Desperate to do whatever it took to put an end to what she imagined was the inescapable – her untimely death in her grandfather and great uncle's beloved tower – Ava obeyed. She closed her eyes tightly and spread her arms out wide. The next thing she knew, she was flying!

But no! I am not flying by myself! I am sitting on something, hanging on for dear life. That something is the one that is flying. I can feel the wash of its wings!

She tried to open her eyes to see what was happening. But she could not. She quickly was starting to lose awareness. The last things she sensed before she blacked out were a series of ear-deafening explosions.

Woosh-bang! Crash! Kaboom! Crash!

The twisted, rusted metal remnants of the former inglorious tower staircase had finally met the bottom of the chasm. Miraculously, less than five seconds later, the twisted wreckage vanished and was replaced.

A new spiraling staircase was reborn.

2

Ava began to stir a half-hour later. It was not like she had fainted or something similarly dramatic. Jordyn simply thought that she had experienced too much up to that point. Hence, she had placed Ava under a knockout spell that put her fast asleep, so she would not have to witness the staircase's demise. Then again, if Jordyn had given Ava a choice in the matter, witnessing the death of the rickety staircase would have been the best part of her harrowing experience. Watching it regenerate to a brand-new staircase would have been (excuse the idiom) the icing on the cake. In any case, she would come to loath spiral staircases. Even today, looking at a spiral staircase gives her the creeps.

Ava realized she was lying on a king-sized bedstead popular during the Victorian era. She recalled examining photographs of similar-looking beds in a book at her school library two years earlier. She had been intrigued with the beautiful, feminine style of the beds in the photographs – as well as the refined boudoir accessories. She even had a few screenshots of the beds on her cellphone.

Her head was resting on a mound of soft, feathery pillows. They were covered with handsome white lace delicately embroidered with lovely red and yellow rose petals. Silken sheets and a soft, fluffy comforter matched the pillows' design. The mattress was lumpy and at least three feet off the floor. Victorian beds had to be high off the floor to avoid drafts from the fireplace. There was a step stool beside the bed. Ava thought it made perfect sense. Otherwise, so she considered, one would have to make a running leap just to lie down. Not to mention having to jump off the bed in the middle of the night to use the bathroom, possibly resulting in twisted ankles or worse.

A seemingly weightless, luxuriously handstitched burgundy canopy was mounted on the bed's five-foot-tall bedposts. It covered the entire bed frame. The bedposts and headboard were made of sturdy mahogany and stained a rich, dark tone. The headboard felt oily to Ava's touch and smelled minty. She presumed it had been polished recently. She was about to get a taste of the oil residue on her fingertips, but common sense and her uncanny memory overpowered her curiosity. She knew that the oil of perilla was sometimes used to polish furniture in the olden days. Perilla is an herb and has medicinal qualities, used to treat nausea, sunstroke, even asthma, whereas perilla mint is poisonous.

Best not she considered wordlessly. She slipped her hand beneath the comforter and wiped her fingers on the sheets. *No sense starting my journey as sick as a dog and suffering panting disease. Given the way things have been going since I started my climb, I would be tasting the perilla mint instead of perilla!*

She got a whiff of a strong, unpleasant odor beneath the comforter after she wiped the oil from her fingers. The stench smelled just like the distinctive odors of a petting zoo or a horse stall. She had read somewhere that horsehair was used to make mattresses during the Victorian era. She reached to the underside of the mattress then sniffed her fingertips. She winced at the strong odor, confirming that the mattress was made of horsehair. She had also felt straw below the mattress. The straw was used to protect the mattress from the bedstead.

There were two chests of drawers against the far wall to her right. The drawers were stained the same dark color as the headboard and bedposts. Partially burned candlesticks set in brass candelabrums were on the tops of both drawers. There were a small serving table and two chairs in the middle of the chest of drawers. An oil painting of an elderly man, woman, and a small child was on the wall above the table. The child was around six or seven years old.

Ava narrowed her eyes. She abruptly drew in a sharp breath.

What the heck! This is remarkable. The elderly man and woman resemble the two magical people in the cave! Well, I guess they were magical because they seemed to be making magic with those sticks of theirs. Or were the sticks wands actually? Anyway, could they be the same? Oh, my goodness! They have elf ears too! She sat up in the bed, her expression one of extreme panic. Oh no! And – no way! She rubbed her eyes. I cannot believe this. The child elf looks just like me! She threw her hands high in the air and shouted, "What in the world is happening to me? What is going on here? Who are those three people, I mean elves?"

In response to Ava's shouts, Steph yelled from the other side of the room. "Ava! Thank goodness you are okay. You had me worried sick!" She was all smiles as she rushed over to stand next to the bed.

Steph's yelling had caused Ava to cringe because she thought she was imagining things once more. That she was still on the staircase. That it did not collapse and would start shaking violently. She was staring at Steph wide-eyed. She genuinely wanted to believe what she was seeing was real. But she was afraid that they would once again turn out to be dreamlike visions. She whispered timidly, "Steph, is it really you?" She rubbed her eyes and said in a hesitant tone, "Please tell me it is you and not a new figment of my totally gone wild, vivid imagination. If it is you, please hop up here and hug me." She added with teary eyes, "Lord knows I could use one."

There was a step stool where Steph was standing. She stepped onto it and leaped onto the bed. She and Ava hugged. They were grinning from ear to ear.

"Yep, it's me," Steph said softly. Her face was beaming with excitement. "Jordyn totally surprised me. She said I am going to accompany you on your adventure. She says you need an Earthly World companion, her words not mine. She also said that company will do you good." She pulled Ava in close and squeezed her in an even stronger hug. "Jordyn told me she was moved by the way you and I seemed to hit it off from the start. I am incredibly happy, Ava, more so than you can imagine!"

In a solemn tone, Ava said, "I was worried sick about you too." She stared at her hands. They were shaking. She unconsciously began to pick at her fingernails. Some had bits of dried mud beneath them from when she had fallen in the muddy water at the tower. "When I looked up at the opening in the tower's floor and realized you had vanished, I panicked. I thought the worst, that a goblin or something eviler had spirited you away. I tried to go to you, but the upper stair treads vanished into thin air. It was the strangest thing I tell you. Stranger than science fiction. It was sort of magical, spooky too." She closed her eyes and whispered to herself softly, "Thank you, Lord, for keeping Steph safe. For bringing her to me. For getting us back together."

Steph said with a heavy sigh, "I am sorry I could not keep my promise, thus scaring you. Before I knew what was happening, Jordyn whisked me from the opening in the floor to this room shortly after you moved down. I have been here for what seems like hours. She said I would be safer here than being anywhere near the staircase." She looked straight into Ava's eyes and gave her a probing look.

"Ava, can you tell me what happened to you while you were on the staircase? Do you remember? How did you get here?" She wiggled her eyebrows in a comical way and laughed. "Oh, yeah, how could I forget. Jordyn's magic. One minute I was sitting alone," she pointed to the left, "way over there in that rocking chair. I must have fallen asleep. When I woke up, here you were, sound asleep. Jordyn told me that I should not disturb you. She said you were under a sleep-induced spell.

"Anyhow, whatever it was that Jordyn had done had placed you sound asleep. You were snoring loudly, obviously deep in REM sleep. It probably was good she had placed you under a spell. Because whatever happened inside the tower would probably had scared you half to death if you had been awake. Because from here, I nearly jumped out of my skin when I heard an enormously loud explosion. A minute or so later there was another explosion. That one was even louder. It was like the entire staircase had crashed to the bottom of the chasm. It went like—

Woosh-bang! Crash! Kaboom!"

Ava said glumly, "Exactly how it sounded to me before everything went dark."

Steph pointed to the chandelier that was hanging from the ceiling in the middle of the room. "That thing shook like crazy, swinging back and forth for the longest time. Snuffed most of the candles, at least nine of the twelve if I recall correctly. But they magically relit a few seconds after the shaking stopped. Probably some more of Jordyn's magic. As the chandelier swung back and forth the entire room shook like an earthquake, although I have not felt one before. It was scary. I can only imagine how it would have looked to you if you had been awake." She grabbed Ava by the shoulders. "So, can you tell me all about it? What you experienced on the staircase before, I guesstimate, it collapsed? As they say in neverland, I am all ears."

Ava swallowed hard and wet her lips. "Well, I saw lots of pretty cool and yes, I must admit some really scary things. At least in my mind, in my imagination. Then again, they could have been real. I just do not know for certain. It is hard to explain, Steph. But at the end, just before I heard the staircase crash to the bottom, I thought I was flying!"

"You were flying?" Steph asked in an incredulous tone. She was staring at Ava open-mouthed. She leaned in closer. "Flying like a bird, flapping your wings, stuff like that? Or like a superwoman kind of flying, or maybe like Diana in the movie *Wonder Woman*, you know soaring through the air while staying vertical?"

Ava rolled her eyes as she said with a laugh, "No, not that kind of flying. Although at first, I did have my arms spread wide like I was an airplane or something. I must have looked totally ridiculous. Then I was holding onto something to keep my balance. No, I was not the one that was flying. I was sitting on something that had a scaly back. Whatever it was, it probably was the one that was flying. I tried to open my eyes, but I could not. It was like they were glued shut." She stopped talking for a few moments deep in thought. She was biting at her cheek. "To tell you the truth, Steph, even though my eyes were shut tight, I felt like I was on the back of a—"

"Like you were on the back of what?" Steph interrupted with a grin. Her eyes were wide with excitement.

Ava said in a purposely slow way, "Like I was riding on the back, on the back of a dragon, Steph! An honest to goodness, real, living dragon! Can you believe it?" Steph shrugged her shoulders. She lifted a single eyebrow and cocked her head like she could not believe what Ava had said. "I was falling through the chasm, somersaulting head over heels. I was following the staircase, perhaps twenty feet above it, as it was collapsing on itself." She took in a deep breath and exhaled a long sigh. "That is because, thankfully I must say, I was blown clear above the hole in the floor when the explosion happened. As I was plummeting to what I thought was my certain death, I could see everything. That is because your lantern had fallen into the chasm and was lighting the way. I also saw that spooky light at the bottom of the crumbling staircase. Anyway, the dragon if that is what it truly was began to speak to me in my mind! I think it was telling me what to do in its foreign tongue."

Ava had suddenly stopped talking. She turned her head and stared across the room at the painting. Her eyes glazed over as she began to rethink her encounter with the people in the cave. She thought to herself; I am certain the dragon was talking to me in my mind in the same strange language that the man and woman were speaking in the cave. That is until the woman spoke to me in English. What was it that she had said as she looked me straight in the eye? Ah yes, she had said in a surprisingly sweet voice in perfect English, 'Will you not join us, dearest Avaïnoĉel? I presume you are ravenous. There is enough for three.' For some curious reason, the tone of her voice seemed to make my heart soar. I wonder why that was? And what did she mean when she said the word Avaïnoĉel? Could she have meant to say Ava Noelle but had mispronounced my name?

Steph remained quiet while Ava was recollecting what happened in the cave. She was observing her with a tolerant, understanding expression. Eventually, no longer able to control her excitement, she waved her hand back and forth in front of Ava's eyes. She snapped her fingers a couple of times to get her attention. While tapping Ava's forehead lightly with her finger, she said in a lighthearted way, "Hello, earth to Ava Noelle. Is anyone in there?"

Ava's head jerked back with surprise. She blinked her eyes. "Huh?"

Steph said, "You were saying before you drifted off to outer space? Something about what you thought was a dragon talking to you."

"Sorry," Ava said in a weak voice. "Yes, I guess you are right. I must have drifted off. Anyway, as I was saying, Jordyn's voice-thoughts asked whatever it was that had been talking to me via voice-thoughts to speak in English. Her words said in my mind – I recall them precisely – 'Speak to Avaïnoḋel in her Earthly World language, Fluescere. She does not yet know Fortunomy!' Soon, whatever it was that had been talking to me in its foreign tongue via voice-thoughts gave me commands in English. It said it would not allow me to die. It had saved me.'" She gave Steph a sweet smile. "Because as you can see, I am here." Grabbing Steph's hand, she added, "And I am so very glad you are here as well."

What Steph said in reply to Ava's words was totally off the mark with what they were discussing. She said, "Ava, I have to tell you that you are utterly amazing! How do you do it? How are you able to recall exactly what Jordyn said to the dragon or whatever it was? I mean, you were tumbling through the air undoubtedly scared out of your mind. I certainly would have been. Heck, I have trouble remembering to do some of my chores. I have to write them down, or I tend to forget some."

Ava rolled her eyes and smiled. "I know what you mean. I wish I could forget to do my chores – like every day and twice on Sunday. I try to pawn them off on my sisters too, but it never works."

Steph said, "I do the same with my sister, Sophia, well, at least I try. So, why do you think Jordyn referred to you by that weird name? The Ava I Noellee thingy, or however you had pronounced it? And what in the world is fort nomy?"

Ava chuckled, and then she said, "Please excuse me for laughing, Steph, but I must correct you. What I said is pronounced *ə-vä-ī-nō'-ĕlō*, emphasis on the fourth syllable. Not Ava I Noellee. I assume Avaïnoḋel is my given name here in the Inner World since it sounds sort of like my real name. Spoken in a weird, foreign tongue as you can probably tell. The other word you mentioned is pronounced *fōr-tūne'-ō-mē*, not fort nomy. Emphasis is on the second syllable."

Steph said, "Thanks for explaining all that. But let me get back to what I had intended to say at the onset. How in the world do you know these things – the Ava I Noelle word and the fort nomy thing? I mean how can you recall them exactly from memory? Again, all the while you were plunging to the bottom of the chasm and probably scared as can be?"

Ava was grinning when she said, "Again, Steph, it is pronounced Fortunomy not fort nomy. And my name, if that is what it is, is pronounced Avaïnoáel. And oh, about the memory thing, it is no big deal. I have a slightly rare skill to recall images and words easily. It is what scientists call an eidetic memory, commonly referred to as a photographic memory. I was tested in a clinic when I was a kid." She rolled her eyes as she tucked in her upper lip. Then she laughed. "But I cheated on the series of clinic-controlled tests. I must confess I cheated quite a bit."

Steph was pressing her lips together tightly. She gave Ava a curious look. "Why did you cheat? How can you cheat on a clinic-controlled test? You do not look the sort that would cheat to make yourself look good. I can tell you just are honest as the day is long. Am I right?"

Ava's eyes seemed to light up. "Oh, I did not cheat to make myself look even more unusual or special. I cheated by pretending I could not recall things, see things. I did not want to appear to be a nut case. You know, a biological specimen for others to study until I am so old, I will not be able remember my own name. Anyhow, after they tested me, I fell in the normal category for eidetic memory cases. I was in the two to ten percent of the preadolescent range of having the ability. But I knew better.

"I think my weird brain is something much more than what others thought at the time. It is much more complex than simply having an eidetic memory. If I want to, I can instantly recall anything I have seen, heard, and physically felt." She touched her nose. "And even smelled. Back to when I was a toddler. It might sound crazy, Steph, but I think I am a borderline clairvoyant with precognition abilities."

Steph said, "What is borderline clairvoyant and precognition? Are those like being able to see things that are not there? Like magic stuff, sort of like Jordyn's ability to do things, like her telepathy and the sort?"

Ava replied, "I do not know for certain if they are like Jordyn's amazing powers." She closed her eyes. "But, like the dictionary definition of clairvoyant, *the mystical power of seeing objects or actions removed in space or time from natural viewing*, I too have that ability. At least I think that I do. Likewise, the definition of precognition is *to predict future events or situations, especially through extrasensory means.*" She opened her eyes and stared at Steph with a blank look. "Extrasensory is just like it sounds, outside of the normal senses such as sight, hearing, and touch. Let me give you an example of clairvoyance."

Steph held her hand up to stop Ava from talking. "Whoa! Hold on a minute. Please tell me all of what you just said weren't the Webster's Dictionary definitions of clairvoyant and precognition quoted word for word."

"Yep," Ava replied evenly. She grinned. "Word for word. The definitions just popped into my head, probably because I had read them at one time." She tilted her head to one side and frowned. "See what I mean? See what I must put up with daily? Happily, things do not come to my mind automatically. I must summon them up in my brain if that makes sense. Otherwise, I would go totally insane with all the junk floating around in my head."

"Dang, Ava," Steph said with a disbelieving shake of her head. Her face was noticeably flushed. "Yes, I see what you mean. But I gotta tell you. You are something else, utterly amazing." She exhaled a long sigh. "Please continue with whatever you were going to say. I didn't mean to interrupt you."

Ava said, "Thanks for your flattering words. They mean a lot to me. Anyway, I distinctly recall the creature's exact words. They were very calm and composed." She closed her eyes tightly. "The creature said," she opened one eye and winked at Steph which made her laugh, "and I will quote its exact words in both English and what I assume is Fortunomy, 'Avaïnoάel, et ego salvum te. You will not die. Close your eyes and hold out your arms to your sides. Like a flying bird. Et no moriatur. I will save you.'" She opened her eyes and shrugged. "Yes, Steph, it had said those things in its language and ours, 'I will save you.' How cool is that, huh?'"

Steph was genuinely impressed when she spluttered, "You are incredible! I have never met anyone more interesting in my entire seventeen years. And do you want to know what else?"

Ava smiled at her. "I think I already know." She wrapped her arms around Steph's shoulders and hugged her. With her eyes closed tightly, she whispered in Steph's ear. "You were going to say something along the lines of 'I am so happy you and I are besties now. I cannot wait to learn more about your other cool talents.'" She backed away from Steph and looked her straight in the eyes. "Was that pretty much the gist of it?"

Steph had flinched when Ava told her pretty much what she had been thinking. She stared at Ava for a few seconds, her eyes blinking rapidly with disbelief. She pressed the palms of her hands to her face. "Wow! Totally amazing!"

"Thank you so much," Ava said with a laugh. "Don't pass out on me, okay? Frankly, it means the world to me that you said that, or, should I say, you were going to say that. That we are besties. She shrugged her shoulders. "What I said to you a moment ago is due to my clairvoyance. Maybe it is precognition. I am not certain. In any event, people commonly refer to it as ESP, extrasensory perception. I am sure you have heard of that term. Yes?"

Steph nodded her head.

"Around forty percent of the world's population believe in such stuff, which would include me evidently. I have never told my parents, sisters, or friends about my abilities, that is, if they exist at all. If I told them, they would put me away forever in a looney bin and misplace the key to the lock. Also, strangely I have to say, my ESP began when I turned thirteen. It was last December, on the fourteenth. By the way, you said you were seventeen. When is your birthday?"

Steph replied, "It is February 14. I turned seventeen this year."

Ava exclaimed, "A valentine's birthday baby! Well, isn't that wonderful? You will make a terrific valentine for some lucky guy someday if you haven't already."

Steph was blushing when she said, "Thank you. That is nice of you." Her eyes rested on the double doors to their left. They were closed. "I have one more question before we beat it out of here through those doors and try to find something to eat." She patted her stomach. "I do not know about you, but I am starving."

Ava said with a grin, "I am as hungry as a fiery dragon. Okay, fire away, no pun intended, with your question and please be quick about it if you can. That nasty moan you heard just now was my stomach growling. All I have had to eat since yesterday morning is one-half of a PB&J. The other half was squished in my backpack. It looked too gross to eat at the time. But I wish I had it with me now because I would scarf it down in one gulp."

Steph said, "Back to my question. What was that other strange word that Jordyn had said? You said it as well a minute ago. It sounded like flue scare or something like that."

Ava replied, "It is pronounced Flū-shĕr ′-ĕ, emphasis on the second syllable, sher. I do not know if you know this, but Fluescere is a Latin word. Do you know what the word Fluescere means in English?"

Steph was giving her an admiring look. "Dang girl! Do not tell me you know Latin as well. You are out of this world incredible!"

Ava said in a nonchalant tone, "I know just a bit of Latin. Greek too. But only those words or phrases that interest me. Words that tend to lend themselves nicely to my fascination with the fantasy world. The make-believe world of magic, spells, and enchantments. Anyhow, Fluescere is the Latin word for flame. Can you tell what I am getting at?" Steph shook her head.

"Steph, the creature that saved me has to be a dragon! I am certain of it. A scaly back on which I was perched. Having the sensation that I was flying. Jordyn referring to the creature as Fluescere, flame in English. It all makes sense!"

Steph was about to say she agreed with Ava's hypothesis when Jordyn's telepathic voice-thoughts abruptly entered her and Ava's minds.

"Ava, Steph. Please excuse me for interrupting. There will be plenty of time later for you to discuss Ava's adventures while she was on the staircase. Regrettably, we do not have much time. I need to be somewhere else in a little while, and you need to get going. Therefore, please allow me to explain why you are here in this enchanting land, the Inner World."

Ava said, "Please, Jordyn, before you continue with your voice-thoughts, and I apologize for interrupting, I must tell you something." She started to tremble noticeably. A flush appeared on her face. "As you probably knew at the time, I was scared out of my wits in the staircase's chasm. What I experienced on the staircase before and after it collapsed almost caused me heart failure." She grabbed Steph's hand and squeezed it firmly. "But I am okay now. Now that I am here in this charming Victorian-era bedroom and with my newfound friend, my bestie, Steph."

Steph said in a whisper, "Thank you, Ava. I am glad you are okay. As I said earlier, you are now my bestie too."

Ava thanked her, and then she said, "Jordyn, as you could probably tell from my thoughts, I wasn't overly scared of being inside the tower before stepping onto the staircase. Just the opposite. That is because the tower is an important part of my family's legacy. Although I must admit there were a few anxious moments when I doubted things." She took a deep breath. She could feel her heart was racing, and the annoyingly dry feeling in her throat had returned.

"You could probably tell as well," she glanced at Steph, "and by what I had said to Steph, that I did not trust you. I hope you understand why I thought and said what I did. I mean, think about it, Jordyn. I was and continue to be mystified how you can talk to us in our minds telepathically. How we can do the same, to converse with you. How you could move Steph from her home to the tower to this room. Even though I must admit all of it is super cool, it sure is baffling, nearly unnatural. Yet I am sort of getting used to it. Moreover, I think it is cool being telepathic and all. So, I am sorry for doubting you." She frowned just as goose pimples sprinted across her shoulders.

"Finally, to tell you the truth, Jordyn," she looked at Steph, "you as well, I must say this. I am afraid that I will not have the ability, nerve, and courage to achieve whatever it is that you expect of me. I am afraid I will not make the grade. I am afraid I will fail and fall short of your expectations. Does that make sense to both of you?"

Steph was nodding her head. "It makes perfect sense to me. I had the same feelings, being scared, doubtful, hesitant, questioning my abilities, all that stuff during my last adventure."

"It certainly does make sense, Ava," Jordyn's voice-thoughts declared. "Your worries and fears are understandable. However, as Steph said a while ago, 'Never listen to your fears. They know nothing of your incredible power.' Why do you think Steph said that to you?'"

Ava shrugged her shoulders. "I dunno. Maybe to make an impression on me. If so, the words did make an impression, I have to admit."

"I know what you are thinking right now," Jordyn said. "You are recollecting what you had said in response to Steph's words as the two of you were side by side in the tower. You had asked, although Steph had not replied, 'My power? What power? To what kind of power are you referring?' You do recall that conversation, yes?'"

Ava nodded her head. She looked at Steph. She too was nodding her head.

"I knew you would remember," Jordyn said. "Yes, Ava, never listen to your fears because they know nothing of your incredible power. In the words of your favorite prophet, Mahatma Gandhi, and I want you to memorialize these words as well, 'Be the change you want to see in the world.' If you try to live up to Steph and Gandhi's aphorisms you will do fine.'"

"But how?" Ava asked skeptically. "How can little ole me change the world? I am a nobody in the grand plan of important things. Just another teenager trying to do what is right and stay out of trouble." She chuckled. "Which is more difficult than it sounds. And what about my powers? I ask both of you again." She looked at Steph. "What powers do I have?"

Jordyn said, "You will learn of your powers soon enough, Ava. For now, please trust what Steph and Gandhi have said, what I have said. Can you do that for me, for us?"

"Okay, I will do as you ask," Ava said with a frown. She puckered her lips and glanced around the room uneasily. "However, just so you know, if there is one thing that I abhor more than anything, it is being held in suspense. Okay, what do you say we move on? Let us start with, what does all of this have to do with me, Jordyn? I mean, why am I here? More importantly, where in the world is here, this Inner World place you referred to?" Steph suddenly doubled over with laughter. "What is so funny?" Ava asked in a grouchy manner. She crossed her arms over her chest and glared. "What in tarnation did I say that was so darned funny?"

Steph grabbed her by the arm. "Ah, Ava, if you will recall, Jordyn was about to tell you *the what, the where, and the why*. Before you said all that stuff you just said."

Ava said with a chuckle, "Yes, I guess she did, huh?" She looked at the ceiling. "Sorry, Jordyn. I guess my interruption took longer than I had anticipated. Okay, I am now ready for what, where, and why. Fire away!"

CHAPTER 10

JORDYN'S ENLIGHTENMENTS

"So comes snow after fire, and even dragons have their endings."
—J.R.R. Tolkien, The Hobbit

1

Jordyn started by explaining the origins of the Inner World.

"Ava, Steph, as the two of you will soon see for yourself, the land you are about to enter is exquisite beyond imagination. It is breathtakingly beautiful and more enchanting than either of your wildest dreams. I will start at the beginning.

"Long before humankind arrived on Earth there was a hidden land deep within the Earth's core. It is a magical land that exists even today. It is called the Inner World, where you are at present. Ava, you witnessed the birth of that land. It was when you saw the cataclysmic explosion that caused the dinosaurs to tumble off the mountain." She paused briefly, so Ava could absorb what she just said. "I do not want to test your intelligence, Ava, just your short-term memory. I need to make certain everything is okay with your recall ability. You did experience some horrific things on the staircase. You do remember them, yes? If so, tell me a bit about them if you please."

"Yes, I do recall them," Ava promptly replied. "Vividly. The images are crystal clear in my mind. I must admit, it was sad to watch the mother and baby brontosaurus, the juvenile, meet their doom. I guess like most of the creatures at the time." She noticed that Steph was staring at her with a questioning, surprised expression. She said, "You know, Steph, when the asteroid impacted Mexico's Yucatán Peninsula? It happened around 66 million years ago."

"What in the world?" Steph shouted. She was staring at Ava warily. "Do you mean to tell me you *actually saw dinosaurs?* Honestly? And you watched as the asteroid hit the earth 66 million years ago?"

"Well, maybe I did and maybe I did not," Ava replied. She smiled. Her eyes had brightened noticeably as she said in an eager tone, "But it felt so real, Steph. It was like I was there watching the entire scene unfold before me. I felt the hotness when the asteroid hit, sensed, and heard the explosion. I saw the huge plumes of fire and shortly afterward an enormous column of water zoomed miles in the air. Shortly thereafter, like the momma and juvenile brontosaurus, I also slipped from the mountain. Boulders, debris, and muddy water were enveloping me. The next thing I knew, I was back on the staircase."

Jordyn's voice-thoughts said, "You were there, Ava. You had witnessed the birth of the Inner World firsthand. At the same time, you were also witnessing the end of an era, the wonderful period of dinosaurs. It took some doing on my behalf, but you were present in person 66 million years ago. So, like everything else you think you had imagined while you were on the staircase, that too was real."

Steph was shaking her head. She looked at the ceiling and said, "Geez, Jordyn, I thought you taking me back and forth across the Atlantic over a couple of centuries was unbelievable. But taking Ava back through time 66 million years and down to the Yucatán Peninsula. Talk about incredible. You are downright amazing; do you know that?"

"Thank you," Jordyn's voice-thoughts replied. "I try. Most of the time I succeed, but occasionally I fail." Her telepathic voice-thoughts seemed to chuckle. "Fortunately, I have never stranded someone where he or she ought not to be. I always manage to get them home eventually, safe and sound."

Ava said, "I guess what I experienced was the death of one wonderful era and the birth of another. Was the birth of the Inner World just as wonderful as the age of dinosaurs when they were alive and roaming the Earth?"

"Yes and no," Jordyn replied. "Yes, there are some aspects of the Inner World that rival, perhaps even exceed, the wonders of the age of dinosaurs, at least in the eyes of humankind. There are other aspects of the Inner World that mirror the history and not so good times of the Earthy World's stories."

Steph said, "This is the second time you have mentioned the Earthly World. When you refer to the Earthy World, are you referring to the world in which Ava and I were born, you know, the world of humans?"

"Precisely," Jordyn replied. "But there is a twist to that as well."

Ava suddenly asked, "Jordyn, please excuse me for changing the subject once again. But is there anything to eat around here? I am starving. I have not had a bite to eat since I partially chomped on the PB&J sandwich. And I know Steph is hungry as well." Steph nodded her head.

"Turn around to your left," Jordyn said. "Also, it is about time the two of you stopped lazing around on the bed. It must be made-up, restored to its original state. The occupants of the room will return shortly."

Ava was about to ask who the occupants were going to be when Steph dragged her off the bed. Then she, like Steph, was gawking with an expression of utter disbelief.

On a small table nearest the double door was a silver tray loaded with a half-dozen, steaming hot McDonald's Big Macs. There also were two king-sized cartons of fries and two huge cups of soda, complete with straws. But the delicious-smelling, Earthly World fast food was not the reason they were gawking awestruck while their stomachs growled noisily.

Standing next to the table and smiling timidly was a slight, female creature. She was bedecked in gold and silver trinkets worn on her wrists. A string of pearls surrounded her neck at the collarbone. She looked to be about three feet tall. She had golden skin and long, sharply pointed elven ears. Her ears were much longer than the ears of the elves in the painting.

The creature's eyes, they were as large as tennis balls, were the brightest shade of dark green imaginable. They seemed to shine with playful mischief. She was clad in a dress that appeared to be made of tanned leather. Her dress was spotted, dirty looking, and covered with sewn patches of fabric in a few places.

"Well, hello," Ava said in a nonchalant tone. She pointed to Steph. "This is Steph. Her name is Stephanie JoAnne Galanos." She pressed her thumb against her chest. "And I am Ava, Ava Noelle."

The creature did not take her eyes off Ava as she curtsied gracefully. She nearly shouted in a squeaky tone, *"Avaïnoćel, O Poica Katharos!"* She curtsied once more. Then she quickly glanced at Steph and said something that sounded nothing like "Stephanie JoSnne Galanos." She was staring at Ava excitedly.

Jordyn's voice-thoughts interrupted Ava and Steph's confused stares. "I know what both of you are thinking. Yes, she is a goblin. Her name is Gklimbopa, but she prefers to be called by her humble nickname, Gklim. Gklim in the Elvish language, Fortunomy, implies *helpful, honest, and true.* Goblins are, at least in the Inner World, weak but cunning. Greedy but magnanimous. They are gruesomely attractive in their own way as you can tell, yet they are forcefully loyal. If you befriend a goblin, you will have a faithful friend for life.

"Gklim is the chambermaid of the bedroom. While you might think the bedroom is of the Victorian era, Ava, it is not. In fact, Earthy World humans of the Victorian era copied this style. They named it Victorian, but it has been an Inner World furnishment for many centuries. Also, until you are outside in the Inner World, Gklim will not be able to understand what you are saying in her language. That is why she mispronounced Steph's name."

Ava gave Gklim a sweet smile as she attempted to curtsy. She never was good at curtsying and all but tripped over her own feet causing her to stumble forward a bit. Gklim quickly looked away. She had covered her mouth with her hand and was giggling. Ava was also giggling because she knew she must have looked ridiculous as she tried to curtsy. She said, "Jordyn, please tell Gklim we are incredibly pleased to meet her. Can you do that for me, for us? And thank her for making up the bed for me. It was quite comfortable."

After a few moments, she had been reading Jordyn's voice-thoughts, Gklim smiled and curtsied once more. With one long, final look at Ava, she slowly backed toward the double doors. She grabbed the door handles and pulled them open. With one final respectful bow to Ava, she disappeared. As soon as she was gone, Ava and Steph rushed over to the food and began wolfing it down.

Steph said, "How in the world did you do this, Jordyn? Dang, there is even ketchup and my favorite, honey mustard sauce for dipping my fries. Thanks a bunch."

Ava took a second, huge bite of her Big Mac and stuffed a handful of fries in her mouth. She mumbled, "Yesh, thank you, Jordyn, I wassh soooo hungrry!"

Jordyn's voice-thoughts said, "Do me a favor and take that tray of food over to the table across the room. It is the table situated directly below the painting Ava was staring at for the longest time a bit ago. Then take a seat. I have more to tell you. Hurry now. Time is wasting."

Once Ava and Steph were seated comfortably and eating, Jordyn's voice-thoughts continued. "Okay, Ava. First, let us address the question that has been nagging you since Gklim spoke to you, okay?"

Ava gulped some soda to wash down another handful of fries she had stuffed in her mouth. She swallowed, licked her lips, and said, "Yes, okay. I assume Avaïnoάel is my given name here in the Inner World. I mean you referred to me by that name when I was in the chasm. And the creature that saved me, Fluescere, called me by that name as well. Is my assumption correct?" Jordyn's thoughts responded that she was correct. "Thank you, Jordyn, for confirming that for me. I also noticed Gklim said the words O Poica Katharos after she said the Avaïnoάel word. What was that all about, Jordyn. Can you tell me, please?"

Jordyn's voice-thoughts said, "Translated from Fortunomy to English, O Poica Katharos means the Purest of Elves."

Ava's hands started to tremble. She nearly dropped her cup of soda in reaction to what Jordyn had said. She whispered in an unsteady voice, "Say what?" She looked at Steph. Her bestie was staring at her with a look of utter surprise. Ava said slowly in a firm way, "The Purest of Elves?" She looked away from Steph and stared at the ceiling. "What in the world does that mean, Jordyn? I am no elf. At least I do not think that I am." With a nervous laugh she gingerly touched her left ear and suggested, "Heck, I do not even have elf ears. And as far as I know, all elves have elf ears!" She hesitated momentarily then whispered under her breath, "Like the threesome in the picture—"

Jordyn did not reply. She had read Ava's mind and knew what she was thinking.

Ava had turned around slowly in her seat. She was staring up at the painting of the male, female, and child elf. Her thoughts were racing. She was thinking, now that I am up close to the painting, I could swear that kid looks exactly like me when I was her age. *Exactly like me!* She unhurriedly got to her feet and moved to stare point-blank at the painting. She did not intend to do it, but she had lost her grip on the cup of soda. It dropped to the floor spilling its contents onto the decorative rug. She appeared oblivious to the mess the accident had caused.

Steph placed her food on the tray and quickly got to her feet. She stood beside Ava. Her hand shot up to her mouth as she stared at the painting. She said in a tremulous voice, "Ava, that – that child there. I do not want to say this, but she looks like you. At least what I would imagine you would have looked like when you were a kid. What is she, six or seven years old, maybe a bit older?"

Ava did not reply. Her knees were shaking. Tingling goose pimples seemed to cloak her entire body. She felt woozy. She had to grab onto Steph's arm to keep from collapsing on the sticky mess of spilled soda. She said in a weak tone, "Jordyn, what is going on here? Do you know? Why does the child in this painting have my features? My eyes, my hair color, my nose, my smile, my everything? And most telling, my distinctive eyebrows of all things? And who are these elderly people? Or should I say elves? All three of them must be elves because they have elven ears." She touched the painting and gently stroked the child's face. As she did, visions of the threesome she encountered in the cave flashed before her eyes.

Will you not join us, dearest Avaïnoéel? I presume you are ravenous. There is enough for three.

"What – what is – is going on here, Jordyn?" Ava stuttered. "Please tell me because I am going to go crazy not knowing!"

Jordyn's voice-thoughts said, "Have a seat if you please." Steph immediately did as Jordyn had requested and sat down. Ava remained standing. Her eyes were glued to the painting. Jordyn said, "You as well, Ava. Also, please finish your meal. It will be the last Earthly World fast food you will enjoy for a long time. I refilled your cup as well. As you probably have noticed, the spill is no longer there. I cleaned it up. Once you are finished eating, I will confiscate the cups, burger wrappers, the whole lot. They do not belong in the Inner World."

Ava reluctantly complied with Jordyn's request. She sat down. She was still staring up at the painting. Her appetite had disappeared, but she picked up her burger and began to nibble on it, nonetheless. She knew that she needed the nourishment.

2

Jordyn's voice-thoughts stated, "Steph, under normal circumstances, what I have to say I should say to Ava alone. However, you need to read my thoughts as well. You must be aware of Ava's history, her birthright, and her ancestry."

Steph nodded her head and said, "Thank you, Jordyn. I appreciate that."

"You are welcome. Please bear in mind what I said to you earlier, Steph, and to you alone. I will say it again. You are Ava's Earthy World companion as she journeys in the Inner World. You are her keeper as well. Therefore, you must care for her to the best of your ability. Naturally, you must strive to keep yourself safe as well. Can you promise me that you will keep close watch over her, over both of you?"

"Yes, of course," Steph said. "I promise." She looked at Ava. She was still staring up at the painting as she sluggishly nibbled on her burger. Her lips were trembling, and she was blinking back tears. Her complexion seemed drained of color. Steph assumed that Ava had not noticed that Jordyn had been conversing with her telepathically. She also assumed that Ava had not even noticed that she had spoken aloud.

"Good, and I thank you," Jordyn's voice-thoughts said. "So, let me begin. Are you ready, Ava?" She waited a few moments for Ava to reply. Then her voice-thoughts seemed to shout. "Ava!"

"Yes, Jordyn," Ava replied listlessly. She looked away from the painting. "I understood everything that you and Steph said to each other. I apologize for looking like I was not paying attention." She looked at her burger for a few seconds then took a big bite out of it. She stuffed another handful of fries in her mouth. Her appetite had returned.

"No apologies needed," Jordyn said. "It is important to focus on everything I am about to say. Also, please do not interrupt me until I have finished. As I said earlier, my time is limited, and you two need to get going." She appeared to be chuckling when her voice-thoughts said, "I know of your tendency to interrupt due to your insatiable curiosity. It is not a bad thing I dare say. However, try to not interrupt until I have finished. Okay?"

Ava sipped her soda, and then she said, "Yes, Jordyn, I understand. Okay."

Steph was happy to see that the color in Ava's cheeks had returned, and she no longer was trembling. She was also relieved that Ava's appetite had come back. She had started on her second burger.

Jordyn said, "After I finish telling you about your birthright and your ancestry, I will briefly discuss the Inner World. I will also say some things that pertain to Steph only. Afterward, I will entertain any questions either of you may have. Does that sound good to both of you?"

Ava and Steph replied at the same time, "Sounds good to me." They burst out laughing and gave each other a high-five.

"See?" Ava said happily to Steph. She had returned to her normal, jovial self. "We are like two peas in a pod, two besties."

Jordyn said, "Ava, you witnessed the end of the dinosaur era that occurred 66 million years ago. Scientists say the dinosaur extinction occurred rapidly. Dense clouds of dust probably blocked the sun's rays. Ultimately, greenhouse gases killed over seventy-five percent of all plants and animals. When the huge explosion occurred, it also created a deep depression in the Earth's crust. It was a fissure. The fissure is called Thávma. Into the fissure, the Thávma, spilled countless microbes of bacteria and other living matter that managed to survive the first few weeks of the ecological calamity that was occurring on Earth. Slowly, over tens of millions of years, the Thávma gradually closed, but not completely.

"All through the millennium, life deep below the Thávma adapted and changed just like it had on Earth's surface. Natural evolution on Earth's surface, what I referred to as the Earthly World, and beneath the Thávma was in full swing. Yet there was one distinctive difference between the two worlds. Prehistoric creatures continued to adapt and change below the Earth's surface, whereas on the surface they perished. Gradually, over time, creatures different from those on the Earth's surface came to be below the Thávma. However, some of the creatures were the same.

"The first primeval creatures to come about in the Inner World were fire-breathing dragons and similar prehistoric beasts. The first dragons were small, perhaps no larger than the Earthly World's red-eyed crocodile, wingless skinks of today. Skinks are the closest Earthly World creatures to Inner World dragons. They look like baby dragons. The creatures are of the Tribolonotus genus, presumably the same genus of the Inner World's dragons. We believe that the earliest species of primitive dragons from the Inner World escaped through the Thávma to the Earth's surface, to the Earthly World. Some of the dragons in both worlds were able to breathe fire. However, while the Inner World dragons continued to adapt and change, the Earthly World dragons did not. Their species died out eventually. The exceptions, conceivably, being the ancestors of the red-eyed, wingless crocodile skinks.

Ava's thoughts seemed to be screaming. Oh my gosh, dragons do exist! Perhaps only in the Inner World. But they do exist! And they can breathe fire. I wonder if Fluescere can breathe fire.

Jordyn had read her thoughts. She said, "You are correct, Ava, with what you are thinking. Just like in children's fairytales, Inner World dragons can breathe fire. So can Fluescere, the dragon that rescued you. But you need to know something else. A handful of Inner World dragons, perhaps simply wandering or suffering as abandoned hatchlings, escaped via the Thávma to the Earthly World eons ago.

"Descendants of the original dragons live with their offspring in the most remote islands and mountains of the Earthly World to this day. Perhaps ordinary humans may have spotted dragons in the past. Which would explain why Chinese, Greek, and other cultures have told legendary tales about dragons for centuries."

Ava and Steph were staring at each other with shocked looks of utter amazement. They simply could not believe what Jordyn had said. Offspring of dragons that had exited the Thávma were living amongst humans in the Earthly World to this day!

Jordyn said, "Now to the most significant part of my story. The most resilient DNA that survived in the Earthly World and evolved was that of creatures that eventually walked upright. Human beings and two distinct species of creatures like human beings. The two distinct species were elves with their distinctive elven ears and winged fairies. The fairies also had elven ears, only less pronounced than those of elves." Jordyn's voice-thoughts paused briefly. "I am not reading your thoughts at present. Even though I can imagine what you are thinking. The answer is a resounding yes!"

Ava and Steph smiled at each other knowingly as if they were sharing a secret known only to Jordyn and them. Elves and winged fairies were real!

Jordyn said, "Yes, there are Inner World-derived homo sapiens, elves, and even fairies that live in the Earthly World amongst humans to this day. Their ancestors had climbed out of the Thávma. I have no way of knowing – nobody does – but if I had to venture a guess, I would say many millions of each species live amongst unsuspecting, ordinary humans. Also, just so you know, the Inner World-derived homo sapiens that I refer to are modern-day witches and wizards. And yes, some have magical powers of which Ava witnessed in the cave. But I will not dwell on this further. You will learn even more when you enter the Inner World.

"Some elves of both Worlds, very few actually, have magical powers. But there are a handful of elves that have utterly amazing magical powers. Ava, you are one of them. I must emphasize that point again. Ava, you are one of the elves that has amazing magical powers. Moreover, you have magical powers that far exceed those of others!" Her voice-thoughts paused once more so Ava and Steph could absorb everything she had said. As she expected, Ava and Steph were staring at each other with incredulity. "In fact, Ava, you, as Avaïnoáel, O Poica Katharos, the Purest of Elves, could be the most powerful elf the world has ever known. I will explain further in a few moments."

By now Ava was squirming in her seat. Her heart was racing a mile a second, or at least it seemed to her. She was unbelievably excited. More so than she had ever felt in her life. She wanted to shout, run around in circles, do anything crazy to vent her excitement. Otherwise, she felt she would go mad with what Jordyn had just said. That she may be the most powerful elf the world has ever known!

She thought to herself, Jordyn knows I abhor suspense. But I promised to keep my mouth shut. After all, if I may be the most powerful elf in the world, I should act like it, shouldn't I? But goodness! I cannot believe what is happening! Everything Jordyn has said is too unbelievable to be true. She looked at Steph and laughed. Steph seemed like she was going to cry with excitement. She was staring at Ava with the widest grin imaginable. Ava was about to jump from her chair and walk around – she needed to do something to ease her tension – when Steph grabbed her by the arm forcefully.

"Shush, Ava. And please stop your fidgeting. I hope you know that you really need to work more on being patient."

Ava knew that Steph was correct. Whenever she got overly excited about something, she had to vent her excitement in some way. So, she remained sitting although she was twirling her thumbs nervously to lessen her jumpiness.

Jordyn's voice-thoughts said, "I know both of you can recall reading about the Salem Witch Trials in school. The trials happened between February 1692 and May 1693 in Massachusetts. Hundreds were accused. Thirty were found guilty. Nineteen were hanged. Even now, ordinary humans believe those that were accused were innocent of sorcery. They suppose witchery cannot exist in a world of ordinary human beings. However, if practicing black magic made the witches and wizards of the time culpable of working magic, they were guilty as charged. Their wizarding ancestors had arrived from the Inner World over thousands of years earlier. After they evolved intellectually and magically, they too practiced magic.

"The atrocities of the Salem Witch Trials were proof that something needed to be done. A secret society was formed to protect the well-being of elves, fairies, wizards, and witches. It is now global. The society came about on October 31, 1675, due to the work of the wizard Reverend Robert Smallgood. The society Smallgood created also vowed to protect the secrecy of the Inner World's existence.

"Smallgood was born in December 1645. He came from a small town called Aberfoyle of modern-day Scotland. He had an active interest in the mystical. Particularly aspects of the mystical that dealt with fairies, elves, and the legendary tales of the people of the Scottish Highlands. Smallgood called the organization that he founded the Society of Fairies, Elves, (and) Wizards,' abbreviated SoFEW. The Society vowed to also protect all Inner World creatures. They include trolls, dragons, pixies, dwarves, and yes, goblins like Gklim. There are many other creatures as well, some good, some evil. You will learn more about these creatures eventually.

"Unfortunately, word of the Society did not reach the American colonies in time to prevent the dreadful Salem Witch Trials. The exchange of information was slow back then. Traversing the Atlantic Ocean was treacherous even in the best conditions. Colonial America had more things on its mind at the time as well, like colonizing the vast lands of the ocean-to-ocean continent.

"Okay, Ava, I will now talk about your birthright and ancestors. I will give you a quick synopsis. A great, magical wizard named Godroh will give you more details when you meet him. Commit his name to your unique memory. You as well, Steph. I say again, the wizard's name is Godroh. However, I must caution you. Others may pretend to be Godroh, to fool you. But there is none as powerful or cunning as Godroh. Therefore, trust only him and those that will greet you when you enter the Inner World.

"Ava, you have great-great-grandparents with the last name of Hall. They reportedly were born in Great Britain and emigrated to the Earthly World country of America at the turn of the twentieth century. I am quite certain your grandfather, James, on your mother's side has mentioned their names. Your great-great grandmother's name was Polly. Her husband's name was James. Your great-grandmother was their youngest child. Your grandfather and great uncle are her direct descendants. As is your mother and down the line to you. While the descendancy of your ancestors after the Halls, both living and deceased are linked, it is not important. At least as it concerns this topic. What is important is the Inner World's Prophecy and how it pertains to you. The Prophecy is a projection of *what once was and what will someday be all over again* as it concerns the mystical aspects of both worlds.

"According to the Prophecy, a female will be born on the 14th day of Dekémvrisom of the Inner World's spiritual year, 2007. Dekémvrisom means December in the Elvish language, Fortunomy. Steph, just so you know, Ava was born on the 14th day of Dekémvrisom, 2007. It was a Friday. Friday is the most blessed day of the week of both worlds. Now I will talk briefly about the number fourteen from both an analytical and spiritual perspective.

"In numerology, which is the analysis of numbers, the number fourteen echoes with an idiom of personal freedom. It also embraces independence and self-determination. Those born on the fourteenth day of the month are exceptionally curious and interested in pretty much everything. As you know better than anyone, Ava, the inquisitiveness element of the number fourteen describes your personality to a T. So do the independence and self-determination values. The number fourteen also has significance in the Bible. It is a symbol of salvation and liberation.

"According to the Inner World Prophecy, a fifth-generation elf, the youngest granddaughter of a third-generation male human – that would be your grandfather – would be reawakened on the Earthly World. She would be known as Avaïnoáel, O Poica Katharos. As I said earlier, O Poica Katharos translates to the Purest of Elves. There is much more for you to learn about the Prophecy. Godroh will tell you everything you need to know at the proper time. Before he does, others you will encounter may mention the Prophecy. Nevertheless, what they know is limited because its contents are a well-kept secret. Only Godroh knows the whole truth. Someday you will know as well."

Jordyn's voice-thoughts paused momentarily as she interpreted Ava's reaction. She said at last, "I can tell by your expression, Ava, that you can hardly believe what I am saying. But what I have narrated is true. Therefore, to prove my words true, I would like you to do something for me. When I tell you, please point the forefinger of your right hand at the chamber bed. Afterward, order the canopy to change color, to any color that you desire. I am blocking your thoughts at present, so I will not know what color you are going to choose. We will only do this little experiment one time.

"After that I must, unfortunately, erase your memory of everything I have told you about being Avaïnoáel, O Poica Katharos, the Purest of Elves. Everything, to include the Prophecy. Everything I have said about your grandparents, the Hall's, of Fluescere, etcetera. The only memory, the only allusion you will retain will be that of the wizard, Godroh. Ava, erasing your memory is for your protection as well as for Steph's. Please trust me. You will automatically recall everything that I have said when the time is right. Your subconsciousness will make it happen. Otherwise, Godroh will reinstate your memory of those things you have yet to recall. Steph, I will erase your memory as well. Except for my mention of Godroh. Okay, Ava, are you ready?" Ava nodded her head. "Please get to your feet and point your finger as I instructed you."

Ava slowly got to her feet. She straight away began to move about randomly due to the tension that seemed to be gobbling up her entire body. She set off with the giggles. She gave Steph a nervous grin and pretended to faint.

Steph jumped up and grabbed her hand and squeezed hard. Her tone was overly concerned when she said, "Are you okay?" Ava nodded her head.

Jordyn's voice-thoughts were once more in both of their minds. "Ava, I want you to say *Presto Chango.* After you say *Presto Chango,* follow those two words with the color you desire by thinking it in your mind. As an example, say *Presto Chango.* After that think of the color violet. There is no need to say or think anything else. You got that?"

Ava nodded her head nervously, and then she did what she typically does. She interrupted. "Jordyn, you told me to not interrupt, but I must." She spun around and pointed to the painting. "Before you erase my memory, I must know something. Because it is driving me crazy." She breathed in deeply and exhaled sharply. "I simply have to know who those three elves in the painting are. The two adults look like the male and female I saw in the cave; except they are much older."

Jordyn's voice-thoughts replied, "The two elderly adults represent your great-great-grandparents, Mary and James Hall. They were two magical elves of the Inner World. Both were pure elves."

Ava asserted, "But you said they *reportedly* were born in Great Britain. That they emigrated to my home country at the beginning of the twentieth century. I do not understand something, Jordyn. Did my great-great-grandparents come from the Inner World? Or were they born in the Earthly World?"

"Ava, you do not miss a thing, do you? You are correct to question me further regarding the descent of the Halls. I had said they *reportedly* were born in Great Britain because that is what they wanted everyone to believe at the time. I will explain.

"Polly and James were actually born in the Inner World. They were youngsters when they traveled with their parents via the Thávma to the Earthly World. From there they sailed with their parents to Great Britain. When they became of age, they wed. When they were in their twenties, they emigrated to your home country, to America. They settled in Long

Island, New York. Just so you know, your great-great-grandfather served in the National Guard of America of the Earthly World. Service to your homeland has a long history in your family on both sides."

Ava said, "Okay, that is cool. They were born in the Inner World. Thank you for clarifying that for me." She pointed to the painting. "But who is the child elf in the painting? Is the child elf me, Jordyn? Is it? Please tell me the truth because the child looks just like me. Exactly like me!"

Jordyn replied, "Yes, it is you. It represents Avaïnoάel, O Poica Katharos, the Purest of Elves."

"But how?" Ava cried. She was wringing her hands. "How can it be possibly? My great-great-grandparents died many decades before I was even born! How is it I am pictured with them? It doesn't make a lick of sense!"

Jordyn's voice-thoughts seemed strained when she replied. "The painting simply is the artist's depiction of what the three of you would have looked like when you were a young child. As I said, your great-great-grandparents were pure elves having been born in the Inner World. In fact, they were the last pure elves of your family tree. Before the Prophecy was fulfilled and you came to be."

Ava's eyes widened. She could hardly believe everything Jordyn had told her. Her great-great-grandparents being born in the Inner World. Emigrating as children to Great Britain through the so-called Thávma that connects both worlds. Afterward emigrating to America as adults. The Inner World's Prophecy being finalized when she was born. When she was reawakened as Avaïnoάel, O Poica Katharos, the Purest of Elves.

At last, after a few moments of silent, innermost contemplations, she had regained her composure. She said in a whisper, "I apologize, Jordyn, but I have one last question. Why now?"

"Why now that you are regarded as Avaïnoάel, O Poiça Katharos?" Jordyn replied having interpreted Ava's thoughts. "Fulfilling the Prophecy? For the simple reason that you are now thirteen years of age. Also, because the world as we know it is in dire danger. Perhaps that is the most significant reason."

Ava discounted what Jordyn had said about the world being in dire danger. She understood that. There was too much crime, pollution, and war. The still ongoing, worldwide COVID-19 pandemic had been deadly, and the Earth was warming too fast. Maybe due to humanity's disdain for the delicate balance of nature. Consequently, she had missed the point that Jordyn was trying to make – that she, Ava Noelle, as Avaïnoάel, O Poica Katharos, had everything to do with the world's dire state.

By reading her thoughts, Jordyn knew that Ava had missed the point. She did not wish to confuse or excite her even more, so she let it go. Ava would learn the truth soon enough.

Looking at the ceiling with a troubled expression, Ava said, "Tell me what is so significant about me being thirteen years old. I mean, what is in a number anyway? Why not 14, 15, or when I am an adult at 18?"

Jordyn replied, "You are now a thirteen-year-old adolescent, a teenager. As you continue to change physically and mentally, you are also changing emotionally and psychologically. Thus, you are ready to face the world as you know it."

Ava was not ready to accept everything that Jordyn had said. She still had many doubts, many more questions too. And she knew that Jordyn understood her reservations and hesitancy by reading her thoughts. Yet for Steph's sake, she figured it was time to move on. Because she knew in her heart that there was no going back, only forward. She also assumed she would learn more in the future.

"Okay, Jordyn, I will accept everything that you have said is the truth." She glared at the painting. "I also accept what I see before my eyes as fact. But you must understand, all of this is a complete shock. I am baffled by all of it." She glanced at Steph and said nervously, "Given what I have seen, felt, heard, and sensed since climbing the tower, I guess that nothing should surprise me." She pushed her shoulders back and jutted out her chest. "So, for the umpteenth time, Jordyn, I apologize for interrupting. Now I am ready to point my finger and say those words, *Presto Chango*, and think the color of my choice."

Jordyn said, "Make certain to point the forefinger of your right hand at the bed as you say and think those three words. You need not point your finger directly at the canopy. Your thoughts will take care of that, and your finger will automatically know what it is supposed to do. What happens next will be exactly in reply to your thoughts."

Ava looked at Steph and could not help but grin. Steph was staring openmouthed at the bed. She was bouncing up and down on her tiptoes slightly. She had crossed her fingers. Ava could tell that she too was hoping all would go well.

Meanwhile, Ava's thoughts were scattering. She inhaled deeply and closed her mind to everything but what Jordyn had told her to do. With a drawn-out exhale she said, "Okay, here goes nothing" and pointed her forefinger at the bed. Her hand was shaking. She whispered cautiously, "*Presto Chango,*" and then she thought orange.

A brief burst of orange sprang from the tip of her finger and zoomed at lightning speed across the room. As soon as the beam struck the burgundy canopy, the canopy switched to bright orange. It had transformed to the orangish color of an overripe Halloween pumpkin.

Steph squealed, "Wooowww! That was like completely awesome!" She punched Ava hard on the shoulder. "Way to go, girl!" She grabbed Ava by the forearms, and they began to dance together in widening circles.

Ava was screaming, "Oh, my goodness! I did it, Steph, I did it! Did you see that cool, brief glow at the tip of my fingertip? Then it zipped across the room in a stream of bright orange! Talk about totally cool!"

Steph hollered, "Yes, Ava, I saw it! What you just did was incredible. See what I told you? Never listen to your fears – they know nothing of your incredible power!" She leaned in and whispered, "Just so you know, Jordyn told me to say that catchphrase to you. It was her way of propping up our bond as recent friends, at least I guess it was. I honestly did not know anything about your powers at the time." She gaped at the orange canopy for a few seconds. "But wow, Ava! Now that I know what powers you have; I honestly cannot wait to see you in real action!"

Ava's expression suddenly went blank. She abruptly stopped dancing and let go of Steph's forearms. She turned about and sat down on the chair. Lifting her eyebrow while cocking her head, she said to Steph in a surprised tone, "See *what* in action? What in the world are you talking about?"

Steph returned Ava's empty stare. She swallowed hard and her shoulders slumped slightly. The way the palms of her hands were splayed out suggested she too was confused. "Beats me, Ava, but whatever it was, it must have been tremendously fantastic." She wiped away the tears from her flushed face. "See? I am crying tears of happiness. You are as well. And my heart is racing like a mile a minute as if I just saw something amazing. How about you?"

Ava ignored Steph's questions. Something was nagging her like something incredible had just happened. But she could not summon it from her subconscious. She looked up at the painting.

Why in the heck does that canvas intrigue me so much? She turned away from the painting and eyed the bed canopy. I could have sworn that the canopy was burgundy, not orange. What is going on here? She shrugged her shoulders and reached down and gobbled up a handful of fries. They had gotten cold, but she did not seem to care. She was famished.

She and Steph finished their meal in silence. They had puzzled looks and occasionally shook their heads with confusion. They were trying to figure out what had just happened. They knew something had, but they could not bring it to the forefronts of their minds. They had no idea that Jordyn had erased their memories of Ava's magical powers. Nor did they know that Ava was the legendary Avaïnoðel, the Purest of Elves. Yet they were able to recall information that Jordyn had allowed them to retain. In addition to a name that she had said was especially important.

Godroh.

3

"Okay, Steph, now it is your turn," Jordyn's voice-thoughts said, thus bringing her and Ava back to the present. "I know you recall from your last adventure how you defeated those horrible Nazis in the cathedral. Even though they outnumbered you three to one and were armed to the teeth. While you were unarmed. How you took them out one by one with your bare hands and kicks of your powerful legs."

Steph smiled and nodded her head. She noticed that Ava was staring at her with a look of admiration. She pretended to ignore her envious stare. Steph is not one to brag – ever. She undoubtedly is one of the most modest teenagers' going. But Jordyn having openly restated her heroic actions to save the Jewish boy, Adalard, made her feel incredibly good inside.

Jordyn said, "You had stepped between the slave, Joseph, and the white overseer, Boss, when the latter was whipping the child. You also faced off with the ruthless slaveowner, Judas Gray, even as he pointed his rifle at you. Lastly, but not conclusively, you helped Christopher. Not only did you befriend him, but you held him up as he walked proudly across the stage to receive his high school diploma. Because of your love and compassion, you gave him the courage to attend Yale University. He graduated a year early and ultimately became a biomedical scientist, despite his cerebral palsy. And Steph, thanks to you, he continues to work tirelessly to this day to find a cure for children with cerebral palsy and other childhood diseases."

Steph's face was the color of a glowing red Christmas tree bulb. Ava was clutching her forearm tightly. She was staring at Steph admiringly with a warm smile. Steph looked at her and managed a weak grin. She shrugged as if Jordyn had not said anything important.

But Ava knew otherwise. She elbowed Steph in the ribs to get her attention. In a whisper she said, "Dang, girl, you *are* amazing! My respect for you has increased a zillion times if that is even possible."

Steph lightly placed her forefinger against Ava's lips. She was grinning as she gestured for Ava to shush. They had promised Jordyn that they would not interrupt.

Jordyn said, "All of that took some doing, Steph. While I was with you part of the time, to guide you, everything you accomplished took guts, courage, and determination. It also took cunning, intellect, and strength. None of it could have happened if it were not for those handfuls of attributes and many more that you possess. Thanks to you, Adalard was saved from certain death by Jew-hating Nazi soldiers. Thanks to you, Joseph and his sisters Hannah and Patsy were freed from slavery. They lived the remainder of their lives as unchained, free citizens and went on to do great things.

"I know what I have said embarrasses you to some degree, Steph. Because you are very modest. But I have my reasons for saying what I did. First, Ava needs to know how lucky she is to have an intelligent, brave companion such as you. Second, it is essential to remind you of your own, unique powers. While I cannot bestow mystical powers on you – nothing of the sort – I have given you some skills that will come in handy. The first skill is owing to your exceptional athleticism and aggressiveness as a rugby player. It is a martial arts skill known as Krav Maga. It was developed by the Israeli Defense Force. Krav Maga is the world's most dangerous form of combat. You will instinctively employ this skill if the occasion presents itself. Hopefully, it will not."

121

Ava and Steph were gawking at each another. They wordlessly said at the same time, "Wow!" As before when they reacted in the same manner, they burst out laughing and gave each other a high-five.

Jordyn ignored their hilarity and resumed her voice-thoughts. "The second skill is comprised of two abilities: archery and swordsmanship. When you arrive in the Inner World, you will be a proven markswoman archer. You will carry a bow – a longbow naturally – and a quiver of arrows. You will also be an adept swordswoman, capable of skillful moves and able to defend yourself effortlessly. Hopefully, you will not need to use these skills, but you will have them all the same. The weaponry will be provided to you as soon as you enter the Inner World."

Ava, with a look of surprise on her face, threw her hands in the air as if asking, "What about me?"

Jordyn said, "Ava, you too will have swordswoman and archery skills. Like Steph's skills, they will come naturally to you even though you have never shot an arrow or picked up a sword in your life."

Ava punched the air with her fist and yelled, "Yes!"

"However, Ava," Jordyn said, "you will not have Krav Maga skills. Sorry."

"Aww," Ava said unhappily. She looked like she was about to ask Jordyn why she would not have Krav Maga skills. But Steph smacked her on the shoulder and told her to shush.

CHAPTER 11

THE FINALITY BEFORE
THE INNER WORLD

"Never laugh at a fire-breathing dragon – unless you want to get burned."
—the author

1

Jordyn said, "At last we have arrived at my description of the Inner World. I will give you a brief review. Trying to describe the Inner World at great length would be like trying to describe the Earthly World at length to an absolute stranger. It would take weeks, perhaps months. It is impossible to do so. There will be much more for you to learn about the Inner World. And learn you shall, in due time. Here we go."

Jordyn began her summary by explaining that the Inner World is made up of three different regions. Each is completely dissimilar in its culture and history. The first region Jordyn described is called Antiquom.

Antiquom is the Inner World's oldest region. It is known by another name as well. Inhabitants commonly refer to Antiquom as the Inner World's Yesteryear. It is a place of incredible prosperity, tranquility, harmony, and great optimism. It also is a land of goodwill and everlasting peace. Nevertheless, like all worlds, and as one would expect, Antiquom has its share of unsavory, greedy, and even evil creatures, and, sadly, conflict.

The second region is called Andron. Andron is commonly referred to as the Inner World's Corridor. Andron, or the Corridor, is a passageway of sorts from the Inner World's Yesteryear to the Inner World's tomorrow. Andron can best be described as the Inner World's present day, the here and now. Like Antiquom, Andron has conflict and unsavory creatures.

The third region of the Inner World is called Ostium. Ostium is the Inner World's future, its tomorrow. It is a world yet to come but may be starting to exist although only a bit. Since Ostium embodies the Inner World's future, Andron may already be, figuratively speaking, passing the baton to Ostium. Jordyn said there is no way of knowing if Andron will cease to exist after Ostium arrives completely. Just like Antiquom and Andron, Ostium has its share of hostilities and evilness.

Jordyn had perceived the perplexed looks on Ava and Steph's faces. As a result, her thoughts quickly followed up on what she had just said about the three regions of the Inner World.

"I understand both of you are a bit puzzled with what I have said. Indeed, all this may sound a bit confusing to you right now. Please trust me when I say everything will make perfect sense as you journey in Antiquom of the Inner World."

Jordyn went on to explain that the Inner World is incredibly beautiful. It is unlike anything Ava and Steph had ever seen in encyclopedias, on the Internet, or in movies. Like Earth's outer crust, the Inner World has similar topographical features. It has lakes, rivers, streams, mountains, grasslands, and deserts. Then again, the Inner World does not have oceans, nor is it divided as continents or distinct landmasses that are separated by immense bodies of water. Despite its lack of oceans, some of the Inner Worlds' largest lakes are briny, but not as much as the Earthly World's oceans and seas.

Jordyn said, "Remarkably, the Inner World's three regions share a common sun, moon, and celestial constellations that are different from those of the Earthly World. Legends state that a mighty body created the Inner World's outer space millions of years ago. Whether or not a mighty body managed to enact such a marvelous miracle is a mystery. But the fact remains. The Inner World's heavenly panorama, like its unique topography, is completely different than that of the Earthly World.

"The Inner World does not have continents. It is one spread-out landmass. Like the Earthly World, the Inner World also has differences in weather patterns with variances in temperature, humidity, and precipitation, some severe. Like the Earthly World, the Inner World experiences rainfall, snowfall, and droughts depending on the location. Also, —"

Having forgotten to not interrupt, or more likely because her curiosity was once more getting the best of her, Ava abruptly disrupted Jordyn's thoughts. "Jordyn, if the Inner World doesn't have continents and is made up of one landmass, how are the three regions divided? Let me see if I remember them correctly from oldest to youngest. They are Antiquom, Andron, and Ostium. Anyhow, are they separated by rivers or mountain ranges or other geographical barriers?"

"That is an excellent question," Jordyn replied. "Even though I asked you to not interrupt. But since you asked, I will respond to your question. The three regions – and you restated them correctly, Antiquom, Andron, and Ostium – are separated by invisible barriers. The barriers are magical impediments. In your modern-day lingo, I guess you could refer to the invisible barriers as, let me think how to put this—" Her thoughts paused briefly. She was reading Steph's mind. "Thank you, Steph. You are correct. The modern-day term of the invisible barriers separating the three regions could best be described as magical force fields."

"Magical force fields?" Ava exclaimed. "That is incredible! The Inner World sounds like something right out of a fantasy novel or sci-fi movie." She slapped Steph's shoulder as she shouted exuberantly, "Magical force fields, Steph! Can you imagine? Our adventure is going to be awesomely remarkable!"

Steph was smiling and nodding her head. She too was excited. But suddenly, with a serious look, she said with a smirk, "Goodness, Ava, suppress your inquisitiveness and please shush!"

Jordyn's voice-thoughts said, "Perhaps it is better if you interrupt as I describe the Inner World. That way you will not forget to ask me questions, some of which could be important if we wait until the end. So, ask away as we go. But please try to keep your questions to a minimum.

"In reply to your sci-fi movie issue, Ava, I must say this. There are no futuristic aspects of the Inner World, no spaceships, astronauts, terrestrial creatures, those sorts of things. At least not at present. Then again who knows? Maybe Ostium will have such things someday, like those of the Earthly World. Yet you are accurate when you associate the Inner World with a fantasy novel. In fact, I do believe you and Steph will find the Inner World to be more magical and make-believe than either of you ever thought possible."

Steph grinned at Ava and said, "Something tells me that our joint adventure will far surpass everything I did on my last voyage. Anyway, whatever it is you are meant to do; I promise you this." She placed her left hand over her heart and raised her right hand high in the air. "I will be by your side no matter what."

"Moving on," Jordyn's voice-thoughts said, "now it is time for me to explain something that should concern you both. For Ava, it is the reason why she is about to venture to the Inner World. For you, Steph, it is the reason you are to accompany her. It all has to do with one word. That word is Wendigorium."

"The word Wendigorium does not sound anything close to being nice at all," Steph said cautiously, "What does it mean actually?"

Jordyn replied, "Wendigorium is the name of a monster that for now dwells in the Inner World. It is a tremendously evil beast. It is a most dreadfully malevolent creature, perhaps of all past and present creatures of the entire planet."

Ava and Steph stared at each other for the longest time. They were shaking their heads with miserable expressions on their faces.

"Is that why I, why we are here?" Ava asked in a tremulous tone. "Is this evil creature, this dreadful creature, Wendigorium, our *objective*, for lack of a more accurate word, in the Inner World? If so—" She looked at Steph who was shaking her head. "—then I am not so certain I want to be here, Jordyn. And I seriously doubt Steph does as well."

Steph did not say anything in reaction to Ava's comments. She simply stared straight ahead emotionless.

Jordyn said, "There is only one way I can answer your question, Ava. Yes."

"Yes, what?" Ava asked curtly. "What do you mean when you just say yes?"

Jordyn replied, "Yes, the reason you are here in the Inner World is to confront Wendigorium. You may have to face him in your world as well. It all depends."

Ava jumped to her feet and stared at the ceiling. She mumbled, "Well, for your information, I do not want to be here." Her tone was defiant. "All I wanted to do was continue my family's legacy by climbing the dagburned tower. I did not ask to be thrust within the tower by some unseen, magical force without my consent. I did not ask to try and descend that stupid staircase, just to be knocked around and somersaulting like a stupid, nonsensical puppet on a string. To see and feel so many terrible things. Frankly, I did not ask anyone to be here!" She was shaking so much she had to sit down.

"Hold on a minute," Steph said calmly. "I am going to be with you. We will have weapons, and we will know how to use them as Jordyn said."

Ava cried heatedly, "Oh yeah? How do we know that for real, Steph? Answer me that!" She jumped to her feet once more. She pointed her finger at the ceiling and began to walk in tight circles. She was scowling. Her nasty scowl appeared angrier than a Canadian goose protecting her nest. She abruptly stopped walking and scolded in a sardonic tone, "Jordyn, I want you to tell me what good are swords and bows and arrows against this Wendigorium thing? The beast sounds vicious. You even said so yourself." She sneered nastily and narrated in a sarcastic, singsong manner what Jordyn had stated about Wendigorium. "'Wendigorium is the name of a monster that for now dwells in the Inner World. It is a tremendously evil beast. It is a most dreadfully malevolent creature, perhaps of all past and present creatures of the entire planet.'"

Ava gave Steph a serious look. "Also, just so you know, I for one am not convinced that what Jordyn said about you and me being able to handle the weapons effectively is true. How in God's name can two people who have never shot an arrow and wielded a sword know what to do when the time comes?" She threw her hands in the air with total frustration. "Answer me that, Steph!"

Suddenly, the image of Ava shooting the orange light at the bed canopy appeared in Ava and Steph's minds. As quickly as it had appeared, it vanished. Jordyn had allowed them to replay the image of Ava's magical power in their minds. Her plan had succeeded. Ava's angry, defiant, and ugly attitude suddenly softened. She appeared to be embarrassed with her display of anger. She sat down and took Steph's hand in hers. She looked into Steph's eyes and said in a calm tone, "Please promise me something, Steph. Can you promise me everything will be okay? Can you do that for me? Can you promise me that much if nothing else?"

"I would be lying to you if I said everything will be okay," Steph said. She gave Ava's hand one of her resolute, reassuring squeezes. "So, I cannot promise you that. But I can tell you this much. As Jordyn said earlier, I faced evil men with guns, both in Nazi Germany, and on an American plantation a year before the Civil War. Jordyn was with me in Germany, but she was not with me in America. But—" she smiled and took a lock of Ava's hair and twirled it in her fingers, "—as you can see, Ava, I survived. It is all up to you, to me, to both of us as a team. I was strong back then, and I intend to be just as strong if not stronger here in the Inner world. I also know in my heart you are strong as well. We must believe in Jordyn. She is the most magical being one could ever imagine. She will not let us down, and she will never deceive us." She smiled. "We got this, Ava."

Jordyn said to Ava, "Like those many times on the basketball court – when you looked up from your five-foot, two-inch, small frame and stared anxiously at the girls who were at least a foot taller than you. You were afraid, rightly so. But you jumped in the fray and matched them with your athleticism, your skills, your cunning, and most importantly, your courage. You had the same fortitude, tenacity, and boldness on the volleyball court. You always have been up for a challenge no matter how difficult it may have appeared at the time. You, like your father, your Grandpa Jim, and your great uncle, are unconquerable."

"I guess you are right," Ava said softly after a few moments' hesitations. She looked at Steph. "But, Steph, why won't you promise me that we will be all right?"

Steph was giving her a sincere smile as she said, "I cannot. I cannot predict what the future may hold for you, for us. But I can promise you this. As I said a few moments ago," she crossed her heart, "I will be by your side through thick and thin. I will never abandon you. That I can promise you, or I will die trying."

Ava said, "Okay, I appreciate that, Steph. Thank you. As for you, Jordyn, I am terribly sorry. It seems like I am forever questioning your abilities, your candor. I should not be so doubtful. Please continue, and

I apologize for interrupting again." She ran her fingers through her hair. "It's just that I am so overly, darned curious!"

Jordyn continued to describe the horrible wrongs of the dreadfully malevolent creature, Wendigorium. She said that Wendigorium and the beast's notorious band of scary *belugas* were terrorizing Antiquom. Wendigorium's terrorism started thousands of years ago and continues to this day.

Jordyn said, "Wendigorium has been referred to by a few other names that describe his brutality. The most notorious is the Latin word "Occisor de Orbis." It translates in Latin to *Slayer of the World.*"

She went on to explain that scholars' characterization of Wendigorium as the Slayer of the World accurately describes Wendigorium's notorious cruelty. She stated that no legendary creature or human being in Earth's history has ever been as immoral as Wendigorium. A few of the more disreputable names she cited in comparison included the mythological beasts Hades, Cyclops, and Medusa. She also mentioned the infamous humans Heinrich Himmler, Josef Stalin, and Adolf Hitler.

Ava would come to realize much later that what Jordyn had said about Wendigorium, due to no fault of her own, was not completely accurate. As if she was confirming this fact, Jordyn's voice-thoughts said, "At this juncture, I must acknowledge something. What I have told you is the extent of my knowledge of Wendigorium, and some of it may not be precise. I expect Godroh will enlighten you more about Wendigorium. I wish I knew more to better prepare you, but I do not."

Steph said, "You know, Jordyn, I think I have heard of the beast. At least I think so, although the evil, fantasy spirit I have read about is called Wendigo. Is Wendigorium the same creature as Wendigo?"

Jordyn's voice-thoughts said, "Excellent question, Steph. But my answer, I am sorry to say, must be both yes and no. Yes, Wendigo was a topic of folk tales told by Earthly World Canadian Algonquian people, particularly those that dwelled along the East Coast, in Nova Scotia, and the Great Lakes region. Wendigo supposedly was a man-eating creature. Nevertheless, as far as I know, the beast was not real. It was an imaginary, evil spirit. In contrast, and this is the no part of my answer, Wendigorium is real and the evilest creature of all time."

From Ava's point of view, Wendigorium did not appear to be a man-eating creature. That was good, at least so she thought. Yet the idea of the beast being the evilest creature ever had terrified her just the same. She said to Jordyn, "So, what you are saying is that there is no connection between the Algonquian peoples' man-eating evil beast Wendigo and Wendigorium that is in the Inner World?" She quickly added in a glad, optimistic tone, "Which is good, right? Because we certainly do not need to have a man-eating creature on our hands. Therefore, there is no connection between the two beasts. Am I correct?"

Jordyn said, "Ava, as I had said when I answered Steph's question, I am obliged to reply yes and no. Please allow me to explain. Wendigorium that is presently tormenting the Inner World is alive, whereas Wendigo of the Algonquian people was fictitious. Nonetheless, and you need to know this; even though the Algonquian's evil spirit, Wendigo, may be fictitious in the Earthly human world, its folklore could be based on reality. It may be based on the evil exploits of Wendigorium if the creature dwelled in the Earthly World at some point. Although once more I must caution you that I am not certain. I am merely speculating.

"Also, it is important for you to know this. I do not know enough to say that Wendigorium lived among humans of the Earthly World. Nevertheless, there is no way to discount that the creature had not. As I said earlier, the fissure between the two worlds, the Thávma, is intact. The Thávma has been open for an exceptionally long time. So, anything is possible. Once more I must say that Godroh will further enlighten you, Ava, on the uncertain areas I cannot address satisfactorily. Perhaps he will enlighten Steph as well."

Ava was completely confused at that point. She was also becoming increasingly worried. Just the thought of confronting an evil creature on which Earthly World legends could have been based was unthinkable. Added to that was a feeling of disgust because Jordyn had said Wendigorium was even eviler than the Nazi dictator, Hitler. And in her assessment Hitler, the evilest abomination the world ever created was the most horrible human ever born! She said rather forcefully, "Okay, Jordyn, please allow me to see if I have a complete understanding of what you have been saying."

Jordyn's voice-thoughts replied, "Please do, Ava. You and Steph must have a complete understanding of everything that involves what you are about to encounter. At least as much as I can tell you given what I know."

"Sounds fair to me," Ava said in a convincing tone although she did not feel happy about the prospects of facing evil at thirteen years of age. "From what you have told us, Wendigorium is alive and well in the Inner World, in Antiquom. That the creature may or may not have dwelled in the Earthly World. Am I correct thus far?"

"You are correct," Jordyn declared. "The creature is terrorizing the Inner World's inhabitants, thanks to its evil ways and with the assistance of belugas."

"What exactly are belugas?" Steph asked a split-second before Ava could ask the very same question.

Jordyn said, "Belugas are mutated, massive elves, nearly twice as tall as normal elves and much heavier. It is said they do not have a soul. They also are practically blind, depending of course on their species of which there are two of the belugas' genus. Despite that, they can perceive things perfectly using an extrasensory perception power like echolocation skills of Earthly World bats."

Ava quickly said, "I have read about bat's echolocation skills." She glanced at Steph and saw her questioning look. She explained, "Bats emit high-frequency sound pulses through their mouth and nose. They listen to the echoes. Thus, they can determine the size and shape of objects in their vicinity." She grinned in response to Steph's surprised expression. "However, unlike the belugas' being practically blind like Jordyn just said, bats have keen eyesight, especially in the pitch-black."

Steph placed her finger to her lips and grinned. She was telling Ava to shush for the umpteenth time.

Ava frowned and quickly said, "Oops, I did it again, didn't I, Jordyn? I interrupted you. Sorry. Please continue."

Jordyn said, "No apology is necessary, Ava. It is good for Steph to know what echolocation is. There are two types or species of the belugas' genus. One type is much smarter than the other and can see much better. It is known as *déxypnos.*"

Ava said aloud to Steph, "Sort of like the Greek word "éxypnos" which means smart. Isn't it amazing how so many Earthly World words are like those of the Inner World?" She frowned because Steph was shaking her head, that she had interrupted Jordyn once more. She silently mouthed, "Oops."

Ignoring what Ava had said, Jordyn exclaimed, "The stupider of the belugas' genera – sorry but that is the only way to describe it – is known as a dud. It is a failed specimen of nature and nearly useless except for terrorizing its prey brutally. However, it is just as cunning and sly like an Earthly World fox as it is dumb. It also is exceptionally strong. While it understands the Elvish language, Fortunomy, it does not have vocal cords. It cannot speak. It just moans and hisses terribly loud, scarily as well.

"The other species of belugas, the déxypnos, is just as cunning and sly, just as strong, but exceptionally smarter than the dud. As I said a moment ago, it also can see much better. The déxypnos is more intelligent as well, due to an abnormal mutation of the genus' genes. The déxypnos has vocal cords and can speak. Unlike its dud brethren, it walks upright most of the time. The dud can stand on its hind legs as well, but it usually walks heavily on all fours like an Earthly World bear.

"Unlike similar species of the same genus the World over, the déxypnos and duds never breed with each other. Therefore, their genetic makeup stays the same within their species. More importantly, and yes, frighteningly, there is no way to tell the two types of belugas apart. They look the same. At least to all but the most trained experts.

"The leader of the belugas is the brutal monster, Strum. The name Strum means *barbarity* in Fortunomy. The name Strum is a derivative of the Latin word "mōnstrum," which means *a thing that evokes fear and wonder.*

"By the way, I forgot to mention something extremely important. Both of you will be speaking and listening to the Elvish language even though what you are thinking and absorbing in your minds will be words in your native tongue, English. If you were unable to communicate or appear to comprehend Fortunomy, you would stand out too much. That is something I do not want to happen. You could be in extreme danger."

Ava was about to ask Jordyn to describe the belugas in more detail, such as their physical features, mannerisms, and the like. However, before she could muster up enough nerve to interrupt Jordyn once more, Jordyn's voice-thoughts continued.

2

"Okay, Ava, Steph," Jordyn said. "It is almost time for the doors that Gklim had exited to reopen. They will lead you to Antiquom of the Inner World."

Steph said, "May I ask a couple of questions before we go?"

"Me too?" Ava added hopefully. Although she knew for a fact, she had like thirty questions or more to ask.

"Certainly. But just a few," Jordyn replied. "You go first, Steph."

Steph said, "Can you give us a few hints or, better yet, tell us what we should expect when we actually enter the Inner World? I mean, how will we know what to do? where to go? who, if anybody, should we try to seek out to guide us? Or will someone meet us once we are on the other side of the doors like you said?"

"You will be met shortly after you enter the Inner World," Jordyn said as she ignored Steph's four other questions. "Do you have any other questions?"

Steph quickly replied, "Yes, I do. I know this may appear to sound trivial, but how will we get our weapons? How will we know which ones are ours, Ava's and mine?"

"Those that meet you will supply you with your weapons. They will know what weapons belong to who."

"One last question," Steph said. She looked Ava up and down, and then she gestured with her hands along her upper body. "As you can see, I am wearing the jeans and tee-shirt I wore in Spirit's barn when you fetched me. Ava likewise is wearing what she had on when she climbed the tower. Will our modern-day clothes be suitable in the Inner World? Or will we be given new clothes, you know, things that fit in with the Inner World's fashion if there is one?"

Jordyn said, "Those that meet you will supply you with a satchel of spare clothes and dried, eatable goods, a flask, and a waterskin. Around the time the doors open to the Inner World, what you presently are wearing will change to Inner World attire. I am confident you will like your new clothes. They will fit you perfectly. Also, most Inner World elves wear jewelry, including the male elves. Hence, your new attire will include elven jewelry.

"One piece of jewelry is particularly important. It is a ring both of you will be wearing on the pinky finger of your left hand. The rings you will be wearing are of an ancient land beneath the sea of the Earthly World. The land is called Spardom. The emblem engraved on the ring represents peace, love, and harmony. There are only four of these rings in existence today. One ring is worn by the Queen of Spardom, Queen Lindsial. One ring will be worn by each of you. Godroh is wearing the fourth ring. When you meet Godroh, make certain he is wearing the ring. If you cannot see a ring on the pinky finger of the wizard's left hand, you can assume he is an imposter."

"Okay, I am finished asking questions," Steph said. "Thank you." She said to Ava with a grin – she was grinning because she already knew the answer – "Do you have any last-minute questions for Jordyn?"

"Do I have any questions?" Ava replied with a loud laugh. "You know me too well, Steph, than to ask that." She began to count on her fingers. "Let's see, question one, two, three, four, five, six, seven, eight—"

"Three should suffice," Jordyn said interrupting Ava's tallying. "I will answer them right now since I know what the three most important ones are that you want to ask. The others can wait because they will be answered sooner or later. Is that okay with you?" Ava nodded her head reluctantly. "Remember what I said earlier. My time is limited, and those that are waiting for you on the other side are getting impatient. I also imagine they are getting a bit worried as well since it has taken us much longer than expected."

Ava said coolly, "But, as you know all too well because you can read my mind, I think I have at least six particularly important questions that need to be addressed right now. Maybe as many as ten."

"I know that you have six questions you deem important," Jordyn said. "And a whole lot more, like over a few dozen. I quit counting after twenty-seven. But not now. You will have plenty of opportunities to answer the questions for yourself in due time."

In due time? Ava pondered silently. How am I supposed to reply to a question to which I probably will never have an answer? Answer me that Jordyn if you please. Her face immediately reddened because she realized Jordyn undoubtedly had interpreted her sarcastic thoughts. Once again, she was relieved that Jordyn had not reacted negatively.

Jordyn said, "In due time, Ava. Trust me. Okay, first, to answer the most important question. I already explained the three elves in the painting to you, to Steph as well. However, I erased your memories of what I had said. Now is not the time for you to know all the details. The Great Wizard Godroh will give you the important details I erased from your memory, or you will recall them on your own."

Ava stared up at the painting. She said in an anxious tone, "Yes, you said you would erase our memories of a few things, but that child elf, she looks—"

Jordyn immediately interrupted her. "Not now, Ava. Please trust me. If you and Steph knew everything that I told you before I erased your memories, both of you would be in mortal danger. That is until you are prepared to defend yourselves. True, there are a few who know some things about you. However, they have sworn an oath to protect you. I must also stress that they only know what they need to know and nothing more. Now onto the second question."

Ava looked away from the painting. She was upset that Jordyn did not go further in detail about the child elf. Yet she understood that Jordyn would not address it further.

Jordyn said, "The tower you climbed, your grandfather and great uncle's tower, was built in the early twentieth century, as you know. But the original tower, its mommy if I can call it that, was built hundreds of thousands of years earlier. That tower is in the Inner World. It is called Gnaèfa by the Inner World's inhabitants. It also is known as the Spire of Time. Therefore, Ava, your hypothesis is correct. The spiral staircase from your modern-day tower descended to the mommy tower, the original tower, Gnaèfa. You and Steph are standing in it right now."

"So, there are two identical towers?" Steph asked. "One in the Earthly World and one in the Inner World?"

"Precisely," Jordyn said. "But the tower in the Inner World looks more like Ava's tower when it was originally built than what her Earthly World tower looks like today. The tower in Buffalo, New York, of the Earthly World was built by elves. So, Ava, onto your third and last question."

Ava exclaimed, "But Steph got to ask four questions! She just asked you her fourth!" She looked at Steph. "Maybe it was her fifth or sixth. I lost count."

"Sorry, Ava," Jordyn said, "but my time is up in a few moments. Which leads nicely to your third, most important question. The answer is no."

Ava shouted, "No what?" She was frustrated because Jordyn had not replied to her question. Her frustration quickly turned to exasperation. Steph was pointing at her and laughing hysterically. She began to feel uncomfortable. Her face had reddened strikingly, and her ears felt like they were on fire, but she did not care. She hated it when someone laughed and pointed at her. It made her feel stupid. She flashed Steph an annoyed look and fumed between clenched teeth, "What is so darned funny, Steph? Why are you pointing at my head? Please stop it. You are embarrassing me!"

Steph said in a jovial way, "Can't you feel it? You have got to be able to feel it! Because I can."

"Feel what? What is it I am supposed to feel? And darn it, Steph, please stop pointing at me. You are making me feel totally stupid!"

Steph pulled back her long hair from the sides of her face to expose her ears.

"Oh my gosh!" Ava screamed. "You have elf ears! And they are simply adorable too. Do I?"

Steph nodded her head and grinned.

Ava gingerly touched her left ear. She screamed, "Awesomesauce! I guess that is why you were laughing and pointing, huh?" She immediately grimaced as a horrible thought entered her mind. "They aren't ugly looking are they, you know, sort of too big for my head like Gklim's odd-looking ears?" She started to fumble with her ponytail. "If so, I am going to cover them right now!"

"Not in the least," Steph replied. "Your ears are adorable! They look great on you. How about mine?"

Ava said, "They look great on you too, honestly." She seemed to be grinning from ear to ear. "I guess we officially are elves now, huh?" She broke out laughing as she declared lightheartedly, "We cannot be true elves without pointy elven ears! Am I right?"

Before Steph could reply, the double doors that lead to the Inner World creaked opened noisily. As Jordyn had said, the Earthly World clothes they were wearing at once shifted to Inner World garb.

In addition to sporting brand new elf ears, they were wearing dark brown cloth skirts called tunics. Their tunics were paired with vests made of leathery dragon skin. Luscious, lightweight cloaks that fell past their shoes covered up their tunics and vests.

Ava's cloak was pure white. It was fashioned with shed unicorn hair. Steph's cloak was a dark green. It also was made of shed unicorn hair and dyed. The cloaks were essential for traveling in the Inner World's forests during late summer. Their satchels, waiting for them on the other side of the opened doors, would include heavier cloaks for the cold winter months. Like her summer cloak, Ava's winter cloak was pure white. Steph's was bright red. Again, both cloaks were made from shed unicorn hair.

A tightly woven brooch of silver in the shape of a unicorn fastened their cloaks just above their breastbones. An extra set of brooches were in their satchels.

Their footwear was the same. The shoes were made of dragon skin. They were open at the sides and laced up along the length of their legs to just below their knees. Their satchels would contain boots of dragon skin for winter wear.

Steph had a golden pearl earring in both of her ears. She also was wearing a white choker made of braided cord, the hide of a unicorn. A single pearl that matched her earrings was in the center of the choker.

Ava had on a choker as well. Her choker was a smooth, black cord from the rind of a dragon's tail. A charming, sterling silver replica of a fierce dragon emitting flames was intertwined on the cord in the middle of the choker. She was not wearing earrings.

As Jordyn had mentioned, they had matching rings on the pinky finger of their left hands. The beautifully etched rings were made of pure silver. Their handcrafted design was that of an Elvish symbol that denotes peace, love, and harmony. They would later refer to the rings as their *secret pinky promise*. The rings denoted Ava and Steph's steadfast devotion to each other as well as their enduring friendship. It also conveyed a contract, a secret pact known only to them. The secret pinky promise pact between them is comprised of three elements.

One, if either is in danger, the one in danger will attempt with all her strength to send her pinky ring to the other. Two, if a situation develops that creates doubt or certainty, and to certify something as being completely true, she will attempt with all her strength to send her ring to the other. Three, if Ava and Steph are together and one senses danger while the other one does not, the one realizing danger will remove her ring and hide it away. Thereby covertly alerting the other of the threat.

Ava and Steph were wearing rich leather archery bracers on their left forearms. The bracers were necessary to protect their forearms when shooting arrows. Finally, they each had a belt, called a baldric, fastened around their waists from which the sheaths and scabbards of their swords would dangle. Ava's sword would be enclosed in a soft leather sheath while Steph's would be enclosed in a more rigid scabbard.

"Well, we sure do look the sort," Steph said proudly. She slowly turned in a circle. "What do you think? How do I look?"

Ava replied, "I love it!" She twirled around two times with her arms held out wide. "I cannot wait to walk over the doors' threshold. How about you?"

"Me neither," Steph said. "But, before we walk through those open doors, I have a question." Ava nodded her head. "What is the story surrounding that *no* Jordyn had said in response to your unasked third question? Do you know?"

Ava whispered in a soft tone, "No, Steph. Jordyn will *not* accompany us to the Inner World." She took Steph's hand in hers. With eager smiles on their faces, they unhurriedly walked toward the doors. Ava said, "Since she will not be accompanying us, I guess we are on our own. Are you ready?"

"Ready as I'll ever be," Steph replied. "You?"

"Yep," Ava said. Her eyes were shining brightly, her tone of voice anxious as never before.

"Let's do this!"

END OF PART ONE

PART TWO

———————————

—————

THE MYSTERIOUS INNER WORLD

"Imagination is the beginning of creation. You imagine what you desire, you will what you imagine, and at last, you create what you will."
—*George Bernard Shaw*

~~~

CHAPTER 1

THE INNER WORLD

"In life the only thing that you can expect is the unexpected."
—*Joan Rivers*

1

The world Ava and Steph were about to enter is nothing like anything they ever could have created in their mind's eye. Or could have seen in picture books and encyclopedias, via the Internet and Netflix, or by watching make-believe movies. Even as far back-when to their childhood, storybook fantasies. Not in their finest, creative imaginings, an area in which Ava dominates given her thirst for knowledge, could they have foreseen such splendor they were about to behold.

Without a doubt, Antiquom, the most ancient of the Inner World's three enchanting, mystical realms, is awash with magical spectacles too fantastic for words. The most creative, Earthly World skilled painters and sculpturers, gifted graphic designers, authors, poets, and thinkers – none could ever create in their minds such breathtaking spectacles as Antiquom holds.

The realm's amazing flora is unheard of in the Earthly World. Delicate flowers of every imaginable size, shape, and color seem to be everywhere – in the open meadows, amongst the forest trees, and below the snowline of towering mountains. Luscious fruits as large as Earthly World watermelons dangle from weight-laden boughs of the forest trees. Strange creatures, beasts, and birds of every conceivable size, shape, and color abound. For the most part, Antiquom's creatures are friendly. Yet there are those, like the mercilessly heartless belugas, that pursue others to bully, overwhelm, and destroy.

There are fire-breathing, ferocious, winged dragons in the snow-capped peaks of the Mystic Mountains and Mountains Cross. Snake-like, flying lizard dragons in the lakes. Gnomes and pixies peeking from inside knots of trees within the forests. Winged fairies flitting here and there, shy, and wild. Secretive unicorns and centaurs in the extreme denseness of the trees. Greedy dwarves hoarding precious gems, silver, and gold in subterranean mines of the most desolate mountains. Mermaids sunbathing on the rocky shores. Witches, wizards, elves, and more.

Welcome to the Inner World.

2

Ava and Steph could not believe what had happened after they stepped over the threshold. The doors they had just walked through had vanished into thin air! There was no sign of the exterior walls of the tower as well. Instead, they were staring straight ahead at a seemingly impenetrable, scary forest of towering, deciduous trees.

Ava supposed the trees bore a semblance to oak trees of the Earthly World. The exception being the color of the leaves. Unlike Earthly World oak tree leaves, which are brown, red, or even yellow, the leaves of these trees were dark blue. Ava thought they were the same color as the flowering hydrangeas in her backyard at home. She bent down to pick up a freshly fallen leaf. It was still moist and pliant. She turned it over in her hand to examine it. She said, "Yep, just like oak leaves back home." She traced the leaf's delicate edge with her finger. "It has the distinctive lobe and rounded serrations like an oak leaf. Like the red oak leaves in the Earthly World, it also has a pointed tip."

Steph said in a low, sarcastic tone, "Yeah, except it is blue. Go figure, huh?" She and Ava roared with laughter.

Ava stuffed the leaf in the pocket of her cloak. She said with a grin, "My first souvenir of the Inner World. Proof that I have been here. I only hope it does not dry out before I get a chance to preserve it."

Steph gestured with a nod of her head to the forest. Not a bit of sunlight seemed to be peeking from within the tightly spaced trees. She said in a flat tone, "Well, you have got to admit that what we are seeing should not surprise us in the least. The tower is gone as are the doors we just walked through. Replaced by a thick forest of blue, as you say, oak trees. But we might as well face the facts. Because something tells me that it will only get weirder as time goes by. What do *you* think?"

Ava replied, "You know, Steph, I think you may be one hundred percent correct." She fanned her face with her free hand. She was pretending to feel dizzy. She said in breathless anticipation, "Okay, are you ready to do this, to turn around and face whatever comes our way?" Steph nodded her head. Ava said, "Me too." She grinned shyly. "Well, sort of anyway. What do you say we turn around together, to face whatever is waiting for us as besties?" Steph nodded her head yet again. "But first, close your eyes on the count of one. I will close my eyes as well. Then we slowly turn around to the right when I say two and open our eyes on the count of three. Sound good to you?"

"Sounds good to me," Steph said. She clasped Ava's hand tightly. "But don't let go of my hand. I do not want to lose you or you to lose me. That would be a terrible way to start our adventure!"

Ava whispered, "Okay, I won't let go of your hand. Here we go. One . . ."

They closed their eyes. Their pulses were fast with a mix of thrill and anxiety. They were ready for whatever faced them in the Inner World – but only if they were together.

Ava strengthened her grip on Steph's hand. She said softly, "Twoooo . . ."

They turned around to the right at the same time.

As a burst of adrenaline coursed through her body, Ava shouted, "Three!" Just as she turned around, her eyes immediately went up as she looked heavenward. She whispered, "Thank you, God!" She had truly expected something dreadful was going to happen. Perhaps that she would be on the ghastly spiral staircase once more. That everything that happened in the bedchamber was but a figment of her imagination. Or worse, she would still be standing on the tower's ledge to the right of the wrought iron gate in the pouring rain.

Steph let out a huge sigh and sagged against Ava. Her voice was shaky as she said, "I cannot believe this! I honestly thought we would see something dreadful. Like we would be in the tower even now staring through the hole in the floor at that stupid staircase. Or I would be back in my horse's barn in Tennessee. But this is amazing!" She cupped her hands beneath her chin and stared reflectively at the scene.

Ava felt great. It was if something had cast all her worries to the wind. Like she had been set free of an insufferable burden. She started to ponder everything that happened after she was pulled from the tower's ledge. Like the top eleven steps of the spiral staircase vanishing into thin air. She considered the steps almost certainly had vanished to make it impossible for her to return to the Earthly World. Thereby leaving her with two choices which she had not even considered at the time. Descend the staircase which led to the Inner World or throw in the towel, conceivably dying as a result.

Moreover, she understood that everything she had envisioned up until that moment had a purpose. The whole lot was a compressed lesson of sorts, meant to prepare her for what was to occur next. Watching the culmination of the dinosaur era and the beginning of the Inner World. Seeing the three people in the cave. Their pointed wands making fire, painting on the wall, the female illuminating her face. The female talking to her in a strange language she now knows as Fortunomy, beckoning her to join them. The staircase imploding. Bolts, rivets, and stair treads exploding, sending her somersaulting wildly. Perched on a flying, fire-breathing dragon she now knows as Fluescere, her very own savior.

Her last Earthly World meal, delicious Big Macs, and fries, along with a refreshing Coca-Cola. The strange portrait of the elderly elven couple and the child that looked just like her on the wall of the bedroom. A Victorian-style bedroom copied by Earthly World humans from Inner World furnishings long ago. Noticing that the chamber bed canopy had changed color from burgundy to orange, but not telling anyone she had noticed.

Finally, and perhaps most importantly, Gklim muttering the strange word Avaïnoćel, and the creature's apparent deference to her as she bowed and curtsied elegantly. That word, unlike just about everything else she recalled that Jordyn had said, seemed to be engraved in her mind. Like it was way more important than everything else she had experienced, seen, or heard.

All of it – everything. The good. And the not so good. All of it had a purpose. To test my nerve. To assess my resolve. And to teach me. So, I could move ahead.

Steph disrupted her thoughts as she said, "I cannot believe this. It is utterly beautiful. What Jordyn had said about the Inner World's charm and allure was one hundred percent true."

They were standing on the apex of a gradually sloping, downward hill. Below them was a knee-high carpet of stunningly beautiful wildflowers adorned with blossoms of delicately soft indigo tones. The lush, bluish-green carpet seemed to breathe as it quietly swayed like waves of a gentle sea in the delicate breeze.

The entrancing landscape reminded Ava of the rising and falling, bluish-green swells of Lake Michigan of the Earthly World. She and her family had visited the lake on many occasions. Like the grandest of the Great Lakes back home, the gently waving grassland sea of azure before them appeared to go on as far as the eye could see. Immense, charming, irresistible. Eager to be floated upon and explored.

The lush, flowering landscape was peppered with enormous boulders. The mammoth sarsens were stained with swirling splashes of color, splotches of white, green, red, and yellow. They were highly polished and echoed the sun's brilliant sparkle. Their sparkling luster reminded Ava of the endless rows of solar power panels lining the interstate in Indiana of the Earthly World. Except the reflecting mirrors of the boulders were gigantic and strewn about at random.

Ava guessed the boulders were made of jasper. She recalled that ancient Egyptians of the Minoan Kingdom used similar-looking stones to fabricate stamps, globules, jewelry, and implements. She wondered if Antiquom's residents fashioned bits of the boulders to make elven jewelry that Jordyn had mentioned. The colossal size of several boulders caused her to think of the mammoth boulder she had read about in fifth grade. The Giant Rock. Giant Rock is in the Earthly World's Mojave Desert of California. She recollected that Giant Rock covers an incredible amount of ground, something like 5,000 square feet, and stands seven stories high.

There was no way of knowing the size of the boulders before her and Steph. Nevertheless, she assumed a few of the boulders were as large or even larger than Giant Rock. One freestanding boulder off in the distance, perhaps five or six miles away, seemed to be several miles in length. Unlike many of the other boulders, the boulder was stocky, maybe a few hundred feet tall at best. Its massive size nearly obscured a grove of giant fruit trees standing tall on a hill behind it. She imagined that the view from its summit would be breathtaking!

There were smaller-sized boulders strewn about the landscape as well. In comparison to the humongous boulders, the less significant boulders were as inconsequential in size as two and three-story houses; others were even smaller, the size of Earthly World cars and trucks. There were also loads of normal-sized boulders the size of trash cans and littler, every day, Earthly World stuff.

Ava was giving off the impression that she was completely mesmerized by the spectacular scene that was before them. Suddenly, her attitude seemed to change. She began to wonder why Jordyn abruptly had said *no* to her question and fell silent. No, Jordyn would not be accompanying them to the Inner World. She considered without a word, did that mean Jordyn will not be here at the *start* of our journey? Or did that mean she will not be here during the *duration* of our journey? And just how long will *we* be here? days? weeks? months? years? Or until Steph and I turn old and gray then fade away? Gosh, I hope not! So many unanswered questions, and all Jordyn had permitted me to ask – well, that she interpreted from my thoughts anyway – were three measly questions.

Oh well, it is what it is. But it seems so unfair in many respects. Here Steph and I stand in the center of a seemingly prehistoric scene, in a strange area surrounded by Giant Rock sarsens. To make matters worse, we have no hint of what we are supposed to do and how we are supposed to do it. Sure, we need to face Wendigorium. Well, at least I must face the beast. We know that much. I do not like the thought of doing so, and I suspect Steph does not as well. But at least we know of one goal – Wendigorium. But how in the world are we supposed to start? What is the next step? Who is going to lead us?

Predictably, Ava was deeply engrossed in her thoughts and looking slightly ill at ease and utterly out of place. Meanwhile, Steph's expression was composed. Unlike the grimace of questioning curiosity Ava had on her face along with her usual searching, furrowed brow of inquisitiveness, Steph was smiling contently. She looked blissfully satisfied and quite comfortable, relaxed in fact, of their surroundings. She also was clapping her hands together nearly imperceptibly. If all that did not suggest her excitement and happiness, and her feeling totally at ease, nothing did.

The valley way off in the distance seemed to stretch to the horizon. It was glittering with an elegant carpet of charming, yellowish-white blossoms that were in full bloom. Ava and Steph will reach the carpet of blossoms at the end of the day. When they do, Ava will remark that the pretty blossoms remind her of buttercups back home of the genus weed Ranunculus. The Earthly World dainty weed thrives from late spring to late summer. She will tell Steph that buttercups back home are poisonous to humans but only if they are ingested. That they are very intoxicating and can cause excessive salivation, colic, and blistering of the intestines, among other nasty ailments. She will say that Earthly World cows instinctively know to not ingest the sweet-smelling blossoms as they graze.

Later, she and Steph will learn that the delicate blossoms are called *sanatios*. Sanatios means healing in Fortunomy. Dried sanatios are used to treat all sorts of ailments, including non-lethal battle wounds. Despite their healing properties, sanatios are highly noxious. One robust whiff of their heady scent is enough to knock one out for hours! Consequently, those that pick the blossoms for medicinal purposes must wear cloth masks. It is only after the blossoms are dried and processed that they are safe to use.

Many weeks later in her journey, Ava will pluck a sanatios from its stem despite being aware of its intoxicating effect. She will inhale its delicate fragrance deeply. The blossom will smell truly divine. Like the delicate scent of a perfumed rose with a dash of the dried bark of the laurel tree, cinnamon. Afterward, her life will change forever.

Ava was shaking her head with disbelief as her eyes explored the landscape. She thought wordlessly to herself; all of this is amazing, utterly amazing! I simply cannot believe it!

"Yes, I agree. It is amazing," Steph said softly.

Ava considered that Steph's tone when she had spoken was startlingly low. Her words were difficult to hear, yet she seemed to interpret them in her mind clearly. She also thought Steph looked peculiarly strange as well.

Like she had finally lost it and was in la-la land. Her eyes were closed. Her lips were pressed together in a straight line. She seemed deep in thought.

"It is like I can read your mind," Steph said surprising her. Her eyes were still closed. "You too?"

"O-o-okay," Ava stammered. She moved backward a few steps. "Steph, I really do not like saying this, but you are starting to freak me out." She licked her lips and swallowed hard. "First off, what is with that crazy look on your face? Also, *what* is amazing? Are you talking about Jordyn when you say that she read your mind? If so, it is what Jordyn does. We did the same thing back there. We read her thoughts. Anyway, that stuff is behind us, at least for now. Story over. Book closed. No more Jordyn and no more mind-reading, telepathic craziness, although I truly wish we could do it even now."

Steph opened her eyes. "No, Ava, what I am talking about has nothing to do with Jordyn. I know it sounds crazy, but I think I can read your thoughts. I could be completely wrong, totally going mad." She gave Ava a calculating look. After considering what she was going to say for a few seconds, she burst out, "But darn it! Try as I do, your thoughts seem to come and go. It is like I cannot focus properly." She shook her head and frowned. "Probably because my brain is still trying to develop the knack for reading your mind. Anyway, I could swear you were thinking about Wendigorium a few moments ago. You were wondering why in the heck we are here as well. Am I correct?"

"Well, yes," Ava replied hesitantly. She was still giving Steph a strange look. "Of course, I was thinking about Wendigorium and why in the heck we are here. It makes perfect sense, at least to me. It should to you as well. Were you not thinking the same things?"

"Not really," Steph replied as she pointed. "I was marveling at all those huge boulders when a strange name suddenly popped into my head."

Ava said indifferently, "I see. Was that name Wendigorium? If it was that name, that is no biggie. That is all I can think about too."

"No, Ava, it was not a name. It was a term that consisted of two words – Giant Rock."

"Giant Rock?" Ava exclaimed with a look of total surprise. "So, what you are telling me is you were also thinking about the Earthly World's largest boulder, Giant Rock? The one in the Mojave Desert?" She gave

Steph two thumbs up and grinned. "If so, I was thinking the same thing. What a coincidence, huh?"

Steph was looking at her with a puzzled expression. She shook her head. "Honestly, Ava, I have no idea where the Giant Rock is." She shrugged her shoulders. "Or where it is, in the Mojave Desert or the Sahara Desert or any other desert for that matter. I have never heard of the thing."

Ava laughed at full volume. "Whoa! Now, this is incredible! That is why you said a few moments ago, that you agreed something was amazing. You had read my thoughts! Just like in the tower and the bedchamber, when you had read Jordyn's thoughts, now you are reading mine." She smacked Steph hard on the shoulder. "I am so happy for you! I guess that is one ability Jordyn gave you, but she forgot to mention." She pulled a face and kicked at the ground with the toe of her shoe. "Well, to tell you the truth, I am a bit jealous you can read my mind. I surely cannot read yours. If I could, I would have done it already."

Steph grasped Ava's hand and gave it a light squeeze. She said, "I would like to try an experiment if you agree." Ava nodded her head. "Think of something, maybe a color or type of food. Maybe even a combination of things. Something simple so my brain can comprehend it. Say it as slowly as you can. But whatever you do, do not say what you are thinking out loud, okay?"

Ava was giving her a doubtful look. She had doubts that Steph's experiment would work but figured she would play along. There was no harm in doing that. She shrugged her shoulders indifferently, rolled her eyes, and thought about a bunch of silly words.

Bright – orange – banana bread – apple pink – yucky tarts.

Steph's eyes snapped wide-open. She bent over at the waist and cracked up. She was all smiles when she shouted, "What the heck are bright orange banana bread apple pink yucky tarts?"

Ava yelled, "Beats me! That stupid stuff just popped into my head."

Steph grabbed her by the shoulders. "So, I did it. Pretty cool, huh?" Ava nodded her head glumly. "Okay, Ava, now you try it. I will turn my back to you and think of something simple like you just did. See if you can read what I am thinking. You got it?"

Ava was kicking the ground with her foot yet again. She had a miserable look. Her lower lip jutted out in a pout, and then she said in a sad tone, "I doubt that I can. As I said earlier if I could I surely would have done so by now." She added with a frown, "It probably is one more skill that Jordyn gave you but did not give to me."

Steph's tone was hopeful as she said, "Oh, I seriously doubt she would give me telepathic abilities and not give them to you. That would not make a lick of sense. After all, what Jordyn said may be happening to us right now but sort of in slow motion. Our words and thoughts could be in Fortunomy. All the while our brains are thinking and interpreting stuff in English. Or completely the opposite. We need to train ourselves, be patient. That is all." She pulled a face and twirled her finger at the side of her temple. Then she crossed her eyes and stuck out her tongue. She was trying to act like she had just gone crazy. "Or whatever I am trying to say about all this absurd telepathic, Fortunomy craziness." She quickly turned around and said over her shoulder, "Give it a try, please! There is nothing to lose. I bet you can read my mind too, except you probably have not developed the skill completely. Maybe because you are so young."

Ava burst out laughing then shouted, "Two plus two are five?" She added in jest, "Are you a mathematical dropout, Steph? Don't you know that two plus two is twenty-two?"

Steph quickly turned around, and then she gave Ava a hearty bear hug. "You did it, you did it! Okay, now I am going to walk behind that boulder over there." She was pointing to a car-sized boulder a dozen or so paces away. "Let us see if this telepathic stuff works at a distance. I will think of something weird, like a strange color or of a fruit, maybe foodstuff. You do the same, okay?"

Ava nodded her head happily. "Got it."

Pinkish-green peanut butter.

Steph peeked from behind the boulder and stared.

Fried apricots in white spaghetti sauce.

Ava stared blank-faced at Steph in return.

Boiled cucumbers in salsa. Popcorn ice cream. Scrambled eggs and spaghetti. Anything stupidly colorful to eat!

Steph returned to stand in front of Ava. She was shaking her head.

"Nothing?" Ava asked, although she already knew what Steph was going to say.

"Nope. You?"

Ava did not have to reply. The letdown expression on her face said it all.

"It's okay," Steph said. Her tone was upbeat despite her disappointment. "At least we know we are telepathic when we are standing close to each other. That could come in handy, don't you agree?"

"Definitely," Ava replied. Knowing that she and Steph were telepathic felt wonderful, even if it did not work over a distance. She cocked her head to one side and said, "I wonder if it will work with others. That too could come in handy, to be able to read others' minds. Especially if we are in danger."

"We will have to wait and see," Steph replied. "But it really doesn't matter one way or the other. At least we can help each other by conversing without speaking, without others knowing we are doing it. Hopefully, we will never leave each other's sides. That would be tragic, don't you think?"

Ava nodded her head, and then she said, "Our telepathic ability could get stronger over time. Because, as you said, our brains are trying to figure out all of this. Then again, maybe, because we are thinking in English rather than Fortunomy is why it only works when we are close to each other. Perhaps it will work over a distance when we converse in Fortunomy after we learn more words."

They spent the next few minutes doing mind-reading experiments. When they were more than ten or so paces apart, around thirty feet give, or take, they could not read each other's thoughts. Although Ava had the feeling her mind-reading ability was getting stronger with each passing minute. At one point she said, "Why do you think we can now read each other's thoughts? We did not seem to have the knack for doing that in the tower or bedchamber. Sure, we could read Jordyn's thoughts, but I never was able to read yours and you, mine."

Steph replied, "I think it is a defense mechanism of sorts. Now that we are here in the Inner World. I suppose it is Jordyn's way of ensuring we can be in contact with each other telepathically. Well, at least when we are relatively close to each other." Her attitude suddenly changed for the worse. She stared at the ground and began to wring her hands. After a few moments of uncomfortable silence that was making Ava feel dreadfully anxious, she looked up. Her eyes were searching as she stared into Ava's eyes. Her upper lip was twitching like she was about to cry. She whispered, "I must protect you, Ava. That is what counts more than anything. I must keep you safe and hopefully never out of telepathic range from me."

Ava cried in an anxious tone, "What in the world is wrong now?" The hairs on the back of her neck were burning. She was rubbing at the goose pimples that had cascaded from her shoulders onto her upper arms. She started to shiver. "You're scaring me all over again, Steph. And what is all this nonsense about us never being out of telepathic range?" She gave Steph a sour look and said in a tone that was overly harsh, "Do you know something I don't?"

Steph replied bluntly, "Yes, I do. Apparently, Jordyn did not tell you what she told me. It was when you were staring at the painting on the wall, the one in the chamber. She and I were having a telepathic conversation. Jordyn had said that I must do everything in my power to ensure you remain safe."

Ava shrugged her shoulders and said in an indifferent tone, "Okay, I get all that. It's no biggie really. I also sensed Jordyn's words when she said something along those lines. So, what is the big deal? She said you had to promise to keep me safe. Fine. I will do the same for you, you know that." She added with a gleeful smile, "After all, we are besties."

Steph was pinching the skin at her throat just as another pained look showed on her face. She looked away and stared at the ground. Ava saw that her attitude had changed suddenly and was now even graver than before. She moved back a few steps. Without looking up Steph muttered, "Ava, it is much more than that. Jordyn said I should be prepared to sacrifice my life for you if need be. She was very straightforward when her thoughts said that." She looked up at Ava. Her eyes had welled up with tears. She took Ava's hand in hers and said in a solemn tone, "Yes, Ava, she said I must sacrifice my life if need be, to protect you."

Ava's face suddenly reddened. Her eyes were cold, hard. She let go of Steph's hand and shouted angrily, "She said what?" She folded her arms over her chest and pulled a face. "How dare she say such a thing to you! That you should be prepared to sacrifice your life for me! You are my friend, Steph. We will look out for each other. That is what friends do." She began to walk in circles. She pressed her fist to her mouth and frowned as she faced Steph. "How dare she say that!" Her tone had deepened. Her look was one of total disgust. "How dare she say you should be prepared to sacrifice yourself for me if need be. That is selfish, and it is wrong! No one's life is worth more than another's. That is the way it is. That is the way it is going to be as it concerns you and me and our friendship. End of story!"

Steph grabbed Ava by the shoulders and stared straight on into her eyes. She looked utterly miserable. Her eyes were still filled with tears. It was obvious to Ava that she was trying hard not to break down sobbing. She said in a solemn tone, "Ava, it is much more than that. As you can tell, what I am saying, what I am going to say is very emotional for me." She blinked a few times, and then she wiped her tears with the back of her hands. "Therefore, I want you to listen carefully to everything I am about to say. Can you do that for me? Please?"

Ava nodded her head. She looked away and stared impassively over the terrain. She did not want Steph to feel more embarrassed than she already was. She also hated it when she got emotionally upset and the dreaded teary-eyed sniffles appeared. It made her feel fragile and weak.

Steph said in a shaky voice, "Jordyn said that if anything bad happens to you, to make you incapable of facing Wendigorium, then the world as we know it will end."

Ava shot her a nasty look. She said in a very sharp tone, "What do I care if the Inner World will end?" Steph's head jerked back, and then she cringed. She was staring at Ava wide-eyed with an expression of utter disbelief.

Ava instantly recognized that her words and tone of voice were overly harsh and uncaring. She felt bad that what she said had caused Steph to cringe. "Steph, I am sorry to sound heartless, but we know nothing of the Inner World. It is our world, the Earthly World, our home that we should worry about. Not this strange place of elves, dragons, fairies, belugas, and Lord knows what else, to include the creep, Wendigorium. Whoever or whatever he or she or *it* is."

"Not just the Inner World, Ava," Steph said slowly. "Our world. The Earthly World. Jordyn said that our homes, our loved ones, and friends, everything that we hold dear to our hearts – all of that will come to an end ultimately if something terrible happens to you."

"What in the world are you talking about?" Ava said as she shuffled back two steps. Her chin started to tremble. She was hoping with all her heart that what Steph had said was nothing more than a bad joke. She suddenly felt lightheaded. She bent over a little and closed her eyes. Then she pressed the palms of her hands against her temples. She wanted to rid her mind of what Steph had said. Yet she could not. Steph's thoughts seemed to be screaming in her mind, "It is true. It is true. It is true."

After a few minutes, she was able to regain her composure if only slightly. She stood up straight and opened her eyes. Her voice was shaking and barely audible as she said to Steph, "Are you saying, what Jordyn said, that if something happens to ordinary me, our families will suffer? Steph, how can that be? I am a nobody, both at home and here in the Inner World. For crying out loud I am only thirteen years old! How can this be?"

Steph whispered in a solemn tone, "Because you are Ava Noelle." She did not say anything for nearly a minute. When at last she spoke once more her tone was sincere and as honest as the look on her worried face. "Jordyn said you are the Protector of the World, of both worlds. She had said those exact words a few times to me, Ava. I would not lie to you or make a joke of this as you know. It is too important." She was nodding her head. "Yes, she actually said you are the Protector of the World."

Ava's expression was one of sheer terror. The rosy color of her slightly tanned face had vanished. It was replaced by a washed-out, sickly color. She suddenly felt cold to the core. Her knees were shaking, and the dreaded goose pimples were now crawling up the back of her legs. They had already covered her shoulders and forearms causing her to shiver for the umpteenth time.

Steph laid her right hand against her breastbone. She was staring at Ava intently. Ava wanted to say something, but words would not come. She merely returned Steph's stare. At last, her voice cracking with emotion, Steph said, "It is true, Ava. Honest, it is. Jordyn said you are the Protector of the World. I swear that is what she said. Obviously, I wordlessly swore an oath to her. I swore that I would do everything in my power to protect you, to ensure you are not harmed. Even to sacrifice my life for you if need be."

Ava was about to reply. Instead, her eyes widened. She screamed forcefully, "Steph, look out! There is something behind you!" She grabbed Steph by the shoulders and spun her around. She was pointing to an odd-looking tree. The tree was less than four feet in height. It was remarkably short given the span of its outstretched limbs. The limbs were at least three times broader than the tree was tall.

Ava initially thought that what she had seen was nothing more than a fleeting image in her mind's eye. Perhaps a blossom or a leaf floating in the soft breeze. Just as she was about to dismiss what she had seen, it reemerged. She spluttered, "St-st-eph, was th-that a h-h-hand that was re-retrieving a hat? A tiny hand and a tiny hat?"

Steph replied coolly, "I think so. It sure did look like a hand to me, and there was an odd-shaped, dinky, red hat too."

Ava said, "What do you say we move over there and take a look?" She grabbed Steph's hand and started toward the tree.

"I think it will be okay," Steph said in a whisper. "Whatever we saw looked to be pretty small, so I doubt it is dangerous." She rolled the fist of her free hand in a knuckle-white ball and sneered a tough-looking grin. "The two of us should be able to handle it quite nicely. Stay close to me, and whatever you do, don't run." She added in a lighthearted manner, "Could be a tiny bear that wears a dinky hat. One should never run from bears. You do know that, yes?"

Ava did not reply as she stared straight ahead. The look of uneasiness had vanished from her face. It had been replaced by a look of curiosity. Her heart began to race with excitement as the adrenaline set off coursing throughout her body.

Before they could take three cautious steps toward the tree, they recoiled at the unmistakable sounds of hushed giggles. The giggles stopped them in their tracks. Then whatever was behind the weird-looking tree giggled again.

Realizing that Steph would read her thoughts, Ava considered wordlessly, Steph, whatever it is must be less than two or three feet tall! Or maybe, just maybe, it is much larger and crouching on all fours! Steph nodded her head. "There it goes again," Ava said in a whisper. The hushed giggles were peculiar, unlike anything she had ever heard – teensy and raspy, almost grainy. They did not appear to be unfriendly sounds, at least she did not reckon so. Quite the opposite. They were surprisingly pleasant to the ear. Melodious in a way, like the cheery, satisfied babbling of a small child at play. Singsong, childlike, and sweet. Also, the giggles were dissimilar in tone.

Ava thought, perhaps there is more than one? Maybe a male and a female? What do you think?

Steph nodded her head and said aloud, "Yes. Two or more, definitely."

Suddenly, the entire hilltop burst out in similar-sounding laughter, giggles, shouts, and gleeful calls! Ava and Steph were about to turn tail and bolt in the forest, just as two small figures emerged from behind the tree. A second or two later, similar figures appeared from behind all the other weird-looking trees in the vicinity.

"Oh my gosh!" Ava and Steph yelled at the same time. They looked at each other and howled with laughter.

"They're fairies!"

3

"Well, aren't you the cutest creature I have ever seen," Ava said without a second thought. She was moving about nervously as she stared at the smaller of the two fairies. "And I love your wings. They are so pretty!" She was referring to the female fairy. She was standing beside a much older male fairy and had her arm around his waist. The male fairy was wearing the hat she and Steph had seen. It was perched precariously on his forehead. Ava was surprised it did not fall off.

"Huh?" the male fairy said in what Ava assumed was Fortunomy, although her brain was hearing it in English. He grinned playfully. "Cute and pretty? Why thank you, milady! In all my years I have not been referred to so nicely."

The female fairy said in a high-pitched, singsong voice, "No, Dad! She was talking about me." She giggled and smacked him hard on his back. "You know that. You are nothing even close to being cute and pretty. You are average, in fact completely dreadful looking." She placed her arm around his shoulder and kissed his cheek. "But I love you just the same despite your conceited ways." She effortlessly lifted in the air. A fraction of a second later she was hovering in front of Ava and Steph. She smiled a silly grin, and then she gracefully curtsied as she hovered.

Ava was bouncing up and down on her tiptoes with excitement. She was wondering how the fairy could curtsy while hovering vertically. To her credit, Ava strives bravely to curtsy. But she barely can curtsy even though she is standing stationary. But to curtsy while winging in mid-air was totally amazing!

The fairy was a tiny, human-like creature with light blue, translucent wings. Her delicate wings were fluttering at the blurred speed of an Earthly World hummingbird. She was no more than two feet tall. Like the goblin, Gklim, the fairy's attire, her skirt, and her slacks, were similarly drab looking. Except her clothing, unlike Gklim's, was well cared for without holes and patches. The color of her skirt and slacks were a dull green, almost the color of green olives. Her cerise hair was done up in one long braid behind her back. She had a pinkish complexion that almost matched her hair. She had freckles like her father, the one she referred to as Dad. She wore no jewelry. She was shoeless, her toenails painted pink.

"Hello. My name is Doo." She pointed to her father. "The old fellow is my father. His name is Ktli, but I just call him Dad. You can call him Dad too if you prefer that name rather than Ktli."

Steph was super excited, even more so than the day she brought her horse, Spirit, home from Ohio. She appeared to be grinning from ear to ear, and her insides were vibrating with unimaginable joy. She exclaimed cheerfully, "Isn't this wonderful!" She looked at Ava. "Doo and Dad. DooDad. What do you think?"

Ava grinned and nodded her head.

Doo smiled at Steph and said, "I like the name you call us." She tilted her head to one side and scratched her chin. "DooDad. Sounds pretty." She turned in the air to look at her father. He was still standing on the ground next to the tree. She cupped her tiny hands together and called out, "How about you, Dad? Do you like our new family name, DooDad?" Dad shrugged his shoulders indifferently. Seeing the impatient, stern look on Doo's face, he pretended to smile and nodded his head. Doo turned around and said to Steph, "And you are?"

Steph gestured to Ava with a slight wave of her hand and said, "This is Ava Noelle. I am Stephanie Galanos, middle name JoAnne."

Doo was staring at Ava and looking her up and down carefully. Ava started to shuffle her feet. She was feeling uncomfortable because Doo was ogling her, her head tilting this way and that. Then Doo smiled brightly which made Ava feel a whole lot better.

"I know who you are, Ava Noelle," Doo said bluntly. "It is nice to make your acquaintance at last. You are the reason Dad and I," she gestured to the other fairies that were surrounding them, "the reason all of us are here. We have been expecting you. We are eager to join you. We have been here a fortnight. We did not wish to miss your arrival."

Ava's thoughts seemed to scream. A fortnight? Two whole weeks? How long has Jordyn and Godroh been planning Steph and my excursion to the Inner World? Two weeks ago, I was sitting at home watching tv or goofing around with my sisters! Steph, you probably were doing something similar with your sister or with Spirit. She had noticed Steph's shrug of her shoulders, so she knew that Steph had read her thoughts. The fairy looked at Steph and smiled. Ava had a sneaking suspicion that the fairy had read her mind as well.

Doo said, "You too, Stephanie Galanos, middle name JoAnne. It is a pleasure to meet you as well." She turned around, cupped her hands, and shouted, "The other pretty elf accompanying Ava Noelle is Stephanie Galanos, middle name JoAnne."

The other fairies clapped their hands and cheered in unison, "Welcome, Ava Noelle and Stephanie Galanos, middle name JoAnne!" A few of the male fairies threw their hats high in the air while the females curtsied elegantly.

Turning in midair to face Ava and Steph once more, Doo said to Steph, "We did not know who if anybody would be accompanying Ava Noelle. But we came prepared with equipment for two just in case." She giggled adding, "Those of my land know we should always be prepared for the unexpected." She curtsied daintily. With a wave of her hand, she said, "Although I assure you, we will give you all the courtesies required of our graciousness." Looking at Ava she offered, "Any friend of Ava Noelle is a friend of ours."

Steph said, "I did not know until recently I would be accompanying Ava. I am glad that I am, and I thank you for your kindness, Doo."

Ava placed her arm around Steph's shoulder to reassure Doo that she and Steph indeed were close friends. Looking up at Steph she said, "And I am so very happy you are."

Doo was nodding her head. "I must say you are just as pretty as Ava Noelle, and I just love your cute dimple." Steph was blushing as she thanked Doo for her compliment. "We fairies do not have such daintiness on our cheeks, nor do Katharos elves."

Doo's saying the words Katharos elves had caused Ava to squinch her eyes. She felt as though she had heard the words somewhere. But try as hard as she did, she could not recall where. Doo seemed to have noticed her reaction, but she did not say anything. She just kept on talking.

"Although I have seen some humans with dimples. Some even have two, one on either side of their faces. Anyway, we are to go with you and Ava Noelle to meet the Great Wizard. He is His Excellency, Godroh of the Mystic Mountains." She placed her hands over her heart. "He is the most powerful wizard in the land. Unlike many other wizards of our land, he is great and kindly. We respect him very much."

Doo once again looked intently at Ava. She said, "We were told, Ava Noelle, that you are a different elf. That you come from the Earthly World. I assume along with your friend, Stephanie Galanos, middle name JoAnne." She bowed deeply in midair. "We vow to do everything in our power to safeguard you." Looking at Steph she added, "You too, Stephanie Galanos, middle name JoAnne. I give both of you my word."

"Please call me Steph," Steph said with a smile. "One word, much simpler than Stephanie Galanos, middle name JoAnne."

"That I shall do," Doo said in a happy tone. "That is a markedly shorter nickname, Steph, and I thank you. It will be much simpler for others to remember than Stephanie Galanos, middle name JoAnne." She abruptly shouted over her shoulder, startling both Ava and Steph. "Dad, hurry up and please fetch their weapons and satchels." Her frustrated expression with her father abruptly changed as she addressed Ava and Steph once again. "We have a long journey, a dangerous journey ahead. You need to have your swords and bows. They are of the highest quality.

They were made by the elves of the Bkotn Tribe. The Bkotn are very brave and skilled." She gave them a mischievous grin. "I wish I were an elf, so I too could fire an arrow and wield a sword." She held her arms out wide. "But as you can see, an arrow is longer than the breadth of my arms." She waved her hands down her sides as she flew, and then she giggled. "Also, the bow is twice as long as I am in height. You see, yes?"

"You do not use weapons?" Steph asked. "How do you protect yourself otherwise?"

Doo laughed, and then she nodded her head and winked. "We have our ways. Godroh told me that fairies of your land are benevolent like us. But they also can be fickle and cruel. We can be both as well, good, and bad. We are Katharos, so we have magical powers. Our magic is not equal to that of wizards and witches, but our sheer numbers make up for our disproportionate weakness."

Once again, Ava had reacted introspectively when Doo said the word Katharos.

Doo smiled at Steph as she looked her up and down like she had with Ava. She said, "I like you, Stephanie Galanos, middle name JoAnne, who prefers to be called Steph." She looked at Ava. "You too, Ava Noelle. Something tells me that the three of us, along with Dad, will become good friends. I only hope I can journey with you until whatever you have to do is finished." She excused herself politely and flew back to where Dad was standing with a group of fairies. She immediately began to bark orders to Dad and the others.

Ava could not help herself, but she was chuckling with Doo's inference that the phrase, "middle name" was part of Steph's name – Stephanie Galanos, middle name JoAnne. Yet she knew she must not forget that she and Steph were in the Inner World, a world where things were undoubtedly much different than at home. She supposed all sorts of things were possible. She considered silently; perhaps creatures of the Inner World do not have middle names. Maybe they do not have last names either. I wonder if Godroh has a middle name. Certainly, a wizard of his renowned standing must have a title, a middle or at least a last name. Maybe his full name is Godroh of the Mystic Mountains? Or could it be everything that Doo had said? She had called him the Great Wizard, His Excellency, Godroh of the Mystic Mountains.

Then again, our first president, George Washington, did not have a middle name. The use of middle names did not come about as a common practice until the nineteenth century. Nowadays, when people refer to George Washington, they simply refer to him as Washington. But he did have a title. President of the United States. But if it were up to his vice president, John Adams, Washington would have been dubbed 'His Highness, the President of the United States, and Protector of the Rights.'

Ava was frowning because of everything she had just considered. She said to herself, I do not like that name. It sounds too much like Protector of the World. Oh well, Godroh is who he is, and I suppose his title or first or last name is unimportant. She heaved a long-drawn-out sigh. But goodness! Why do I always have to overthink things? Ugh! After all, we are here in the Inner World, so anything is possible!

Steph had not said a word as she was reading Ava's excruciatingly long, rambling thoughts. Without looking at her, she said aloud in a joking tone that had a hint of sarcasm, "Ava, once you figure out all that crazy nonsense you have been thinking to yourself, please let me know, okay? And you are right. You do overthink things!" She reached out and lightly smacked Ava on her upper arm. "Get a grip, girl! We are here in the Inner World like you said, so anything is possible. We need to go with the flow!"

Ava and Steph turned their interest to DooDad. They could not help but overhear Doo and Dad's conversation. The fairies were shouting at each other.

"Please, Dad, we do not have much time," Doo said irritably. She was waving her hands in the air with evident frustration as she zoomed back and forth.

"Where are they, Doo?" Dad replied heatedly. "You never informed me where Godroh told you to hide the equipment." He scratched his head. "Besides, I thought only one of them was coming. Do we have enough for two?"

Doo moved in close and whispered something to him. She was shaking her finger beneath his nose. Then she soared back to where Ava and Steph were standing. She said in a squeaky whisper, "Please excuse my father. He was about to embarrass me with his haranguing about only one of you showing." She smiled at Steph and curtsied. "Sorry, Steph.

As I said, we did not know you were accompanying Ava. I am only glad we have spare weapons and extra clothes in your satchel that will fit you proper. Anyway, Dad knows where everything is hidden. He merely is dismayed because Godroh told me where to hide the stuff instead of telling him. Males of my kind do not like to be inferior to females. But it is too bad for Dad and other males of my kind. We females are their equals." She glared and shouted over her shoulder to Dad, "You know where they are. Please ask the others to help you." She rolled her eyes at Ava and Steph. "What is worse, Dad does not like it when I know matters that he does not. Ever since my mother died, he has been impossibly ill-tempered." She smiled and placed her hands over her heart. "But he is my Dad, and I love him. Yet he can be difficult at times and hard to live with." She glanced over her shoulder once more and growled orders at her father.

Ava and Steph exchanged telling glances. They were thinking the same thing.

Without a doubt, Doo was the boss in the DooDad family.

*****

10 Septémvriosom (September), 2021

Ava, Steph, and DooDad had been traveling for a little over a month. Early on, nearly all of the paths they strode were surrounded by wide-ranging pastures of edible grain. Ava had plucked one of the kernels from a stalk early on to examine it. She commented to Steph that the kernel resembled an Earthly World wheat berry. She described the milling process of the wheat berry. Steph, as usual, listened to Ava's explanation with great interest. She believed Ava's unnatural ability to recall just about anything she had seen, read about, or heard was nothing short of incredible. She also considered that Ava's brain must be a prolific storage area of boundless knowledge.

Ava had said, "Gristmills separate the berries from the chaff and grind them to a fine powder. Your mom probably has the result of something like this in her cupboard. I know my mom does. This is like the wheat berry that makes wheat flour." She went on to say in a grouchy tone, "But give me a break, will 'ya! Walking through these stalks – they have to be over five feet tall – is really getting to be a pain." She patted her rear end. "Right about there in my caboose! The only thing I can see is the tops of the mountains and these endless stalks of grain."

In response to what Ava had said about the endless stalks of grain, Steph began to sing. Ava had never heard Steph sing before that day. She was pleasantly surprised with the rich quality of Steph's alto voice. Nevertheless, she did not think much of Steph's satire with the words she sang and her non-verbal gestures. Steph started off singing the lyrics to the Earthly World, American patriotic song, "America the Beautiful." Then she began to improvise which seemed to tick Ava off royally.

"O beautiful for spacious skies," Steph looked at Ava and grinned, *"for endless stalks of grain."* She pointed at the towering peaks of the mountains off in the distance. "For purple mountain majesties," she slowly waved her hand in the air, *"above the fruited plain! An-ti-quom, An-ti-quom, please shed thy grace on thee. Then crown thy good on Ava's hood, from grain to grain'n tree!"*

Steph promptly doubled over with laughter. Her face was bright red and she was slapping her knees with her hands. She was having a good time of it.

Conversely, Ava was not amused. She stared at Steph for a few moments unblinking, the look on her face deliberately emotionless. She said in a sarcastic tone, "Ha-ha, ha-ha. Well, aren't you the epitome of real humor, Steph!" With a loud "harrumph!," she promptly walked away leaving Steph in fits of laughter.

Even though Ava had pretended to be annoyed, Steph had read her thoughts before she scurried off. She could tell that Ava thought her Antiquom version of the Earthly World's American patriotic song was cool. Although Ava would never admit it and has not done so to this day.

Afterward, anytime a pathway guided Ava and the others through one more endless field of grain, Ava would walk far behind Steph on purpose. She could tell that her bestie was quietly singing her song, "Antiquom the Beautiful" to herself. She did not want Steph to read her thoughts, to know she genuinely enjoyed her catchy tune. In fact, she would sometimes find herself quietly humming Steph's song as she walked. But never when she was within Steph's telepathic range.

Steph's telepathic power had not changed since they arrived in Antiquom. Whereas Ava's telepathic power had increased more than three-fold. She could detect others' thoughts from a distance that surpassed one hundred feet.

Despite the numerous paths through grain fields, their travels included forested trails as well. It was there, deep inside the forest, that Ava's curiosity was at its highest point. For certain, there were the rather unexciting spheres of lichen, moss, and ferns along the wooded trails. There were normal-looking trees and groves of dreary shrubs and weeds. Typical flora one would expect to see along a similar forested trail of the Earthly World. But there were also loads of amazingly exciting things. As a result, Ava had the tendency to scamper off the trail and disappear inside the forest quite often to investigate something that had caught her eye.

Scaring the others half to death!

4

Steph chided Ava almost daily about her tendency to vanish. How much it frightened her to know that she had disappeared if only briefly. Ava nearly always had a sound, ready excuse that went something like the following. "My alleged propensity for vanishing in a blink of an eye is not due to mischievous or ill-behaved motives. Quite the opposite. I am a passionate, wholehearted campaigner of the pursuit of knowledge far beyond ordinary aspirations. While others go with the flow and trek aimlessly without purpose, I always have a goal and a keen interest."

In that instance, Steph had rolled her eyes because of Ava's particularly verbose excuse. She also focused on the offhand way in which Ava had expressed herself by using utterly baffling language and superfluous expressions. "What in the world are you doing, Ava? Accessing the online dictionary and thesaurus in your mind as you talk? I did not understand but five words that you said!" She smiled and turned about to walk the trail.

In defense of Ava's inquisitiveness, something must be said about Antiquom's forests. Ava and Steph were continually bombarded and besieged by uncountable, unimaginably miraculous phenomena in each of their waking hours. Everywhere they looked, fresh, exciting, and curiously interesting wonders greeted them. And those fascinating wonders needed exploring, at least in Ava's opinion. Even if the others seemed to not care.

It did not matter what she noticed that had stirred her interest. Off she would go hurriedly in pursuit. As Steph was fond of saying, with no regard for her well-being or the concern of others. She said that Ava seemed to be indifferent to the potential, negative consequences of her impulsive, investigative endeavors. One particularly dreary day – it had been raining for over twenty-four hours – Steph sat her down and delivered one of her mild scolding's.

"Ava, you know how much I admire your intelligence, your gumption, and your spirit. How much I love you as a friend too. But how in the heck are we supposed to keep you safe if you keep scurrying off like that? You need to control your impulsiveness, your curiosity. If you cannot, you will find yourself in real danger." She went on to say that Ava had the bad habit of chasing every single sprightly, oversized Antiquom bug that she saw. She admitted that it was no big surprise that Ava was fascinated by the bugs. She was equally fascinated because Antiquom insects were unlike anything she had ever imagined. Not even in their science classes or in nature books had either of them seen such strange-looking, extraordinary bugs.

The Antiquom butterflies – Ava believed they were the greatest sight to behold – seemed to be in a curiosity-satisfying class all to themselves. Doo had explained that there are over four hundred diverse species of butterflies on Antiquom. The brilliantly painted, kaleidoscopic Antiquom butterflies seemed to be everywhere. Doo had said they are in the murkiest of dark forests and sail endlessly over the sunshiny, flowering fields. What is more, Antiquom butterflies are gigantic. Almost all adult butterflies are larger than the greatest Earthly World butterfly, the Queen Alexandra's Birdwing. Ava recalled reading that the Birdwing's wingspan stretches roughly one foot across when fully grown.

The rarest of Antiquom butterflies is the brilliantly colored, blue, and gold-checkered Tartan Ymni. Ava saw one that very day. It has a two-foot wingspan, easily twice that of the Birdwing. Naturally, she chased after it in the rain until it soared out of sight high in the treetops.

Whenever the foursome stopped to rest, Ava liked to clamber up a tree. Steph did not seem to mind her doing so. "At least I know where she is," Steph told Doo at one point as she looked up at Ava. "As long as she doesn't jump from limb to limb and disappear, all is well." She added with a frown, "Or tumble to the ground."

As it concerned her tree-climbing, Ava asserted that when she climbed a tree she could see everything all the way to the horizon. One time she had said to Steph, "I can explore for miles around without ever leaving my lofty perch. Without disappearing and getting you upset. You should climb the trees with me, Steph. You would be amazed at what you can see from high up. The view is incredible!"

Ava insisted that the tastiest, sweet bear fruits were the ones highest in the boughs of the trees. She claimed that the fruit at the lower branches was overripe and too tangy for her taste. Surprisingly, Steph agreed with her. Ava knew that Doo and Dad could zoom up to the higher branches to pick fruit for her and Steph. But in her inquiring mind, and given her tenacity, she insisted there was something wonderfully satisfying about plucking one's fruit from a lofty bough. Even if it involved climbing a towering tree and risking a plunge to the ground.

"It is like being in a huge candy store," she offered at one point. "All sorts of delicious yummies, gummy bears and jellybeans, chocolates, and toffee. Then asking someone to pick out a bag full of the stuff for you instead of doing it yourself. That would be like totally wrong!"

Steph had replied in an anxious tone, "Stop talking about candy. Especially toffee! You know I love the stuff!" Then she went on to scold Ava once more. She said that Ava had disappeared briefly five times earlier on that very day.

Doo had chimed in which she seldom did. She said that no one keeps records of such things on Antiquom, like strange disappearances and their rate of recurrence. She stated there are far more vital issues to consider when trekking in any of Antiquom's forests than mundane, statistical record-keeping. The priority being one's continued existence in an extremely hostile, unpredictable environment. She said forcefully, "Even so Ava, Steph is correct. You have already gone missing fifteen times in less than a week." Ava had given her a doubtful look. "Yes, I counted them," Doo exclaimed. "On seven occasions you inexplicably reappeared before we could conduct an extensive search. All that has to be a record. Just ask any Antiquom explorer, traveler, merchant, farmer, or even an ordinary village resident. They will confirm what I am saying."

Doo went on to say that nearly all voyagers that go missing in Antiquom's forests are never found. Sometimes a follow-on explorer or traveler will discover what little is left of the unfortunate voyager's remains scattered far and wide on the forest floor. More often, the victim's remains are never recovered. She ended her part of the mildly scolding conversation with words of warning.

"Any lost voyager whose remains were never found certainly had been spirited away by any number of mystical whatever's that lurk in the mysterious forests. They probably vanished when the mist appeared. The mist is evil magic. In my land, the incredibly old realm of Antiquom, mystical, evil creatures are everywhere." She placed her tiny hand on Ava's arm and said warningly, "So, please be more careful, Ava Noelle. I do not want to be the one to tell the Great Wizard Godroh that you had vanished without a trace." With a stern look, she added, "Remember the first time you disappeared?"

Ava's face had flushed markedly. She had to look away because she was very embarrassed. She was shivering. Just the thought of what had happened gave her the heebie-jeebies. It still does to this day.

CHAPTER 2

THE METAMORHIRÍO

"In my land, the incredibly old realm of Antiquom, mystical, evil creatures are everywhere."—*the winged fairy, Doo*

1

The first time Ava had "vanished" (the others' definition, not hers) was fewer than ten minutes in duration. In Ava's opinion, her temporary absence before she was discovered was a relatively short period. Even so, Steph and DooDad sought to keep a close watch on her after that first incident. They were extremely concerned for her safety.

Their excessive watchfulness sort of riled Ava. Yet she knew they had every right to be concerned. Antiquom is, unquestionably, a dangerous land. Nevertheless, Antiquom is a truly fascinating place as well. She did not want to miss a thing or allow anything to go undiscovered while she was there. She had said to Steph, "Who knows if I will survive my encounter with Wendigorium? And if I do manage to survive, which I certainly hope and pray I do, what will happen after that? Will Jordyn scoop us up and shoot us back to our normal lives? Okay, it will be wonderful to see my family and friends once more. And I cannot wait to meet yours too. But having to end this amazing adventure will be terribly boring, especially after all you and I have been through, are yet to go through.

"I could visit Niagara Falls a dozen more times, go on countless African safaris, climb the Alps and Mount Everest – heck they could even send me to the moon as the first youngster in outer space! But nothing,

nothing at all in the Earthly World could ever compare to what I have experienced in Antiquom. Sure, it has had its boring moments, particularly," she pulled a face and snickered, "as we walked in your endless stalks of grain. But all the rest, Steph, all of it has been exciting and interesting. Am I right?"

Steph said that she agreed with her.

Ava's first vanishing act occurred when she and the others were traveling a forested trail. They were on their way to a community of elves a little more than six miles distant. Ava was the last in the line of their small group. Being last in line was pretty much routine for her. She usually lingered for a few moments at the rear to gape at something interesting that had caught her eye. After satisfying her unquenchable curiosity, she hurried along the trail to catch up with the others. Therefore, there was no need for alarm that she routinely took up the tail end of the small procession to look at interesting things. Besides, the area in which they were traveling was one of the safest in Antiquom.

However, that was before Ava's first so-called vanishing act. Afterward, the others kept a close eye on her. She no longer was permitted to trail at the rear of the procession. She was stuck in the middle, either right behind Dad or Doo, and with Steph taking up the rear. When she dawdled, admittedly she did quite a few times, Steph would tell the others to stop. Once Ava had satisfied her curiosity, off they would go. Sometimes, Steph would have to take her by the hand and pull her along. She was that reluctant to turn away from whatever had interested her.

Later, Ava considered that she could not fault Steph for pulling her along the trail. If it were up to her at the time, given her dawdling, their journey would have taken a week. That is how curious she tended to be, slowing them down. Thus, instead of a week-long journey, it only took three and one-half days to trek the trail.

It is also essential to say something at this point about Steph and her own dallying and stopping along the trail. She caused the march to come to a standstill on many occasions. For she too found her curiosity had been piqued. However, since she gave off the impression that she was in charge, she usually told the others it was time for a break. Then she would go off and investigate whatever it was that had interested her. She tried to keep a good distance from Ava whenever she did so. However, most often Ava could read her thoughts and knew the reason they had stopped. But she never let on that she knew. She did not want to embarrass Steph. Moreover, she knew that Steph's dallying was nothing compared to her own.

The trail they were hiking the first time Ava vanished was dark, damp, and gloomy. Each step was treacherous and difficult. The footpath was laden with unstable, razor-sharp rocks. Knotted tree roots hidden beneath the forest floor caused stumbles which resulted in Ava and Steph getting minor cuts and bruises. DooDad did not have a problem, well, most of the time. The fairies were able to fly above the trail while Ava and Steph had to walk. But sometimes the fairies were forced to walk as well. That is because the boughs of the trees along the trail were sometimes weighed down with huge leaves and fruit, so much so they drooped low over the footpath. Ava and Steph continuously had to bend over to avoid smacking their heads on low-hanging branches. In other places, fortuitously not many, they were compelled to crawl on all fours on top of jagged rocks. DooDad, being much shorter than Ava and Steph, usually were able to walk upright but not always.

For anyone who has trekked a rocky trail, having to crawl on all fours on jagged rocks is one nasty experience. Pulling a heavy satchel behind and carrying a longbow and sword makes the effort nothing short of brutal. But Ava and Steph managed. They had no other choice.

Hiking the gloomy trail that day felt like being inside a suffocating, opaque tunnel of endless green, gold, brown, and yellow. Owing to the canopy's dense closeness, extremely little of the mid-morning sunshine reached the forest floor. Besides being dark, damp, and gloomy, the footpath was unpleasantly cold.

At one point the trail skirted an expansive, foul-smelling, mucky swamp. A sizeable section of the swamp covered the trail, so they had to slosh through the mucky mess, which added to their discomfort. The muddy body of swampy water was packed with ugly, surface-skimming, ten-legged, green bugs. The whole area smelled dreadfully disgusting. Ava thought it was very fascinating, nonetheless.

Swamps are interesting, to say the least. At least in Ava's opinion. Yes, she realizes that they can stink to high heaven. But the creatures that live in the swamp are amazing. Once again, in her opinion. Moreover, she thinks that swamps always seem to get a bad rap. Even if they are among the most important ecosystems of the Earthly World. Surely, of the Inner World as well.

Ava knew that back home in the Earthly World, swamps perform as massive sponges or pools. Swamps absorb excess water during heavy rain, thus lessening the effects of flooding. As the old-timer fishermen and women of Louisiana readily will say, swamps are crucial, especially during hurricanes and coastal storms. That is because they prevent fertile soil from washing away from the vulnerable coastline.

Because the swamp Ava and the others were next to reeked of decomposing plants and stagnant water, they began to speed up their pace markedly. The others — not Ava certainly — wanted to leave the swampy area as quickly as their legs could travel or their wings could fly. As one would expect, she wanted to dawdle, to stop for a few moments, and explore. Without uttering a word or making a sound, she did just that. She crossed her fingers and said a silent prayer. She was hopeful that the others would not notice she had stopped.

Because she was in the back of the group, the others were unaware she no longer was following them. She quietly placed her weapons and satchel on the soggy forest floor. She undid the laces of her shoes which she thought seemed to take far too long. Then she gingerly strode into the malodorous swamp. Much to her surprise, the water was pleasantly warm. The squishy whatnots of rotting vegetation and decayed organisms below the surface felt good beneath her feet. She thought it was wonderful to be walking on something squashy after trekking the rocky trail.

She was not overly concerned about what could be skulking below the opaque surface of the unctuous water. She knew from her science book readings that water-logged plants and forest waste were the worse things that she would probably encounter. Indeed, there could be leeches, but sucking parasitic worms did not bother her in the least. She understood that the leeches can be annoying, and their bites tend to itch, but they are not threatening. Doo later explained that leeches have been used by Antiquom fairies and elves, and other creatures, to treat diseases over the millennium.

As far as Antiquom reptiles were concerned, venomous snakes, crocodiles, and alligators (if there were any in Antiquom), well, regrettably, the existence of these dangerous creatures did not enter Ava's thoughts. Looking back maybe they should have. If they had, perhaps she would not have entered the swamp. Then she would not have caused so much grief for the others. Nonetheless, Ava being Ava, she probably would have ventured into the swamp despite the negative effects.

Her quest in the swamp was an Antiquom amphibian. It was an unusually large, bright blue creature that resembled a frog. It had leaped from the fringe of the trail to the swamp as she passed it by. The creature looked positively familiar to her at the time. She was sure she had seen a doppelganger frog in a science book back home. So off she went wading in the swamp, slowly, carefully, contemplatively. Never once taking her eyes off the creature as it slowly did little breaststrokes on the water's face.

About eight minutes after Ava had vanished – once again, the others' definition, not hers – Steph realized that she was not behind her. She had asked Ava a question and had not received a reply. She and the others speedily retraced their steps.

When Steph and DooDad arrived at the swamp, they spotted Ava. She was chest-deep in the swampy water, her long brown, pony-tailed hair trailing behind on the filthy water's surface as she waded. Her back was to Steph and the others as they stood staring at her in disbelief. At that precise moment, the creature Ava had been pursuing was perched on a partially submerged log. The log was in the middle of the swamp. It did not appear to be overly frightened. It just sat there; its large, dark blue eyes riveted on Ava.

Now, everyone knows from natural science books and everyday life that frogs cannot smile. Okay, yes, ceramic garden frogs sometimes have a silly grin painted on their faces. And they truly do look adorable and quite harmless sitting upright on their hind legs, their front feet (called hands) clutching their potbellies lovingly. However, at least in the Earthly World, actual, real, living frogs do not smile.

Despite this, if any living frog in the universe could smile, the Antiquom frog-like creature Ava had been pursuing was the one that was smiling. In addition to giving the impression that it was grinning from ear to ear, the creature had an unfettered air about it. It seemed to be beckoning her on, wanting her to draw nearer as it sat motionless on the log. Naturally, she complied.

Looking back, Ava was convinced that the creature had hypnotized her and had placed her under a spell of some sort. She was that enthralled as she stared awestruck into its bulging eyes. Nothing else was in her mind but the creature's adorable blue eyes and its alluring smile. She was not scared. She also had no inkling of what was going on around her. A vicious, jaw-snapping alligator of the Antiquom variety could have been inches away, and she would not have noticed. Nor would she have reacted if it had attacked her.

Afterward, Steph told Ava that she was very anxious as she watched from the trail. Perhaps anxious is not the right word. Steph was outright livid! She was angry because Ava had vanished from the trail without a word, but she was also distraught because Ava had waded into the swamp. Her reddening face had clearly emphasized her rage. But to her benefit, she somehow managed to keep her cool. She was equally concerned for Ava's safety. Worried beads of sweat were breaking out on her forehead. Her powerful leg muscles were tight like she was about to dash into the swamp at the first sign of danger.

Steph yelled, "Ava, I want you to turn around right now! There must be leeches or other nasty water critters in there! You are going to be stung by something or worse. Maybe you will be bitten by a huge fish with sharp teeth. Darn you, Ava, there could be alligators or crocodiles in there! Perhaps even poisonous snakes. Get out of there right now. Now I tell you!"

Ava had no clue that the others had returned to the swamp until she heard Steph yelling at her. She was charmed at the time, so Steph's screams sounded indistinct, far off, like a soft echo of a whispering voice in an empty room. She was thinking of nothing but the creature. It was staring at her steadily as it smiled affectionately.

Ava shook her head defiantly in reaction to Steph's distant yelling. She continued to push her way further in the swamp, her eyes never leaving the creatures. She thrust her forefinger high in the air, probably signaling, "Just one more minute." She gave a thumbs up. She undoubtedly was implying, "Remain calm! Everything is fine! No need to worry. I got this!" When she was roughly twenty feet from the creature, she stopped wading. The shadowy water was now lapping at her chin. She was vaguely aware that if she waded further the water would be over her head. Then she would have to swim to the creature and grab onto the log.

"It's okay, little froggie," Ava later recalled she had said in a low, sugary voice. She had been staring spellbound into the creature's eyes. "If you do not mind, I am going to get a wee bit closer. I would like to see if you are in fact like the blue poison dart frog back home." She smiled nonsensically without even knowing that she had. "The blue poison dart frog in my world inhabits a place called Suriname." She druggily waved her hand in front of her adding, "In swamps just like this. Although to be perfectly honest with you, I don't know where Suriname is actually."

Without warning, her feet began to sink into the tangled, mushy undergrowth. The muck was gradually sucking her in. She seemed to awaken from her enchanted state with being sucked into the gunk, at least for a moment. She began to panic a little. She lost her footing and briefly vanished beneath the murky water. When she reappeared a few seconds later, she had her hand high in the air signaling a thumbs up. Once again, she probably was implying something along the lines, "Everything's okay here. No need for panic. I got this. So, chill!"

To Ava's surprise, the frog did not leap off the log despite her panicked splashing and drawing even nearer. She did a slow breaststroke toward the creature then stopped. Now she was standing in water that was just below her eyes, so she was forced to hold her breath. She was bouncing up and down on her tippy toes so she could breathe. All the while she remained under a hypnotic spell. Her eyes riveted as before. Her brief panic when she slipped beneath the surface soon forgotten.

Steph later told her that she had been horrified when Ava had slipped beneath the surface. She said that when it happened, her entire body froze in place. She had struggled to form words on her lips, but nothing escaped her dry throat. She swiftly unlaced her shoes and moved closer to the swamp's edge. She was determined to put an end to Ava's madness because it was scaring her half to death.

Before she entered the swamp, Steph briefly glanced down at Doo and Dad. The fairies' tennis ball-sized eyes were riveted on Ava and the creature. It was at that moment Steph noticed that Dad was removing his wand from the pocket of his chestnut brown cloak. He promptly pointed it in the direction of Ava and the creature. The wand was emitting tiny, dark green sparks from its tip. He had an unsettled expression on his freckled face. He muttered, "I would rather you not follow her into the water, Steph. You will only confuse things."

In reply Steph cried crossly, "But what is to be done? Ava is not going to return to the trail until she accomplishes what she has set out to do. But I refuse to allow her to disappear beneath the water again! Plus, she looks like she is holding her breath! That is because the water is right below her eyes! Cannot either of you do something because, as you can see, she is not listening to me? If you cannot do something, I will!" She stepped into the swamp and began walking in the murky mess toward Ava.

Dad rocketed in the air without another word or a moment's hesitation. Three seconds later he was hovering a few inches above Ava's head. He pointed his wand at her and muttered something that vaguely sounded to Ava like silly gobbledygook. But then, considering her entranced state, what he said may have been words she normally would have understood. She was still bouncing up and down on her toes, taking deep breaths each time that her nose was above the water. Without looking up, she shook a finger at Dad threateningly. Her voice inflection was strange, totally different than her normal voice when she spoke. Her words were drawn-out and sounded strangely distant even to her.

"Shooooooo, Daaaaad! I am going to be okay." Then her mouth was under the surface. She bounced up and yelled, "Just so you know, I heard you muttering your fairy babble under your breath!" Her head disappeared briefly below the surface. Bouncing up high on her toes yet again she yelled, "You better not have cast a spell or hexed me. If you did, undo it." She disappeared beneath the surface for a moment. It was twice as long as before. She suddenly bounced up and screamed, "If you do not undo it, you will be sorry. I promise you!" She disappeared beneath the surface.

Whatever it was that Dad had done with his wand seemed to counteract the creature's mesmeric magic. Although it was not easy to do so, Ava briefly refocused her attention from the creature's glowering eyes to Dad as she continued to disappear and reappear from beneath the water's surface. Dad's round eyes seemed to be gigantic as he glared intently at the creature. She saw that his wand was emitting dark green sparks from its tip.

She abruptly shouted in a terrified, high-pitched screech as she bounced up and down frenetically, her flailing arms splashing water everywhere, "Oh my God! What in the world am I doing out here? I am going to drown! Help me, Dad, please! My lungs feel like they are going to burst. I cannot breathe properly!"

The creature captured her attention yet again. It had countered Dad's magic. She set out dogpaddling toward the creature! In the same, strange tone as before, she suddenly growled at Dad, "And stop pointing your wand at my frog! He is not dangerous or anything. You are going to scare him. Do as I ask, or I am going to, I swear to God—!" Before she could complete her thoughts, or grasp what was happening, she had abruptly stopped dogpaddling. Her body became vertical in the water. She began to turnabout slowly against her will. All the while she was bouncing up and down on her toes to gasp for air. In a matter of seconds, owing to Dad's magical spell, her legs began to slosh through the muddy water by force. Soon she was chest deep in water and rapidly wading in the direction of the trail against her will.

Despite her continued, robust, vocal objections and impassioned struggling, and even with her semi-conscious frightened state, she and the creature could not compete with Dad's magic. Her legs were moving on their own while a strange voice in her brain was screaming silently. The creature was the one screaming words of defiance in Ava's head. Although she did not realize it at the time.

"Stop walking impudent moron! I am the one in control here, not that stupid fairy! Turn around, elf. Do it now! If you do not return to me, I will kill you and your friends!"

At that moment, Ava's inner thoughts were completely conflicted. Part of her psyche, her normal self, was scared almost senseless. She could not wait to get to the shoreline as quickly as Dad's magic could compel her. Nevertheless, another part of her psyche wanted to obey the creature's screaming pleas inside her head – to turn around. She later recounted to Steph and the others that she wanted to turn around and swim back to the creature! Luckily, Dad's enchantment was too powerful. She steadily waded toward shore, her legs moving in compliance with his magical spell.

Yet the creature was not giving up that easily. It continued to influence her mind. She shrieked crossly in her strange, semi-hypnotized tone of voice, "What in the world did you just do to me, Dad? I was not in any danger. I know how to swim! So, what if I had dropped beneath the water's surface a half-dozen times, huh? It was no big deal. The water was just over my head, that's all! Let me go right now! I have to return to the creature!"

She resumed struggling, desperately trying to fight the unseen, magical force that was forcing her legs to stride forward. But her efforts were futile. She was splashing through the muck at an even faster pace. Soon she would be in waist-deep water, further along out of harm's way. A minute or two later she would be back on the trail safe and sound.

Part of her psyche was relieved, yet she unconsciously fought Dad's spell in vain. The creature did not want her to give up. It was not giving up on her either. Its intentions continued to scream in her head, trying to force her to struggle against Dad's spell, to turnabout.

Ava roared in a nasty tone, "Geez, Dad! I cannot believe you hexed me. How could you? And all this time I thought we were friends!" She unexpectedly looked up at him. She did not want to, but she could not help herself. She began to laugh hysterically. The creature's hypnotic spell had been broken completely at last. Probably because she was too far away for its mystical magic to hold her captive any longer. Her thoughts about the creature vanished.

She considered that Dad looked incredibly silly as he flew above her. He was fluttering backward clumsily. His wand was in one hand while his other hand was yanking at his trousers. They were slipping down his butt. Despite his comical appearance, he continued to exhibit a serious-minded, stern expression. His large eyes remained pointedly fixated on the creature. His look was outright murderous. And his wand continued to produce threatening sparks. Ava had the sense that if the frog moved even an inch along the log or leaped into the water, Dad would zap it to smithereens.

"Well, I hate to admit it," Ava said in a cheery tone. "But I think it is very cool that I am wading through the water even though I am not moving my legs deliberately. This must be a scientific marvel; I kid you not! Also, I must say you are one totally cool fairy, Dad. I never knew fairies could fly backward. You look like a gigantic, two-foot-tall, white-bearded Earthly World hummingbird hovering up there, except, "she giggled lightheartedly, "except I can see the crack of your adorable, itsy-bitsy, fairy butt! It's soooo cute too!"

In response to what Ava had said, Dad nervously tried to pull up his trousers even more. At the same time, Ava was laughing hysterically as she slowly waded ever closer to the trail. The panic and confusion had left her. In their place was a whole lot of shame for what she had done – wading into the swamp. She also felt a tad bit of resentment for what Dad had done, that he had hexed her.

He had placed me under a magical spell without my permission!

The more that Ava considered that reality, the more it ticked her off.

2

Once Ava was standing on the trail, she began to explain the reason she had waded into the swamp. But Steph was not having any of her excuses. She was shaking her head reproachfully, her expression incredulous. She had cracked her knuckles, flexed her fingers, and stretched her muscular arms. She roughly grabbed Ava by the shoulders and squeezed hard. Her grip smarted, so much so that Ava flinched and said softly, "Ouch, Steph! Not so hard, huh!"

As a forceful rugby player, Steph is exceptionally strong. Ava was quite thankful at that moment that she did not rear back and punch her square in the nose. Naturally, Steph would not have acted in that manner. She is too kind for anything even close to that. But looking back, Ava knew that she certainly deserved a swift kick in her sopping wet rear end if nothing else.

"I cannot believe you, Ava!" Steph chided heatedly. Her dark brown eyes were riveted on Ava's mud-streaked face. Gooey gobs of muck and swamp undergrowth were stuck in Ava's hair. Steph glanced irritably across the swamp at the creature Ava had been following. She later said that something about the creature gave her the creeps. When Ava was in the swamp she had thought, is it because it keeps staring at her intently? Or is it something else? And I must wonder – is it really a frog?

Ava quickly mumbled a few more excuses to explain why she had pursued the frog into the swamp. Interrupting her panicky excuses, Steph suddenly barked disapprovingly, "Stop talking, Ava!" She was shaking her head with disbelief. "A stupid blue poison dart frog you say?

Of the dying poison dart frog species? Tell me you are not serious! You thought that ugly thing was like the poison frog that you had read about in a library book? A frog that already was dying and ready to shoot poisonous darts at you. What were you thinking? You could have been poisoned if you got too close or touched it!" She looked Ava up and down angrily, and then she spun her around roughly on her heels. Ava nearly fell flat on her face. That is how forcefully Steph had spun her around. She stared at Steph wide-eyed, completely shocked by her friend's anger.

"You are lucky that no leeches are sticking to your skin, sucking your blood!" Steph exclaimed as she examined Ava's scalp. She leaned in close then swallowed hard and backed away. She pinched her nose. "Darn you, Ava! You stink to high heaven, not to mention your clothes are slimy and sopping wet! It will take hours to get that crud out of your hair. If I had access to a straight razor or scissors, I would shave your head or, at the minimum, cut your hair." She snatched something from Ava's scalp and tossed it to the ground. It was wiggling as she stomped on it angrily. "Darn you girl! Whatever that it is has to be the grossest thing I have ever seen!" Then she did something that Ava had least expected given her fury. She wrapped her arms around Ava's shoulders and hugged her tightly in her typically strong bear hug fashion.

Ava could not help but notice that she was trembling and rocking back and forth.

"Goodness, Ava, you have no idea how you frightened me! You scared the bejesus out of Doo, and Dad as well! When I turned around on the trail and saw that you had vanished, I did not know what to think. I imagined some horrible beast had snatched you or worse! Honestly, Ava, I do not know what I would do if you were hurt, or if I were to lose you. You are my only Earthly World friend. Please, Ava, please – never do something like that again."

Ava gently pulled back from Steph's powerful embrace. She took a deep breath then smiled. It was one of her charismatic, innocent-looking smiles. Her light brown eyes were flickering naïvely. Just as they always seemed to do whenever she had been caught doing something she should not have. In a sincere tone she said, "Oh, Steph, that was so sweet of you to say. I would not know what to do if you were, likewise, hurt or taken away from me. For sure, I adore and love Doodad, but you are my only Earthly World friend too. Even so, you worry too much about me, don't you know that? I would not have touched it. I know better than to do that. I simply was curious, that is all. I wanted to see if it was, in fact, like the blue poison dart frog back home." She added with a shaky laugh, "Also, please excuse me for correcting you. But the frog is not dying as you implied. It is not ready to croak, no pun intended." She grinned nervously.

"That is just part of its name, dyeing, spelled d-y-e-i-n-g like in coloring, not dying like in death. Also, the species, which includes the blue poison dart frog, do not shoot darts. That merely is a part of its name. But you are correct. I could have been poisoned had I touched it. But, as I said, I knew better than to do that." She turned and gazed thoughtfully across the slimy water. The creature was staring at her with its blue, unblinking eyes. To her surprise, but inwardly to her delight as well, the creature began to leap back and forth along the length of the log in response to her looking at it. It appeared to be agitated. The creature stopped moving then eyed Ava straight on. It started to croak low, grumbling, mournful moans that swept across the swamp in ghostly echoes.

Ava pointed and said in a put-on, miserable tone, "See, Steph? He is upset because I did not get a closer look at him. But now I will never know if he is like the blue poison dart frog from Suriname." She spread her arms out wide. "And darn it! I was this close to him. How sad he looks, poor fellow. He even is croaking to me, begging me to return to the swamp. See? He wants to be my friend." She made a timid move toward the swamp. She was not going to go back into the water. It was just that she wanted to prove a point. I am in control here, none of you. She said aloud, "Maybe I should—"

Before she could say anything further or move an inch, Steph grabbed the back of her collar. She asserted in a threatening, matter-of-fact whisper, "Do not even think about it! If you even step a millimeter of an inch into the swamp, I – I - I do not know what I will do, but I most certainly will do it!" She spun Ava around and stared at her straight on. Her eyes were darting back and forth as she searched Ava's eyes. Less than a foot separated their noses.

"I was only teasing you," Ava declared in a shaky tone. She gave Steph an anxious grin. "There is no way I am going back in the swamp. I apologize if I have upset you." Given Steph's staring, she was quite certain that Steph had not heard a word she had said.

Steph whispered in an angry tone, "Yes, Ava, I most certainly would do something to you that both of us would regret later. So, you better not think of going back into that swamp! I will have a heart attack if you do." She made a fist and placed it close to Ava's nose. She was grinning. "And you will be one hurting elf too." She dropped her hand to her side. "Of course, you know I would never hurt you, but I swear to God I would do something." She looked away from Ava, her eyes welling up with tears.

Ava wanted to say something as a defiant retort, but nothing came out of her mouth. She knew better than to make things worse by arguing with Steph. She knew that Steph was one hundred percent correct. She sniffed the collar of her tunic and spluttered, "Gawd, I do stink to high heaven!" She promptly gathered her belongings from the ground. She slipped on her shoes and quickly laced them up. Then she set out on the trail in the direction they had been traveling a half-hour or so before.

Dad was standing next to Doo. He looked extremely annoyed; his brow was drawn in an angry frown. Ava glared at him as she passed. But she deliberately flashed a cheerful smile at Doo. Doo smiled in reply and winked. Ava was about to wink as well, but she knew Dad was watching her closely. She did not want to give him the satisfaction of knowing she no longer was angry, that she was faking. She muttered over her shoulder, "Thanks for nothing, Dad. I'll never know if it is like the frog back home because of the hex you gave me."

Dad flew to hover mere inches above Ava's head as she walked away from the swamp. She knew that he was not going to let her out of his sight. That he was following her started to annoy her once more. She tried to shoo him away with pathetic, impolite waves of her hand. But he easily dodged her waves and remained above her head. She glanced up at him and made a face. His upset look troubled her greatly and hurt down to the pit of her stomach. He suddenly bellowed in his creaky, low-pitched, fairy voice, "Okay, Ava, I have had enough of your pouting. I want you to stop walking, turn around, and return to Doo and Steph. There is something you must see."

Dad's tone was startlingly enraged which made Ava feel even lousier. But she continued her pretend ruse of being angry with him. She countered glumly in a heartbreaking tone, "Please leave me alone. I feel miserable right now." She shook her head defiantly and sped up her pace. "Besides, I am not like Doo. I am not your daughter, well, an offspring fairy child, or whatever I am trying to say. I do not like it one bit when you holler at her, and I certainly will not tolerate you raising your voice to me." She glanced up at him. "So, I ask you to never raise your voice to me again. You got that?" She began to walk even faster. "Also, just so you know, I am not going to turn around, nor am I going to stop. You can fly above me until your wings fall off from tiredness, but I am pressing on."

She glanced up at Dad once more. Her tone was unarguably grave when she said, "Also, do not hex me again. Yes, I must admit it was sort of cool moving through the swamp without deliberately trying to. On the other hand, having my strength of mind ripped from me without my consent did not feel, well, to be honest with you Dad – it did not feel right. Friends are not supposed to make friends feel like that. Period. So, please, never do that to me again. I want to be in control of my body, my actions, and my thoughts. Not you or anyone else!"

"Ava, you must stop walking and turn around," Dad said. His tone was more pleasant, less commanding which made Ava feel a bit better.

"I am not turning around," she replied gloomily. "This is the direction we were walking previously, so I am continuing. All of you can come with me if you like, or you can stay here. It is your choice. But I am moving forward and putting all that happened back there behind me." She heard the unmistakable flutter of Doo's elegant, nearly translucent wings as she flew toward her.

Doo always seemed to know what she was thinking and how she was feeling. Similarly, Doo also seemed to have just the right words whenever she was feeling down in the dumps, like when she was missing her family and friends back in the Earthly World. She even wondered at times if Doo could read her mind. She could read Doo's thoughts, so it was possible that Doo could read hers. She considered asking Doo about it on more than one occasion, but she always wavered. She did not want to embarrass the lovely, winged fairy. Besides, what difference did it make actually?

Doo was hovering mere inches in front of her face. She was flying backward, although not nearly as clumsily as Dad had flown over the swamp as he tried to pull up his trousers. The cute freckles on her nose and around the creases of her lips bunched together as she smiled. Yet Ava noticed that her forehead was furrowed. She said in her high-pitched, squeaky voice, "Ava, you must turn around. You must see the – *frog.*"

Doo's odd pause before she said the word frog did not escape Ava's notice. Likewise pausing before saying the word frog, she replied sarcastically, "What is wrong with my – *frog?*" She suddenly realized Steph had been calling out to her, but she had not been paying attention. She stopped walking.

Steph called out, "I have no idea what this is, *but you are darned lucky to be alive!*"

Ava pretended to ignore what Steph had said. She faked a yawn, shrugged her shoulders, and started walking yet again. Her lips were tightly pursed in a stubborn, resolute scowl. Even so, she was becoming more alarmed the further she walked. Steph's anxious tone and what she had said were bothering her. She began to read Steph's mind. What she interpreted from Steph's thoughts were confusing her.

Steph yelled again. "Ava, you must see this. There is a lesson to be learned here, not only for you but for me as well. Please turn around. I am begging you."

Ava stopped dead in her tracks. That Steph had said she was begging Ava to turn around sounded creepy. Steph was not the sort to beg anybody to do anything. And that included Ava.

3

"Yes, Ava," Dad bellowed. By the far-off sound of his voice, Ava assumed he had returned to wherever Steph was standing. "You are lucky to be alive. Your cute frog could have torn you apart and gulped you down with four or five hungry swallows! Then all that would have remained of you, our friend who we love and admire, would be nothing more than a memory."

Ava's heart began to thump loudly in her chest. Her face felt hot, flushed. Tasting a tinge of blood in her mouth caused her to cringe. She was not aware that she had been biting on her lower lip. She licked her lips and closed her eyes. She whispered in a subdued way, "Doo, please take me back to Steph. I will open my eyes when I get there. Even though I do not want to see whatever it is I know I must. Can you do that for me?"

"Certainly," Doo replied. "Anything you ask. Just be careful as you go, okay? I do not want you to trip over the rocks and roots." She reached down and clutched the forefinger of Ava's right hand. As she flew, she slowly led Ava to where Steph and Dad were standing. A few moments later she said softly, "Okay, Ava. You can open your eyes now. The swamp is to your left."

Ava turned, opened her eyes, and gawked. She tottered slightly and had to lean against Steph to keep her balance.

Her darling blue frog had disappeared. In its place, towering like a behemoth over the submerged log the frog had set on, was a massive, ferocious-looking beast. It was more terrifying than anything Ava could have ever imagined. The creature had the identical shade of blue as the frog she had pursued. It had the same, bulging eyes. Yet its eyes were ten times bigger than the frog's and riveted on Ava as she stood shaking from head to toe.

The beast was over ten feet in length and stood at least four feet tall. It was a hideous mixture of a vicious Earthly World alligator and a gargantuan hippopotamus. Its snout was long, rounded, U-shaped like an alligator. But the balance of its enormous body was barrel-shaped like a hippopotamus. Its skin was fibrous, leathery. Its snout was closed tightly. The beast's bottom teeth jutted from inside its upper jaw. They looked frighteningly sharp.

Ava instinctively began to back away. She was breathing hard. Her mouth was wide-open. In reaction to her backward movement, the beast opened its mouth. Repulsive, rose-colored spittle dribbled in disgusting globules from its upper jaw. Its tongue was frothy. Two rows of ivory teeth flashed terrifyingly in the soft sunlight. The beast suddenly snarled raucously. It stomped its feet irritably causing huge splashes of brown water to spray far and wide.

Ava and Steph jumped back just as they grabbed each other's hands. They were trembling uncontrollably. In reaction to their backing away, the beast suddenly crouched low on its haunches. It was poised to pounce, ready to strike. Its bulging, blue eyes were still focused on Ava. Watching her every move. Her every gasping breath. It was expecting her to turn away and run. If she did, it would rush across the swamp with five or six gargantuan leaps and seize her in its massive, bone-breaking, flesh-tearing jaws.

"Oh my gosh! It is going to attack us!" Steph wailed. "What should we do? Should we remain here, or should we run for it?"

In a scarcely perceptible, shaky voice, Ava murmured, "Let's get the heck out of here before it attacks!" She grabbed Steph's hand and yanked her close. "On the count of three. One, two."

Before she could say three, Dad abruptly yelled, "Stop! Do not move. If you run it will attack. It is agile and quick. It will be upon you before you can take ten steps – perhaps less."

In reaction to Dad's shout, the beast looked away from Ava and stared at him. Then its bulging eyes focused on Doo. The fairies were hovering about ten feet in the air on either side of Ava and Steph. Doo was to Ava's left. Dad was to Steph's right. They were pointing their wands at the beast. Dad's wand was emitting blue sparks. The sparks of Doo's wand were red. The beast gradually became more rigid and slowly raised up on its haunches. It instinctively knew that the fairies, even with their puny size in contrast to its own, were threatening.

"Stay where you are!" Doo commanded. "It eventually will tire, turn away, and leave us be."

Dad quickly said, "If it does attack, Doo and I can destroy it. But we are loathed to destroy anything, even something as hideous as that treacherous beast. So, stay where you are as Doo and I have commanded."

Ava gulped in sheer panic as she pointed at the beast. Her hands were shaking. She looked up at Doo through her teary eyes. Doo was staring at the beast with a look of utter disgust. Ava stammered, "Doo, wha – wha - what is that thing? Please tell me that thing is not what I had waded after into the swamp. Please tell me that thing is not the innocent-looking, blue frog that was squatting on the submerged log!"

"I am sorry to say it is the same," Doo replied. She softly landed on the ground beside Ava. She placed her right arm around Ava's thigh. At a little more than two-feet tall, Doo could not give Ava a customary embrace around the shoulders. Her one-armed fairy hug around Ava's thigh would have to do. She kept her eyes riveted on the beast. Her wand continued to discharge red sparks from its tip. Without looking up at Ava, she said, "It is a metamorhirío. Metamorhirío in Fortunomy simply implies transmuted beast. The metamorhirío is but one of a dozen or so creatures on Antiquom that can transform from one beast to another, sometimes even three or more. We believe the metamorhirío can transmute to at least five or perhaps six different creatures, all in a matter of a few moments. It can transmute from something as small as an insect to its true, gigantic self, and perhaps a few other creatures in between. What you are seeing is its true form. It cannot transmute to anything larger than itself.

"As you have undoubtedly supposed, it intended to lure you as its likely prey to draw closer. Then it would strike you and drag you under the water. Deepwater is where the beast resides. I would imagine it was as tiny as an insect when the three of us passed it by on the trail. It must have transmuted when you passed it by, oblivious to the rest of us.

"The metamorhirío can read another creature's thoughts. That is one of its ploys, to mimic something another creature may have been thinking about. It can invade one's thoughts as well." She looked up at Ava. "Were you thinking about something like the Earthly World blue frog when you first saw the metamorhirío, perhaps in its third shape, maybe as an insect or something small like that?"

Without taking her eyes off the staring creature, Ava replied, "Why yes, Doo, as a matter of fact I was. I was wondering if frogs lived in Antiquom's swamps like frogs live in ponds and marshes back home. For some strange reason, my thoughts focused on the blue poison dart frog. Why I do not know. The thought just occurred to me." She looked down at Doo. "Probably because I was fascinated when I read about it in the Earthly World.

"I heard a slight splash as the frog, I mean the metamorhirío, must have leaped into the water. When I looked back to see what had made the noise, that is when I saw the blue frog swimming away from me. I was intrigued totally, probably because I had thought of the blue poison dart frog. And, lo and behold, there was one before me! So, naturally, I pursued it. Now, I am terribly sorry that I did. I acted stupidly; I must admit."

Ava bent over and kissed the top of Doo's head. She glanced up at Dad. He was pointing his wand threateningly at the metamorhirío as he hovered in place. She said in a sincere, apologetic tone, "Dad, I am terribly sorry for the way I acted toward you. Thank you for hexing me, for saving my life. Please forgive me for the way I acted." She looked down at the ground and added in an apologetic tone, "And I am sorry for telling you that you had breached my self-control. If you had not done what you did, I probably would be dead."

Dad did not reply. When she looked up at him, he nodded his head and smiled. She could tell he was no longer angry with her, that he had forgiven her despite her rudeness. His smile had made her feel a bit better. As she stood next to Steph and Doo, she was extremely embarrassed, nonetheless. She was also feeling more sheepish than she had ever felt in her life. Thoughts of dread, of what could have happened, were racing through her mind. Steph, interpreting her thoughts, was nodding her head knowingly.

Ava thought to herself for Steph's benefit, what I did was so stupid, Steph. What would have happened if you had not discovered me missing, not turned around when you did? If Dad had not hexed me? Pointing his wand at the metamorhirío to keep the beast from attacking me as I returned to the trail? I would be dead if Dad had not saved me!

Steph placed her arm around Ava's shoulder and squeezed lightly. She said in a calm, understanding voice, "Now you know why you cannot go wading in waters like that. We are not of this world. We do not know of the dangers that surround us. When you want to go into a body of water, ask either Doo or Dad if it is safe to do so, okay? And whatever you do, never go into a stinky swamp, not here or even at home." She glanced at Ava's matted hair, shook her head, and said, "Yuck! What a mess."

Ava and the metamorhirío continued to gawk at each other for the longest time. Then the creature looked away from Ava to Dad. The fairy continued to hover in the air, his wand radiating blue sparks. His eyes were centered on the beast, his spirited expression unrelenting. At last, the creature looked away from Dad and gave Ava a final, enduring look. It opened its mouth wide and roared vociferously causing Ava and Steph to jump back. It unhurriedly turned around and splashed noisily through the swampy muck. A few moments later it submerged and disappeared out of sight.

Ava and Steph stared at the spot where the beast had gone under. When at last the tiny ripples on the water's surface caused by the beast's underwater swimming ceased, Dad touched down. He walked over to Ava and kissed her hand. Ava expected him to scold her. Instead, he said in moving words that will be forever etched in her mind.

"Never forget, Ava Noelle. Never forget who you are."

CHAPTER 3

DOO'S EXPLANATIONS
AND A REVELATION

*"To be yourself in a world that is constantly trying to make you
something else is the greatest accomplishment."*
—Ralph Waldo Emerson

1

A few days after Ava's so-called first vanishing act, Doo sat her and Steph down to tell them a bit more about Antiquom.

"As you probably know Antiquom is the Inner World's Yesteryear, its history of long ago. It is a long-forgotten, ancient land, or so the fables say. But as you also know, it is alive and thriving with unimaginable wonders. Antiquom is referred to as the Realm of Peace and Tranquility. However, that is a misleading term. Antiquom is anything but peaceful and tranquil. Surely, many ages ago it was a peaceable land. But things have changed for the worse over time. There also are two other realms of the Inner World." She looked at Ava and Steph in turn. "If I am repeating things that you already know, please tell me. Thus, I will move on to other topics."

Steph said, "Frankly, Doo, at least in my opinion, I think it is fine if you tell us everything about the Inner World, about Antiquom. Even if what you are about to say we have heard before." She looked at Ava although she already knew Ava had agreed with what she had said. But she and Ava did not want to let on that they could read each other's minds. So, she said to Ava, "Do you agree?"

189

Ava nodded her head eagerly. She was frustrated because Jordyn did not address the dozens of questions that were zipping in her mind. Before she and Steph left the bedchamber. Thus, she knew that the more she understood the happier she would be. Despite her thoughts, she said in an enthusiastic tone, along with a huge smile, "The more you can tell us, Doo, the better."

Doo said, "The central, or middle realm of my land is called Andron. Myths refer to it as the Inner World's Passageway, the Inner World's Corridor to the third realm. The third realm is called the Ostium. It is the Inner World's Future and Tomorrow. I have never been to the second and third Inner World realms, Andron and Ostium. Therefore, I cannot vouch for what the myths and fables say. I do not even know if the realms exist. Quite frankly, I often wonder how Ostium can exist if it is our future, our tomorrow." She looked at Ava and then at Steph. She was shrugging her tiny shoulders. "How can something be that is not already? It does not make sense."

Ava and Steph shrugged as well. They also had no idea how something that had yet to be could be real.

Doo said with a cute grin, "All I know about those two realms is what I have been told by Dad and the elders. But I know quite a bit about Antiquom." She reached out to touch Ava's hand briefly. Ava read Doo's mind and knew that the next portion of the talk had everything to do with her, with her curiosity.

Doo said, "As you already know, Antiquom is a perilous land for those who do not grasp its many hazards. It is teeming with vicious beasts, venomous flora, swift-flowing rivers, and fathomless bodies of water. Some of it you have seen and experienced for yourselves. But there are many other dangers you have yet to encounter. Antiquom's bleak and mysterious forests are mostly treacherous for inexperienced voyagers such as you. Please allow me to explain further."

Doo started by describing the shifting fields of steamy, bubbling tar pits prevalent in Antiquom's forests. Ava noticed that Doo's squeaky voice trembled every so often.

"The tar pits unwearyingly pass the time as they have over the millennium. Ever since the fissure, Thávma, opened nearly 66 million years ago. They patiently wait. Ready to ensnare a careless traveler who wanders off the path onto their sand or leaf-covered wickedness." She wiped away a tear that had trickled from her eye. "The oily tar quickly grabs hold of the traveler's ankles as firmly as an unyielding, stretched knot. There is no escape. As little as four inches of the tar's depth is enough to ensnare even the largest of creatures. Smaller creatures, even fairies do not stand a chance. That is because the tar is sticky. All it takes is one drop, and you are ensnared." She wiped away another tear. "The moment the horrified traveler begins to panic, they nearly always do, the pasty sludge gives the victim's fear a willing, helping hand. It slowly elasticizes and draws the fighting traveler deeper into its bowels. Its gooey, methane-infused reservoir greedily metamorphoses inside-out until the victim is completely trapped. Then the victim's body is gradually transformed to more tar." She suddenly buried her face in her hands and sobbed. After a few moments, she looked up. Her face was streaked with tears. She quickly wiped them away.

She said, "Oh, I am sorry. I always get emotional whenever I describe the tar pits. It is how my dear mother died. She accidentally stepped in one. I watched horrified as she slowly disappeared beneath the surface. There was nothing I could do."

Ava quickly enfolded Doo in her arms. She said, "Oh, Doo, I am deeply sorry. You do not have to tell us anything more about Antiquom. We can just sit here, talk about other things."

"No," Doo quickly replied. "I would like to continue with my story if it is okay with you." Ava and Steph nodded their heads. "As I said, there are those that enter Antiquom's forest but never come out. Some pointlessly perish while attempting to cross over what they wrongly assumed was a tranquil stream. Only to be pulled beneath the deep water by its swift undercurrents. Then some unwisely walk headlong into a thick blanket of enchanted mist from which nearly no one can escape. Antiquom's mountain ranges are equally treacherous. Take one wrong step, and the traveler may plunge head over heels into a bottomless crevice or tumble off a precarious cliff. And yet, despite its many hazards, Antiquom is a magical land of truly fascinating, mystical wonders. The diverse flora is especially spectacular as you have already seen. It is a colorful display of incredibly overwhelming, unbelievably vivid, dazzling colors."

Ava had to agree with Doo. Everywhere she looked, juicy fruits dangled from weighed down tree limbs by the hundreds. Several tree fruits, like the tasty, bright orange-colored *thkao*, were massive. The thkao is about the size of a ripe, round watermelon. Ava enjoyed devouring the sweet thkao fruit, almost as much as she used to enjoy gorging on scrumptious gummy bears.

One tree, termed the *thboma*, is comparable to an Earthly World cacao tree. Doo told her and Steph that its seeds are used by elves, fairies, witches, and wizards to make tasty beverages and sugary sweets. Other creatures feed on the succulent thboma seeds that fall to the forest floor. The creatures' droppings are the primary reason why the thboma thrives in every area of Antiquom, apart from the snowy mountain peaks.

Doo continued with her storytelling. "Creatures of every size, shape, and manner imaginable inhabit Antiquom. Several probably are familiar beings of your Earthly World fairytale lore, like those you have described to me. Fire-breathing dragons and forest-dwelling gnomes, trolls, centaurs, and unicorns." She smiled gleefully. "Except here they are real."

Ava had to agree. Other amazing Antiquom creatures bore no resemblance to Earthly World beasts. They even did not come close to resembling fairytale lore. She knew of many, although she did not know what all of them were called.

Take for instance the woolly, bushy-tailed *yhioh*. The yhioh is around the size of a fattened-up muskrat but with eight spidery legs instead of four. It has short, thick fur, which ranges from a light blue to dark purple. As the yhioh ages, its fur changes to a murky-colored bluish black. It has a pair of razor-sharp, two-inch fangs that protrude from its upper jaw. Despite its relatively small size, the yhioh is as ferocious as a ravenous Earthly World tiger. It is common for the yhioh to hunt prey many times larger than its size.

Then there is the gorgeous, Earthly World butterfly doppelganger called the *bltale*. The bltale has four iridescent eyes, no antennae, and a wingspan that is nearly twelve inches in width. When it folds up its wings, the bltale blends in perfectly with its environs, regardless of the surrounding's hue or form. Through this scheme, the bltale is virtually unseen by predators. The bltale inhabits the immense, wind-blown seas of Antiquom's rolling plains in its search of flora. Given its gigantic size and an insatiable passion for sweet nectar, the bltale is a crucial pollinator of fruit, flower, and vegetable plant life throughout the realm.

Ava also considered something else Doo had said. Given its ancient physiognomies, Antiquom lacks traditional safety mechanisms with which she and Steph were familiar. There is no Internet, cellphones, computers, or any means to call for help, short of shouting. Therefore, in such a primitive, hostile land, survival skills are paramount. Skills of which, at that point, she knew that she and Steph did not even come close to possessing.

Ava considered silently, yes, we have our swords and bows and arrows. And we are skilled at using them. Steph is a more skilled swordself. But I am more accurate with the bow. All the same, we lack the knowledge, the experience, and the know-how to trek through Antiquom on our own. Thank goodness we have DooDad to keep us safe.

Steph had read Ava's thoughts. She nodded her head without looking up.

As if she had read Ava's thoughts as well, Doo surprised them when she said, "One's continued existence on Antiquom depends on a few vital areas of expertise. First and foremost is instinct – the ability to recognize the impending danger and to react accordingly. Next is warfare brainpower – the means to outsmart one's adversary, to strike successfully before being struck severely. Which includes the ownership of superior fighting skills – to crush an opponent despite his or her strengths. Finally, there is the camaraderie – the reliance on group bonds and the will and ability to support others. If one has all these skills and qualities, one has a relatively good chance of surviving. Simply having one or two of these skills and qualities does not imply success."

Ava considered it was the third area of expertise that she and Steph possessed, without a doubt. They were loyal and totally supportive of each other. As far as the other skills were concerned, she considered only time would tell if they could enhance them.

Doo looked at Ava and Steph in turn. She said, "Even so, despite your unfamiliarity with Antiquom and its many perils, both of you have noteworthy, fundamental traits. They will serve you well. Ava, yes, you may be overly curious, yet you are unobtrusive. You are also clever and expressive. You are determined and tireless. Blend these positive traits with your tenacity, courage, and resolve, and astonishing results are possible." She looked at Steph. "You too are clever and expressive. You are highly intelligent. Most of all, you are strong, determined, and unyielding."

2

Doo changed the subject to tell Ava and Steph about something referred to as Elven Truths. There are nine Truths. She gave them a quick summary.

Elven Truth one concerns mystical beings in general. The Truth maintains that mystical beings have coexisted with ordinary humans since the beginning of time. Doo said that for the most part mystical beings are defined as elves, fairies, wizards, and witches. The second Elven Truth addresses other mystical beings: dragons, pixies, unicorns, centaurs, gnomes, and dwarves, to name a handful. Like elves, witches, and wizards, some of the creatures are good and some are evil.

Doo said, "Which leads me to address Elven Truth three. It concerns a secret society to protect the well-being of creatures such as elves, wizards, and my kind."

Steph stated, "Jordyn told us a bit about the secret society." She looked at Ava. "What was it called again?"

"It is SoFEW^2," Ava replied. "The Society of Fairies, Elves, Witches, and Wizards." She grinned at Doo. "Steph and I prefer to call it SoFEW^2 with witches mentioned before wizards. It is a broadminded, female idea common today in the Earthly World. Like you said earlier, females are males' equals. So, Steph and I skipped the wizard's aspect of the term and replaced it with witches and wizards."

"Oh, so you know about SoFEW," Doo said. "Or, as you refer to it, SoFEW^2. Well, I will provide too much detail about it then. Godroh has been to the Earthly World on many occasions. He explained the society's existence when I visited with him. It was when he gave me and my companions your weapons and satchels." She grinned. "I often wondered why he had given us one more set of weapons and another satchel. Now I know. He probably knew that you were going to be here too, Steph. After all, he is the Great Wizard. Anyway, I have since joined the SoFEW^2 organization. Unlike on the Earthly World, not too many of us belong to the society. However, I am proud to say that I now belong.

"Then again, we do not need as much protection here in the Inner World as our kind requires in the Earthly World, among ordinary humans. Godroh told me about the murder of witches and wizards many centuries ago in your world. It is horrible to think about such atrocities. Just the same, things of that nature happen here as well, but from a different perspective." She grimaced. "Wendigorium and the belugas, to mention but two of the horrible things that dwell here."

"Yes, we know about Wendigorium and the belugas," Steph said with a frown.

Doo told Ava and Steph a bit about the next Elven Truth, number four. Because of their genetic makeup, fairies, like Doo and Dad, cannot marry or produce offspring with ordinary humans, elves, wizards, and witches. Thus, their offspring and descendants are considered Katharos. They are pure.

Ava's mind began to race. She thought to herself; why does the word Katharos sound familiar to me? This is the third time Doo has said the word in casual conversation. She glanced at Steph. Steph did not seem to be interested in the word. She also did not react outwardly to Ava's inner thoughts.

"Which brings me to Elven Truth five," Doo said. "The offspring and descendants of elves, wizards, and witches that do not intermarry and produce offspring with ordinary humans are also Katharos. They too are pure."

Ava noticed that Doo was looking at her suspiciously. It was if Doo were reading her thoughts as she tried to remember what she knew about the term Katharos.

Doo went on to say, "Elven Truth six says that offspring and descendants of elves, wizards, and witches that intermarry with ordinary humans are considered Akáthartos. They are impure. Thus, the mystical powers of Akáthartos descendants gradually diminish over time and with each successive intermarriage. However, the mystical powers of Akáthartos descendants can be bolstered to a limited degree when offspring are produced with a Katharos.

Doo said that the SoFEW, Ava, and Steph's SoFEW², has an organizational hierarchy as well. Details of the society's hierarchy are contained in Truths seven and eight. But she had lost Ava's interest after the sixth Truth because her mind was wandering. She was still trying to recall something, anything about the Katharos term Doo had used when describing creatures' mystical purity.

Why is that term so familiar to me? Could it have been something that Jordyn had said? Before she erased our memories?

Doo said, "Which leads me to the ninth and most significant of the Elven Truth's. It concerns a legendary, fabled elf that all of us in the Inner World reverently refer to as Avaïnoáel."

At Doo's mention of her assumed name in Fortunomy, Avaïnoáel, Ava's thoughts immediately began to race once more. She glanced over at Steph. She was polishing her sword. She had an impassive expression on her face although Ava presumed that she had been listening.

Doo said softly, "Avaïnoáel is avowed to be the Purest of Elves here in the Inner World and your Earthly World as well. Her rightful title is Avaïnoáel, O Poica Katharos – the Purest of Elves. The ninth Truth is based on the Inner World's Prophecy which is extremely significant. The Prophecy is a sacred testament, a projection or prediction of *what once was and what will someday be all over again* as it concerns the mystical aspects of both worlds. I do not know much else about the Prophecy other than what I have said." She smiled adding, "Except for one very important fact."

Ava's posture unexpectedly stiffened just as her muscles tightened. She could feel the warmth as a flush of red raced from the back of her neck to her face. She did a doubletake and grabbed Steph's arm. Her thoughts continued to race.

Steph, I just know I have heard that phrase, O Poica Katharos somewhere before! But where? Steph did not reply. Ava was gawking at Doo. Her mouth was open wide with anticipation. She did not want to miss a single word the fairy was saying.

Doo said, "The legendary O Poica Katharos, the Purest of Elves, is also known as the Protector of the World." Doo's mention of the phrase Protector of the World immediately caught Steph's attention. She stopped polishing her sword and stared at the fairy attentively.

Taking Ava's hand in hers and squeezing it lightly, Doo said, "Avaïnoáel is the Protector of your world, the Earthly World. She is also the Protector of my world, the Inner World. From what the legends say, the Prophecy portends Avaïnoáel will come again, to be reborn in another's body to save all of us from evil. From Wendigorium, the belugas, and even eviler forms that are yet to be unearthed in both worlds." She leaned in closer and whispered, "I have also heard that Wendigorium is likewise reborn. Perhaps reincarnated is a better word as it pertains to the evil beast. But this is purely speculation on my part and is based on stories told by the elders over the millennium."

All the while Doo had been talking, Ava had been reading her thoughts. Therefore, she had already grasped everything she needed to know. But she pretended otherwise. She did not want Doo to know she could read her mind. She would tell Doo about her mind-reading abilities much later.

Steph placed her hand on top of Doo's tiny hand then squeezed both hers and Ava's lightly. Then she turned and looked Ava straight in the eyes. Her breaths were fast, and all the color in her face had vanished. She said in a trembling voice, "Ava if you will recall—" She paused briefly and giggled. "But of course, you can recall everything when considering your amazing memory. What Jordyn had said to me? That you are the Protector of the World?"

Ava nodded her head, more for Doo's benefit even though she realized Steph had read her mind and knew her answer.

Steph looked at Doo with an expression that was a mixture of shock and bewilderment. With carefully chosen words, she said in a hushed tone, "Doo, are you telling us that our dear friend, Ava, is the Protector of the World? That she is also the legendary O Poica Katharos, the Purest of Elves? That the Inner World Prophecy proclaimed her as such? That the Prophecy predicted her return, to be reawakened in another's body. As you said, 'what once was and what will someday be all over again?'" She gave Ava a sincere smile. "Our sweet, super inquisitive Ava?"

Never taking her eyes off Ava, Doo nodded her head and said, "Yes, Steph. I honestly believe she is. Our dear friend is Avaïnoäel, O Poica Katharos, the Protector of the World." She sighed softly then nodded her head and smiled just as a teardrop caressed her pretty, freckled cheek.

"She simply has forgotten."

CHAPTER 4

BKOTN ELVES AND OTHERS OF THE UNSEEN VALLEY

"O, what a tangled web we weave, when first we practice to deceive!"
—Sir Walter Scott

1

Ava and Steph wordlessly chatted about everything Doo had told them about Antiquom as they moved along the trail. About its many dangers, Elven Truths, Katharos, Akáthartos, and other topics relating to the fascinating world in which they were traveling. Naturally, their telepathic discussions focused largely on Doo's assumption that Ava was the legendary Avaïnoάel, O Poica Katharos. But Ava and Steph agreed they would not discuss the topic openly, in words spoken aloud. Jordyn had said they should trust only Doo and Dad, and naturally, Godroh.

As they rounded a sharp curve on the trail, their spirits rose markedly. They could see their destination off in the distance. It was an elven hamlet set back in a spacious, V-shaped clearing. It would be the first and only dwelling where they would spend the night off the trail during their trek. The hamlet was surrounded on three sides by the dense forest. It was much smaller than the hamlets they had passed previously.

Ava counted three dozen roofed huts before her tallying was interrupted by the sounds of familiar cackling. She pointed and said excitedly, "Check 'em out! Tell me they don't look exactly like Earthly World chickens!"

Doo said as she giggled, "They do because they are."

"They are?" Steph asked with a dazed look. She playfully slapped Ava on the back. "Totally cool! But how did they come to be here in Antiquom?"

Doo replied, "According to legends, an adventurous elf that lived many generations ago was responsible for the Inner World's fowl, the chickens as Ava referred to them. The adventurous elf, like many before and since then, had ventured to the Earthly World via the Thávma. Naturally, he met up with groupings of elves. Many elves live in the vicinity of the Thávma, in modern-day Mexico of the Earthly World.

"Legends say the explorer elf was smitten with the delicious flavor of the bird, to include its cooked eggs. When he returned to Antiquom, he carried with him a large canvas sack filled with eggs." Her eyes seemed to smile playfully. "Imagine his surprise a few weeks later when he heard peeping noises inside the sack. He opened the sack and there they were – dozens of baby birds! Not only was the adventurous elf an avid explorer, but he was a shrewd businesself as well. He bred his flock of birds and sold or bartered them locally. Over time the birds became commonplace throughout Antiquom. Now they are everywhere and an important staple in all places of the Inner World."

"Why hadn't we seen them or heard their cackling before now, along the trail?" Ava asked.

Doo said, "Oh, they were there in the other villages. We simply did not get close enough. Godroh had not obtained permission for us to venture into those villages. Also, many villagers keep their chickens penned both day and night to keep predators from stealing them."

Steph said, "What do you call them, you know, in Fortunomy?"

Doo replied, "They are called pollo." She looked at Ava and Steph quizzically. "Maybe because that is what the elves on the other side of the Thávma call them in their Spanish language?"

"Makes perfect sense to me," Steph said. "Pollo is the Spanish word for chicken."

Doo said, "We must stop here." She pointed to the pathway up ahead that led to the hamlet. "We cannot go any further until I obtain permission from the hamlet elder. Her name is Yavanna. You should address her as Lady Yavanna. Godroh told me she is an age-old elf. She has lived nearly one thousand years." As was her custom before she flew away from Ava, Doo curtsied and excused herself politely. Then she flew along the pathway toward the elder's hut.

ED KIGHTLINGER

Ava and Steph watched anxiously as Doo knocked on the elder's door. When the elder appeared at the doorway, they were astounded. Yavanna looked like a typical Earthly World grandmother. Maybe 65 or 70 years of age but not a day older. She was standing erect and appeared physically fit. Her strawberry blonde, pale yellow hair had but a hint of gray.

Ava noticed that Dad looked upset when Yavanna reached down and shook Doo's tiny hand. He was deeply offended because he knew the elder would not converse with him. Doo later explained that Yavanna was observing the Unseen Valley elven custom by greeting her instead of Dad. Female fairies, elves, and humans alike converse with female elders. Males converse with males. There are no exceptions to the time-honored custom.

"What happens if there are no females to confer with a female elder?" Ava asked Doo when they were back on the trail the next morning. "If there only are males in their group."

Doo replied bluntly, "Then the male travelers are on their own and are not permitted to stop. If they stop without permission, they will be dealt with accordingly." She frowned. "Elves are very territorial."

After speaking with Yavanna, Doo flew back to them. She said, "We have been granted permission to stay the night. At first, Lady Yavanna was hesitant. Fortunately, when I reminded her of your mission to confer with Godroh she relented." She looked at Ava and Steph in turn. "However, you are not allowed to speak with her. She considers you to be ordinary, everyday elves. You will sleep in an empty hut." She looked at Dad. "You and I will sleep where we normally do," she pointed to the trees, "in there." She addressed Ava and Steph once more. "It is important for you to bed down in a more comfortable place tonight. So, you can rest well. The next portion of our journey will be exceedingly difficult and fast-paced. Please follow me and whatever you do, do not speak to anyone."

Ava and Steph obediently followed Doo as she flew along the pathway. Dad did not go along. All he did was scowl, mumble angrily, and then he disappeared into the forest.

While Doo and the elder conferred inside the hut, Ava and Steph were sitting on a log next to a large communal firepit. Ava was trying to eavesdrop on Doo and the elder's conversation telepathically. But she

200

and Steph were too far away from the hut. She could only discern bits and pieces of what Doo and Yavanna were saying. So, she gave up.

If only they knew who you were, Steph's thoughts said. They would be jumping up and down like crazy. You would be the one talking with the elder instead of Doo. She laughed. Heck, I bet Lady Yavanna would let you sleep in her hut tonight. It looks a whole lot better than all the other huts in this tiny hamlet.

Ava purposely blocked her responding thoughts from Steph and said nothing in reply.

Happily, despite their everyday elvish status, Lady Yavanna treated Ava and Steph somewhat courteously, but not overly so. They dined separately from the hamlet elves. They ate dried fish, vaotz mixed with tangy herbs, salted vegetables harvested from the garden, and a goblet of water. Dessert was a sweet, gooey cake that tasted like cinnamon.

That night, Ava was incredibly happy to be lying on a cushiony bed. Her back was sore from sleeping on beds of leaves and twigs. Steph likewise was thankful for the chance to sleep indoors for a change.

The next morning, after a delicious breakfast, Ava and the others resumed their hike. An hour later they merged onto a new trail where they met up with a large group of serious-looking elves. The elves were armed to the teeth and looked dreadfully intimidating. Ava was glad the ferocious-looking elves were on their side and not the other way around.

2

The new trail was a rambling, up and down, back and forth footpath. It was a tough hike, gradually moving uphill despite a few welcome downhill spots. Ava's calves and thighs were aching because of the gradual incline. Their previous treks were relatively flat. Steph seemed to be faring better, although she too was groaning and moaning. Happily, after a couple of days of conditioning, their muscles would no longer ache as much.

Unlike their previous journeys which were comparatively safe, they were heavily guarded. The added security was owing to their location. They were in the sprawling, nearly impenetrable, bewitched Forest of Artonia. Artonia is considered the most dangerous of places in

Antiquom. It is chock-full of mystical beings and unexplainable, magical phenomena. The disappearances of travelers and explorers Doo had mentioned a while back occur most frequently in Artonia. Also, there are many unseen hazards including the dreaded tar pits like the one that had claimed Doo's mother.

Three dozen Bkotn elves were guarding Ava's group. They were posted to the front, middle, and rear areas of the procession. The elves' composition was the same as a tactical company of Earthly World soldiers. It had the strength in numbers and weaponry to fight on its own without outside assistance. Doo told Ava and Steph that the Bkotn and other warriors throughout Antiquom refer to their company as an *Etanpioa.*

The term Etanpioa makes perfect sense to me, Ava considered wordlessly. The Greeks back home refer to their military groupings or companies as an "etairía." She looked at Steph as her thoughts continued. It is truly remarkable that many words in Fortunomy vaguely resemble words from Earthly World languages.

Steph's thoughts replied, Ava, you are amazing. Are you now telling me that you know words in Greek? You must know that you are something else!

Ava did not reply. She honestly wanted to answer Steph's question. But she had no clue how she understood what she had said. She blocked her thoughts from Steph. I know Greek too, huh? Well, this is the Inner World, and I supposedly am the O Poica Katharos. Therefore, I guess anything is possible. But all of this is too inexplicable. Even for me, and I probably have one of the wildest imaginations going!

The Bkotn elves accompanying Ava and the others dwell in the Unseen Valley of Artonia. Like DooDad, the Bkotn elves were given notice that Ava and perhaps two or three others would be arriving. That they would have to escort Ava to confer with Godroh.

Ava assumed they knew nothing of her true purpose, to face Wendigorium ultimately.

The mysterious Unseen Valley where the Bkotn elves reside is aptly named. That is because it is virtually impenetrable to land travelers. The only reliable way to enter the Unseen Valley safely is by sailing the Solenom River. If Ava and the others had tried to enter the Unseen

Valley by themselves via land routes, they would not have been successful. They would have been forced to turn around or worse. They could have perished without a trace. Like the bewitched Forest of Artonia, the Unseen Valley is just as dangerous.

The Solenom River is the lengthiest waterway in Antiquom. It covers the entire length of Artonia's forest. Solenom is fed by melting glaciers that lie on the towering peaks of Antiquom's northern mountain ranges. Flash floods in the central part of Artonia add to Solenom's volatility – and unpredictability.

Monsoons in the Forest of Artonia during the Antiquom rainy season cause the Solenom to burst over its banks by dozens of feet. The river itself becomes a churning torrent of white water during the monsoon season. When the northern glaciers melt is when the Solenom is the most treacherous. Then the river is nearly unnavigable, but skilled mariners manage to surmount its fury even so.

The mariners must be prepared for swift-flowing, perilous currents when navigating the Solenom. Not to mention there are hazardous, rock-strewn rapids, and suddenly appearing waterfalls. Hull-crushing sand bars can appear seemingly out of nowhere. If navigating the mighty river is not difficult enough, boat travelers must contend with inhospitable creatures that line the shore along the way. Predictably, it takes a highly skilled, well-armed, courageous mariner to navigate the unpredictable Solenom River successfully.

Early death is commonplace in the ancient realm of Antiquom due to natural phenomena and hostile beasts. In the bewitched Forest of Artonia, especially when traversing the Solenom River, inexplicable fatalities and accidents occur too often. Mercifully, despite sailors' river-borne nightmares, and seemingly endless hostilities, trade flourishes between elves of the Unseen Valley and other villages.

The Unseen Valley elven society is comprised of three separate, diverse categories of elves. They are the Bkotn, the Mkleon, and the Smbot. The Bkotn escorting Ava and the others are the Unseen Valley warriors. They mercilessly defend the Unseen Valley and adjacent terrains.

The Mkleon elves are farmers and orchardists. Along with herbs and spices, the Mkleon farmers cultivate starchy grass crops. The grass crops thrive in the peaty, fertile wetlands that lie alongside the Solenom. The main crop that is grown is a lot like the Earthly World grain "oryza sativa" (Earthly World Asian deep-water rice). The Antiquom variety is called vaotz. It is the same herb-infused grain that Ava and Steph happily devoured the night before.

Because of its availability – it grows everywhere along rivers and streams – vaotz is a sustenance grain throughout Antiquom. Other wetland grass crops are cultivated in the Unseen Valley as well, primarily to make beverages and medicines. Mkleon orchardists also cultivate the various, succulent fruit trees and berry bushes that grow in the forest.

The third category of Unseen Valley elves is the Smbot. The Smbot harvests fish, mollusks, and similar creatures from the Solenom River. Like the warrior Bkotn elves and the farmer and orchardist Mkleon's, the Smbot have darker skin pigments than most Antiquom elves. Also, like the Bkotn and Mkleon, Smbot elven ears are much shorter than other Antiquom elves. Their ears also have a noticeable hook on the tip.

The Mkleon and Smbot barter or sell their goods to other elven communities that live along the Solenom River. A limited amount of selling and bartering is done with residents of wizarding towns and villages to the south. Every so often, the Unseen Valley merchants will conduct trade with dwarves that work the metallic mines in the mountains. However, seeing that elves and dwarves seldom get along well, commerce with the dwarfish communities is rare.

The greater part of the Bkotn Etanpioa escorting Ava and her companions had exquisitely adorned elven longbows and quivers of sharp, poisoned-tipped arrows. The tips of the arrows were fashioned from animal bones. A few carried lances and shields. The lance-carrying elves did not have bows and arrows. All the elves had a scabbard fastened to the outside of their left thigh. It held a razor-sharp blade.

Others carried swords like the Earthly World Egyptian sword known as the "khopesh." The khopesh is a curved sword derived from battle axes. The bold-faced Bkotn call their lethal swords the *tkalakn*. The word tkalakn translates to "deadly" in Fortunomy. The tkalakn is a destructive hacking weapon and exceptionally sharp. It is around twenty to twenty-four inches in length.

One of the guards allowed Ava to examine her tkalakn. Ava later told Steph that it was very sharp. She said it was weighty as well, perhaps weighing more than five pounds. Much heavier than their swords which were wretched in comparison.

The Bkotn elves are some of the most courageous elves in Antiquom. They are second in fearlessness and skill only to the unarguably intrepid Timere elves. The Timere elves dwell in the perilous, steep, mountainous cliffs that overlook the Solenom River to the north. The mountains are called the Mystic Mountains. The Timbre territory also extends to the Solenom below.

Ava and the others in her group, escorted by the Bkotn, were on their way to meet up with the Timere elves before they journeyed to meet up with Godroh. Because large communities of evil beasts thrive in the northern parts of the mountains, reinforcements were essential.

The Bkotn hardiness is perfectly understandable. From the day they are born Bkotn infants are exposed to harsh conditions. Bkotn elves eat and sleep in the open amongst the huge boulders that line the Solenom. It has been their custom for a millennium. Their only shelters in the freezing winters are poorly built, drafty thatched huts.

The Bkotn cultivate and harvest their own food and barter little with other elves. Given their harsh lifestyle, they do not use fire to keep themselves warm in winter or for cooking food. They prefer to eat raw and sundried fish. Seedlings harvested from the banks of the Solenom, and freshwater algae are basic elements of every meal. The freshwater algae Bkotn elves harvest is similar in flavor to Earthly World Japanese nori. Because it is a freshwater alga, it has little to no salt content. It is also packed with protein and other essential vitamins.

The Bkotn believe that living a hard, austere way of life out in the open reinforces their toughness and fiercely powerful combat spirit. They also say it furthers their determination, tenacity, and related mental skills.

Adding to their legendary bravery, the Bkotn elves truly are the most unique of all Antiquom elves. Because they have an unusually distinctive tradition. The Bkotn community, or *Tribe*, as they refer to their closed society, consists of female elves only. Female Bkotn elves marry and breed with male elves when they become of age, typically with the Mkleon and Smbot. They marry and produce offspring with elves from outlying communities as well. Occasionally, Bkotn elves marry humans that live in the southern portion of Antiquom. Those that marry humans are then banished from the Tribe.

Notwithstanding their conjugal bonds with their Bkotn elven brides, male elves are strictly forbidden to reside within the Tribe. Similarly, as soon as a young male elf loses its need to suckle, he is handed over to his father. There he will be raised according to the customs and traditions in his father's village.

Regular visitations between Bkotn elves and their mates and offspring are encouraged. With one proviso. Visitations must be performed in a neutral area called a *Netrum*. The Netrum is a shared area to the east of the Bkotn Tribe's region. It is a rather contemporary spot, at least in the eyes of the Bkotn elves who live in the open. It has numerous, basic cottages made of timber where Bkotn elves, their mates, and their male and female offspring can enjoy privacy. Visitations between Bkotn elves and their mates and offspring are limited to two days a month.

Despite the Bkotn's stern, *no males allowed* lifestyle, the Tribe gets along exceptionally well with other elven communities both within and beyond the Unseen Valley. This undoubtedly is owing to the Bkotn's fearless skills instead of other elven societies' willing acceptance of the Bkotn's untraditional way of *no males allowed* existence.

The Bkotn guarding Ava and the others were commanded by a mighty elf called Elbereth. Her name means Heroic Leader. Elbereth is the natural-born leader of the Bkotn Tribe. She was accorded her name at birth for a few reasons. All of which have to do with Antiquom elven folklore.

When she was born, Elbereth was considerably longer and much heavier than other Bkotn newborns. She came to be on the sixth day of Ioúniosom, the sixth month of the Inner World. The number six is a magical number in the elven world. The number denotes flawlessness. Finally, and surely the most significant, Elbereth was born on the birthday of the Inner World's famous elf heroine warrior by the same name. Essentially, Lady Elbereth's stature, as well as her prominence, afforded her an indisputably compelling eminence both within and outside of the Tribe.

Bkotn elves are beautiful. There was not one common place-looking elf in the Etanpioa escorting Ava and the others. Bkotn elves are slender with thin waists and long limbs. Yet despite their lean stature, they are well-nourished and exceptionally powerful. They have well-toned athletic physiques. Most have long black or dark brown hair that they wear in tightly knotted flowing braids. There are a handful of Bkotn elves that have blond hair and a few elves that have red hair.

One elf in Elbereth's Etanpioa had pure white hair. Her name is Haleth. She is the same age as Ava. Like all the Bkotn warriors, Haleth wears her hair in braids. Her close friends refer to her as the Exalted One because of her strikingly beautiful, pure white hair.

Another distinct feature of the Bkotn's extraordinary athleticism is exhibited by their strikingly well-developed, skin-tight thighs and calf muscles. Ava imagined the two muscle groups were essential for leaping from boulder to boulder in the Unseen Valley. The Bkotn's shoulders are broad, and their necks are elongated. Their biceps, triceps, and forearms are well built with no visible flab.

When the Bkotn elves' emotional and mental competency is linked with their unique strength and skilled warriorship, they are practically invincible. They are a daunting force with which any foe must think twice before confronting.

The trail that Ava and her companions had been hiking is known as the *Kuoino*. The Kuoino is the lengthiest, most journeyed trail of Artonia. Because of its nonsensical zigzagging, up and down, and back and forth course, the Kuoino is aptly named. The word Kuoino stems from the Fortunomy words kuo and ino. Kuo translates to whacky, and ino means snake. Whacky snake – Kuoino.

As everyone expected – they had been forewarned by Dad – Ava would sometimes stop along the trail to look at something that interested her. Whenever she did, it caused the entire column to come to a halt. Most of the Bkotn warriors were not concerned when they stopped for a short time. They welcomed it.

Elbereth was an exceptionally strict leader. In addition to the nighttime halt, she allowed only two official stops per day, a brief stop at mid-morning and mid-afternoon. She also did not allow talking among her warriors or eating while on the march.

"We have a timetable," Elbereth said to Steph irritably at one point. "The timetable decides whether or not we reach our destination before nightfall. You must persuade your companion to cease her tarrying. She is slowing us needlessly."

Steph simply asked Elbereth to follow Dad's instructions. Ava was to dawdle as much as she wanted but not excessively. "Besides," she had said without a hint of emotion, "I think you know how important she is. So, I implore you to let her be. After all, no one is being harmed." Elbereth simply nodded her head and walked to the front of the Etanpioa.

3

"Well, I do not like her. I do not trust her!" Siofra said angrily as she looked askance at Ava.

Ava was studying a small grove of fruit trees just off the trail. Her curiosity had once again caused the Etanpioa to stop for a few minutes. She was a few dozen paces from where Siofra was sitting with ten of her subordinate warriors.

There usually were eleven warriors in the group that made up the rear of the column. One elf, Haleth, the Exalted One, was at the front of the column. Siofra had disciplined her for disobedience. As punishment for her penalty, Haleth had to carry more supplies than the others.

Siofra glanced around at the others in her group. She said in a blunt tone, "No matter how many times Ava allows us to stop and talk. Besides, she is slowing us down." She leaned in close and laughed. "If I thought I would not be caught, I would wring her neck and leave her for the birds to fight over her worthless bones. Better yet slice her open with one slash of my tkalakn. I could care less if she is going to see Godroh. Big deal. He is overrated in my opinion. There are more powerful wizards out there."

Like Haldir of Mountains Cross. He is ten times more powerful than Godroh! Besides, he is my friend, and I trust him.

Siofra was the third in command of the Etanpioa. All the warriors reported to her. She in turn answered to the second in command, Morwen. Morwen was Elbereth's immediate subordinate. Siofra was the Tribe's consummate archer and the most proficient swordself. Moreover, she was even more proficient in weaponry than her superiors, Elbereth and Morwen. Siofra became third in command primarily due to her skillful weaponry abilities and proven toughness. As well as her strict approach to discipline.

At first, Elbereth was not keen with the idea of making Siofra third in command. However, Morwen worked hard to convince her.

"We need someone strong, knowledgeable, and competent," Morwen had said during a heated discussion with Elbereth. "Most of all, Siofra is well-organized and disciplined. The others have become lazy. They are not focused as they should be. Siofra will bring them up to our standards. I guarantee it."

Eventually, Elbereth relented although she swore, she would keep a close eye on Siofra.

Another thirteen-year-old elf named Galadriel was seated in Siofra's group. She, unlike most Bkotn elves, the majority have dark brown or black hair, has bright red hair. In the Earthly World, humans nowadays would classify Galadriel as a ginger. Like other elves her age, she has a skin condition resembling acne, the curse of teens the world over, both elven and human. She also has freckles seemingly everywhere on her body – her face, back, arms, shoulders, and even on her lips and the tip of her nose. She is exceptionally articulate, extremely intelligent, and highly skillful despite her young age. She is very opinionated as well.

In reaction to what Siofra had said about Ava, Galadriel asserted, "Oh, she seems to be okay." She purposely did not look at Siofra. She could tell that her superior was glaring at her for speaking up. "Sure, maybe she stops way too often to look at interesting things. I cannot blame her. I wish I could as well. There are many curious things in Artonia, much more than in the valley back home."

"I bet she is an Outsider," another elf said in a nasty tone. She was Vena, the Etanpioa's renowned mischief-maker. She was also Siofra's favorite subordinate. The other elves in the Etanpioa did not like her. Yet they had to pretend that they did. Or else they would have to suffer Siofra's wrath which would be intolerable. Siofra tended to get physical when she got angry. Sometimes kicking and punching her subordinates when Elbereth was not around.

Vena's tone was insulting as she said, "I bet the other one is an Outsider as well, the elf that calls herself Steph." She doubled up with laughter. "What kind of names are those? Ava and Steph? They are hideous names and sound oddly foreign to me. Yes, they definitely are Outsiders of the worst sort." She glanced at Siofra. "I also do not trust them, and I would like to get rid of both of them."

Siofra was still staring at Ava with an expression of outright disgust. Her eyes were cold and flat. She pursed her lips, and then she said, "I have to agree with you, Vena. They certainly are Outsiders as you say. Maybe I should ask them." She glanced around at the others. "What do you think?" All but one of the elves nodded their heads in agreement. Galadriel was the sole dissent.

"I do not think that you should," Galadriel said in a cautious tone. "Lady Elbereth said we are not to have extensive talks with either of them, to never ask them questions. To simply say hello or answer by saying yes or no. Besides, Ava is on a special mission to visit the Great Wizard Godroh." She smiled feebly. "That is what makes her and the others special, especially in Lady Elbereth's eyes." She gave Siofra a hesitant look. "In my eyes as well."

Siofra was scowling at Galadriel with a nasty expression, but she did not say anything. She did not want the others to know that she was upset with the young elf for being unruly, for speaking her mind.

But I will get back at you for speaking out against me! How dare you!

Galadriel quickly looked away. She appreciated from too many thrashings Siofra had personally administered on her small frame that the older elf had a vicious temper. She also did not want to give Siofra any excuse to give Elbereth and Morwen a negative report on her performance.

"What makes them so special?" Vena said in a disgusted manner as she gave Galadriel a glancing dirty look. "Look at the other one, the one who calls herself Steph. She is talking to the fairies. If two lowly fairies can talk to the two elves, why are we not allowed to do the same?" She glanced around at the others. "We ought to teach them a lesson or two about civility!" She stood up and pretended to make a move toward Steph and DooDad. "Why is it we cannot talk to them? It is not fair!"

"Because orders are orders," Siofra barked harshly. "And sit down, now!" She cackled, "When I asked for your opinion, I was referring to myself. I am third in command, so I have a privileged status. The rest of you are nothing but load bearers. It is I who will speak to them. It is I who will learn of their so-called special mission." She grabbed her tkalakn and jumped to her feet. She said in a hushed tone to Ava, "Hey you!" She did not want Elbereth and Morwen to hear her. They were at the front of the column with two of Siofra's subordinates, Lia and Haleth. "Hey, you with the weird, Outsider name, Ava. I want to talk to you." She gestured to the log on which she had been sitting. "Come here if you know what is good for you."

Ava gave Siofra a skeptical look then said in a sarcastic tone, "And why do you want me to go to you?"

"I would like to thank you personally for stopping every once in a while," Siofra lied. She faked a smile. "You must be aware our leader, Elbereth, is extremely strict. She does not allow us warriors to talk during our march. But thanks to you we get more breaks. Come sit with us, so we can talk, to get to know each other better." She flashed another fake smile. "We do not bite."

Ava gave Galadriel a fleeting glance. The pretty, redheaded elf was shaking her head a little. Ava looked away from her and glared at Siofra. Just as Ava placed her hands on her hips in a defiant gesture, Siofra crossed her arms over her chest. She still had her tkalakn in her left hand and was moving it up and down in a threatening manner. She was glaring. It was apparent to Ava that they had reached a standoff. One she was determined to win.

Unbeknownst to Siofra and the others in her group, Ava had many private conversations with Galadriel. She also had conversations with another warrior, Nessa. Their talks usually occurred after the older elves were fast asleep and out of earshot and when the young warriors were on watch. Steph sometimes joined in. Doo did as well. The four elves had become good friends. Ava trusted Galadriel and Nessa. So did Steph and Doo.

As she continued to faceoff with Siofra, Ava was thinking, I have seen the way you treat your subordinates, especially Galadriel, Haleth, and Lia. What you are doing to Haleth and Lia is inexcusable. I doubt they will last through the march because you have overburdened them. You like to berate them, embarrass them, and beat them with your fists. Not only have I seen you thrashing others when you think we are not watching, but I have also read Galadriel, Haleth, and Lia's thoughts. Their thoughts speak of your cruelty. You and Vena have physically punished Haleth four times on this march alone!

And if I ever catch either of you beating her again, or hurting Galadriel or Lia, you will regret it!

Wanting to break the impasse and allowing Elbereth to have the Etanpioa move on, Ava was the first to speak. She dropped her hands to her side and said in a curt tone, "Well, you just thanked me, Siofra. Therefore, I have no reason to join you and the others. Quite frankly I do not want to give you the satisfaction of talking to me one on one." She turned around and strutted toward the front of the column. She cried out in a strong voice, "Thank you, Lady Elbereth, for stopping. I promise I will not delay any more today."

Siofra pointed her tkalakn in Ava's direction as she walked off. She whispered in an angry tone, "I am going to destroy you!" She brusquely sat down on the log in a bluster just as Morwen approached them.

Morwen shouted, "Okay, we are moving on. Resume your positions."

The warriors got to their feet, bowed slightly, and then they gathered their possessions and departed. Siofra did not move. Her eyes were cold and hard. Her lips were flattened in a curl once more. She was shaking with rage as her mind raced with hatred.

The Ava elf is rude. She showed me great disrespect. Hah! I also saw the way she looked at Galadriel. They think I had not noticed, but I saw Galadriel shaking her head at her! Almost certainly some of the others did as well. I will kill them. I swear if it is the last thing that I do!

When the others of Siofra's group were out of earshot, Morwen said quietly, "We need to talk, privately." She glanced around, and then she pointed to a clump of high bushes beside the trail. "In there. Now."

Without looking up at her superior, Siofra nodded and stood up. She retrieved her weaponry and satchel from the ground. She followed Morwen obediently. She was unsure if Morwen was going to give her a chewing out for speaking to Ava. Then again, or so she hoped, Morwen was probably going to enlighten her with more details of their risky scheme.

But I swear I will destroy Ava and her conniving friends no matter what!

CHAPTER 5

FRIENDS, RIVALS, AND DISAGREEMENTS

"Not until we are lost do we begin to understand ourselves."
—*Henry David Thoreau*

1

Many of the Bkotn warriors were very fond of Ava. Particularly the young warriors. They respected her insouciant, carefree, and curious manner and readily dismissed her inquisitiveness. Most had never ventured beyond the Unseen Valley until then, so they were similarly amazed at just about everything on the Kuoino. Except they, unlike Ava, could not stop the march along the trail to satisfy their curiosity. They had to pretend they were indifferent to what they saw and heard no matter how interesting and exciting. It was merely one more aspect of maintaining discipline and part of, as they liked to say amongst themselves, "the Etanpioa game." Moreover, the young warriors had to prove their worth to the Etanpioa leadership, so maintaining military decorum was of utmost importance.

But that did not stop the young warriors from gossiping about Ava and Steph every chance that they got. They were curious as to why the Etanpioa was guarding two young elves. They also gossiped amongst themselves why Elbereth tolerated Ava's ceaseless dallying along the way. Their leader was profoundly disciplined, and she tolerated little nonsense within the Etanpioa. More surprisingly, she frequently invited Ava to march with her in the front of the column. No other warrior, except for the second in command, Morwen, could join the Etanpioa leader at the front of the column. Even so, they were not jealous of Ava's seemingly important status. They were more curious than anything.

The young warriors, as well as the older warriors, were not privy to Ava's legendary status. Elbereth was the only one that knew Ava's identity. Godroh had told her in confidence that Ava was the O Poica Katharos. He made her take an oath that she would protect Ava at all costs. She purposely did not tell Morwen and Siofra of Ava's identity. She did not feel she could entrust her subordinates with such guarded, incredibly important information.

Like Vena had said, Galadriel and many of the others believed that Ava and Steph were Outsiders. So did Galadriel's best friend, Nessa. Like Ava and Galadriel, Nessa was also thirteen years old. However, she was far less experienced than Galadriel. Galadriel had made three previous excursions to the Forest of Artonia before then. Nessa was on her second voyage. Furthermore, Nessa was less disciplined and more carefree than Galadriel. Yet she was just as courageous as her friend.

Unlike Vena, Siofra, and some of the older elves, the young elves did not consider that being an Outsider was a derogatory characteristic. They believed that Ava and Steph most likely were from a faraway elven village well beyond the Unseen Valley. Possibly as far away as the fabled Missing Land or perhaps further than that land if one existed at all. Considering the unusual manner that the Etanpioa was guarding Ava and Steph, it was not surprising that the young warriors would consider that possibility.

By all fabled accounts the Missing Land, or *Leípei* as it officially is known, lies to the south on the far side of Eastern Antiquom. Leípei purportedly is a charmed realm of many mysteries, peculiar secrecies, and phantastic beasts. Legends say the transfigured creature Wendigorium and the Great Wizard Godroh were born in Leípei.

Age-old elven tales speak of the skies of "Parádeisos" opening and casting forth light and happiness upon Leípei (Parádeisos means Paradise in the Earthly World Greek language.). It was at that moment, when the skies opened, that the Great Wizard Godroh was created. Many generations later, because there was no potent being that could counter Godroh's great powers of benevolence, the Parádeisos skies opened once more. This time they brought forth the evil creature, Wendigorium.

Because Godroh was first born and all-powerful, the skies also brought forth vile beasts to support Wendigorium, to counteract Godroh's vast powers. The beasts were the ghastly belugas. Two species of belugas were created. One, the duds, were malevolent of the beasts while the other species, the déxypnos, was more intelligent. Their intellect was important to manage the duds' brutality. Over time, the belugas spread far and wide and to all parts of Antiquom, including the Forest of Artonia. Shortly after Wendigorium and the belugas came to be, Antiquom's second realm, Andron, was conceived. At least that is what the legends say.

Elven legends also maintain that few creatures have journeyed to the Leípei. By all accounts, those that enter Leípei never return. Legends declare they are forced to join either Godroh or Wendigorium's ranks and thus are expelled from the normal lands of Antiquom. Those that refuse to join either's ranks are exiled to dwell forever in the *Deep Realm*.

The Deep Realm is where all living Inner World creatures go after they die. It is a transitory land comparable to the Earthly World's Purgatory. If creatures were benevolent as living beings, they move on to Parádeisos. It is there that their innermost essence, their souls, will revel in everlasting peace. If the creatures were evil as living beings or undeserving of Parádeisos' forgiveness, they will wander endlessly in despair as ghosts and shadows. Legends also say that some benevolent creatures remain as ghosts or shadows, at least temporarily. Because they have unfinished affairs in the world of the living. Once they conclude their unfinished business, they enter Parádeisos to dwell in everlasting peace.

Toward the end of Ava's journey in Antiquom, we will discover that the foregoing, legendary elven tales are mostly hogwash and are based on wild imaginings. Particularly those that concern how Godroh, Wendigorium, and the belugas came to be. The exception being the Missing Land, Leípei. Leípei actually does exist, and it is to the south on Eastern Antiquom. It is inhabited by elves, humans, and other creatures. Furthermore, regarding elven legends' mention of the Deep Realm and Parádeisos, there is no evidence that they are real. Yet there is no evidence that they are not.

Some of the young warriors would say things like the following when they spoke of Ava's inquisitive idiosyncrasy. "What difference does it make if she is overly curious? She is showing us respect. Nearly all elves and travelers from distant lands barely even talk to us. Some are so indifferent they even will not look at us."

Despite Elbereth's orders that they were to not engage in lengthy discussions with Ava or Steph, some of the warriors, again primarily the young ones, would occasionally strike up a conversation with them. Naturally, they would ensure that Elbereth and the other leaders were not nearby.

Given her carefree manner, Nessa was not discreet regarding her conversations with Ava and Steph. She considered it was okay to converse with them. At one point she said to her fellow, young warrior friends, "Ava strikes me as being highly intelligent. She knows so much about so many things of the Earthly World. Those of us who have traveled in the interior of Artonia previously should share our knowledge with her. Who knows? Perhaps someday she can be a Bkotn warrior. She is muscular and strong. So is her companion, Steph. I would welcome them into our ranks. I do not consider them to be Outsiders. Rather, I consider them to be our equals. We should accept them as such and go out of our way to be friendly."

Despite many of the warriors' fondness for Ava, they always kept her in their sight whenever they stopped. Elbereth had warned them repeatedly. If Ava ever became missing, for even a few moments, all involved would suffer the penalties.

2

Dusk was about to settle on the trail. Nessa was preparing to assume the first night's watch at the tail end of the Etanpioa when Siofra shouted her name causing her to cringe.

"Nessa, I want you to get over here. I must speak with you!"

Nessa immediately felt unsteady just as her stomach churned in painful knots. Despite her nervousness, she struggled to act normally. Showing fear as a Bkotn warrior is unheard of. She turned around slowly and winced. Siofra was scowling at her. She bowed deeply, not because she was required to but owing to the way Siofra had spoken to her. She said in a nervous tone, "Yes, Siofra. What is it?"

"Walk with me a bit," Siofra said in a nasty manner. "You and I need to have a discussion concerning your earlier, inappropriate comments." She gave Nessa a spiteful look. "Comments you should never had made to the others."

"Okay," was all Nessa could say as she followed behind Siofra. She was barely able to keep pace with her superiors' brisk gait. Her legs felt oddly unsteady, and she was trembling. A nasty dryness was in her throat. It quickly spread to her lips. She licked her lips nervously.

The other elves watched as Siofra and Nessa walked off. Because of what Nessa had said earlier about Ava and Steph, they expected she was about to be punished, most likely thrashed. They started to discuss her fate in hushed, blathering whispers.

After a hundred or so paces, Siofra stopped. She turned around. Her clenched fists were at her side. The expression on her faultless, blemish-free face was impassive.

Nessa felt certain she was in for a severe beating for speaking her mind earlier about Ava and Steph – how she would gladly welcome them into the Etanpioa.

Siofra's tone was strangely calm as she said, "I understand you hold Ava in high regard. Is that correct?" Nessa swallowed hard then lowered her head and nodded. "That you would not have an issue with her or the other elf, Steph, becoming Bkotn warriors. Am I correct with what I have been told? Did you say those things to the others? That you would welcome them into our Etanpioa?"

Nessa rubbed her hands down her legs nervously. She wanted to flee, to escape the maddening nightmare before her. But she knew it was a crime to turn her back on Siofra, on any of her leaders. Doing so could result in the most severe penalty imaginable. Perhaps even expulsion because of flagrant disobedience. She cleared her throat and said in a whiny tone, "I am sorry if I offended you, Siofra. I was simply asserting—"

"Oh, I am not offended at all," Siofra said. Then she gave Nessa a surprisingly pleasant smile.

Nessa was gawking at Siofra. She was shocked by what her superior had said. And the way she had said it along with a smile was even more shocking.

Siofra said, "In fact, I agree with you," she rolled her eyes, "despite Ava's obsessive curiosity." She leaned in closer and said in a whisper, "And stopping our march far too often, although the more frequent breaks are refreshing. Yes, I also like her. Perhaps not as much as you, but I like her just the same." She straightened up and furrowed her brow. "But do not tell anyone, okay?" She laughed. "It would ruin my reputation."

Nessa was nodding her head. She managed a feeble smile. She could feel the tension that had been gripping her body and the emptiness in her stomach were slowly melting away. But she remained cautious. Siofra was a cunning warrior. Despite feeling like she was going to throw up, she said in a pretend, happy tone, "Thank you for not being angry with me. I honestly think Ava is a highly intelligent elf. I like her. Many of the others do as well. Her companion Steph is also genuinely nice."

Siofra said, "How many times have you been in this forest, in Artonia?"

"One time in the past. This is my second excursion. The first time was as far distant as the village of Knoki. As you know, Knoki is a six-day march from our valley."

"Ah, wonderful," Siofra said. "So, I assume you know about the Crostim Ledge? It is in a clearing that overlooks the mighty river, Solenom. I have heard it is the finest outlook of the valley just off the Kuoino."

"Indeed, I do," Nessa said enthusiastically. "I even visited it. The view is breathtaking!" Thinking that Siofra may think she visited the ledge without her former leader's permission, she promptly added, "My superior gave me and a few others in our Etanpioa her consent to visit the ledge. May I ask if you have been there?"

Siofra was shaking her head. Her mouth fell open slightly. Then she said in a gloomy tone, "Regrettably, I have not. However, I would like to see it. Before I am too old to ascend its steep pathway. I have heard the view of the Solenom as well as the surrounding valley is spectacular. We should arrive in the vicinity tomorrow, an hour or two before dusk." She laughed quietly. "That is if our dear friend, Ava, does not slow us down too often." She placed her hands on Nessa's shoulders and looked the young elf straight in the eyes.

"I would like for Ava to see the Crostim Ledge. Thus, she will have something to boast about after she arrives at her destination. She may even tell Godroh. In return, he may look upon us more favorably, perhaps provide us increased assistance." She shook her head and gave Nessa a sad look. "I was very curt with her earlier because I was upset that she had caused us to stop so close to dusk. Hence, it will be my way of apologizing to her for my rudeness. Regrettably, I am not familiar with the pathway to the ledge." She clasped her hands in front of her chest. "Perhaps you could be our guide?"

Nessa did not reply, but she was already feeling giddy. It would be wonderful to visit the ledge once more and even better to accompany Ava.

Siofra shook her head and stared at the ground. She said in a pessimistic tone, "But no, I am foolish thinking such things. Unless we can convince Ava to not gawk at things along the way, we will never reach the ledge tomorrow before nightfall. Then our opportunity will be lost. Elbereth will want to get an early start the next morning, so we cannot do it then. She lightly touched her throat in thought." If only there were a way to get Ava to—"

Nessa exclaimed, "Pardon me for interrupting, but I could talk to her, to Ava. Only for a moment or two, I assure you. I could tell her that you would like me to escort you and her to the Crostim Ledge. I also could ask her to not delay along the way tomorrow so we can make good time. We might even arrive earlier than expected."

"You would do that for me, for us?" Siofra said excitedly. "Really? If so, that would make me incredibly happy. Finally, after so many voyages in Artonia," she breathed in deeply and closed her eyes, "I will see the spectacular view from Crostim Ledge."

Nessa said eagerly, "It would be my honor to escort you and Ava, truly."

"Then it is settled," Siofra said. She embraced Nessa taking her completely by surprise. "You, Ava, and I will venture off the trail and trek to the Crostim Ledge tomorrow." She stared dreamily at the trees. "I cannot believe it. And after all these many voyages. But you must not tell anyone except Ava. And you must caution her to not tell her companion, Steph, or the two fairies that accompany them. Also, you must tell her that I permitted you to take her to the ledge. However, do not tell her that I will accompany you. That will be our little secret, between you and me. If word of our exciting adventure were to be discovered, well, I must say Elbereth would be furious." She grimaced. "And I do not think your fellow warriors would be too happy with you, knowing you are a favorite of Siofra."

"But why must we keep our secret from Elbereth?" Nessa whispered sheepishly. "I would never do anything to betray our leader, you must know that. Indeed, I respect you dearly, Siofra. But we should not hide our intentions from Elbereth. It would be disloyal and discourteous."

"You are correct," Siofra cried which resulted in Nessa backing up a few steps with alarm. "Well done, Nessa. I am extremely proud of you! And I am pleased to say you have passed a crucial test."

"I have?" Nessa muttered with complete surprise. A fluttering feeling formed in her belly as the adrenaline started to race through her veins. She said with a beaming smile, "I assume that is a good thing. Am I correct?"

"Indeed, it is. I was testing your loyalty to our Etanpioa leader as well as your discretion. You have passed the test. I fully intend to tell Elbereth that you will escort Ava and me to the Crostim Ledge. I will tell Morwen as well." She placed her finger to her lips. "Naturally, the others would be jealous if they were to find out. So, we will keep this a secret. A secret among us five. You, Ava, Elbereth, Morwen, and me. And you must not tell Ava that I will accompany you. Only that you have my permission, and it is my way of apologizing to her for my rude manner. Got it?" Nessa nodded her head. "Then swear to it," Siofra whispered. "Can you do that for me? We do not want the others to become jealous."

"I swear."

"Okay then, off you go," Siofra said cheerily. "I will remain here for a few moments. That way the others will not get suspicious. And bear in mind, you vowed to not tell anyone but Ava. And one other thing, Nessa?"

"Yes, Siofra."

"When the others ask what I have said to you, and trust me they will, tell them I gave you the worst scolding you have ever had in your life. Because you talked so highly about Ava. That you would welcome her and Steph into our ranks. Tell them you will now walk a straighter line than ever before. Yes?"

Nessa nodded her head and giggled. She bowed deeply and skipped along the trail. Her heart seemed to be singing as tears of joy rushed from her light blue eyes.

3

"I do not care if I am making you upset," Steph said furiously in a quiet voice. Her tone was surprisingly rude. She was glassy-eyed, her expression unfocused as she had just awakened. She took a sip from her goblet and resumed scolding Ava. "I do not want you to go. Period. Everything you said sounds too fishy. We hardly know these warriors." She flashed Ava another nasty look. "As you so properly put it, I cannot stop you from going. But if I could, I would. Without beating around the bush, I must say I forbid you from going as if you care what I have to say anyway. You are too young to make such critical decisions by yourself." She was shaking her head as she looked Ava up and down with a hurtful expression. "Too immature as well." Then she turned up her nose and laughed in a snooty way. "Remember what happened with the metamorhirío? One would think you would have learned your lesson after that."

Ava and Steph had been arguing for at least five minutes. The dispute started after Ava told Steph telepathically about her trip to Crostim Ledge the next evening. Steph's words were surprisingly nasty. Her attitude was disturbingly unpleasant as well. Nevertheless, Ava was trying her best to remain calm. She knew that allowing Steph to rile her up would not solve anything and probably would make things worse between them.

"But the third in command is coming with us," Ava whispered in a pleasant tone. "I will be okay."

"How do you know that as a fact?" Steph replied heatedly. "You are inexperienced in such things, too young as I said. You have no clue what you are doing."

Ava noticed that the vein on the right side of Steph's neck was pulsing severely. The last time she saw that vein acting up was after she exited the swamp. Steph was mightily angry with her then. She purposely blocked her thoughts from Steph's mind. She grasped a while back that she could block her thoughts as easily as she could interpret the thoughts of others. She did not like to keep her thoughts from Steph. But the way Steph was acting, she thought it prudent to do so.

Goodness, Steph is even angrier with me now than before. But why is she being so mean, scolding me the way she is? This is unlike her, totally unlike her. What is going on? I certainly do not deserve this kind of treatment, from her or anyone! She really is starting to tick me off!

She said to Steph in a quiet, purposefully calm tone, "But I *do* know what I am doing, Steph. Because I interpreted Nessa's thoughts. She was thinking that she was particularly happy that Siofra was making the gesture as a way of apologizing to me." She let out a long sigh. "You know I can do that, that I can read another's thoughts. I have told you many times that I can." She touched Steph's forearm. "Words may sometimes utter untruths, but thoughts cannot lie."

Steph forced a laugh. The laugh had a particularly nasty edge to it. Her face reddened a great deal as she considered what she was going to say next. Mimicking Ava's words in a horrid-sounding, sarcastic tone, she said, "Because I interpreted Nessa's thoughts. Wow. Isn't that wonderful? You interpreted her thoughts. Whoopie!" She looked daggers at Ava.

Ava pursed her lips. She was unblinking as she stared at Steph. After a minute or so of staring, Steph was forced to look away. Without looking at Ava she said, "And how do you know that Nessa is not deceiving you with her thoughts, huh? I mean, think about it, Ava. You and I can verbalize telepathically and, as you say, you can read others' thoughts too. Given all of that craziness, and everything else that is happening to us right now, how can you be so stupid as to think—" She abruptly stopped talking because of Ava's sudden reaction to what she had just said.

At that point, it was apparent that Ava had enough with Steph's rude words and her offensive tone of voice. Her mouth was wide open. She wanted to say something, but no words formed.

Steph waved her hands from side to side. Her manner was contrite as she said, "Please, Ava, do not get upset, okay? I did not mean what I said."

Ava was furious. She was nervously shifting her weight from one foot to the other. She buried her clenched fists deep inside her cloak. She also blocked her thoughts from Steph once more. She truly felt like punching something. Not Steph – she would never strike out at her bestie despite her horrible attitude – but something, anything to vent her anger.

"Please?" Steph said as she looked up at Ava. "I am sorry. I do not know what is happening to me."

Ava had squared her shoulders and was baring her teeth as she glared at Steph. She slowly pressed each finger together, thumb to thumb, index to index, pinkie to pinkie. Then she placed her index fingers on the tip of her nose. Her eyes narrowed to slits and locked onto Steph's panicky stare. She hissed between clenched teeth, "Stupid? Did you just say I am stupid, Steph? Did you?" Then with an ugly scowl, she growled, "How dare you!"

Steph did not reply. She simply stared up at Ava with a blank expression. Ava noticed that she was trembling which is something Ava never saw her do before that night.

"I may be a lot of things," Ava stammered, "but not that." She continued with a nod of her head, "Yes, I may be overly inquisitive. I must admit it. Yes, I may be almost four years younger than you and not as learned. But that is life. I may not be as strong or agile as you. Because I am more petite. I may be naïve in many ways as a measly, inexperienced, immature thirteen-year-old as you imply. I may not yet have your incredible, adventurous experiences owing to Jordyn's magic. And I did not do all those fantastic things you *allegedly* did to help others." She glowered furiously.

"But if there is one thing I am not, Steph – it is *stupid!*"

Steph threw her hands in the air. She stood up and moved to hug Ava, but Ava quickly backed away. "I said I am sorry! I honestly do not know what has come over me. I never get this angry. Never! Especially with you, Ava. I swear!"

Ava backed up a few more steps. She turned away from Steph to look at Doo. She said in a sugary voice, "Goodnight, Doo. I am going to sleep now. Please tell Dad I said goodnight. I look forward to seeing you in the morning, bright and early." She held out her hand. "Unless you would like to join me? Maybe have a snack before we retire?"

Steph felt miserable. She grabbed Ava by the arm.

Ava slapped her hand away. She silently mouthed, "No! Leave me alone!"

Steph said, "Ava, you and I should sit down and discuss this further. I told you I was sorry for what I said. You must understand that. I did not mean to say the word stupid. I meant to say silly. I meant to say how can you be so silly as to think—"

"Silly?" Ava growled disrupting Steph's words. She murmured, "Now I am silly? Imagine that!" She was clenching her teeth as she pondered what she should say next. She feigned a laugh that had an unpleasant, haughty, and taunting sound. Then she yanked her closed fists from her cloak and slammed them to her side.

"Give me a moment to ponder what you just said, Steph. Let me see. What is the best definition of silly I can conjure up?" She lightly poked Steph in the chest with her finger. "For your information, miss know it all," she snapped, "silly means having or showing a lack of common sense or judgment; being absurd and foolish." She tilted her head and looked to the forest canopy. "Whereas, let me see. Ah yes, stupid merely implies having or showing a great lack of intelligence or common sense. Imagine that. Lack of judgment – me being silly. Lack of intelligence – me being stupid." She waved her hands in the air on both sides of her face and gawked at Steph.

"Wouldn't you know it? Silly and stupid are just about the same thing! So, that is what you think of me – that I am silly? That I am stupid? Why not call me empty-headed, Steph? How about simple-minded? Or better yet call me a simpleton. That should work. Or perhaps even brainless, huh? I believe all those are synonyms for silly and stupid!"

Steph reached down and took another sip of her goblet. She said, "I am sorry, Ava. I really care about you. And I worry about you too. You know that better than anyone. But I am adamant. You should reconsider going. You are too important to our causes to make these decisions on your own. I do not want you to go." She giggled nervously. "Anyway, I guess this is our first argument, huh?"

Ava shouted, "And our last!" Her shout caused the other elves to look in their direction. "I am going to bed down beside those who care for me more than you do. With those who hardly know me but know I am anything but stupid and silly. I am going to sleep beside my real friends, Nessa, Galadriel, and Haleth." Turning to Doo, she said in a soft tone, "Would you like to join me?"

Doo looked at Steph with a questioning expression. Steph nodded her head slightly.

Oh, I know what you are thinking, Steph," Ava's thoughts said. She had unblocked her outgoing thoughts. I saw you nodding at Doo. I had read both of your thoughts as well. You are hopeful she will try to talk me out of accompanying Nessa to the Crostim Ledge tomorrow. Well, good luck with that. Because I am going whether you like it or not. And nothing is going to happen to me because the third in command, Siofra, is going to go with us. It will be her way of apologizing to me." Then she said out loud in a whisper, "Also, while I did not make an issue of what you said earlier, it wounded me terribly. But if you will recall, you had said some nasty, insulting things. And yeah, Steph, stupid, silly me can quote what you said from memory. Do you want to know why?"

Steph was shaking her head as she stared unemotionally at the ground.

Ava raised her voice slightly and said, "Because I am very smart. And I am anything but stupid and silly! I will restate some of the nasty, insulting things you said to me. Let us see if you would have liked the words if I had said them to you. You said in a nasty tone, 'I do not want you to go. Period. Everything you said sounds too fishy. We hardly know these warriors . . . I must say I forbid you from going . . . you are too young . . . too immature as well . . . remember what happened with the metamorhirío? One would think you would have learned your lesson after that.'" She glared at Steph. Steph was avoiding her eyes. "Do you recall saying those words?"

Steph shook her head and mouthed, "No, I do not."

"Too bad. Nevertheless, I would like you to try and stop me. Would you like to know why?"

Steph forced a grin, and then she mouthed, "No, I do not." She was still staring at the ground.

"Because, Steph, if you try to stop me, three dozen elves who have sworn an oath to protect me will wrestle you to the ground." She smiled deviously. "Pure and simple." She abruptly spun around and whispered over her shoulders, "So, have yourself a restful sleep. That is if you can. Because I, Miss Sillily Stupid, your former simpleton bestie, is going to sleep like a baby tonight. And tomorrow evening I am going to see Crostim Ledge with my true friend. Someone who doesn't insult me!"

She was about to walk off, but she hesitated. She was crying as she turned around slowly and faced Steph. "Gosh, Steph. I do not know what in the heck you were thinking. Just so you know, no one in my entire life has insulted me the way you did tonight." She wiped her tears on the sleeve of her cloak. "And that includes my worst enemies!" She was shaking her head unhappily as she stared at Steph for a few more moments. "Steph, how could you be so mean to me? You have hurt me more than you will ever know!" Then she turned on her heels and marched off into the darkness.

As soon as Ava and Doo were out of hearing and telepathic range, Steph buried her face in her hands. She began to sob and said to herself in a whisper, "My God, what just happened? I think we just destroyed our friendship! Ava has never yelled at me like that. Yeah, I made a mistake, said stupid things. I admit it. But the way she responded." She suddenly frowned. "But what am I saying? It is not her fault. It is *my* fault. Why in the world did I say those horrible things to her in the first place? It is like something made me say those things because I never talk like that to anyone, especially to her!" She instinctively could tell that someone was close by. It was Dad. "Dad, why did I say all those nasty things to her?"

"I am not certain," Dad said. "But I have a suspicion. Please hand me your goblet." He swirled the contents of the goblet and then sniffed it. "I think some evil power may have put something in your drink. Not a surprise. This is the most enchanted forest in all of Antiquom." He handed the goblet to Steph. "Smell it. But first, swirl its contents. Its odor is clear."

Steph said, "Goodness! This stuff smells weird, like licorice or something just as spicy. I thought it was water. Do you think someone has tried to poison me?"

"It is not poison," Dad said. "It is bad magic. I believe it will wear off soon." He placed his hand on Steph's knee. "Do not fret, Steph. Doo will discover what is happening." He rolled his eyes. Then he smiled.

"She always does."

4

The Etanpioa was roughly ten minutes from their destination. It was a large clearing just off the trail in the forest. They would spend the night in the clearing after another day's grueling march.

Earlier, during the midday break, Elbereth had said they would arrive at the night's destination more than three hours earlier than expected. That assertion made Ava quite happy. She and Nessa would have plenty of time to climb the steep incline to the Crostim Ledge. Then they could return to the Etanpioa well before dark.

Ava was the reason for their scheduled, early arrival. She had not caused the march to stop but one time during the day's trek. Elbereth was especially gratified. She was so pleased she asked Ava to join her at the front of the Etanpioa where they chatted away nonstop. Ava told Elbereth about her hometown in Illinois and some interesting aspects of the Earthly World. In turn, Elbereth provided Ava with more information about the two other Inner World realms, Andron and Ostium.

The only time Ava had stopped along the trail, thus halting the march, was to observe a large creature. It was laying its eggs. The creature bore a resemblance to an Earthly World tortoise. Except the Inner World creature had six muscular legs instead of four. Like the Earthly World tortoise, the creature had the characteristic, flecked pattern of blotchy yellows and honey browns.

The younger elves were equally interested in the creature. They had formed a wide circle around the creature as it laid its eggs. There were twenty-two eggs in all. They were about one and one-half inches in diameter. Much to their surprise, Elbereth joined their curious assembly. She told them that the creature was a wyknonm.

"The wyknonm is a rarity in the Forest of Artonia, in fact all of Antiquom," she said in her robust, imperious voice. "Sadly, the wyknonm in these parts is nearly nonexistent. The Great Wizard Godroh spoke to me of belugas favoring the wyknonm's eggs. Like all creatures they stalk and persecute ruthlessly, the belugas are just as obdurate when hunting for the wyknonm, to include digging up its unhatched eggs."

Elbereth went on to explain that the wyknonm migrated from the banks of the Solenom River over the millennium. It was owing to the glaciers up north growing in volume, thus forcing the Solenom River to flood its banks more than usual. Many of the freshly laid wyknonm eggs were wiped out year after year, threatening the species' survival. The slow-moving wyknonm were unable to adapt, so they gradually moved deeper to the protective forest.

She added that creatures in both the Inner and Earthly Worlds depend on their environments to sustain their species. The physical qualities of their habitats help them to find food, build homes, endure weather, and produce offspring. She briefly explained the Earthly World's ongoing global warming phenomena that may be caused by human activity. One of the warriors asked if the phenomena were occurring in the Inner World.

Elbereth said with a smile, "I asked Godroh the same question. He replied that it is not occurring here in our world. He also told me that the Earthly World's gradual rise in temperatures is destroying some species. Other species are relocating, several further to the north to cooler areas to escape the steadily rising temperatures. Perhaps other species will adapt over time as they have over the millennium." She picked up one of the eggs and handed it to Ava so she and the other elves could examine it. "It is okay to handle the egg," she said when Ava gave her a doubtful look. "The beast will bury it along with the others. It too will survive."

Ava examined the egg briefly then gave it to Nessa. Nessa passed it down the line.

Elbereth said, "Also, the species will survive as well, despite the belugas. Godroh said that he and other kindly wizards maintain a protective area for imperiled beasts such as the wyknonm. So, if their kind perishes here in the forest, they will live on elsewhere."

As soon as the wyknonm began to bury its eggs, Elbereth told everyone it was time to move on.

Ava and Steph were not speaking. Steph had tried to engage Ava in conversation a few times earlier, but Ava had ignored her. Steph felt horrible because she argued with Ava the night before.

"She is angry with you, that is all," Doo said to Steph as they walked in the middle of the group. "Logically, because you were extremely unpleasant to her. She was equally unpleasant but not as insulting. Your words offended her greatly. I can tell her heart is hurting."

"But it wasn't my fault," Steph said glumly. "Dad told me a magical potion was put in my goblet. That is why I acted the way I did. He told you that too, yes?"

"Yes, he did," Doo replied. "He also told Ava. But she was hurt by your insulting words and your tone. Perhaps when we stop tonight, she will come to you. Then she will forgive you."

"I hope so," Steph said. "Have you figured out who could have put the potion in my goblet?"

"Not yet," Doo replied. "But it must have been one of the warriors." Her expression changed. "That is if it was actually something in the goblet and not an evil wizard in our vicinity. Anyway, have any of the elves taken a misliking to you? Have any said anything whatsoever to make you suppose they do not like you?"

"Not a one," Steph answered. "Gosh. I only hope Ava and I will bury the hatchet soon."

"Bury the hatchet?" Doo asked with a skeptical expression. "Did you and Ava plan to bury a weapon?"

Steph replied with a laugh. "No, bury the hatchet is a catchphrase in my world. It means the same as make peace, settle our differences."

"Oh, I see," Doo said with a straight face. "Stay strong, Steph. I am confident you two will, as you say, bury your hatchet. Perhaps tonight. In the meantime, I am going to talk with some of those who were on guard last night. Because I truly do not think it was something in the goblet. I think it was something else." Steph was about to ask Doo to explain, but Doo had flown off.

Earlier, before Ava was summoned to walk alongside Elbereth, Nessa told her more about their plans to visit Crostim Ledge. She said, "You and I will go off when the others are distracted. Siofra told me she would inform Elbereth, so our excursion is approved. Even so, we must be wary the others do not notice our departure. Siofra said Morwen will distract the others by announcing a fun contest. It will be followed by a special meal. The contest is one where we conceal at the back of trees and wide bushes. Others have to discover us."

"Oh, like hide-and-go-seek," Ava said. Nessa gave her a quizzical look. "It is a game, Nessa; a contest that Earthly World children play. We too hide behind trees and other things, and others have to try and find us."

Nessa had nodded thoughtfully. Then she provided more details about their excursion to Crostim Ledge. She ended their brief talk when she said with a grin, "We will return well before dark. No one will miss our absence. You will enjoy our trip. The view from the ledge is spectacular. You will see."

*****

Siofra was standing in a thicket just off the trail as the column marched by. Once she knew the other warriors were out of earshot, she whispered, "Nessa! I want you to come in here. We need to talk."

Nessa was at the rear of the Etanpioa. She dutifully stepped into the forest. She was all smiles thinking that Siofra was going to give her more information about their Crostim Ledge adventure.

As soon as Nessa was standing next to her, Siofra yanked her roughly by the forearm. Then she slapped Nessa's face hard. Tears immediately welled up in Nessa's eyes. Siofra said in an outraged tone of voice, "Why did you tell Ava that I would accompany you to the ledge?" She was utterly enraged and paced back and forth as she glared at Nessa with a look of complete disgust.

Nessa swallowed hard. She cleared her throat. Her voice was husky, shaky, and barely discernible when she said, "Siofra, I swear. I did not tell Ava that you will accompany us."

Siofra slapped Nessa again even harder causing her head to snap brutally to the right. With an ugly smirk, she grabbed Nessa by the collar of her cloak, nearly yanking her off her feet. She seethed between gritted teeth, "Do not lie to me! I will destroy you if you lie to me. You know the penalty for deceit to one's superior." She turned up her nose. "It is banishment, Nessa, and exile! Vena overheard Ava and Steph arguing last night. The stupid fairies may also have heard the argument. Vena was certain that Ava had said I was going to accompany you to the ledge!"

Nessa struggled to release herself from Siofra's grip, but she could not. She was trembling too much, and her arms felt weak. She cried, "I am not being dishonest! I swear. I am a loyal warrior. I do not lie. I would never betray you. I would rather die than to betray you." Her lips were quivering. Her face was ashen white. She suddenly felt dizzy because Siofra had reached down and unsheathed her blade. She stared at the blade and cried, "Please, believe me, Siofra! You must believe me. I did not tell Ava!"

Siofra's look of hatred suddenly diminished, completely shocking Nessa. She released Nessa from her powerful grip and sheathed her blade. She did not want to risk Nessa backing out of the upcoming trip to the ledge. If Nessa refused to take Ava to the ledge, that would ruin everything. She pretended a smile. "Okay, I believe you, but it is unimportant, nonetheless. Therefore, I apologize for accusing you of dishonesty. It must have been Elbereth that informed Ava of our secret plan. Yes, it must have been her. Ava was at the front of the Etanpioa. It makes perfect sense because I told Elbereth our secret."

Nessa stumbled back a few steps. She was on the verge of tears and trembling wildly. She jammed her hands into her armpits to stop them from shaking. With tremors in her voice, she said, "Yes, that must be the cause." She added in a panicky tone, hoping more than anything Siofra would believe her, "Because I swear to you, Siofra, I did not tell Ava about your plan to accompany us. You must believe me. I may be young and inexperienced, but there is one thing I would never do. I would never lie to you."

"It does not matter anyhow," Siofra said in a casual tone. "So, clear your mind of what I have said. In any event, I cannot accompany you although I wish I could."

"Oh, I am deeply saddened," Nessa said in a lie. Her voice was breaking, but not because she was sad that Siofra was not going to accompany them. She was scared almost senseless. All she wanted to do was get out of Siofra's sight. She pretended a smile. "I know how much you wish to visit the ledge."

Siofra said, "I do, but I will have many more opportunities. As you undoubtedly know, Elbereth has taken a liking to Ava. She wants to please her just like us. To thank her for making today's march much shorter than usual. By treating her to look over Crostim Ledge. Hence, here is what you are to do." She glanced around to make certain no one was nearby. She leaned in close and whispered, "Shortly after the contest begins, you will hide with Ava. Make certain it is on the right side of the clearing. That way you will be closer to the pathway that leads to the ledge. Then off you go. Can you do that for Elbereth, for me, for your friend, Ava?"

"Yes," Nessa said excitedly. She was a bit more relaxed even if the left side of her face was throbbing from Siofra's forceful slaps. She wanted to reach out and hug Siofra, anything to mollify her, but she knew she could not. The older elf probably would beat her to death if she did.

"Okay then, off you go," Siofra said with a smile. "Be careful and make certain you return before nightfall. And whatever you do, ensure Ava is well protected."

Nessa bowed deeply, and then she exclaimed, "Yes, yes, yes! And thank you!" She was eager to be getting away from Siofra, more so than the upcoming trip to Crostim Ledge. When she stepped onto the trail, she bumped into Morwen nearly knocking her off her feet. The second in command had been standing just outside the thicket where Nessa and Siofra had been talking.

"Oh, I am sorry, Morwen," Nessa cried. "I did not see you!"

Morwen gave her a dirty look. "It is quite alright." Then she barked an order that caused Nessa to jump back with alarm. "Get back to your post. Now! And at a run."

Nessa turned to run up the trail as fast as her legs could move. She wanted to get as far away from Siofra and Morwen as possible.

"Is everything in order?" Morwen asked Siofra as she stepped into the thicket.

"Yes. The foolish child believed every word. But I wonder how Ava knew I had lied to Nessa, that I would accompany them?"

"It must have been Elbereth like you said," Morwen said with a haughty laugh. "It makes sense, does it not? Ava is at the front of our formation. Perhaps Elbereth truly has taken a liking to the young elf because she is going to meet with Godroh."

Siofra said in a skeptical tone, "Oh, you honestly do not believe that do you? That Elbereth has taken a liking to Ava. I seriously doubt it, and so do you. Anyway, there is no way Elbereth can know possibly. I never told her about our plan, that Nessa and Ava were going to the ledge. I told Nessa to not tell anyone about the ledge either, the exception being Ava." She scratched her head. "Given her reaction, I honestly believe that

Nessa did not tell Ava about my accompanying them. If she had been lying, I would have seen it in her eyes. But it baffles me how Ava could know about my initial, stated intent to accompany them.

"It is not important," Morwen replied flatly. "So, no one knows of our plan except you, Nessa, Ava, and me, correct?"

Siofra replied, "The older one, Steph, as well as the two fairies, they might also know of the plan. Vena snuck behind Ava and Steph when they were arguing last night. She thought Ava mentioned my name and had said something about me going with them. So, what should we do about the two fairies?"

Morwen gave her a dirty look. She crossed her arms over her chest and glared. Then she said in a sarcastic manner, "So, it looks like there is one other who knows of our plan – Vena. It looks like you made a mistake after all, Siofra."

"Morwen, you and I both know we do not have to worry about Vena. She would do anything for me. She is one hundred percent loyal. I am confident she will not say a word to anyone."

Morwen said, "Well, I hope you are right. When Ava does not return, we will muster the Etanpioa. When we discover Nessa is missing, we will tell the others that we suspect that she took Ava to Crostim Ledge. It would make perfect sense since everyone knows Nessa has been there one time before." A wicked grin appeared on her face. "Naturally, we will say that Nessa scooted off with Ava without our permission and knowledge. We will also pretend to be livid with her insubordination. After everyone starts to panic, especially Elbereth, you will offer that the two of them probably are lost. Because it will be dark, we will be unable to start our search until morning. I will inform Elbereth that I have doubts that we ever will find them. Practically no one returns from the forest after getting lost, especially those as inexperienced as Ava and Nessa. Elbereth will understand, although she probably will search anyway. But her search will be halfhearted. She has gone astray many times in Artonia. You and I have as well. You have had horrible experiences in this forest. We also have given up our share of good warriors to this godforsaken place."

"Regrettably, we have," Siofra said in a sad tone. "Warriors more skilled than Nessa and nowhere as rude as Ava. Ava has no worthy warrior skills that I can see. Is our wizarding friend ready? Our plan will not work without him." She smiled adding, "It was particularly good to see him after all these years. He has not changed a bit."

Morwen grinned then said, "Like you, I have not seen him since yesterday's dusk. When, thanks to you allowing him to get close to our ranks, he placed the spell on Ava's friend, Steph." She broke out laughing. "That stupid male fairy suspects that one of us slipped a potion into Steph's drink. All the while it was Haldir doing what he does best – black magic. Your wizarding friend is one tricky soul! But let me ask you this, Siofra. Should we leave everything up to him? Is that wise?"

"We have no other choice," Siofra replied offhandedly. "Once Haldir does what he needs to do with Ava, we collect our treasures, our rewards. Then we sneak away from the Etanpioa and travel southeast, perhaps to the border of Leípei. There we will live our lives in opulence henceforth." She smiled. "And marry, have children, and finally be allowed to live with our husbands and children like normal elves. Our Bkotn tradition of not living with our husbands and sons is deplorable. I cannot wait to break those bonds."

Morwen said, "And the others, Steph and the two fairies, the DooDad as Steph refers to them?"

Siofra said, "They are irrelevant. Ava is the most important of the two elves. Why I do not know. But she must be valuable to seek counsel with Godroh and for Haldir to be interested in her. No ordinary elf or human can seek counsel with Godroh without a critical cause. The others, Steph and the two fairies, I suggest we allow them to roam endlessly in Artonia until their dying days or we show them generous Bkotn mercy."

"Show them mercy?" Morwen said as she tilted her head to the side. "How?"

Siofra shoved the point of her tkalakn into the thick bark of a young sapling. She laughed hideously, and then she narrowed her eyes.

"Mercy of the blade, Morwen. The mercy of the tkalakn blade."

5

A half-hour later, Ava and Nessa were hiding behind a broad tree as the contest began. Nessa was peeking from behind the tree trunk anxiously. She was waiting for the right moment when she and Ava could dash to the forest undetected. She knew that the best time to run off would be when the first warrior was found. All eyes would be focused on the discovered warrior which usually resulted in boisterous shouts and calls from the others. Thereby forcing the game's two seekers to scramble off in numerous directions in search of the others that were hiding. No warrior wanted to be found first. Being the first would result in a good form "penalty." To serve up her penalty, the warrior would have to distribute drinks to the entire Etanpioa during the celebratory dinner. It was all in good fun and just part of the Bkotn way of life.

Ava was not reading Nessa's thoughts although later, she wished that she had. Then she would have known the reason Nessa's left cheek was pink, that she had been slapped by Siofra. She also would have known to ask Nessa probing questions. After all, what Steph had said the night before was still nagging her. It was like Steph knew something that she did not. But she was so excited to be accompanying Nessa to Crostim Ledge, her mind was distracted. As a result, she was careless and simply took things in stride, thereby allowing Nessa to make all the decisions.

Nessa grabbed Ava's hand and pulled hard, jerking her back to reality. She whispered, "Okay, now we go. They will not notice we are gone. The contest takes an especially long time. We Bkotn warriors are stealthy. We know how to avoid others – to include our own. I honestly expect that we will return long before the contest finishes." With a huge grin she added, "And just in time for the special dinner!" She and Ava sprinted from the clearing to the forest. They arrived on the pathway that leads to Crostim Ledge in less than two minutes. They did not stop running until they no longer could hear the shouts and calls of the other warriors.

"Stay close behind me," Nessa said. She was searching the forest with her eyes, her tkalakn held out in front of her as she walked.

Ava's longbow and quiver were slung over her shoulders. She had unsheathed her sword and was carrying it in her right hand. At that point, she had not used either of her weapons in anger to defend herself.

She had practiced with them many times with the Bkotn warriors. Even so, she seriously doubted she would know how to use them properly if necessary. She hoped she never would. Just the thought of hurting or, God forbid, killing something or someone made her stomach turn.

"We must be careful," Nessa whispered over her shoulder. "There are many dangerous beasts in the forest before dusk falls. This is the time of day when they are on the prowl in search of their dinner." She and Ava continued walking the pathway until, around ten minutes later, she told Ava to stop. She said in a whisper, "Strange."

"What is strange?" Ava asked. Her heart began to race because of the anxious look on Nessa's face. "Are we lost?" She abruptly winced in reaction to a rustling sound to their right. Like something was walking on twigs and dried leaves. "Did you hear that?"

"Yes, I did," Nessa replied in a whisper. "And yes, Ava, I think we may be lost. We may be going around in circles. But how that is taking place, I have no idea." She turned around and looked past Ava. "I do not recognize the pathway we just traveled on. Look for yourself, and please tell me I am wrong." She pointed to their right. "Moreover, I had not noticed all that mist before now. Did you?"

Ava turned and stared along the pathway. Nessa was correct. What she saw looked unfamiliar. Yet she wondered how that could be since they had just strolled upon it. The mist that was gradually creeping up from the ground was even more startling. She recalled word for word what Doo had said about the mist.

"Any lost voyager whose remains were never found certainly had been spirited away by any number of mystical whatever's that lurk in the mysterious forests. They probably vanished when the mist appeared. The mist is evil black magic."

Ava was very much trying to remain calm, but her thoughts seemed to be racing a mile a minute. She thought to herself; what happened to our pathway? I do not recall all those boulders and thick shrubs. We must be lost! But common sense is telling me there is no way it could have happened! Has something sinister, something magical placed a spell on this part of the forest? Is that mist a foreshadowing of what is to come? She could tell Nessa was overly concerned as well. To lessen her friend's anxiety, she said, "It could be the light, Nessa. You know, from the setting sun as it casts weird shadows through the treetops. But I must agree it does not look familiar to me either."

Nessa did not say anything, but Ava had read her thoughts. Her thoughts seemed to be screaming frantically inside Ava's head. "We *are* lost! But how. And my goodness, why? Why did I accept Siofra's suggestion? I should have said no. How could I have been so careless? I know better! Even so, I must not allow anything to happen to Ava. I must not!"

"Did you hear that?" Ava whispered in reaction to an odd moaning noise. It seemed to be coming from the other side of a sharp turn in the pathway. Nessa replied that she had heard the sound as well. Ava grabbed Nessa's cloak sleeve and pulled her close. She whispered, "I cannot be certain, but it sounds like someone is whimpering, perhaps saying a strange word over and over. What do you say we get out of here before something terrible happens? I no longer care about visiting the ledge."

Nessa said in a miserable tone, "A Bkotn warrior is calling out for help. I am certain because what she said is our secret word, Axiui. We are taught early on to say the word when one of us is in trouble." She grabbed Ava's cloak at the shoulders forcing her to her knees. Ava tried to resist, but Nessa pushed down on her shoulders even harder. "I apologize for doing this, Ava, but you must remain here and stay hidden. I vowed to protect you, so I will be the one to aid my fellow warrior. I will return after I have done what I need to do." She added with a smile, "Everything will be okay, I promise you."

Ava had read Nessa's following thoughts after she spoke. Like her, Nessa was thinking it could be a trick by an evil wizard or worse – a metamorhirío trying to lure them along the path.

"But then again," Nessa had thought to herself, "metamorhirío's do not know how to speak. So, it must be a Bkotn warrior in distress! Perhaps one of the hiding warriors got lost up here then was injured somehow. It has happened before during the games. Not too often, but it is not unheard of."

Nessa's discounting a metamorhirío's trickery should have made Ava feel better, but she was becoming more anxious, nonetheless. Mirroring Nessa's thoughts she said, "Maybe it is a trick! Maybe an evil wizard or some other sort of nasty magic." She started to get to her feet, but Nessa forced her to her knees once more.

The uneasy look on Nessa's face did nothing to allay Ava's nervousness. She wanted to take control of the situation, to persuade Nessa to leave with her. To return to the safety of the Etanpioa. But she knew nothing of the path they were on. Besides, the pathway looked totally unfamiliar. She grasped, reluctantly, that she had to trust Nessa's instincts and experience. But that did not keep her from trying to persuade Nessa to beat it out of there with her. She said, "Nessa, my fairy friend, Doo, said this is the most enchanted forest in Antiquom. She also said that the mist may precede something terrible that is about to happen. Perhaps you should stay here with me, at least for a few more moments. Then we will wait to see what happens next. I do not want you to get hurt." She was about to get to her feet, but the disapproving glare Nessa was giving her kept her on her knees. "Maybe we should stay together. Two is better than one. Please do not go on alone."

"Ava, only Bkotn know of the secret word, Axiui. It is a magical word borne of our ancestors. No spell, no enchantment, no powerful wizard, no stranger can speak the word. Only Bkotn." She flashed Ava a quick, reassuring grin. "Even you, Ava, you cannot say the word correctly with the proper voice inflection." Her optimistic expression disappeared in a flash as her tone of voice changed markedly. "You must stay here. You must remain safe. I swore that I would protect you. And I am prepared to do so with my life if need be. I will return to you in a moment." She turned about and slowly moved up the pathway in a low crouch.

Ava immediately got to her feet and rushed to a large boulder further up the pathway. She slipped behind it and waited. Beads of nervous sweat appeared on her forehead. She was going to follow Nessa but thought better of it. She did not want Nessa to think she did not trust her intuition. Looking back, she wished that she had.

After a few dozen or so paces Nessa abruptly stopped walking. She had heard something that sounded like crunching leaves to her left. The sound was barely noticeable. She instinctively knew that the wind did not cause the sound. There was little to no breeze deep in the forest. Only something that walked upright could make such a sound. She sheathed her tkalakn and grabbed her bow. She swiftly strung an arrow onto it.

Just then Ava detected another's thoughts. They were not as clear as Nessa's, but she could sense them, nonetheless. She grinned with the knowledge that Nessa's hunch of another Bkotn in distress had been correct. Good! The Bkotn in distress is nearby. It will be nice to have another in our little group. She glanced behind her then scowled. The ominous mist was growing opaquer and getting closer. I just hope the other warrior can be moved. We need to get out of here as soon as possible before the mist gets any closer. She suddenly detected fleeting thoughts of a third entity. Those thoughts seemed to be expressing words that were unrecognizable to her. Like phrases of a peculiar language. The thoughts were also repetitive, almost like they were incantations. Then, as quickly as they had materialized in her mind, the third entity's thoughts stopped. She would discover much later that while she could, strangely enough, detect the being's incantations, she would never be able to understand its ordinary thoughts.

Nessa was on the other side of the sharp turn in the pathway and out of earshot. But Ava could still read her thoughts as she said in a low voice, "Hello? Is someone there? If so, show yourself. Axiui? I say again, Axiui?" There was no reply. Nessa called back to Ava in a shout, "There is no one out here! Just us."

Despite Nessa's reassuring shouts, Ava could tell by her thoughts that she was alarmed. She was also confused because she and Ava had heard the spoken words of one who was in distress. Ava stepped from behind the boulder and began to walk toward Nessa. She shouted, "Yes, there definitely is someone out there! I am certain of it! I am coming to you, Nessa, so please stay put."

Nessa rushed along the pathway toward Ava. She hollered, "Get back there, Ava! Please do as I ask!"

Ava stopped walking. She said in a soft voice, "Nessa, I know there are at least two something's out there, not far from you. I am positive! Will you please allow me to come to you?"

"No!" Nessa shouted. "Please stay where you are, where it is safe!" She turned around and disappeared on the other side of the bend in the pathway. She suddenly pulled hard on her bowstring. Someone or something had emerged from the dense undergrowth behind her. Whatever it was had tapped her on the shoulder. She swiftly spun around and aimed her bow. Then, with a long sigh of relief, she lowered her bow and grinned.

Ava was grinning as well. She could tell that the originator of the second set of thoughts knew Nessa and that Nessa knew her. Unexpectedly, the third set of thoughts restarted its strange incantations. She stepped from behind the boulder and gasped. The mist was now where she supposed Nessa and the other warrior were standing on the other side of the turn in the pathway! She was also getting bad vibes concerning the third being's continuing incantations.

"Oh, this is wonderful, Siofra!" Nessa lied as she pretended to smile. "You decided to accompany us. I am so happy!"

Siofra placed her finger to her lips. "Shhh." Then she gestured with her eyes past Nessa. She was nodding her head, suggesting that Nessa should turn around.

Nessa believed one of their fellow Bkotn warriors was standing behind her. Maybe her best friend, Galadriel. She spun around eagerly. Then she staggered forward and collapsed face-first to the forest floor. Her arms were spread out beside her. Her legs were bent curiously, one twisted beneath the other. The back of her cloak was stained with bright red blood that steadily spread.

Ava covered her mouth to stifle a scream. She had discerned Siofra's thoughts as she thrust her tkalakn deep into Nessa's back. By reading Siofra's well-honed, killer-instinct thoughts, she knew that Siofra had thrust the blade skillfully. It had struck just below Nessa's seventh thoracic vertebrae, piercing her heart. She had died almost instantly, but not before she addressed her dying thoughts to Ava.

Ava saw that the mist was racing along the pathway toward her! She leaped from behind the boulder and crashed recklessly through the thick forest to her left. She had purposely sidestepped the pathway, somehow knowing that continuing along it would spell her doom. She tripped over the stump of a fallen tree, then she picked herself up and resumed running. She could hear the crashing sounds of Siofra as she chased after her. Siofra was calling her name, telling her to stop, that she will not outlive the forest's magic. And of all things, she was shouting that she would not harm her! Another elf was shouting as well. Ava recognized the cold, commanding voice as Vena's, Siofra's favorite subordinate. She looked over her shoulder as she ran. The mist was still chasing her and getting closer! She quickened her pace.

Thorns and low-lying branches were cruelly raking her legs as she crashed through the thick forest. Nonetheless, she kept running as fast as her tormented legs would move. She was oblivious to the pain in her lower extremities. Her head was pounding. Dribbles of blood were seeping from the many cuts and scrapes. She was terrified, but she was more stricken with grief. Tears were gushing from her eyes like the drowning water of an angry sea. The unreal shock she had just suffered in her mind was horrendous. Knowing that her friend Nessa had been murdered compelled her to race even faster. With one objective – to avenge Nessa's death as soon as she could.

As she ran blindly through Artonia, Nessa's final reflections and her dying thoughts were coursing through her mind.

"Ava, Steph told me this afternoon that I should protect you with my life. She told me a secret as well. She told me who you are. Thus, I have been blessed to have known you. Goodbye, Avaïnoáel, O Poica Katharos. I love you. Now run! Run as fast as you can. Please!"

*****

Owing to her uncanny power of telepathy, Ava's heart had been shattered with what she had sensed. She was certain Nessa was dead. Positive that Siofra had tricked her to turn around. So, the ruthless third in command could callously thrust the blade of her tkalakn deep into Nessa's backbone. Cruelly piercing her heart. Extinguishing her life almost instantly.

Yet even with Ava's thoughts and assumptions. Despite her telepathic visions as she perceived Nessa's death. Even with her overwhelming grief and heartache. Thinking all the time of Nessa's dying thoughts.

Nessa was alive!

The carefree and spirited brave warrior was lying unconscious, face down on the forest floor. Her arms splayed to her sides. Her legs bent curiously. Scarcely breathing. Her heartbeats imperceptible. Yet she was just as alive as before. Under the influence of a magical spell.

Siofra likewise was ensorcelled. Even as she assumed that she had murdered Nessa against her own will. Thus, violating her oath as a Bkotn warrior – *to forsake a Bkotn is to forsake oneself.*

Ava continued to crash recklessly through the forest. Siofra's traitorous thoughts as she murdered her comrade, thus violating her Bkotn oath. Nessa's dying thoughts even though she did not die. The third set of thoughts chanting incantations nonstop. Vena's voice calling after her even though she was far afield participating in the Etanpioa game with her fellow warriors.

Every one of Ava's thoughts was based on falsehoods. Each was a deception of a differing ambiguity. With one simple explanation.

The bewitched Forest of Artonia was, and still is, in control of all things that enter its realm. Controlling what living beings may think. Or dream, see, hear, or even believe is true – or untrue. All the time in complete control.

As is the evilest wizard of the ancient realm of Antiquom.

Haldir of Mountains Cross.

CHAPTER 6

ARTONIA AND BLACKMAGIC IN CONTROL

"Words may sometimes utter untruths, but thoughts cannot lie."
—*Ava Noelle, (Avaĭnoáel, O Poica Katharos)*

1

Ava was relieved that the sun was rising. The scattered light as it filtered through the leaves reminded her of softly flickering tree lights at Christmastime. The morning haze added to the enchanting spectacle.

I must have been moving for over twelve hours now. No wonder I am way past exhausted. Thank goodness the sun is almost up. Trying to find my way in the pitch-blackness was nearly impossible. I was lucky I did not fall into a void, walk dead-on into a tree, or tumble headfirst down the mountainside.

Ava briefly stopped running hours ago when she no longer heard Siofra and Vena's voices. Weariness wanted to overwhelm her many times, to force her to stop moving. But she kept on no matter what. She only stopped to tend to her cuts and scrapes. One gash, high on her inner left thigh, was quite deep. She poured water from her flask into the wound. It hurt like crazy, immediately causing her to feel dizzy. She resisted the urge to yell out in pain and shook her head vigorously to ward off vertigo. She wrapped the gash and the other more troublesome cuts on her legs with strips of cloth she had ripped from the lining of her cloak.

She came close to falling asleep after wrapping her wounds. She nearly nodded off one other time as well when she stopped to rest for a few moments. But she scrambled to her feet both times and pressed on. Shortly after she attended to her wounds, Ava noticed a nagging pain in her knees. The outside of her legs and knees seemed to be screaming with discomfort. She realized she needed to make trekking poles. The poles would reduce the strain on her legs.

She stopped to cut down two tree limbs with her sword. The limbs were crooked, oddly shaped, and very skinny. But she did not care. If they were rigid enough to support her weight they would work nicely. She whittled at the branches as she pressed on in the darkness. Afterward, as she walked, she purposely kept a slower gait, and she stayed more upright rather than bending forward. Those deliberate measures, along with the makeshift trekking poles, seemed to cure the knee pain almost at once.

She had no idea where she was headed. But she knew that she must strive to move downhill as best as she could. She found herself walking in circles a few times in the darkness – the terrain looked vaguely familiar – but she refused to panic. She knew from the nature books she had read that panicking would do nothing but frighten her even more. So, she kept walking, and eventually, she found herself in new terrain.

Luckily, the full moon was at its highpoint. While everything around her was blurry and shadowy, she could see well enough to keep from crashing headlong into the trees. She heard many odd noises as she walked, but she kept her sword unsheathed and at the ready just in case. Thankfully, nothing odd or scary approached her in the middle of the night.

She kept saying to herself silently – downward. That is the keyword for my survival. Sooner or later, I will stumble upon the Solenom or one of its many tributaries. There I can replenish my hip flask and hopefully find something to eat. Maybe I can seek out help from friendly elves. But I need to be ready to hide too. I will have no way of knowing what I will find when I get to wherever I end up.

Ava correctly assumed that the Crostim Ledge is a high point off the Kuoino Trail, the trail she and the others had been hiking the day before. The ledge is not the highest point but towering nonetheless, along with the most stunning, wide view of the Solenom.

She pondered; if the ledge is even close to the highest point in Artonia, and considering it overlooks the Solenom valley, moving downhill should eventually take me to the river. Nessa and I were nearly as high as the ledge before she was murdered by her superior. She felt like crying as she recalled for the umpteenth time bits and pieces of Nessa's dying thoughts.

She told me who you are. Thus, I have been blessed.

Ava shook her head vigorously to drive Nessa's heartbreaking thoughts away. But the courageous warrior's final, unspoken words kept on in the back of her mind.

Goodbye Avaïnoáel, O Poica Katharos. I love you. Now run! Run as fast as you can. Please!

Later, by the position of the sun shining through the leaves, Ava guessed it was midday. She was ambling along, barely able to stay on her feet. She was extremely tired, way past exhaustion. She had stopped earlier for a short nap – perhaps thirty minutes, maybe longer. Then she continued to stumble bone-tired through the forest.

She suddenly let out a hushed squeal of delight. She had stepped out of the forest onto a small clearing. Her elation had nothing to do with entering the small clearing, although it was nice to sniff the clean, unforested air. The cause of her elation had everything to do with what she saw on the other side of the clearing.

It is a trail! It even has a cairn at its entrance. So, it probably is an important trail. At least I hope it is. And maybe, just maybe it is a downhill trail that leads to the river.

Ava knew from her nature books that a cairn is a manmade pile of stones. Or, in this case, placed by some Inner World creature, probably a witch, wizard, or elf. Cairns are used by trail markers and hikers, sometimes at the beginning of trails or pathways. They also are used in barren landscapes where trees and other forms of identifying signs for marking the trail are impossible.

She glanced around the clearing to make certain no one was nearby. Then she dashed to the trailhead. She noticed it was a well-trampled trail. To her relief, it appeared to trek downhill gradually. She just started out walking the trail when she perceived something soaring through the air. Whatever it was started to hover mere inches above her head and slightly behind her. Her heart seemed to sprint with excitement.

"DooDad? Is that you?"

Then realizing she would have detected either Doo or Dad's thoughts, she intuitively knew it was not one of her fairy friends. She stopped walking, slowly turned around, and looked up, not certain of what she would see. Then she howled with laughter.

2

Ava's eyes were gleaming with excitement. "Well, hello there you darling, beautiful thing! From where did you come?" She straightened out her left arm to allow the small, magnificent bird to alight onto the sleeve of her cloak.

In one of her many discussions, Doo had portrayed the khni bird. Her description matched the vivid colors and oddly shaped beak of the bird that was on Ava's sleeve. Consequently, Ava knew for certain it was a khni.

The khni are about the size of the fully-grown Earthly World American robin. The robin is a common sight in the continental United States. The khni have dazzlingly brilliant, dark red feathers with purple faces and pink, yellow, and green wings. Their oddly shaped beaks are black. They are recognized as the most beautiful bird of the Inner World and are likewise revered by their inhabitants.

Some time ago, Ava had spotted a khni when she was on the Kuoino Trail. It was flying above an elf that had passed them by. Ava asked one of the Bkotn warriors the reason that the bird was flying above the elf's head. It seemed to glide in step with each of the elf's footsteps. The warrior – a particularly nasty older elf – gave Ava a dirty look and ignored her question. But later, Galadriel told her a bit about the species when she and Ava were alone.

Galadriel had said, "Owing to the khni's harmonious and loyal nature, the bird's resemblance is the official icon of Antiquom. Because of its loyal spirit, it emphasizes peace, love, and harmony. Elves, fairies, witches, and even wizards, wear an image of the khni on their garments or as jewelry accessories. The khni symbol is supposed to bring the bearer good luck." She had opened her cloak and proudly pointed to the broach on her tunic. It was the replica of a golden khni. Ava could tell that the broach was made of pure gold.

"The khni are extremely sociable birds. Nevertheless, they have a startling, curious character. They prefer to live a life apart from their kind during most of the year, seeking to befriend other creatures such as the elf you saw earlier. The exception is during the khni mating season which occurs in late winter. During the mating season, they are nowhere to be found in the Forest of Artonia. According to elven legends, when the khni disappears from the forest during the mating season, they have flown to *Paravem*. Paravem is an elven, mystical world of angels. Perhaps that explains why the species is called the khni. Khni means winged angel in Fortunomy."

The bird that had just befriended Ava flew from her arm and hovered above her head. It seemed to oblige Ava to resume her trek. So, she did. She recalled that Galadriel had also told her that the khni would never leave her side, night, or day. Except, naturally, during the mating season when it would fly off.

"That is not so bad," Ava said to the bird. "Winter is still a ways away." She looked up over her shoulder and said cheerfully, "I will call you Fidelium. How does that sound to you? Fidelium is the Latin word for friendship." She bowed slightly as she walked. "Hello, Fidelium. My name is Ava, Ava Noelle." She knew that Fidelium would remain with her no matter what. And, as Galadriel had said, she knew he would squawk loudly whenever danger was near, or whenever she was about to do something stupidly dangerous. Like touch or sample a poisonous plant or berry or sniff a noxious flower.

3

Ava was humming softly as she walked the trail. Fidelium was flying a few inches above her head. Despite her nearly crushing tiredness, having Fidelium to warn her of dangers was reassuring. His presence was uplifting as well. She could not interpret his thoughts. She assumed he was unable to interpret hers. Therefore, there was no banter between them. Yet she was thrilled to have the company. Especially after what happened on the path to Crostim Ledge. She had been traumatized by Nessa's death.

She was thinking, I miss Steph. And DooDad. Galadriel and Haleth too. But most of all I miss Nessa. Why did she have to die? She was so young, pretty, full of spirit. She was my best Bkotn warrior friend! And why did Siofra slay her, stab her in the back? That was so cowardly! Surely, it was not because Nessa was taking me to the ledge. I had read Nessa's mind the night before. Siofra was supposed to accompany us. Could it be Siofra, maybe others, were involved in a scheme to kidnap me? to prevent me from seeing Godroh? to stop me from doing what Jordyn said I must do? to confront Wendigorium? She shuddered. Or worse, kill me? If so, why? I have not hurt anyone! And what about Steph? Is she in danger? Gosh, I hope not. DooDad as well.

Then again, could all this be because Nessa spoke with me occasionally? Elbereth had cautioned all of them not to engage Steph and me in conversation. But a few had. We had become friends. Gosh, poor, poor Nessa. I wonder if someone will tell her mother. She loves – loved her mother so much. She said her mother was enormously proud of her too.

*****

Pleasingly melodious chirps, beeps, and tweets of gorgeous, multicolored songbirds seemed to accompany Ava as she walked. The songsters were calling out to each other as they flitted playfully amongst the towering trees bordering the trail. Their delightful songs helped to uplift her spirits as she plodded on.

Because she is a musician and loves music, Ava appreciates musical harmony. Thus, the countless chirps sounded to her like a woodwind ensemble. But there was one small problem. Because of her weakened, irritable state of body and mind, the carefree songs of the feathered ensemble started to sound like an inharmonious mishmash. They began to get on her nerves. She unexpectedly shouted at one point, surprising even herself with the nasty tone of her voice.

"Shut up! Everyone shut up now. You are driving me insane!" In reaction to her loud shouts, a hush fell over the nearby trees of the forest. She was relieved that Fidelium did not seem perturbed by her shouts. He continued flying above her head. She quickly realized she had rudely squashed the comforting choruses that had initially brought her smiles.

"Oh, now I feel so darned stupid – for shouting at you like I am a maniac or something equally absurd. Sorry, guys. It is not your fault I am hopelessly irritable and drained beyond words. Please resume your singing and all. It makes me feel better."

The birds' songs resumed a few minutes later.

Ava was thinking to herself; I should be scared senseless. Here I am all alone not knowing where I am headed. And what I will find when I get to wherever that is going to be. But, oddly, I do not feel frightened in the least. But gosh, I feel so incredibly sad. All I can think about is poor Nessa and all the Bkotn warriors that will miss her vivacity. This is the first time I have witnessed death – or perhaps envisioned it in my mind. Will these unhappy thoughts ever leave me?

Ava knew it was important to keep her mind occupied, to help her forget the tragedy that had occurred and her ever-increasing tiredness. She started to whistle the happy birthday song. "Because it is a new day," she said to no one as she quickened her pace. "And hopefully it will lead to even brighter days."

She smiled when she heard the unmistakable whistle of a *yuki* that was darting in and out of the tree branches as she walked. The large, exceedingly shy bird mimics whistled songs of other birds and the simple melodies of elves and wizarding humans. Nessa had told her that when elves and humans trek the trails alone, they usually whistle tunes. The yuki's copycat whistles afford the traveler's much welcome company. Like the khni, the yuki also tends to warn travelers of impending danger. If the bird stops whistling, one can assume that danger is afoot.

"Tweedy-tweet-tweet-tweet-toot," chirruped the yuki. "Tweedy-tweet-tweet-tweet-toot," and so on until, mimicking Ava's melody, it repeated the tune once more.

Other yuki's soon followed along, creating an endless string of melodies. A few seconds later the combined whistling began to sound like a round (such as the round row, row, row your boat.). But before long, Ava's original happy birthday melody turned in to a cacophonous disaster. Even so, she thought it was wonderful to hear the birds' songs, chirps, and cheeps. It made her feel a bit happier.

As she walked the downhill trail, she saw many creatures. Some she recognized; others were unfamiliar to her. Most scurried to the forest as she approached. Unlike before when she was with Steph and the others, she did not stop to pursue them. She dared not give in to her curiosity since she was alone with only Fidelium for protection. Now and then, one of the more intelligent-looking creatures stopped and watched as she passed. She assumed they were sizing her up, deciding if she was hostile or friendly.

She was thinking; surely, they have seen elves walking this trail. Probably witches and wizards as well. After all, this is a well-used trail. Considering the way they are staring at me; I wonder if they know I am not of the Inner World. Animals are more intuitive than humans in the Earthly World. I would imagine they are more intuitive in the Inner World as well. More so than wizarding humans and elves, probably fairies too.

Ava has similar physical characteristics of other elves. Her similar features have to do with her physique. Like many elves of the Inner World, her slim and well-toned body bears out her athleticism and powerful muscles. This despite her standing five feet two inches tall. Similarly, she has shoulder-length, light brown hair with a reddish tint along with light brown eyes and eyebrows – all common physical qualities of Inner World elves. Therefore, to other intelligent creatures, wizarding humans, elves, and fairies, she looks just like one more, ordinary elf of the Inner World.

On the other hand, Ava has features that easily distinguish her from other Inner World elves. The first noticeable difference has to do with her facial attributes. Her face is heart shaped. She has a prominent chin. She also has charming folds in her cheeks, commonly known as smile lines or laugh lines. Elves of the Inner World have square faces. There are no folds visible in their cheeks when they frown or laugh. She is also the spitting image of her grandfather Jim and great uncle as it relates to their prominent noses. Their dad, her great grandfather, had a prominent nose as well.

The next noticeable difference in comparison to other elves concerns Ava's eyebrows. Male and female elves of the Inner World have distinctive, S-shaped, thick eyebrows. While Ava's light brown eyebrows are thick, with a reddish tint like her hair, they are straight. Her eyebrows also have a soft but noticeable, full arch over the center of her eyes. This slight difference is particularly obvious to observant creatures of the Inner World. Because they instinctively focus on another's eyes and facial features for any sign of hostility – or friendliness. Dogs of the Earthly World do the same thing. They look directly into humans' eyes to read their countenances.

Another difference is the way Ava wears her hair. She always wears her shoulder-length hair in a low ponytail. Many Inner World female elves wear their hair in a bun that is tightly wrapped at the base of the neck. Others allow their hair to fall straight. The Timere female elves that live high above the Solenom River wrap their hair in two buns worn at either side of the head. Sort of like the actress, Princess Leia, of the movie *Star Wars.*

Lastly, the most obvious distinction between Ava and other elves of the Inner World has to do with linguistics. She was raised in the northern American state of Illinois of the Earthly World. Therefore, whenever she converses with others in Fortunomy her Earthly World North American accent is evident as soon as she opens her mouth.

At one point Ava had a brief encounter with a family of gnomes on the trail. There were four gnomes, a mother and father, and their two children – an adolescent male and a toddler female. Gnomes are secretive creatures, and one seldom sees them along any of Artonia's trails. They instantly duck into tree trunk crevices or hide behind rocks when strangers are nearby. The tallest adult gnomes are only two feet tall, so they can easily hide from sight. Females are usually a few inches shorter. Gnomes are so stealthy given their small stature; entire tribes of gnomes can encircle their prey without detection.

The little boy gnome was as handsome as he was charming. He wore a bright red cloak that hung to his knobby knees. He also sported a bright red hat with a dark red quill feather protruding from its rim. The feather was probably from a khni bird. No creature of the forest would ever harm the khni. Ava assumed that the gnome had plucked the feather from the forest floor.

The boy was undeniably spirited as he was brave. He gleefully dragged his mother by the hand to get a better glimpse of Ava as she approached. With his reluctant mother in toe, the gnome fearlessly stepped onto his side of the trail with an air of triumph. He let go of his mother's hand. Then he spread his legs wide apart and placed his hands on his hips. With a huge smile, he said hello in Fortunomy.

Ava did not want to alarm the youngster's mother even more. So, she moved to walk on the other side of the trail. "Well, hello, young sir," she said gaily. "It is a grand day for a stroll, isn't it?" She yearned to stop and chat with the interesting, brave gnome, but she thought better of it. It was a good thing she did not stop. As soon as she was a few feet from the youngster, his frantic father grabbed him by the collar of his tunic and pulled him in the thicket. The foursome was well out of sight a few seconds later. But they were not out of hearing distance. The young gnome's mother was scolding him like there was no tomorrow.

4

It was a little after midday on the Kuoino. The Etanpioa had stopped for the midday meal.

Steph was hollering at Morwen. "You tell me where she is or so help me God, I will beat you to a pulp. I am fed up with your procrastinating. Tell me right now where Ava is and what you are going to do about it. Or I will speak to Elbereth myself!"

"You may not speak with Elbereth without my permission," Morwen asserted. "I have told you that at least five times now. I will handle this matter on my terms. Perhaps I will dispatch a party to find out where your friend, Ava, has disappeared to. Perhaps I will not. In any case, there is no need to bother Elbereth. Furthermore, it is my understanding that this may not be the first time your friend has disappeared." She cocked her head to one side and let out a gratifying groan. "Am I correct with what I am saying?"

Steph stared at her indifferently and did not reply. She looked furious. Her jaw was clenched, and her hands kept opening and closing at her side in powerful, white-knuckled fists. She felt like punching Morwen in the nose because of the older elf's incompetent attitude.

Morwen said with a nasty grin, "So, I presume she will return eventually, unharmed I expect."

"No, this is not the first time she has gone missing," Steph said in an angry tone. "Not that it matters. But this time she has gone missing with one of your warriors. She is with Nessa. I told you that repeatedly. Therefore, I would expect you would be concerned for Nessa if not for Ava."

Steph had been hesitant to tell Morwen that she knew where Ava and Nessa may have gone. She did not want to get Nessa in trouble. But she and Ava had been missing since the night before. And she was getting more worried as the minutes ticked by. As a result, she figured it was time to reveal everything that she knew. But only bit by bit. She did not trust Morwen. She trusted Siofra even less. The duo always seems to be gossiping, warily glancing around to make certain no one was eavesdropping on their conversations.

She thought to herself; why is that? What are you too scheming? Are the two of you somehow involved in Ava's disappearance? Nessa's as well? By the way, where in the heck is your number three in command anyway?

"And I think I know where they are," Steph said in a sarcastic tone. She eyed Morwen suspiciously. "And I think *you know as well.*"

Morwen said angrily, "Oh, you do, do you? Why are you telling me this now? And what makes you think I know where they have gone off to? Why would I concern myself with a disobedient warrior that violates orders and your foolish, repeatedly vanishing friend, Ava?"

Steph said flat out, "Because the third in command of your Etanpioa, Siofra, may be with them, that is why!" She moved forward a few steps. She was inviting Morwen into her personal space. She was taunting the older elf to do something that would give her cause to reveal the powerful energy of her rugby kicks. "And if you are as good as a leader as you think you are," she said with a sneer, "then you will know the whereabouts of your subordinate, Siofra." She moved in even closer until they were standing less than a foot apart. She looked up into the much taller elf's eyes. "Unless, you are a poor leader, Morwen." She chuckled. "Could it be, Morwen? Are you a poor leader? It seems that you are since you lost contact with your immediate subordinate."

Morwen had been glaring at Steph with unblinking eyes. She had a loathsome expression on her face and was shaking with fury. Steph returned her stare unflinchingly.

Morwen angrily hissed in a whisper, "You do not frighten me; you are nothing more than a disrespectful, worthless Outsider elf! How dare you speak to me in this manner. I could run you through with my blade right now, and no one here would speak a word. You and your ridiculous friend, Ava, and the two absurd fairies, they are nothing to me, to us Bkotn warriors." She coughed up phlegm and spit it at Steph's feet. "The four of you are nothing but a major inconvenience, something to discard with the gnawed bones of our dinner, to rid ourselves of your rotting stench. You are nothing more than garbage to me."

Steph said flippantly, "So, you are telling me you do not know where your subordinate and one of your warriors have gone off to. Well, if that is the case, I will take matters into my own hands." She stepped backward. "Because you are not capable of doing so considering you are a useless leader." Before Morwen could reply or make a move, she turned on her heels and raced to the front of the column. She was shouting as she ran. "Elbereth, may I please have a word with you? It is a matter of great urgency. It involves Ava, the Great Wizard Godroh, and one of your warriors."

In reaction to Steph's shouts, the entire Etanpioa pointed their weapons at her. Steph stopped running and slowly walked toward the leader. The others were attentive to each step that she was taking. They were justifiably anxious. No warrior or even another elf could approach their leader without expressed permission. It was only because Steph was Ava's companion that they did not shoot her straight away.

Vena abruptly stepped in front of Steph. She held her hand out motioning for Steph to stop. She yelled, "You may not; I repeat that you may not call out to Elbereth in this manner! You may not approach her as well. Back away now, or I will be forced to stop you!"

With one powerful, forceful jab, Steph roughly elbowed Vena aside. Vena stumbled and plummeted to the ground. She grabbed her lance and scrambled to her feet. She was about to advance toward Steph when Elbereth's commanding voice roared, stopping her midstride.

"You will not harm her, Vena! Lay down your weapon. Now!" Vena gave her a questionable look. "I said lay down your weapon now! The rest of you as well. And Vena, I want you to report to Siofra immediately."

Steph said casually, "She cannot report to Siofra." Elbereth was staring at her with a curious expression. "That is because Siofra, as well as Ava and Nessa, are missing. They have been missing since last night. Morwen and I were just discussing their disappearance. In fact, we have been talking about their disappearance since yesterday. Also, Morwen has refused my request to seek an audience with you on five occasions. She has done nothing to find Ava, your third in command, or Nessa."

"What?" Elbereth said in a dumbfounded manner. She glared at Morwen. Her second in command was standing directly behind Steph. Unbeknownst to Steph, the tip of Morwen's tkalakn was mere inches from the back of her neck.

"Is there anything you wish to tell me about this, Morwen?" Elbereth shouted. "Is what Steph has told me the truth? If so, why have you not informed me of their disappearances? You know that we must do everything possible to protect Ava." She glanced around at the others. "And since last night? All the while we have been marching since dawn, opening the distance between her and the others, and I was not told? Also, Morwen, sheath your tkalakn. Do it now!"

Morwen did not reply. She was staring at Elbereth with a blank-faced expression. After a few moments she carefully sheathed her tkalakn. Even so, she did not move away from Steph.

Elbereth speedily reached behind to her quiver. She placed an arrow on her bowstring and aimed it in Steph and Morwen's direction. Her actions were so speedy, she completely caught Steph and the others by surprise. Steph's eyes widened in panic. She started to tremble.

Oh my God! Is she going to shoot me? Because I am talking to her without permission?

Elbereth said to Steph quietly in a commanding tone, "Steph, move away from Morwen now, now I tell you!"

Steph, at last aware that Morwen was standing behind her, turned around. She quickly sidestepped to her left and glared at Morwen. Her face had reddened but not because Elbereth had pointed her armed bow in her direction. She was livid that Morwen had snuck up behind her without her realizing it!

Elbereth said in a firm tone, "Steph, I want you to come and stand beside me." She glared at Morwen and then at Vena. Vena was standing next to Morwen. The young elf's expression was defiant, hostile. She was staring at Elbereth straight in the eyes. Elbereth instinctively knew what was about to occur if she did not retain control. Morwen, with Vena's assistance, was on the threshold of a coup d'état.

Lia, who was being punished by Siofra, snatched a longbow from the ground and an arrow from its quiver. She quickly placed an arrow on the bowstring. She aimed the arrow at Vena and slowly moved to stand beside Elbereth. Her eyes were riveted on Vena as she yanked back on the bowstring.

Steph moved to stand beside Lia. She hesitantly placed an arrow on the bowstring of her longbow. Like Ava, she had never shot an arrow in self-defense or anger. She was reluctant to do so right then. But she knew she would shoot if she had to. Like Elbereth, she sensed that an attempted coup was in progress. She loosened the tension on the bowstring slightly and pointed her longbow at the ground. She dreaded the thought of accidentally shooting one of Elbereth's warriors without provocation.

In response to Lia aiming her arrow at her, Vena lifted the lance high above her head. With a repulsive snigger and cold, bulging eyes, she aimed the lance at Elbereth. Then she looked straight at Steph and redirected the lance at her.

Elbereth cocked her head to one side. She raised one eyebrow and gave Vena a glassy stare. She broke out in an arrogant laugh. She was not intimidated by Vena's threatening look or actions. Vena was no match for her quickness. Before Vena would even cock her arm to hurl her lance, Elbereth would have pushed Steph out of harm's way. A split-second later her arrow would have flown true and hit Vena square in the chest before she even threw her lance. She was about to say something to Vena then stopped short. Instead, she shouted, "Haleth, Galadriel, Aredhel! Relieve Morwen and Vena of their weapons. Do it now!" She glared at Morwen and then at Vena. "Elanor, Yavanna! Assist them, and then bind them."

Before Vena could react, Haleth and Aredhel grabbed her from behind and roughly shoved her to the ground. Haleth knelt on her back. She withdrew Vena's knife from its scabbard and hurled it to the forest. Yavanna grabbed Vena's lance and tossed it out of her reach. Then Haleth removed a coil of rope from inside her cloak and set out to bind Vena's wrists.

Galadriel, Elanor, and Yavanna hesitated. They were uncertain about confronting Morwen, to relieve the second in command of her weapons and to constrain her.

"Elbereth shouted, "Morwen no longer is my second in command. She is relieved forthwith." She glanced over at Galadriel. "Galadriel, you are now my second in command. At least until we know the whereabouts and condition of Siofra. So, take charge as I instructed you." She pulled back on the bowstring. "If Morwen makes a move to harm any of you, it will be her last." Then glancing in Lia's direction, she said in a soft voice, "There are traitors among us. Shoot the prisoner, Morwen, if necessary. To disable. Not to kill. Do not wait for my orders if she makes a move toward Galadriel and the others. Do you understand?"

Lia nodded her head and stood solidly at the ready.

CHAPTER 7

HALDIR OF MOUNTAINS CROSS

"One can always repay a debt of gold. But one is eternally indebted to evil."
—the author

1

"She is dead, murdered," Siofra exclaimed miserably. Her grimy face was streaked with tears. She was sitting on the forest floor, her back resting against a tree. She had been in the same position since nightfall, going on twelve hours. She had not slept a wink. Nessa's head was cradled on her lap. She had undone Nessa's braids some time ago and was stroking the long strands of her hair lovingly. She looked up at Haldir.

The Mountains Cross wicked wizard stared down at her with an empty expression. He had not said a word since he arrived some time ago.

Haldir's seemingly uncaring attitude made Siofra feel even gloomier. She muttered without looking up, "And I am the one who killed her." She kissed Nessa's pallid cheek then spoke to her lovingly in a whisper. "I never intended to harm anyone, Nessa. I never intended to kill. I truly am sorry." She looked up at Haldir again. "But I did kill her – because she is dead! Strangely, I do not recall consciously doing it, thrusting my blade in her body. But I did it all the same. How could I have done such a thing, Haldir? Her back was turned to me. I behaved like a coward. I have violated my oath as well. An oath I took eons ago. I have forsaken a Bkotn. I have slain an innocent warrior."

That was the second time in her life that Siofra had come across Haldir. The first time was nearly two hundred years earlier. She was not in a position of command at the time. She was a typical, underling Bkotn warrior. It was her first journey on the Kuoino. She understood the stories, had heard them for generations. Stories about the mysteries surrounding the notorious trail of Artonia. Travelers vanishing without a trace. How the ghostly mist seemed to pull the unsuspecting inside its hold, never to be seen again. She knew that Artonia was otherworldly, bewitched. But she never believed she would watch every one of her fellow warriors vanish. That she would be the last remaining soul. To survive and to recount her horrific story to others.

She and the others of her Etanpioa had purposely gone off the trail in search of food and water. Up to that point, they had gone nine days without a drop of water. Earthly World humans cannot go three or four days without water. But elves are more resilient. Yet they too must have water after eight or nine days, or they will die. Three warriors of Siofra's Etanpioa had already succumbed to dehydration.

The Etanpioa leader, her name was Elva, had no other choice but to seek sustenance in the bowels of Artonia's murkiness. As if by chance, the skies opened the next day with a four-day deluge. At least Siofra and the others had drinking water. Yet they still had nothing to eat. The forest seemed empty of creatures they could hunt. There scarcely was edible vegetation to scrounge from the forest floor. The lichen and moss were known to be poisonous. Soon they were too weak to move on or to defend themselves properly if attacked. They made camp and stayed put to await their certain fate.

Two more warriors perished in the ensuing days of suffering. They had been fighting over the decayed, stinking carcass of a bird. Both died from their critical wounds. The Etanpioa was down to eight warriors. Then on the twelfth night, Elva walked off into the murky mist. They called after her, but they were too weak to stop her. They never saw her again.

Elva's absence left Siofra in charge of what remained of her starving, tattered Etanpioa. Despite her weakened condition, she tried to rally her warriors, to encourage them to press on. However, she was largely unsuccessful. They were too weak to travel. So was Siofra. She quickly lost hope.

The belugas that had been stalking the Etanpioa for days began to close in. They knew that the elves were starving and too weak to defend themselves properly. Nevertheless, they realized that even a dying, famished Bkotn is ferocious, and she will never surrender without a fight to the death. It is in keeping with their code of honor.

The belugas, obviously of the intelligent species known as the déxypnos, crept up on the elves as they slept. Then they stealthily subdued the elves one by one. They gagged them, and then they stole them away. Within three days, Siofra was the only warrior remaining in her Etanpioa. Still, she was determined to resist to her dying breath.

The night Haldir saved her, the belugas had crept up on her silently as she slept. There were just about to grab and gag her when Haldir appeared.

Siofra, awoken when Haldir muttered a few unintelligible words, gawked at him awestricken. He was pointing his wand at the terrified belugas. There were five of them. They tried to flee, but he said a few more words, and they froze in place. A split-second later a green light discharged from the tip of his wand. The petrified belugas' bodies fell apart immediately and formed countless clouds of minuscule, grayish splinters. Then the splinters merged as one and unhurriedly drifted like an eerie ghost to the treetops where they disappeared.

After regaining her strength somewhat over two days – Haldir had fed her morsels of food – Siofra recounted her story to him. She told how she and the others were slowly dying of thirst. Then starvation took over. With tearful eyes, she recounted how the belugas had stolen her comrades in the night one after another. Until all that remained of her Etanpioa was her.

It was then that Haldir stated the belugas did not slay her comrades. "Quite the opposite. They will nourish your fellow warriors until they are healthier and stronger. They will treat them with civility. Then they will sell them as slaves to the Joini."

Siofra had never heard of the Joini.

Haldir explained that the Joini are the nastiest, most self-serving, corrupt dwarves of the Inner World, including Antiquom. He had explained, "Dwarves and elves do not get along well, at least commonly. It has been this way since the beginning of time. There are some exceptions of course. A few elven communities get along nicely with communities of dwarves. But elves never get along with the Joini.

"That is because the Joini is a different breed from all others of the dwarfish type. They do not work the gold, silver, and gem mines themselves. Rather, they use forced labor – elves, fairies, trolls, even gnomes. The same creatures must tend to their needs as well. Making clothing. Preparing food. Performing domestic tasks. I must admit, the Joini feed, clothe, and shelter their forced labor reasonably. They do not beat or whip them. Yes, there are punishments, but nothing physical thank goodness. But their decent treatment of slaves does not apply to those they meet in battle. In battle, the Joini are ruthless and cruel. They are even known to slay the wounded unfit to work their mines."

With a furrowed brow he added in a disgusted tone, "Anyway, despite their cruelty in battle, to use others as forced labor, as slaves, goes against the Inner World's Code of Peace, Love, and Harmony. Every civilized creature knows that. Then again what is a wizard such as I to do? I alone cannot confront the Joini. They are a million strong at least and, as I said, heartless in battle."

Siofra was grateful that Haldir had saved her life. He had nourished her until she was strong enough to walk. Then he had led her out of the forest so she could travel the trail to the Unseen Valley. It was then, when they were standing on the trail, that Haldir voiced his warning words. He had looked at her straight on when he spoke.

"I hope you know, my dear elven, Siofra, that you now owe me a debt, an obligation for saving your life."

Siofra replied, "I imagine repaying another for saving one's life comes at a great cost?"

"Indeed, it does," Haldir answered coolly. "Indeed, it does." Then he walked off into the forest.

Siofra had seldom thought about Haldir over the hundreds of years and only then whenever she retold her story. That was until the Etanpioa was commissioned to escort Ava when Morwen told her that Haldir wanted to kidnap the young elf. As she lovingly cradled Nessa's head, Siofra sensed that the time for repaying her debt to Haldir finally had arrived.

As if he had read her mind, Haldir nodded his head and smiled. The lines of his aged forehead seemed to smile as well. His green eyes were sparkling, full of life and joy. The strands of his scrabbly white beard that hung to his waist wiggled as he laughed raucously. His laugh was icy cold, taunting, unpleasant to the ear.

Siofra started to shiver.

"My dear elven, Siofra, yes indeed. You are correct. The moment has arrived for you to fulfill your obligation." He glanced down at Nessa. It was the first time he had looked at the slain warrior.

"I regret to say not doing so will result in you taking her place."

2

Haldir gestured to Nessa's lifeless body. His tone was cavalier as he said, "She is not dead."

"What are you talking about?" Siofra exclaimed as she gawked at him. Her tone of voice was gloomy, incredibly sad. "I killed her, Haldir. The back of her cloak is covered in blood. She is not breathing. There is no heartbeat. She is dead I tell you! She has been dead since last night!"

Haldir removed his wand from his cloak. He smiled deviously and began to tap the palm of his hand with the wand. "You have seen death many times, my dear elven, Siofra, yes?" Siofra nodded her head hesitantly. "So, you know how the coldness of death feels. Is she cold? Are her joints rigid? Have her muscles hardened?"

"Why no, none of that," Siofra replied. She looked flabbergasted. "But how, Haldir? What does all this mean? How can it be? Why has death not set in?"

"It is sorcery, my dear elven, Siofra. Effortless wizarding sorcery."

"And what about the other elf, Ava?" Siofra said. "Has she been found? Have you captured her?"

Haldir shook his head. The look on his weary face was one of mystification. He replied, "No. She was too quick. She vanished before I could hex her. She is a slippery one, she is. She moves through the forest effortlessly as a winged creature moves through the air. If I did not know better, I would say that she is magical." He pointed his wand at Nessa's forehead. Green light radiated from its tip. Together, Siofra and Nessa were gradually swathed in an ever-growing, soft, greenish glow. Siofra's blue eyes started to glaze over. Her eyes had a strange, distant look as she stared at Haldir out-of-focus.

Nessa all at once turned her head to one side and started coughing and sneezing, breaking Siofra's hypnotic stare.

Ahem. Cough-cough. Atishoo! Cough-cough. Atishoo!

Nessa's eyelids fluttered, and then she opened her eyes and stared up at Siofra. She was smiling a little, like a child who had just awakened from a nap and sees her mother's face.

Cough-cough. Atishoo!

Siofra gently stroked her cheek and smiled. It was a forced smile since she dimly recalled she had murdered Nessa. She also recognized that Haldir had deceived her agonized mind with his gruesome, cunning spell. She said in a gentle, loving tone, "That is good, Nessa. Cough it up. Clear your lungs."

Nessa turned her head to the side once more.

Cough-cough-cough. Atishoo!

"Are you feeling better?" Siofra asked in a soft-hearted manner. Nessa nodded her head. "For some reason, you fainted. Then you must have hit your head when you fell. You have been asleep since yesterday evening. I have been tending to you ever since. I never left your side." She stretched her arms and yawned. "I too must have fallen asleep. I feel so strange."

"I fainted?" Nessa exclaimed in a shaky, disbelieving tone. Her voice was unsteady, nearly imperceptible. She stared up at Haldir. His back was turned to her and Siofra. Her eyes suddenly widened with a worrisome realization. With a voice that was elevated in pitch and volume, she sat right up and cried, "Where is Ava? Is she here?" She looked around anxiously. "Where is she, Siofra? Do you know what has become of her?"

"She ran off," Siofra said in an untroubled manner. She pointed to her left. "Right over there. I called after her, but she would not listen. She took off after you fell. Probably because she wanted to see Crostim Ledge with or without you. You know how curious she tends to be. She probably returned to the Etanpioa, leaving you here to die." Her lips curled upward in a smile. "I had to tend to you, so I did not bother myself with her. She is nothing to me."

Nessa tried to get to her feet. But she was too weak and unable to stand. She laid her head against Siofra's chest.

"Remain motionless," Siofra said in a soothing tone. "You must not move too quickly. Give your body time to recover from the fall."

Nessa wailed, "But Ava, Siofra. We must find her. She is—" She stopped midsentence because Haldir had abruptly turned around. He was staring down at her. His brow was furrowed. Nessa did not like his questioning look.

"She is what?" Siofra said coolly in a flat voice.

Nessa noticed that Siofra's attitude continued to be indifferent as it concerned Ava. Even though she respected Siofra, more so because she *had to* rather than the older elf *deserving* it, she would not reveal Ava's identity. Especially in front of the man she assumed was a wizard. She swore an oath to Steph that she would not disclose Ava's identity to anyone.

She is too important for others to know the facts. The more that know her secret, the more danger she will have.

Nessa stared into Siofra's eyes. She was searching to find a clue to explain everything that had happened. Especially why Siofra seemed unmoved by Ava's fate.

But why would Ava run off after I fell? Had something frightened her? She would never run off if I were injured. No, I am certain she would have remained with me. She is too loyal, too courageous, too much of a friend. Did I faint, or did something else happen to me? Hmm, I wonder—

Nessa's eyes suddenly widened.

And I recall speaking to Ava in my mind. Telling her to run away. To escape. Because I had felt a sudden, excruciating pain in my back, and I did not want her to be in danger. Oh, my goodness! I was speaking to Ava in my mind before I died! Had Siofra murdered me, but somehow, I was brought back to life by this evil-looking wizard who is staring down at me?

"Do not worry about Ava," Siofra said tersely. She closed her eyes to shut out the dreadful, murderous thoughts in the back of her mind. She opened her eyes after a few moments and stared blank-faced at Nessa. "She is nothing to me, to us. Just another lowly elf." She moved a lock of hair from Nessa's eyes. "In contrast, you are a fellow Bkotn warrior. You are priceless to me. We will find Ava sooner or later." She looked at Haldir. "One way or the other we will find her. I promise."

"We must seek to find her!" Nessa said in a low voice. She gripped Siofra's cloak and tried to pull herself up. She gasped, "We must find her." Her face abruptly paled as she whispered, "But Siofra what if we cannot find her?"

"Then we do not," Siofra said indifferently. She stood, and then she helped Nessa to her feet. "Then the forest will have claimed another of its prey." She winked at Haldir.

"Such is life, Nessa. Such is life."

3

"Please sit next to me," Elbereth said to Steph. "You as well, Galadriel. There are many things we must discuss." She shouted to Lia. "Lia, please come here!"

Lia rushed over to Elbereth and bowed. She said in a humble tone, "Yes, ma'am?"

"You performed admirably today. You are hereby relieved of your punishment."

With a cheery smile that highlighted her youthful face, Lia said, "Why thank you. Thank you. I am honored by your words, your praises." She bowed deeply. She looked at Steph and then at Galadriel. "If you desire nothing more of me, I shall leave you three to discuss your affairs." She glanced over her shoulder. "To assist the guarding of the prisoners."

"No," Elbereth said softly. "Your loyalty and courage inspired me despite your youthful age and innocence. You deserve to know what caused these unfortunate events. I will highly regard your opinions as we talk." She motioned to the ground next to where she was sitting. "Please sit next to me." Then she said to Steph, "Please begin. Tell me everything."

Steph took a deep breath. Then she began to summarize the heated conversation she had with Ava the previous night. It was when Ava told her that she, Nessa, and Siofra were going to sneak off and visit Crostim Ledge. It was to happen during the Etanpioa game. At first, she was not going to tell Elbereth about Siofra's involvement. She had read Ava's thoughts that revealed Nessa was not supposed to tell Ava about Siofra accompanying them. Then, making certain no one knew of Siofra's intentions, Ava had whispered that very same fact. Consequently, considering that Ava had said what she did out loud, Steph did not think she was revealing their telepathic powers. Also, considering Morwen's suspicious behavior, she assumed that Siofra almost certainly was involved in the conspiracy. That is if there was a conspiracy in the first place.

Steph also considered there was everything to gain by telling Elbereth all that she knew. The more than Elbereth knew, the better their chances of finding Ava. She knew that the Bkotn warriors gossiped like a flock of cackling female hens. Therefore, eventually, the entire Etanpioa certainly would guess that Ava was the revered O Poica Katharos. That is if they already did not suspect it given the deferential treatment Elbereth bestowed on her.

I would not doubt anything at this point, Steph considered silently. I told Nessa of Ava's identity. She could have told everyone, including Morwen and Siofra, although I doubt that she did. She swore an oath to protect our secret. Nevertheless, anything is possible. Despite everything, I should assume Elbereth already knows Ava's identity. If I were Godroh, I would have told her. It makes perfect sense.

Elbereth said to Steph, "Do you believe Siofra is involved, that she too is working on a secret plan? A plan that involves your friend, Ava?" She glanced over at Morwen.

Morwen was sitting on the ground with her wrists bound behind her. Her head was hung low. Vena was sitting beside her. She was equally sullen, yet she was giving Steph nasty looks. Elanor and Yavanna were guarding them.

Elbereth said, "I have never trusted Siofra completely. Then again, I have no cause to distrust her motives. Only her poor judgment." Addressing Steph once more she said, "Your thoughts?"

"I have no reason to suspect Siofra's motives," Steph replied in a forthright tone. "She is in your charge, not mine. All I know is that we must find Ava. I have no other purpose than to protect her, protect her with my life if necessary. I took an oath. I promised."

Galadriel glanced at Elbereth for consent to speak. Elbereth nodded her head. Galadriel said to Steph, "I have a few questions. First, please give us more details about your fairy friend telling you that your goblet was hexed."

Steph restated everything she knew about the possible magical spell. She ended by saying, "Maybe that is why I acted so cruelly toward Ava. I had never insulted or scolded her in that manner like I did last night."

"Where are your two friends, Doo and Dad?" Galadriel said. "I have not seen them today."

Steph replied, "They are searching for Ava. They left after sunset, yesterday evening." She frowned. "When Ava did not return. They knew that she was with Nessa. I also told them I suspected Siofra was with her as well."

"I see," Galadriel said. She leaned in closer to Steph and whispered, "Why is it you vowed to protect her, your friend, Ava?" She was staring which caused Steph to feel a bit uncomfortable. "Yes, we have been told that Ava, like you, has a purpose. However, I suspect Ava's purpose is much more vital than your own. She is the one who must seek council with the Great Wizard, not you." She eyed Steph suspiciously, and then she said with a sincere smile, "So, Steph, please tell us why she must confer with Godroh. Do you know?" She calmly moved a wisp of her scarlet hair from her dazzling blue eyes. "I think you know her real purpose. You do, do you not? Am I correct?"

As Steph returned Galadriel's stare, she wordlessly considered that the young elf was as cunning as she was intelligent. In addition to being stunningly attractive, with facial features and a hair color completely different than her colleagues, she was shrewd.

An excellent choice as second in command too. A born leader with evident qualities to take the lead of others.

"I have no idea," Steph lied. "All I know is I am to protect her. That is all."

"I see," Galadriel said in a low voice. Her tone of voice and the raising of one eyebrow suggested she was skeptical despite Steph's words. "I shall abide your word." She shrugged her shoulders. "What more can I do? Even so, if you know more about Ava than what you are telling us—" she paused briefly. "Then," she looked at Elbereth who was nodding her head, "I urge you to tell us when you know when it suitable for you to do so. You can trust us, Steph." She gestured at Elbereth and

Lia in turn. "We too have sworn an oath in this matter. We believe the oath Godroh made us swear through our leader is exceptionally unique. Quite unusual actually."

"And what oath was that?" Steph asked dubiously. She looked at the others. "What made it so unusual, so unique?"

Elbereth said quietly, "Like you, I also pledged to sacrifice my life to protect Ava. The Great Wizard Godroh made me swear that I would forfeit my life as well as those of my Etanpioa to protect her. Then I made my warriors take the same oath. Moreover, Godroh said that if required, we should be willing to witness the death of all Bkotn elves, our entire Tribe, if we do not adhere to our oath, to protect Ava."

Steph said in a weak voice, "You know who Ava is, am I correct, Elbereth?"

Elbereth nodded her head and said, "Yes, I do know Ava's identity. But no one else does. As Ava's best friend of the Earthly World perhaps you should be the one to tell the others starting with these two." She looked at Galadriel and Lia in turn. "In that manner, they will double their efforts to find Ava. She will have their unquestionable loyalty as well."

Steph briefly gazed into the eyes of Galadriel and Lia one by one as she chewed on her lower lip. She was deep in thought. As her gaze rested on Elbereth once more, a single tear squeezed from her eye. She had to look away as her face blushed. She lowered her head, swallowed hard, and whispered.

"Ava is Avaïnoάel, O Poica Katharos – the Purest of Elves."

In reaction to what Steph had said, Lia stared at her with a look of astonishment. Galadriel and Elbereth exchanged knowing smiles.

Galadriel said, "Steph, thank you for telling us that. I suspected as much given Ava's mannerisms. The way she wears her hair. A couple of her facial features, her eyebrows for example. Her strange accent. Her accent is unlike anything I have ever heard." She smiled. "Like your accent, Steph, but of a slightly different variety than Ava's. Like she was raised in a different part of the Earthly World than you. Moreover, perhaps more revealing, Ava's strange curiosity is overly mystifying, at least to me. Her strong, inexhaustible interest in just about everything she sees, hears, and touches. Her desire to know about all things."

Galadriel stood up and then moved to sit beside Steph. She wrapped her arm around Steph's shoulder and pulled her close. Steph was trembling. Galadriel gently rubbed her upper arm. "It almost is like Ava unconsciously, impulsively is struggling to reclaim her identity. Although she does not know that she is doing so." She looked at Elbereth and Lia in turn. "It is like our blessed Avaïnoćel has forgotten who she is."

Steph recoiled in surprise. She said in a soft tone, "You are amazing, Galadriel. Doo said the same thing. That Ava has forgotten who she is." She managed a meek smile adding, "Also, congratulations on being selected as the second in command. I am confident you will perform wonderfully and uphold the finest traditions of the Bkotn Tribe."

4

"Elbereth, Galadriel!" Lia shouted excitedly as she scrambled to her feet and pointed. "Look! Siofra and Nessa are coming!"

Steph stood up and straightaway began to shout. "Where is Ava? Tell me where she is, Siofra! What have you done to her! Why is she not with you two!" She quickly positioned an arrow on the bowstring of her bow. She aimed it directly at Siofra. The telltale vein in her neck that appears whenever she is angry was pounding frantically. "Tell me what you have done with Ava, or so help me God I will shoot you!" She sneered. "And I suspect I will be a lousy shot because I am very angry, so the arrow could strike you anywhere!"

Galadriel got to her feet and gently pushed down on Steph's bow, so it was pointing at the ground harmlessly. She said in a commanding whisper, "Steph, no. Please unstring your arrow. Now is not the time to react excessively. If you were to shoot Siofra, the consequences for you would be severe."

Steph glanced over at Elbereth. Unlike the others in the Etanpioa – they were standing, some with their weapons unsheathed – Elbereth was seated. The Bkotn leader appeared relaxed and surprisingly calm. She gestured with a nod of her head for Steph to sit beside her.

Steph gave Siofra a dirty look as she sat beside Elbereth.

"Where is Ava?" Galadriel said in a booming voice. She was eyeing Siofra and Nessa guardedly. "What have you done with her?"

"How dare you speak to me in such a manner, Galadriel!" Siofra growled as she drew nearer to the group. She roughly pushed Nessa aside as she pulled her tkalakn from its sheath. Her eyes darted from Steph to Elbereth and back again to Galadriel. "Move aside Galadriel or I will cut your throat!"

"You will do nothing of the kind!" Elbereth commanded. She got to her feet. Steph did as well. "Galadriel is now my immediate subordinate. She is the second in command of this Etanpioa. You, Siofra, remain third in command, at least for now. Therefore, I insist that you give your superior the respect she deserves. Sheath your tkalakn now."

In reply to what Elbereth said, Siofra smirked. Then she pointed her tkalakn in Galadriel's direction. Galadriel remained calm and unflinching. She walked closer to Siofra as if she were inviting her to start something.

In the blink of an eye, Elbereth positioned an arrow on her longbow and fired. She aimed her shot, so it impacted less than an inch from Siofra's right foot. Elbereth positioned another arrow on her longbow before the others even knew what was taking place.

Siofra gradually moved even closer to Galadriel. She was taunting Elbereth with her bold moves. She looked over at Morwen. The former second in command was smiling and nodding her head. Vena was smiling as well. Siofra could tell they were coaxing her to stay defiant.

Elbereth's eyes darted in Morwen's direction. A sly smile creased her lips because right then and there she knew what was being planned by the trio. Siofra and Morwen, along with Vena's assistance, had been contemplating a coup d'état. Elbereth contemplated that Nessa possibly could be involved as well, but she seriously doubted it.

"Siofra, drop your tkalakn now, or you die," Elbereth commanded. She glanced at Nessa. "Move aside, Nessa. Drop your weapons as well." Nessa instantly complied and hurried away from Siofra. Siofra slowly moved even closer to Galadriel. She was glowering at Elbereth.

Elbereth shot another arrow in a blink of an eye. It grazed Siofra's left ankle drawing blood before it impacted the ground.

Siofra did not flinch. She took another step, and then her eyes widened. She had felt a slight prick on the back of her neck and could sense that blood was seeping from the wound.

"Take one more step, milady, and you will die."

Siofra realized it was Lia. She had encircled the group when the others were distracted. Her tkalakn was resting against Siofra's neck.

"Then you will die as well," Siofra said with a grin. "Remember your oath, Lia."

"I will be forgiven," Lia replied defiantly. "If you were to harm our leader or second in command because, like me, you are their subordinate."

Siofra glanced around the Etanpioa and scowled. She saw that all the warriors had their weapons trained on her. She gave them a disgusted look. Then she unsheathed her blade and threw it and her tkalakn to the ground. She glared at Elbereth, coughed up a wad of gunk, and spit.

Elbereth said, "Lia, Steph, retrieve their weapons and bring them to me. Galadriel, guard them."

Galadriel promptly armed her longbow.

Steph and Lia quickly retrieved Siofra and Nessa's weapons and dumped them on the ground next to Elbereth.

Siofra said in a weak voice, "Elbereth, please allow me to—"

Before she could utter another word, Elbereth shouted, "Silence! I will not speak to either of you." She nodded her head in Galadriel's direction. "She is your superior. She will decide when and if I will have a hearing with you." She glared at Siofra and Nessa briefly, and then she slowly turned around, so her back was to them.

In the Bkotn Tribe, turning a back on another is the most profound sign of loathing and disrespect. The other Etanpioa warriors turned their backs to the pair as well, the exception being Galadriel. She was smiling because she saw that all the warriors had their backs to Siofra and Nessa. She walked over to Elbereth and whispered, "My lady, it is over. You have the Etanpioa's loyalty."

Nessa was sobbing and shivering because the Etanpioa had turned their backs to her. She was staring at Elbereth and Galadriel through tear-streaked eyes. Her hands were splayed at her side as if she were saying, "Why me?"

Elbereth remained motionless for a few more seconds. Then she walked off and called over her shoulder, "Steph, Lia, bind the prisoners. Galadriel keep them safe as they do. Then move them to sit with the other traitors. Post one additional guard as well. I do believe Calen is a good choice. But that is your decision."

"I am not to blame!" Siofra screamed. She scowled at Nessa and pointed a trembling finger at her. "It is her fault, not mine. The traitorous, insubordinate Nessa is the one to blame. I saw her and Ava leave the camp during the contest. I followed them to see what they were doing. We are lucky to be alive. If it were not for me—"

"Shut up," Steph yelled angrily, interrupting Siofra before she could say anything else. "You are a despicable liar. I know for a fact of your scheme because Ava told me personally. So, shut your trap, or I will stick my shoe in your mouth and jamb it down your throat!"

Nessa collapsed to her knees. She closed her eyes and lowered her head until it was touching the ground. Steph rushed over to her. She said in a soft voice, "Nessa, please place your hands behind your back. I must bind you." Nessa did as she was told. Whispering close to Nessa's ear as she fumbled with the ropes, Steph said, "You are going to be okay. Elbereth and Galadriel, Lia too; they know the truth. I told them everything."

"Nessa spluttered in between sobs, "Every-everything, St-Steph? You-you-you told them everything? Do-do you mean that—"

"Yes," Steph said. "I told them who Ava is. But Elbereth already knew. Godroh must have told her. And Galadriel guessed the truth. But do not worry about that right now. Ava is strong, resilient, and she is super smart. She can conjure up things, amazing things in her mind that will aid her. I am certain of it. Plus, someone told me she has powers of which she has no clue that she possesses. She may not know it right now, but her instincts will kick in automatically if she is in real danger. I also told the others what Siofra had asked you to do. I told them all about Crostim Ledge. Placing you under arrest is a scam, I am quite certain. They already know that Siofra is the guilty party. That she told you what to do. So, you will be okay. I promise."

"Thank you," Nessa managed to whisper. She let out a huge breath, and her eyes went skyward. She was thankful for Steph's reassuring words about her fate. But most of all, she was encouraged by what Steph had said about Ava. That Ava would persevere despite the dangers of being alone in Artonia.

Steph gently wiped at Nessa's tears with her hands. Then she continued to fumble with the ropes through her watery eyes. "Listen up, Nessa. There is no way I am going to bind your hands. You are innocent.

I am just going to loop the rope around your wrists. So, please do me a favor and hide the ends of the ropes in the palms of your hands. Pretend that I tied them securely, okay?" Nessa smiled meekly and nodded her head. Then Steph helped her to her feet and led her to where the other prisoners were sitting. Although she purposely told Nessa to sit some distance away from the others. She had noticed that Siofra was giving Nessa dirty looks. So was Vena. She said to Calen, "Do not allow the others to draw near to her. If they do, shout out. Understand?" Calen said that she understood.

After Nessa was sitting near the other prisoners, Galadriel said, "It is time to question the two prisoners, Siofra and Nessa."

Siofra shouted in a nasty tone, "Galadriel, since I am third in command, I demand to be summoned before you first." She glared at Nessa. "You must not believe the lies that this disrespectful, wayward warrior is about to tell you. She is going to lie, to try and involve me in her insubordinate scheme."

Completely ignoring Siofra's request, Galadriel said, "Calen, bring Nessa to me." Then she walked a dozen or so paces from where the prisoners were sitting and sat on the ground. The other warriors in the Etanpioa sat down to watch the proceedings from a distance.

Galadriel had made certain the prisoners and their guards as well as the curious onlookers were well beyond earshot. She did not want the others to hear something they should not. Especially if Nessa or Steph were to say something about Ava's identity. Although she figured the entire Etanpioa would know the truth soon enough. Once Nessa was sitting and had composed herself, she said, "Thank you, Calen. Please take a break." She looked at Lia. She would serve as an impartial observer. "Are you ready?" Lia nodded her head and sat down. Then Galadriel said to Steph, she would serve as a witness, "And you?"

Steph replied with a shrug, "Yes, I guess so. But I do not have much to offer that I haven't already told you."

Addressing Nessa, Galadriel said, "I believe you should start. Please start at the beginning."

Nessa began to summarize everything that happened after Siofra told her that she and Ava could visit Crostim Ledge. Somewhere in the middle of her deposition, Steph noted that Nessa had not yet mentioned

Siofra's intention to accompany her and Ava to the ledge. Steph assumed it probably was because of her ingrained loyalty to the Bkotn hierarchy, likewise to Siofra as third in command. Or perhaps she was hesitant to associate Siofra in some alleged, insane conspiracy without evidence or collaboration.

Steph cleared her throat and said casually, "Excuse me for interrupting, Nessa. Perhaps you are omitting a key point." She glanced at Galadriel. She was nodding her head, implying that Steph should continue. "Ava told me that Siofra planned to accompany the two of you to the ledge. That you should not tell Ava or anyone else about her intent. Ava also said that Siofra had obtained Elbereth and Morwen's permission and that the three of you had to be discreet." She smiled at Galadriel and Lia in turn. "Being discreet would ensure that the others would not be jealous of Siofra's scheme; her obvious favoritism of one of her subordinates; and that she wanted to reward Ava." She beamed a sly smile. "You know, for stopping only once during yesterday's march."

Steph knew that Nessa had not told Ava about Siofra's intent to accompany them. That she was obeying Siofra's order, to keep Siofra's connection a secret. Nevertheless, Ava had read Nessa's thoughts concerning Siofra's implied objective. Therefore, Nessa would presume that Ava had telepathic skills and had read her thoughts. But it was a risk Steph was willing to take. If Nessa did not talk about Siofra's involvement, it would weaken her argument considerably. Then the whole thing would boil down to Nessa's word against Siofra's and vice versa. As it turned out, Steph was correct with her assumption.

Nessa had given Steph a curious look, and then she started to tell the truth about Siofra's original intent to accompany her and Ava to the ledge. To Steph's relief, she prudently did not speak to Ava's mind-reading abilities.

The Bkotn typically do not conduct a hearing for warriors that are accused of even the most serious infractions. The Bkotn leader or her second and third in command dole out penalties if warranted. The exception is the murder or the unintended, accidental death of a fellow Bkotn. Then the entire Tribe gets involved. The Tribe decides the punishment with a majority vote, and it never ends in death.

However, given the seriousness of Ava's disappearance, Elbereth decided to conduct an informal hearing. There also was the issue of the alleged, failed coup. But even addressing that possibility or trying to prove a coup had occurred was next to impossible. Especially considering it seemed that only Morwen, Siofra, and Vena were involved. So, Galadriel did not even consider the matter.

After nearly an hour of Nessa's deposition, and back and forth dialogue between Nessa and Galadriel, along with Steph's statements, the hearing was concluded.

Galadriel said, "Nessa, I have decided your fate. You are free of culpability. You were responding to Siofra's orders, her desires that you escort Ava to the Crostim Ledge." She looked at Steph. "And her original, stated intention to accompany you and Ava to the ledge. Please stand up and turn around."

Nessa was staring at Galadriel. She was struggling to speak, to say the right words. She was rocking back and forth unsteadily. She stammered, "Could you please say that again, Galadriel. Just so I know it is true."

Galadriel smiled, and then she said, "You are free of charge. You have done nothing wrong. You simply were following orders of your superior. Now please stand so I can untie your bindings."

Nessa covered her mouth with her hand and sighed deeply as she stood up. She whispered, "Thank you, Galadriel. May you be protected at every turn as Our Lady's second in command." She looked over at Lia and Steph. They were smiling. Steph winked at her. Nessa said, "How can I ever thank you enough, Steph?"

Galadriel started to untie the rope that was binding Nessa's wrists. As she did, Nessa released the ends of the rope she had clutched in her hands. Galadriel managed to maintain her composure and pretended to untie the rope. She looked at Steph and shook her head. "Nice move, Steph," she said softly with a grin. "Not tying the rope. I hope that you know that you would make a horrible Bkotn warrior, yes?"

Steph's face blushed, and then she laughed. She replied in a squeaky tone, "Indeed, I would. I know that better than anyone."

Galadriel walked over to Elbereth. The two of them had a brief discussion. Then Galadriel walked over to Lia and whispered in her ear.

Lia suddenly stood and shouted to the Etanpioa, "Galadriel has decided that Nessa is free of culpability!" Lia was now the third in command, having been told by Galadriel that Elbereth had relieved Siofra of her position.

Steph assumed the others in the Etanpioa would react outwardly in some fashion to Lia's proclamation. However, surprisingly, they did not. They seemed to take Lia's pronouncement in stride. They slowly began to gather their weapons, and then they formed a long line.

Lia shouted, "Release the prisoners."

"Is that it?" Steph said to Galadriel as she watched the guards untie the prisoners' bindings. "What about Siofra? Is she not going to have a say in all of this? To give her side of the story. To defend herself. And what about Morwen and Vena? Are you going to let them go free as well? Also, why are the others in the Etanpioa forming a row?" Steph knew that she was out of line. She felt embarrassed for asking a string of questions. She also judged that how the Bkotn conducted their tribunals was none of her business.

Galadriel said calmly, "It is our custom, Steph. It is the way of the Bkotn Tribe. Watch closely what happens next. Then I will address your concerns."

Steph stared in wonder as Morwen, Siofra, and Vena slowly gathered their belongings, including their weapons. The others in the Etanpioa, except for Elbereth, Galadriel, and Lia, were standing in a row. They were staring straight ahead at attention. Morwen, Siofra, and Vena slowly walked past them in a single file. After they passed the last warrior in line, Morwen and Vena entered the trail and walked in the direction of the Unseen Valley. Their heads were hung low.

Siofra did not join them. She purposely walked into the thickness of the forest and disappeared.

Steph turned around and noticed that Elbereth, Galadriel, and Lia had their backs turned to the threesome. They did not turn about until Lia shouted, "Prepare to continue on the orders of our leader!"

"What in the world just happened?" Steph cried. "Why did Morwen and Vena enter the trail even as Siofra entered the forest?"

As Galadriel gathered her belongings, she said, "Elbereth had a conversation with Morwen while I conducted Nessa's inquiry. Morwen and Vena were guilty of disobedience. Disobedience is a minor infraction. So, Vena was set free. Morwen also was at fault for conspiracy and conduct not fitting a Bkotn of her leadership position as second in charge.

"Morwen admitted to conspiring with Siofra to lure Ava into the forest. Siofra was in contact with the evil wizard, Haldir. She knows him quite well. Haldir is known as the Wizard of Mountains Cross. He is the evilest wizard of Antiquom. When questioning Morwen, Elbereth learned that Haldir has a special interest in Ava. He is determined to capture her before she can have a council with Godroh."

"Wow, okay," Steph said.

Galadriel continued to explain what had occurred. "Siofra was guilty of many crimes – conspiring with Morwen, coercion of a subordinate warrior, Nessa, the kidnapping of another elf, Ava, and placing her in harm's way. She was likewise guilty of conduct not fitting her position as third in command. Most grievously, she was guilty of stealing Haldir within our midst's, so he could hex you as well as the contents of your goblet. He may have hexed Ava as well. Anyway, if Haldir had wanted to, he easily could have hexed or slain us all. It would have been difficult for him to do so, but his being close to our ranks and undetected is worrisome. Consequently, Siofra was at fault for imperiling our entire Etanpioa, a most severe Bkotn infraction. She had violated our sacred oath – to forsake a Bkotn is to forsake oneself.

"Fortunately for all of us in my Etanpioa, Haldir only wanted to turn you against Ava and, likewise, her against you. He was the cause of your argument with Ava. Haldir's purpose – at least Elbereth and I assume – was to give Ava the greatest reason for accompanying Nessa to the ledge. That reason was you, to protest your words.

"Ava is tough, and she is resilient as you know. She is stubborn too. When you fought her with your words and insults, she was resolved to go to war with you in return. Employing the only means she knew how at the time, by rebelling. By going to Crostim Ledge with Nessa despite your objections." Galadriel nodded her head then said in a serious tone, "She is Avaïnoáel, O Poica Katharos. Hence, it is not in her nature to concede. She will never surrender. She will never abandon her principles, in this case, as I said, going with Nessa to the ledge despite your aggressive misgivings."

"I feel rotten," Steph said grimly. "But I know everything that happened was not my fault. As you say, it was owing to the wizard's nasty spell. He certainly knew how to get at Ava all right. Through me. He knew my insulting words would compel her to rebel. But I have a couple more questions." Galadriel nodded her head. "Why is Morwen accompanying Vena on the trail? You said her infractions were profoundly serious. If they are that serious, why is she allowed to walk the trail with Vena? Why did she not go with Siofra into the forest? Also, how did they know what they were supposed to do? What they must do now?"

Galadriel said, "Vena and Siofra were close friends. Vena was wrongly influenced by Siofra as third in command and due to the many favors afforded to her by her superior. Given Vena's only charge, disobedience, she is free to rejoin the Tribe. After a probationary period, she will be given another opportunity in another Etanpioa. I am confident she has learned her lesson and will perform satisfactorily.

"Morwen, despite the seriousness of her charges, must accompany Vena until she arrives safely in the Tribe. Walking the trail by oneself is too dangerous. Vena is inexperienced, while Morwen is not. Once Morwen sees Vena safely home to the Unseen Valley she will return to the Forest of Artonia unaccompanied. Both she and Siofra, because of their grievous crimes, are now expelled from the Tribe. They no longer are Bkotn warriors."

"But-but-but what if they regroup?" Steph stammered. She looked deeply troubled. "What if they rejoin with Haldir, regroup to cause Ava even more danger? Are you not worried about that?"

Galadriel clasped Steph's hand and led her to join the others of the Etanpioa. The other warriors were already on the trail. They soon would be dispatched to look for Ava. But Steph would not know that until later in the day.

"As I said, Steph, Ava will prevail. I am certain she will. If she encounters true danger, her amazing powers will shine clearer than the most dazzling gems of the dwarves' kingdom. Our Avaïnoðel will know what to do – instinctively. As for us Bkotn, well, we will concern ourselves with that possibility when the moment in time comes. At the end of the day, no matter what happens, we are Bkotn." She grinned mischievously.

"We worry not."

CHAPTER 8

THE WELCOMING SOLENOM RIVER

"Never confuse a single defeat with a final defeat."
—*F. Scott Fitzgerald*

1

2 Októvriosom (October) 2021

It was the third day since Ava had gone missing. She correctly assumed that the Etanpioa were out looking for her. Nonetheless, she figured the best thing to do was to proceed east, toward the Solenom. Then she would be out in the open, thus increasing her chances of being found. She would be able to refill her hip flask. She had finished the last drop of water hours ago.

The first night she spent alone in the forest she kept on moving. She wanted to increase the distance between her and Siofra and Vena. She had stopped briefly but a few times. To tend to her cuts and scrapes and to cut the tree branches for her trekking poles. She did not sleep a wink, although she almost nodded off on two occasions.

The following morning, she stopped a few times in the thick of the forest to rest. She was not tired actually, at least not too much, even though she had been awake for over twenty-four hours. She had stopped walking to contemplate everything that had happened over the previous two days.

She wondered about the depressing argument she and Steph had about the Crostim Ledge fiasco. How Steph had insulted her, how she all but ordered her to not accompany Nessa. However, even after Doo told her that Steph's drink may have been messed with, something in her psyche wanted to fight back. For some unexplained reason, she wanted to defy Steph's strong assertions. So, she had pressed on with her plans to accompany Nessa to the ledge.

She pondered why she would react in such a way. Yes, she knew Steph was a real pain that night. Her words were insulting, demeaning, and demanding. They hurt her to the core. But when she found out Steph's drink may have been placed under a spell; she should have conceded. However, she did not. She turned a blind eye to the obvious, the real reason Steph had acted the way she did. In the end, Steph's reproving words had proven correct.

Why was that she wondered? Was I somehow destined to be on my own in the Forest of Artonia? To prove my worth. Was all that had happened nothing more than fate? Or was everything carefully planned, just a few miserable episodes of a much larger story, a well-thought-out scheme? Could it have been that I, like Steph, had been hexed? Is it possible that Siofra had been hexed as well? Why else would she murder one of her warriors?

No matter the reasons for her predicament, Ava was heartbroken by Nessa's needless death. And she was as angry as a swarm of yellowjackets after their nest had been disturbed. She was geared up for vengeance, ready to fight. Furious at Siofra for slaying Nessa coldly while her back was turned. Outraged at Siofra and Vena for chasing her through the forest like two rabid foxes pursuing a scared hare.

But, despite everything, the thing that bothered her the most was not being around Steph. She missed her Earthly World friend, her bestie. She missed her a lot. She also missed DooDad. And she could not help but imagine that they were upset with her vanishing – once again.

After Ava had entered the clearing and met up with Fidelium, she resumed walking on what she hoped was the trail that would lead her to the Solenom River. She was optimistic because it gradually sloped downward. She was pleasantly surprised with her stamina. In addition to her heartened spirit and enhanced resilience. But mostly with her amazing ability to keep walking with only a few short breaks.

She assumed her toughness had everything to do with her transformation from a human to an elf. Doo had said the genetic makeup of elves' metabolism is vastly different than that of humans. The coolest thing, at least to Ava, elves supposedly are immortal. Elves can go on longer than humans without food and drink. They likewise are known to remain awake for days and press on with only occasional, brief breaks.

She had noticed the last elven phenomena firsthand with the Bkotn. At the onset, she had thought the warriors were happy to rest when she stopped to gawk curiously at interesting stuff. But after a while, she realized they were more thrilled with even more opportunities to chitchat with their fellow warriors. Elbereth pushed the Etanpioa hard. She did not permit the warriors to engage in conversations as they walked. They had to stand four-hour rotating watches after dusk which afforded them few opportunities to relax and chat with their colleagues.

All in all, Ava was quite pleased to be an elf.

Even if I have odd elf ears that will make my friends gawk at me in wonder! That is if I ever get to return home . . .

The following afternoon, after she and Fedelium had met up, she continued walking almost nonstop. As she walked the trail, she noticed she was starting to become progressively more sluggish. She could not concentrate properly on what she was doing, where she was walking. Her thoughts kept drifting to the scene in her head when Nessa was slain.

Because of her unfocused state and increased lethargy, she tripped over hidden roots and rocks more frequently. One time she tripped over a stump and collided with the ground painfully. After nearly four more hours of continuous walking, taking but three brief breaks, she finally heeded to her tired body and perplexed mind. She had been awake for over thirty-six hours. Consequently, she and Fidelium stopped hours before sunset to make camp.

Perhaps camp is not the right word to describe Ava's encampment. Sleeping under the stars is a slightly better description, or, more accurately, roughing it in the open. She had roughed it up before when she was with the Bkotn and even before then. But she and Steph had slept beneath a tarpaulin made of the skin of some beast. It was a reserve tarp that was used by the Bkotn to cover their supplies when it rained. The tarp she and Steph slept under was open on both ends. It was damp and drafty inside. But it was a comfy roof over their heads. To Ava it almost was like sleeping in the tent she and her sisters shared at the COW campground.

She thought with a laugh, without the insufferable snoring!

She had walked a couple of dozen paces inside the forest to set up her campsite. She did not want to sleep near the trail. If someone or something ambled along the trail and discovered her and Fidelium, she would have little time to react – to defend them. But she wanted to make certain she was close enough to the trail to flee on it if necessary. She had had enough of running through the forest in the dark.

She also liked sleeping off the trail. Being in the forest at night comforted her, more so than sleeping on the trail. Besides, she had survived one night alone amongst the towering trees as she walked nonstop. She felt secure beneath their leafy, welcoming embrace. She also had Fidelium with her. He would warn her of any impending danger.

The wide trunk of a tree served as the back wall of her crude shelter. She had chosen the tree because it did not appear to have any dead or rotting limbs. She knew from reading outdoor and camping magazines that camping out under dead limbs could end one's camping ventures forever. She had gathered leaves and what looked like pine needles from the ground for bedding. She placed them at the base of the tree. Then she collected limbs and twigs and built a makeshift upside-down, V-shaped shelter.

The shelter was rickety – she had no cord to reinforce the joints – but she did not care. The crude shelter offered her the uplifting sense of being protected from above. She covered the top of the shelter with the lining of her torn cloak. Then she settled in, rested her back against the tree trunk, and wrapped her cloak around her torso. She had placed her sword and bow and arrows beside her. Fidelium perched on the ground at the shelter's opening.

She had fallen asleep almost immediately. She did not awaken until morning, well past sunup. She stretched with a long yawn and started walking the trail as before. Fidelium hovered above her as she walked.

She suddenly yelled, "Oh, goodness, yes!" Then she happily sprinted along the trail. Just as she ran by the cairn denoting the trail's entrance, or, in this case the way out, she stopped running. She tossed her makeshift trekking poles into the forest. She removed her bow and quiver of arrows from her shoulders and unsheathed her sword. With her arms held out wide, she started to skip in place. Her eyes were dancing with happiness. It was the happiest she had felt in three days.

She dropped to her knees, closed her eyes, and said a silent prayer of thanks. As soon as she had finished praying, she thought of Fidelium and opened her eyes. What she saw caused a warm glow to touch her heart. She felt relieved like a weight had been lifted from her heart despite everything that had happened.

Fidelium seemed just as excited as she felt. He was flitting back and forth wildly in the air. He looked down and noticed she was staring up at him. He playfully performed a nosedive straight at her. Before he collided with her head as she ducked, he rocketed high in the air and set off to fly in spreading circles.

She suspected Fidelium was delighted to be out of the woodland as he glided high above the unforested, wide-open area. Indeed, Fidelium was pleased to be able to spread his wings. Even so, as Ava's defensive bird, he was living up to his reputation as a protecting khni. He was searching the area warily. He would not stop searching until he was satisfied that no danger was present.

She yelled up at him, "Yes, Fidelium, we finally have reached the Solenom. Isn't this wonderful?" She stood up and gathered her weapons. She walked further in the wide open, seemingly limitless area and began to scrutinize the scene. She was happy to be out of the gloomy forest. Yet she knew that the environs of the ferocious Solenom could be just as deadly as the forest. She took an arrow from her quiver and positioned it on the string of her longbow. She pointed the bow toward the ground. She began to walk slowly toward the raging river, her eyes watchful as she looked to the left, to the right, and back again.

No trails or pathways were leading to the river. Just large boulders and rocks were strewn about haphazardly. She had to look down as she walked to keep from tripping on rocks and slipping on the moist sand. She paused every few steps and glanced about, her longbow at the ready. After a few dozen awkward steps, because the arrow strung on her bow was making her unbalanced, she stopped. She pushed the arrow inside its quiver and slung the bow over her shoulder. She unsheathed her sword.

It was much easier for her to move without tripping. She reckoned the sword would serve as an improvised trekking pole, so she could remain upright if she were to trip.

2

Ava was staring at the untamed Solenom. Its turquoise blue, whitecapped waves were lapping the washed boulders lining its peaceful banks. She felt happy and relaxed.

There is an old elven proverb that is worth repeating as it pertains to the Solenom.

> *"No river is supreme. No river too wide.*
> *No river boundless. To make its further side.*
> *Yet tread you not your two feet bare.*
> *For rocks and stones are ever there.*
> *To trick you up, to take ahold.*
> *To drown your life, to seize your soul."*

Ava knew nothing of the ancient proverb as she moved nearer to the river's swollen banks. Yet she appreciated that the Solenom's raging torrent could not be crossed. Doo had told her that even when the Solenom appears tranquil, its sky-blue surface of gently rocking ripples outwardly tame, the undertow is perilous. And deadly.

"Many have succumbed to the Solenom," she recalls that Doo had said. "Despite its breathtaking magnificence, its irresistible serenity, its overwhelming allure."

With Doo's words fresh in her mind, she stared at the river with uncertainty. She swallowed hard. She turned around and glanced up at the perimeter of the thick forest. The cairn of the trail's entrance was barely visible. She knew that returning to the trail was unthinkable. She had to refill her flask and find something to eat. She turned around slowly, gazing somberly at the flat, rock-strewn shore. A feeling of dread, of outright hopelessness, seemed to overwhelm her. Her body suddenly felt heavy. Because she realized there was no means of escape. She was trapped, figuratively speaking.

But I must find a way to escape if it becomes necessary. Even though I am trapped by the Solenom on one side, the forest on the other, and the endless banks of the river on the two other sides. After days of trekking through Artonia, there must be a way out of my predicament. But how?

She sat down on a squat boulder. Her gaze once again returned to the forest.

Perhaps, after finding food and quenching my thirst I should return to the trail. Perhaps the trail I was on will take me to the Kuoino, the trail we were on before the stupid Crostim Ledge disaster. Maybe Steph and the others are waiting for me up there. Or, better yet, maybe they are looking for me, hiking the trail that leads to here. Abruptly, what Steph had said about her powers entered her mind. However, the words were slightly different, like something Jordyn would have said to her via her voice-thoughts.

The world knows not of your power. It merely knows your name.

"And what exactly *is* my name?" Ava said aloud. "And what exactly *is* my power?"

Her gaze returned to the river. She licked her dry lips and walked to the shoreline. She knelt on all fours and filled her flask. She gulped down the water. It was cool and refreshing. She hoped it was just as clean and bacteria-free as it was invigorating. She refilled her flask and returned to the boulder on which she had been sitting. She slung her bow and quiver over her shoulders and sheathed her sword. Fidelium set down beside her.

"Oh look," she said to Fidelium. "It is a bouquet of sanatios." She smiled. "Back home we call them buttercups. I wonder. Doo told me they have healing properties. Maybe I should take a few and push them in my cut." She reached down and plucked a blossom from its stem.

Suddenly, Fidelium began to screech loudly nearly scaring her half to death. He was eyeing the blossom she was holding in her hand.

"Oh, do not worry yourself, Fidelium. I know I cannot eat it. I just wanted to see, "she moved the delightfully fragrant blossom to her nose, "to see how it smells—"

She suddenly felt lethargic and struggled to complete her thoughts but could not. The next thing that she knew, but only just, she was lying face down in the sand. Fidelium, meanwhile, was high in the air circling above her. She could vaguely hear him as he screeched frantically.

Without warning, something seemed to grab her roughly. The powerful force lifted her high in the air. A few seconds later she was sailing over the forest. She was in a vertical position, her lifeless arms hanging limply at her sides. A minute later she was gently set onto the ground feet first. Then she was standing upright, lifeless, unconscious because of the sanatios' noxious, sleep-inducing effect.

*****

Ava awakened an hour later. The peacefulness of the sunshiny, mid-afternoon had evaporated in a blink of an eye. In its place roared the bleakest, most terrifying, chaotic blackness imaginable. Muddy, somersaulting clouds were colliding viciously; their howling tormented moans boding unspeakable evil. Their terrifying savagery a prediction of what was yet to come.

Uninterrupted streaks of dreadful, bloody red lightning flashed cruelly within the swimming, murky gloom. The ruthlessly exploding lightning stretched out in all directions. Like the gruesome, skeletal fingers of a vicious, evil murderer possessed by Satan himself. A brutal killer at the ready to pounce on its unsuspecting victim. Mercilessly. Ruthlessly. With no sense of right and wrong. No caring of good and bad. A heartless assassin without a soul.

She slammed her eyes shut to escape the shocking horror. But there was no escaping the sinister scene. The gory flashes of lightning continued to flame cruelly beneath her tightly sealed eyelids.

She wanted to cover her ears. To oust the raucous, thunderous groans of the ferociously roaring clouds. But she could not. She could not move her hands. Her arms were stretched brutally and painfully behind her back encircling a thin sapling. And her hands were attached at the wrists. She wiggled her fingers to feel what had bound her wrists, but she could not feel anything.

She also could not move her legs at the ankles. They too were bound to the sapling. She opened her eyes and looked at her feet. Nothing was binding them. Just like her wrists. She rightly thought it must be magic, evil magic, the evilest magic imaginable! Not shocking given everything that had happened to her since Siofra murdered Nessa.

But why is this happening to me! What is it that I have done that is so horribly wrong to deserve this terrifying nightmare!

She crouched slightly at the knees to stretch her legs. Bending over just a little and leaning forward against the flexible sapling. Her arms simply slid up and down on either side of the sapling. But her wrists remained tightly bound. Her ankles remain firmly locked in place, unmovable. Fortunately, she was able to wriggle her toes and stretch her calves. If she were unable to move them even a little, she knew that her legs would fall asleep. Then she would be nothing more than a calcified, breathing corpse of an immovable statue.

She screamed angrily at the chaos swirling above her. Her tone was alarmingly desperate yet enraged.

"Why are you wicked clouds, thunder, and lightning directly above me and only me?" Her eyes warily darted to her left and then to her right. "Why are you not at the outside edges of this clearing or above the forest? Why only here above me!" She inhaled a long breath then exhaled sharply.

"I feel so vulnerable. So alone—"

She started to shiver. Her lips trembled. She lowered her head and asked for forgiveness.

Tears welled up in her eyes. She tried to blink them away. But they continued even so. Straight away her tears cascaded down her cheeks.

Then she stared, utterly confused as a soft, greenish light slowly enveloped her trembling body. She started to feel drowsy but not in a normal way. It was an odd sensation. Almost like she was being forced to somnolence. She tried to open her eyes—

She shrieked, "Why can I not open my eyes! I must open my eyes! And what happened to Fidelium? What did they or whoever do to him?"

She struggled fiercely against the invisible bindings. But her struggles were in vain. She continued to call out, even though the odd lassitude was overpowering her senses gradually, making her words vague.

"And where is Steph, DooDad, and the—?" She yawned against her will just as her chin dropped to her chest. She remained like that for a few moments. Then she snapped conscious, but just scarcely. She lifted her head. Her lips barely moved as she tried to talk.

In a scarcely lucid, weak whisper she said, "Why haven't they come. Rescue me? And you (sigh) Siofra – more of your – nasty trickery? Do you intend to – me as I (yawn) here defenseless? Do you? You just – ahead and try. Because (sigh) I never – give in to you. I will – to your evil ways! I swear if it (yawn) – the last thing I do. Will avenge (sigh) Nessa's death!"

As if on impulse her head snapped back against the sapling, and then it gradually slumped until her chin was resting on her chest once more. What was left of her pathetic vitality essentially was used up. Yet somehow, she continued to struggle mentally, her subconsciousness not about to give in. She whispered vague, questioning words chock-full of utter hopelessness. They would be her very last words for a long time.

"None of this would have – I hadn't tried – climb Grandpa's tower." Her head slammed back against the sapling where it remained suspended momentarily. Then it gradually set out to fall toward her chest.

"And you, Jordyn, I must – you this. Why am – here in the Inner World? What I – deserve this hor – hor – ble – night – night – nightmare?"

END OF PART TWO

PART THREE

A PHANTASM WORLD
OF MAKE-BELIEVE

"It always seems impossible until it's done."
—Nelson Mandela

~~~

CHAPTER 1

AVA NOELLE'S TRANSFORMATION

"Be the change you want to see in the world."—*Mahatma Gandhi*

1

Ava gradually reawakens hours later. She is not consciously aware that she is doing so. Although her subconsciousness is struggling to overcome the lethargic paralysis shrouding her body and paralyzing her mind.

Her brain is in total disarray, at a complete loss of her surroundings. The rhythmic beating of her heart is much slower than normal, thus depriving her cells of vitality. Her short inhales and exhales are causing her breathing to be shallow, scarcely filling her lungs with life-sustaining air. Her senses are listless, somnolent, barely functioning. She is powerless to focus her fogged-up eyes. Her sense of hearing is sensing no sounds. Her mouth is wide open, dried out, pasty white spittle at its corners. The tip of her tongue is distended, resting limply on her lower lip. She is unable to speak.

All the while her subconsciousness seems to understand she is aching from the top of her head to the end of her toes.

With great effort, together with soft, tormented groans of anguish, she tries to lift her head little by little. Even this uncomplicated, natural act is a slow, agonizing endeavor. Consuming too much energy. Her eyebrows are squished together, her ruddy face an odd expression of uncertainty. She instinctively narrows her glazed-over, dull-looking eyes, frantically trying to focus. But for now, her attempt is futile. Her eyes' photoreceptors are a labyrinth of mixed messages. Sending chaotic, mumble-jumble electrical pulses to their optic nerves. Creating confusion in her disarrayed brain. Rendering her intellect unmindful of what she sees.

Oddly, however, Ava's subconsciousness understands what she is seeing.

The heavens have absolved themselves of their earlier, dreadfully murky pessimism. Their terrifying foretelling of her imminent day of reckoning has vanished, at least for now. She manages to nod her head appreciatively in a heartbreaking, sluggish way.

Bringing her one step closer to reality.

She stares out-of-focus at the sky for the longest time. Yet her subconsciousness is determined to comprehend what she perceives. All at once, her glassy eyes begin to move together as they track one, two, then three fluffy cumulus clouds that are drifting lazily in the sky. Next, a couple of million neurons in her brain finally start to communicate electrochemically. Then her brain begins to register recognition of what she is seeing. Thanks to her powerful subconsciousness as it fights valiantly to reawaken her senses.

Bringing her one step closer to reality.

The clouds look like fluffy cotton balls floating in the dark blue sky. She continues to stare blankly at them but with a less faraway look than before. Thanks to her subconsciousness. Suddenly, a couple million more neurons are set in motion. They send a pleasant memory from her subconsciousness to her awareness. The memory sets off millions more electrical pulses in her stultified brain. Enabling her brain to spring back to life wholly. At last, her mind unhurriedly sets out to behave like it is supposed to with reenergized conviction.

Bringing her one step closer to reality.

A thin smile appears on her lips as she remembers.

I remember. Something. Dear to my heart. I was staring at clouds. Just like these. At the beach. On vacation. With my family. Sitting upright. On a lounge chair. A dozen or so feet from the water's edge. I could hear – I could hear the frothy waves. Lapping the sand delicately. I was reading—

Her mind tries to remember. What was it? What was it you were reading?

She listlessly smiles with recognition. I was reading the novel *Puppet.* I had placed it on my lap while I looked at the sky. Imagining animals and other unique images. They were on the horizon. Created by the gently floating clouds.

The electrical neurons in her brain continue to correlate. To make sense of what she is seeing.

Bringing her one step closer to reality.

She smiles once more, this time more broadly, more knowingly.

They were imaginative clouds just like these, weren't they? But somehow in a different world. I wonder where that different world was. Other than the one I am in right now? If so, what world could it be possibly? Am I now in that different world or another one? I cannot remember—

Her mind lazily continues to focus. Shortly, the pleasant memory of fleeting clouds slips away to nothing. Even so, her subconsciousness knows that the hopeful sky is trying to uplift her spirits. The balmy sunshine is trying to paint one more smile on her upturned face. The gentle breeze is trying to brush her confused, muddy thoughts away.

She subconsciously inhales deeply and involuntarily smiles yet again.

Bringing her one step closer to reality.

Then she abruptly tilts her head to one side. A ridiculous looking, far off, childish grin shows on her face. Her tongue protrudes from her mouth and rests on her lower lip like before. She dreamily gazes skyward, her eyes once more unfocused. The neurons of her brain are slowing down. Yet again sending and receiving jumbled electrical messages. Whatever had caused her lethargy is coursing through her body, affecting her mind. Yet her subconsciousness struggles on.

Ava remains in this half-asleep, half-awake, languorous state for over an hour. Unthinking. Unfeeling and unaware. Staring up at the sky blank-faced with expressionless eyes. Her subconsciousness realizing that she is aching all over. Fighting gallantly to bring her back to awareness, so she can live.

When suddenly, every tingling nerve in her body begins to send electrical impulses to her brain. Causing her to suffer the unmistakable sense of something is dreadfully wrong!

Quickly bringing her one step closer to reality.

A slight chill abruptly causes an itchy prickling on her scalp. Goose pimples cover her shoulders which makes her shiver. She swallows hard then draws her mouth in a straight line and bites hard on her tongue. She tastes blood.

At last, her mind awakens to reality.

To the here and now. With alarming comprehension.

Oh my God, I am standing in the same spot!

She realizes she is still restrained at the wrists and ankles by the magical bindings. Her head is pounding fiercely from the side effects of the sanatios toxicity or whatever caused her to fall asleep through the night, for nearly twelve hours. Her outstretched arms are dangling limply on either side of the sapling. They are as stiff as boards and hurting something awful. The tips of her fingers are numb and tingly from hanging lifelessly for so long.

Her feet are fast asleep, and her toes feel petrified, unable to move. Her feet and toes have that deadened, uncomfortably itchy-tingling feeling. Sort of like when you cross your legs at the knee and one foot falls asleep. Then as you stand up to walk without first waking up your foot, it tends to flop to one side at the ankle bone. The ankle can even snap. It has been known to happen.

Ava grasps every muscle of her upper and lower limbs would be useless if she were forced to use them right now. They feel rigidly taut, like rigid anchor chains of a moored ship during a raging cyclone. Tight, stiff, utterly unyielding. Yet ready to give way and split in two if set in motion. That is if she could free herself from whatever in the heck they are! And if she were to try and use her arms and legs without stretching properly.

She knows she cannot escape the invisible bindings that are imprisoning her wrists and ankles. But she can stretch out on her toes and perform partial knee bends along the sapling's length. She also can flex her hands at the wrists and wiggle her fingers.

She immediately sets out to do just that.

Her chin had been resting on her chest while she slept. As a result, her neck and shoulder muscles are sore. Especially at the back of her neck. Her neck has the same achy feeling when one wakes up after sleeping the wrong way. Then having to put up with a stiff neck all day long that aches no matter which way you move it.

She concentrates on stretching her neck and shoulder muscles while she warms up the rest of her sluggish body. Her neck gradually becomes less stiff.

When her upper and lower muscles feel more alive and relatively useful once more, she begins to bend over at the waist. She starts slow, steadily bending lower and more forcefully with each successive bend. As far down as possible. Until her outstretched arms seem to scream for her to not bend any further. Because of the excruciating pain in her triceps.

The supple sapling against her back submissively bends as well.

She is hopeful that her repeated bending actions will cause the thin sapling to snap in two, setting her free. Or even better, overwhelm the bindings of the invisible ties that are holding her captive at the wrists and ankles.

She struggles to overpower the sapling's elasticity by robustly bending over at the waist even lower. Ignoring her screeching arms and shoulders.

Despite her repeated efforts, she cannot break free. The sinuous, yet strong sapling simply bends to a certain point every time, no matter how vigorously she bends over. Then, like a heartless, brutally controlling rubber band, it rudely snaps back to its original, upright position roughly yanking her vertical along with it.

But she does not give up. She continues bending at the waist for ten additional minutes. Until her forearms, shoulders, and stomach muscles can no longer take the strain. Then she is forced to stop. She realizes she would be in a world of hurt if she were to injure her upper arm and shoulder muscles. Trying to wield her sword – or even yanking it out of its sheath for that matter – or grabbing an arrow out of the quiver – or pulling back on the bowstring – all would be tricky if not impossible.

Ava has been listening to the unmistakable, mighty roar of the Solenom as she stretches. She could not hear the river's deafening roar before she fell asleep due to the raucous commotion created by the stormy clouds. The raging river is on the far side of the forest. Knowing that the mighty Solenom is close by gives her hope, but only slightly.

Her thoughts abruptly wander to the split second when she sniffed the sanatios blossom. Before her bird friend, Fidelium flew off. Before her life changed from a smidgen of elation and hope to total despair. Before she ended up here. Bound to a sapling by magical things. Weak, helpless, and vulnerable. Completely at someone or something's mercy. Unable to stand up for herself. Unable to do anything at all but scream bloody murder.

With what good it would do me! But why in the world did I sniff the darned thing anyway? I knew that it probably was poisonous to ingest, just like the buttercups back home. But common sense should have warned me it could have been noxious to smell as well. So, because of my stupidity, my crushing curiosity, smelling the blossom knocked me out cold. My fault for being clumsy and overly nosy – again. She grins shrewdly.

Although it did smell pleasant despite its nastiness. I wonder if there is any use for the blossoms here in the Inner World other than for medicine. Maybe making perfume because it sure does smell heavenly. I would not mind dabbing a bit of its perfume on my neck from time to time.

Yep, I got myself in a fix by smelling that darned thing, didn't I? But how in the world did I end up here? what brought me here? what are these, these *whatever-they-are's?* and how are they binding me to this darned sapling? what is going to happen next? where is Fidelium? I hope he is okay. Lastly, *why* am I here in the first place?

She suddenly shouts in a ghastly tone, "And will you look at what I just said? Over and over repeatedly, again, and again, and again! Asking myself so many stupid, unanswerable questions even I cannot keep track of them! Darn it. What is the use of being curious and asking questions if you cannot satisfy your curiosity and get some answers!"

She knows that she had better get an idea of her surroundings. She was unable to do so earlier because she was heavy-eyed. She strains her neck as best as she can and looks around. She can only look ninety degrees to both her right and left sides. She has no idea what could be happening beyond her line of sight and directly behind her. The knowledge that over half of her surroundings cannot be viewed is giving her the creeps.

She usually is a very calm, albeit overly inquisitive being. She does not get upset easily or without cause. However, now that the effects of the blossom's toxins have worn off completely, she gradually is starting to feel uneasy about what is to come, and with it, the dreadful unknowns. Her heartbeats accelerate as her gaze nervously begins to dart in all directions. She must blow out a series of short breaths to control her nervousness. Surprisingly, she is wishing that she were sound asleep once more.

At least I would not know what is going to happen to me if I were asleep. And I am certain something is going to happen. Why else am I bound to this spot? But gosh, not knowing what is going to happen next is scaring me half to death.

She imagines strange noises are surrounding her. They seem to be coming from every direction. Most seem to come from behind her. She twists and turns in place. Her eyes frantically trying to scan every inch of terrain within her line of sight.

Without warning, Steph's prophesizing words she said a long time ago enter her mind. She is deeply puzzled by the sudden thoughts. Moreover, she is frustrated that they are appearing right now. Because she has more important things to consider.

Like escaping and staying alive!

"Never listen to your fears, Ava. They know nothing of your incredible power."

Her eyes continue to dart everywhere, enquiringly, searchingly. She shouts out loud in a tone of voice that is outright unpleasant, "But what powers do I have, Steph, huh? You never did answer my question. Neither you nor Jordyn explained my supposed powers! Jordyn had said but never explained; and I quote what she said, 'You will learn of your powers soon enough, Ava.' Thus, I must ask again. What powers, huh? Also, what about all that rubbish, what Jordyn told you about me being the Protector of the World! How am I supposed to be whatever that is supposed to mean if I do not know what powers I have if any?'"

She is looking up and scowling at the sky. Her mood is darkening as the second's tick by.

"Quite frankly, I think all of that, all of this, is nothing more than a stinking pile of rubbish! Because if I were a protector of anything I would not be here! Would I? I would not be bound to this stupid tree by these stupid bindings. Would I? Unable to move. Would I? Incapable of looking in all directions, looking behind me! Would I?"

And beginning to feel deathly scared, frightened out of my wits! Even more scared than being on the tower's staircase. Or imagining Nessa had been murdered by her superior, Siofra! No, not that scared. Another's life is worth much more than my own. Poor Nessa . . .

As she thinks for the umpteenth time of her dear friend Nessa, her shoulders gloomily droop forward. She lowers her head and begins to grumble.

Yeah, all-powerful. What a bunch of garbage. If I were powerful, I would figure out a way to escape. Wouldn't I? Instead of standing here sniveling like a baby and shivering from my head to my toes.

Her shivering quickly intensifies, so much so she is starting to feel cold. She also feels lightheaded. She closes her eyes to ward off nausea crawling in her head and roiling inside the pit of her stomach. Grief-stricken tears continue to escape from her closed eyelids. The teardrops slowly drip onto her ashen cheeks then flow like minuscule tributaries until they silently sprinkle the ground with sadness.

Moooaaaaannnn!

Her head draws back quickly in reaction to the loud, moaning sound. Her muscles suddenly go weak just as a tightness grips her chest.

Her eyes snap wide open as she screams forcefully, "What in the world was that!"

She once again is frantically scouring every inch of the terrain in her restricted line of sight. She does not see anything out of the ordinary. Just the open clearing with an encircling line of forest trees. She should feel a bit relieved that nothing is obvious. Yet her panic intensifies markedly. Now she is shivering uncontrollably.

I cannot see what is happening behind me!

Moooaaaaannnn!

"Oh no! Go figure! Whatever it is that is making that dreadful noise is right behind me!"

She fights to turn her upper body in a desperate, but unsuccessful attempt to locate the source of the noise.

Sssss! Ssss!

Noises that seem like hisses of an angry serpent are now coming from her right, once again out of her line of sight.

Sssss! Ssss!

Then the dreadful *Moooaaaaannnn!* Screams from her left! The sounds seem to be multiplying in intensity! Like they are getting closer! Within a matter of seconds, she imagines she is being encircled by countless wails of terrifying moans and hisses from every inch of the encircling forest!

Sssss! Ssss! Moooaaaaannnn! Sssss! Ssss! Moooaaaaannnn!

"Oh my God! Please, somebody, help me!"

She begins to sway slightly. Her eyes slam shut once more. Her terrified mind's eyes do not want to witness what she is certain is going to happen next.

Unexpectedly, Steph's voice and her prophetic, yet extended words seem to crash in her tortured mind yet again. Her words oust every other thought and every sound from her brain.

"Always remember, Ava. Never listen to your fears. Because your fears, as well as all beasts, know nothing of your incredible power. Muster up your inner strength, Ava. You got this. I believe in you."

Then Jordyn's excerpt from Mahatma Gandhi's phrases zooms in her mind.

"Ava, be the change you want to see in the world."

Steph's voice returns.

"Because you are the Protector of the World, Ava. Yes, you are she."

Instantaneously, wave after wave of epinephrine rapidly courses throughout Ava's body. Her body's amazing, chemically induced energy induces a startling sense of euphoria. It promptly crushes and overcomes her intense trembling. She instantly reclaims her tenacious, equanimity. Her self-confidence.

Her face and neck immediately flush with color. Her arm and leg muscles begin to flex involuntarily. She unconsciously clenches her hands to tight-fisted balls, turning her knuckles pure white. Her nostrils flare. Her lips set in a straight line. Her appearance is now one of undeniable resolve and courage.

She appears ready for a fight to the finish.

Her eyes open wide. Her gaze is alert. Her jaw set. She stares straight ahead and shouts a thunderous roar of triumph.

"Yeeeessss!"

Her booming shout was raucous, clear, and powerful. It quickly resonates like an invisible tsunami scouring the land in swells just as an unseeable, powerful hurricane-force wind springs forth with an explosion. The airstream's velocity and authority cause the trees to sway violently at their tops. A few trees give way and break in two and fall over with a rumbling *snaaaap-crash!*

Her immensely forceful shout continues to echo over and over, past the forest onto the opposite rocky shore of the Solenom. Then her echoing shout swiftly rebounds off the distant hilltops. Trees bend over violently in the opposite direction. Again, snapping more than a few in two.

Then suddenly, the vociferous wind ceases to be. Everything goes silent. Birds of the forest alight on the ground to observe. Creatures scamper from the forest and line up on its perimeter to stare. The clouds floating in the sky fade away briskly as if the heavens were swept clean. The rustling of leaves goes silent. A ray of sunshine from the heavens illuminates Ava's upturned face.

A split-second later she savagely lunges forward at the waist with the power and resolve of an enraged, ferocious, leaping tigress. The unseen, magical bindings dissolve to powdery clouds of pallid dust and float to the ground. Then the malleable sapling breaks in two with a roaringly deafening *crack!*

She is free!

2

Ava all but fell flat on her face when she unexpectedly broke free. As luck would have it – she needed some good luck at that point – she kept her balance. If she had not, she would have tried to break her fall with her outstretched arms, possibly injuring them along with her wrists and fingers.

She cannot believe *what* has just happened that allowed her to break free. Or *how* it happened. She merely is glad that it *did* happen. She also appreciates that now is not the time to dwell on what, how, and why.

There is not a second to lose. She straightaway stretches her arms, legs, and fingers and stomps her feet in place to restore life to her lower limbs. Then she spins around on her heels.

What she is looking at should scare her senseless. But for some odd reason, she is not panicky or frightened in the least. Quite the opposite; she is calm and unruffled. Her balled-up fists are at her sides. Her eyes are ablaze with piercing daggers. Her lips are curled in a wicked sneer. Her breathing is even, exuding calm, keeping time with her slowly beating heart.

Surprising even herself, she stares for the longest time at the thing that had caused the horrible sounds. A mystified look is on her face. Because her memory banks are struggling to recall something forgotten long ago. Trying to place a name, a label on what her eyes are seeing. Then out of the blue, the realization unexpectedly comes together in her mind. She slaps her thigh and breaks down with a mocking hoot.

"You are a beluga, aren't you? The source of all the ridiculous moaning and hissing noises." She pinches her nose and winces. "Also, you have to know that you stink royally too. Just like I expected you would. Given the stupid look on your face, I guess you are a dud. Am I right?" She plants her feet wide apart. "If you come any closer, I warn you—"

The beluga stares at Ava with a dull-witted expression.

She sets out to taunt the beast. She closes her right hand to a fist and rudely beckons with three slow curls of her index finger, "Come and get me if you dare, stupid." The beluga does not react. She shouts, "What are you waiting for, huh? And you thought you were so bad with all those scary moans and hisses, didn't you?" She glares at the beluga and shouts, "Well, I am not scared one bit! So, let's you and I get it on!"

Ava's bow and quiver had slipped from her shoulders when she was bound to the sapling. Her weapons are on the ground on either side of the sapling. She bends over and picks them up. She slips the fastenings over her shoulders.

Roughly sixty feet separate her and the beluga. It starts to walk on all fours toward her warily, its snake-like eyes riveted on her face. Its powerful shoulder muscles are swelling with tensity like it about to hurtle towards her.

Eyeing the beluga cautiously in case it makes a sudden move – she will plunge her sword in its heart if it does – Ava swiftly grabs an arrow from her quiver. She speedily positions the arrow on the center of the bowstring. Then she raises the nock of the arrow to eye level and gradually pulls back on the string. She is aiming at the beluga's forehead. She knows that hitting the beast in the forehead is one sure way to destroy it. It probably would survive if the arrow were to strike it elsewhere. Then, just like a wounded Earthly World grizzly bear driven by torturing pain, the beluga would strike her down wildly, ripping her apart from limb to limb.

To the voracious beluga, Ava is nothing more than raw, fresh meat to be devoured. Even so, and oddly enough, it stops striding toward her. It intuitively knows that she is nothing like any other elf or forest creature it has encountered or slain. Ava's tenacity, her manner of speaking, and the scornful sound of her voice set off to make it fluster.

Now the beluga is concentrating its look on Ava's expression. It is trying to read her feelings, her intentions. Its yellow, unblinking, keyhole-shaped, snake-like pupils dilate slowly. A few seconds later the pupils cover the eye's bright red sclera that encircles them. Then the pupils slowly contract to barely discernible slits. The creature's eyes repeat this process two more times as the beast instinctively evaluates her intentions. All the while it remains frozen, staring, contemplating, hesitant to advance, yet impulsively yearning to attack. To kill.

Ava realizes she could slay the beast with one arrow and in the blink of an eye. She has practiced enough to know that at this distance she could neatly slice an Earthly World apple in two at its core. The beluga's hairy head is huge, perhaps twice the size as her own. Striking it square on the forehead is a sure way to slay it. Yet she is hesitant to do so. She loves all living things. She would never intentionally harm anything. She lowers her bow slightly and looks away while continuing to watch the beast with her peripheral vision. With these two, non-provocative acts, she is gesturing that she means the beast no harm. Hence, with any luck, it will turn away.

"I do not want to hurt you, my dear beluga. So, why don't you run along and find something else to stalk, huh?"

The beluga has read her manner, and through her tone of voice, it has detected weakness if only slight and ephemeral. It opens its mouth wide menacingly. Blood-spattered drool drips from its huge jaws that are lined with sharp canine teeth. It moans and hisses loudly causing Ava to walk back a few feet.

Moooaaaaannnn! Sssss! Ssss!

Ava speedily raises her bow to eye level and aims. "Do not think for one second that I will hesitate! I *will* shoot you!"

The beluga has been on all fours. It suddenly stands upright on its weblike, rear feet. Now it is over twice as tall as Ava. It cries out once more in its sickly moaning and hissing sounds.

Moooaaaaannnn! Sssss! Ssss!

It is trying to intimidate her, so she will turn and flee in panic. Then it will drop on all fours and sprint after her as quickly as an Earthly World cheetah. In the end, leaping on her viciously from behind and breaking her neck before she can even take five or six steps.

But then Ava is not intimidated. Nor does she shudder, flinch, or even bat an eyelid. She merely stares at the beast straight on, the arrow of her bow aiming at the center of its forehead.

The beluga cries out hideously once more. *Moooaaaaannnn! Sssss! Ssss!* Remaining upright, it advances slowly. One step. Two steps. Three steps. Four steps—

Ava pulls back hard on the bowstring and yells, "One more step and you are a goner!"

The beluga rears back its head, moans, and hisses, and then it drops down on all fours and pounces forward with quantum jumps with an energy of four tons!

Steadfast and unmoving, Ava coolly draws back on the bowstring and releases the arrow. It flies true and finds its mark in a nanosecond – in the center of the beluga's forehead. The beast immediately collapses to the ground, face first with a revolting, vile-sounding *ka-thump!*

As life quickly ebbs from its massive body, the beluga slams its head to the ground repeatedly. It is trying to dislodge the arrow from its forehead, the source of the excruciating pain. The arrow snaps in two causing Ava to wince. Now she is down to nineteen arrows.

The dying throes of mortality rapidly devour the beluga's last moments. Its torso, arms, and legs erratically flop from side to side. Its moans and hisses become more pathetic, weaker with each passing second.

Ava can no longer stomach watching the beast as it thrashes brutally on the ground. She quickly looks away. Then she doubles over and vomits. Besides being sick to her stomach, she wants to cry. But for some strange reason, the tears will not come. She does not give the lack of tears a second thought. She picks up her satchel from the ground, slings it over her shoulder, and walks in the direction of the Solenom's raging sounds. Before she can take more than five steps, the whole forest comes alive with uncountable screeching moans, and hisses.

Moooaaaaannnn! Sssss! Ssss! Moooaaaaannnn! Sssss! Ssss!

The belugas are emerging from the forest in groups of ten or more. In less than a minute there are so many of the creatures, Ava could not count them even if she wanted to, which she does not. She would like to make a mad dash toward the forest. With any luck, she could shimmy up a tree before the belugas could catch her. She knows they cannot climb trees. Then again, the outer edge of the forest is at least fifty yards from where she is at present. She may be quick on her feet, but the beasts would be on her like a throng of furious yellowjackets in no time. Also, even if she somehow managed to outrun them, she still would have to find a suitable tree for climbing which seems doubtful. So, she continues walking at a pace just short of a run. Almost immediately her path is blocked by at least three dozen of the ferocious, hungry-looking beasts. They begin to encircle her slowly causing her to stop walking.

Her tone is irate as she shouts, "Darn it all! I thought my slaying one beluga would be enough to warn the rest of you to stay away." She swiftly grabs arrow after arrow from her quiver and shoots at the beasts as she spins in a tight circle. Her quiver is empty in less than twenty seconds. She draws her sword from its sheath and raises it high above her head menacingly. The surviving belugas continue to draw closer until she is completely encircled. Now they are less than fifteen paces from where she is standing.

"Okay, come and get me. If you dare! One of us is going down, and it ain't gonna be me!"

CHAPTER 2

THE BELUGAS YIELD TO
FLUESCERE'S RAGE

"Come not between the dragon and his wrath."
—*William Shakespeare, King Lear*

Before Ava realizes what is happening, the belugas unexpectedly start to scramble in every direction. She is taken by surprise by their sudden, erratic behavior. She cannot grasp what is influencing the beasts to act in such a fashion. She slowly turns around in a circle and watches them as they run around witlessly. Not seeing anything out of the ordinary that caused the commotion, she slips her sword in its sheath.

"Hah! It is about time you came to your senses. Thankfully, you have. I am out of arrows, and there is no way I could fight all of you with my sword."

She only takes two steps in the direction of the Solomon, and then she abruptly stops walking. She brandishes her sword once more. She had mistakenly assumed the beasts were hurrying away because of her bravado. Yet they are quickly reforming, this time in two sizeable groupings. One group is forming directly to her right, while the other is taking shape in front of her.

Suddenly, like what happened just moments ago, the belugas set out scampering in all directions. This time she does not re-sheath her sword. She hollers, "What in God's name are you stupid creatures doing? Make up your minds. Either stay and fight or get the heck out of here and leave me alone!"

Maybe they are trying to confuse me. If so, it is working. Then again, perhaps they do not want to attack me. Although that appears very doubtful. I wonder; could it be? Are they trying to stop me from returning to the river? Or are they doing something else entirely? Attempting to delay me because they know something dreadful is on its way.

Eyeing the beasts carefully, she heads in the direction of the river yet again.

When suddenly—

Whoooooooheeeeeee-Aaaahhhhh! Whoooooooheeeeeee-Aaaahhhhh! Whoooooooheeeeeee-Aaaahhhhh!

The dreadfully vulgar, excruciating reverberations sound like the tortured, drawn-out gasps and respires of a dying monster.

Ava stabs the tip of her sword in the ground and covers her ears with her hands. But it is pointless. The hideous sounds are too loud and cruelly ear-piercing. She feels her eardrums are about to explode with the pressure. Likewise, if the horrible sounds do not stop soon, she is sure she will go completely mad.

The horrendous sounds go on nonstop for a least another minute.

Whoooooooheeeeeee-Aaaahhhhh! Whoooooooheeeeeee-Aaaahhhhh! Whoooooooheeeeeee-Aaaahhhhh!

Then a voice echoes over and over from tree to tree until its threatening words shroud the entire area in miserable sadness.

"Aaaahhhhh, Avaïnoáel! He has you at last! And there is no escape. After waiting so long. You are his . . . "

Ava instinctively understands that the voice belongs to Wendigorium even though he is referring to himself in the third person instead of the first person.

"He is coming, Avaïnoáel. Yes, it is he, Wendigorium. Your admirable opponent. He will be there momentarily to join you and his loyal servants."

She glances around at the belugas. There must be hundreds of them. They are squatting on their hindquarters with their eyes closed tightly and heads bowed. They seem spellbound, totally submissive to a god, too terrified to even move a muscle. She sees this as a chance to escape. She grabs her sword and makes a mad dash toward the tree line. To her surprise and delight, the belugas do not move. She runs right past those that had encircled her.

"I refuse to be held captive by your belugas, Wendigorium. I would rather die. Besides, when we face off with each other, it will be on my terms, not yours!"

Wendigorium shouts, "Stop her! She must not leave the clearing! He commands you!"

The belugas lining the forest quickly scramble to their feet in response to Wendigorium's command. They moan and hiss hideously as they hurriedly regroup in a curved line. Ava immediately changes direction and sprints to her left. But she is forced to stop after running less than ten yards. The belugas that were to her right and behind her have somehow reformed on that side. She is outflanked, trapped!

"To run, to try and escape is futile, Avaïnoάel," Wendigorium roars. "You must realize that he is all-powerful. Even from some distance away, he mocks you as you tremble in fear of his coming. Yes, soon you shall—" His mocking words are unexpectedly drowned out by voice-thoughts screaming in Ava's head.

"Et no moriatur! I will save you, Avaïnoάel!"

The belugas start to panic. Most start to run frantically in all directions. Others run around in large circles like they are utterly confused. A few hurriedly scamper off into the forest, hissing and moaning as they flee for safety.

"Remain where you are!" Wendigorium's booming voice commands. "He will arrive before long."

The new voice-thoughts shout inside Ava's head, "Avaïnoάel, you must lie down on the ground!"

Knowing fully well that the owner of these voice-thoughts saved her life once before, Ava falls to the ground. Then she looks skyward and shouts, "Oh, my God, it really is you, Fluescere!"

The dragon is crisscrossing the clearing a mere fifteen feet above Ava's head. She is just as gigantic as she is impressive. Her massive body is at least thirteen feet in length. Her brawny neck is around one or two feet shorter than her body. Her whiplashing tail is around eight feet in length, while the wingspan of her enormous wings is easily twice as long. She is a truly breathtaking spectacle to behold.

The pupils of Fluescere's eyes are serpent-like, not unlike the belugas' eyes. Except for the hue of her pupils that are light blue to purple. The solid sclera surrounding her pupils has a glimmering, golden pigment.

Like dragons in Earthly World fantasy movies and picture books, Fluescere has tough-looking, steel-hard scales of armor. They are of an unusual tint and shade, a blending of colors like ombre. The scales gradually change from blue to black. Ava believes the colors of the dragon's fibrous scales are fascinatingly beautiful!

Fluescere's four, three-toed legs are folded beneath its underbody as she soars back and forth in the sky at lightning speed. Jagged nodes, or spikes, of varying lengths are on her head. They run along her body onto the tip of her tail. Her serrated jaw is wide open displaying row after row of razor-sharp teeth. She looks powerfully ferocious, and she is.

Ava has researched fantasy books about dragons to a great extent. She knows that the skeletal structure of Fluescere's wings helps her to fly high and fast. Curiously, Fluescere's wing structure is like a human hand. It has four fingers, a wrist joint, and a humerus, the long bone that extends from the shoulder to the elbow. Unlike a bird that only has two parts to support its wings, Fluescere's wings are supported in four places. Thus, she can carry more weight, get more lift, and glide effortlessly in the sky as she scoops up air beneath her wings, thus pushing her upward amazingly fast.

Ava has never dreamed or even imagined anything could be so beautiful, so spectacular, so smoothly gliding in the sky like a graceful bird in flight. And so extraordinarily strong as well! Moreover, she is looking at a dragon in real life!

The belugas are becoming more agitated as Fluescere soars above them. Their interest no longer is focused on Ava as their upturned heads warily watch the dragon's movements. A few more flee to the safety of the forest.

"He commands you to seize her! Seize the elf now!" Wendigorium shouts.

Ava is thinking to herself; I guess this is it. Wendigorium is going to have me whether I like it or not. Oh, how I wish there were a way out before I am captured. He will be here soon. And I will have failed before I have even begun.

In response to what Ava had thought about Wendigorium – and before the belugas can even move to comply with Wendigorium's command – Fluescere angrily blasts intense, blistering hot flames from her mouth. Ava knows that the temperature of its flames is more than 2400 degrees Fahrenheit. Consequently, Fluescere's searing flames are hot enough to cut through stone. The flesh and bone belugas do not stand a chance.

The belugas directly assailed by the flames instantly crumble to billows of smoking white ash. Others on the fringes of the flame's passion are critically burned. The charred belugas are running in circles and rolling on the ground in a desperate but unsuccessful attempt to extinguish the broiling flames. They will die from their injuries in less than a minute. The lucky few that managed to escape the dragon's swooping spurts of flames fled to the forest.

Once it is over, less than two minutes after it began, Ava is the only living being in the clearing. She gets to her feet and looks at the carnage with a blank expression. She is rather sad that so many belugas have died. However, she does not feel deeply sorry for them. She knows it all boiled down to two possible outcomes. Her being captured or her staying alive. Either outcome, there is one thing she knows for certain. She would not have allowed Wendigorium to take her alive without a fight to the end of one of their lives.

She watches curiously as Fluescere gradually descends toward her in narrowing circles. The way she effortlessly flies reminds her of an Earthly World hawk circling the sky in search of prey. After a dozen or so gentle turns, she briskly flaps her massive wings and quietly sets down a few dozen paces from where Ava is standing.

Ava is staring awestruck at the incredible creature as it slowly strides toward her. Like humans, dragons are thought to have five basic senses – sight, hearing, smell, touch, and taste. Ava considers Fluescere may have an additional sense, the capability to read another's mind or their intentions. At least she hopes so! But one thing is for certain, she can read the dragon's mind which is wonderful. After all, she had interpreted the dragon's thoughts as she tumbled head over heels in the tower's chasm.

Fluescere's voice-thoughts say, "We meet again, Avaïnoɗel. I am Fluescere." She briefly turns her head just as a puff of ashen smoke discharges from her nostrils. "Please excuse my manners. I will suffer from the effects of my flames for a while longer. It takes some time for my body to smother its fumes. It is the curse of my fire-breathing species."

"Oh, it is okay," Ava says with a smile. "Honestly, I think it is somewhat cool, curiously interesting as well. Does it hurt? You know – when you spew out the fire?" Then, recalling something she had thought about a while back, she says, "Do you mind if I call you Flame. Flame translates to fluescere in the Earthly World dead language, Latin."

"Certainly, Avaïnoŏel, please feel free to call me Flame. I like that name." She turns away as another puff of smoke discharges from her nostrils. "No, it does not hurt in the least when I spew fire. It is natural for fire-breathing beasts of my kind. We start young emitting wisps of smoke, shortly after our egg hatches. The young cannot breathe flames because if they did, they would catch on fire. They have yet to grow scales, and their skin is as delicate as yours. As we mature, the older we come to be, our armor thickens. Hence, the intensity of our flames increases accordingly."

"Are there others like you, Flame, other fire-breathing dragons?"

"There are many," Fluescere replies as another puff of smoke emits from her nostrils. "Those of my kind live in the northern mountains of Antiquom. There are others as well. They dwell in the mountains to the south. Then some live in the deepest parts of the lakes. Unlike us mountain-dwelling dragons, they do not breathe fire. Nor can they fly. They do not have wings, yet they can breathe under water and can stay submerged indefinitely."

Ava's curiosity is nowhere close to maxing out. She is just getting started. She is about to ask another question when Fluescere cuts her off.

"I presume Wendigorium may be here shortly. Although I expect with the belugas dead or gone, the wicked beast may not appear. Either way, we do not have much time. Please climb onto my back. I will keep you safe." With a second thought, Fluescere offers, "Be cautious of my barbs. They are sharp. Wrap a cloth around your hands. I can fit up to five on my back. All the same, the middle of my back is the safest. You need not take my barbs in your hands once we are aloft. I will keep you balanced throughout our flight. You will not fall off, I assure you."

Ava quickly reaches inside her satchel and removes a pair of rawhide gloves. She pulls them on her hands. She is grinning from ear to ear because she cannot believe this is happening. It is like a miracle; like a wonderful dream has come true. She steps onto Fluescere's right wing.

Then she grabs onto one of the barbs and pulls herself on top of the dragon's broad back. A moment later she is soaring through the air high above the Forest of Artonia. As the wind rushes through her hair hopelessly tangling it, she is screaming.

Yes! Yes! Yeeessss!

CHAPTER 3

SUCCESSION OF SERIOUS MISSTEPS

"There is magic everywhere. Akin to you.
Kind-hearted, phantastic, and true."
—Fluescere to Avaïnoάel

1

Ava and Fluescere are high above the Solenom River as it meanders within the winding woodland of Artonia. The river stretches in both directions as far as the eye can see. Numerous, smooth flowing streams and creeks empty in the river along its sides. Wherever the tributaries and the Solenom meet, the river's usual greenish-blue color is replaced by a swirling sea of muddy brown.

Ava can see moving shapes of living beings and small boats in some of the inlet coves where the bodies of water meet the Solenom. She correctly assumes that what she is seeing are fisherelves, most likely Smbot elves of the Unseen Valley. She also appreciates why outsiders call the seemingly dense area the Unseen Valley. This part of the valley is heavily wooded, overflowing with massive boulders, and bubbling pits of tar at the rim of the dense forest. She cannot see a single path or trail. The area looks incredibly rugged and virtually impenetrable by foot.

She considers everything Doo had said about the Solenom's potency and danger is true. White-capped waves are visible in many places. They look exactly like tumultuous waves ocean-going sailors of the Earthly World experience during violent storms. Some of the white-capped parts of the river are many miles in length. She can tell it is in these areas where the Solenom's notorious, nearly unnavigable rapids are prevalent. The rapids are caused when the riverbed suffers a steep descent. From her vantage point high in the sky, she can see where this phenomenon is occurring. The gradient is creating an increase in water velocity and turbulence. As the water churns violently, it creates a white-capped, frothy foam. Then further down the river, the water calms itself to crystal clear currents of bluish white.

She spots a narrow boat directly below them headed downstream. It is navigating the white foam of the churning rapids. It is laden amidships with barrels of foodstuff. There are three figures on board. One is standing on the bow and two are on the stern. Those on the stern are steering the boat. The boat sometimes flies high in the air then slams onto the angry water forming huge splashes.

She ponders silently; I imagine this portion of rapids is no greater than a category one on the Earthly World scale that quantifies a rapid's intensity. One being the easiest to navigate and where little steering is necessary. Whereas a five, or even a four on the scale can result in loss of life. Then again, by the intensity of these rapids, what I am looking at might even be a category two or three. In any event the sailors down there must be courageous. There is no way I would want to do what they are doing. I saw enough of the violently churning rapids of Niagara Falls to stay away from white-water rapids forever!

Fluescere's voice-thoughts say, "I agree, Avaïnoáel. Those that travel along the mighty Solenom are some of the bravest elves and wizarding humans I have ever met."

"Flame, where are you taking me?"

"We are going to the Mystic Mountains much further north. It is there in the highest peaks of Artonia where the mighty wizard Godroh dwells. Sadly, Godroh is not there at present. He and King Poldo are searching for you. They do not know you and I are together. Once you are greeted by those in the Mystic Mountains, I suspect they will dispatch a dragon to locate Godroh and the King – to tell them you have been found."

"Flame, who is King Poldo?"

"King Poldo is the ruler, King of the Timere. They are the elves that dwell in the Mystic Mountains."

Ava says, "I have heard of the Timere elves. They are supposed to be fierce, much more so than Bkotn. But why are Godroh and King Poldo looking for me? Surely, they must know by now that you and I are together. Also, how did you find me, Flame? In the nick of time, I must add. I am indebted to you for doing so. The belugas had me surrounded, and I had expended all my arrows. As you know, Wendigorium was getting closer."

"Avaïnoḋel, my finding you was providence. I flew speedily to the last location in the forest you were known to be. It was the night you and your friend, Steph, had argued. Up to that point, Godroh had been following your travels since the day you arrived in Antiquom. I flew back and forth over the forest for three days looking for you."

Ava is biting her lower lip. Her back muscles begin to tighten because she is annoyed knowing that Godroh had been following her movements all this time. She says in a critical tone, "And just how has he been doing that exactly, watching my travels?"

"The Great Wizard has a mysterious globe in his possession. I have never seen it, but its existence is renowned. The globe can see things others cannot. That is how he observed your travels. There are other globes as well in my land. Sadly, some are in the possession of unkind witches and wizards."

Ava is getting angrier with each passing second. She very much tries to shake it off but is not successful. What she says next reveals her intense outrage. "Flame, I could never be angry at you. You saved me, not once but twice. Although I cannot say the same about Godroh, at least as it concerns my anger. I am furious at him! Are you saying he followed my journey meticulously, watching my every move?"

Fluescere says, "Yes, Avaïnoḋel, he did."

"How did he not know I was in danger? That an elf named Siofra had taken the life of one of her own warriors, my friend, Nessa, when she and I were together? Why did he do nothing when I had run off to escape the same probable fate? Also, why did Godroh not know that I was, in some magical way forced to sniff the sanatios blossom? Even though I suspected it was toxic! That I knew better not to do it. Finally, why did Godroh not do something after a magical force had whisked me from the Solenom? Then that same magical force hexed me! Magically bound me to a sapling!"

Fluescere is about to reply when Ava says in a shout, "Flame, you said there are similar globes to the one Godroh possesses! That some of the globes are in the control of unsavory witches and wizards." A lopsided curl appears on her lips as her expression changes to disgust. "If that is the case, it would take someone with an IQ less than zero to figure out what happened to poor Nessa, to us." She shakes her fist in the air. "Someone or something besides Godroh was watching my every move!"

2

Fluescere decides to give Ava a few moments to bring her anger under control. Once she senses Ava has calmed down, she says, "Shall I tell you the story, what I know?"

"Please do. I apologize for my angry outburst. Thanks to you, I am safe and sound and very much alive. But because of Godroh's inexcusable oversight, Nessa is not. I hope you understand why I am furious with the so-called great wizard."

Fluescere's voice-thoughts say, "Yes, Avaïnoáel, I understand. Everything that has happened dates to your thirteenth birthday." Ava is hanging onto Fluescere's every word as the dragon narrates everything she knows up until now.

"The Great Wizard makes pilgrimages to the Earthy World a few times a year. He has been doing the same for generations. I do not know the reason he journeys. Some say he consults with leaders of the Earthly World's human hierarchy, its presidents, and monarchs. Even so, others' words may be nothing more than hearsay or efforts to appear important. Despite this, I do know one fact. Since your thirteenth birthday, Godroh has made twenty-two pilgrimages to the Earthly World."

Ava's eyebrows rise with surprise as she says, "Why so many visits, or pilgrimages as you say; do you know? And how do you know the number twenty-two is accurate?"

"My sisters and brothers take Godroh to the Thávma every time he visits the Earthly World. They linger near the Earth's opening on this side until he reenters Antiquom. Then they return him to the Mystic Mountains."

"Hmm, I see," Ava ponders aloud. She is shaking her head. "So, twenty-two visits to the Earthly World since my thirteenth birthday. I guess, as Jordyn had said, my thirteenth birthday was important. Have you also taken Godroh to the Thávma or returned him to the Mystic Mountains?"

"No Avaïnoάel, I have not."

"Why is that? Have you been busy doing other things?"

"No, Avaïnoάel. I have been waiting for your arrival. I intend to carry you and only you. Naturally, there are exceptions during times of emergency or when others are in danger – and I am the only means of conveyance available."

"Goodness! That is wonderful, Flame. I am truly honored."

Fluescere continues narrating her story. She describes how Godroh had summoned her one morning shortly after Ava turned thirteen years of age. Godroh told her that he had been mentoring her since the day she was hatched for one special purpose – to look after Ava because she was O Poica Katharos. Godroh also said she was to keep Ava safe or die trying. That she must obey Ava's every command, and to convey her anywhere she wished to go.

"I always wondered the purpose of Godroh paying such close attention to me," Fluescere says. "He would give me special training, teaching me things that the others never had to learn. I owe my vast knowledge of the Inner World to him." She goes on to explain the reason behind Jordyn's participation. This part of her story interests Ava greatly because she always wondered why Jordyn was involved.

Fluescere says Godroh told her that Jordyn was a young, mystical being who aided Earthly World children in need. He and Jordyn had many private discussions concerning how Ava should enter the ancient realm of Antiquom. After many months of planning, they decided there were only two possible approaches. One approach was for Jordyn to relocate Ava to the Thávma where she would be met by Godroh. The other was for Ava to descend the spiral staircase in her grandfather and great uncle's tower. The staircase links the Earthly World tower with the Inner World Gnαèfa, the Spire of Time.

Both approaches had their good and not so good features.

They believed relocating Ava to the Thávma and having her enter the Inner World in that manner was the easiest of the two approaches. However, unless Godroh placed her under a hypnotic spell, which both he and Jordyn did not want to do, they knew she would refuse to go with him freely. Despite how much he would try and play up to her inquisitive personality. Moreover, if he were to hex her, he would lose her trust going forward. And absolute trust between the two of them was the most important ingredient in the recipe of success. Finally, both he and Jordyn knew Ava would be severely upset with suddenly finding herself with an unfamiliar person in a strange land – on the Yucatán Peninsula, Mexico – only to be asked to go inside the perilous, rocky Thávma. Godroh felt certain there was no way she would have consented to any of that, no matter how much he tried to convince her.

In contrast, the spiral staircase that connected the two worlds was even more treacherous than the Thávma. Not only was it perilously unstable, but it had not been used in over two thousand years. Therefore, Godroh did not know if it could still be walked upon successfully. He also said the staircase's chasm was fraught with mysterious enchantments, none of them kind-hearted. Still, both he and Jordyn felt that if everything went according to plan, the tower approach would work out simply fine.

Nevertheless, there were two problems posed by using the tower.

The first problem was how to get Ava inside the tower, so she could access the staircase. If they somehow solved that problem, the second and much larger and more complex problem would ensue. How could they persuade Ava to descend the rickety staircase voluntarily? Only if she agreed to descend the staircase voluntarily would her enormous powers counteract the chasm's magical enchantments – powers of the mind that she would not yet realize she had.

Fluescere says via her voice-thoughts, "Obviously, as you know, Avaïnoáel, they decided on the tower approach. Godroh told me it was – how did he put it? Yes, he said it was the lesser of the two evils and much safer."

"Well, Godroh was correct when he said I would not be pleased if I found myself on the Yucatán Peninsula with him, a stranger. I would have been outraged. Also, looking back and not knowing then what I know now, I would have not descended inside the Thávma. There is no way. No matter how hard he would have tried to persuade me or played up to the inquisitive side of my personality." She laughs then says with a frown, "In fact, I would have been screaming so loudly, Godroh would have had to place me under a spell just to shut me up!" She pats Fluescere's scaly neck with sincere affection. "Thank you for explaining all that. Please continue with your story."

Fluescere begins to explain Jordyn's involvement further. Jordyn knew that Ava's immediate family, except her father, he had to work, were planning a road trip to Buffalo, New York. It was to occur near the end of the month of Ioúliosom of last year. Consequently, Jordyn magically compelled Ava's grandfather to take a circuitous route from the local Walmart to their campground. He was to drive around his childhood neighborhood, pointing out the sites as he drove. With one specific purpose: To stop along Grider Street where the tower was located, the very tower he and his brother had climbed as youngsters.

Predictably, as Jordyn had expected, Ava had already used Google Maps to explore her grandfather's childhood neighborhood. Naturally, she had no idea her grandfather was going to stop to look at the tower. That was Jordyn's doing. Also, as Jordyn had anticipated, Ava's grandfather excitedly told Ava everything that he had experienced when he and his brother climbed the tower. Finally, as Jordyn had hoped Ava had (excuse the idiom) swallowed the bait, hook, line, and sinker.

Godroh told Fluescere that Jordyn knew that Ava could hardly think about anything else but the tower for nearly a year. She became fascinated with the belief that she would someday climb the tower like her forebears. She researched the Internet for information on the tower's history. She explored Google Maps, again and again, to view the tower at different angles and from the satellite's perspective. She took screenshots of the massive structure from above and at street level that were projected on Google Maps. She studied the screenshots whenever she had the opportunity. Ultimately, she started to dream about climbing the tower. Of how fantastic it would be to live up to her ancestors' legacy. The dreams lasted three months. Once again, like Jordyn had done to Steph previously before her adventure, Jordyn had caused the dreams.

Finally, on 9 Ávgoustom of this year, Jordyn placed Ava under a spell just as she had with Steph before her journey. She transported part of Ava's psyche to the tower while the other half carried out its normal activities at home. Then at the precise moment when Ava found herself standing outside the tower, Jordyn released her from the magical spell. Thus, everything that happened *outside* the tower, including Ava's climbing the ledge, was her doing. Because she needed to *choose* to climb the tower rather than being *forced*.

Finally, only if Ava somehow managed to reach the tower's wrought-iron gate could Jordyn whisk her inside. If she had quit before reaching the gate, the entire plan would fail. Then Godroh and Jordyn would enact the Thávma approach. Happily, she did reach the gate which resulted in the most difficult part of the plan. How to persuade Ava to descend the staircase voluntarily!

Ava says, "That is an incredible story, Flame. So, not only were two approaches considered, the Thávma and tower, Jordyn had pre-planned everything that ultimately happened. She hexed my grandfather to take the circuitous route. But she left it up to him to stop at the tower. And I am awfully glad that he did and told me all that fantastic stuff. Then, because Jordyn knew I would naturally be curious to learn more about the tower, she hexed me. No wonder I dreamed about the tower just about every night! Finally, she created my double then unhexed me leaving me to climb the tower on my own. That is until she hexed me once more when she whisked me inside the tower. Everything that happened is very incredible!" She suddenly shouts, "No wonder I left my cellphone and wallet with the ID back home. My double needed it! Wow! Simply amazing. Thank you for telling me all this, Flame. Did Godroh tell you anything more?"

Fluescere replies telepathically, "You are most welcome, Avaïnoáel. Yes, Godroh told me much more. He had said that Jordyn worked hard to have you reach the gate even though she could not hex you. That you had to do it voluntarily. That is why she stopped the rain in the areas where you had already walked. To make your efforts easier. So, you would not be further burdened, frustrated, and then give up your climb."

"I always wondered about that," Ava says. "How and why the rain stopped, and the sun was shining where I had climbed. Jordyn is incredible. Please go on, Flame."

"This is where your Earthly World friend and companion, Steph, joins the story. But first please allow me to say something about the twelve hours that you slept on the tower floor."

Jordyn had caused Ava to sleep for three reasons. One, she had to resurrect the opening in the tower's floor that led to the staircase. It had been closed for more than two millenniums. Two, it was necessary that Ava get some well-deserved rest after her climb. She had a long, daring journey looming on the staircase. And three, she and Godroh, he was standing outside the Thávma, needed to finalize their plans. Godroh is a powerful wizard, but he cannot read minds. So, Jordyn was communicating with him telepathically. It was at that point that Jordyn explained she would need to get Steph involved, even though Steph and Ava had never met. She was certain that Steph would be willing to assist.

Steph is always up for a challenge whether on the rugby field, academically, or socially. She volunteers often to help children in need in the local community. She also loves adventure and yearns to experience new and exciting things. Moreover, she had performed admirably when she and Jordyn worked together earlier. Hence, Jordyn was hopeful that she would assuage Ava's worries about the tower's spiral staircase. That Ava would come to trust her if she narrated some of what she and Jordyn had done together in the past. Then, with any luck, Ava would be persuaded to descend the staircase. Jordyn felt that without Steph's involvement, Ava would have refused. And Jordyn could not compel her because Ava – although she did not know it at the time – was much more powerful than Jordyn. In the end, because Ava and Steph hit it off so well from when they first met, Jordyn decided to have Steph accompany Ava in the Inner World.

Ava wordlessly thinks to herself, well, she is right about that! If it were not for Steph, there was no way I would descend the staircase. I trusted Steph from the onset, and I still do. Yes, there is no way I would have done what an unseen person told me to do via her voice-thoughts if it were not for Steph. Then Jordyn would have had to let me go, or I would be inside the tower even now. And most likely dead because of starvation or lack of oxygen.

She says to Fluescere in an offhand manner, "Well, given the way I feel right now, perhaps I am a bit more powerful than Jordyn. Then again, I seriously doubt I could take Jordyn on. I may be able to break magical bonds with a vicious lunge forward and stand up to belugas. But there is no way I could ever move people across oceans and through time. Or from one world to another for that matter." She rolls her eyes and considers silently, like from the Earthly World to the magical world of here and now.

Her anger returns as Fluescere tells her more about Godroh's magical globe. Fluescere explains that he would consult the globe one or two times a day. He did not need to watch Ava's movements continuously. Godroh had said that the globe can flashback through time. Consequently, he was offered glimpses of where she had been throughout each day.

Ava says, "So, Flame, can I assume he knew exactly when Steph and I crossed the Gnæfa threshold? And from that point going forward?" Fluescere replies that Ava's assumption is correct. "If so, why did he not stop Siofra from doing what she did? Stop her from slaying Nessa. Why did he not intervene?"

Fluescere's voice-thoughts reply, "Godroh's magical globe no longer could see what was happening."

Ava's tone of voice is becoming more heated as she says angrily, "And why not? If the globe was tracking me since the moment I arrived in the Inner World, why not then? Why did it not track me during the most critical part of my journey up to that point?"

Fluescere voice-thoughts reply, "Unbeknownst to Godroh, at least one other wizard was observing your movements. Before he departed to search for you, Godroh told me that he suspected Haldir of Mountains Cross. He suspected Haldir was the one that caused his globe to cloud over."

Ava's head jerks back with surprise. "Haldir of Mountains Cross? I have never heard of that individual before now. Who or what is he or she?"

"Haldir is the evilest wizard in our land. He is the ruler of Mountains Cross. It is a desolate mountain range in the southeastern part of Antiquom. Mountains Cross is where the three realms of the Inner World come together. Haldir is aligned with Wendigorium and Strum. Strum is the leader of the belugas. She too lives in Mountains Cross."

Ava says, "I see. Thank you, Flame. So, this evil wizard, Haldir of Mountains Cross may have clouded the crystal ball – I prefer to call it that – so Godroh could not see what I was doing. Am I correct?"

Fluescere replies that she is correct. "So, let me see if I have this straight, Flame. Godroh lost sight of Nessa and me when we left the contest to visit Crostim Ledge. Am I correct?"

Fluescere says, "Avaïnoǽel, please pardon my disrespect, but you are incorrect. Godroh was unable to see you or the others in the crystal ball much earlier."

"When was that?" Ava asks. "Do you know?"

"The last thing Godroh was able to see was when the elf, I presume she was your friend, Nessa, told you that she was going to take you to Crostim Ledge. Shortly thereafter the crystal ball clouded over and Godroh could see you no more."

Ava shouts, "But Flame, I think that was the evening *before* Nessa was slain! She was slain by Siofra the *following* evening. Do you have any idea what happened?"

"I do not know for certain, Avaïnoǽel, but Godroh mentioned that someone may have hexed one or more of you afterward. It was after your conversation with Nessa. Once Godroh lost your movements, he and the king took flight to look for you. I followed shortly thereafter." Fluescere's thoughts cease briefly then she says, "I did not seek Godroh's permission to search for you. I expect he will be angry with me upon my return."

"Oh, I doubt he will be angry since you found me," Ava says. She rubs the back of her neck. "But if he does get angry too bad for him." She laughs then rolls her eyes. "I will give him everything that I have and more!" She takes a few moments to consider silently everything that Fluescere had said. She begins to work backward in her mind from the moment Nessa was slain and when she ran away from Siofra and her collaborator, Vena.

Ava thinks to herself; just as she gets ready to take up her nightly watch, Nessa whispers to me that we are to climb the trail to Crostim Ledge. I had read her mind as well. Her thoughts reveal that Siofra gave her permission and that Siofra would accompany us. I eat dinner with Steph and DooDad. Afterward, I tell Steph about Nessa, Siofra, and my plans. Steph, strangely, gets all hot and bothered. We argue. It is a horrible one. I go off in a huff. I avoid her the next day and refuse to speak to her. Dad tells me that someone put a magic potion in Steph's goblet. He explains that is why she was so nasty to me. I said I could care less.

A few days later I am hexed! I was chucked from the banks of the Solenom to that blasted clearing and bound to that stupid sapling. I wonder. Could it be that the hexing started the night Nessa told me about the following evening's trip to Crostim Ledge? Is that the reason Godroh's crystal ball went blank shortly thereafter? That must be the explanation for everything that occurred afterward! Steph's odd outbursts of anger and insults. The incorrect theory that someone hexed her goblet. Siofra murdering Nessa. Vena appearing out of nowhere. My being allowed to escape and trek through the most bewitched forest of Antiquom, unmolested for two days. Then smelling the sanatios even though I knew better than to do so. Falling dead asleep. Waking up bound to the sapling. Belugas appearing out of nowhere. And this is the real kicker, the most surprising event of all this magical craziness.

Wendigorium knowing exactly where I was. Probably because Haldir of Mountains Cross had told him!

All of what happened makes sense now! It all boils down to magic. Except, of course, Nessa's death. But maybe, just maybe she was not slain. Perhaps what I thought I envisioned, Siofra brutally thrusting her tkalakn in Nessa's back, was a farce, just one more spell. I hope and pray I am correct. That Nessa is alive.

Fluescere has been eavesdropping on Ava's thoughts all this time. She says, "Avaïnoåel, I have been examining your thoughts. I must say that everything you have been thinking almost certainly is true. All that occurred from the moment Nessa told you about the Crostim Ledge was owing to magic. And, as you say, Haldir of Mountains Cross may be the wizard responsible. He may have been with you and the Bkotn as you traveled. Then again if he were observing you by using his magical crystal ball, he most likely was hexing you and the others from a distance.

"He may have sensed an opening to change the course of events – after your friend, Nessa told you about Crostim Ledge. So, he hexed Steph's mind to cause her to argue with you. Then he followed you and Nessa on the path that led to the ledge. He watched as you ran through the forest after Nessa was struck by Siofra. He must have kept you safe because, as you say, Artonia is dangerous. Then he forced you to sniff the sanatios blossom. Finally, he used a spell that carried you to the forest clearing then bound you to the sapling.

"Five days have passed since Godroh's crystal ball clouded over, and he could no longer observe you. Therefore, I believe you were under the sleeping spell for more than a day. Finally, Avaïnodel, I honestly believe that Nessa was not murdered by her superior, Siofra. The Bkotn take an oath when they become warriors. Slaying a fellow Bkotn is the same as slaying oneself, slaying one's soul. Hence, if I am correct, Nessa is alive. If she is not, if Siofra murdered her, then Siofra is cursed. She will not live much longer, at least not as a Bkotn.

Ava says in a soft tone, "Thank you, Flame, for your thoughtful words. While I may be correct that everything was due to magic, I pray Nessa is alive as you imply. Also, please stop referring to me as my lady and calling me Avaïnodel. Please call me Ava. All my friends do. You are my friend. Therefore, please refer to me by my rightful name, okay?"

Fluescere suddenly emits a short-lived snort of fiery red sparks from her nostrils as she laughs.

"Yes, my Lady, Avaïnodel, I shall call you by your rightful name. Because Avaïnodel, I am your servant and loyal friend. I am honored accordingly with your charm and magic." She pauses briefly then says something that stirs Ava's heart. The touching words will remain with Ava forever.

"Yes, Avaïnodel, I must say this. There is good magic everywhere. Akin to you. Kind-hearted, phantastic, and true."

Ava is grinning from ear to ear. Because she truly respects Fluescere's choice of words. She also recognizes that her beloved dragon intends to refer to her by her rightful name from this day forward – as my Lady, Avaïnodel.

3

Ava and Fluescere's discussion lasted thirty minutes or more. All the while Ava was staring indifferently at the Solenom as it snaked in the valley below. She did not notice that the river was turning out to be much further away as time went by. Now the river looks like a pencil-thin, bluish-white line that is meandering through a chasm of olive green. Ava has been oblivious that Fluescere has been ascending higher in the thin air gradually. She shivers and realizes it is uncomfortably cold. She looks to her left and then to her right. She is surprised at what she sees.

"My goodness, Flame! I had not noticed until this very second. We are nearly as high as the mountaintops." She reaches inside her satchel and pulls out her winter cloak. She changes clothes, and then she removes her shoes and slips on her fur-lined boots. "That feels much better. How far are the Mystic Mountains from where we are now?"

"We are in the Mystic Mountains at present, Avaïno&el. We should arrive at our destination shortly." Fluescere abruptly changes course to the left and begins to descend bit by bit.

Ava throws her hands high in the air and shouts gleefully. "Look Ma! No hands!" Ava also considers what Fluescere had said about keeping her balanced as she flew is valid. She probably could not fall off the dragon's back even if she wanted to.

Fluescere snorts a fiery laugh from her nostrils. She says, "I am pleased you are happy, Avaïno&el. Just so you know, the dwellings of the Great Wizard and the Timbre are much lower than we are right at present. They are below the barren snowline ridges. Happily, for me. The cold does not bother me. But my flames are not as searing in the colder climates." She snorts another brief, fiery flame of laughter from her nostrils. "Although I would not want to be the one attempting to thaw within their much cooler blazes."

Ava sees that many mountain tops have inhospitable-looking, bone-white, snow-bleached crests. The irregular rows of sky-piercing, jagged peaks remind her of the sharp tips of her arrows that are now impeded in belugas. Perilously menacing and dangerous, hard-hearted, and merciless, anxious to destroy all in their paths. Wrinkled, rocky plains of rugged, precipitous brown are below the frosty snowlines. The plains are speckled with patches of green where unfamiliar creatures, at least in Ava's judgment, are grazing. Occasionally, one of the creatures looks up at them and stares.

Glaciers of gleaming, pure white are reflecting the sun's setting rays. The frozen patches of ancient ice look deep, narrow, and dangerous, cold-hearted, and bitterly barren. Ava knows from her science classes that the glaciers' foundations consist of fallen snow from the beginning of time. Then over the millennium, the fallen snow compresses to massive, solidified mounds of nearly impenetrable ice. She supposes these glaciers melt during Antiquom's hottest seasons and form slow-moving rivers of colorful sediment-engorged, icy cold streams. Then the mineral-rich, life-sustaining streams eventually drain into the Solenom resulting in the flooding of its banks.

Fluescere disrupts Ava's gawking. "Avaῖnoάel, do you see that towering mountain to your left? It is the one enveloped in the cloudy mist."

"Yes, I see it!" Ava exclaims. "Why does the mist have a purple haze to it?" She narrows her eyes. "I can also see blotches of red and yellow. What is creating those colors, do you know?"

"It is a 'mons igneus,' a fire-breathing mountain."

Ava recognizes the term mons igneus as the Latin word for volcano. Once again, she is surprised to know that many words in Fortunomy are derived from Earthly World terms. She considers it makes perfect sense since the Thávma connects both worlds. Then again, could it be that some Earthly World words are derived from Fortunomy of the Inner World and not vice versa? I have got to take a course in etymology when I go to college!

"It is the birthplace of my kind, the fire-breathing species," Fluescere says. "We are created from the flaming fires of the enchanted molten streams that flow down the mountainside."

Ava says, "But I cannot see any lava, molten streams of rocks flowing along the mountainside as you say. Why is that? Why is it I cannot see the lava flows?"

"They disappear inside a deep opening. Legends say the molten rocks spread beneath the Inner World's crust far and wide. They also cause the boiling tar pits of Artonia."

"Oh, I see," Ava says. "Do you have a name for the mons igneus? After all, it is, as you say, where dragons are born. Seeing that is the birthplace of you mighty dragons I assume it has a special name."

Fluescere replies, "We call it *Mégisti Koryfí*. Legends of my kind say the Mégisti Koryfí was created by the fabled goddess, Artemis."

Ava exclaims excitedly, "Artemis? This is amazing, Flame. If I recall correctly, the name Mégisti Koryfí is a Greek term that means the mightiest peak. Also, according to mythology, Artemis is the daughter of Zeus, the god of the sky, and Leto, the goddess of motherhood. In Roman mythology, Artemis is known as Diana. Both Artemis and Diana can talk with animals and, I suppose here in the Inner World, with dragons. Like you and I can talk – telepathically, in our minds."

Fluescere opens her wings wide and slows her rate of speed. She is starting a downward spiral.

"We are almost there. A few moments more."

CHAPTER 4

THE FABLED MYSTIC MOUNTAINS

"I may be a prince. But you are my queen."
— *Prince Earendil to Avaïnoάel*

1

When Fluescere lands, Ava is surprised that the temperature is comfortably warm. She quickly changes clothes. She is likewise surprised that the immense clearing in which Fluescere has landed is surrounded by lofty trees. Then she remembers something Doo had told her about Antiquom's geography. They are still in the Forest of Artonia, only at a greater latitude than the remainder of the forest to the south. She wonders why it is so warm here despite being so high up.

Fluescere has read her thoughts. "This area is warmed by the mons igneus. It is visible from here. I will turn, so you can see its cloudy haze."

Ava notices that the fabled Mégisti Koryfí is even less obvious from the ground than it is from the air. Yet from her vantage point, she can make out the slowly moving red and yellow lava flows through the haze. She instantly becomes enthused as her mind conjures images and descriptions of famous volcanoes of the Earthly World. She says to Fluescere, "This is spectacular. I have read a lot about Earthly World volcanoes. Vesuvius of Italy, Mount Saint Helens and Kilauea of my country, Mount Pinatubo of the Philippines. But I never dreamed that I would be this close to one. Does it ever violently erupt, you know, shoot molten rocks and flames in the air?"

"Not that I have been told," Fluescere replies. "I noticed that you have changed clothes. That is good. If you were to descend further downhill, you would have to put on your cold-weather attire once more. It is very cold, but it gradually warms the further you go down." She abruptly bellows a raucously loud boom scaring Ava half to death.

Ava is pressing her hands against her ears as she shouts, "What in the world was that for? You scared the dickens out of me!" In reaction to Fluescere's thunderous roar, chimes ring out from everywhere within the forest. Now her eyes are darting in all directions. "And what is with all those bells I am hearing?"

A snort of fiery red flames emits from Fluescere's nostrils as she laughs. "Please pardon my rudeness, Avaïnoáel. I did not mean to startle you." She snorts another short burst of flames from her nostrils. "It is all part of a special display. As you soon shall see."

Ava's mouth falls open just as throngs of smiling elves emerge from the forest. They are the ones that are clanging the bells, hundreds of them. By the telltale jewelry bracelets that they are wearing on their wrists, Ava knows they are elves of the Timbre clan. Doo had described the lovely bracelets to her some time ago.

The glimmering bracelets are made of agate and crystal beads mined by the dwarves of the Mystic Mountains. The clasps, also fabricated by the dwarves, are made of sterling silver, and formed in the shapes of a heart and arrow. The Timbre call their symbolic bracelets Confident Protection. It is the emblem of the Timbre's steadfast courage and loyalty. The Timbre elves are the most powerful elves of the Inner World, more so than the Bkotn.

All the elves, except for the youngsters, are armed with longbows. Rawhide quivers chock-full of feathered arrows are slung over their shoulders. Ava will be given twenty-two of the Timbre arrows to replenish her quiver. Unlike the Bkotn, the Timbre elves are a diverse group of families. Ava is delighted to see there are quite a few handsome males in the group.

Ava covers her mouth and gasps because of what she next observes. Walking slowly behind the elves as they approach her and Fluescere are at least a dozen dragons! They include utterly adorable baby dragons. The baby dragons do not have scales. Likewise, they do not have teeth which is why elves refer to them as tiny teethlings. Unlike Fluescere's ombre scales that gradually transform from blue to black, the scales of the adult dragons are solid black. A few of the dragons are much larger than the others. Ava correctly presumes they are males.

A few seconds later, she is entranced once more with what she is seeing. She exclaims eagerly, "Oh, my goodness, Flame! You never told me that the Mystic Mountains have centaurs! Look how priceless they are. I cannot believe what I am seeing!"

The centaurs, like the elves and dragons, are still a good distance away. Ava is narrowing her eyes as she stares. She shouts once more. "Wait a minute here! You have *got* to be kidding me! Centaurs, or hippocentaurs, as they are called in Earthly World's fables and Harry Potter books, mostly appear as half horse and half man. They have the lower body of a horse and an upper body of a man. There is an exception, the "centaurides" of Greek mythology. They are female centauresses. But these centaurs are half horse and *half-elf!* And I am happy to see there are female centaurs as well! I simply cannot believe this! Who would have thought—" She is unable to complete her sentence. That is because she is even more astonished than before. She nearly slips from Fluescere's back with excitement. She throws her arms up high along with screams of delight.

"Flame, there is no way I am seeing this for real! This is like a dream come true! It is like I died and went to heaven. I can see unicorns! They simply are gorgeous, Flame. Indescribably so." She lovingly caresses Fluescere's back with her hands and plants a kiss on one of the spikes. "Now I know why you had laughed with your flaming bellow and the reason for all the ringing bells; that you said they were all part of a special display." She breathes in deeply and shakes her head with amazement. "Dragons of every size, elven male and female centaurs, and magnificent unicorns along with the formidable, legendary Timbre elves. Utterly amazing and what a wonderful spectacle to behold. Thank you, Flame."

Fluescere says, "The leader of the centaurs, we refer to them as *kéntauros*, is Lord Wlknoo. He is the one holding the lance. As you can see, the other kéntauros are carrying elven bows. The arrows in their quivers are of elven origin. Elves and kéntauros are the closest of friends, just like the unicorns."

Ava grins as she silently ponders, that yet again a Greek word spoken in Fortunomy is the same. "Kéntauros" translates to centaurs in Greek. And, unlike centaurs in Greek mythology, embodying savagery and rampant madness, these centaurs look calm and friendly. They must be caring since they are walking next to the dragons and directly behind the Timbre elves.

Fluescere says, "The leader of the unicorns as you referred to them – we call them *monókeros* – is Lady Blissia. She is the one walking alongside Wlknoo."

The immense gathering of elves and enchanting creatures slowly draws nearer. Ava barely can contain her excitement. She is grinning from ear to ear. She suddenly notices a rather young male elf has emerged from between the centaur, Wlknoo, and the unicorn, Blissia.

The elf, perhaps three or four years older than Ava, is smiling as he draws nearer. His sturdy, dark brown eyes seem to be smiling as well. He has a trim, muscular physique. His jaw is strong, and he has a prominent, Romanesque nose. Ava notices he is dressed differently than the other elves. His simple tunic of white cloth hangs from his shoulders to just above his knees. The other elves' tunics are a dull grey. His chocolate-brown hair is tousled. Locks from his hairline cover his forehead, just above the eyebrows. Ava notices a glint of silver from beneath his bangs.

She says in a whisper, "He must be royalty!"

Fluescere says, "Yes, he is a monarch. He is Prince Earendil. His father is the king of the Timere. Please dismount so you can greet him, Lord Wlknoo, and Lady Blissia with respect. Please leave your satchel and weaponry on my back. You can retrieve them later."

Ava crawls off Fluescere's back. She turns around and smiles. The trio is standing a dozen feet away. Prince Earendil bows at the waist. Wlknoo and Blissia place one leg in front of them as they kneel. Ava is about to bow or curtsy, she has not decided which one when Fluescere's voice-thoughts seem to shout in her mind.

"My Lady, please do not bend over at your waist or curtsy! Merely turn your head to one side and nod!"

Ava does as she is told.

"Avaïnoάel," Earendil says as he bows deeply once more. His tenor voice is strong and confident. "I am Earendil, son of Poldo." Ava does not know how to respond. So, she thinks she should at least offer her hand so he can shake it. She is about to reach out with her hand when Fluescere's thoughts again seem to scream inside her head.

"He shall not shake your hand! He and the others of his kind cannot lay a hand on you."

Goodness, gracious! Ava's mind ponders. What is going on, Flame? Why am I not allowed to bow or curtsy, and I cannot shake hands either? Fluescere does not reply.

Earendil gestures to the unicorn that Fluescere had said was the ruler of her kind. "I am pleased to present Lady Blissia."

Blissia's spiraling, pointy horn touches the ground as she bends on one leg and kneels. She looks up and says, "My Lady, Avaïnoάel, we are very relieved you have arrived safely. We were worried." Then she stands upright and looks at Fluescere. "I thank your dragon for carrying you to us unharmed." Fluescere does not react. Addressing Ava once more, Blissia says, "We are honored to have you here at last, my Lady."

Before Ava can say anything in reply, Earendil gestures to the centaur. He is the one carrying a lance, so Ava knows he is the leader. "My Lady, I present Lord Wlknoo."

Wlknoo says, "On behalf of us kéntauros, I welcome you to the Mystic Mountains." He lowers his head.

Earendil says, "My Lady, we expect that the Great Wizard Godroh and my father will return later today. They are searching for you. I have asked for a dragon rider to be dispatched to locate them." He smiles and nods his head a little as he looks at Fluescere. "I too thank the mighty Fluescere for saving our Lady's life. We are indebted."

Ava turns around and smiles at Fluescere. Like before when she was praised by Blissia, and to Ava's wonder, Fluescere does not react to Earendil's compliment.

Earendil slowly turns in a circle and holds his arms out wide. He shouts in a robust, truly majestic voice, "My comrades of Mystic Mountains. We welcome Our Lady, Avaïnoάel!"

The entire assemblage of elves, centaurs, and unicorns they bow their heads. Then looking up they yell, "Our Lady, Avaïnoάel!" The elves once more ring their bells.

Ava is surprised that all the dragons do not react at all. Nor does Fluescere. In an eager tone that mirrors her joy, she says, "Prince Earendil, I am very happy to be here and pleased to meet you." She looks at Blissia and Wlknoo in turn. "I am honored to meet you as well. Your reception is, well, I must admit, I am at a loss of words – utterly amazing. Thank you so much!" Turning to Earendil she says, "Prince, or should I say, Lord Earendil—"

Before she can say anything further, Earendil lowers his head with respect. His hands are tilted outward slightly reflecting the honesty of his words. "My Lady, Avaïnoćel, I may be a prince, but you are my monarch." His eyes are twinkling. "Please call me Earendil. When you meet my father, Poldo, he is the king of the Timere, please refer to him simply as Poldo."

Fluescere has read Ava's interpreting thoughts, and she senses Ava's confusion. Her voice-thoughts say, "My Lady, you reign supreme here in Antiquom and the entire Inner World. None are your equal. Please do all that Lord Earendil has requested. Enjoy the honors you richly deserve."

Ava excuses herself from Earendil and the others then turns to face Fluescere. She looks at the dragon kindly, and then she walks over to her. She strokes Fluescere's muscular neck for a few moments. Then she whispers in a soft tone so the others will not hear, "I am sorry, Flame. But I cannot do as you ask. I hope you will appreciate my position. Please?"

Once again Fluescere has read Ava's thoughts of what she intends to say to the others. She says via voice-thoughts, "My Lady, I truly respect your position. That is why you are Avaïnoćel, O Poica Katharos. For your humbleness and humility set you apart from all others of excellence. I am duly honored to serve you. You may tell them what you wish; however, as I said earlier, I shall call you by your rightful name."

Blissia says, "My Lady, please gather your belongings from the dragon. If you would prefer, we can carry them for you."

Ava presses her lips together as she briefly ponders Blissia's offer. She is not comfortable having others carry her belongings. She does not want to do anything that will make her appear too snooty, high, and mighty. That is the last thing she wants to happen. She silently ponders that Blissia's kind offer is well-timed. It is an opening to declare her position regarding the others' pageantry toward her. She turns around.

"Thank you, Blissia, for your kind offer. But it is okay. I will carry them." She looks at Earendil and Wlknoo in turn and back again at Blissia. "I truly respect your deference, to refer to me as my Lady and to address me as the same. I am truly honored. Honestly. Nevertheless, I respectfully ask that you dispense with the title my Lady as it pertains to me. I strive to be unassuming in everything that I do. I was brought up humble and humble I shall remain. Therefore, will you please abide by my wishes, to dispense with referring to me as my Lady?" Earendil, Blissia, and Wlknoo nod their heads reluctantly. "Also, I see no need for you to lower or nod your heads when addressing me. Or bowing. Will that be acceptable as well?"

Earendil is looking at Blissia who is looking at Wlknoo, who is looking at Earendil. Then the three of them look at Ava at the same time. They seem to be confused.

Ava recognizes they do not know how to reply. Because, per her request, they are not supposed to bow, nod their heads, or say "yes my Lady." She says with a smile, "It is okay simply to answer by saying yes or no to me. I will do the same to you."

Blissia says hesitantly, "Is it okay if we call you Avaïnoάel, O Poica Katharos?"

Ava says, "To my face when we are alone, just the four of us, or one on one, please call me Ava; or, if you are more comfortable saying it, Avaïnoάel. But leave out the O Poica Katharos stuff." She looks at the leaders one after the other. "I learned something from my father a long time ago. He was a United States Marine." She sees they are confused with the term Marine. She ponders how to best describe her dad and his service to her Earthly World country.

"My dad was sort of like Elbereth, the leader of the Bkotn Etanpioa. He was a fighting warrior. Does that make sense?" The leaders' expressions confirm that they understand what she has said. "Anyway, when my father would carry on a private conversation with his fellow warriors, or in a group such as ours right now, he would refer to the others by their first names. Sort of like Earendil, Blissia, Wlknoo." She points to herself. "And Ava. Are you following me?" The leaders nod their heads.

"But when my father was with others outside of his small group," she waves her hand across the clearing at the hundreds of elves and creatures standing behind the three leaders, "he would refer to his fellow warriors by their official title. Sort of like My Lord Wlknoo, Lady Blissia, My Lord or Prince Earendil, King Poldo, and Avaïnoάel. Does all of that make sense?" Much to her relief, the leaders appear to understand what she has said. She smiles at them. "So, what do you say we dispense with all the formality except, of course, when we are around others."

Earendil and Wlknoo are hesitant to reply, so Blissia says, "As you wish, Ava. Please allow us to escort you to the part of the forest that leads to a trail. We have prepared a feast in your honor."

Ava ponders excitedly, a feast! This is wonderful. I did not realize it until now, but I am starving! I have had nothing but dried fish to eat for days. She turns away from the others to remove her belongings from Fluescere's back. Her mind is racing, and for some odd reason, she is getting the shivers.

2

Ava leans in close to Fluescere as she grabs her satchel. "Flame, why did you not react to their compliments? When they thanked you for rescuing me and delivering me safely here to the Mystic Mountains? You are richly deserving of their kind words and their thanks. I do not know for certain, but maybe you should have acknowledged their kind words. What do you think?"

"Goodness, I did not realize they had thanked me," Fluescere replies via her voice-thoughts. "Please, my Lady, tell them I am deeply honored with their good wishes."

"You didn't know?" Ava asks in a disbelieving tone. "Why did you not know, Flame? You were standing a few feet behind me. Surely, you must have heard them."

Although she does not want Fluescere to confirm her suspicions, Ava supposes Fluescere is deaf. She is heartbroken with knowing that her beloved dragon will never hear her voice. Tears suddenly gush forth from her eyes like rushing water of a shattered dam. They start to spill down her face. She can feel the sides of her chin quivering like when she was a child. Running to her mother wailing because she had cut her finger, and it hurt terribly bad. Or one of her sisters had punched her in the arm. She purposely takes her time gathering her things to hide her anguish from the others.

Fluescere replies that she, along with all other Inner World dragons, does not have the sense of hearing. They also cannot speak. They are trained to respond to hand gestures and kicks on the sides of their backs by their riders. Yet there is one exception, at least as it pertains to Fluescere. She says, "Godroh combined the Mégisti Koryfí magical alchemy with his mystic charms when he nurtured me as an embryo. After I was born, he made it possible that I can interpret the thoughts of two supreme beings – you, my Lady, and him, the Great Wizard. I cannot interpret the thoughts or respond to thoughts of spoken words of anyone else."

Ava does not want to face the facts even though they are (excuse the idiom) staring her in the face. She persists in arguing, to reject what Fluescere has said. "But you must have heard the words of Wendigorium! How else would you know the beast was approaching? Please tell me you heard Wendigorium speaking out loud to me and the belugas!"

Fluescere's voice-thoughts say, "I regret once again, Avaïnoάel, I must reply that you are incorrect. I read the thoughts of your mind word for word. If you were not at hand in the clearing, I would never have known Wendigorium was speaking, that the fiend was drawing nearer to you. Like the others of my kind, I do not have the sense of hearing. Therefore, I am unmoved by spoken words. Once again, I react only to the thoughts of you, my Lady, and those of Godroh."

Ava is embarrassed by her tears. She always has been since she was a child because she thinks crying denotes weakness. Then again, she supposes that her tears also convey love and compassion that are swelling in her bosom. Along with a bit of sadness because she loves Fluescere so much. Therefore, she considers that being sad and crying, at least in this case, are acceptable reactions to how she is feeling.

In response to Ava's sobs, Fluescere gently folds her within her wing. Ava's trembling gradually lessens. She feels secure, safe, and treasured thanks to Fluescere's tender embrace. And at this very moment, she grasps a few important things. She has undergone many odd changes since arriving on Antiquom. She left her beloved Earthly World family and friends behind, but they certainly are not forgotten. Then brick by brick her former self was unraveled and then slowly rebuilt over time. To what she now recognizes is a mighty elf. She can go many days without sleep or rest and with no food and water. She is tougher, braver, and more resolute than ever before. Also, she is an expert shot with her bow and arrow and handles her sword skillfully. Although she truly regrets that she had slain twenty belugas in self-defense. But she knows it was either them or her.

She also presumes, correctly, that she has not become fully aware of all her abilities. That more powers will come to her soon. More importantly, she suspects that Steph's portending words have likewise come true. That Doo's knowing stares were wholly comprehending for she also knew the truth. And here and now Ava fully realizes the truth as well.

She positively is Avaïnoάel, O Poica Katharos – the Purest of Elves.

She places her forehead on Fluescere's massive body and lovingly caresses her scales. She is still sobbing a little. Her heart is breaking. She feels overwhelmed with the unhappy knowledge that her beloved dragon will never grasp her adoring emotions wholly through her spoken words. That her beloved Flame will never harken to her honest words of admiration and deepest love. That she will never truly feel Ava's thankful feelings spoken aloud – for saving her life two times and for being one of her closest friends.

Flame has interpreted her thoughts. She says, "Do not weep, my Lady. I am fearsome. I am happy and content. Also, I am blessed—

Because I have you."

3

Ava assumes that the Timbre elves and enchanting creatures of the Mystic Mountains dwell in the Forest of Artonia itself. She is partially correct with her assumption. The dragons, unicorns, and centaurs do live in the dense forest. So do the Timbre, at least in theory. Each species rules or occupies different areas of the forest that encompasses the Mystic Mountains just below the snowline. They also defend their respective zones with a common goal – the security of the whole Mystic Mountains and the surrounding, forested area.

Blissia and her fellow unicorns reside in the southern portion of the forest of the Mystic Mountains. It is in Blissia's domain that the forest is the densest. The woodland is practically impenetrable, essential to protect the graceful, peace-loving creatures. Unicorns do not need to eat. Their vitality and magic, along with the positivity all around them, sustains them to an adequate degree. Although they do enjoy munching the plentiful grasses in open areas that are coated with early morning dew.

Wlknoo and his fellow centaurs occupy the eastern area of the forest. The forest is less dense there and wild animals are plentiful. Thus, the centaurs' domain affords them abundant open space to hunt game. The big game that they gather is traded for weapons and other supplies with the Timbre.

Fluescere's relatives live in a vast, open clearing in the northwestern part of the forest. It is the region nearest to the mighty Mégisti Koryfí volcano with its flowing rivers of steaming lava. Dragons revel in being close to the sweltering hot lava and sizzling springs, their natural habitat.

The Timbre elves of Mégedale live in the middle portion of the settlement. The elven city is surrounded on three sides by friendly creatures with the volcano to the north. In essence, the Timbre's domain is virtually inaccessible. Due to the unicorns, centaurs, and dragons' communities to the south, east, west, respectively, and the Mégisti Koryfí to the north. The only vulnerable entrance to the city is from the sky.

Once Ava and the leaders are ready to move on, she notices that the unicorns stay put where they are standing. She will later learn that the clearing is within their southern section of the Mystic Mountains. They will return to the forest after she and the others enter the pathway on the other side of the clearing. She watches as the centaurs move to their right in an easterly direction. They disappear within the forest a moment later. Then the dragons immediately take flight and fly in a northwesterly direction to her left. They, like the centaurs, and in a few moments the unicorns, are returning to their domains. Only Ava, the three leaders, Fluescere, and a handful of Earendil's assistants and warrior guards will walk the path.

Ava says to Fluescere in her mind, "Aren't you going to accompany your fellow dragons to wherever they are off to?"

"No, my Lady. I shall remain with you, at least for now. I want to ensure you are safe for a while longer."

Ava says to Blissia, "Are you and Wlknoo coming with us?"

"Yes, we are to accompany you. We know you have been away for far too long. Once Godroh arrives with Poldo, you will recall many things you have forgotten. Many important things."

Ava is shocked by what Blissia has said. She is about to ask, what things? What important things will I learn? But she remains silent. Fluescere once again advises her to not ask probing questions until later. The dragon had said via her voice-thoughts, "As they say, just go with the flow."

After ten or more minutes strolling single file along the wide forest path, Earendil halts the procession. He walks back to Ava. She is in the middle of the group. With a charming gesture of his hand, he says, "If Ava will accompany me to the head of our convoy."

Ava replies respectfully, "Why of course, Earendil. I would be delighted to accompany you." As soon as she is at the front of the procession, her pulse suddenly quickens. Her insides seem like they are vibrating. She is nearly speechless with a feeling of enormous excitement. Because of what she is looking at in the valley below.

Earendil holds his arms out wide. He says in a robust tone, "Avaïnoåel, on behalf of my father, King Poldo, and all elves, humans, and creatures of Antiquom, welcome. Welcome home to Mégedale!"

Although she somehow manages to feign a smile, Ava feels like she is going mad. She is trying to make sense of what Earendil just said, welcoming her home. She is secretly repeating to herself; it is going to be okay. It is going to be okay. Just go with the flow. Just go with the flow. But how? Why? *Welcome home?* I have never been here before! She struggles to speak, to find the right words. Happily, despite feeling faint and dizzy, she quickly surmounts her shock. Her voice is elevated in pitch and volume as she says, "Earendil, it is simply gorgeous, too beautiful for words."

Going along with what Earendil said about her being back home, she says in a lie, "I am incredibly pleased and happy to be here once more. I know you and your father, and all of your Timbre families are very delighted with Mégedale's grandeur as am I." She leans against Fluescere for support. Fluescere gently enfolds Ava in her wing, but just to some extent. Fluescere's refreshing embrace causes Ava to let out a huge sigh of relief. She utters a weak thank you under her breath.

Earendil is staring at her with a worried look. "Ava, are you okay? You look faint."

"Oh yes, I am quite fine," Ava says as she steps from Fluescere's embrace. "I am amazed by Mégedale's beauty. I simply cannot believe my eyes." Then, like a bolt from the blue, long-forgotten scenes flash in her mind. They are recollections she never knew existed in her amazing subconsciousness. Her eyes abruptly widen with renewed understanding. She begins to feel incredibly rejuvenated. She turns her head to one side and considers to herself; I am remembering things! But how is this possible? I was born in Illinois! Or was I? Doo had said something about me being reborn. She says to Earendil as she points, "I distinctly recall the waterfalls, but the arches," she narrows her eyes, "for some reason the arches look different. Why is that?"

The waterfall's spectacle to which Ava is referring is extraordinary. There is nothing like it anywhere else on Earth. Its spectacularism is due to how the falls cascade down the mountainside. The torrent starts at the pinnacle as two distinct, slow-moving rivulets. As the rivulets gain speed and fall robustly along the mountainside, they interweave again and again. Like a tightly twisted rope or snugly plaited locks of hair. Thus, creating the look of one breathtaking waterfall comprised of countless silvery sparkles. Then, just before the interwoven cascade madly plunges to the frothy pool below, its entwined plait separates in to two distinct waterfalls once more.

The intertwined, plaited waterfalls are called *Katarráplexouktes*. Again, the term is like words of the Earthly World Greeks. "Plexoúdes" means braided in Greek; and "katarráktes" means waterfalls. Braided waterfalls. Katarráplexouktes.

Ava says, "I do not recognize that archway of gracefully curving indigenous trees to the left of the Katarráplexouktes. Yet I assume it leads to the king's mansion. Although it used to be an archway made of stone. The archway is stunningly gorgeous. Am I correct when I say it used to be made of stone?"

Ava is shocked by what she just said. She considers wordlessly, how in the world did I know that Katarráplexouktes is the given name of the waterfalls? No one, including Earendil, even said that strange word in their thoughts. Moreover, how could I even pronounce it? It consists of eight syllables! And how did I know that the king's mansion is behind the archway? Could it be – could everything be true? Was I born here? Or was I reawakened, reborn as Doo had said, even though I was born back home, and now I have returned? It is so confusing!

Fluescere is laughing. Puffs of smoke are billowing from her nostrils.

Ava silently considers with a smile as she looks at the dragon, I know, Flame. I know. I must go with the flow.

Earendil's look of anxious worry has been replaced with an aura of sheer joy. His eagerness to confirm Ava's words is apparent when he speaks. He says in an eager tone, "Yes, you are correct. The former archway failed during an earth tremor many years ago. My father arranged to have the trees planted. They were nurtured to form an arch as you can see." He directs Ava's attention directly below them. "Do you notice something different, perhaps unusual about one of the *diádromosphere?*"

Once again to her complete surprise, Ava finds herself saying, "Are you referring to the larger set of steps, the bridge?" She points. "The one directly below us? If so, yes, I do! If I recall correctly, a similar diádromosphere used to run horizontally from east to west. But this one runs from the top of this ridge to the valley below."

"You are correct once more," Earendil says happily. "We dismantled the old one many years ago. Connecting the valley below to the ridge on which we are standing is more practical. That way we can easily access the unicorn and centaurs' domains." He gestures with a gentle wave of his hand. "If you will follow me, we shall descend the modern diádromosphere to Mégedale."

At first, Ava hesitates. Her thoughts are flashing back to the dreadful tower staircase. However, within a few seconds, she is walking on the diádromosphere a few steps behind Earendil. She is recalling from her readings that this bridge, or set of stairs, is a stressed ribbon bridge. The wooden deck lies on the main supporting ropes rendering it stiff. Unlike the infamous tower staircase and a primitive, swinging suspension bridge, the diádromosphere is very safe to walk upon. If it were not safe, Ava would have asked Fluescere to fly her to the valley below.

She has had enough of rickety spiral staircases to last her a lifetime.

CHAPTER 5

HOSTAGE TAKING

"For Conspiracy, I know not how it tastes,
though it be dished for me to try how."
—*William Shakespeare, The Winter's Tale*

1

Despite being banished from the Tribe and exiled to roam the Forest of Artonia, Siofra had returned to the trail. She waited until the Etanpioa warriors were well out of sight as they spread out to search for Ava. Then she quickly walked along the trail in the opposite direction, toward the Unseen Valley. She caught up with Morwen and Vena a couple of hours later. She immediately began to talk about turning around and getting revenge.

"Why are you doing this?" Morwen had exclaimed. Vena was standing at her side. "Are we not in enough trouble? You and I have been banished from the Tribe, but we are alive. And Vena will eventually be forgiven for her minor infractions. If Elbereth knew you were with us now, Vena and I would be imprisoned instantly. So, would you. No questions asked!"

Siofra said, "We have unfinished business, Morwen. You too, Vena. You know that as well as I." Her tone of voice became harsher. "And do not dare to talk to me in that manner, Morwen! I too am a preferred warrior as former third in command."

"You are no longer in command of anything," Morwen hissed in a defiant tone. "Neither am I superior to anyone. We are outcasts, expelled from the Etanpioa. Do you not understand what that implies? Besides, our returning to the Etanpioa can end one way and one way only! I do not know about you but being a prisoner for the rest of my life is the last thing I want to happen." She glanced at Vena. Vena was nodding her head.

"Isn't it bad enough that we were exiled in disgrace, with dishonor? If we return to anywhere even close to the Etanpioa, we will be as good as dead! Elbereth will insist on it. She will bestow on us no mercy. You will be the first to go because you were banished forever, to walk Artonia until you perish. None of our former warriors will come to our aid. Is that your idea of revenge, Siofra? Is it?" She removed her tkalakn from its sheath and pointed it at her fellow, former warrior.

Siofra snickered a disdainful laugh. "What are you going to do now, Morwen? Kill me?"

Morwen replied angrily, "No, but maybe you can do it yourself like you thought you had done to Nessa."

"I did – I did not slay her!" Siofra stammered. "Haldir hexed me to think that I did. You know that. You heard it yourself. She is alive. You saw that as well."

Morwen crossed her arms and glared at Siofra. She tilted her head to one side and said, "How did it feel, Siofra, huh?" Her tone of voice was firm, confident, bitter. "I bet it felt good at the time. Am I correct? Especially after that insolent, poor excuse of a supposedly important elf's friend, that Ava, insulted you. Not once but repeatedly! Admit it to me, Siofra. I know you enjoyed doing it. You lust after the blood of our enemies just like me. Although Nessa is not and never will be our enemy. Ava is our enemy!"

Siofra pondered for a few moments what Morwen had said. "At the time I thought it had occurred, well, I must admit I was overjoyed. I felt betrayed because Nessa had befriended Ava. So, when I thought I had slain her, I felt vindicated." She sighed deeply, and then she said in a flat, emotionless voice, "Afterward I felt horrible. I had violated my oath as a Bkotn. At least I thought so at the time."

Morwen muttered, "It is not the first time you have violated your oath, Siofra. When we conspired with Haldir, you and I violated our oaths. Many others have violated their oaths, time and time again. Nevertheless, Elbereth does nothing. She is weak."

Siofra said, "Enough of this bickering. We need revenge! Let me ask the two of you one question. What is Ava's weakness, besides not being particularly good with her bow and sword?"

Morwen rubbed her forehead as she considered Siofra's question. At last, she said, "I do not know."

"How about you, Vena, my trusted, loyal friend? One who would sacrifice her life for her best friend. Do you know Ava's weakness?"

Vena immediately bared her teeth. Her tone was scathing as she said, "Indeed, I do. It is that overbearing Outsider, Steph. Along with those two worthless fairies. Ava is loyal to them and them to her. It disgusts me because none of them is worth anything."

Siofra leaned in close to Vena. "Exactly." She looked over to Morwen. "So, think, Morwen. You are wise as well as cunning. How do we get our revenge against injustice? First, starting with Ava? How do we make her vulnerable? To seek us out."

Morwen replied with certainty, "We snatch Ava's friend, Steph. Maybe the two fairies as well. Although fairies are difficult to catch."

Siofra said in a devious tone, "Exactly." Addressing Vena, she added, "And whose friendship do we bring about to help us?"

Vena hunched her shoulders.

Siofra looked at Morwen questionably.

Morwen timidly replied in a questioning, unsure manner, "Haldir?"

"Exactly," Siofra said with a wily grin. "I suspect Haldir will try and snatch Ava if he has the opportunity. If so, he will be following Steph, along with the two fairies in case they rejoin."

Vena said, "But what if Ava already is dead?" She looked at Morwen. Morwen was nodding her head. "You said that Ava ran off in the forest. Artonia is deadly as you know. I doubt she would have survived. But what if she did survive and Haldir has already snatched her? Perhaps even killed her? Or taken her to Mountains Cross?"

Morwen said, "What Vena says makes perfect sense, Siofra. So, is all this worth the risk, trying to infiltrate the Etanpioa and snatch Steph?"

Siofra replied, "I believe it is a risk we will have to take. If Ava is dead or missing, we try to snatch Steph and the fairies. We can hold them for ransom. Then again, Ava may be alive and in hiding. Snatching Steph and the two fairies will bring her out in the open."

"But for what purpose?" Morwen said. "Ava was the one seeking out an audience with Godroh, not Steph or the others. Ava is the important one. Not them. They are her companions only."

Vena cautiously entered the discussion. "Morwen has presented a good argument. If Ava is dead or missing, of what worth are the others to us?"

"Then all is not wasted," Siofra said in an impatient tone. "We slay Elbereth or at the minimum detain her or even expel her from the Etanpioa." She laughed. "Or from the Tribe itself. After all, she suspected the three of us were attempting a coup, so there is nothing to lose."

Morwen said with a surprised expression, "On what grounds do we detain or expel her, Siofra?"

"For violating her oath as our leader," Siofra replied. "Proving she no longer is fit to serve. After all, she is the one that allowed Ava to disappear. A true leader would never have allowed that to happen." She laughed. "Despite her mutinous subordinates' recklessness that was attempting a coup."

2

Morwen, Siofra, and Vena are observing the Etanpioa from their hiding spot deep in the Forest of Artonia. They have been observing the Etanpioa ever since the three of them rejoined. The Etanpioa has spread out in all directions and is searching for Ava. Siofra and the others have been able to avoid detection due to Siofra and Morwen's unmatched evasive skills.

"So, what was that all about?" Siofra whispers to Vena. Vena has just returned to their hiding place in the darkening forest. A messenger had appeared on the trail a few moments earlier. Vena, as the most agile of the three elves, had crept closer to eavesdrop. She can hardly control her emotions as she strives to catch her breath.

"Ava is alive! Alive I tell you!" Vena says with vigor in a hushed tone. She is delighted to see her good friend, Siofra, is grinning. Knowing that Siofra is pleased with what she has said makes her happy. Morwen, although she is not smiling, looks satisfied with her good news as well.

"How can you be certain?" Siofra asks. She gives Vena a disbelieving look. "Perhaps it is a ploy. Perhaps they knew you were spying on them, and they tricked you. Tell us more and do not leave out any details."

Vena says, "I know nothing more except that Ava is in Mégedale. At least that is what the messenger said. Ava supposedly arrived in the city by way of a dragon. The Great Wizard and the King are looking for her even though she is safe. They have not received word that she is in Mégedale. According to what the messenger said, Prince Earendil has dispatched a dragon rider. For what purpose I could not tell. I could not understand what he was saying after that. He and Elbereth had moved beyond my hearing. I wanted to crawl closer, but I could not. So, I turned around and hurried back to you."

"I assume the dragon rider was dispatched to inform Godroh and Poldo that Ava has been found," Morwen says. She looks at Siofra. "How close are we to the Mystic Mountains?"

"Less than a four-hour march to the base of the mountains," Siofra replies. "At least another day's trek to the city if not more." She looks up at the treetops. "But you and I know it is too late to travel at this hour. It is too dark despite the full moon. Surely, Elbereth will be overly cautious as usual. She will not risk continuing along the trail in the dark. Therefore, we must act tonight."

Morwen says, "But what if it is a ruse? Perhaps the messenger is not an envoy. Perhaps Elbereth suspects we are following them." Her brow furrows with displeasure. "Also, Siofra, we must concern ourselves with Haldir. He may be nowhere close to where we are. We cannot do anything without his aid."

Siofra is thinking to herself that Vena referred to the messenger as a male. There are no males in the Bkotn Etanpioa. Also, Elbereth would never try to ask another Etanpioa's messenger to tell lies. She is about to refute what Morwen just said when a shout is heard from the trail. The shout confirms that the messenger's dispatch from Mégedale is authentic.

Steph is calling out excitedly, "Galadriel, Nessa! Lady Elbereth just told me the most awesome news ever. Ava is alive! She is alive and safe! She is in a city called Mégedale. Elbereth said it is a one and one-half day's march from where we are. Isn't that the greatest news ever?" Galadriel and Nessa scream with delight in response to what Steph has shouted.

Morwen saw that Siofra had cringed when Steph called out to Galadriel and Nessa. Knowing that Steph had befriended two of her former warriors caused Siofra's stomach to churn with disgust. Yet she managed an evil grin.

She says to no one in particular, "Ah, perfect. We now have two other hostages to consider."

3

Uuugghhhhh!

"Shut up or I will slit your throat," Siofra quietly says in Galadriel's ear. Her hand is clenched tightly over Galadriel's mouth. She has her knife in her other hand. It is pressed tightly against Galadriel's neck, close to her rapidly throbbing jugular vein. Tiny drops of blood are oozing near the tip of the blade.

Galadriel is struggling frantically to break free of Siofra's hold. She is a powerful elf, but she is no match for the heavier, more seasoned, muscular warrior. She suddenly lets out a muffled scream as Siofra pokes the tip of the blade deeper in the skin of her neck. Now the blood is dripping from the puncture. If Siofra pushes the tip of her blade deeper, the blood will begin to spurt. Perhaps causing Galadriel to hemorrhage.

Naturally, Siofra knows this. She does not intend to kill Galadriel just yet. She merely wants to humiliate her as the Etanpioa's second in command. Moreover, Siofra wants to embarrass Elbereth for banishing her from the Tribe. To appease her revengeful feelings.

"Keep moving like that," Siofra says with a revolting grin, "and you will be nothing but fodder for the belugas. Do you understand?" Galadriel nods her head to some extent. She stops struggling and quickly presses her hand against her neck to lessen the bleeding. She sighs with relief knowing that Siofra did not pierce her jugular vein.

Siofra whispers, "Where are the fairies, Steph's stupid, winged friends?" Galadriel shrugs her shoulders. "Are they here, or did they go looking for Ava?" Galadriel is unable to reply to Siofra's question since it requires two distinct answers. She looks up at her with a puzzled expression. "Oh, perhaps I should rephrase that," Siofra says with a sardonic snicker. "Did they go looking for Ava?" Galadriel nods her head. "So, they are not here with the Etanpioa. Am I correct?" Galadriel nods her head once more. Siofra notices that Morwen is standing beside them. She says to Morwen, "Do you know where Nessa is?"

Morwen appears to be puzzled by Siofra's question. She replies, "No, I do not. What difference does it make? Galadriel was the rear guard. The forward guard, if it is Nessa – I do not know for certain – is too far away to bother us here. Nessa is not a problem unless we encounter her when we grab Steph."

"I want you to find Nessa!" Siofra seethes.

"Why do you want Nessa?" Morwen says. "She is unimportant." She looks at Galadriel. Despite having a blade against her neck, and blood seeping from her fingers, Galadriel looks like she is ready to fight a whole army of rebellious warriors. And that look in her eyes, Morwen considers silently. The way she is staring at Siofra and me one after the other! She would not hesitate to slay both of us if given the chance. She grins. We trained her well.

"They are collaborators," Siofra says with a mocking smile. "And I want my revenge as do you. So, I want Nessa to come with us along with Galadriel and Steph. One or all three of them will be useful if everything goes according to plan." Morwen is about to protest when Siofra says, "Tell me where she is, Galadriel. Tell me. Is Nessa on guard? If not, do you know where she is sleeping?"

Galadriel shakes her head. She will not divulge the whereabouts of her closest friend. She would rather die than put Nessa in harm's way or to violate her oath as a Bkotn.

In the blink of an eye, Siofra slices Galadriel's right hand with her knife. Before the blood even begins to flow, her knife is close to Galadriel's jugular vein once again.

That Galadriel did not cry out or flinch does not go unnoticed by Morwen. She considers silently; Galadriel is a brave second in command despite her youthful age. I am immensely proud of her.

Galadriel continues to shake her head courageously. She is willing to forfeit her life for Nessa.

Siofra speedily moves her knife from Galadriel's neck and jabs it in Galadriel's cloak, penetrating the fabric slightly. Galadriel does not react even though the tip of the blade had pierced her skin. She can feel the blood oozing from the puncture.

Morwen shouts in a whisper, "No, Siofra! Do not do it! Our quest is Steph. Slaying Galadriel will only aggravate and complicate things even more. Remember your oath, Siofra!" She glares adding, "Besides, she is young and has done you no harm!"

Siofra flashes Morwen a dirty look. "My oath? I am no longer loyal to my oath or the Tribe." She pushes Galadriel away. "Neither are you. Gag her and bind her wrists and ankles. She is coming with us whether you agree or not." She glares at Morwen. "And I could care less if she is young!"

Morwen immediately does as Siofra had ordered.

Siofra says to Vena, "Do you know where Nessa and Steph are?" Vena replies that she does. "Good work. You are an excellent spy. Do you think you can handle Nessa on your own?"

Vena grins and snaps to attention. She swiftly moves her lance, so it is diagonal in front of her body. A Bkotn that moves her weapon in such a manner is signaling she is prepared to fight to the death. To sacrifice her life if necessary – for her honor and the Tribe.

Siofra says, "Good. Be wary and as silent as the softest wind. I will find Steph myself." She says to Morwen, "Take Galadriel to our hiding spot. Do away with her if she refuses to cooperate."

Morwen leads Galadriel away and whispers, "I will not allow her to injure you further. You have my word." She removes a strip of cloth from her pocket and hands it to Galadriel. "Use this to suppress the wound on your neck. I will bind your wrists once the bleeding has stopped." Galadriel takes the cloth and places it against her neck. Morwen looks at Galadriel's other hand, the one Siofra had slashed, and says, "It is a superficial wound. The bleeding has already ceased."

Less than fifteen minutes later, Steph and Nessa are in the rebellious warriors' hiding spot. They are wide-eyed and struggling even though they are bound at the wrists and ankles. Both are gagged as well with bits of torn cloth Vena had stuffed in their mouths.

Siofra says to Vena, "Guard them. Keep your tkalakn at the ready." Then she looks at Morwen and commands, "Remove their gags." She looks at Nessa and Steph in turn. "If either of you calls out, Vena will slit your throat." Her lips form a hateful grin. "Trust me. I know her well. She will not hesitate to end your lives."

Siofra slaps Nessa on the face three times. She leans in close and whispers in her ear, "Do you not know you are a disloyal traitor? Indeed, you are. You should know better than to testify harmfully against your superior. I ought to kill you right now." She slaps Nessa's face two more times. She grins wickedly then says in an appallingly hateful tone, "But in due time my precious, rebellious friend. In due time. And please trust me when I say this. Yours will be a slow, agonizing death but only after I have you watch Galadriel die as I slice her up bit by bit."

Siofra leans in close to Steph until only a hair's breadth separates their faces. She says in a mocking, contemptuous tone, "I see your close friend, Ava, has abandoned you, yes? She went off running petrified, cowardly like a clucking pollo runs from the butcher's carving knife."

Steph gives her a disgusted look. Two offensive words escape her lips then she looks away.

Siofra slaps her hard across the face. "Do not look away from me again and how dare you curse at me!"

Steph slowly turns her head and glares. She is shaking her head and inwardly thinking; it will take much more than a couple of dozen, even a hundred slaps to suppress my spirit. She says aloud, her expression one of pure loathing, "Is that all you got, Siofra, huh? Slapping Nessa and me while we are bound at the wrists. Unable to fight back. Let me ask you this, Siofra, as the banished, humiliated, traitorous Bkotn. Are you afraid of me and Nessa? I certainly hope that you are. As for me, if I ever get loose from these ropes, I will make you regret that you slapped me!" Siofra does not give her the satisfaction of replying and merely glares. "In any event, Siofra, I hope you are afraid because I will never concede to you." She glances at Morwen and gestures with a nod of her head at Vena. "Or to them as well. And I swear, Siofra, someday you will regret what you have done. You have my word."

Siofra is visibly surprised by Steph's boldness. She whispers between clenched teeth, "Tie them to the trees and gag them once more."

Morwen and Vena pick up the clumps of cloth from the ground. Vena stuffs the filthy tuft of cloth in Nessa's mouth. Morwen moves to do the same to Steph, but Steph lunges forward and bites down hard on three of Morwen's fingers. Morwen rears back and cries out with pain.

Siofra reaches over and slaps Steph across the face repeatedly and as hard as she can.

Slap – slap – slap – slap! Slap – slap – slap!

Even though Steph is stunned, and her face is already coloring from the hard blows, she does not cry out. Nor does she react outwardly. She simply stares at Siofra and grins. She wants to stick her tongue out at the disgusting warrior but thinks better of it. She silently considers that Siofra just might cut out her tongue if she does!

Vena moves behind Steph and speedily places her tkalakn against her throat. She whispers in Steph's ear. "You move, you die." She looks at Morwen. Morwen is shaking her injured hand up and down; blood is splattering all over. "How dare you injure my fellow Bkotn." She gestures to Siofra.

Siofra picks up the filthy pieces of cloth from the ground and roughly stuffs them deep in Steph's mouth. Steph's eyes immediately widen in panic as she starts to choke. Her face is bright red. Siofra declares in a hateful tone, "Oh, I am sorry, Steph. Did I put them in too deep? Does it hurt? Do you feel like you are going to choke? Maybe die? Good." She turns away and storms off to control her anger. She wants to kill Steph for her belligerent attitude, for biting Morwen. But she knows that Steph is her most important bargaining chip when dealing with Ava and Elbereth.

Morwen looks over her shoulder to make certain Siofra is not watching. She pulls the cloth from Steph's mouth, just enough so she is no longer choking. She says to Vena, "Steph is no good to us if she is dead." Vena is giving her a dirty look, but she does not say anything.

Siofra returns to where Steph and the others are standing. She says to Morwen, "We might as well get some sleep while we can. You take the first watch. And stop shaking your hand like that! Your blood is splashing everywhere!" She reaches in her cloak pocket and withdraws strips of cloth. "Use these. Vena, you take the second watch." She stretches her arms out wide and yawns. "As for me, wake me at daybreak. If you need to wake me earlier, make certain it is important." She gestures to the sheathed blade on her shinbone. "Or else." She notices that Morwen is giving her a dirty look. She says in an annoyed tone, "Too bad, Morwen. You had your chance to be number one of our clandestine group. But you chose not to. How does it feel that I am now *your* superior in crime?"

4

"Siofra, wake up," Vena whispers as she pushes lightly on Siofra's shoulder. She immediately backs away. She knows that her good friend has a bad reputation of thrusting out angrily with her tkalakn when she is aroused during the middle of the night.

"This had better be important," Siofra says in a grouchy, threatening tone. She sits straight up, yawns, and rubs her eyes. "Come on, Vena, spit it out. What do you want? And for your sake it better be good."

"The wiz-wiz-ard, Hal-Haldir is he-here," Vena stammers.

Siofra jumps to her feet and gathers up her longbow and tkalakn. She shoves her tkalakn in its scabbard and shoulders her quiver. "Where is he?"

"He is with Morwen," Vena replies. She is pointing to the area where Steph and the others are sitting. "Over there, in the thicket behind the prisoners."

Siofra quickly walks toward Morwen and Haldir. Vena follows closely behind. She says in a deferential tone, "My Lord, thank you for coming."

"Siofra!" Haldir whispers as he shakes her hand. "The conditions of our meeting once more could not be any finer than at the moment."

Siofra says, "How did you find us?"

"I have my ways," Haldir replies with a sly grin. "I make it a habit to know the whereabouts of my dear friends." He stares at Siofra for the longest time with a bemused expression. His stare is making her feel nervous. She unconsciously shuffles her feet and looks at the ground.

At last, breaking the silence, Haldir says, "My dear friend, Siofra," he gives Morwen a quick look, "I must ask the two of you something important. Now that you have the Earthly World companion of Ava as a prisoner, what are your plans? I hope for the sake of your continuing long lives," he glances at Vena, "and the hopeful long life of your young companion, that your plans are sensible." He tilts his head to one side and grins. "After all, one would not want you three to suffer the wrath of Avaïnoάel, O Poica Katharos. When the powerful, legendary elf discovers you have bound and gagged her good friend, how do you think she will behave?"

Siofra lets out a soft gasp in reaction to what Haldir has said about Ava being O Poica Katharos. She seems frightened, anxious. She looks at Morwen and Vena in turn. They appear equally alarmed and nervous. She says to Haldir in a spiritless tone, "Do you mean to say, my Lord; are you telling us that Ava is Avaïnoáel, O Poica Katharos? If so, that would explain her intended audience with Godroh and why the Etanpioa was guarding her."

Haldir replies curtly, "Indeed, she is the same. Thus, I dread that you have unleashed a power you shall never keep under control."

Vena suddenly exclaims in a trembling tone, "Siofra, what have we done? If Ava is O Poica Katharos, we are finished!"

Haldir turns and looks at Vena and says bluntly, "I must agree, Vena. Perhaps the three of you have set in motion your assured, premature deaths. Or, at a minimum, life imprisonment. As you know from the legends, the O Poica Katharos is most powerful."

Siofra says, "Haldir, what do you propose?" She looks at Morwen. "I am certain Morwen and I will follow any course you desire."

"Perhaps you should dispense with the two warriors," Haldir says without a hint of emotion.

"What are you saying, my Lord?" Morwen stammers. "Surely, you are not suggesting—"

"I am not suggesting anything, Morwen," Haldir scolds as he interrupts her. "I simply am replying to Siofra's query."

Siofra says straightforwardly, "If we dole out their punishment as collaborators, perhaps no harm will result. They are nothing to Avaïnoáel. They merely are acquaintances like others of the Etanpioa. I suspect she will never remember their faces nor their names."

"I beg to differ!" Morwen protests with earnest. "Nessa accompanied Avaïnoáel on the path that leads to Crostlm's Ledge. She will never forget Nessa's face or her name. Especially after running away from what she presumed had occurred, that you had murdered Nessa!" She glances at Haldir. "When she too, as I suspect, was subjected to Haldir's enchantments. Otherwise, why would she have run off?" She glares at Siofra. "No, Ava, I mean Avaïnoáel will not forget Nessa's friendship. Also, I noticed that she often talked to Galadriel as well. I suspect that the threesome has become good friends." She shakes her head and says adamantly, "No, Siofra. We cannot do anything further to harm any of them, especially Steph."

Siofra is frustrated with what Morwen has said. She says, "Shut up, Morwen! We will discuss Nessa and Galadriel's fate in private." Morwen is about to protest, but Siofra cuts her off with a boorish glare. She turns away from Morwen and says to Haldir, "Avaïnoάel's Earthly World friend, Steph? What do you recommend?"

Haldir replies, "Perhaps you should allow me to decide her fate."

"No way!" Siofra declares in an irate tone. "I want my revenge! And I will have it no matter what."

Haldir's head rears back as he laughs. Then he leans in close and says with rage, "You want revenge? You want revenge against what? Against whom?" He shakes his head and sneers. "Against O Poica Katharos?" He abruptly stops laughing. "Are you out of your mind?" He looks at Morwen and Vena in turn. "Please tell me your former Etanpioa third in command has not lost her mind! That she is not seeking revenge against the all-powerful Avaïnoάel! A mere warrior elf going against the most powerful elf of all three realms of the Inner World!"

Morwen and Vena do not reply. Siofra does not say anything either.

Haldir says in a fiery tone, "No, Siofra, you may seek your revenge by dealing with your fellow Bkotn warriors in any fashion you and your conniving cohorts desire." He slams the base of his staff onto the ground. The crystal at the top of the staff gradually burns light blue. "I will deal with Avaïnoάel's Earthly World friend myself. In my fashion."

"But Haldir," Siofra stammers. "I want my re—"

"Shut up you insolent fool!" Haldir growls in a command. Morwen and Vena are standing to his right. He turns his head somewhat and winks his left eye completely surprising Siofra. Wisely, she does not react. She understands that everything Haldir has been saying, along with his feigned, angry disposition toward her, is nothing more than a stunt. He is trying to deceive Morwen and Vena. After all, she thinks to herself, we go back as friends hundreds of years.

Haldir says angrily, "You disgust me, Siofra. You and your laughable idea of revenge. Do you not realize you have sealed your fate and perhaps those of Morwen and Vena? All the same, at least in your scheming friends' state, I can thwart the inevitable. Therefore, you must get out of my sight, and I command you to bother them no more. If I wanted your input, your advice, or your support," he winks yet again, "then I would ask for your help. But I no longer need it. So, go. Now!"

Siofra does not move. She bares her teeth as her nostrils flare. She stares at Haldir pretending to be unafraid. She is about to say something when Haldir points his staff at her heart.

"I said get out of my sight now! Before I banish you from the living!" He winks a third time.

Siofra takes a long look at Morwen and Vena. Then she turns around. A minute later she steps out of the small clearing into the forest.

Haldir barks to Vena, "Bring Stephanie JoAnne Galanos to me." Vena gives him a puzzled look.

"That is Steph's rightful Earthly World name – Stephanie JoAnne Galanos. She prefers to be called Steph. Bring her to me." Vena walks off to fetch Steph.

Haldir looks at Morwen straight in the eyes. "You and Vena do as you wish with your former warrior colleagues. But I must caution you, my dear friend. If you continue to join forces with Siofra, your fate is forever in her hands. She is controlling, manipulative, and vindictive. She will take you down a path on which I fear you will never escape. She and I go back many years to when she was a young warrior. Her revengeful ways are the reason you and Vena are in this predicament. Once Avaïnodel discovers what you have done, neither of you will be safe."

"What shall I do?" Morwen whispers. "Please, Haldir. I seek your advice."

"Elbereth sealed Siofra's fate with her dictum days ago," Haldir says. "Thus, compelling Siofra to roam the forest unaided. Forsake her, Morwen, for she deserves nothing more. After you return Vena to the Tribe, you too will have to reenter Artonia. But then, perhaps with a bit of luck, you can travel east where you can live free. I suspect it is what you desire."

"But how? Siofra surely will follow Vena and me. I am her unequal, Haldir. She can easily overpower me. She is ruthless as well as vengeful."

Haldir is lying as he says, "I have caused Siofra's memory of everything that has occurred to be empty. From the moment she returned to the trail after being banished until now. I will force her to return on the trail and reenter the forest at the exact spot she was banned. Then Artonia and its savage creatures shall decide her fate. I wish her well despite her detestable quest for revenge." He adds with a sigh, "After all, I have known her for many years."

"You can do all that?" Morwen says. Haldir nods his head. "But what about Nessa and Galadriel?" Haldir flashes her a bad-tempered look.

"Morwen, do not try my patience. As I said, you will decide their fate. You must, and you shall. Now that Siofra is gone, you are in charge once more."

"My Lord," Morwen says quietly. She glances at his staff. Her eyes are pleading. "Please, Haldir. When this is over once I have decided Nessa and Galadriel's fate. I must end this tragedy with dignity, with honor. It is the only way I can uphold my oath to the Bkotn code."

Haldir looks at her curiously for a few moments. At last, he nods his head with recognition. He says in a soft, somewhat miserable tone, "Are you certain, Morwen? What you ask of me cannot be undone. You do realize that, yes?"

Morwen nods her head. "Yes, I understand, Haldir. There cannot be any other outcome. Please do as I desire. All of this must end with dignity, at least for me. As punishment for everything I have done."

"As you wish, my dear friend," Haldir says in a gentle tone. He lowers his head reverently and whispers, "May you find solace in the Deep Realm." Then he points his staff at Morwen's heart.

Morwen's upper body shudders slightly just as her cloak seems to catch a windless breeze. She mouths a nonverbal, "Thank you."

Vena returns with Steph in tow. Steph has a large gash on her left cheek. Blood from the wound is trickling onto her cloak. She is struggling brutally even though she is bound tightly at the wrists and ankles. She glares at Morwen and then at Haldir.

Morwen and Haldir are ignoring Steph's glaring stares. They are gawking at Vena. She is covered from head to toe with leaves and broken twigs. Her hair is a disheveled, tangled mess. Twigs and dirt are sticking to her forehead. Her left eye is nearly swollen shut. Her right eye is already starting to discolor with a bluish-black tint. She will be sporting two black eyes for nearly a month. Her lips are cracked, bleeding, and already starting to puff up. She is trembling slightly.

Morwen says in a startled tone, "What in the world happened to you, Vena? You look terrible! Like you just faced off with a pack of belugas."

Vena gives Steph a dirty look. She punches Steph hard in the small of the back with her fist, obliging Steph to stagger forward. She points to Steph's bound legs. "That is what happened to me. She has some magical power in her legs. I have never seen such strength."

"How is that?" Haldir says without looking at Vena. He is staring at Steph's feet. "She is bound at the ankles." He moves to the side and sees that Steph's wrists are bound behind her back. "Her wrists are bound as well."

Vena's tone of voice is exceptionally angry as she says, "When I approached her, she dropped to the ground. Then she tripped me and began to pummel me with her bound feet." She points to her left eye. "She did all of this to me in a matter of seconds. I almost passed out, it hurt so bad." She pushes Steph with her open hand causing Steph to stagger forward. Steph gives her an ugly look and sticks out her tongue.

Vena ignores her as she resumes describing what had taken place. "Then she opened up her legs at the knees and placed me in a chokehold between her calves." She opens the collar of her cloak and shows the others her neck. It is swollen and even now is a shade of pinkish blue. "She did this to me too! So, I reached down and grabbed my blade from its sheath." She pulls up the hem of Steph's cloak. There is a small jab wound on Steph's right calve that is bleeding slightly. "I stabbed her in the leg as you can see. I only scratched her, but it was enough to get her attention. She loosened her grip a little, and I reached up with my blade and cut her face." She gives Steph a spiteful look then says with a grin, "I was aiming for her throat." She pushes Steph yet again, only harder this time. Steph falls to her knees, but she manages to scramble to her feet straightaway.

Vena says, "I managed to roll away and stood up. But once more, I barely escaped. She was on her feet in no time. She is quick I tell you, and like I said she has a secret, magical power in her legs. That is when I reached over and grabbed Galadriel by the hair. I placed my tkalakn against her throat." She kicks Steph hard in the back of her knees. Steph collapses and falls flat on her face. Even so, she is back on her feet before Vena can continue with her story.

"'I had Galadriel in a chokehold. I told Steph that if she were to make one more move toward me, I would slit Galadriel's throat. Then I looked at Nessa and said I would slit her throat as well. Next, I asked

Steph if she was going to go with me quietly, and do you know what she said?" The others shake their heads. "She actually said, 'Only because of them; otherwise, Vena, I would make you pay.' Can you imagine she said that while bound at the wrists and ankles?'"

Before Siofra and Morwen can reply, Steph's eyes suddenly close. Her shoulders slump forward. Then her head drops to her chest just as her entire body goes limp. Morwen, and Vena stare at her in disbelief. They had no idea that Haldir had placed Steph under a spell without uttering a single word. He had stealthily done so by using the wand that was hidden in the roomy pocket of his robe.

Haldir says to Vena, "Unbind her. She will dutifully walk along beside me." He gives her a cross look and seethes, "Also, do not push or kick her again. I despise those who injure others who cannot defend themselves. What you did was uncalled for. It is a mark of cowardice. If you push or kick her again, you will wish you had both legs to walk upon instead of relying on a stick for support!"

Vena quickly cuts the cords binding Steph at the wrists and ankles and backs away from Haldir. She stares at Morwen for a few moments because the older warrior is shivering uncontrollably. When she looks away from Morwen, she is astonished to see that Haldir and Steph are nowhere to be found. She turns around in a full circle and says to Morwen in a dumbfounded tone, "It is like they vanished into thin air! How is that possible?" Then, after turning in a complete circle yet again she is facing Morwen. "What are we supposed to do now?"

Morwen replies, "We deal with Nessa and Galadriel ourselves as Haldir had suggested." She walks toward where Nessa and Galadriel are standing some distance away. Vena follows her. "Cut their bindings at the wrists and remove their gags, starting with Galadriel. I want them to die one by one but with a bit of dignity. They deserve that much even though they are collaborators as Siofra had said." She unbuckles the sheath of her tkalakn, but she does not remove the blade. "I will guard them as you remove their bindings and gags."

As Vena leans in to cut the cord that is binding Galadriel's wrists, Morwen snatches her from behind. She immediately disarms Vena just as she places her in a disabling chokehold. Morwen does not intend to choke the life out of her; rather, she only wants to knock her out.

Nessa and Galadriel remain motionless and stare with panicky eyes. They are stunned at what Morwen is doing to her fellow collaborator.

A few seconds later, once Vena is unconscious, Morwen gently lowers her to the ground. She places her finger to her lips and says to Galadriel and Nessa, "Shhh. Remain quiet. I am going to set you free." She hurriedly removes the gags from their mouths. Then she cuts the cords binding their wrists. She commands in a whisper, "Go! Leave!" Nessa and Galadriel stare at her with disbelieving expressions. "Tell your story about Siofra and me any way you desire." She looks down at Vena. Even now she is regaining consciousness. "As for Vena, I see no reason why you cannot be misleading. For her sake. As you probably know, Siofra led her astray for so many years. Siofra and I abandoned both of you as well." She nods her head at Nessa. "Now two times you have been forsaken by a fellow Bkotn, Nessa. I am dreadfully sorry. I cannot ask you for forgiveness because I do not deserve it."

"Why are you letting us go?" Galadriel asks incredulously. She is bending over to untie the cord at her ankles. She looks up. "You easily could have slain us. No one would have known."

"Because I could never slay another Bkotn," Morwen replies. "I could not live with the nightmarish visions, the profound remorse, the horrible knowledge that I had murdered a comrade." She looks at Nessa. "Knowing I betrayed my fellow Bkotn is bad enough, two times in your case, Nessa. I am terribly sorry. Now both of you go! Be safe. Say as you wish to Elbereth concerning me and Siofra. But please tell untruths about Vena. She deserves a second chance. I beg of you to do as I ask."

Nessa and Galadriel hurriedly race in the direction of the trail to join up with the Etanpioa.

Morwen watches them go. She lets out a long sigh and begins to weep as she recalls her and Haldir's accord. She kneels beside Vena and gently caresses the young warrior's long, chestnut brown hair. She removes the twigs and leaves from Vena's hair and straightens out the tangles with her fingers.

Vena is wide-awake. She looks up at Morwen and smiles. Her eyes are questioning, yet she understands what has happened. She also suspects what will happen next. She sits up and wraps her arms around Morwen's neck and hugs her close. She begins to cry.

Morwen whispers, "I love you, Vena. You are a fine warrior and a good friend. I am sorry that Siofra and I led you off course. Go home to the Tribe. They will forgive you and speak not of what happened tonight. May my blessings be with you always." She kisses Vena's cheek. "I pray going forward you will carry on as straight as an arrow flies true. Do it for me. For us and our fellow Bkotn." She abruptly clutches at her chest and collapses onto Vena's lap.

With one closing smile of eternal peace, Morwen closes her eyes for the last time.

CHAPTER 6

FOOLISH TRICKS AND TREACHERY

*"Tricks and treachery are the practice of fools
that don't have brains enough to be honest."*—*Benjamin Franklin*

1

Steph is stretched out on the floor, her back against the wall, one leg crossed over the other. She thinks she has been sitting in this exact spot for hours. Then again, ever since the man – she knows for certain he is a wizard but does not know his name – led her to the dingy cabin, time seems to have stopped. She considers it is unimportant in any case. The most important thing is trying to figure out a way to escape. She must return to the Etanpioa, so they can take her to Mégedale, to link up with Ava once more.

The floor on which she is sitting is made of soft planks of wood. It is spotted here and there with numerous patches of black mold and olive-green shards of mildewy straw. Discarded skeletons of what looks to Steph like fish bones are scattered everywhere. She stifles a yawn then flicks away a purple bug that is crawling along her shin. The bug lands a few feet away then sets out to crawl back to her. She reaches out with her leg and smashes it to smithereens with the heel of her boot. Nasty, yellowish slime seeps from its crushed abdomen.

If she had to cry right now, she could not. Her tears are all washed up. When she was walking beside the wizard, she was barely awake. But she wept quite a bit. She was thinking of home, her parents, sister, and Spirit. She was also thinking about Ava even though she knew that Ava was safe with the Timbre elves. Moreover, she was particularly worried about Galadriel and Nessa's fate.

She doubts the trio of collaborators allowed Galadriel and Nessa to go free. If they freed them, the two young warriors most certainly would have alerted the Etanpioa. That Siofra and Morwen, along with Vena, had rejoined just as she feared that they would. She even had stated that very probability to Galadriel. Therefore, she believes that Galadriel and Nessa must be dead. To keep secret that the wizard had abducted her and is holding her prisoner.

Steph knows that Vena is cruel and mean-spirited. She also knows that Vena is Siofra's sidekick and pretty much does whatever the older warrior wants. As for Siofra, well, Steph realizes that she is even worse, horribly vindictive, and cruelly heartless to the point of behaving illogically. She is not so sure of Morwen. Morwen seemed upset every time Vena had smacked or kicked her. She also noticed that Morwen shivered quite a bit which is uncharacteristic of a seasoned Bkotn. Thankfully, she had pulled the gag from her throat as well. If she had not, Steph is certain she would have choked to death. Moreover, and surprisingly since she used to be the second in command, Morwen allowed Siofra to boss her around.

Steph also suspects that Siofra's supposed departure from the area was a scam. She would not be surprised if Siofra and the wizard linked up once more. Back in the forest, she could not tell what the wizard was saying to Siofra most of the time. She was too far away. But she did see him wink at her two times. She is certain of that. Then just as he pointed his staff at Siofra's chest he winked a third time. She could also hear him as he said forcefully, "Siofra, I said get out of my sight now!" She watched as Siofra grudgingly walked away from him and the others. But Siofra did not leave the vicinity. Instead, she hid behind a clump of trees and may have been watching what was going on, including her and Vena's brief scuffle.

Haldir's cabin is sparsely furnished. The only furnishings are a rickety cupboard against the wall; a round table with a soiled tablecloth in the center of the room and one chair; a beaten-up wicker chair in front of the hearth; and a small, dust-covered end table. The hearth is layered with darkish ash. Firewood is stacked high next to it. A rolled-up straw mat is to the left of the hearth. Probably where the wizard sleeps Steph guesses.

The cupboard is filled with pottery jars and assorted dried foods. A rotting pile of fly-infested, stinky fish bones and guts in a wooden bowl is sitting on the end table next to the cupboard. There is an oil lamp beside the bowl along with a nearly burnt-out candle.

The cabin is bordering on the obscene. Steph can think of no better word to describe its filthy, insect-infested condition. The ceiling and every piece of furniture is covered in cobwebs, and a thick coat of dust is everywhere. Steph assumes nobody has stayed in the cabin for a long time.

There are only two ways that she can escape from the room. Dashing through the wooden door, which is closed and seems to be locked from the inside – she saw Haldir slip the key in his pocket – or leaping headlong through the open window. Also, the odds of her getting past Haldir seem to be pretty much impossible. She had attempted to escape two times earlier. Both attempts ended miserably but, happily, without her being thrashed or even receiving a reprimand.

The first time she tried to escape was when Haldir had fallen asleep at the table where he is sitting at this very moment. His arms were folded on top of the table. He had lain his head on his arms, his face turned away from where Steph was sitting. Once she heard his slow, rhythmic breathing, joined by the random snorting snores, she made her move. She silently crawled on all fours toward the door. As soon as she reached for the doorknob, her heart seemed to skip every other beat. She panicked and began to shake uncontrollably. She slammed her back against the wall as if doing so would make her invisible. Somehow Haldir knew what she was doing.

"I would not do that if I were you, Stephanie," Haldir mumbled without looking up. His head was still turned away from her, cradled in his folded arms. "I have the key in the pocket of my robe. If you wish, you can try to get it from me. But then again if I were you I would not."

Steph's first impulse was to race back to where she had been sitting. Instead, she remained where she was, sitting on the floor next to the door. She was trying to be as quiet as she could, slowly breathing in and out and just barely. Striving to ignore her shaking legs and to slow the cadence of her loudly beating heart. Her throat felt abnormally dry, and she had to keep licking her lips. Although she was very scared and nervous, she was determined to try once more to escape.

After a while, by the sound of Haldir's rhythmic breathing, she could tell he had fallen fast asleep. She quietly crawled to the window, desperately trying to calm her bursting, nervous breaths. Once she got to the window, she sat underneath it for a few minutes. She continued to watch Haldir closely. He did not stir and seemed to be sound asleep. She was just about to grab the windowsill and pull herself up when Haldir spoke, causing her stomach to feel rock hard.

"I would not do that either if I were you, Stephanie. No sooner would you place your hands on the sill, and I will have slammed the window shut, latched it, and, regrettably, smashed your fingers as well. I truly do not wish for you to be injured, either physically or psychologically." Then he mumbled in a pleading manner, "My dear, Stephanie, I beg of you. Will you please allow me to get some sleep? I pray you will do the same. We have a long journey ahead of us."

Steph got to her feet in an angry bluster and quickly walked to her spot against the wall. She stuck her tongue out and silently cursed Haldir as she passed him by. Although she had failed at her first attempt to escape, she did not give up hope. She tried a second time to escape.

That time she planned to sneak up behind Haldir and attack him as brutally as she knew how. She figured the best way was to grab him around the neck and choke him until he fell unconscious. She assumed even if he fought back, she could have the upper hand. Jordyn had said she had Krav Maga skills. She seemed to have applied them quite well against Vena even if she had no clue what she was doing. But she only stopped pummeling Vena because the warrior had threatened to slit Galadriel and Nessa's throats. If she had not stopped, she is certain she would have eventually knocked Vena out cold.

When she tried to escape the second time, Haldir was sitting at the table eyeballing the crystal ball like he is doing right now. His back was to her. He was trying to shield whatever he was looking at from her prying eyes. She was certain he was not paying a lick of attention to her. She quietly crawled toward him, inch by inch. Then she gradually got to her knees. Thankfully, her knees did not crack as they tend to do from time to time. Her hands were a mere hand's width from the back of his neck. Before she could even fathom what was happening, she was sailing backward in the air! She landed hard against the wall to where she had been sitting before her foolish attempt to strangle him.

364

Haldir had not even turned around, yet he had somehow hexed her! He had murmured, "Sorry, Stephanie, I hope you are not hurting too badly. I made certain you sailed so your back would hit the wall instead of your head. If I were you, I would not try that trick again as well." He resumed toying with the crystal ball without another word.

So far, other than forcing Steph to sit on the floor, Haldir has been kind and respectful toward her. Well, mostly. After he woke up from his brief nap, he had placed a pitcher of water and a goblet on the floor beside her. He said in a kind voice, "You must be thirsty, Stephanie. Tell me if you need more." Then he went to the cupboard and returned with a wooden dish piled with confections. She gobbled them up and asked for more. He readily obliged and added a dozen pieces of fresh fruit he had sliced for her.

After thanking him she faked a gullible smile then said in an innocent tone, "Sir, what if I have to, you know, if I have to go, you know, use the—?" She began to blush for real because of her inference to doing what comes naturally for every living creature.

Haldir stared at her for a few moments deep in thought. He was biting the inside of his cheek, trying to figure out what she was implying. At last, grasping what she was trying to say without saying it, he nodded his head and smiled. "Oh, I understand what you are saying, Stephanie. Use the pitcher if you must do what comes naturally. Afterward I will rinse it clean of your waste."

That was the only time Haldir was even close to being impolite to her.

Steph has been sweating profusely for a while now. Not because it is hot inside the cabin. Although it is rather stuffy with only the open window for fresh air. Her profuse sweating is due to her ever-increasing, angry mood. Her face and neck are bright red. She keeps opening and closing her hands into fists. Her eyes are cold and hard as she stares at the back of Haldir's head.

She wants to leap to her feet and attack him like a rabid dog, biting the back of his neck if she must. But she knows she has no chance of escaping. Not if he is in the room. Just the same, she knows she must do something to vent the anger building up inside her. Otherwise, she will jump to her feet and try to strangle him no matter how he reacts. Either he gives in or she is forced to do the same. Or he throws her across the room to slam against the wall once more. Knowing that the chances of surprising him are futile, she eventually decides on a different tactic. She says in a sweet, singsong tone, "Sir, can I ask you a great big favor?"

Haldir chuckles then says in a sardonic manner, "Stephanie, I do believe you are in no position to ask me for favors."

"Okay then," Steph says. She remains silent for a few moments to consider what she should say next. "Okay, I will rephrase my question. Will that put me in a better light?"

"Perhaps. Go ahead and rephrase. Then let us see if the light shines brightly enough to interest me."

Steph says in a quiet, polite manner, "Where are we, sir?"

"Here."

"No, darn it!" Steph cries, trying as best as she can to stifle her growing anger. She breathes in deeply then says in a polite tone, " *Where* are we? Where is *here?*"

"In my cabin."

She can no longer control her anger. She stands up and screams, "Darn you, whatever your name is! Stop being an absolute idiot. You are not funny at all. A child could give better answers than you! I think I have a right to know where I am and who you are. So, cut the (expletive)!"

"I am not trying to be funny, Stephanie. And my name is Haldir – Haldir of Mountains Cross. Surely, you have heard of me?"

Steph has not heard of him. Nevertheless, she figures now that he is talking, perhaps she can get some answers to her questions. She unconsciously rubs her backbone. It is sore from sitting so long and being tossed against the wall.

"Haldir, it is a pleasure to meet you. Before you even start to think of tossing me through the air again, I want you to know I am not planning to escape. I am not going to try and harm you." She chuckles. "At least not yet. I promise. Although I swear if the opportunity presents itself, I will try once again. I can assure you of that. Can I come across the room, so we can talk?"

Haldir says with a laugh, "Well, I hope for your sake that you do not try to escape. As far as harming me, Stephanie. That is impossible."

"Okay, I am going to walk across the room and stand next to you. That way we can talk face-to-face. Will that be okay?"

Haldir turns around in his chair. He cocks his head to one side and raises an eyebrow. "Why?"

Steph shouts defiantly, "We need to talk face-to-face, Haldir! I am not the sort to be sitting on the floor while you do whatever it is you are doing and treat me like a speck of dirt to be scorned and kicked around, metaphorically speaking. Flung through the air like a discarded, stuffed toy. That is why! Either you allow me to talk to you decently, or I swear I will start throwing things around inside this dinky cabin of yours, and then – then – then I will think of something else to irritate the heck out of you until you decide to talk to me!" She glares at him for a few seconds then spits out, "Because I need – no I demand answers! And you are going to give them to me one way or another!"

Haldir's eyes widen. He grins, and then he breaks out laughing. When, after a half-minute or so he has composed himself, unlike Steph, she is still shaking with rage, he says, "I like your courage, Stephanie. It is no small wonder you are the best friend of Avaïnoáel."

Steph does not intend to do it, but she involuntarily gasps at Haldir's mention of her being the best friend of Avaïnoáel. The best friend of her sweet Ava. She blurts out, "If she knew I was being held prisoner, you would be destroyed for certain!"

Haldir shows no emotion after her outburst. Instead, taking her completely by surprise, he walks to the other side of the room. He grabs the wicker chair next to the hearth and drags it across the filthy floor. Little tracks of fine dust and mildewy straw trail the dragged legs of the chair. The zigzagged tracks remind Steph of scribbled chalk marks etched on a sidewalk by a child. He positions the chair on the opposite side of the table.

"Come, Stephanie, sit down with me at the table. We shall talk."

"Only if you say please," Steph says nervously as she stares at him. "You have got to want me to sit with you for your own good, not because I asked you. You have got to say please. It is the only polite way to start a decent conversation." She tilts her head to one side. "Do you not agree?"

Haldir gives her an annoyed look. He crosses his arms over his chest and shouts angrily, "You want *me* – to say please – to *you?*"

Steph nods her head. Then she crosses her arms over her chest and glares. "Yep."

Haldir doubles up with laughter. He abruptly turns his back to Steph, sits down, and begins to tinker with his crystal ball once more.

Steph remains standing for a few moments. She is staring at the back of his head. She is about to sit on the floor when Haldir whispers.

"Please, Stephanie. I honestly would like you and I to discuss a few things of importance." He turns in his chair and grins. "Would you mind fetching me a goblet of water along the way? I am quite thirsty."

Steph says, "Why thank you, Haldir. Would you like some sweets too? I do. I am starving!" She walks over to the cupboard and pours a goblet of water. Out of the corner of her eye, she sees that Haldir is draping a clutch of cloth over his crystal ball.

Obviously, he is looking at something he does not want me to see!

2

Steph is sitting at the table across from Haldir. She is cradling a goblet of herbal tea that he had brewed. The tea is sweet with a tangy hint of anise. The anise flavor reminds her of the cookies her mother bakes during the holidays. Her stomach churns as she thinks of home, but she tries to ignore the sad feelings.

I must remain strong for Ava. She is the reason I am Haldir's prisoner. She gulps down what remains of her tea then says, "This is delicious. Thank you for making it for us."

Haldir smiles and says, "You are welcome. I am glad you enjoy it. Surely, you know something about the elves of the mysterious Unseen Valley?"

"Yes, my fairy friend, Doo, told us all about the elves that live there. The Bkotn, the Mkleon, and the Smbot." She grabs another sweet confection from the plate sitting on the table between her and Haldir. "By the way, Haldir, these are delicious. Are they made of the same grain cultivated by the Mkleon? I forget the name—" She rolls her eyes and laughs. "Although Ava, I mean Avaïnodel; she surely would remember what the grain is called." Her expression changes immediately as she looks Haldir straight in the eyes. She says in a flat-out tone, "As you undoubtedly know, Ava has a photographic memory. She also seems to know things that constantly amaze me, like words in Latin and Greek. Probably more languages too."

Haldir is nodding his head slightly as he calmly returns her gaze. "Yes, Stephanie, I know all about her memory recall ability and much more. By the way, the grain you are referring to is vaotz. It is like your Earthly World rice. And yes, you are correct. Vaotz is cultivated by the Mkleon. So is the brown, powdery substance on top of the confections. It is called *zácharium*. It is like the Greek word "záchari." Zácharium is a common, natural sweetener for many confections as well as delicious beverages. It comes from a bean pod. The Mkleon grind the pods to a fine powder.

"Also, you are correct when you say that Avaïnoάel may know words in more languages. In addition to Latin and Greek as you mentioned, she knows French, German, and Spanish just to name a few. She may not be aware of her linguistic ability consciously; but if the situation were to present itself, she would understand what is being said in just about most of the world's languages. She would also be able to respond in the same languages because she is fluent in all of them. She is fluent in Fortunomy as well, although once again she probably does not realize it.

Steph is trying hard to hide her emotions, but she cannot. She is utterly amazed by what Haldir had said about Ava's linguistic ability. She is shaking her head and thinking to herself; goodness, no wonder Jordyn referred to her as the Protector of the World!

Haldir says, "There is one additional aspect of Earthly World etymology that many believe, I included. We passionately believe that Earthly World languages are spinoffs of the Elvish language Fortunomy. Not the other way around. Especially the older languages, Sumerian, Egyptian, Latin, and Greek. In essence, Fortunomy may be the basis of all the Earthly World's languages.

"Wow! That is amazing," Steph says in an enthused tone. She gives Haldir a grim look. Trying hard to not cry, she says in a miserable tone, "Haldir, please be honest with me, okay?" Haldir nods his head. "Why am I here? Why are you keeping me against my will?"

Haldir flashes Steph a nasty grin that reminds her of the creepy dancing clown, Pennywise, in Stephen King's scary novel, *It*. His evil-looking grin causes her to cringe just as goose pimples cover her upper arms. She rubs her arms vigorously.

"I said a few moments ago you are free to leave, Stephanie. But if you leave, you will get lost. Getting lost in Artonia is not wise even for someone as skillful as I. We are far and wide from civilization. There are no elves, humans, or fairies anywhere close. No one will come to your aid if you are lost or injured. There are belugas, many of them, mostly duds, and thousands of other nasty creatures." He places his elbows on the table and bends forward somewhat. "And the dreadful, enchanted mist."

Steph tilts her head to one side and looks up at the ceiling. She had not noticed it earlier. The ceiling is covered with grotesque-looking insects. Most are crawling while others are mere skeletons, forever encased in sticky cobwebs. She purposely does not look at Haldir when she speaks. "Okay, I get all of what you said. I will not try to run off, you know that. Doing so would be plain stupid, something I am not. Moreover, I am of no use to Ava if I am devoured by something in the forest, or if I fall in a tar pit, or worse, being consumed by the enchanted mist. I have heard about that as well as the tar pits!" She folds her hands on the table and looks Haldir straight in the eyes. "Therefore, what do you say we get to the point, Haldir. Tell me the reason I am here! And no lying, okay?"

"You are here because I need you to assist me."

Now Steph is drumming the table with her fingers nervously. Then she begins to rock back and forth in her chair. She is still staring at Haldir unblinking.

Haldir says, "I need you to assist me in saving Avaïnoáel's life. She is in danger."

"Oh, come on now, Haldir!" Steph shouts in a sarcastic tone. "You – you want *me*," she points the thumb of her left hand at her chest, "to help *you* save Ava?" She rolls her eyes and laughs. "This I cannot believe. You, Haldir of Mountains Cross wants *me* to help *you* save Ava, the renowned, all-powerful Avaïnoáel!" She slams the sides of her fists on the table and glares. "Are you nuts? Or do you think I am stupid or something? You only want me to help you because you want to hand her over to Wendigorium. End of story, pure and simple!" She leans across the table and shouts, "Right?"

370

Haldir gives her a solemn look. He is shaking his head. He says in a gloomy tone of voice, "I am sorry, but you are incorrect, Stephanie."

Steph's face reddens. She is still staring at Haldir, her eyes cold and hard. She pounds the table with her fists once more. Then she leans in close and seethes, "Oh yeah, Haldir? How is that, huh? How is it I am incorrect?"

"You are incorrect that I have some nefarious purpose as it concerns your friend. Even if what you say about my being a comrade of Wendigorium is correct. But in this case, I cannot abide with Wendigorium and my accords with him." His tone rises with unmistakable unease. "I will not allow Wendigorium's ill-treatment of your beloved friend to continue any longer! You and I must work together to try and save her!" He reaches to the middle of the table and snatches the cloth that is covering the crystal ball. He throws the cloth onto the floor. Then he gives the ball a vicious look of contempt. "Look for yourself, Stephanie JoAnne Galanos."

Steph shakes her head and looks away. She is staring at the wall. She feels lightheaded, and her stomach is grumbling angrily. She says in a strained voice, "No, Haldir. I do not want to look." She rubs her upper arms because the goose pimples have returned. She is shaking nonstop but manages to squeak out in a whisper, "I am afraid of what I am going to see."

Haldir says, "You must, Stephanie. I implore you to look."

Steph glances down at the globe. It is cloudy, but she can make out a figure. The figure is becoming more pronounced as the clouds slowly separate. She is certain the figure is Ava. She looks up at Haldir and pleads, "Please, I beg of you. Do not make me look further. Just explain to me what you see."

Haldir says irritably, "Look as I request of you! You must see what is happening! Only then can you agree that we must do everything we can to save her. Later, the three of us – you, Ava, and I, the three of us can come to some sort of agreement. We can decide on a plan going forward that does not involve Wendigorium." He forcefully pushes the globe across the table nearer to Steph. "Look for yourself what Wendigorium has done to your friend, Stephanie! I beg you to look now!"

3

Steph can hardly breathe as she stares at the globe. Now that the clouds have dissipated, she sees that the hazy figure most certainly is Ava. She is standing in a grassy field. There is a line of trees to her left side. Steph correctly assumes the field in which Ava is standing must be a clearing in the forest, almost certainly Artonia. She stares for a few moments longer, and then her entire body seems to freeze. Her leg and arm muscles suddenly go weak. She slouches back in her chair. A painful tightness in her chest causes her to grimace. She squeezes her eyes shut and shakes her head in denial. She does not want to look anymore. She would rather run out the door, flee inside the forest, and risk her life. Do anything no matter the danger to herself. Anything other than looking at Ava's image in the crystal ball!

Then again, she knows that she must go on looking. She must know what is happening to her friend! Otherwise, how can I help Haldir? If I do not know what is happening to my dear Ava!

She halfheartedly opens her eyes. Her shoulders droop and her chest caves in as she stares at the scene. She looks away briefly, and then she manages to refocus her attention. Ava is glaring up at the sky, looking dreadfully scared. Steph immediately realizes why.

The sky above Ava is pitch-black. It is filled with murky clouds that seem to be rolling on top of each other. Surprisingly, it does not look like it is raining, at least not now. Steph is shocked to see there are no clouds in the sky above the forest. There it is sunny. The terrifying, crashing black clouds are above Ava only!

Streaks of blood-red lightning are flashing violently inside the murky clouds. Steph figures she must be imagining what she is seeing because the streaks of lightning look like emaciated fingers dripping with gore! Even worse, the fingers seem to be reaching out from all directions in the sky like they are struggling to grab Ava, to stab her heart with their pointed barbs!

Steph's anguished thoughts cry out; why aren't you moving, Ava? Get out of there! You are going to get hit by lightning! And those bloody-looking fingers of lightning. They look like they want to grab you, snatch you away or impale you with their sharp spikes. Move Ava. Move now!

A sudden shudder sweeps through Steph's entire body. She sees that Ava's back is touching a thin sapling. Her arms appear to be stretched out behind her on either side of the sapling. Her wrists seem to be pressed together as if she is tied up. Unable to move. Unable to break free. Steph narrows her eyes. She shouts out loud in a feverish voice, "There is nothing, Ava! I cannot see anything binding your wrists. You can break free. I am certain of it. You must run Ava, run to the forest before it is too late! Before those bloody fingers in the sky grab you!"

Now Steph sees that Ava is talking. She leans in closer and turns her head to the side. She can barely understand what Ava is saying. However, she knows enough to realize that Ava is speaking to her.

"Steph, where are you? You promised you would do anything to keep me from harm. I beg you to come and help me. Please, Steph, please!"

Suddenly, the crystal globe slowly clouds over. Steph screams, "No, don't go, Ava, please. I will help you. I promise." Then the clouds start to dissolve. Ava's figure is gradually rematerializing. She is still standing in the same place. Steph is relieved that the nasty clouds and bloody-finger streaks of lightning have vanished. The sun is shining brightly, even above Ava. Steph looks away from the globe and gives Haldir a puzzled look.

He says, "I sped up the scene by a few hours. We have little time to waste. As I said earlier, we have a long journey ahead of us."

Steph asks in a tentative tone, her voice shaking, "So, what I saw with the lightning, the ugly clouds, and such already happened? They were in Ava's past as she stood alone in the clearing?"

"Yes," Haldir replies. The deeply troubled look on his face causes Steph's stomach to knot up. "What you are now seeing," Haldir gestures with a slight wave of his hand at the globe, "is the present. What your friend is experiencing at this very moment as you and I speak." He shrugs his shoulders. "I had to speed up the scene, Stephanie. Otherwise, we would be here watching nothing, thus wasting our time, precious time when we could be saving your friend." He glances at the globe. "You must look, Stephanie, even though you do not want to see inside. I will try to zoom in on Ava's face." He passes his hand over the globe.

Steph peers into the globe. Then she instantly pulls away, and shrieks, "Oh my God, no!" She looks at Haldir. "Ava looks horrible, so dreadfully pitiful! Her hair is a tangled mess. Her shoulders are stooped." She stares at the close-up of Ava's face. She whispers in a shaky voice between grief-stricken sobs, "Please tell me she isn't dead, Haldir." She looks up from the globe at Haldir and stares at him through her tear-filled eyes. In a pleading tone, she says, "Please tell me she is going to be okay. That she is merely unconscious or something."

Haldir gestures to the globe with a slight nod of his head.

Steph looks again. Ava's eyes are closed. Her head is bent low, her chin resting on her chest. The tip of her tongue is sticking out of her mouth, overhanging her lower lip. Steph can tell that Ava is breathing, but only just. She gapes at Ava's face, barely able to see her friend's image through her steadily flowing tears. She struggles to breathe as she watches Ava attempt to lift her head. Ava's efforts are painstakingly sluggish, but her head is moving just the same. Steph sighs with relief. Then she watches happily as Ava slowly stretches and turns her head from side to side.

Steph wipes her tears with the back of her hand. She is smiling because Ava is doing uncountable deep knee bends. She is tempted to clap her hands as Ava gallantly tries to snap the sapling in two with her repeated, forceful bends. Then her heart seems to smile as she watches Ava's lips form to a slight smile. Then she cries out in a panicky tone of voice, "Oh my God, no, please no!" Without looking away from the globe, she screams at Haldir, "What is that thing? That thing slowly walking on all fours toward Ava, stalking her from behind! She cannot see it, although by her reaction I think she can hear that it is drawing nearer."

Haldir leans in close and peers in the globe. Steph has a sinking feeling in her gut as she watches his eyes widen with a look of alarm. Her hands quickly move to her mouth when he shouts. "Oh, my goodness, Stephanie! It is a beluga, a dud!" Steph shrieks, "Can't we do something, Haldir? Can't you help her? You must help her. You must! The beast is huge. It is going to slay her. I just know it!"

As he continues to stare intently in the crystal ball, Haldir says in a blunt tone, "I doubt the beast intends to harm her. Not after Wendigorium has gone to all the trouble of capturing her." He pauses and stares intently in the globe for the longest time. Then his brow furrows as his troubled expression changes to one of total confusion. He says in a questioning tone, "Why is she not moving? Can you tell? She must know that the beast is behind her. We have got to do something and soon! Otherwise, either the beluga or Wendigorium will have her." He jumps to his feet. "We must do something now, Stephanie. Now!"

Steph stammers nervously, "She – she – she cannot move, Haldir! I am amazed you had not noticed it before! She has been like that since the beginning. Something is preventing her from escaping. She is bound at the wrists by something invisible. So, she cannot use her weapons even though they are on the ground next to her. Her hands, Haldir! Look closely at her hands!" Haldir sits down and looks at the globe.

Steph moves in closer as she continues to stare in the globe. Something she noticed about Ava a few seconds ago did not seem right. But whatever it did not register in her mind at the time. She tries to recall what it was when she unexpectedly considers what she just said to Haldir.

Her hands, Haldir! Look closely at her hands!

Making certain that Haldir is not observing her closely, she cautiously looks away from the globe and quickly glances at her right hand and then at her left. Just to make certain she is not imagining things. Not going crazy. Which she realizes is possible given her current emotional state.

Just as I thought, she says to herself. I have a pinky promise ring on both of my pinkies. I am wearing my promise ring on my left pinky finger as always; Ava's ring is on my right. It all makes sense now. Haldir is trying to trick me. Everything I am seeing already happened – before Ava somehow got to Mégedale!

Unbeknownst to Haldir and everyone else, the Mégedale messenger had stealthily presented Ava's pinky ring to Steph. It was shortly after he told Elbereth that Ava was safe with the Timbre elves. The messenger had moved close to her when no one was watching. He had said in a whisper, "Ava sends you her best, loving wishes, Steph." Then he opened his hand revealing Ava's pinky ring. "She said to give you this, so you would know that she is safe. She said for you to do the same, to remain safe."

Steph peers in the globe once more. She narrows her eyes and stares fixedly at Ava's left hand. She looks at Ava's right hand as well. Then her lips form to a sly, but fleeting grin with what she sees. She quickly replaces her grin with a fake grimace and pretends to shiver.

Ava in Haldir's magical crystal ball is still wearing her pinky promise ring!

CHAPTER 7

DECEPTION'S REVENGE

"Injustice is achieved in two ways: either by violence or deceit."
—*Marcus Tullius Cicero*

Steph is finding it extremely difficult to pretend she is upset with everything she just witnessed in Haldir's crystal ball. Especially now given that she knows that Ava is safe in Mégedale. She is also livid that Haldir had tried to deceive her to think otherwise. At first, she was going to confront him with the facts. But the more she thought about it, calling his bluff seemed impractical. She realizes that he is holding her hostage for a reason. That Ava will try to rescue her sooner or later. She is confident that once Ava knows her whereabouts, she will do exactly that.

Then again, she considers silently, he might have something else up his sleeve to entice Ava. I will have to wait to see how this plays out. Yet there is one thing I know for certain. In the end, I am one hundred percent expendable. So, if I am alive and well, and Ava assumes that I am okay, the safer I am going to be. That is why I must fake everything going forward. At least until I make my move against him. I just need time to think things through.

Steph makes it a point to never lie. She also has trouble faking things, pretending things exist when they do not. Whenever she feels the need to tell untruths, it usually is to avoid insulting someone. Like the time she was roller skating, and a friend asked if she liked his spin. He had been practicing it for weeks, at every Friday night skate. Steph thought her friend's spin was something straight out of a comic strip. Arms flailing, off-balance, only four revolutions – barely, and every revolution slithering across the floor like skidding pucks of a backyard shuffleboard. Even though she felt like doubling over with laughter, she had lied. She told him that the spin looked great. She had said, "A wee bit more practice (actually a lot she thought), and it'll be perfect (which she seriously doubted)." She had rationalized that what she had said was not a real lie or being untruthful. It was what they call a white lie. A harmless fib to avoid hurting her friend's feelings.

Besides, she thought at the time, who knows? Maybe he will get better, and my little white lie will have helped to make it happen because I gave him added conviction. Years later she discovered that his spin did get better. Lots better. It was almost perfect.

Haldir is pacing back and forth. He occasionally peers in his magical globe. It is tucked in the crook of his arm.

"So, what should we do now?" Steph says in an anxious tone as she pretends impatience. "What is the next step? Have you figured it out? Please tell me that you have a plan to help Ava before it is too late." She is wringing her hands nervously. "I am getting more anxious here as the minute's tick by."

Haldir replies politely, "I am thinking how we should handle this."

Earlier, Steph noticed that every time she got close to Haldir; he would walk away or turn his back to her. She figured that whatever he was looking at in the globe was not for her viewing. She sat down at the table and devoured more of the delicious confections. Soon afterward she unrolled Haldir's sleeping mat and took a short nap. Now that she is refreshed, she is ready to confront Haldir more aggressively with her plan.

"Haldir, you mentioned earlier that we have to be in a hurry. That we have a long journey ahead of us." She stares at the crystal ball. Like earlier, it is firmly tucked in the crook of his arm as he paces back and forth. Without taking her eyes from the ball, she says in a calm tone, "Have things changed? Because of what you are seeing in that magical globe of yours?"

Haldir says softly, "Perhaps they have, Stephanie." He appears to smile but only slightly. "I no longer can see the beluga. Thus, Avaïnoåcl appears to be out of harm's way for now. We shall have to wait and see what will happen next." As an afterthought he adds, "I am watching closely to see if Wendigorium will arrive on the scene."

Steph abruptly jumps to her feet. She pretends an ecstatic smile. Even though she wants to rush over to Haldir and slap him hard across his face for deceiving her once more. For she knows Ava is nowhere on his stupid crystal ball. Maybe she was at some time, but she is no longer. She is safe with the Timbre! She exclaims, "That is awesome news! That the beluga is gone. Is Ava bound to the sapling even now? Has she managed to escape?" She slowly walks toward Haldir and stretches out her hand. "Can I look? Please?"

Haldir walks backward, turns, and ambles toward the window. He peers outside. He says, "The sun will set in a few hours. Perhaps we should get moving." He turns around and is visibly surprised to see Steph sitting at the table. She has her hands folded before her and is grinning. He gives her a puzzled look.

"Okay, Haldir, you are the boss, and you are in charge." She glances around the room. "Should we pack some supplies?" She snatches a confection from the plate and holds it up. "Do you have more of these?" She pushes the chair away from the table, glances down at her cloak, and pulls at a button. "I do not have anything to wear other than what you see. Siofra would not allow me to bring my satchel to their hiding place." She rolls her eyes. "I cannot blame her. I would do the same. They were in a hurry when they snatched me." She pauses momentarily then says in an excited tone, "Does anyone live nearby where we could purchase some extra clothes for me? That would be nice. Do you agree?"

Haldir's eyes seem to cloud over. He again appears confused. He tilts his head to one side, purses his lips, and says, "Stephanie, are you feeling okay?"

"Why do you ask?" Steph replies with a faint smile. "Do I look like I am not well?" She touches her forehead. "Well, I feel okay. No fever." She grins. "How do I look to you?"

Haldir says, "You do not appear to be ill. However, I thought you would be more upset than you are."

"Aw, I am not upset in the least," Steph replies with a long, pretend yawn. She stretches her arms out wide. "Just tired. That's all." She stares at Haldir straight on. "Why would I be upset? Have you done something wrong?" She flashes a grin. "Because I have not." She suddenly stands up and walks over to Haldir. She reaches inside the pocket of his robe and removes the door key. She is both surprised and relieved that he does not react. She walks to the door, turns the key in the latch, and opens it. She shakes her head and breathes in the fresh air. Patting her rear end, she says, "Haldir, do you mind? I must – you know – go. I really would like to have some privacy. Unlike the other way when I used the pitcher, this requires more solitude. I hope you realize what I am saying."

Haldir says, "I understand. Just do not take too long."

Steph says, "I won't. Thank you." She is about to walk over the threshold then turns about. "Oh, my goodness I almost forgot. Do you have something to – you know?" She glances at the cloth that Haldir had tossed on the floor. It was the one he had used to cover the crystal ball. "Something like that to – you know." Her face blushes for real.

Haldir walks over and picks up the cloth. He is about to toss it to her when she cries out in an angry tone, "No, not that one! It is filthy, Haldir. Full of bacteria and other yucky stuff from the floor. Maybe you would use it, but I refuse to, even to – you know." She pats her rear end yet again. "Do you not have something spotless that I can use? Something a bit more sanitary?"

Haldir gives her a knowing smile and walks over to the cupboard. As soon as he turns his back, Steph grabs the fire iron lying beside the hearth. She slowly creeps up behind him, the poker in her hand held high above her head. She stands unmoving, trying to remain as quiet as a peaceful, nighttime hint of a summer breeze. She watches as Haldir gathers up a bundle of sticks.

Steph recognizes the sticks as *xylosgium*. Its name is like the Earthly World Latin words "xylospongium" and "tersorium" (sponge on a stick). As the name implies, the sticks have sponges attached to them. The sponges are dipped in acidic solutions or salt to disinfect them before and after use. Steph knows the purpose of the sticks firsthand. She and Ava have used similar, primitive lavatory gadgets on many occasions since entering the Inner World. As repulsive and unseemly as the crude devices may appear, they attend to the essential, nasty business quite satisfactorily.

"Just be sure to not share them," Doo had said to her and Ava. They were staring innocently at the things with an appalled expression at the time. "You do not want to catch another's germs."

Haldir turns around. When he sees Steph lowering the fire stick to smack him, he tries to duck out of the way. But Steph is too fast. She smacks him hard on the side of his head one time. He cries out just as his hand rockets to his forehead like a shot out of a cannon. Blood immediately seeps between his fingers from the wound. He looks at Steph with a bemused expression and then falls to his knees. He collapses to the filthy floor and lies motionless, moaning and groaning.

The magical globe he had placed on the cupboard tumbles and rolls across the floor. It crashes against the far wall. Thinking it might be of some use later, Steph runs over and grabs it. She is surprised by its lightness, assuming it weighs no more than an Earthly World softball despite its soccer ball size. She quickly covers the globe with the cloth lying on the floor and enfolds it in the crook of her arm.

She snatches a large knife from the pantry and stuffs it in her sheath belt. Then she grabs the wood ax next to the hearth. She tries to stuff the ax in the belt, but the handle is too broad. After considering it for a few seconds, she decides to take it with her just the same along with the fire iron. The knife, fire iron, and ax might come in handy as weapons since hers are with the Etanpioa.

She cautiously walks to where Haldir is lying unconscious and stares down at him. He is breathing which makes her feel a bit better. She notices the red stain on his head where the fire iron struck but is surprised the wound is no longer bleeding.

Hmm, he looks unconscious enough, dead to the world. However, he could be faking it like a Virginia opossum pretending to be dead. I did not think I hit him hard enough to knock him out. For sure I could have if I wanted to, but I drew back at the last moment. I did not want to hurt him too badly. Yet he does not appear to see me standing here. But why did he not try to stop me? Surely, he must have known what I was about to do before I did it. Just like the two times before when I tried to escape.

She nudges him in the ribs with the fire iron a few times. He does not respond. Then she places the tip of the fire iron against his throat. Just in case he was to lunge at her unexpectedly. She leans in close and whispers. "I ought to destroy you, you good-for-nothing scoundrel. For holding me hostage against my will. But you were relatively decent to me. I also could sense that you were as frightened of Wendigorium as I. Therefore, I shall allow you to live. So, the two of us can see how this plays out going forward."

She turns away and rushes toward the door, stops, and then she hurries to the table. She stuffs the seven remaining confections in her pocket. She is about to dash toward the door once more but runs to the cupboard instead. She grabs a goblet and crams it and dried food and confections inside her cloak pockets until they are overflowing. She also grabs a handful of xylosgium. Just in case she must – you know. She stands in the doorway and glances over at Haldir. Then she does a double take because she imagines that his eyes are open slightly. Like he is looking up at her.

But no, it must be my imagination. She shrugs her shoulders and supposes if he does not follow her, everything should be okay. She takes one last look around the dingy cabin. Then she dashes through the doorway and melts inside the forest.

A few moments later Haldir pushes himself off the floor. He brushes the grimy filth and mildewy bits of straw from his robe. He opens the cupboard drawer and removes a small looking glass. He is grinning as he stares at his reflection in the glass and dabs at his forehead with a cloth.

The red substance on his forehead may have looked like blood to Steph, but it is nothing more than red-colored cream. He had concocted the cream from the rotting fish guts when he was standing at the cupboard, pretending to fidget with the xylosgium's. When Steph struck him with the fire iron, or so she thought, he had pressed his hand with the cream to his forehead. The cream stained his head and seeped between his fingers.

In addition to the pretend blood, Steph's blow did not strike his head. He had placed a hex on the fire iron a split-second before it connected. If he had not hexed it, Steph would have rendered him unconscious for real. Her intended blow was powerful enough to do just that. Even though she had held back a bit because she did not want to hurt him seriously.

Haldir sits at the table and fills his goblet to the brim with tea. Then he reaches below the table with his hands and gropes for the secret latch. The latch opens a hidden compartment built beneath the table. It is where he hides his magical crystal ball. He twists the latch sideways. The crystal ball rolls to the palms of his hands. It is the same magical, see all crystal ball that he and Steph had gazed in hours before. The ball Steph is carrying with her is fake. He had swapped the real one with the one Steph is carrying while she slept. Nevertheless, the ball she is carrying is also magical but not as powerful as the one on the table. Not even close. Nevertheless, if Steph has the crystal ball in her possession, he can track her every move. It is sort of like an Earthly World modern-day tracking device. Except the ball is even more magical. It can see everything even though it is covered with a cloth.

Haldir places the crystal ball on its stand and waves his hands in a circular motion above it. An image of a young elf running through the forest begins to show through the gradually dissipating, cloudy haze. She is holding an ax in one hand and a fire iron in the other. She stops running every so often to look around or to retrieve something from the ground that has fallen out of the stuffed pockets of her cloak. Then she resumes running, instinctively zigzagging through the forest like a frantic creature trying to avoid its menacing pursuer.

"Ah, my precious, conniving, foolish, Stephanie. I do respect your intelligence, courage, and tenaciousness. Most of all your cleverness. But trouble attends as you unwisely run through the forest. The magical ball you carry pursues you faithfully with every twist and turn and each new way. Thus, I will know precisely where you are at all times." He leans back in the chair. A knowing smile appears on his face as he watches Steph. "I noticed the way you looked at your hands beneath the table. Just to look in the globe and pretend to stifle a smile. I do not know the reason you did that, but I shall find out sooner or later. Thus, I shall keep you safe as you travel. I am obliged to. For sooner or later Avaïnoáel will come out of hiding to seek you out. And when she does, I shall know." He laughs spitefully and peers in closer at Steph as she runs as quickly as her legs will travel.

"As will you, Stephanie – for it will be then you shall breathe your last because you are nothing more than a useless burden."

CHAPTER 8

MÉGEDALE

"The future belongs to those that believe in the beauty of their dreams."
—*Eleanor Roosevelt*

1

As she walks behind Earendil on the gradually sloping diádromosphere, Ava is thinking she must be in the middle of an enchantingly fantastic dream. Her senses have been inundated day and night by fabulous sights, smells, and sounds. Just about everything she has seen, experienced, and felt since arriving on Antiquom is far beyond description. Thrilling, amazing, and certainly, incredibly unbelievable.

She considers if she were to live for a hundred years, there would not be enough time to tell others of her exciting journey up till now. She laughs inwardly, wise to the realization that no one would believe her back home anyway. That is, only Steph. Thanks to Jordyn's miracle, Steph also has tales worthy of the greatest Earthly World fictional books ever written. Twice as many as Ava given her exploits two years earlier.

Undeniably, some parts of Ava's supposed dream have been frightening. Descending the tower's spiraling staircase is one example. Encountering the deceitful metamorhirío in its original state is another. Above all, standing stupefied and helpless in the clearing. Bound at the wrists and ankles by magical evilness! Alone and vulnerable. It was then she thought she was certainly going to die.

But she knows she has yet to encounter the most terrible things. When, how, and in what form they will show themselves, she cannot even begin to imagine. Strangely, not knowing what is going to happen next excites her. Her curiosity is fervent, eagerly anticipating what she is going to see, hear, and experience. Especially as it concerns Wendigorium. She knows facing the evil being is inevitable. She truly is not looking forward to it. But strangely she is excited, nonetheless.

And yes, there were those times of late when she thought she would not live up to her dream's wonder. That her dream would turn to a demoralizing nightmare from which there was no escape. Like when she ran out of arrows and the belugas surrounded her. Watching in her mind as Siofra so callously murdered Nessa while Nessa's back was turned. Running through Artonia, not knowing if she would harken to the next day's sunrise. The horror of being carried aloft against her will from the rocky shore of the Solenom by some unseen force.

Now the rumbling sounds of the famous twisted waterfalls, the Katarráplexouktes, are more evident. The Katarráplexouktes is nowhere as spectacular as Ava's favorite cascades, the Earthly World Niagara Falls, but she believes they are a close second. Besides, the Katarráplexouktes waterfalls are unique. There is nothing like them on the planet.

As she walks along the diádromosphere – they have only ambled a fourth of the grand stairway – Ava can distinguish the figures in the vast pool in which the Katarráplexouktes empties. Elven and human youngsters of all ages are splashing in the water as they slide from the crown of a winding wooden chute. She can hear their giggles of glee as they throw their hands high in the air. They look like roller coaster enthusiasts of the Earthly World screaming down the tracks as they plummet seemingly weightless.

Others in the pool are playing the elven game of *vóleïtioro*, or water-style volley. There is an elven land version of the game by the same name.

Earthly World volleyball players use a ball with an inflated bladder. The bladder is surrounded by eighteen panels of artificial or real leather. Elves use a comparably sized ball made of animal skin stretched over stalks of straw. The stalks are tightly spun to a solid sphere. The elven vóleïtioro is much heavier and harder than the Earthly World volleyball. Therefore, if an elven player's face is smacked by the leather laces, he or she will know it – for a long time.

Other elven children, and some adults as well, are wrestling beneath the water. They are playing a competitive water sports game like Earthly World aquathlon (underwater wrestling). It is where two opponents try to remove the cloth from the other's ankle. If one succeeds in doing so in the allotted time – timed by a referee with an hourglass – he or she wins the bout. If neither wins it is a draw, but they get to compete later.

But that is in the official underwater wrestling games that are held in the springtime. The wrestling games in the pool below are not official, nor are they timed. Also, unlike aquathlon competitors of the Earthly World, who wear fins and masks, elves do not wear special gear. That is because they are more resilient and agile than humans, even under water.

A rush of excitement suddenly sends color to Ava's cheeks. She stops walking and points to a small pond to the left of the larger pool of water. She cries out, "Are those mermaids?"

Wlknoo is walking alongside her. He says, "Yes, they are mermaids or, more precisely, a mermaid and a mérlin. The one with the long blond hair was named after you. Her name is Avaiä." He adds with a chuckle, "She will tell anyone who will listen how proud she is to bear a resemblance to your name. Her official title is Avaiä, River Goddess of the Solenom. The mérlin at her side is Lord Mérino. He rules over the *Konoanlia*."

"I seem to have forgotten what Konoanlia is," Ava says. "What is it? Where is it located?"

"Konoanlia is a large, freshwater lake in the center of Antiquom. It is extremely far away. The Solenom drains in it."

Ava says, "How did they get here? They could not have swum here possibly. The Solenom is far below the Mystic Mountains and, as you say, Konoanlia is far off as well. Also, I seriously doubt they could walk on land with their fins unless, and I assume it is possible, they can grow legs."

"No, Ava, they did not swim to the Mystic Mountains," Wlknoo says with a grin. "Only one of them has fins – Avaiä. Mérino walks the same as you, with his two legs. He traveled upstream on the Solenom. One of our dragons flew him up here. He will return to the Konoanlia in the same manner. Only his return trip shall be much quicker since he will be traveling downstream."

"Okay, I got all that," Ava says. "Thank you. But how did Avaiä get here?"

"With her magic," Wlknoo replies. "She is akin to the Great Wizard Godroh of the Mystic Mountains and the evil wizard Haldir of Mountains Cross. Like them, she is charmed."

Ava says, "Why are Goddess Avaiä and Lord Mérino here? Do you know?"

Wlknoo replies to her question without a hint of emotion. "To celebrate your return, Avaïnoɑ́el. And to seek your counsel."

Ava is about to ask Wlknoo why they would want to seek her counsel, for her to give them advice or direction on any topic. After all, I have nothing to offer them she thinks to herself. But I better not say anything more. Flame said I should not ask too many probing questions at the onset. That I should go with the flow.

Now Ava and the others are midway on the diádromosphere's length. This stretch of the footpath gradually veers to the right – in the direction of the eastern portion of Mégedale. The further they walk, the more the *katállilosly* gradually comes in view. The katállilosly is where the ordinary Timbre elves live, work, play, and youngsters, as well as adults seeking higher education, attend classes. A community of humans also lives in the area.

Whereas the portion of the city Ava was looking at earlier is called the *plateíazan*. The term plateíazan implies piazza or square. With its expansive park, large pool, shops, and recreational amenities, a plateíazan is comparable to an Earthly World town square. King Poldo's mansion overlooks the grandeur of the sprawling plateíazan.

The ancestors of the present-day Timbre elves existed in the wild, in the dense Forest of Artonia surrounding the Mystic Mountains. Over time they began to live in treehouses. The treehouses afforded them protection from wild animals and the feared belugas. It also raised their dwellings high above the snowdrifts during the winter and the rivers of mud caused by melting glaciers in late spring and summer.

Like the World over, the Timbre elves harvested the plentiful forest trees of the surrounding areas for lumber. However, unlike Earthly World humans at the same time, the Timbre elves practiced sound forest preservation techniques. Their worthy conservation efforts continue to this day. For every tree that the Timbre lumberelves cut, they plant two seedlings in its place. Thus, the adjoining forest not only survives, but it also continues to expand in size, guaranteeing lumber for future generations.

The Timbre treehouses started simple enough. At first, they were straightforward dwellings designed for small families, perhaps four to six elves. Then they grew as well as in grandeur to accommodate larger families. Eventually, owning to the Timbre's architectural prowess, the treehouses became colossal structures. The larger structures can accommodate entire extended families on one platform laid across the branches of many trees. But the ingenuity of the Timbre architects did not stop there. They eventually built solid treehouse structures that are the size of town halls. The structures can accommodate hundreds of elves at one time.

Timbre elves maintain careful records of their history, as well as the all-inclusive history of Antiquom. The earliest records reveal that a Timbre architect by the name of Ckiotn ventured out of the Thávma 40,000 years ago. He went on to teach Earthly World humans how to build treehouses. The timeframe of his teachings correlates to when humans began to build treehouses in the Earthly World. Remarkably, the treehouses of today's Earthly World Indonesian treehouse-dwelling tribes, the Korowai and Papua, are like the most basic Timbre treehouses of Mégedale.

Given her intense curiosity, Ava, as usual, is at the rear of the procession. She is still walking beside Wlknoo. She notices there is a segment of the diádromosphere that leads to the katállilosly. Her eyes widen as her stomach seems to flutter with delight. She whispers excitedly, "Are we going to visit the katállilosly? So, I can see inside one of the dwellings?" She grins then says, "Perhaps we should slip away, you and me, just to take a quick peek."

Wlknoo says, "It does not look like we are going to stop. Although I think we should because it is beautiful to behold. The architecture is amazing. It is difficult to imagine how so many structures can be supported on tree limbs." He glances to the front of the procession." Perhaps you should ask Earendil if you and I can slip away."

Earendil is at least ten to twelve paces in front of them. She stops walking and stares down at the katállilosly. Then she yells, "Earendil, excuse me, but aren't we going to stop so I can take a quick tour of the katállilosly? This would be an excellent opportunity to visit it. Especially since we are this close."

Earendil walks back to where she is standing. He says, "We hope to allow you later to meet some of the residents and to tour the katállilosly. I am certain you will find its architecture amazingly wonderful." He motions with a wave of his hand to his left. "However, as you can see by the turn of the diádromosphere, we are nearing the King's dwelling. It is there, in the King's Great Hall we shall feast."

Ava's mouth falls open. She swallows hard with disappointment that they are not going to take a quick tour of the katállilosly. She is anxious to see how the common Timbre elves live. She says in a sad tone, "Well, okay, I guess. If we get to visit it later. I sure would hate to miss out visiting it." Something in the back of her mind is nagging her. And that something is telling her that she will not visit the katállilosly for an exceedingly long time.

Earendil says, "Thank you for your understanding, Ava." He turns about and walks to the front of the procession.

Ava, as usual, remains where she is standing. Wlknoo remains behind as well. Her curiosity is overpowering her consciousness once more. She stares nostalgically at the katállilosly for the longest time. At last, she turns away and sprints up the diádromosphere to join the others. She cries out to Wlknoo, "The last one to the rear of the procession is a rotten egg." Wlknoo does not reply, but he makes certain he does not outpace Ava's fast sprint– although he could do so in two quick gallops.

2

As she gets closer to the procession, Ava notices there is a bit of commotion at the front. A messenger is sprinting up the steep incline of the diádromosphere. Earendil tells the procession to halt. The messenger confers with Earendil. Ava is happy about the delay. She turns around and looks at the charming katállilosly for a few moments.

When she turns to the front of the procession, she notices that the messenger is staring at her as he confers with Earendil. She is not surprised by the messenger's actions. Others stare at her as well, like she is a goddess or something special to behold. Which she knows she is not and hopes never to be. But then again, their stares make her feel uncomfortable like she is on display.

She is reminded of what Steph had said when they first met. Steph said that people had stared at Christopher, the boy with spastic cerebral palsy that Steph befriended in the 1960s. But the people back then also ridiculed him and tauntingly pointed their fingers even as they stared. The stares she must endure are quite the opposite. Unlike Christopher's stares, hers are stares of warmth, adoration, and love.

Ava ponders to herself, what was that Steph had said about those that stared at Christopher? Ah, yes, she had said, "Of course, they did not know better. People with disabilities were hidden from public view during the 1960s." So, I guess I should not complain because others stare at me. They simply do not know any better. All the same—

A realization suddenly seems to dull her senses. Just as time seems to pass her by sluggishly, in slow motion. Blocking out everything but what she is staring at. Her heartbeats abruptly quicken, and she can tell that she is starting to blush.

She considers silently. Gosh! He is handsome! And the way he is standing there with his hands on his hips in front of Earendil, his prince, his boss. Confidently bold and so sure of himself!

Ava is ogling the messenger as he speaks with Earendil. He has the same shade of red-colored hair as Galadriel. Ginger heads, as Ava likes to refer to redheaded elves, are a rarity in Antiquom. Hence, they tend to stand out noticeably amongst other elves. He is a little less than six feet in height, perhaps five foot ten inches. Ava supposes he is around her age, maybe a bit older. Perhaps as old as fifteen. He is slender, not wiry but well-built. His calf and thigh muscles are especially muscular. Like Galadriel, he has a ton of freckles that seem to shine beneath the blazing sun.

No surprise he is thin and muscular, Ava considers. After all, he is a messenger. Running as fast as he can while carrying important messages is his way of life.

She takes in deep breaths and continues to stare wistfully. She does not realize she is doing it, but she is slowly walking nearer to the front of the procession like she is in a trance. She instinctively wants to get a better look at the strikingly handsome messenger elf. She starts to daydream about how it would be like to sit and talk with him beneath a half-moon. Maybe holding hands. Divulging teenage secrets. When suddenly, she is detecting tidbits of the messenger and Earendil's conversation via telepathy.

"As well as her . . . Steph," the messenger's thoughts say as he speaks. "Galadriel . . . Nessa . . . my Lord."

Steph and Galadriel? Ava's mind seems to scream. Nessa? Oh my gosh, no! Are Steph and Galadriel – are they dead? Nooooo! She wants to run up to the front of the procession. To demand what is going on. Wisely, she stops walking and stares at the messenger. He looks away from her as soon as he realizes she is staring at him. From this distance, Ava can only understand snippets of what they are saying. She slowly moves in closer, so she can comprehend the entire conversation.

". . . Godroh and His Excellency as well." The messenger says. "After the feast. In the King's chambers."

Earendil says, "Thank you, Voronwe. I shall inform our Lady, Avaïnoáel. Please return to the mansion and await further orders." Voronwe bows his head respectfully. He glances at Ava one last time, and then he turns and sprints down the diádromosphere toward the King's mansion.

Earendil gathers his four aides around him in a tight circle. He says, "When do you advise we tell Avaïnoáel of the news?" Earendil does not know that Ava is standing directly behind him. She is smiling and trying to control her emotions. She knows she is not supposed to do it, but she could care less right now. She taps Earendil on the shoulder. Earendil turns around and stares into her eyes. He looks nervous. She says, "Tell me what? What news do you have for me?"

"It is nothing that cannot wait, my Lady." Earendil gestures with his hand, motioning the others to move forward. "Perhaps we should continue?"

"No, we shall not continue," Ava says flatly. Her tone is stiff. She does not intend to do it, but she places her hands on her hips. "Not until you tell me what the messenger said as it concerns me."

Earendil fakes a smile as he says, "The Great Wizard Godroh has returned. He looks forward to meeting you as soon as possible. Unfortunately, my father has been delayed. It appears that his dragon has fallen ill. Godroh had offered up his dragon for my father, but my father said no. He insisted that Godroh meets with you. He, as well as I, knows that Godroh has much to tell you." With a sincere smile he adds, "While I know my father is disappointed that he cannot be here, he wishes you well."

Ava says, "I understand. I am pleased Godroh has returned safely. But I am sorry your father is delayed." She tilts her head to one side and raises an eyebrow. She stares at Earendil with her questioning expression for a few moments. "Is that all that the messenger said, Earendil?" Earendil does not reply as he shifts from one foot to the other.

Ava knows he has more to say. His dilated pupils and slight tics below his right eye are a dead giveaway. Besides, she has already read his thoughts. She is thinking to herself, Earendil, now is your chance to prove your loyalty to me and every creature in Antiquom. If you tell me the truth, you and I will go forward as close allies. I will have your back, as I know you will have mine in return. However, if you dare to lie to me—

Before she can finish her train of thought, Earendil clears his throat. He is about to say something. After a few moments he says, "Yes, my Lady, there is more."

Ava breathes in deeply and exhales with a long sigh of relief. She is happy Earendil has admitted he has more to say. He has passed the test. As she reads his thoughts formulating in his mind, she wants to run to Fluescere. Hop on her back and soar off to search for Steph. But she keeps her emotions in check. She is standing emotionless, pretending she does not know what Earendil is about to say. She says in a nonchalant tone, "By your actions, Earendil, I can tell what you have to say is not pleasant. I do not care. Speak." She knows she has been too curt with her demand. She adds with a sincere smile, "If you please."

"My Lady, your friend Steph has been kidnapped by Haldir. Her location is unknown. Galadriel and Nessa were kidnapped as well, but they are now safe. They somehow managed to escape. The Bkotn Etanpioa is searching for Steph. Scouring every inch of the trail's forest. They are but a day's march from here. But Elbereth will not proceed any further until they find your friend. Or you instruct them to do otherwise. A Bkotn messenger informed us of this tragic news. As soon as the news arrived in Mégedale, a Timbre messenger, as you saw, was sent to me."

Ava continues to read Earendil's thoughts. But she continues to play dumb. Revealing to the others that she is telepathic would be a mistake. She says in an angry tone, "How do we know that Haldir kidnapped Steph? Who told what to whom, Earendil? I must know everything! And what is this news about Nessa? I thought she was dead!" She manages a slight smile. "I am extremely happy to know she is okay. She is a close, loyal friend and a gifted Bkotn warrior."

Earendil gives Ava a quick overview of everything that happened since she disappeared on the trail to Crostim Ledge. How Nessa was not murdered by Siofra. That Haldir undoubtedly cast a spell on them. He briefly summarizes the Bkotn trial. Siofra's banishment from the Tribe. Morwen and Vena's exile from the Etanpioa. That Morwen had to reenter Artonia later as punishment just like Siofra. Galadriel being promoted to second in command. How Morwen, Siofra, and Vena must have rejoined forces and stalked the Etanpioa. Kidnapping Steph, Galadriel, and Nessa. Siofra walking off after arguing with Haldir. Morwen allowing Galadriel and Nessa to go free. The discovery of Morwen's body. That there were no visible signs of trauma. Elbereth assuming that Morwen was murdered by Haldir. That they found no trace of Siofra or Vena and assumed the duo had linked up with Haldir.

Earendil grins when he describes how Steph pummeled Vena and almost overcame her. Knowing that Steph effectively used her martial skills given to her by Jordyn causes Ava to grin as well. He finishes his quick overview by saying, "Both Galadriel and Nessa watched as Haldir vanished before their eyes with Steph walking beside him. Steph looked like she was under a spell. There was nothing Galadriel and Nessa could do. They were bound at the wrists and ankles, gagged, and tied to trees. Vena was guarding them."

So, Nessa is alive! Ava ponders silently. But Steph is in danger. Kidnapped by Haldir, probably knowing that I will do everything in my power to find her, to set her free. I am glad Galadriel and Nessa are okay. However, I feel compelled to do something right now. Especially considering that Siofra and Vena are on the loose and might link up with Haldir once more. But then again, I need to think this out. I will talk to Flame. She will have some good ideas. She always does.

Ava is making a Herculean effort to hide her emotions. She wants to cry out in anger. She wants to sprint down the diádromosphere. Hop on Fluescere's back and find Steph! Nevertheless, she knows everyone in Mégedale is looking to her for leadership, to guide them during these troubling times.

Leadership that I, as a thirteen-year-old elf do not possess, Ava thinks angrily. How am I supposed to react to Steph being kidnapped? Nessa being alive? And after all this time I thought she was dead. What should I say to everyone? To express my concerns while trying to control my emotions? Not crying like a baby even though I want to!

She still is looking at Earendil with a blank expression. She turns about and faces the others. They are looking at her with anxious faces. She says in a confident tone, "There is nothing we can do right now about Steph's disappearance. Nevertheless, I must say that I am both relieved and happy to know Nessa of the Bkotn is alive and that she and her fellow warrior, Galadriel, are free." She turns around and says to Earendil, "I would like to send a word or two to Elbereth of the Bkotn Etanpioa as soon as possible."

Earendil replies, "Certainly, as you wish."

"And I would like to use the same messenger that delivered the news about Steph and the Bkotn elves to you." She cocks her head to one side and winks. "I believe his name is Voronwe?" Earendil does not say anything. He merely nods his head. She is thankful that he is effortlessly concealing his surprise that she knows Voronwe's name, especially considering she was well out of earshot when he dismissed the messenger. She can also tell by his thoughts that he now knows she is telepathic, and that he will not tell a soul.

As she and the others resume walking, she is thinking to herself; I leaked that info, just so you know I have more powers than you think. It is also my way of letting you know that I respect your honesty. That I had read your thoughts before you told me everything truthfully. More importantly, that you are now in my confidence, and I hope I am in yours as well.

She can tell that Earendil is considering that he will dispatch Voronwe early tomorrow morning. After Voronwe has had sufficient nourishment and a good night's sleep. She tugs Earendil's sleeve and winks once more, merely to let him know that she can read his thoughts. Just in case he had any doubts. "Tomorrow morning will be simply fine. Naturally, he needs to have sufficient nourishment and a good night's sleep. Will that be agreeable?"

With a sly, knowing grin, Earendil says, "Indeed, Ava, as you wish."

Ava thanks him, and then she says, "I also appreciate your honesty, just so you know." She stops walking to address the group. With a curl of her lip and a sneer, she says, "I forgot to say this as well. We will find my loyal friend, Steph. We also will find the Bkotn traitors, Siofra and Vena. More importantly, we will do what we must so we can find Haldir. To punish him for his evilness!"

Much to her surprise, the others are grinning and nodding their heads eagerly. Their combined expressions of wonder and respect for what she just said are apparent. She is relieved that her short speech, spoken from the heart, was what they wanted to hear. She is also relieved she did not start to cry – although she wanted to. She says with a pleased smile, "Okay then. I do not know about you, but I am hungry. I am told a feast awaits us." She glances at Earendil. He nods his head slightly and grins. "And we must make haste to welcome the Great Wizard back home." Then, with an air of renewed self-confidence, she slings her satchel over her shoulder and briskly leads the others down the grand stairway to the king's mansion.

CHAPTER 9

CREATION OF AN ALLIANCE

"Be slow to fall into friendship; but when thou art in, continue firm and constant."—Socrates

1

The feast was everything Ava had hoped for and more. There were five long tables in the Great Hall, including the king's table. The hall was filled with nearly a thousand cheerful, sincere-looking elves of every profession as well as hundreds of humans. There were royals as well as common elves and humans. Laborers as well as shop keepers. Young and old. And bunches of giggling youngsters of all ages whispering words of delight as they glanced in Ava's direction shyly. The youngsters' noisy chatter and laughter seemed to fill the hall with fantastic happiness. Ava had never imagined she would ever experience anything quite like it.

The king's table at which she was seated was on a raised platform at the northern end of the hall. She was sitting in the chair of honor in the center of the table. Her table must have had one hundred or more guests of all ages. Most were immediate family members and close friends of the royals.

From where she was sitting, she could see everyone in the Great Hall. Those that were facing her could see her as well, which caused her to feel a bit uncomfortable at first. Some diners whose backs were to her would turn their chairs around and look at her and the royals between courses. She considered their actions to be particularly weird. Then she recalled that at many Earthly World dinner theaters, patrons whose backs are to the stage must turn around to see what is happening. So, after a while, she became more comfortable. She would smile or wave, mostly to the youngsters looking at her and sometimes to the random, handsome elf around her age. Whenever she waved to the handsome males, she would blush to cause her to look away quickly.

She was sitting directly opposite an elderly elf named Wade. His back was to the others in the hall. Wade is King Poldo's stepbrother. Earendil normally would be sitting in the chair. Since Earendil was attending to other affairs at the behest of Ava, Wade had to shoulder his and the King's responsibilities. Ava was pleased that he did.

Wade is a hearty elf, full of life with an infectious smile. Ava rightly assumed her stepbrother, Poldo, has an opposite personality. Poldo is more reserved and formal. Wade's long, gray-speckled beard dropped below the tabletop. His hair was tousled and hanging far below his ears. His table manners were a bit sloppy which made Ava feel even more comfortable. He tended to eat with his fingers more often than he should have instead of using the utensils. Whenever he did, his wife would poke him in the ribs and give him an annoyed look. Then he would look at Ava and shrug his shoulders. She, in turn, would smile and occasionally do the same ill-mannered thing that he had done. Just for fun.

Wade is a jokester. His quips and funny short stories caused everyone at the table to break out with laughter during the feast. Ava could tell he was trying to put everyone at ease, especially her. She, as well as some of the others at the table, knew that more serious issues for discussion were imminent. But those discussions would be held privately. Just herself, Earendil, the Queen, Earendil's advisors, Godroh, and a few others.

She was not looking forward to meeting Godroh. She intended to give him a piece of her mind. For tracking her via his crystal ball. Thus, giving Haldir and perhaps unknown others the ability to track her actions as well. That is if her being tracked caused everything untoward to occur in the first place.

Shortly after the appetizer was served, Wade started in with his quips. His quips and jokes continued throughout the meal. He looked across the table and smiled at Ava. "Avaïnoáel, please excuse me for interrupting your meal." Ava nodded her head. She would have answered him, but her mouth was full. She really was enjoying the delicious appetizer.

Wade's face was serious as he spoke. "As you probably know, Avaïnoðel, we Timbre have a keen interest in the education of our youngsters. We teach them all sorts of things that will prepare them for the future. Do you know the most important subject that is taught in school?" Ava shrugged her shoulders as she continued to chew her food. Wade grinned and looked up and down the table. Then, with his eyes twinkling and his chubby cheeks grinning delightfully, he reared back in his seat and bellowed, "We teach them the 'elf-abet!'"

Ava nearly choked on her food. Yes, admittedly, the joke was as corny as the day is long, but she appreciated Wade's mirth. She also thought the joke, although very much clichéd, was funny.

Wade also enjoys telling dragon jokes. Ava will later repeat some of them to Fluescere.

"Hey everyone," Wade shouted at one point during the meal's second course. "Why are dragons so good at making music?" He looked up and down the table. The others were either shrugging their shoulders or shaking their heads.

Ava could tell some of them already knew the punchline. But they too were smiling.

Wade's chubby cheeks rolled with laughter again as he cried out, "Dragons are good at making music because they really know their scales!"

Ava could tell that Wade and Blissia are the closest of friends. Blissia was at the end of the table enjoying a bowl of whatever it was she was eating while standing up. Wlknoo was standing beside her.

"Excuse me, Lady Blissia," Wade hollered down the table during the third course of the meal. "Do you know where all the naughty unicorns go?" He glanced up and down the table like before.

Blissia yelled in a spirited, joking manner, "No, Wade, I do not. But something tells me you do."

Wade bellowed, "Naughty unicorns go to unicourt!"

The feast was comprised of four courses – hors d'oeuvres (fresh fruit), an appetizer (*saganakiza*), the main course (baked pollo with stewed vegetables), and dessert (confections sprinkled with powdered zácharium).

The appetizer, saganakiza, was Ava's favorite course. It was served on a medium-sized plate. The delicious appetizer is made of garlicky-flavored fried bread. The crusty bread is coated on the top with a creamy sauce of cheese and sprinkled with spicy herbs. Chefs take freshly baked bread like Earthly World rolls and slice them in two horizontally. Then they dredge the slices of bread in powdery vaotz and fry them. Just before the bread is fried to perfection, the chefs sprinkle on the sauce and herbs. Saganakiza is served hot.

Ava gulped down her appetizers. King Poldo's wife, the Queen, an incredibly attractive and gracious hostess, was sitting to her left. Her name is Estel. She noticed that Ava had finished her appetizers before anyone else. She pushed her plate toward Ava. "Here you go, Avaïnoάel. I know you are very hungry. You have been going for an exceedingly long time without proper nutrition." Ava shook her head politely. "I insist, Ava," Estel whispered in a soft voice. "Please. No one will care. We do not like food to go to waste. Besides, "she patted her belly and smiled cheerily, "we are full."

Ava saw that Estel was pregnant. She looked like she was ready to have her baby right then and there. She had not noticed it before because Estel remained sitting when she arrived at the table. She smiled and said thank you. Then she grabbed one of the scrumptious appetizers and took a big bite. She pointed to her mouth as she chewed. "Sorry. I am really hungry as you can probably tell." She glanced down at Estel's stomach and mumbled, "How far along are you?"

"Nine months," Estel said in an excited tone. "Poldo and I are hoping for a female. Should be any day now."

Ava reached down and touched Estel's belly. She closed her eyes, and then she smiled. She opened her eyes and said in a joyous tone as she looked at the Queen straight on, "Congratulations, Estel. Your wish will come true. I am positive it will be a girl." Estel was wide-eyed as she gaped at Ava with a quizzical expression. Ava glanced around the table, and then she leaned in close and whispered. "Please do not tell anyone, but I sometimes have visions whenever I touch something." She flashed a quick grin. "But only when I want to, you know, consciously summon them in my mind. Otherwise, I would be half crazy by now."

"Of course, Avaïnoðel," Estel said in a whisper. She pressed her finger against her lips. "It will be our secret, and I thank you so very much!"

Ava grabbed another saganakiza from the plate and nearly swallowed it whole. She winked at Estel and said, "Thank you for keeping our little secret." She pulled up the tablecloth and glanced at Estel's belly once more. "Trust me. She is a girl, and something tells me she will be as pretty as you."

The food was delicious. The company was wonderful. The jokes and laughter were exhilarating. Ava felt at ease. She finally had arrived at her initial destination – Mégedale of the Mystic Mountains. Yet she was worried about Steph. More worried than she had ever been about herself, her safety, and welfare. Though she understood there was nothing to be done – at least not now. She would have to put Steph's fate in Haldir's hands. And retain complete confidence in Steph's intelligence, resourcefulness, cunning, and skills. She considered that Steph had experienced worse dangers, far greater than hers. That she would fight and endure.

Ava reveled in every facet of the four-course meal and its welcoming pleasantries. Her stomach was satisfyingly full. To include gobbling the three saganakiza's that Estel had given her. Yet strangely, she felt an odd fluttering in her stomach like it was empty. Her heart was racing as well. Also, from time to time her mind would go fuzzy. But she was not surprised by her emotions. Because she knew precisely why she was feeling the way that she was. Her giddy, love-sick feelings were owing to the elf that was seated at her right. It was none other than Voronwe, the incredibly handsome royal messenger.

Earendil had seated Voronwe beside Ava, so they could carry on a conversation. He knew it was important for her to gauge the messenger's intelligence, courage, and devotion. After all, she, as the all-powerful Avaïnoðel, had requested that Voronwe personally deliver her words to Elbereth. Earendil understood that her request was the equivalent of a command. Nonetheless, if he did not have complete faith and trust in Voronwe's capability to deliver her message discretely, he would have stated as much. Then he would have suggested that she choose another messenger.

Earendil considers Voronwe to be intelligent and resourceful. He also recognizes that Voronwe is a strong runner in addition to being an excellent marksman. Most importantly, Voronwe is loyal. He knows that Voronwe would not hesitate to sacrifice his life rather than divulge sensitive information. The young warrior messenger has proven his worth on many occasions. Also, equally important as his loyalty and skills, Voronwe is one of the finest spies of all Timbre warriors. None come even close to his infiltrating abilities. Not even Earendil who had taught Voronwe all that he knows.

Also, Earendil could not help but notice the way Ava and Voronwe had looked at each other on the grand stairway. He is hoping that they will become close friends. Especially considering Ava could benefit greatly by having a good friend right now. Someone with whom she can confide.

After all, Earendil considers, it can get tremendously lonely at the top.

2

Ava and Voronwe are sitting across from each other at a small table at the fringe of the plateíazan. Like it was earlier in the day, the plateíazan is crowded. Youngsters are playing on swings and slides. Elves and humans of all ages are engaged in watersport games in the pool. Others are sitting on benches enjoying the late afternoon sunshine. Large and small groups of families and friends are picnicking on the lush, manicured grass. While romantic couples seek a few minutes of privacy as they stroll the winding paths holding hands.

Earendil wanted to close the plateíazan from others while Ava and Voronwe met. She had said no, insisting that the others should be able to enjoy themselves after the feast. Earendil was about to say he was concerned for her safety in such a wide-open area. Especially now that half of Mégedale knew she was in the city. She had read his mind and said before he could verbalize his thoughts, "There is no need to clear the area. Trust me when I say I will be fine."

Earendil then proposed that guards be posted to keep an eye on things as she and Voronwe conferred. He said in a reassuring tone, "They will be in discreet stations. You will not even know they are there." She asked if guards are normally posted in the plateíazan. He replied that they were not. Only in extreme situations when the city was on high alert.

With one eyebrow raised as she looked at him doubtfully, Ava said, "Then I see no need for guards as well." She added shrewdly, "But that is your call, Earendil. If you want to alert the entire city that there is danger just because I am here." She gave him a questioning look and grinned. "If so, go ahead and do what you must to cause a small panic." Earendil dropped the subject, but she knew that he was going to have guards at the ready – just in case.

Ava is not at all concerned with her safety. Fluescere is high in the sky keeping an eye on things below. Having her loyal dragon close at hand makes it possible for her to relax even more. Knowing that Fluescere will zoom from the air and whisk her and Voronwe away at the first inkling of danger.

She and Voronwe have been talking for more than an hour. Ever since the feast ended. After their talk, Voronwe will get some much-needed sleep. He has a day-long journey ahead of him tomorrow. To deliver her message to Elbereth.

"So, you will do as I ask?" Ava asks him.

Voronwe leans across the table. He looks at her straight on and says in a dutiful tone, "Yes, Avaïnoðel, anything you request is my command."

Ava smiles heavily and slouches in her chair. Then she rubs at the back of her neck just as a slightly upset expression appears on her face. She shakes her head three times, and then she says, "Voronwe, what you said is not the proper answer. Also, as I have said repeatedly, please call me Ava." She rolls her eyes and frowns. "Unless we are in mixed company. Then, although I do not like all the pageantry and the formality, please refer to me as my Lady or call me Avaïnoðel. When we are alone, I am merely little ole me, Ava. Okay?"

Voronwe bites his lip and tilts his head to the left, and then he tugs at his ear. He shrugs his shoulders and says, "What I said is not the proper answer? I am sorry, Avaïnoðel, I mean, Ava. I do not understand what you imply. Please tell me why my answer was not proper."

Ava presses her lips together. She is trying to stay focused as she dreamily stares into Voronwe's deep blue eyes. She leans across the table and takes his hands in hers. She immediately feels giddy all over, but she keeps her emotions in check. She is surprised to see that his hands are calloused yet soft to her touch. She looks down at their hands and smiles. "We are friends, agreed?" Voronwe nods his head. He is blushing two shades of red which make the freckles on his face stand out even more.

Ava says, "Not close friends like having affection for each other or anything even remotely similar. We just met. We have many years ahead of us to nurture such things if they are to be. Right now, there are more important things to consider. All the same, we *are* friends. I value that." She lets go of Voronwe's hands and leans back in her chair. "Voronwe, I must tell you something about friendship. At least the way that I see it. True friends do not *command* friends to do *anything*. Nothing at all. Does that make sense?" Voronwe nods his head. He is still blushing but not as much. "Good. I am glad you understand. True friends *ask* friends if they will do something. I enquired if you would do as I *asked*. By asking, I am giving you a way out. Unlike a command that your Etanpioa leader gives you, you do not have to comply with what I ask of you. Therefore, Voronwe, you can say yes. You will do as I ask. Or you can say no. You will not do as I ask." She scrunches her nose and grins. "But if you say no, you better have a good reason."

Both she and Voronwe lean back in their chairs and laugh.

Voronwe says, "I understand, Ava. I will gladly do as you ask."

Ava's eyebrows raise with questioning. She sits back, crosses her arms over her chest, and looks Voronwe straight on. "Even though what I ask of you and the others to do is dangerous? That if you are discovered it could fail? That I would not want you and the others to be hurt or worse? That if I could think of another way going forward I would?"

Voronwe eyes are unwavering as he stares at Ava for a few moments. She notices his breathing is even. Her respect for his courage and resolve steadily increases as the second's tick by. As of late, her own courage and resolve have increased ten-fold. She knows that Voronwe, along with her and the others, will make a good team.

No, not a good team she reasons to herself. We will make a fantastic, powerful, *great* team!

Voronwe reaches across the table and takes Ava's hands in his. He gives them a firm grip and once again blushes. Ava blushes three shades of red as well. His voice is firm and strong when he says, "Ava, I understand the risks involved." He looks at their hands and grins. "Along with everything else you have asked of me. I will ensure the others understand the dangers as well – before I obligate them to accompany me. Also, as a friend to a friend, I will do everything in my power to complete the task successfully. For I understand its importance." He gestures with a broad sweep of his head from the left of the plateíazan to the katállilosly at its right. "Not only to you but to all of Mégedale as well." He lets go of Ava's hands and places his hands over his heart.

"I promise you Avaïnoáel. I will not fail."

3

Ava had asked Earendil for the private discussion with Mégedale's leadership to be held outdoors. She was relieved when he said yes. He explained that many meetings are held in the plateíazan when the weather permits. Although he would have to miss the feast to make it happen. He said with a wide grin, "But I will enjoy my feast later in the day. Now and then the leftovers are better than the main course. Because the chefs tend to keep the good stuff to themselves. That is why I cater to them as I do." He patted his lean stomach. "It is wise to never hold back on special favors for the ones who fill your belly."

Ava does not know the reason why she requested the meeting be held outdoors. She also asked Fluescere to be close during the meeting, just in case. The dragon is soaring amongst the gathering nighttime clouds. But one thing Ava knows for certain. She has had a nagging feeling that the meeting will go dreadfully wrong. That something is not right.

Although it is a few hours after nightfall, the temperature is pleasant. There is a slight breeze. Torches have been strategically placed around the meeting place. Ava suspects there are a few Etanpioa's at the plateíazan periphery, strategically posted in the shadows. However, she is incorrect. The Etanpioa's are gathered inside the walls surrounding the king's mansion. They are prepared to mobilize when Earendil gives the order. So, the plateíazan is deserted except for those who are attending the meeting.

Wade is sitting to Ava's right. Godroh is to her left. The king's first assistant, a young elf named Melian, is sitting to Wade's right. She has a bundle of parchment paper on her lap. Her chair has a special holder for the ink of her quill. The quill already is in her hand poised above the paper, ready to transcribe everything of importance that is said. Estel is to Melian's right. An ottoman has been placed before her chair so she can keep her feet up. She is smiling at Ava as she lovingly caresses her belly.

Earendil is sitting to Godroh's left. Two humans, situated to Earendil's left, are at the meeting. They are the mayor and vice mayor representing the human domiciles of the katállilosly. The mayor's name is Noble. He is a squat, chubby man dressed in typical elven attire. Deroinde is the vice mayor. She is a tall, thin blonde. She is wearing a lovely, dark blue dress with a string of pearls surrounding her neck. She is wearing matching earrings. Her attire and jewelry surprise Ava since she has not seen other humans or elves dressed in such a fashion. She will later learn that Deroinde was born in the Earthly World to wizarding parents. Her parents visit Antiquom once every two years via the Thávma.

Earendil says, "Avaïnoáel, would you like to begin our conversation?"

"Thank you," Ava says as she glances around the circle. "First, I want to thank all of you for the wonderful reception and delicious meal." She pats her stomach and grins. "I have had nothing substantial to eat for a while. I am happy to say, now I am pleasantly full." She is pleased to see the others nod their approval and smile. "Second, as is my custom, while we are here together as one, I respectfully suggest we dispense with the pageantry. I am a humble elf. Although I sincerely appreciate your politeness, please call me Ava going forward."

Wade laughs. He says in a jovial way, as is his custom, "As you wish, Ava. But only if you refer to Estel as Estel, and Earendil as Earendil, Earl for short." He throws back his head then says with a grin, "You may call me Wade."

"Agreed," Ava exclaims gleefully with an accompanying chuckle. She glances around the group once more, pausing briefly to look at each member one by one. "You know why I am here." Everyone nods his or her head. "But the extent of what we know at this time is unknown." She looks at Earendil. In the absence of his father, he oversees the meeting. "So, Earendil," she glances at Wade and giggles, "I mean, Earl if you please let us begin."

The discussion takes much longer than Ava had anticipated. It started cordial, but after a while, it became more heated. Earendil and Godroh could not agree on some of the ideas proposed by others in the group. Ava purposely kept quiet, but she thought Estel's plan to confront Wendigorium at Mountains Cross was the best approach.

"What do you think?" Earendil says to Godroh. "Do you think my mother's approach is sound?"

Godroh gets up from his chair in a huff. He begins to pace. The others are forced to turn their heads to keep up with his obnoxious pacing. "Quite frankly, Earendil," he says in a rebellious tone, "I think your mother's approach," he looks at Estel and sneers, "is not the proper way going forward." He resumes his pacing and nearly screams the basis for his opposition to Estel's idea. Finally, after ten or more minutes of subjecting everyone to his insufferable pacing and shouting, he says, "I think the best approach is to wait. Wendigorium will come to us eventually. Perhaps next year around summer. We should not risk anything to go to Mountains Cross. Our supply line will be too extensive. There is the issue of Wendigorium's newly formed alliances as well. They are too numerous and formidable for us to confront them on their territory."

Ava is watching Godroh's hands as he waves them back and forth in the air. She cannot help but laugh inwardly. How he is waving his hands frantically reminds her of multicolored, wedge-shaped flags flapping in the wind at curbside car dealerships back home. Then suddenly, her stomach seems to knot up. Her eyes narrow to an icy scowl as she looks at his left hand. She is zeroing in on the pinky finger.

Her thoughts seem to scream, he does not have on the pinky ring like he is supposed to!

She stands up. She points at Godroh and shouts in an outraged, biting tone, "You are not Godroh! You are an imposter. What have you done with the wizard?" She crosses her arms over her chest. "If you have done anything to harm King Poldo," she glances over to Estel, "I will make you regret it!"

The others, except for Estel, are now on their feet. They are staring at Ava with expressions of utter disbelief.

The imposter exclaims in a shout, "Oh, so you think I am not Godroh?" He moves a bit in Ava's direction. He is scowling at her. "If I am not Godroh, then who am I?"

"Do not step any closer!" Ava screams as she points her finger. "Or I swear, I will, I will—"

The imposter throws his head back and laughs. "If I continue to step closer, what do you intend to do to stop me? You do not have power over me. You cannot cast spells. You are nothing but an Earthly World elf with a fancy name." He grins cruelly and adds in a loathsome tone, "Despite the exaggerated, deceiving Inner World legends that are nothing more than ancient lies! You are nothing more than rubbish to me!"

Earendil aims to put an end to the disagreement even though he has no clue what had precipitated it. He looks at Ava and the imposter in turn and says in a persuasive, calming tone, "Ava, Godroh. I do not know what caused this unexpected disagreement. Nevertheless, please cease your quarreling! We must resume our dialogue with decorum and civility." He looks at Ava. "May I suggest, my Lady that you and Godroh settle your differences in private after our meeting is adjourned."

The imposter pulls a wand out of his robe. He points it at Earendil and shouts, "Sit down and shut your mouth, you useless prince!"

Now Earendil is shaking with rage. He remains standing, places his hands on his hips, and says in an energetic, commanding manner, "Godroh, *you* sit down, and *you* shut up! How dare you speak to Avaïnoáel and me in such a manner." He glances at Ava adding, "I demand that you give O Poica Katharos the respect she deserves. I will not abide—"

Before he can complete his sentence, a soft, blue glow appears at the tip of the imposter's wand. Earendil's eyes widen with disbelief. He mockingly gestures with his hands, seemingly daring the imposter to go ahead and do what he intends to do. He whispers, "I do not know what has come over you, Godroh. But one thing I know for certain. You do not dare to put a spell on me! Because if you do anything to me or the others, you will die!"

Ava jumps to her left and stands in front of Earendil to block the spell, that is, if one is going to be directed at him. Instead, to her horror, the imposter suddenly turns around and aims his wand at Estel!

Ava moves in the direction of Estel and shouts, "No! No! Not the baby!" Just as she shouts, a blue beam silently gushes from the tip of the wand like a flash of cloud to ground lightning. Luckily, Estel instinctively had shifted her hands to cover her stomach. The beam smashes her wrists immediately causing the sleeves of her robe to ignite.

Earendil screams, "Mother!" He sets out to help her, but before he can take a single step, a beam from the imposter's wand strikes him in the face slamming him back in his chair. He closes his eyes and slumps forward unconscious.

The others are watching horror-struck as Estel tries to extinguish the flames by waving her arms up and down forcefully. But her actions are only causing the flames to spread. The flames are creeping up the sleeves onto her shoulders. She tries to undo the buttons of her robe but cannot because the flames are spreading too quickly.

Ignoring the imposter and the others, Ava grabs two pitchers of water from the center table. She rushes over to Estel and douses the flames with the watery contents. Then without a second thought, she slaps the residual embers with her bare hands. Estel is clutching her stomach with both hands. Her face is ashen, her eyes wide-eyed as she stares. Ava grabs her by the shoulders and whispers, "Are you okay, Estel?" Estel does not reply.

Then to Ava's shock, Estel nearly falls forward just as she is encased in a cloud of blue mist. The magical mist from the imposter's spell has rendered her unconscious. Ava manages to catch her just before she collapses to the ground. She gently lowers her to the chair and places her legs on the ottoman. She spins around just in time to see the imposter is turning in a slow circle as he points his wand at the others. Then they, like Estel, are enveloped in a cloud of blue mist one by one. Some, including Wade, fall back in their chairs from where they were standing. Others that were standing astride of their chairs are less fortunate. They flop face-first onto the ground unconscious.

The imposter points his wand at Ava. She genuinely wants to react, but for some reason, she stands immobile, her expression one of total defiance. Surprising herself, she grins just as the cloud of blue mist wraps around her body. Amazingly, unlike what happened to the others, the mist evaporates a split-second later. The imposter points his wand at her another time. Like before, the cloud of mist disperses almost immediately.

Ava shouts, "How dare you! You almost hurt a defenseless elf carrying an unborn child. The child of a queen no less!" Then without realizing what causes her to do it, she spins around in a circle and points her finger at the others one by one, and shouts.

Reversio!

She shakes her head incredulously with what she has said and done. Miraculously, the others in the group have regained consciousness. Most of them are staring at her wide-eyed with astonished expressions. She rushes over to Estel and kneels in front of her. She gently grabs her hands and examines them. She whispers, "Estel, are you okay? Is the baby okay?" Gesturing with a nod of her head at Estel's hands, she says, "They are only burned to some extent. You will recover nicely once they are attended to."

Estel manages a smile and says in a weak voice, "Yes, thank you, Avaïnoάel. The baby is kicking up a storm. She is okay." She begins to cry. "You saved my life and the life of my daughter. How can I ever repay you?"

Ava gives the queen a reassuring smile. She is about to reply, but she cringes instead. The last thing she wanted to occur is happening. Earendil is yelling at the top of his voice. He is mobilizing his Etanpioa's. Ava believes his doing so could worsen the situation and result in a disastrous outcome with needless deaths. She jumps to her feet and turns around to look at Earendil, to state that he should repeal his shouted orders. Her face instantly flushes with dismay.

Earendil and the imposter are standing side by side. The imposter's wand is against Earendil's throat as he grins evilly at Ava. He says between clenched teeth, "Make a move and the prince will die." He glances in Estel's direction. "You will cause the queen and the baby's death as well because my next spell will not render them unconscious. I will slay them." He smiles at Ava as he leans in close to Earendil and whispers in his ear, "Now prince, do as I say. Sit down and shut your mouth. If you do not, you can say goodbye to your mother and her unborn child."

Ava whispers to Earendil, "Earl, please do as he says. He is not Godroh. He is an imposter. Please trust what I say. Please sit down. If you do not do as he asks, he will hurt you and the queen further." She steps in front of Estel, shielding her. She is hopping mad as she stares at the imposter for a few moments. "But before he hurts your mother again, he will have to go through me!"

Earendil nods his head and sits in his chair. He is staring at Ava with a questioning look. She ignores his stare. For two reasons. One, she does not want the imposter to read anything in her expression. And two, she has no idea what she must do to disarm the imposter. Nevertheless, deep inside, she is confident she will figure it out soon enough.

The imposter screams as he glances around the group, "Not just the prince. All of you sit down, now!" He waves his wand back and forth threateningly. Those that were standing immediately sit in their chairs. Noble is the exception.

The mayor is lying face down on the ground and is out cold. He had smacked his head hard as he fell forward when the cloud of blue mist covered his body. Ava's enchantment reversed the imposter's spell but could not bring the mayor out of his unconscious state. Unrecognized by Ava and the others, Noble is near death because of massive bleeding inside his brain. He will die before the night is over. His passing will turn out to be Wendigorium and Haldir's first casualty of an imminent war. It will be a horrific conflict that will encompass all Antiquom and result in many more deaths.

"You too," The imposter growls as he points his wand at Ava. "Sit down or I will disable you." He sniggers spitefully as he declares in an ugly tone, "Then off you and I will go to Mountains Cross. So, as you have hoped all this time, you will meet your archenemy, Wendigorium." He throws his head back and yells to the clouds, "There I will relish in your death!"

Ava is unmoved by his threatening words. She glares at him with daggers. If her glare were a deadly weapon, the imposter already would be nothing more than a lifeless memory. She remains standing and places her hands on her hips defiantly. In a controlled voice, she demands, "Who are you? What have you done with Godroh?" She glances in Earendil's direction. "And once again I warn you. You had better not have done anything to harm the king!"

The imposter says in a bold tone, "Who I am and what I have done if anything with Godroh is none of your concern. Now sit in your chair and shut up." He gives Ava a dirty look and slowly moves his wand up and down. "Or would you prefer that I make you sit?"

Ava remains standing. She looks up at the sky. She is speaking to Fluescere in her mind, telepathically. Only she knows that her loyal friend is high in the sky above the clouds, ready to zoom down in a split-second.

The imposter follows her gaze.

In response to Fluescere's anxious thoughts, Ava replies telepathically, "Not yet, Flame. I will tell you when. But move closer. It will be soon, I assure you."

The imposter hisses at Ava in an acerbic tone, "What are you doing?" He lets out a nasty laugh. "Calling the gods and goddesses to assist you? I wish you luck." A blue glow emerges at the tip of his wand as he points it at her. In response, Ava says, "Clearly, you must know that you do not scare me, whoever you are."

She glances around the group. Unlike her, the others appear anxious. Most look like they want to run away, the exceptions being Earendil and Wade. They are glaring at the imposter. Despite her burned hands, Estel is clutching her stomach and glaring at him as well. Ava is enormously proud of her because she is instinctively protecting her unborn daughter as best as she can. Just like any other expectant mother the world over.

Ava notices that at least three Etanpioa have arrived on the scene. They are moving slowly as they surround the group. Most of the warriors are aiming their weapons at Ava, not knowing who she is and because she is standing along with the imposter. A few warriors' weapons are trained on the imposter, even though they, wrongly, recognize him as the Great Wizard. After all, Godroh is a resident of the city and often chats with the warriors. He is well-liked and regularly shares his knowledge of the Earthly World with them.

Ava knows that if an overzealous warrior were to fire, she could perish in a flash with an onslaught of many dozens of arrows. There is no way she could avoid so many arrows coming at her at once. Maybe later when she learns all her powers from the real Godroh but certainly not today. She says to Earendil in a steady tone, "Please ask your warriors to back away, to stand down." She glances over at Noble. Blood is seeping from his nose and mouth. "There is no need for further bloodshed." She pretends to smile adding, "Because, as you can see, most of them have their weapons trained on me."

Earendil is not right after being hit in the face with the imposter's spell. He narrows his bloodshot eyes to understand what is happening. Once he realizes the Etanpioa have assembled as he commanded, he shakes his head. Ava recognizes that he still does not realize that most of the arrows are aimed in her direction. If he did, he most certainly would do as she asks. She also suspects that he is presupposing that only he and his Etanpioa can resolve the situation successfully. In the end, his primary purpose as it concerns Mégedale is to command the Etanpioa's and protect the city.

"Earl, I have this under control. There is no need to risk the lives of your seventy or more warriors." She glares at the imposter. "I just know he is itching to slay them all." She silently considers to herself, and the warriors, me . . .

Earendil looks at her doubtfully. He does not want to give the order for his warriors to stand down.

Ava says in a whisper, "Earl, please do as I ask of you."

Earendil slowly nods his head as his renewed awareness finally grasps that he must obey Avaïnodel. No matter how forcefully he wants to challenge her words. Before he can issue a command, however, and just as Ava had feared, an obsessive, young warrior at the imposter's rear releases his arrow. She notices that the warrior seemed to be aiming his weapon at her before he let it fly. Whether he released the arrow intentionally or accidentally; no one ever knew. Mercifully, the seventy or so others of the three Etanpioa hold their fire.

Amazingly, and to Ava's great relief, the imposter knows that the warrior has released his arrow. He abruptly spins around, and his wand flashes once more. The arrow bursts in flames mid-flight. Its sandy, bluish brown, flaming debris falls a few feet in front of Ava. A second flash from the imposter's wand hits the warrior square in the chest. He clutches at his heart and falls. He is dead before he hits the ground.

The young elf's fellow warriors automatically pull back hard on their bowstrings and aim their weapons at the imposter. The three Etanpioa leaders are looking at Earendil anxiously. They are waiting for him to give the command, to open fire.

Once again, thank goodness in Ava's opinion, Earendil is slow to respond due to the earlier spell that had rendered him unconscious. She takes advantage of his sluggish response. She slowly turns in a wide circle with her arms held out wide as she shouts, "Stand down! Stand down I say!"

Every one of the warriors is ignoring her shouts because they have no idea who she is. They take orders only from their Etanpioa leaders, King Poldo, or Earendil, rightly so. She is shocked to see that at least half of them if not more are now pointing their weapons at her!

"Brave warriors of the Timbre Etanpioa's I command you as Avaïnoáel, O Poica Katharos to do as I say." She nods her head because she sees that all the warriors are staring at her. "Yes, I am she! I am Avaïnoáel, O Poica Katharos. Some of you must have heard I am in your city. There is no need for further bloodshed." She turns in a slow circle as she points her finger at the encircling Etanpioa's. "Now do as I command and stand down!" She is relieved to see that all the warriors except the three leaders do as she has ordered.

She knows if the three leaders release their arrows, their actions will result in an automatic, unspoken command for the others to release their arrows as well. Then seventy-plus arrows will fly possibly striking others in the group. Afterward, many if not all the brave warriors will perish without reason due to one wide-ranging blast from the imposter's deadly wand. She places her hands over her heart and says to Earendil, "Earl, there is no need for anyone else to die. I will handle this. Please trust me. Tell the leaders to lower their weapons."

Earendil hesitates for a few moments, and then he nods his head half-heartedly. His tone is intense, solid, and commanding. "Do as Avaïnoáel has ordered of you!" The three leaders immediately comply and lower their bows.

Ava looks skyward. The imposter follows her gaze once more. Okay, Flame. Now. Be careful. Especially of the Etanpioa's and the others in my little group.

Just as the imposter is about to look from the sky and say something to Ava, Fluescere whooshes from the clouds in a blurred blast of bluish black, exploding rage. In reply, the imposter calmly directs his wand at her. A continuous stream of blue sparks sails through the sky striking

Fluescere on every inch of her armored torso. The spells bounce off her rock-hard scales and ricochet everywhere. Happily, none of the exploding blasts strikes anyone on the ground.

A moment later Fluescere knocks the imposter flat on his back with one solid flick of her wing. The force of her mighty blow knocks the wand from the imposter's hands. It lands at Ava's feet. She stares at it for a few moments. It is glowing ever so faintly, like it is talking to her, telling her to retrieve it. She reaches down and picks it up. An odd, blank-faced look appears on her face. It is a look of total disbelief at what she is doing. Of what she is about to do. Because she fears she will not know how to perform what she is supposed to do properly.

She closes her eyes for a few seconds. She is striving to recall something in her past, to have her subconsciousness bring it to the forefront of her awareness. Then her eyes suddenly snap wide open. She walks to stand beside Fluescere. She looks down at the imposter with an unwavering gaze. Her face is flushed, full of life. She grins a smile that reflects the prevailing tenacity of her heart and mind. Of her powerfulness. Of her magic. Of her wonderous talent as Avaïnoáel, O Poica Katharos.

The imposter is staring at the wand, unsure what he should do. He looks up at Ava and scowls. "What do you think you are going to do with that? You are no wizard. Moreover, that wand belongs to me. It answers only to me." He jumps to his feet with an effortless leap. Ava backs up instinctively. "Using it will merely result in your shame." He reaches out to grab the wand from her grasp. She pulls her hand away. When suddenly, without consciously realizing what she is about to do, she points the wand at his chest and yells.

Anaísthisom!

The imposter's eyes slowly close then his head snaps toward the back. A second later he drops to his knees then collapses sideways to the ground. Ava gently nudges him in his side with her foot. He does not respond. She can tell that while he is still breathing, he is out cold.

What Ava had just said to render the imposter unconscious seemed vaguely recognizable to her. Like her subconsciousness knew exactly what she had to do. But then, what she says next is wholly familiar to her awareness. She directs the wand at the imposter and yells yet again.

Presto Chango!

Immediately, the imposter is wrapped in a soft, yellowish glow that was expelled from the tip of his wand. His torso lurches up a bit just as he lets out a sharp sigh. It sounds like the pained moan of a child.

Ava stares stunned as his body gradually changes. Her legs suddenly feel heavy like they no longer can support her weight. She starts to shiver. A feeling of dread is overwhelming her because she has no inkling of what she has done. Or how, what, or why she had said what she did. Or what is going to happen next.

The imposter's scraggly beard of gray steadily disappears. His full eyebrows shrink in length and viscosity. Then they begin to change color. The length and color of his head hair change as well. His hair, like his eyebrows, gradually transforms from grayish white to a golden, chestnut brown. Soon his facial appearance progressively turns to that of a younger look, smaller, less full, and absent facial hair beneath the nose. His torso at once sets out to shorten as do his arms and legs. His markedly slighter upper body gradually withdraws inside the interior of the long, brown robe. Then his shortened arms and legs disappear inside the robe as well. Now the only thing noticeable is the imposter's shaggy, uncombed head hair. It is only just poking out from the robe's collar.

Ava drops to her knees and sets out to stroke the imposter's disheveled hair. She opens the collar of the robe and nearly falls backward. Her hands fly to her mouth. She shrieks, "Oh, my goodness! He is only a boy, perhaps no more than ten or eleven years of age. What have I done? I have hurt an innocent child!" A miserable, cold shiver runs down her spine. She feels like something dreadfully evil has clutched her heart turning her to the same wickedness. "What kind of evil would subject a young wizard to such madness as this? My God, what have I done!" She is shaking all over, rocking back and forth. "I have hurt a child!"

After a few moments, Fluescere's voice-thoughts enter her mind. She is enfolding the boy gently in her wing to keep him warm. "Ava, he is going to be okay. You simply stunned him and allowed him to return to his original life. You had no idea he was a child, that some evil wizard had brainwashed him with a dreadful hex. Please get to your feet. You must show resolve, dignity, and insight." Her voice-thoughts pause for a few seconds. "Although your initial reaction of compassion and grief have achieved more loyalty and respect than you may ever know."

Ava does what Fluescere has asked. Except for Estel, she is seated, the others are kneeling with their heads bowed. She sees that the warriors are also kneeling, the exceptions being the three Etanpioa leaders. They are staring straight ahead at attention, their longbows held vertical across their breasts. They, like their warriors, are saluting her.

Ava notices that Estel is looking at her with watery eyes. She has her clasped hands over her heart. Ava reads her thoughts.

"Thank you, Avaïnoάel, for saving my daughter, for saving all of us! Indeed, you are the all-powerful O Poica Katharos!"

CHAPTER 10

LOYALTY BRINGS FRIENDSHIP HOME

"When sorrows come, they come not single spies, but in battalions."
—*William Shakespeare, Hamlet*

1

Three days later

Galadriel and Nessa are sitting together on a log some distance away from the rest of the Etanpioa. It is nearing nightfall. Nessa is sharpening her knife after using it to whittle a sculpture that vaguely resembles a flying dragon. Her cloak and the entire area around her are covered with wood shavings. She knows that dragons are Ava's favorite creatures. So, she intends to give the figurine to her on her fourteen birthday. That is, she considers if I can ever finish it or get to see her again!

Suddenly, a movement to their right catches Galadriel's attention. Her tone is extremely nervous as she whispers, "Goodness, no! Elbereth is standing over there! Someone is with her. It looks like a Timbre warrior, but I cannot be certain. Oh no, they are looking at us! Maybe they will come this way." She jumps to her feet and lets out an anxious sigh. "I am in trouble now! Elbereth told me not to hang out with you now that I am second in command. Act like I am teaching you something or other." She reaches down and grabs Nessa's knife.

"Hey, give that back!" Nessa growls in a voice that is much too loud.

Galadriel gives her a dirty look. "Keep your voice down! You are going to get me in trouble!" She snatches the sharpening stone from

416

Nessa's hand. Nessa is about to protest but does not say anything because of Galadriel's nasty scowl.

Holding the knife and sharpening the stone in her hands, Galadriel sets out pretending to demonstrate the proper technique for sharpening a knife. She says in an excessively loud voice, "Position your blade at a twenty-degree angle like this. Then move the knife back and forth across the stone in a flowing motion."

Nessa reaches up and snatches the knife and stone from her hands. She shouts, "What in the world is wrong with you, Galadriel? I know how to sharpen my blade." Her face suddenly goes pale as she looks to her right. "Goodness! You are correct! They *are* coming this way." She glances to her left. "Must be because no one else is around here." She lowers her voice and says in a whisper, "It *is* a Timbre warrior, a male at that! Act normal."

"Darn you, Nessa!" Galadriel moans under her breath. "I was *trying* to act normal by pretending to show you something. But no, you had to go and ruin it. Thanks for nothing! Get to your feet to greet Elbereth and the visitor properly."

Nessa ignores her and says excitedly, "I bet he is delivering a message from Ava!" She looks up at Galadriel with wide eyes that are overflowing with joy. "Why else would he be here?"

Galadriel whispers between her clenched teeth, "I said get up!" At last, Nessa gets to her feet. She starts to brush the wood shavings from her cloak.

As Elbereth and the Timbre warrior draw nearer, Galadriel's outward appearance is pleasant, despite she is feeling weak at the knees. Swallowing hard she says in a feeble voice, "Good evening, Elbereth, sir. May we be of assistance?"

In opposition to Galadriel's cordiality, Nessa is still busily brushing at the wood shavings. She seems completely oblivious that her leader and the visitor are less than twenty feet away.

Galadriel is hopping mad. She says in a whisper, "Stop doing that! And darn you, Nessa, take your hands away from your butt. You look ridiculous."

Nessa says, "Okay, okay, calm down. I was just trying to get the sticky shaving from the back of my cloak!" She is about to say something else but stops mid-thought. She is staring googly-eyed at the Timbre warrior. He and Elbereth are now less than ten feet away. She sees that he is perfectly handsome from head to toe. But his flawless handsomeness is not the reason she is staring. It is because of his flaming red hair. It is the same shade as Galadriel's. What is more, he seems to have Galadriel's pointy nose, her round face, and her freckled lips too, or so she thinks. She squeezes Galadriel's arm hard and whispers out of the side of her mouth. "I cannot believe this, Galadriel. He looks just like you! Like he is your brother or cousin. Goodness, he is handsome too, don't you think?"

Galadriel yanks her arm away and growls, "Shut up! You are embarrassing me, us!"

Elbereth says in a cordial tone, "This is a messenger from Mégedale of the Timbre. His name is Voronwe. Voronwe, these are the two to whom you wish to speak, Galadriel and Nessa. Both, as I said, were held captive by the wizard of Mountains Cross along with traitorous others. They somehow managed to escape. I am immensely proud of their courage and tenacity."

Both Galadriel and Nessa's faces redden. Galadriel knows better than to say anything. She simply lowers her head and smiles. Nessa, on the other hand, is less disciplined and impulsive. She looks to the side and giggles. Then she says shyly, "Aw, shucks, it was no big deal. We were just doing what you have taught us." Her face brightens markedly, "In fact, Voronwe, it was thrilling. You should have seen—" Before she can say anything further, Galadriel elbows her in the ribs.

Voronwe extends his hand. "It is a pleasure to meet you." Galadriel and Nessa shake his hand in turn. With a slight, deferential nod of his head, Voronwe says to Elbereth, "My Lady, with your permission." Elbereth smiles and nods her head at him, and then she walks off.

Galadriel is the first to speak. She is blushing, and her tone is unusually shaky. She feels like she is going to faint straight away. Her tone is nervous. "You and I have the same color hair. Very unusual, would you not agree?"

Voronwe grins but does not say anything. He too is blushing.

"And the same nose, lips, eyes, and round face!" Nessa shouts. By how the others are looking at her, she quickly realizes she should not have said what she did. However, instead of apologizing, she shrugs her shoulders.

"But both of you must admit that you do have similar features. It is rather obvious I dare say. The hair, nose, eyes, lips. Even your freckles! You are the same height as well. You could be related, brother and sister, maybe first cousins or even twins!" She eyes Galadriel suspiciously and says, "You had better hope you two are related before you fall madly in love or something equally weird and Elbereth finds out."

Without taking her eyes off Voronwe, her lips creased in a straight line, Galadriel nudges Nessa hard in the ribs with her elbow once more. She whispers out of the corner of her mouth, "Be quiet. You are embarrassing all of us."

"Well, it is true," Nessa says matter-of-factly. "And the way you are staring at each other. Both of you are blushing ten shades of red as well!"

"You must be Nessa," Voronwe says with a sincere smile. "Avaïnoáel told me all about you. Her description of you and your mannerisms were spot-on flawless. There is no doubt in my mind who you are. Cheeky, outspoken, and unquestionably brave." Galadriel is staring at him with a puzzled look. She is about to ask what the legendary Avaïnoáel has to do with all of this when Nessa smacks her hard on the shoulder.

"See, Galadriel? What did I tell you!" She tilts her head to the side adding in a sarcastic tone, "And you did not believe me, huh? Our friend, Ava, *is* Avaïnoáel!" She giggles and pumps her fists. "I always knew that she was because Steph would not lie to me." She says to Voronwe, "What an honor that she has remembered me."

Voronwe nods his head then looks at Galadriel. "And you are Galadriel. Like your friend, Nessa, Avaïnoáel holds you in the highest regard as well. She said you were a very professional warrior, a true leader. One of a kind, especially considering both of you are the same age."

"I am deeply flattered," Galadriel says. "Thank you. She is a wonderful friend." Her expression unexpectedly turns serious. The inspiring, powerful leadership element of her personality is now in charge. "What news do you have for us, Voronwe?" She cocks her head to the side. "Hopefully, a message from Ava? Perhaps that she has found our friend, Steph? Maybe that they have captured Haldir? Is she safe?"

Voronwe is shaking his head as he says, "There is no news about your friend Steph, unfortunately. Nor of the wizard, Haldir. But yes, your friend, Ava, is well. She has a special message for you and Nessa."

"What is it?" Nessa exclaims impatiently. She looks at Galadriel and instantly gets the giggles. Her eyes seem to be dancing with joy once more. "Does she have a secret plan for us?"

In what Galadriel and Nessa will later discover is a lie, Voronwe replies, "I am not aware of a secret plan. Only that she would like you to accompany me to Mégedale. She values your friendship and seeks your aid."

"This is incredible!" Nessa says to Galadriel. She smacks her on the shoulder once more. "We are going to assist Ava. Is this not grand? I have always wanted to visit Mégedale!"

Galadriel drops her head and swallows hard. "I am afraid I cannot accompany you, Voronwe." She looks up at him. Her eyes are watering. "I am second in command of the Etanpioa. I am positive Elbereth will not permit me to accompany you."

Voronwe says bluntly, "She already has given her permission."

Galadriel looks up. She is grinning. "She has? This is wonderful news! How did you manage to persuade her?"

"I did nothing to persuade her. I simply told her that Avaïnoðel insisted that you and Nessa should accompany me. Your leader has no other choice but to obey."

Galadriel is looking at Nessa as she stammers, "But – but – but who will be her second in command? Yes, many are just as qualified; some even more. But our Etanpioa is already short of warriors. Elbereth will be five warriors short if you and I leave."

Nessa exclaims with a straight face, "Who really cares? Elbereth will do simply fine, even if she has no second in command." She is bouncing on her toes with excitement. She says to Voronwe, "When do we leave?" She picks up her sword and quiver. "I am ready to go right now."

Voronwe says, "We cannot depart on our journey until more warriors arrive. They should be here sometime the day after tomorrow if they march throughout the night."

Galadriel asks, "More warriors? Do you know from where?"

"They are Timbre warriors," Voronwe says proudly. "Four fully armed Etanpioa. They will subordinate to your Etanpioa leader. When she gives the command, they will assist in searching for your friend, Steph." He turns up his nose and says in a nasty tone, "The wicked wizard, Haldir, as well. I would hate to be him if he is found by the Timbre."

Nessa looks at Galadriel and says, "Well, so much for worrying about who Elbereth will select as her second in command, huh? She will have at least forty-eight Timbre warriors from which to select."

"You are right," Galadriel says. "It is customary for the leading warrior to select her second in command from the subordinate Etanpioa." She suddenly reaches out and takes Voronwe's hand in hers, completely taking him and Nessa by surprise with her kind, albeit coquettish gesture.

Nessa knows that Galadriel will release Voronwe's hand before they are anywhere close to the others. It is strictly forbidden for an active Etanpioa warrior, regardless of the tribe, to display affection to one of the opposite sexes. Hence, she is astonished by Galadriel's boldness. She is a bit jealous too. Then again, she considers Galadriel's holding hands with a male elf is but one of the many reasons she was selected as Elbereth's second in command. Principally considering she is young and relatively inexperienced. She was selected because she is intelligent, daring, unafraid, and gutsy, with a boldness burning in her bosom as fiercely as her flaming red hair.

Nessa is following closely behind Galadriel and Voronwe as they stroll hand-in-hand along the trail. She, just like Galadriel, is keeping an eye out for the others. Neither of them wants Galadriel to get caught. That would result in severe penalties to include Galadriel forfeiting her position as second in command. As she walks, her arms swinging at her side, Nessa is listening to Galadriel's sweet, flirtatious words. She cannot help but grin at her good friend's cheekiness.

"So, what do you say you and I compare ancestries, Voronwe? After all, we can assume that we are somehow related. Nearly all Antiquom elves with our shade of red hair are related in one form or another." She gives him a sly grin. "Then again, perhaps we are not."

Nessa is silently pondering Galadriel's flirtatious words. Then, as her thoughts turn to the upcoming adventure to Mégedale, she begins to skip along like she is at ease with the world.

2

The supporting Timbre Etanpioa's from Mégedale arrive at the Bkotn campsite shortly after daybreak two days later. As soon as they are settled in, Elbereth calls for Galadriel, Nessa, and Voronwe to join her at breakfast.

"Galadriel, as you know I must select one of the Timbre Etanpioa leaders as my second in command. When you return from your mission you will resume your duties. That is if the supporting Etanpioa has departed. If they are still here when you return, you will relieve Lia as third in command, temporarily. Afterward, I will reassign her to third in command when you assume your rightful position. Do you understand?"

Galadriel replies, "Yes, I understand, and I thank you for your trust."

Elbereth says to Voronwe, "Are you prepared to depart? If so, I shall dismiss my warriors with parting words." Voronwe replies they are ready to leave.

Elbereth takes Galadriel's hand in hers. "You oversee Nessa. You shall protect her to the best of your ability. Do you understand?" Galadriel replies that she does. Then she clutches Nessa's hand. "I admire your spirit. I also respect your skills and tenacity. Someday you will lead your own Etanpioa, I am certain of it. But for now, you must follow Galadriel's orders. Do you understand what I am saying?" Nessa replies that she will comply with Galadriel's orders.

Elbereth looks at Galadriel and Nessa in turn. Her expression is solemn. "Voronwe will ask you to accompany him on a special mission. You can refuse his request. However, if you agree to do as he asks, you may not break your word. You must do exactly as he says as it concerns your official duties. He will oversee you totally, once again as it pertains to your duties that he sets forth given Ava's guidance. Do you comprehend everything I have said?"

Galadriel and Nessa are giving each other bewildered looks.

"We already told Voronwe that we will accompany him," Galadriel exclaims. "Surely, you have allowed us to do so?" Elbereth nods her head. "Well, if you have given us permission how is it now that we can refuse him?" She looks at Nessa and Voronwe in turn. "I am sorry, Elbereth, but I am confused."

"Me too," Nessa says.

Elbereth replies, "Voronwe informed me there is more he must tell you. Things that your friend, Ava, does not want anyone but you two to know. I am not pleased with that part of Ava's plan. However, I must obey because she is my superior. Even though I realize that giving my consent may put you at risk." She glances at Voronwe. "And just so you know, I trust Voronwe's judgment and competence." She pats the pocket of her cloak. "Prince Earendil of Mégedale presented me with a letter detailing Voronwe's outstanding credentials." She looks around to make certain no one is nearby. She lowers her voice appreciably and says in a whisper, "I assume you know that your friend, Ava, is the Avaïnoἀel, O Poica Katharos? That Voronwe has told you this?"

Nessa's eyes brighten. She says in an exuberant tone, "Yes, we have—" She abruptly stops talking because she notices that Galadriel is shaking her head forcefully. Galadriel does not want her to tell Elbereth that Steph had informed her of Ava's identity some time ago. That information potentially could embarrass Elbereth, thus putting Nessa in a bad spot. Armed leaders the world over are supposed to know mission-essential secrets before their subordinates. Every seasoned warrior knows that. Besides, Elbereth is already distraught because there is more to their mission than Voronwe can confide in her.

Elbereth lets go of Galadriel and Nessa's hands. She says to Voronwe, "Take care of them." Then she says, "You two stay safe. Remember to uphold the Bkotn code in all that you do going forward. Also, when you see our Lady, Avaïnoἀel, please give her my kindliest regards." With a final nod of her head, she abruptly turns away and walks off to talk further with the Mégedale Etanpioa leaders.

This is the last time the three Bkotn warriors will stand eye to eye.

*****

As soon as Elbereth is out of earshot, Galadriel grabs Voronwe by his upper arm. She spins him around roughly then pushes hard on his chest with her open hands. He steps backward to keep from falling on his rear end.

"Hey! What was that for? Why did you push me?"

Galadriel is pacing back and forth and glaring at Voronwe. Her eyes are blazing with anger. She stops walking and says, "What is going on, Voronwe, huh?" She cracks her knuckles. Then she moves to stand close to him until their noses are almost touching.

Nessa whispers, "Galadriel, calm down."

Without looking away from Voronwe, Galadriel says, "Stay out of this, Nessa. Before we accompany him to Mégedale, I want to know all the details. If there is something that we should know, now is the time to know it. He has something to tell us that even Elbereth does not know." She says to Voronwe, "Tell us what is going on before I smack you so hard you will wish I hadn't."

Voronwe says as he backs away from Galadriel, "We are not going to Mégedale. At least not yet."

Nessa cries in a shocked tone, "We are not going to Mégedale to see Ava? But you promised us, Voronwe. You said she needed our assistance – in Mégedale. You said she values our friendship and seeks our aid, all that other stuff too!"

Galadriel exclaims, "Please hush, Nessa. Let him explain." She is shaking her finger in front of Voronwe's nose in a threatening manner. "Did you lie to us? To Elbereth as well? Did you? As Nessa said, you stated that Ava needed our assistance. That we should accompany you to Mégedale. So, what has changed in two days? And why could you not tell our Etanpioa leader?" She gives him a nasty look and jabs him in the chest with her finger. "Did you lie to her as you did to us? I hope for your sake that you did not!"

Voronwe whispers, "I can understand your concerns. But if you will recall lady Elbereth said—"

"My concerns?" Galadriel hisses interrupting Voronwe. "What do you know about my concerns? I must ensure Nessa's safety since she is in my charge. You heard what Elbereth said." She glares at him and clenches her hands to fists. "Now talk before I beat the daylights out of you!" She laughs then looks Voronwe straight on. "Well, maybe not since you are a fellow redhead." She cocks her head then says with a sly grin, "But you never know, do you? We Bkotn are very unpredictable as you probably have heard."

Voronwe moves in a complete circle and throws his hands high in the air. He gives Galadriel an impatient stare then curses under his breath. He is frustrated, more so than at any other time in his life. Carefully and gently, he says, "Galadriel, I am trying to explain. If you will remain quiet for a few moments, perhaps I can!" He throws back his head and chuckles. "Yes, we must be related. You remind me so much of my mother. She has the same feistiness, only a much smaller amount than you obviously have."

Galadriel does not respond. She says to Nessa as she points to a thicket off the trail, "What do you say we go over there? No one will see us." She and Nessa walk toward the thicket. Voronwe is doubled over in laughter. Galadriel turns around and stares at him. She growls, "Stop standing there like an idiot and come with us. And you had better stop laughing too, or else!" She rolls her eyes and whispers to Nessa in an exasperated tone of voice, *"Ándreste!"* Galadriel's annoying use of the word *ándreste* simply implies (stupid) male elf!

Once they are off the trail, Voronwe says, "Ava and I had a long talk. She made me swear that what I am about to say will go no further than us three." Galadriel is still furious as she impatiently stares at him. Conversely, Nessa is leaning in closer. She is eagerly anticipating what he has to say. "She also made me promise that what I am going to ask you is because you are her friends. Not out of some crazy loyalty to her as Avaïnoóel. That you can refuse to do as she asks of you. Moreover, she promises that she will remain your loyal friend through thick and thin no matter what you decide."

"I will do anything she asks," Nessa says.

Voronwe looks at her and then at Galadriel. "Even if it means sacrificing your life?" Galadriel and Nessa reply at the same time, "Yes." Voronwe says, "Can both of you give me your word?"

Galadriel says, "You have my word."

"Mine too," Nessa hurriedly says to Voronwe. She is giving him an annoyed look. "Enough of this giving our word and loyalty stuff! We would do anything for Ava; you must know that by now. So, what is it we are supposed to do? Hurry up and get to the point because you are driving me crazy!"

Voronwe begins to narrate some of what Ava had told him. "She was held captive by some unseen force a few days after she ran off from the Crostim Ledge path." Looking at Nessa he adds, "It was after she thought you had been murdered by Siofra. Siofra and Vena were calling after her." He reaches out and touches Nessa's hand. "She said that I should tell you that she was deeply moved by your feelings toward her. She knew that you had said that you love her. She was encouraged by your words that she should run away and as quickly as possible. That you also had mentioned Steph. She thanks you from the bottom of her heart for your kindness. She told me to tell you that she loves you in return and is very relieved to know you are alive and well. That what she thought happened to you was nothing more than a hideous, repulsive stunt."

Nessa is weeping. Galadriel gives her shoulders a firm squeeze and whispers, "She loves you, Nessa, as much as you love her. So, do I. The three of us are lucky to have each other."

Voronwe says, "Ava hiked the forest for nearly three days. Then shortly after she reached the Solenom, she was knocked out and whisked from the shore. She woke up to find herself bound to a small tree at the wrists and ankles. She does not know for certain, but she suspects it was Haldir's magic. There was nothing physical binding her. She fell asleep while standing up, and then she was attacked by a beluga."

Galadriel says excitedly, her eyes wide open and glowing, "She was attacked while she was bound to the tree?"

"No, she had somehow managed to break the magical bonds holding her," Voronwe replies. "She is not certain, but she thinks it is the precise moment that her mind, heart, and spirit recognized who she was – that she was Avaïnoðel, O Poica Katharos."

Galadriel and Nessa exchange glances of pure joy. "She destroyed one beluga with a straight and true shot of her arrow. It was stalking her from behind. Then she walked toward the forest even though she knew many others were slowly surrounding her."

"Were they the dud belugas or the more knowing kind, the smarter ones?" Nessa asks.

Voronwe says, "Ava is fairly certain they were duds. Hundreds of them, probably with a few of the smarter variety, the déxypnos, in their ranks. She expended all her arrows within a minute. She was outnumbered. So, she drew her sword and prepared to fight them to the death."

Nessa lowers her head briefly and murmurs, "Ava is so brave. Just like the legends say." She shivers and looks up. "I wish I were as brave as her."

Galadriel says, "What happened next? She must have destroyed them; otherwise, she would not be in Mégedale. Am I correct?"

Voronwe is shaking his head. "No, she told me that even with her brand-new, vast powers, she could not fight them all. As I said, she guessed that one or more among them was of the smarter variety, the déxypnos. That they would command the duds to imprison her. Anyway, she thought that she would give it a go, to fight them to the death; but she felt in her heart she would lose the battle in the end." He shudders and stares at the ground. He places his cupped hands below his chin and stays silent for a few moments. He is thinking hard about what he is going to say next. After a few more moments of contemplation, he looks up and smiles.

"When suddenly, a booming voice appeared out of the heavens. Ava said it was piercingly loud. She covered her ears, but she said the powerful voice entered her head unmercifully, wracking her brain with throbs of pain. The belugas heard the evil creatures' words as well. They stopped attacking and bowed reverently." Voronwe's face turns grim as he looks at Galadriel and then at Nessa. "Wendigorium said he was coming."

"Oh my gosh," Galadriel cries. "Wendigorium. How dreadful." She notices that Nessa is now shivering with the mere mention of Wendigorium's name.

"Did she fight Wendigorium?" Nessa says in an unsteady tone of voice.

Voronwe says, "No, fortunately, she did not have to fight the beast. With so many belugas surrounding her, she surely would have been captured as I said. When out of the blue her faithful dragon, Fluescere, appeared. The dragon annihilated most of the belugas with his fiery flames. A few escaped to the forest. Then she scooped up Ava and flew her to the Mystic Mountains, to my city of Mégedale."

"Wow, what a story?" Galadriel says. "Truly amazing."

"There is more," Voronwe says. "According to Ava – she can communicate with Fluescere telepathically." He grimaces because he accidentally divulged Ava's telepathic powers. "Goodness, I was not supposed to tell you that. However, now it is too late." He smiles in a submissive way. "Please do not tell anyone, okay?" Galadriel nods her head, but Nessa does not say or do anything. Voronwe says to her in a worried tone of voice, "You are not going to tell anyone, are you? Ava could get incredibly angry with me if you do, although I guess she will not."

Nessa replies, "Of course not. I already assumed she can read minds, but I kept my beliefs to myself."

"How is that?" Galadriel says with a disbelieving expression. "How did you suppose Ava can read minds?"

"Because of what Voronwe said earlier. He had said that Ava was moved when I said that I loved her." She frowns just as a spasm runs up her spine and across her shoulders causing her to shiver. "When I thought Siofra had stabbed her tkalakn in my back. Voronwe also said Ava was encouraged by my words that she should run away and as quickly as possible." She looks at Galadriel and then at Voronwe and shrugs. "I never *said* those words. I was in too much pain. I could not have opened my mouth even if I had wanted to. But I thought those exact words including a mention of Steph. Therefore, it is obvious that Ava had read my thoughts, that she is telepathic." She shakes her head and grins. "Ava is something else!"

Voronwe says, "Well since you already know about her abilities, I guess there is no harm done. Anyway, as I was saying, while Fluescere was searching for Ava, she had noticed a small clearing in the forest. Unlike other clearings she had seen, those attended by farmers and where elves live, this clearing looked oddly different. All the trees in the vicinity, perhaps a few dozen yards surrounding the cabin, had blackened treetops. Also, the clearing was not circular, rectangular, or square in shape. It resembled a crudely shaped pentagram. As we know, the pentagram is the symbol of a wicked witch or wizard. Anyone entering the area on the ground would not notice the pentagram-shaped clearing. Only those flying high above it could discern its features.

"Ava said that Fluescere dared not descend lower to take a closer look. The dragon did not want to alert the owner of the cabin. But she continued circling the clearing. She was about to depart the area to resume her search for Ava when she spotted a carriage tucked beneath a thicket. She immediately recognized the carriage as one belonging to a wizard. The carriage had curvatures on its sides to propel it quickly across the land. Unlike normal carriages used by ordinary men, carriages of that type are self-propelled, undoubtedly spurred on by wizardly spells.

"Fluescere continued to circle high above the clearing. She watched as a man exited the cabin then walked to the carriage and mounted it. The carriage then speedily took off on a path. The path headed in a westerly direction, away from the Solenom. Fluescere followed the carriage for a few seconds. Then rightly thinking that the wizard may have had something to do with Ava's disappearance, she sped off in a westerly direction as fast as her wings could fly. Moments later she spotted Ava. She was surrounded by the belugas. Fluescere destroyed most of them then whisked her to safety. Happily, before the carriage could arrive Ava was on her way to Mégedale." Voronwe's blue eyes widen markedly. They seem to be glowing in the morning sunlight. He moves in closer and says in a whisper, "This is where the three of us enter Ava's amazing story."

Nessa does a fist pump and yells, "Yes!" She gives Voronwe a dirty look. "What you have told us up until now is exciting; however, I must say this. It is about time you got to the juiciest part of the mission! Hurry and get on with our part!"

Before Voronwe can reply, Galadriel says, "Ava wants us to spy on whatever wizard it is that owns the cabin. Am I correct?"

Nessa takes her cue from Galadriel and offers with a sly grin, "Because she suspects it is Haldir's cabin, the one that her dragon saw? Because she believes that Haldir kidnapped our friend, Steph? That he might be holding Steph there?" She notices that Galadriel is nodding her head, encouraging her to continue. "Perhaps Ava also assumes it was Haldir that put her under the spell, binding her to the tree as you said? And she wants her revenge. Am I correct?"

Voronwe agrees with everything Nessa has said. "I have to say you two are amazing. You already have everything figured out. Now I have to say something important. Ava said for me to tell you at this point, given the information I have provided, that you may refuse to help. You may say no that you will not come with me. To spy on Haldir and to try and find Steph."

"There is no way I would say no," Galadriel says in a frank manner. "How could I possibly say no to our friends?" She looks at Nessa and tilts her head. "How about you? Although I think I already know your answer."

"Unh-unh," Nessa says earnestly. "I am not missing out on this. If Ava picked us, she must believe in her heart it just might work. We have to find Steph." She says to Voronwe, "So, when do we start?"

Voronwe says, "We will gather our things and head north along the Kuoino. Once we are out of sight of the Etanpioa's, we will enter the forest. We will double back through the forest staying parallel to the trail. When we are well beyond where the Etanpioa's are searching, we will reenter the Kuoino and head south."

Galadriel says, "But how will we know where to turn inside the forest? Where Haldir's cabin is if it truly is his in the first place?"

Voronwe says, "It should take us a full day, perhaps less if we travel quickly, to arrive in the vicinity of the cabin. It is not far from Crostim Ledge. At least that is Ava's belief. She also told me that Fluescere will return to where she had been bound by the wizard's magic. The dragon will search the trail looking for us. Once she finds us, she will tell us where we should go back inside the forest in search of the wizard's cabin."

Nessa says, "How in the world will the dragon tell us where to reenter the forest? Dragons cannot speak, and I have been told they are deaf as well. They merely react to visual clues."

Voronwe shrugs his shoulders. "I have no idea. I just hope Fluescere figures out a way to give us a sign. If not, our mission will fail." His eyes are watery as he stares past Galadriel and Nessa. "We must not fail our good friend, Ava."

3

Ava is eating breakfast in her bedchamber when there is a knock on the door. She rushes to the wardrobe and throws on a nightgown. It is the same gown she has been wearing the past four days. But she does not care. It is warm, soft, and she likes the stitched flowers. The flowers remind her of her mother's garden back home. She looks in the mirror and quickly removes a few tangles in her hair with her fingers. Then she sits on the edge of the bed.

"Please come in. The door is unlocked." As soon as the door opens, she lets out a soft squeal of delight. "Queen Estel, King Poldo, Prince Earendil, and the Great Wizard Godroh, good morning!" She sees that Estel's hands are bandaged from the slight burns she suffered when the imposter hexed her. She hurries over to her. "Estel, how is our little girl doing today? How are your hands? Are they almost healed?"

The Queen replies with a wide grin, "She is kicking like she is more than ready to join us. I am thinking today, perhaps tomorrow at the latest. As far as my hands are concerned, thanks to you they will be simply fine as you had said they would. The doctor says I should be able to remove the bandages tomorrow."

Ava steps back from her and says, "Wonderful. I am extremely excited for you. Happy too." She offers her hand to King Poldo. He hesitates briefly, and then he grabs her hand and pulls her in a hug. She is genuinely surprised, but she does not mind. After all this time it feels good to be hugged by someone. Her stomach churns a bit as she is reminded of the loving hugs of her parents. She is also thinking about why she and Voronwe did not hug when they went their separate ways. Now she wishes that they had.

Poldo says, "My dear, Avaïnoáel, we are very blessed you have returned. May the sunshine sanctify your upcoming journeys with warmth and love." He releases her from his embrace and smiles delightfully. "I only wish I were here for your welcoming feast. Likewise, please pardon Godroh and my untimely arrival. It seems we missed a bit of excitement as well." He glances at Godroh. The wizard is smiling. "How is the boy that impersonated him? I do not know all of the details; however, I was told it was an interesting attempt of deceit." He looks at Godroh and laughs. "I am surprised anyone could look, well, as interesting as our wizard friend."

Godroh is smiling as he extends his hand to Ava. He says, "I finally have the pleasure, my Lady."

Ava does not shake his hand. Instead, she leans in close and says in a whisper, "First, I need to see your other hand if you please. If you truly are Godroh you will know why I am asking you to do this."

Godroh nods with purpose and shows her his left hand. The peace, love, and harmony promise ring is on his pinky finger.

Ava takes his right hand and clutches it with both of hers with a firm handshake. She says in an earnest tone, "Thank you, Godroh. At last, we meet." She tilts her head and says in a more solemn tone, "You and I will talk later." She quickly looks away to address the king. "The boy is fine, Poldo."

At this point, Ava purposely dispenses with the rituals as it pertains to statuses. She is grateful that the king did not react negatively when she referred to him by his first name. She correctly assumes Earendil must have told him how she feels about all the ridiculous but necessary solemnity of titles. She says to Earendil, "Perhaps you would like to explain what we know about the Godroh imposter."

Earendil says to his father, "The boy's name is Jason. He is from the village Nebolom. It is a human village close to Mountains Cross. He is unaware that he impersonated Godroh. Or how he came to be here. He also does not know who transformed him to look like Godroh. But whoever it was that hexed the boy, he or she knew exactly what Godroh looked like. To include the wizard's mannerisms and tone of voice. Whoever it was also had inserted the boy's brain with acute knowledge of our quest to confront Wendigorium. That is obvious because the boy acted out the part perfectly. He looked exactly like Godroh at the time, except his behavior was somewhat strange – understandably. I admit that I was duped until Ava confronted him." He looks at Ava. "How she was able to figure out he was an imposter is beyond me. Especially considering she had never met Godroh."

Ava and Godroh give each other knowing glances but say nothing about the pinky rings.

Ava says, "Jason and I spoke at length. The poor child is but ten years of age. The last thing he recalls, he was walking with his dog in the forest. He does not even know that he flew to Mégedale on a dragon. But strangely, he knew exactly who I was but did not seem to know any of you. All of us have agreed to not tell Jason what happened. He is shocked that he is here. But he seems content. All of us are optimistic that his life will change for the better."

Poldo asks, "How will he explain to his parents, assuming he has any, that he was here? I can only imagine they are sick with worry."

Earendil says, "He is an only child, an orphan. He was used to wandering alone in the forest with his dog. He is bright, unassuming, polite, extraordinarily strong for his age. He is very skilled with the bow. We will train him to be a good warrior. But first, he shall live with a modest human family to adapt to his new surroundings."

Poldo says, "Well, I am glad the young boy is okay. Too bad his dog was left behind. I am certain having his dog would help in his recovery. We should try and get him another."

Ava laughs as she says in a happy tone, "He brought his dog with him!"

"He did?" Poldo exclaims. "How did he manage that as an impersonating Godroh?"

Ava replies, "We have no idea. All we know is that a day after the incident he was walking in the plateíazan. He was wobbly from his double transformations, so a doctor was accompanying him. He scared the dickens out of the doctor when he suddenly shouted, 'Cassandra!' The dog, she is brown and has spots all over her torso, came running up to him, her tail wagging like crazy. Having her with him will help greatly with his speedy recovery as you said.'" She grins and shrugs her shoulders adding, "I suspect that he carried his dog with him as he was astride the dragon. He probably let her go somewhere in the forest before entering the city."

Estel is beaming. She places her arm around Ava's shoulder and squeezes. She says to her husband, "Ava saved Jason's life with her enchantments." She touches her belly. "She saved our daughter's life as well. She may have saved all our lives, those of us attending the meeting. As well as many warriors."

Ava is tempted to tell the others she had no clue how she performed the spells on Jason. Or how she brought the others back to consciousness. But she decides now is not the time to admit it. She notices Godroh is nodding his head as he looks at her. She knows the Great Wizard will tell her all that she needs to know. Jordyn had predicted it. She says, "It was my pleasure, Estel." She looks at Poldo and says with a smile, "I am very happy that you will be here when your daughter arrives."

"So, you are certain the baby is a female?" Poldo says. Ava nods her head. "Then we shall call her Ava," the king says, "to honor the one who saved her life." He smiles at Estel. "Estel and I have already agreed on the name for our daughter."

Estel is nodding her head exuberantly. "Indeed, we have. We also are overjoyed and honored that she will have your name."

Earendil notices that Ava has not touched her breakfast since they arrived. He says, "Father, mother, Godroh, I think we should leave Ava to finish her morning meal." He winks at Ava and chuckles. "Mother told me you have a voracious appetite. We shall talk later."

After a few departing words, the foursome leaves Ava with her thoughts.

Still no word on Steph! Otherwise, Earendil would have told me. Gosh, I hope she, Voronwe, Galadriel, and Nessa are all right!

4

"Look, look up there!" Nessa cries out in a whisper. "Do you see the shadow in the sky above the trees? It is difficult to make out what it is. But it is a shadow of something large flying in the air."

Voronwe and Galadriel look up to where Nessa is pointing. The fleeting shadow is to the east of the trail and almost directly above them.

"I see it," Voronwe says. "If it Fluescere she should signal us soon."

Galadriel says, "But if it is a dragon, how do we know it is not carrying something else, something evil?" Voronwe and Nessa look at her with surprised expressions.

"I never thought of that," Voronwe says. "I should have known better. Thanks, Galadriel. We need to be extremely careful going forward." He pulls out a map of the terrain from his pocket. The map features the territory from Mégedale to the Unseen Valley. He unfolds the map and studies it for a few moments. "I doubt it is the dragon. Look at this."

Galadriel and Nessa move in close to study the map. Galadriel places her arms around Voronwe's neck as she looks over his shoulder. Her closeness causes him to blush noticeably. He shivers a bit then says in a creaky voice, "See this mark I made on the map?" Galadriel and Nessa nod their heads. "This represents the start of the ascending path that leads to Crostim Ledge from the Kuoino." He glances at Nessa. "Where you and Ava were before everything happened. And here," he places his fingertip on a zigzagging line, "is where I believe we are right now. The north-south line represents the Kuoino. As you can see, we are north of the ledge, at least one day's journey away." He traces a short, squiggly line on the map that runs east to west. It terminates on a hill that overlooks the Solenom. "This is the trail that I think Ava was on that led to the river. It is the only trail that leads to the river in this vicinity. As you can see, she was well south of Crostim Ledge. I am thinking at least two days away from where we are now. She traveled quite a distance which is impressive considering she was in the middle of the forest.

"She was whisked from the head of the Crostim Ledge trail," he points to the map, "to somewhere around here, to the west of the Kuoino. She said that she could hear the Solenom, that it was to her east. She confirmed her assumptions when she was on her dragon's back. She saw the clearing where she had been held and the river at the same time. Therefore, she suspects Haldir's cabin is somewhere around here." He points to an *X* he had inked on the map.

Galadriel and Nessa are staring at him with blank faces. Galadriel says, "I do not understand what you are telling us."

"Me neither," Nessa says. "How can we be here," she places her finger on the map, "when Ava said we should be somewhere around here?"

Voronwe stares up at the canopy of trees with a look of complete annoyance. He says in a dismissive tone, "I do not know." He quickly changes the subject. "But whatever was up there above the trees has departed. Maybe it was nothing more but a passing cloud. Perhaps we should discount Ava's dragon being anywhere around here." He folds the map. He is about to stuff it in his pocket when a large shadow is above the trees once more.

Galadriel shouts, "Not so fast, Voronwe. There it is again!"

Nessa says, "Maybe we should try to find a clearing to see it more plainly."

Voronwe unfolds the map and examines it. "There is a clearing to the south of us. Maybe an hour's hike away. What do you think? Should we head there?" Before Galadriel and Nessa can reply the threesome is startled by the booming rumble of a crashing tree deep in the forest.

"Well, that got my attention," Voronwe says with an unsteady laugh. "Must have been a dead tree that met its fate finally."

A split-second later another tree falls with a crash. Like the first fallen tree, it was to their right, to the east of the Kuoino. Then a third tree falls with a mighty boom. It is followed almost immediately by a fourth, fifth, and so on until fourteen trees have fallen.

Galadriel exclaims, "Now *that* is no coincidence!"

Nessa's eyes are bulging with excitement. She says with a questioning look, "Maybe the first tree caused the second one to fall and so on. Do you think that is possible?"

"I seriously doubt it," Galadriel says. "What do you think, Voronwe? Should we get off the trail and enter the forest to see what happened?"

"I think we should," Voronwe says. "It cannot hurt. No creature could cause fourteen trees to fall like that." Nessa is staring at him wide-eyed. She says in a shout, "Unless that creature is a dragon! Besides, I need the two of you to consider something."

Voronwe declares, "Well if it is Ava's dragon then it cannot be where Haldir's cabin is located. There is no way the wizard could miss the racket of all those crashing trees." He turns to step off the trail inside the thickness of the forest. "Follow me and stay close."

Before he can take a single step, Nessa grabs his arm. "How many trees did you say fell?"

Galadriel says, "He said fourteen trees fell; why do you ask? What difference does it make if it were fourteen or forty?"

Nessa's eyes excitedly dart from Galadriel to Voronwe and back again. "Because fourteen is Ava's lucky number. She told me so when we were hiking the path to Crostim Ledge."

Voronwe asks, "What makes the number fourteen so special to her?"

Nessa replies earnestly, "Because Ava was born on the fourteenth day of Dekémvrisom (December)!" She grins and stomps her feet. "And I would bet tonight's dinner that Ava somehow told Fluescere to cause fourteen trees to crash so I would know it was her!"

5

"Well, it looks like this is the place," Voronwe says as he stares at the enormous pile of what used to be stately, towering trees. "I cannot believe this! They have been pulled out by the roots. No creature except a dragon or giant could have achieved this incredible feat."

Galadriel murmurs, "Or an evil wizard trying to lure us to his domain." She looks at Nessa and frowns. Nessa is pointing to the fallen trees one after the other. "What in the world are you doing, Nessa?"

"Counting them just to make sure," Nessa says. She sees that Voronwe is laughing at her. She says indignantly, "What are you laughing at?" He does not reply. She says, "Well if you must know I am making sure there are fourteen trees. As I said, fourteen is Ava's lucky number. Something tells me it is our lucky number as well. Also, as I said I am certain it is Ava's way of telling me, telling us that the fallen trees were caused by Fluescere. There is no doubt in my mind." She is about to say something else when another tree crashes to the ground. Like the other fallen trees, this one is to the east of the Kuoino and deeper in the forest.

"If it is Ava's dragon, I bet it is telling us to follow the fallen trees," Voronwe says. "This part of the forest is less dense than before. We can walk abreast. Nessa, ready your bow. Stay to my right. Galadriel, please do the same to my left." After Galadriel and Nessa are ready, he says, "Okay, let us move on. Stay alert."

A few moments later they arrive at the most recent fallen tree.

Nessa whispers as she looks skyward, "Look up there. It *is* Ava's dragon, at least I hope it is."

"It could be anyone's dragon," Voronwe says matter-of-factly. "If we are close to Haldir's cabin, it could be his, anybody's. That is if he has a dragon and not a magical carriage like Ava had said. So, it could be a ruse, a trap. Hopefully, the dragon will uproot another tree."

Fluescere is circling overhead. She quickly flies diagonally to the southeast.

Galadriel says to Nessa, "If your hunch is correct, the dragon should be pulling up another tree from the roots shortly."

Nessa says in a shaky voice, "Yeah, if it *is* Fluescere. If it is not her, we could be in a world of hurt fairly soon."

Fluescere's shadowy figure appears above the trees once more. She circles above the warriors a few times, and then she flies to the southeast.

Voronwe says, "I think she wants us to follow her." He points in the direction that Fluescere had flown. "Let's go. I am going to walk ten or so paces ahead of you. Stay behind me. If you must shoot, do not hesitate. And whatever you do, do not call out. We will hear the strum of your bowstring. Be careful."

Galadriel appears smitten as she watches Voronwe walk in front of her. She admires her fellow, redheaded warrior. She considers him to be well-trained in addition to being a crafty spy. She believes he is courageous and daring as well. And she knows he must run as fast as the wind blows. She likes him a lot, a whole lot. She is not certain if he likes her in the same manner, yet she hopes he does. But there is one thing both know for certain. They are not closely related. They, like their parents, do not have siblings. Furthermore, the chances of a Timbre having offspring with a Bkotn probably is one in a million. At least in Galadriel's hopeful, propitious opinion given her love-struck state.

Nessa is also thinking about something precious to her as she searches the forest with her eyes. It is a hopeful desire. She is hoping that Ava will ask her to accompany her on her next journey. After all this spying business is complete.

Meanwhile, Voronwe, like Galadriel and Nessa, is also pondering something dear to him. It is making him to feel giddy all over. He is remembering when he and Ava were holding hands in Mégedale, not once but twice. He cannot wait to see her once more. But he also considers that Galadriel is sweet as well. And he knows that she likes him a lot. Then again, he believes that having a chance to be either's close, male elffriend probably is next to impossible. Because Ava is who she is and due to the Bkotn's strict male-female socializing restrictions.

Voronwe abruptly stops. He motions for Galadriel and Nessa to stop as well. He crouches low and gestures for them to do the same. Then he presses his finger to his lips telling them to stay silent.

The second's tick by slowly. They turn to minutes. All the while the warriors are listening intently, their eyes anxiously scanning the forest. Voronwe crawls back to Galadriel and Nessa.

Nessa whispers, "What is it? What do you see? Is it Haldir's cabin?"

"I do not think so," Voronwe replies in a soft voice. "It is not large enough to be a dwelling. But whatever it is, it is enormous. I cannot make out what it is because it is encircled by thick hedgerows. It is too risky to approach from one direction. So, here is what I want you to do."

Voronwe clears a small patch of ground with the palm of his hand and draws a circle in the dirt with a twig. "This is the clearing surrounded by the hedges." He draws an *X* in the dirt. "This is us." He looks at Galadriel and draws a semicircle. "I want you to advance in this direction in a wide circle." He etches another half circle. "Nessa, you do the same to our right. Once I know you are in place, I will move forward from my last position. Then I will signal you to move forward cautiously. Stay hidden behind the trees as best as you can. If what I saw is a creature, and it moves toward you menacingly, shout out." He gives them a stern look. "Release your arrow at the same time. Just be careful you do not miss. You do not want to hit any of us. Any questions?"

"Yeah, I have a question," a strong voice commands from behind a nearby tree. The three warriors immediately jump to their feet and aim their weapons at the tree. "Do you have anything to eat? I ran out of food yesterday. And whatever you do, do not shoot me after everything I have been through! That would be a dreadful way to go!"

Steph is the source of the spoken words. She briefly peeps from behind the right side of the tree trunk. She is grinning happily, highlighting the cute dimple in the middle of her right cheek.

Nessa calls out, "It's Steph! Lower your weapons!"

Steph moves from behind the tree. Her face is dirty, and her cloak is frayed. Her long hair is tangled and overflowing with twigs and leaves. She looks very tired. Nevertheless, despite being alone in the forest for nearly four days, she is grinning from ear to ear.

6

Galadriel and Nessa are hugging Steph tightly. Voronwe steps forward. Steph reaches out between Galadriel and Nessa and shakes his hand. He says, "Steph, it is wonderful to see you once more. I am awfully glad you are safe. You must be famished. Would you like to take a few moments to eat something and regain your strength before we move on?"

Steph pulls away from the Bkotn warriors and says, "Yes, please! I am as hungry as a bear." In reaction to the others' inquiring looks, she says, "The bear is a large, hairy animal of the Earthly World. It is immensely powerful. There are many species, eight if memory serves me correctly. The most common are the black bear, grizzly bear, and polar bear." The others still look confused. Steph grabs a hunk of dried fish that Galadriel has offered her and stuffs it in her mouth. She mumbles in between chews, "I guess you could equate a bear to a beluga, although I have not seen a beluga ever, and I hope I never do."

As Steph eats, Nessa, as is her curious custom – she could pass as Ava's twin given her intense inquisitiveness – asks Steph question after question.

After a while, Steph says humorously, "Nessa, I must say that you remind me so much of Ava with your nonstop questions. You are super curious just like her."

Nessa blushes and says, "Aw, really, Steph? That is so nice of you to say. Thank you."

Galadriel squeezes Voronwe's shoulder tenderly and says, "What is our plan now, Voronwe? Should we continue to look for Haldir's cabin?"

"Oh, are you looking for the wizard, Haldir?" Steph says. She points to her right. "His cabin is due south. I managed to keep the rising and setting sun to my east and west as I traveled. Ava told me at one point that the Kuoino proceeds in a generally, northward direction. Even though the trail lives up to its name and zigzags most of the way. His cabin is more than four days from here." She shrugs her shoulders. "But that is through the forest like I traveled. It probably is a good three-day hike or even less on the trail."

Voronwe looks at the others one by one. "The only reason Ava wanted us to scope out Haldir's cabin was to rescue you." He adds with

440

a grin, "And here you are. But we did not find you, you found us which is terrific. Ava will be quite pleased you are safe."

Galadriel says, "In fact, Ava's dragon, Fluescere, led us to you, or at least close to you. If it were not for Fluescere, we would be looking for you even now."

Steph says, "I owe everything to Ava's dragon as well. Because if it were not for her yanking all those trees out of the ground, I still would be heading north. Naturally, I followed the sounds since there were so many. I would not have reacted to one or two trees falling. But I just knew that hearing so many falling trees was not natural. I hoped for the best and here we are."

Nessa says, "Well, I say we head back to Mégedale. I cannot wait to see the smile on Ava's face when she is reunited with Steph. What do you think?"

"Ah, Nessa," Galadriel says in a gloomy tone. "I think you are forgetting something. If you recall, you and I must return to the Etanpioa now that Steph is with us. I must assume second in command."

"Oh, I completely forgot about that," Nessa groans. She is shaking her head miserably. "And I wanted to see Ava and watch as she reunites with Steph." Her eyes brighten. "Maybe Elbereth will allow us to go to Mégedale?"

Galadriel says, "I do not want to disappoint you, Nessa. But the only reason our Etanpioa was going to Mégedale was to escort O Poica Katharos to confer with Godroh. I expect, after we rejoin our fellow warriors, we will return to the Unseen Valley." She notices the sad look on Nessa's face. "But we will have so many stories to tell our friends back home, will we not?" Nessa pouts and looks away.

"You have been in the forest for quite a long while. Are you ready to travel?" Voronwe says to Steph. "Strong enough?"

Steph nods her head. "I was in the forest for four days actually." She glances over to Fluescere. The dragon, Steph, and the others are in the clearing. Being inside the hedgerow provides them a bit of protection. Having Fluescere close by is even better. "But what do we do about Fluescere? Do you think she will stay here, or do you think she will follow us?"

Voronwe says, "I guess once we return to the trail the dragon will return to Mégedale. But it would be nice to have her along with us until we meet up with the Bkotn Etanpioa. Which reminds me. We are wasting time chatting here. We must tell Lady Elbereth that you are safe and sound."

"And perhaps give her this," Steph says as she opens her cloak. She removes the cloth that is covering Haldir's crystal ball. "I have not had the chance to look in it since I ran from Haldir's cabin. Pretty cool, huh?"

The others' eyes are riveted on the ball. Cloudy images of indistinguishable forms are circling within its center.

"What is that thing?" Nessa shouts as she jumps back. She appears frightened. "It looks creepy. Things are moving about in it. They look gross." She unexpectedly leaps to her feet and whispers nervously, "Steph, maybe you should—"

Steph interrupts her as she says in a boastful manner, "I have this as well!" She removes a knife from her waistband. Voronwe and Galadriel look away from the ball and smile with wide eyes. They recognize a quality blade when they see it. "I stole it from Haldir. It is handmade and very sharp too. I am going to keep it as a souvenir."

Without warning, Nessa grabs the ball from Steph's lap and hurls it with all her strength to the thicket. She is shivering from head to toe.

Steph gets to her feet and shouts, "What did you do that for, Nessa?"

Nessa looks at Steph and then at Galadriel and Voronwe. Her words are soft and shaky as she says, "Steph, those hazy, moving figures in the ball are us! I could see the four of us and Fluescere as well. The evil wizard, Haldir, must have been tracking you, and he probably knows where you are! He undoubtedly knows we are with you as well!"

Galadriel suddenly shouts, "Quiet!" Her expression is overly anxious. She looks at the others one by one. "Do you hear those faint sounds?" The others are nodding their heads as they look in all directions. The sounds are still far off but getting closer with each passing second. They also seem like they are coming from all directions within the forest! Then the distant sounds become more distinct.

Sssss! Ssss! Moooaaaaannnn!

"Those are belugas!" Voronwe shouts as he stands and pulls Galadriel to her feet. "I know by their groans and moans and hisses. We have a few belugas captive in Mégedale, so training warriors can recognize the beasts' unique sounds."

Nessa's face is ashen. She seems to be looking in all directions at once. Her powerful leg muscles have tightened as if she is ready to run. She shouts, "What are we going to do?"

Voronwe says in a commanding voice, "Hurry and gather around in a tight circle. We must prepare to fight them!"

Galadriel cries, "But by the many sounds there could be hundreds of them. We will run out of arrows in no time."

Voronwe says, "Then we fight them warrior to beast with our blades." Beads of sweat are pouring from his forehead. He suddenly gives Steph a worried look. She is chuckling, and her eyes are damp and overly bright. He considers that perhaps she has lost her mind. It would make sense since she was held captive by Haldir and alone in Artonia for four days. He grabs her by the shoulders. "Steph, are you going to be okay?"

Steph holds out her hands and says in a casual tone, "All I have is this fire iron, a hatchet, and a knife. So, count me out until they get really close for hand-to-hand fighting. But by then I honestly think it will be too late, at least by the number of hisses and moans we are hearing!"

Nessa abruptly screams, "Look at Ava's dragon, Fluescere!" The others turn around and gawk. Fluescere's wings are slanted toward the ground. She is staring at them. Puffs of grey smoke are leaking from her nostrils. Nessa says, "I think she wants us to climb on board."

Voronwe says in a gloomy tone, "It is Ava's dragon. She was groomed by Godroh to carry Ava and only her." He looks away from Fluescere. "Never mind the dragon. The belugas are drawing closer. We must get prepared to fight." He cocks his head as he hears a new sound. Then he scowls.

Galadriel is staring at him wide-eyed. She cries, "I hear it too. It is the sound of a carriage. Haldir is on his way! He will hex us as he did to Ava. Then we will have no means to escape!" She grips Voronwe's muscular arm so tightly her knuckles turn white. Her eyes are pleading. "What are we to do, Voronwe?"

Before Voronwe can reply, Nessa cries out, "Steph, Galadriel, Voronwe!" The others turn their heads and stare. Nessa is sitting on Fluescere's upper back. Her eyes are sparkling, and she is beaming a silly grin. "Hurry and hop aboard before Haldir and the belugas get here."

The others quickly ascend Fluescere's wing and climb on her back. A moment later the gratified, immensely relieved foursome is soaring high above the forest in a northerly direction toward Mégedale.

Voronwe shouts, "We did it! We got you Steph! Well, I should say you got us. We escaped the belugas and Haldir too! What a story we have to tell everyone when we get home."

Voronwe is sitting behind Steph. Steph is sitting behind Nessa. Nessa had insisted that she sit up front because, as she had shrieked jubilantly, "So I can see everything first! Besides, it was my idea to hop on board!"

Galadriel is sitting behind Voronwe. She is hugging him tightly around his waist. She moves her hands and places them loosely around his neck. Then she plants a lingering kiss on his right cheek. Using his nickname, she whispers in his ear, "Thanks to you, Vone, we are safe. Thanks to your courage and expert map reading skills. Not only have you saved Steph, but you have also saved Nessa and me." She kisses his cheek once more and rests her chin on his shoulder. "I thank you from the bottom of my heart." Then she whispers in his ear, "I really – I think you are wonderful."

Voronwe is blushing because of Galadriel's kind words and admiring kisses. Abruptly, his thoughts turn to Ava, when the two of them held hands, not once but twice! The way she had smiled at him. How it made him feel. Then he touches his cheek where Galadriel had just kissed him, not once but twice too! He feels the warmth of her cheek against his. He grins a knowing smile because he adores two charmingly lovely, fearless warriors. He also recognizes he is in a sticky situation as old as time.

Steph, oblivious to what is happening behind her yells, "Hey you guys, how are we going to tell Elbereth to call off her search for me? Surely, Fluescere cannot land on the trail, can she?"

Nessa shouts above the rushing wind, "Who cares? We are on our way to Mégedale to see Ava!" She throws her arms high in the air. "Look at me, Galadriel! No hands!"

Yaaayyy!

END OF PART THREE

PART FOUR

BEFORE ONCE MORE

"In a gentle way you can shake the world."
—Mahatma Gandhi

~~~

CHAPTER 1

AVAÏNOÄEL, O POICA KATHAROS

*"Life is a tragedy to those who feel
and a comedy to those who think."*—Horace Walpole

1

1 Noémvriosom (November), 2021

Ava is standing at the base of the spiral staircase that leads to Godroh's laboratory. She has a twisted, disgusted look and is biting her lower lip. Her eyes are cold, empty, and flat. She starts to rub her forearms because goose pimples have appeared out of the blue. At the same time, her mind is replaying in agonizingly short-lived, frightening clips when she descended the tower's staircase. The staircase that led to where she is right now – the Inner World. Despite the graphic visions of the other staircase whirling in her mind, she assumes everything is going to be okay. Because there are two striking differences between this staircase and the other one.

This staircase seems cheerily optimistic as it appears to spiral gracefully toward the heavens. Like it is heading for a happier, more exciting place. A place where her insatiable curiosity and intense intellect will be fulfilled. It is well-lit with kerosene lamps conveniently spaced to provide adequate lighting. There are niches randomly placed in the walls. The niches contain lovely, handmade, plaster statues of exotic Inner World birds and small creatures.

447

In contrast, the staircase connecting the two worlds was dismal. It descended like it (literally) was nosediving straight to the evil eye of the other, "unmentionable place" – eager to carry Ava along with it. Mercifully, it eventually led to the Inner World. Furthermore, even though it was surrounded by a spacious corridor, the corridor was eerily claustrophobic, gloomy, and poorly lit. There barely was enough illumination for her to keep from falling even though she strode cautiously. Not to mention that the stair treads were ridiculously narrow.

The other staircase was exceedingly unstable as well. It lacked handrails and balusters. Nothing was supporting it on either side of the stair treads; it seemed to be floating in the air and supported solely by its base. It trembled and swayed and was prone to give way completely. As it ultimately did, assertively – taking Ava along with it. Almost to her death, or so she thought at the time.

Whereas this staircase is constructed solidly of concrete slabs fitted to the walls. Because the corridor is narrow, she can slide her hands along the walls as she climbs. Not because she must. But because she can. It just adds to her comfort level which is crucial given the former staircase's horrors that remain fresh in her mind.

"Well, if this isn't déjà vu," she whispers after a few tentative steps, "I don't know what is. But I must admit it is nowhere as scary as the staircase in my grandfather's tower. Still, climbing it brings back nasty memories I would rather forget."

Ava is speaking to Fidelium. Her loyal bird is perched on her left shoulder. He returned to her two days earlier. All that time she thought he was dead or had given up on her. When she told Godroh the news, that Fidelium had returned, the wizard said his return was nothing short of a miracle. Khni birds seldom stray from those they befriend, except during the mating season. But to have one return after such a long time and over a long distance is unheard of.

Ava is feeling mixed emotions as she slowly climbs the fifty stairs. She is excited to visit Godroh's laboratory. That is a definite yes. But she is not overly thrilled about conferring with him one on one. That he and Haldir used their magical, crystal balls to track her moves causes her to feel upset every time she thinks about it. Pestering her like a lead balloon.

Unable to sail away. Ready to come crashing down at any moment. She worries that moment will occur today.

Earendil told her that Godroh's laboratory comprises an expansive test center where he conducts amazing enchantments and experiments. He said the laboratory is everything one would expect from one recognized as the Great Wizard. It is crammed with row after row of shelves laden with all sorts of jars, bottles, boxes, and wooden containers. There are live specimens of strange creatures, dead specimens of many more. Some of which Earendil never knew existed. Butterflies, bugs, and tiny reptiles mounted on pins seem to be everywhere. Bits and pieces of herbs, roots, and other, indescribable matter cover the shelves. Bubbling cauldrons of steaming unknowns make the laboratory humid and malodorous. Rolled-up charts of parchment are scattered all over the place. And there is a myriad of tattered, old books. Earendil said many of the books are laid open, their pages smeared with gobs of only the gods know what. He figured the books had been soiled when Godroh consulted them to conduct his dangerous experiments.

"I have been up there three times," Earendil offered. "On each occasion, I was both shocked and mesmerized. The first thing you recognize is the peculiar smell. It is a strange, ever-changing smell that seems to shift in odor and intensity. It all depends on where you are standing in his laboratory. Others have been up there as well. They, like me, have smelt the odor, and they describe it differently. So, prepare yourself for that strange odor as soon as Godroh opens the door." He had paused for a moment then whispered like it was an Antiquom mystery, "He has a secret, mysterious-looking glass as well."

Ava could not help but notice that Earendil's eyes seemed to sparkle when he mentioned the looking glass. She had given him a quizzical look. After all, she thought to herself, looking glasses, or mirrors, are commonplace, at least in the Earthly World. Although now and then looking glasses can be magical, like in the fairytale book *Cinderella*. Harry Potter likewise carried a shard of a looking glass, or mirror given to him by his godfather Sirius in *Order of the Phoenix*. The image Harry saw inside the two-way-looking glass was Professor Dumbledore's brother, Aberforth Dumbledore.

"Yes, there is a secret, mysterious looking glass," Earendil had said in response to Ava's inquiring look. "I recognized it as such even though it was covered with a cloth. I asked Godroh about the purpose of the looking glass and asked if I could see it. He said no. I was both disappointed and a bit offended. I recall his words exactly as he moved to stand in front of the glass. 'My deepest regrets my Lord, but it shall be seen by Avaïnoǽel and her alone.'"

Earendil had mentioned that Godroh's ridiculously small sleeping quarters – he had said, "more like a storage closet" – has no furnishings. The only thing in the room is a straw mat laid on the floor. He went on to explain, "We have only seen the Great Wizard a few times throughout the year. We assume he was working with his Earthly World counterparts for your return to the Inner World. Before that, he would be around most every day."

At first, when Earendil said that she would have to climb a spiraling staircase, Ava refused. She told him how unstable the staircase in her grandfather's tower was. How she thought she was going to die each time it shook violently. Then it had finally disintegrated within itself like a controlled, demolition building implosion.

"Except, Earendil," she had exclaimed with an uneasy look, "the staircase implosion was not controlled. Everything fell apart at its seams, steel bolts and rivets blasting everywhere, echoing off the walls. Shooting like errant tips of countless arrows in every direction threatening to pierce every part of my body. Scaring me half to death. Then I was somersaulting head over heels through the air. Knowing for certain I was going to die. Obviously, I survived. But only because Flame had come to my rescue. If she had not saved me, I would be here talking to you as a ghost if at all."

Ava has now reached the outer door of Godroh's laboratory. Her clothes are dripping with sweat but not because she just climbed the staircase. Before heading off to Godroh's imposing tower, she was with Earendil for a bit of jousting with their swords. She shot a couple of quivers of arrows too. She felt she needed the practice. Moreover, she wanted to blow off some steam before seeing Godroh. Not bothering to change her clothes or freshen up, she went straight from the warriors' practice field to Godroh's tower. She sniffs her underarms. Thankfully, the delicate perfume she had dabbed on her body is still working. Ironically, the perfume is made of the toxic sanatios plant that had caused her first encounter with Haldir's magic and the dreadful belugas.

She knocks on the solid wooden door then steps back somewhat when Godroh opens the door. The odor that Earendil had mentioned hits her square in the face like a gust of stale wind. She wants to pinch her nose but manages to keep her hands at her side. She believes it smells like roses at first. Then the scent seems to change dramatically from good to bad then back again to almost pleasant.

Is it cow dung? Burnt hay? Recently cut grass or fresh flowers? Or something totally out of this world? She shrugs her shoulders and smiles at the Great Wizard.

Godroh lowers his head to one side elegantly. Then he gestures with a gentle wave of his hand for her to enter. His tone is cordial as he says, "My lady, Avaïnoáel, thank you for coming. Please make yourself comfortable." He lifts one eyebrow. "Will you not join me with a goblet of thkao? I arranged to have some freshly squeezed. I understand it is your favorite fruit juice."

Ava nods her head, gives Godroh a gracious smile once more, and enters the room. She places her weaponry and satchel against the wall to the right of the door after Godroh closes it. Her curiosity is piqued immediately when she turns around. Her eyes sweep the expansive room, seemingly exploring every inch from where she is standing. What Earendil had said about the allure of the laboratory is one hundred percent true. It is crammed with countless rows of mysterious-looking things, more so than she could ever have imagined.

Fedelium flies from her shoulder and alights on a nearby shelf. Not surprisingly, he is perched on a shelf filled with glass jars of tiny bugs. Some of the bugs are moving.

The first things that catch Ava's attention are the balls of light floating in midair. She is staring at them open-mouthed. They are truly fascinating to behold! Godroh says he calls them fairy lights. Because they float in the air delicately like gracefully hovering fairies. She can relate to his comparison. Doo seems to float in the air just like the lights when she hovers. Elegantly, gracefully, effortlessly, more so than even an Earthly World hummingbird. Remarkably since Doo is around two feet in height, very much larger than the fairy lights. They are about the same size as a standard Earthly World lightbulb.

Her sudden thoughts of Doo cause her heart to sink. She has no idea where her sweet fairy friend and Dad might have gone. She has not seen them since just before she accompanied Nessa on the path to Crostim Ledge. All she knows is she misses them dearly. She quickly dismisses thoughts of DooDad from her mind. She should remain focused. Besides, there is an interesting laboratory to explore!

Nine fairy lights are floating a few inches below the ceiling. They are cleverly arranged to illume the entire laboratory. The balls of light do not have ampoules as one sees with oil lanterns. They merely are swirling balls of light magically floating in midair. One fairy light is directly above Ava's head. It is following her as she wanders around the laboratory.

Godroh calls this light his subjective aide. He says, "My eyesight has worsened over the centuries. Thus, I opted that this fairy light should accompany me throughout the laboratory." He slowly waves his hand up and down and back and forth. The light magically follows the precise movements of his hand. He returns the light to its original position above Ava's head with a slight flick of his wrist. He also has caused the light to change color. Ava is shrouded in a pinkish glow.

"Wow! This is totally cool," Ava exclaims as she looks up. Her eyes are wide open with wonder. "You can make it change colors too! Can you do the same with the rest of them?"

In reply, Godroh waves his hand. All the lights change color. Some are blue, some are white, others are pink, green, yellow, and so on. Then to Ava's amazement, a few lights begin to blink intermittently. It almost is like they are keeping beat to a fast-tempo, soundless song in Godroh's head.

Ava says, "You probably know Godroh, there is a fairly recent craze in the Earthly World involving lights somewhat like these." She throws her head back and laughs. "But of course, they do not float in midair and magically change colors with the wave of one's hand. They are called LED strip lights. They consist of flexible circuit boards of surface-mounted light-emitting diodes. They can change colors and keep beat to the music. Yet one must use a remote control or another device. Some even respond to your voice; an example is when you say, Alexa." Godroh nods his head appreciatively.

"Hmm, I wonder about something," Ava says as she looks at the lights. Now they are moving up and down to a slower beat. "Maybe your magical fairy lights have inspired the LED strip lights of the Earthly

World?" She looks at Godroh. He does not say a word, but she notices the twinkle in his eyes and his shrewd grin. *Just as I thought,* she considers without a word. *The two worlds are more interconnected than anyone could imagine. I just hope some of the Earthly World's bad habits like pollution, plastic in the oceans and lakes, and horrible weapons of mass destruction are never introduced to the Inner World.*

She continues to explore the laboratory. Scorch marks are everywhere, on the walls, on the shelves, and even on the polished, wooden floor. She correctly considers they were caused by Godroh's wand when experiments had turned out wrong or creatures had gone awry. She also spots the looking glass Earendil had mentioned. It is perched on a tripod in the far corner of the laboratory and covered with a heavy cloth.

Godroh steps over to a small table on the left side of the room. It is brimming with goblets, confections, and a tall jar of thkao. He begins to prepare the drinks and snacks.

Ava is feeling bright and breezy as she explores the laboratory. She has not felt inquisitive about anything whatsoever in such a long time. It feels good to be interested in something other than tragic news, doom, and gloom. And leaving on the other end of the staircase all the doubts about her being O Poica Katharos and what that means going forward.

Godroh hands the goblet of thkao to her. She nods her head appreciatively and tastes the beverage. "Wow, Godroh! This is delicious. Thank you." As she takes another sip, she is reminded of a quote she read back home in Illinois. *It seems so long ago since she was home.* The quote was, "Depending on where you are from Illinois, it's either soda, coke, or pop." She laughs inwardly as she considers silently, *but thkao? A sugary, but surprisingly sour, fizzy drink made of bright orange fruit the size of watermelons that grows on trees? Who would have thought?* She sets the goblet on the side table. "Godroh, do you mind if I continue to look around?"

"Why of course, my Lady."

Ava winces visibly as he says *my lady* for a second time.

Godroh says, "If you have any questions, please let me know." He walks over to a set of wicker chairs facing the hearth. He turns one chair around so he can face Ava as she roams around the laboratory. He aims his wand at the hearth. The firewood ignites spontaneously.

The flames' dancing, yellow-red flickers instantly cause Ava to feel right at home. She picks up a jar of crawling insects from a shelf and examines it. "Godroh, you have probably heard," she says over her shoulder, "I do not like all the pageantry." She turns around. "You know the formality of addressing me as my lady or Avaïnoàel."

She places the jar of crawling insects on the shelf and picks up a heavy bottle of bubbling, frothy liquid. The bottle is surprisingly heavy. It is extremely interesting to her as well. The foamy liquid is tinted dark blue at the top with red color at its bottom. She is tempted to shake the bottle to see if the bubbling liquid mixes. But she does not because she is afraid it might explode or do something just as creepy.

"So, please call me Ava when we are alone or with those we consider as our confidants." She turns around and gestures to the bottle with a slight nod of her head. "What is this stuff?"

Godroh replies in an impartial tone, "I shall do as you ask, Ava. I shall dispense with the formalities but only because you have asked me to do so." He adds with a slight nod of his head, "What you are holding is the blood of a beluga."

"All this bubbly, foamy stuff is the blood of a beluga?" Ava says. "Is the beluga's blood bubbly like this and made up of these two colors? I would think that the colors blue and red would combine naturally, you know, to a purplish color."

"I am sorry, Ava, but it appears I may have misled you. The blood of all belugas is red as you undoubtedly know. The blue color is a potion I concocted. When the potion interacts with the blood, it bubbles up as you can see. As you stated correctly, the two colors should combine to make a purple color. However, the beluga's blood will not mix with the blue potion. I still have not figured out the explanation."

Ava carefully sets the bottle on the shelf. She spies an astrological chart and picks it up. She says, "So, what is the purpose of the potion, the mixing serum? Is it poison or something?"

"Heavens no," Godroh says with wry amusement. "We hesitate to destroy belugas purposely unless they first attack us. I am attempting to make a serum to convert the duds to the more intelligent variety."

"Why would you want to do that?" Ava asks. She has a disbelieving look in her eyes. "Would that not be more dangerous, riskier, having many more intelligent belugas with which to contend?"

Godroh replies, "Perhaps. Then again, the more intelligent belugas we have on Antiquom, the better our chances for peace. We cannot negotiate with the duds because they are unintelligent. All they know is how to follow Wendigorium and Strum's orders, as well as those of the déxypnos species. And, as you know better than anyone, to attack carelessly. The duds also have voracious appetites as you can well imagine."

"Oh, I think I understand what you are saying," Ava says with a nod of her head. "The more intelligent they are the more possibilities for level-headed thinkers. Saturate their numbers with many more smart belugas, the déxypnos, thus increasing our chances for peace. Am I correct?"

"Exactly," Godroh replies.

Ava declares, "But would it not be easier to cross-breed them? Maybe we would end up with more intelligent creatures that way. Simpler, less complicated, probably less troublesome as well. As you probably are aware, scientists in the Earthly World breed sterile insects to reduce the numbers of their destructive counterparts. Eventually, at least they hope, the destructive insects will die off. A good example is the tsetse fly that causes trypanosomiasis or sleeping sickness."

"We have tried the cross-breeding method with the belugas we have in captivity," Godroh says. "Unfortunately, when we crossbreed the belugas their offspring die. Without fail. I would imagine the sterile technique would take too long if not being impossible to achieve."

Ava holds up the astrological chart in front of her. She has unfolded it. "What is this all about? I do not recognize any of these celestial constellations. They are not in the Antiquom or Earthly World nighttime skies. What do they represent? Can you tell me?"

Godroh gestures to the table between the two chairs. Ava notices her goblet is on the table. He stands and turns his chair around to face the hearth. "If you do not mind, bring the chart here, and I shall tell you everything about it."

A huge grin suddenly appears on Ava's face. Before she arrived in Godroh's laboratory, she intended to tell him off, to scold him about using the crystal ball to track her. Thus, allowing Haldir to do the same, to watch her every movement. But now that she is in this amazing laboratory she is feeling right at home. Like she is back in her science class at school. Basking in the remarkable topics of physics, biology, chemistry, and natural science. Moreover, once again her inquisitiveness is soaring like it did when she and Steph first arrived in Antiquom. Making her feel normal again. Like her old self, but much wiser, experienced, and yes, more powerful.

Then again, she considers wordlessly, I just might tell him off. We shall wait and see.

2

Ava exclaims, "I must say, Godroh, that this thkao is delicious! Where did you get the fruit?"

"I carried a few of the thkao fruit back with me after my journey with King Poldo. They are from the Unseen Valley and were selected especially for you. The Mégedale chefs brewed them excellently as you can see."

"Well, I certainly appreciate you and Poldo looking for me." Ava purposely emphasized Poldo's name and left off the king part. She once more wanted to drive home her feelings about the primness when referring to others in their close group. Looking at Godroh dead on she says, "If you do not mind me asking, where did you conduct your search? It must have been extensive considering you were absent for a long period."

"Initially, our dragons took us as far as Mountains Cross. I thought that perhaps Haldir would have taken you there to meet up with Wendigorium. We did not suspect that he, Haldir, would detain you in an open clearing so close to the Unseen Valley and Mégedale. That he would arrange for Wendigorium to come to you."

"Almost exactly in between, I imagine," Ava says. "Probably why he chose the spot. He must have thought you would not consider that he would detain me so close to either area. I think his cabin is close to where I was detained. Perhaps on the east side of the Kuoino. Am I correct with my assumption?"

"Yes, you are correct. It is one of his many cabins in Artonia. Now, looking back at what happened, that you were detained south of Crostim Ledge, your hypothesis makes perfect sense. We simply did not consider it at the time. I never suspected he would be so foolish to detain you close to Mégedale. I should have known better."

The issue of the crystal balls is continuing to nag Ava. Now there is this latest information about how close Haldir was to Mégedale and that Godroh did not consider the possibility. To curb her building irritation, she quickly changes the subject. "Godroh, you raised Fluescere from the day she came to be as a little hatchling. Am I correct?"

"Indeed, I did," Godroh says with a broad smile. "She is one of my finest innovations, although I did not create her, really. I just raised her. I am happy she told you. She is one of a kind and extremely loyal. As soon as she discovered you had disappeared near Crostim Ledge, she went looking for you. My first reaction was to tell her to return, but I knew she would not listen. She serves you and only you. She must have told you that."

Although she did not intend to do it consciously, Ava gives him an annoyed look.

Godroh suddenly sits up straight. He sighs heavily and says, "Ava, something tells me you are a trifle angry with me. I cannot read minds or anything similar, but I detect that you are irritated. Is it about my not considering that Haldir would select a place so close to Mégedale in which to detain you?"

Ava says in a tone that is overly firm, "At first no, but now, yes. It does concern me that you did not consider that option. I would have. It is so obvious it stands out. Like we say in the Earthly World, it stands out like a sore thumb. There is also the issue of the crystal balls that allowed Haldir to track me." She gives him a questioning look. "Have there been other mistakes as well? Maybe involving my dear friends Steph and Nessa; perhaps even the presumed traitors, Sofia, Morwen, and Vena?"

Godroh clears his throat and swallows hard. He settles back in his chair then says in a glum tone, "I must say, Avaïnoáel, you are one worthy opponent."

Ava sits straight up in her chair like she was just struck by a bolt of electricity. She is scowling. "An opponent, a rival? To what are you referring, Godroh? Also, tell me this. Are we on the same side or not?" She pauses briefly and adds curtly, "Also, as I asked please call me Ava."

"I apologize. It was a slip of the tongue."

Ava stares at him for a few moments. "What part? Calling me Ava or referring to me as a worthy opponent?"

Godroh sighs and rolls his neck to the side. He is visibly frustrated with the way the conversation has turned. He stares at the ceiling for a few moments, and then he looks at Ava straight on. He says in a sorrowful but forthright tone, "You are a worthy opponent to your enemies – *as well as to your friends!*"

Ava appears stunned by Godroh's words. She slumps back in her chair and looks angrily at him.

"You heard me correctly, Ava. You are so strong-willed now, thus intensely daunting, that even you do not recognize what has happened to you. You are exhibiting the calmer, congenial aspects of your wonderful, caring personality to the extreme. So much so you are always striving to prove to others that you are not who you are, of who and what you have become." He exhales a long sigh. "But Ava, I must tell you that you indeed are her. You are Avaînoáel, O Poica Katharos, the most powerful elf the planet has ever known. Whether you like it or not! "Hence, as I said, you are a worthy opponent to your friends as well as to your enemies." Ava is about to say something. He gestures with his hand for her to remain silent.

"Please allow me to explain. Then you can rebut if you would like. First, I implore you to cease telling others how to address you. If they want to compliment you, to recognize what you have become, who you truly are, let them do it. If they call you Avaînoáel, does it truly matter? If they call you O Poica Katharos; is there any harm in that? If they call or refer to you as my Lady, let them do it. No injury is done and if it makes them feel good so much the better. They respect you, Ava, and they want you to know it." He leans in close which forces Ava to slide back in her seat unconsciously.

"Second, the fighting elves and humans of our allied Etanpioa's must adhere to decorum. Their leaders, King Poldo, Prince Earendil, and Lady Elbereth, and many others, must adhere to decorum as well. They *must* be formal. Therefore, they *must* observe your so-called pageantry whether you like it or not. It is the soldierly way the world over. Addressing one's leaders properly is essential for good order and discipline. To follow orders unselfishly if those orders are legal. To sacrifice their lives if necessary, in carrying out those orders."

Godroh settles back in his chair. His eyes remain riveted on Ava's face. His tone is much softer as he says, "You say you do not like all the pageantry, the formality of addressing you as my Lady or Avaïnoáel. Nonetheless, you too must adhere to the fighting forces traditions and customs." He searches Ava's eyes. "And why do you think that is?" Ava shrugs her shoulders.

"Because Ava and this is most important, you, as Avaïnoáel, O Poica Katharos, are the commander-in-chief of every fighting warrior of the Inner World. You have supreme command and control over their actions. You are the Inner World's head of state. King Poldo, Lady Elbereth, and Prince Earendil report to you. Lady Blissia and Lord Wlknoo report to you. Lady Avaiä, the River Goddess of the Solenom and King Mérino – they too report to you. Likewise, there are many other warrior leaders you have yet to meet that report to you. Everyone ultimately reports to you and to no one else."

Ava touches her fingers to her parted lips as her eyes widen with astonishment. She is shocked by what Godroh has said. She never considered she was like the President of the United States back home, that she too is a commander-in-chief. That she exercises supreme command over the Inner World's friendly fighting forces. Now she is shaking her head in disbelief.

"Ava, please allow me to speak of something closer to home, to further explain what I am saying. Your father was in the United States Marines of the Earthly World. When he was on active duty, he, like all others in uniform, addressed his seniors formally. His superiors did the same both up and down the chain of command. It is no different here in the Inner World. It is but one especially important element of Etanpioa discipline." He sits still for a few moments and does not say anything as he stares at the dancing flames in the hearth. Ava does not say anything. Her face is pasty white, and she is staring at the floor.

Without looking away from the hearth, Godroh says in a whisper, "Always remember this, Ava. Perception is ninety-nine percent of one's success or failure in the eyes of others. To be perceived as a leader, you must act like a leader. Tolerating the pageantry is just one part of it – as unimportant as it may seem to you." Ava is looking at him with tearful eyes. She is nodding her head in agreement because she knows that everything Godroh has said makes perfect sense.

Godroh walks to the table with the thkao and confections. He calls over his shoulder, "Would you like some confectioneries, Ava? They are particularly sweet and tasty."

Ava replies in a shaky voice, "Yes, please. They are my favorites. Thank you."

When Godroh sits back down, Ava takes hold of a confection. She is nodding her head and smiling. Her complexion has returned to something close to normal. She wipes at her eyes and says, "Godroh, I apologize for being rude earlier. You are correct. I am so entranced by what I have become I have been downplaying it to my detriment. I now know that thanks to you. Thank you for setting me straight."

"No need to apologize, Ava. You are powerful. You are insightful. You are intelligent and yes, as inquisitive as the day is long. All wonderful qualities. But you are young too. Relatively inexperienced when it comes to world affairs. Unknowledgeable of the dangers that face you. That is why you are here with me today. So, I can assist you in obtaining all the knowledge that is possible. I promise I will do exactly that. I will also remain faithful to you until my dying breath." He smiles brightly as he hands the plate of confections to Ava. She places the plate on her lap. She is still contemplating everything that Godroh has said. He says in a whisper, "Ava?"

"Yes, Godroh."

"All of Earth is depending on you. You are our last hope."

3

Godroh gets up from his chair and walks to the far side of the laboratory to where Ava's weapons are resting against the wall. He unsheathes her sword and reads the inscription on the flat side of the blade. "This is a beautiful sword, Ava. Do you know what the inscribed words on the blade say?"

She replies in a sure tone, "Yes I do, surprisingly. Correct me if I am wrong, but I believe it says *to forsake a Bkotn is to forsake oneself.*"

"You are correct," Godroh replies. "Almost nothing quite like an exquisitely crafted Bkotn sword. Their artistry is amazing. Almost as fine as the Timbre." He runs his fingertip along the blade. "Sharp as a knife too." He waves the sword in the air.

Woosh, woosh, woosh!

"Ava, do you know how it is you understand what the inscription says?"

"No, not really. Perhaps someone told me. But if they had I surely would have remembered, but I do not." She indifferently shrugs her shoulders. "It does not matter because I know what it says now that you have confirmed it."

Without turning around Godroh says, "Do you realize you are fluent in Fortunomy?"

Ava gets to her feet and stands beside her chair. She raises her eyebrows with surprise. "I am?"

"Indeed, you are. Your mind no longer must translate things from Fortunomy to English and vice versa. You are also fluent in many other languages: Mandarin Chinese, Japanese, Hindi, Greek, Italian, German, French, Arabic, Russian, and Spanish. They are but a few crucial languages as far as I am concerned. There are a hundred more including those no longer spoken by Earthly World humans. The dead languages as they are referred to."

"No way!" Ava says with a hearty laugh. She is shaking her head. Then she crosses her arms over her chest in a cheeky stance. "There is no way I can understand all those languages. Okay, I must half-heartedly agree that I may be fluent in Fortunomy but not ten other languages in addition to English." She gives Godroh a quizzical look. "And dead languages plus a hundred more." She shakes her head again. "Nope. Unh-unh. There is no way."

"Onamae wa nandesuka?"

"My name is Ava," she replies in an unemotional manner. "Why would you ask such a silly question?"

"Yīnwèi n? xūyào zhīdào."

Because she thinks Godroh is kidding around, Ava says with a laugh, "And why do I need to know, Godroh?" She gives him a strange look.

He replies flatly, "Einen Punkt beweisen."

Ava slaps her thighs and roars with laughter. "What are you doing, Godroh? What do you mean when you say, 'to prove a point?'"

Godroh carries her longbow, quiver, and sheathed sword to where Ava is standing. He sits in his chair. She seems slightly worried because of his serious expression and his furrowed brow. She sits in her chair and stares at him.

In a tone of voice that is firm and direct, Godroh says, "I just spoke to you in three languages. The first was Japanese. I asked you in Japanese what your name is. As you know, you replied. The second language I spoke was Mandarin Chinese. I said in Mandarin, 'because you need to know.' The last language was German. I said 'einen Punkt beweisen,' to prove a point.'"

Ava's hand moves to her mouth in surprise. After a few moments, she says at last, "Do you mean to tell me you said all that stuff in three different languages?"

Godroh nods his head. "Yes, I did. You replied in identical languages as well. You replied in Japanese when I asked your name in Japanese. Likewise, in Chinese and German. No matter what words you hear or read in any of those languages, plus over a hundred more, you will respond in kind in the same language instinctively. Without a second thought or a moment's hesitation. You can also read and write in a hundred languages and those no longer employed today. They include the so-called dead languages such as Latin and Akkadian. They were spoken in the Mesopotamia era from the 3rd to the 1st millennium BCE. Even Coptic and many others."

Ava's tone is frenzied as she shouts, "Coptic? No way! Coptic – the combination of Demotic and Hieratic languages that include Hieroglyphics? I cannot believe this!" She folds her arms over her stomach and bends over slightly. She remains in that position for a few moments. Then she straightens up and stares into Godroh's eyes. "Really, Godroh? Honestly? Even Akkadian of Mesopotamia and Hieroglyphics of the Coptic language? Perhaps even Biblical Hebrew?"

Godroh is nodding his head. "Honestly and yes, all of them to include Biblical Hebrew."

4

Ava is still trying to absorb everything Godroh has said about her linguistic ability. Her introspective thoughts are interrupted when he reaches down and picks up her quiver. He places the quiver on his lap and withdraws an arrow. Without warning, he snaps it in two.

"Hey! What did you do that for!" Ava exclaims in a shocked, agitated tone. "I only have twenty of those." She gives Godroh an annoyed look. "Darn you — now nineteen!"

"You will not be needing this and any of the others," Godroh says.

"Gosh, Godroh, you just broke one of my arrows! What is wrong with you? Furthermore, what do you mean I will not need my arrows any longer? Gimme that before you break the others!" She reaches out to grab the quiver. Godroh suddenly throws the quiver to the floor. Arrows scatter everywhere. Now Ava's eyes are reddening. She is staring at him intently. She is taking in deep breaths and exhaling them sharply to keep her emotions in check.

Unexpectedly, Godroh thrusts the pointed shaft of the broken arrow at her chest!

Without making a sound, Ava leaps high in the air and lands in a crouch in front of him a split-second later. She is glaring at him with a face of sheer anger. Her teeth are exposed, and her nostrils are flaring. Beads of sweat are forming on her forehead. Every muscle in her body is twitching like she is ready to fight!

Without realizing what she was doing in reaction to Godroh thrusting the arrow at her, Ava had leaped from her chair and soared five feet in the air with ease. As she was leaping effortlessly in the air, she had snatched both shards of the broken arrow from his grip. She landed in a crouch directly in front of him. She shouldered her quiver and speedily grabbed the sword from the floor and unsheathed it. Then she shoved the tip of the sword against his throat instinctively without piercing the skin.

The whole thing had occurred in the blink of an eye, in less than a second.

Her lips are pressed together tightly. Her eyes have narrowed to slits. She is gawking at Godroh. Abruptly, just as her grasp of what occurred enters her awareness, her eyes widen markedly. She calmly places the sword on the ground. She slides the quiver from her shoulder. Then she drops to her knees and presses her palms on the floor to keep from falling over. She starts to shiver. She looks up and sees that Godroh is grinning. She reads his thoughts and is shocked to realize that he is proud of her, of what she just did. That she behaved as she should have as the all-powerful O Poica Katharos!

Unknowingly revealing that she can read his mind – although she will learn afterward that he already knew – Ava says in a stunned, disbelieving tone, "You are proud of me that I acted as I should have as the all-powerful O Poica Katharos? But my goodness, Godroh, I could have hurt you seriously! I am so deeply sorry I reacted the way that I did! I did not mean to point my sword at your throat."

Godroh's thoughts say, but you did not hurt me. You acted precisely as I knew you would. I am a friend. You instinctively knew that. So, there is no way you would have injured me.

Ava has a bewildered expression on her face even now. She says, "I do not know what came over me." Her eyes suddenly flare. "Hey, wait a minute here! Why did you thrust the tip of the arrow near my chest in the first place? What was all that about? Also, why are you thinking that I acted precisely as you thought I would?" She makes a face. "If you must know, what just occurred scares me half to death, actually." She looks at her hands. "See what you made me do? I am shaking still."

Godroh says, "So you will know, Ava."

"Know what for crying out loud?" Ava cries. "That you tried to stick an arrow in my chest? That I somehow jumped back then high in the air and landed in front of you in one quick movement? Then I somehow grabbed both parts of the broken arrow from you. Shouldered my quiver. Grabbed my sword from the floor and unsheathed it. Then pointed it at your throat without realizing what I was doing! Goodness, Godroh, what is going on?" She eyes him suspiciously for a few moments. "Okay, Godroh, now is the time to fess up! What is happening to me? How did I just do what I did? I reacted so swiftly before I even knew what I was doing!" She wipes at the beads of sweat on her forehead and examines the palms of her hands.

"Instinctively—"

CHAPTER 2

ETANPIOA'S UNDER ATTACK

"Victorious warriors win first and then go to war,
while defeated warriors go to war first and then seek to win."—*Sun Tzu*

"Hey, look over there!" Steph yells above the roaring wind as she points. "Dead ahead of us and a little bit to the right. Do you see that?" She is pointing to three enormous columns of smoke that are rising from the dense forest. The smoke is to the east of the winding Kuoino. The trail is visible from this altitude as Fluescere soars at top speed toward Mégedale.

Galadriel cries, "Oh no! That is roughly the area where the Etanpioa's looking for Steph should be!"

"Etanpioa's like plural?" Steph asks showing surprise. "Is there more than one?"

Galadriel answers, "Yes. There is Nessa and my Etanpioa and those of the Timbre warriors. They are looking for you."

Nessa points at little specks off in the distance. She screams, "What are those flying in and out of the smoke? They look like dragons. There must be at least five of them!" She narrows her eyes and points to the north of the columns of smoke, "And what in the world are those other, smaller flying things?"

Galadriel's tone is unusually concerned as she yells, "Oh goodness! I cannot be completely certain from this distance, but they look like *gryphons!* Gryphons are some of the most ferocious creatures of the Inner World. I have never seen one. Few have since they are furtive creatures. However, my mother told me all about them when I was a child. They have a body of an exceptionally powerful "liontári" and the head and formidable wings of an "aetós." They have sharp, extraordinarily long talons like the aetós and strong, razor-like beaks too. Their talons and beaks can rip an elf or human, any prey actually to include belugas, to pieces."

Steph shouts, "I have never heard of gryphons before now. From where do they come, Galadriel? Do you know?"

Galadriel replies, "They live in the mountains. Dwarves throughout the Inner World use them to guard their gems, gold, and silver that they mine. Usually, armed dwarves are mounted on them during conflicts. Look. There must be dozens of them!" She narrows her eyes for a few moments then shouts. "This is terrible! There appears to be a dwarf on each of them. The dwarves must have declared war on the Timbre and Bkotn, maybe all elves and humans!"

"Maybe the dwarves are going to the Etanpioa's assistance," Steph shouts over her shoulder. "What do all of you think?"

Voronwe yells, "I seriously doubt it. Dwarves and elves have not had good relations for generations. Either way, we must get down there! Those dragons and the gryphons, or whatever they are, will decimate the whole, combined Etanpioa!" His look of alarm abruptly turns to one of exasperation. "But we cannot do anything but watch as we pass by and hope for the best. That is because Ava told Fluescere to locate you, Steph, to return you directly to Mégedale! The dragon will not respond to any of our commands. She obeys Ava and Godroh only!"

Nessa hollers, "But we have to do something! Maybe Fluescere will figure out what is happening. Then she will get close enough so we can jump off her back."

Steph shouts, "See if you can locate a clearing close to where the smoke originates." As the others search the horizon, Steph notices that Fluescere is veering to the left gradually to avoid the columns of smoke. In a desperate attempt to get the dragon's help she shouts, "Fluescere, we need for you to get lower. We must find a clearing. We must do something to help them!" Fluescere does not respond and continues to turn gradually to the left. "Fluescere! You must listen to me. If we continue this course, we will be unable to help. Besides, the other dragons are sure to see you. Then they will see us as well. If they are loyal to Haldir then all of us are at risk. There will be no way for you to maneuver."

"Steph, it is of no use," Voronwe moans in a shout." Fluescere cannot hear you. She is deaf. All dragons are deaf."

Nessa cries out, "But we have to do something. Otherwise, all our friends will perish! Your companions as well, Voronwe!"

Fluescere has increased her speed. Steph leans in close to Nessa. "Nessa, I want you to do something for me. It will be very tricky and perhaps dangerous as well. Are you willing to do as I ask?"

Nessa shouts over her shoulder, "I will do anything to help my friends! Do you want me to jump? Maybe Fluescere will catch me before I hit the ground."

Galadriel yells, "Hey! What is going on up there? You better not be asking Nessa to jump, Steph. I forbid it! And Nessa, I command you to do no such thing!"

"No, I would never ask her or any of you to do that," Steph hollers over her shoulder. "However, I have an idea that may compel Fluescere to fly toward the smoke." She rips a long strip of cloth from the lining of her cloak. Then she removes Ava's pinky finger ring from her right hand and ties it to one end of the cloth. She ties the other end of the cloth near the hook of the fire iron she stole from Haldir's cabin. She hands the fire iron to Nessa and shouts above the wind, "Please creep onto the middle of Fluescere's neck. Something tells me she will keep you balanced but be extra careful all the same. I will cling onto your cloak to make certain you do not slip. Once you are far enough along her neck, reach out with the fire iron and dangle the ring in front of her eyes. After a few seconds lower it to her nose and let her sniff it for a few moments." She crosses her fingers. "Hopefully, she will respond to it. It is our only hope."

"What in the world is all that supposed to accomplish?" Voronwe shouts. "I seriously doubt Fluescere will respond to a ring dangled in front of her eyes."

"Oh, she will respond all right," Steph shouts. "There is no doubt in my mind. The ring belongs to Ava! While it may look the same as mine, I am confident she will instinctively know it is her ring." She whispers in Nessa's ear, "Once she responds, and I hope with all my heart she does, quickly pull back on the fire iron and hand it to me. Then scoot back here to where it is safer. Can you do all of that?" With a frown, she adds, "And whatever you do, stay safe and do not lose the ring!"

"Yes, I certainly can do all of that," Nessa says in a confident tone. She starts to slide her body onto Fluescere's neck slowly. Fluescere at once compensates for the sudden shift of weight. Now she is flying markedly less smoothly. Fortunately, Nessa and the others remain balanced.

Steph thinks to herself, thank God Fluescere is compensating for the weight shift. She still has her fingers crossed. I can only hope and pray this silly idea works! If it does not, everyone down there is going to die. And all because they were looking for me!

Once Nessa is far enough on Fluescere's neck, she does what Steph had asked. She dangles the ring in front of the dragon's eyes. After a few moments, she reaches out further with the fire iron, so the ring is in front of Fluescere's nose.

Fluescere abruptly bellows loudly. Red-hot flames shoot out of her mouth. She begins to fly erratically. Fortunately, she stays balanced enough so the others, including Nessa, do not tumble off her back. Although all of them are tightly gripping her spikes with their gloved hands.

Luckily, Nessa had withdrawn the ring from Fluescere's nose just in time so that the cloth was not burned to a crisp. She quickly scoots back to her original position on the dragon's back and hands the fire iron to Steph. Steph unties the ring and shoves it on the pinky finger of her right hand. Then she throws the fire iron over the side to her right. As she had hoped Fluescere zooms right after it.

The powerful dragon is near the fire iron in a matter of seconds as it sails end over end in the air. She lets out another powerful roar that is followed by a short burst of blazing flames from her mouth. The cloth instantaneously disintegrates to a wisp of grey smoke. The fire iron glows bright red and melts down a split-second later. Then it disappears in a sparkle of white ash. Once the fire iron disappears, Fluescere does exactly what Steph had hoped. She cranes her neck and looks at Steph and the others.

Steph thrusts her right hand high in the air and makes a fist so only the pinky ring is showing. She points with her left hand to Ava's pinky ring. Fluescere looks from the ring to her and back again a few times. Steph is starting to feel dismayed when the dragon suddenly lets out a burst of grey smoke from her nostrils. Steph correctly assumes the burst of smoke was her recognition of Ava's pinky ring. She stares into Fluescere's eyes as the dragon continues to fly erratically. She expressly enunciates each syllable slowly and says, "I am Steph, Avaïnoáel's Earthly World friend. I too was in the tower when you saved her as Jordyn had asked." She points to the billowing columns of smoke on the trail. "You must obey me as you would Ava. Those are Ava's friends down there, and they are in peril. We must save them!"

At first, Fluescere appears uncertain of what Steph has said. Then, to everyone's relief, she nods her head deliberately and immediately dives toward the trail. All the while she is puffing snort after snort of grey-white smoke.

Nessa shouts, "Oh my goodness, Steph! You did it!"

Steph answers back, "No, *you* did it, Nessa. You are incredibly brave. I know Ava will be even more proud of you when she finds out what you have done!"

CHAPTER 3

ON THE CUSP OF ALL-OUT WAR

"Only the dead have seen the end of war."—Plato

1

Godroh exclaims, "Ava, are you feeling okay? You look a little pale. I apologize if I upset you. I just thought that surprising you the way that I did would draw out your remarkable powers. If I had simply told you about your abilities, perhaps you would not have believed me." He smiles then says in French, "Le voir et le faire, c'est le croire." He looks at Ava expectedly. "What I just said was in the Earthly World French language. You did understand it, yes?"

"I am okay, really," Ava replies in a convincing tone. "And yes, what you just said in French, 'seeing and doing it is believing it' is one hundred percent correct. If I had not done it and seen it, I would never have believed it. All the same, I must admit that I am still trying to come to terms with everything that occurred.'" She chuckles and shakes her head as she asserts, "You know, Godroh; I have always prided myself with my quickness and dexterity because I am only a bit taller than five feet. Especially on the basketball and volleyball courts. But to jump four or five feet in the air and quickly take hold of things before I even realized what was happening is surreal. It will take a bit longer for me to process everything." She throws back her head and chuckles. "Also, that I was able to translate what you just said in French so easily still astonishes me. I heard the words in French as they entered my ears, but my mind automatically translated them to English. I was going to answer in kind, in French, but you kept talking. All of what you have taught me is utterly amazing!"

"I just wanted to ensure you retained your translation abilities," Godroh says. "Just so you know, I taught you nothing, yet I appreciate your compliments. Everything you discovered was already part of your psyche. Moreover, everything you learned up until now is very shocking to your psyche as well. I know that for a fact. So, I must ask once more. Are you feeling okay despite the shocking revelations of your superpowers?"

"Yes and no," Ava says with a frown. "I sort of am okay with everything that happened. I must admit it is totally cool too. However, something else is bothering me." She taps her temple with her forefinger. "As you may know, I am marginally clairvoyant—"

Godroh interrupts. "I believe that your extrasensory abilities are much more than *marginal*, Ava. I would define them as *extraordinary*."

"Perhaps you are right," Ava says softly. "All the same, something seems wrong. "I cannot put my finger on it, but it is like something is happening or is going to happen. Something that demands my attention." She is staring at Godroh. "Something terrible. Maybe it is happening even now. I just do not know for certain."

Godroh says with intense conviction, "Well then, there is no time to lose."

2

"As soon as Fluescere gets close to the ground, jump," Voronwe shouts. "But be extra careful and do not get hurt." He taps Steph on the shoulder. "Will you be okay jumping from Fluescere's back? The Bkotn and I routinely practice such procedures, but I do not know about your experience."

Steph says, "If the three of you can do it, so can I. I am a rugby player. Rugby is an Earthly World vigorous sport. Powerful legs are everything. So yes. I will be okay. However, I just wish I had something to fight with other than this stupid fire iron, ax, and knife. I wish I had my longbow and arrows."

"If things on the ground are as bad as they look from up here," Galadriel shouts, "grab any weapon on the ground that you can. That includes an extra quiver, perhaps even two."

"Hold on!" Nessa yells loudly just as Fluescere zooms to the right to avoid a collision with another dragon.

"Fluescere is overloaded with us on her," Steph yells. "She will get cremated by the other dragons if we do not get to the ground soon."

Voronwe shouts above the wind, "Not to worry, at least I do not think so. At least as it concerns her getting cremated as you say. Dragons seldom fight one another, even if they are on opposing sides. But you are correct when you say she is overloaded. We need to get off her as soon as possible, so she can destroy the belugas."

Galadriel shouts, "Perhaps the dragons are not a danger to her, but the gryphons are!"

"She should be okay," Nessa says in a shout. "She has tough scales and can breathe fire."

"But the gryphons intuitively go for the eyes of their prey," Galadriel counters. "That includes dragons, large and small. Considering how many there are, she could easily be overwhelmed."

"Everyone, pay attention," Voronwe commands. "After studying Fluescere's trajectory, I think she is going over there." He points to a small clearing in the forest on the left. "There is not enough room for her to land, so jump as soon as she loiters over the clearing. But be extra careful to jump from the base of her neck. If you do otherwise, you will be knocked out cold by her flailing wings. Nessa, you go first on my command." A few moments later Fluescere is just about fifteen feet above the ground.

Nessa does not wait for Voronwe's order. She hurls her satchel and weaponry over the side and jumps a few seconds later. When she hits the ground, she automatically rolls to prevent injury to her body. Bkotn warriors are taught the roll technique early on in their training by leaping off towering boulders.

Steph scoots to the base of Fluescere's neck. She tosses the tools she stole from Haldir's cabin over the side and jumps. When she hits the ground, she follows Nessa's example and rolls. She immediately gets to her feet and grabs her tools. Voronwe and Galadriel jump to the ground one by one a second or two later.

As soon as Fluescere is free of her passengers, she soars in the direction of the columns of smoke. She aims to attack the belugas. Dragons and belugas have fought one another since the beginning of time. The belugas always end up losing.

3

Ava is still trying to figure out what is bothering her. She is suffering vivid, even if quick, short-lived, blurry images in her mind's eye. Belugas running through the forest. Dragons spraying fiery flames. Columns of smoke rising in the air. Elves shooting arrows. Desperate shouts and cries of pain. Bizarre creatures with the bodies of lions and heads of eagles.

The images that the mystic, clairvoyant section of her mind is envisioning are coming and going too quickly. Thus, she cannot process them properly. Because the region in front of her brain, the prefrontal cortex, is slowing her awareness purposely. The prefrontal cortex is acting as it should – as her brain's master regulator, its protective watchdog. Allowing her mindfulness sufficient time to process what she has already discovered about her remarkable physical and language abilities. If the prefrontal cortex were not doing as it should, Ava's brain would be "flooded," utterly overwhelmed emotionally and mentally. Thereby rendering her inefficient in both body and mind if only for the time being.

I need to focus on something else, she thinks to herself. Otherwise, I will go totally insane. She shakes her head forcefully to clear her mind. Shaking her head in this manner seems to help a little but not as much as she wants. She is determined to try a different approach to clear her mind. She will focus on a brand-new topic entirely.

"Godroh, can you tell me more about my magical skills? As you know I enacted strange spells and said odd words when I faced up to your imposter, Jason. Oddly, I did not have to think about what I was going to say. Nor did I have to consider what would happen after I said what I did. I just said the words and things happened. Do you know if I possess more magical spells? Also, does a wand help when I produce them, that is if I have more magical, spell-inducing powers?"

Godroh says openly, "Honestly, Ava, I have no idea how you came to know those magical words that you said – *Presto Chango, Reversio,* and *Anaísthisom* – that resulted in magical spells and changes. I was not aware that those enchantments even existed. Magic and the mystical world of spells and enchantments are greatly unknown. Yes, we wizards and witches know – that is the key word here, *knowledge* – of magic. Despite that, we are not magical per se. Whereas *you* are magical, extraordinarily so. I suspect your subconsciousness knows of many more magical spells. I can only hope that when the occasion avails itself if it ever does, you will summon them from the inner depths of your mind to realism."

Ava asks, "Are wands necessary for me to conjure magical spells? That is if my subconsciousness knows more than the three spells I have already exhibited? The reason I ask is that I used Jason's wand when I rendered him unconscious and when I caused him to transform to his original self."

Godroh shrugs his shoulders and says, "Once again I must say I do not know, honestly. Yet you did not use a wand when you used the *Reversio* spell. You simply pointed your finger at the others one by one and rendered them conscious once more. Perhaps employing a wand will enhance your magical abilities. Then again, perhaps a wand is unnecessary. I simply do not know for certain."

Ava glances around the laboratory. "Do you have an extra, magical wand? Something I could use just in case?" She adds with a sly grin, "In the event my unconsciousness compels me to use another magical spell? Perhaps I may even have to protect myself someday. Who knows?"

Godroh's expression abruptly turns serious. "It is funny you should ask. I do not have an extra wand, but I have something else. I have been waiting for the proper time to present it to you. And now is the time." He stands and walks over to a nearby bookcase. He rummages around in the bookcase for a few moments. Then he grabs a long wooden box from the top shelf. He blows at what looks to Ava like two centuries of dust from the top of the box. He turns around and says, "It is not an *extra* wand as I said. Although it is something special, something to protect you." He walks across the room and hands the box to Ava.

Ava's hands are shaking with excitement. She lets out a gasp, and her eyes widen as she reads the handwritten, calligraphic lettering on the outside of the box. The gilded lettering consists of three words. The first two words are in the Ancient Greek Attic dialect from the reign of the Macedonian kings, circa 5 BCE. The words are *Hellenes* (in Greek, *Goddess*). However, these two words are not the cause of her excitement. It is the third word that has captured her attention and ensuing exhilaration.

"Aθήνα."

In a hardly perceptible whisper, Ava says with great delight, "Godroh, does the inscription on this box imply what I am thinking? That whatever is inside the box is a mark of respect to the mythological Greek Goddess, Athena, the Goddess of War, Wisdom, and Handicraft."

Godroh says, "I do not believe it is a mark of respect to the Goddess."

Ava gives him a quizzical look. Her elated expression quickly changes to one of misery. She is about to say something when Godroh holds up his hand. He is smiling as he says with a twinkle in his eyes, "I know for a fact that it *belonged* to the Goddess of War."

Ava takes a deep breath. Then she says in a faint whisper, "It *belonged* to her? How do you know?" She lifts one eyebrow then says in a cautious tone, "Are you telling me that Athena was real? That she was not a mythological goddess?" She is shaking her head. "Godroh, no offense, but I find that hard to believe, frankly."

"Oh, you find that hard to believe, do you?" Godroh says with a grin. "You, the O Poica Katharos having a conversation with a wizard inside a castle in a land beneath the Earth's crust. A land you never knew existed until recently. A land of elves, wizarding humans, belugas, dragons, and a king and queen of centaurs and unicorns. A haven for bizarre creatures of the mind's wildest imagination. Having yourself been subjected to magic, bound to a sapling. Finding within your inner self a means to break free of those bonds. Battling belugas and hearing the voice of Wendigorium. Being whisked away to this city on the back of your dragon, Fluescere. Conversing with her telepathically. A few moments ago, soaring feet in the air and acting offensively before you knew what was happening." He shrugs his shoulders and declares with a smirk, "Need I go on to prove my point?"

"I see your point," Ava says after a few moments of reflection. "And so, I guess anything is possible. I can accept that Athena was real. Although, like everything else that has happened since I arrived in the Inner World, it will take some time for it to sink in. So, she lived two thousand, five hundred years ago I would imagine. Am I correct?" Godroh nods his head. "But how is it," she looks down at the box sitting on her lap, "you came to have this in your possession after nearly two and one-half millennium?"

"It was passed down by other occupants of this laboratory. Before my predecessor died, she gave it to me for safe-keeping." A distant look appears on his face as he stares straight ahead. "She was an amazing wizardess, full of knowledge, especially of the Earthly World's presumed mythological history, much of it which is genuine. I owe my knowledge of wizarding spells to her. I have kept the box safe for over two hundred years, and now I am honored to give it to you." He throws his hands up in delight. "For what are you waiting? Make haste and open it!"

Ava opens the wooden box gingerly and is immediately stunned at what she sees.

4

"Okay, gather around," Voronwe says.

The others assemble in a small circle around him. Gritty looks of resolve are on their faces. Voronwe and the two Bkotn warriors have been training all their lives for this moment. They are mindful of the history and conflicting ethos of the Inner World that have led to the current situation. They have heard stories told by elders of the atrocities of Wendigorium and Strum as well as others. Furthermore, although they are relatively young, just teenelves, they are willing to sacrifice their lives for what they believe to be good and honorable.

Steph has not received combat training. Nor is she closely mindful of the Inner World's troubles like the others. Nevertheless, she too is eager to join the battle, to defeat injustice. Because she has faced crushing evil two times before – the revulsion of slavery a year before the American Civil War and the bigotry of German Nazis. Both were scourges of the humanity of the Earthly World. Moreover, she wants revenge for Ava being held captive and nearly being captured by Wendigorium. And, of course, she wants revenge for being held hostage by Haldir.

Voronwe is looking at his map. "If this is anywhere close to being accurate, the trail is fairly close to this clearing." He looks at the sky. Wisps of smoke are visible between the leaves. He folds his map and tucks it away. "I guess I will not be needing this any longer. We need only to follow the smoke trails." He looks at the others one after the other and says, "May the gods be with you." Then he turns and rushes toward the trail. Galadriel quickly follows him.

Steph is about to follow them when Nessa grabs her hand. "Steph, stop." She removes the quiver of arrows from her shoulder and offers it and her longbow to Steph. "You will need these." She glances at the fire iron and axe that Steph is clutching in her hands. "Those are useless except for hand-to-hand combat."

Steph says, "I appreciate your offer, Nessa, but I cannot accept them. I have watched you practice. You are a more skilled archer than I am. I could not even get close to your accuracy even with many more years of training."

Nessa stares at Steph for a few moments. Then she drops the quiver and bow to the ground. She gives Steph one last glance then turns around and scurries after Voronwe and Galadriel. She yells over her shoulder, "Oops. Looks like I dropped my stuff! I guess they are yours now, Steph."

Steph tosses the fire iron and axe in the underbrush. She picks up the bow and quiver of arrows and rushes after Nessa. She is only a dozen or two paces from the clearing when she sees her. The spirited Bkotn warrior is leaning against a tree and grinning.

"Oh, good for you, Steph. You found my stuff. Well, I guess they now belong to you." She takes Steph's hand in hers. "Seriously, there was no way I was going to allow you to walk in battle without proper weapons. And I would not allow you to proceed further alone. That is why I waited." She glances at her longbow in Steph's hand. "Besides, I wanted to make certain you had retrieved my weapons from the ground." A few minutes later, she and Steph are standing beside Voronwe and Galadriel a few feet off the trail.

Galadriel's face is buried in Voronwe's shoulder. She is moaning softly. Voronwe is staring shell-shocked at the carnage. Steph feels like vomiting as she stares at the bloodbath before her on the trail. She never could have imagined such a sorrowful sight. Nessa drops to one knee and closes her eyes.

The bodies of dozens of dead Bkotn and Timbre warriors are on the trail. Many have bloody shafts of arrows jutting from their torsos at all angles. They undoubtedly were fired by dwarven archers riding on the backs of gryphons. Others were slain by dwarves in hand-to-hand combat. A few of the warriors have long, blood-stained gashes on their torsos where diving gryphons had slashed them cruelly. Some were disfigured horribly by the gryphons' sharp claws. Then others are unrecognizable as former living beings. Their charred bodies were scorched by dragons' flames.

There are also numerous dead dwarves. It appears if most of the dwarves perished after falling from the sky. A few are impaled by arrows meaning they fought bravely on the ground. There are at least four dozen lifeless gryphons although no one bothers to count them. Etanpioa archers had managed to shoot the creatures from the sky despite their crushing numbers.

Nessa jumps to her feet. She calls out, "Does anyone see Elbereth? We must find her at all costs. We must reorganize if there are others still alive!" Her shouts seem to wake the others from their momentary stupor. "We also need to move further inside the forest to see if anyone managed to escape – if others can fight!" She raises her sword high in the air and shouts, "Follow me!"

CHAPTER 4

THE PROPHECY'S UNVEILING

"When the truth is known all doubts shall perish."
—Anonymous

"I cannot believe that I am holding these in my hands," Ava says with an expression of disbelief. She is breathing deeply. "That they belonged to Athena." She looks up and sees that Godroh is not sitting in his chair. He is on the other side of the shelves and noisily rummaging in them once more.

He peers around the column of shelves and says, "They are yours now, Ava. Go ahead and put them on. Let me know if they fit your forearms. You are not as tall as Athena is alleged to have been. She was purported to be five feet, ten inches in height. Although, like you, she was slender. So, even though you are shorter, I believe they should fit."

Ava slips the manica's, sometimes referred to as bracers or bracelets, onto her wrists one by one then fastens them with the leather straps. "Godroh, they fit perfectly. Although it may take me a bit of time to get used to wearing them. Are these leather straps new? They look like it. And what are the bracelet's purpose anyhow?"

Godroh walks over to where Ava is sitting. He is carrying two wooden boxes. One is quite large and looks moderately heavy. A smaller, square box is balanced on top of it. Both boxes are coated with dust and seem to be ancient, just like the one that held the manica's. He sets the boxes on the floor in front of their chairs then sits.

"Yes, I had the leather straps replaced last year. The original ones were nothing more than shards of woven dust. To answer your other question of their purpose, by all accounts the manica's, or bracelets as you referred to them, are magical." Ava gives him a quizzical look. "By magical, I am implying that when *you* wear them, they will protect you from harm."

"How in the world can they do that?" Ava exclaims. "Yes, they may be made of bronze, but they cannot possibly do anything like that."

Godroh reaches in the quiver lying on the floor and pulls out an arrow. He is giving Ava a sly look.

Thinking he is going to jab it at her as he did a while ago, she backs away instinctively. She is waving her hands in front of her face. "Whoa! You have already proven your point. There is no reason to do it again." Recognizing he does not intend to poke the arrow at her, she says lightheartedly, "Move one step closer sir, and the arrow is mine!"

Godroh hands the arrow to her and says with a chuckle, "I will never do that again because if I did you may not be as forgiving as last time. I want you to do something for me, to see if your wrist guards are magical. You are right-handed, so try stabbing the tip of the arrow at the left manica with your right. Let us see what happens."

Ava gives him a doubtful look. "What do *you* expect will happen?" She is shaking her head sluggishly. "Because I do not want to stick an arrow in my arm, you know just in case the bronze shield does not stop it."

Godroh shrugs, "I do not know for certain. But if my predecessor was correct – and there is no reason to doubt her words – we should expect some sort of response. At least I expect that we will." He frowns. "If I were you, I would not push too hard just in case."

Ava grips the shaft firmly just above the arrowhead and gently pushes it at the left manica. Her eyes widen with complete surprise as sparks fly from the wrist guard. She plunges the point of the arrow at the manica again but much more forcefully. Sparks fly from the wrist guard once more. She says softly with an air of outright thrill, "This is so cool; I mean awesomely so! The manica is deflecting the point!" She jabs the tip of the arrow at the manica over and over with the same results. Then she switches hands and jabs the right manica. She gets the same results. With a puzzled expression she says, "What does all of this mean?"

Godroh is grinning cleverly. He says in a frank tone, "I believe it implies three things. One, if *you* are wearing them then they are enchanted." He points to a small scratch in the center of the right manica. "I caused that scratch over a century ago just to find out if the manica was magical. I wanted to see if it could deflect the tip of my blade as my predecessor had claimed. As you can tell by the slight scratch it did not deflect the blade's point. This leads me to number two of my hypothesis. When *you* are wearing the manica's, they will protect you from harm. From an arrow, blade, sword, or spear thrust at you or even from an Earthly World bullet aimed in your direction. Finally, number three. If you are not the one wearing the manica's, they simply are ordinary, albeit ancient, bronze wrist guards."

Ava's tone is cynical as she says, "Yeah, right – ordinary wrist guards. I seriously doubt that." As a new thought enters her mind she exclaims, "Whoa! Just like in *Wonder Woman!*" Godroh is giving her a curious look. She counters his look by exclaiming excitingly, "*Wonder Woman* is the name of a movie in the Earthly World. It features an Israeli actress. Her fictional character Wonder Woman has extraordinary, superhuman powers." She curls her fists and crosses her forearms. As the two manica's make contact, little sparks appear just as they vibrate slightly. Her eyes widen with delight. "Now *that* was super awesome! Anyway, as I was saying, the fictional character Wonder Woman wears magical bracelets like these. She and other Amazon warriors referred to them as Bracelets of Submission. They likewise stop projectiles that were aimed at her. She has other cool weapons too." Her excitement abruptly evaporates because she realizes that Godroh appears upset. "Have you not seen the movie? Or is something else bothering you? You do not seem as excited as before."

Godroh replies in a soft tone, "Ava, I have not seen the movie, but I am familiar with the magical aspects claimed by a fictional Earthly World superhero that goes by that name." He leans in close and looks at Ava directly in the eyes. "I need to ask you a particularly important question. Do you know what attire Athena of Greece wore, what weapon's she carried, those sorts of things?"

Ava takes a few moments to consider Godroh's questions. "From the photos I have seen of how she supposedly looked, I believe she wore a full-length chiton and sometimes a peplos for warmth." She glances at her satchel near the door. "I have a white peplos in my satchel to wear over my cloak when it gets colder. I am only glad I am wearing a cloak instead of a chiton. Otherwise, I would have trouble wearing it. Furthermore, I think she carried a lance, or maybe it was a spear. I recall she carried a shield as well." Her eyes brighten markedly. "Yes! Just about every picture I have seen shows her carrying a shield." She notices that Godroh still looks upset. "Okay, Godroh, what is it you are not telling me?"

"Your descriptions of Athena are correct, Ava. She carried a spear and a shield. The spear was an offensive weapon. The shield, like your manica's, was for her protection. The shield could serve as an offensive weapon as well." His expression changes then he says glumly, "I am unhappy to say that this is where your nemesis, Athena's Ares if you will, Wendigorium, comes in to play."

Ava is gawking at him. Her tone is both circumspect and uncertain as she says, "Wendigorium? What does Wendigorium have to do with Athena? Yeah, I know from Greek mythology that Ares was the exact opposite of Athena. He purportedly was despised by the other gods and goddesses while Athena was favored. Thus, just like Diana in *Wonder Woman* the movie, Ares is Athena's nemesis, her foe." She gives Godroh an anxious, questioning look. "But what does all of this have to do with Athena, with Ares, with Wendigorium, and especially – me?" She is staring at Godroh. Then after a few moments, her hand flies to her mouth in complete shock. She has read his thoughts. She can feel her heart is starting to race and that her face is flushed. The nape of her neck seems like it is on fire just as her ears start to burn.

"Oh my God, Godroh! Is it true that Ares was alive, just like Athena? That Ares was more than a Greek mythological, fairy-tale being?" She turns her head from side to side slowly then stares at the ground. She remains like this for a few moments. When she finally looks up, she says to Godroh, "Are you telling me that Wendigorium is the reincarnated Ares just as I, Avaïnoάel, O Poica Katharos, am the reawakened Athena?" Godroh's expression is blank as he nods his head. "My God, Godroh! I cannot believe this! Is it true? Is there proof? Because this is too crazy to believe!"

Godroh reaches down and opens the large box that he had taken from the shelf. Ava sees there are four rows of scrolls stacked on top of one another. There appear to be twenty scrolls in all. He says, "These are the ancient scrolls of the Prophecy. Surely, you have heard of the Prophecy as it pertains to you?"

Ava is nodding her head as she stares at the scrolls. "Yes, my fairy friend, Doo, told me a bit about the Prophecy." She closes her eyes and murmurs, "I seem to recollect, although it is not distinct, that Jordyn may have mentioned the Prophecy as well."

Godroh says, "I thought you may have heard about the Prophecy since arriving in the Inner World. Jordyn told me she was going to tell you a bit about the Prophecy as well. However, in consideration of your safety, she said she planned to erase your memory of the Prophecy's existence. I must also add that Jordyn, like practically all others of both worlds, does not know everything that the Prophecy reveals."

Ava considers silently, so that is why I cannot recall what Jordyn had said exactly. Because she had erased my memory. Now I recall she had intended to do just that!

Godroh says, did your fairy friend happen to mention that the Prophecy is a prediction of *what once was and what will someday be all over again*? It is a fairly common aphorism of the Inner World, especially for those who believe in a better life." Ava replies that she does, that Doo had said those exact words to her and Steph. Godroh continues as he says, "The Prophecy dates to the death of Athena, perhaps even before her passing. Greek gods and goddesses were alleged to be immortal, just like elves are immortal. Nonetheless, just like elves when it comes to their mortality, gods and goddesses could allegedly perish. As you probably know, elves can perish at the hands of another elf's weapon or from a wizarding human's evil spell. In the case of gods and goddesses, they could die only at the hands of another deity. What we have learned over the millennium about Athena and Ares is not accurate. Or so it seems. I will not dwell on the numerous, varied legends of Athena and Ares," he gestures to the box of scrolls, "because everything as it pertains to them, as well as to you, is covered by the Prophecy."

Ava is shaking her head with wonder as she reaches down and removes a scroll from the box. She is about to unroll the parchment when Godroh says, "You are welcome to read all the scrolls of the Prophecy at your leisure. But now is not the time if you agree. There is much more for you to learn from me." Ava nods her head indicating she agrees. She returns the scroll to the box.

"Thank you for your understanding. Even so, there is something I must tell you now. The legends regarding the origins of Athena and Ares are true. Zeus, the god of the sky, lightning, and thunder, was Athena and Ares' father. Zeus was also the father of Artemis, Helen of Troy, and others you undoubtedly know. Thus, Athena and Ares were siblings with Ares being the oldest of the two. Yet as you correctly stated, one deity was good, Athena, while the other, Ares, was evil – at least in the eyes of the other gods and goddesses. Also, both perished in battle at the hands of each other which is contrary to legends. Although the details of their deaths are sketchy."

Godroh gives Ava a few moments to absorb what he just said. Then he says, "Despite the disparities of how they died, one aspect of their lifetimes is known." He gestures to the Prophecy. "Both Athena and Ares proclaimed that they would be reborn, reawakened if you will. As you stated a few moments ago, Athena was reawakened in your body. Ares was likewise reincarnated."

Ava is stammering when she says, "Are – are – are you telling me that I am not who I thought I am, that I was? That I am Athena but in a former human body that is now of the elven species?"

"Not exactly," Godroh says. "Reincarnation is the rebirth of *some* qualities of an entity whether it be awareness, thinking, the soul, or some other aspects of an individual. Since you are reawakened – a word that I prefer in your case to reincarnated – you have inherited Athena's intelligence, linguistic ability, intuition, and other strengths and skills. You have also inherited her unique capabilities and powers. They were demonstrated recently with my imposter and a few moments ago when you performed amazing things in the blink of an eye. Also, you demonstrated unique capabilities back at the clearing when you escaped those magical bonds. Although I am not certain, perhaps your capabilities come from Zeus or even other, close relatives of Athena. There is no way of knowing for certain." He shrugs his shoulders. "Perhaps you have more powers than you will ever know."

"So, I am still me?" Ava says softly as she folds her hands. "Still Ava Noelle, born of my parents, sister of my siblings, granddaughter of my grandparents, and so on; although I am likewise somehow Avaïnoel, O Poica Katharos at the same time, the reawakened Athena." She shakes her head glumly and stares at the ground. After a few moments of reflection, she looks at Godroh. "All of this is just too incredible to consider.

"First, I am climbing my grandfather's tower – trying to emulate him and my great uncle – then I am tumbling from an imploding staircase. With Steph in the Inner World discovering new and exciting things. Then learning I am something other than plain ole me, Ava Noelle. And today discovering I am the reawakened Athena." She adds with a frown, "And what Doo had told me about Wendigorium is not entirely true. But it makes sense since she never had access to the Prophecy and its truthfulness."

Godroh smiles at Ava. Then he places his hand on her right manica and says in a soft, caring tone, "Ava, you still are the same thirteen-year-old teenager who hails from Illinois of the Earthly World." He points to her heart and then to her head. "In there . . . and in there. No matter what you have come to be, nothing can change your origins. Even as you mature physically, expressively, mentally, and forcefully as O Poica Katharos. Also, as you know from what Jordyn had said, a part of you – your twin if you will – continues in the Earthly World even now as if nothing has occurred."

Ava gives him a curious look that has nothing to do with what he just said. Then her expression abruptly changes to one of concern.

Godroh throws his head back and laughs. "As you undoubtedly could tell from my thoughts, yes, what I am contemplating is true. I am sorry to say Wendigorium knows who you are. He similarly knows who he used to be. And yes, he stole Athena's shield and spear from this very laboratory nearly nine hundred years ago. Thankfully, he was unaware that the sacred scrolls of the Prophecy had been relocated to a safer place. Otherwise, he would have tried to take them as well. If he had, I would not be able to show them to you as proof of what you are, of what you have become. However, mercifully, even without the Prophecy I would be able to tell you everything. That is because the information was handed down over the millennium by my predecessors then ultimately to me." He reaches down and picks up the smaller box and hands it to Ava. "Miraculously, Wendigorium did not find this. If he had, he would have stolen it as well."

Ava opens the box. Her expression brightens markedly. "Oh my God! It is the headpiece, the golden tiara worn by Athena when she was not wearing her battle helmet!" She looks at Godroh. "And yes, I do understand what you are thinking, Godroh, and what you thought. I realize the significance as well." She positions the tiara on her head. Then with a shrewd grin she thinks to herself; after all this time . . . finally—

I know who and what Wendigorium is!

CHAPTER 5

DEATH AND DESTRUCTION

*"Life and death are one, even as
the river and sea are one."*—*Khalil Gibran*

1

Ava has been walking around Godroh's laboratory for the past half hour. She is sipping a second goblet of thkao. As she examines curious articles, part of her psyche is trying to compel her subconsciousness to revisit the visions she sensed a while ago. The fleeting, mental pictures of belugas and elves battling. Strange creatures with the bodies of lions and heads of eagles. Dragons spewing forth red-hot flames. Moreover, just a few moments ago a new vision popped within her head. It too was a fleeting scene but unexpectedly involved dwarves of all things. The dwarves were encircling a small group of elves. Then as quickly as the vision appeared it had vanished.

For now, she is consciously blocking the visions. For two reasons. One, she is not certain if the visions are of events that occurred in the past. Or if they are ongoing. Then again, they could be a prediction of the future. If they are forecasting the future, she possibly could do something about them. Two, she realizes she is powerless to do anything, at least right now.

There also is a third item to consider. She has learned a lot in the past several hours. Much more than she thought possible. But she knows there is more to learn. She is also fully aware of a famous, Earthly World axiom employed by strong leaders. She believes it undoubtedly pertains to her current situation: *Knowledge is Power.* Thus, she must obtain all the knowledge possible to understand fully her maximum power going forward. She purposely moves to stand beside the covered looking glass. Because her subconsciousness seems to be saying that the glass will tell her everything she needs to know. She says, "Godroh, what is the purpose of this looking glass and why is it covered?"

Godroh walks over to her. "Ah, I see that Earendil mentioned it to you." Ava nods her head. "He probably told you that I would not allow him to look at it even though he is the Prince of Mégedale." She nods her head once more. He holds out his hand and says, "Please, let me take your goblet." She hands it to him, and he places it on a nearby side table. When he turns around and faces her, his expression is severe.

Ava unexpectedly feels goose pimples all over in reaction to his serious look. She is finding it hard to breathe. Because she somehow knows what she is about to discover will far outpace all the amazing things she has already learned this day. She purposely blocks his thoughts so his emotional words can reflect his actual candor.

Given her mind-reading skills, Ava considers that thoughts are nothing more than silent, inner reflections of another's mind that are interpreted by her own. Whereas spoken words can genuinely express one's feelings, reason, as well as candor or just the opposite. In emotional situations, spoken words can also convey fear, love, and even loathing, all of which are essential sentiments of one's heart. Therefore, Ava blocks others' thoughts far more often than she reads them. Because she feels reading others' thoughts continuously is an invasion of their privacy.

"Ava, as you know better than anyone, you have experienced many wonders on your journey. Starting from the moment you initially crept along the ledge of your grandfather and great uncle's tower. Even as you tumbled on the tower's treacherous staircase seeing amazing events and witnessing the birth of the Inner World. Even while bound magically and suffering the evilness of misplaced magic and the brutality of belugas. Discovering you are Avaïnoдel, O Poica Katharos – the Purest of Elves. And even here, today, as you have come to understand your phenomenal abilities, your capacity to do things in a twinkling. Even as you have learned the inconceivable, that you are the reawakened Athena, thus inheriting her powers, abilities, and phenomenal linguistic skills.

Everything you have learned, discovered, witnessed, and experienced up until now is nothing compared to what you are about to see." He clutches the base of the cloth covering the looking glass. "Are you ready?"

Ava closes her eyes. She is breathing deeply. She says a silent prayer then opens her eyes. With a convincing smile, she says, "Yes, Godroh. I am ready, as ready as I will ever be, I guess."

Godroh yanks the dust-covered cloth from the looking glass. As it falls to the floor, Ava steps back. She is waving her hands in front of her face vigorously. "Goodness, Godroh! That cloth is filthy! How long has it been on the looking glass? Since the beginning of time?"

"Around two hundred years, give or take. I looked in the looking glass briefly, shortly after assuming my position as Mégedale's chosen wizard. Not noticing anything unusual other than myself," he laughs lightheartedly, "which I rather not look at, I covered it. It has remained this way ever since."

"The looking glass must be old," Ava says. "The mirror itself appears to be made of polished metal instead of glass. Which makes sense since mirrors of the modern era were not invented until 1835. She runs her fingers on the beautifully preserved, lightly stained wooden frame. "The frame looks ancient as well. How old is this, do you know?"

"I am not certain, but I believe it dates back at least to the time of Athena and Ares. Hence, it is at least two and one-half thousand years old. Like the scrolls of the Prophecy, it too should tell you what you need to know. I am not certain but perhaps it has other magical powers just like you. Powers that only you can unleash."

Ava exclaims with a disgusted look, "Well, whatever powers it may have had at one time must have died long ago. All I see are wavy images of you and me."

"Talk to it," Godroh says.

"Oh, you have to be kidding," Ava says in a joking way. "Talk to a looking glass, a polished mirror? I may have done weird things in my past but talking to mirrors is not one of them."

"Then think of what you want it to show you. You said earlier that you had brief images of skirmishes. I suspect more of the visions have come and gone since then. I also suspect you consciously blocked them because your gaze seemed distant at times. Am I correct?"

"You are correct," Ava replies. "So, what you are telling me is that I should think or ask the looking glass questions?"

"No, not questions," Godroh says. "Think or talk to the glass like it wishes to tell you what it knows. At least that is what I have been told."

Ava says with a sly grin, "Oh, I get it. Maybe like the evil queen in *Snow White* when she asked the hand mirror, 'Mirror, mirror in my hand, who is the fairest in the land?' only for the mirror to reply, 'My queen, you are the fairest in the land.'" She bends over and slaps her thighs as she roars with laughter. She looks up at Godroh and says, "If the looking glass answers in that fashion, I am outta here! No ifs, ands, or buts!"

Ava is a bit upset that Godroh is not smiling in reaction to her attempt to ease the tension. Her attitude changes as well. She purses her lips and says in a soft tone, "Sorry. I guess I got carried away with all of that. My childhood fantasies tend to sneak inside my more mature psyche from time to time. So, I should talk to the looking glass, yes?"

"I believe you should," Godroh replies. "Please always remember, Ava, what the written Prophecy portends: *What once was and what will someday be all over again.* The looking glass is but a visual component of the Prophecy. That is why it is referred to as the Prophecying Looking Glass." He gestures with a wave of his hands. "Give it a go. You have nothing to lose."

"Yeah, nothing to lose but my insanity, perhaps even my life," Ava mutters to herself. "Okay, here goes nothing." She faces the looking glass straight on. "Mirror, can you tell me what I need to know?" Nothing happens. Her wavy image in the looking glass does not change. She looks over at Godroh and grins. "Nothing." He gestures with his hand for her to try once more.

"Mirror, I need to know what is going on. Can you please show me?" Nothing materializes. "Mirror tell me what is important. Can you do that?" Again, nothing. Now visibly irritated, she suddenly shouts, "I must know what once was and what will someday be all over again!" She quickly backs away just as her hand flies to her mouth in shock.

"Oh my God, Godroh! Can you believe what we are seeing? It looks like New York City of the Earthly World is on fire! I can tell by the topography that it is New York. Jersey City, even parts of Long Island are on fire too!" She turns away from the glass. "I have seen aerial photos of the residual, massive columns of smoke after the collapse of the two World Trade Center's." She turns to face the glass. "But nothing compares to this. This is dreadful!"

"Compel the glass to do more," Godroh shouts. "Not through your words but by way of your reflections, your deepest, innermost thoughts."

The scene in the glass magnifies in response to Ava's thoughts. She now sees a closeup of the borough of Manhattan, New York City. It is like she is looking at the devastation from a circling drone. The upper stories of the iconic 22-story, triangular Flatiron Building are ablaze. The entire thoroughfare of Broadway to the east of the Flatiron Building, from the Theater District to the north to Union Square in the south, is ablaze. Of the more than one million buildings in New York City, most in Manhattan, many remain untouched. However, the Empire State Building is nowhere to be seen, nor is the World Trade Center. They have collapsed!

The scene shifts further north to Central Park flanked by the Upper East Side and Upper West Side neighborhoods. The elegant, suburban Upper East Side is unrecognizable. Its elegant restaurants and chic shops along Madison Avenue are nothing but smoldering residues. The Upper West Side has fared no better. The posh neighborhood is ablaze. Famous landmarks such as the Lincoln Center and the American Museum of History are hidden beneath the smoke. Ava assumes that the historical structures, like the neighborhoods that border Central Park on either side, did not survive the destruction.

The landscape shifts to Central Park itself. She can see the figures of countless people running in all directions randomly. Projectiles from the sky that look like thunderbolts seem to be chasing them as they run. Whenever a projectile strikes the figure of a person, it evaporates in a curl of greyish-black smoke.

She falls to her knees. Tears of utter anguish are flowing down her cheeks. As if she has willed it, the scene changes to Washington, D.C. of the Earthly World. Gone are her beloved icons of American democracy – the Capitol, the Washington Monument, as well as the Lincoln and Jefferson Memorials. They are nothing but crumpled stone. The bridges leading in and out of the District have collapsed. Arlington National

Cemetery is a scorched, smoking meadow. The ruins in and around Washington, D.C., are not smoldering like those of New York City, so Ava assumes the Nation's Capital was attacked first.

Next, fleeting scenes of the Earthly World's other capitals appear in the looking glass. Tokyo, Japan; Moscow, Russia; London, UK; Berlin, Germany. All are ablaze. The scene of Paris, France, is the most disturbing to Ava. The Eiffel Tower has fallen and is lying on its side, now nothing more than a crumpled artifact of what it once symbolized – the celebration of the French Revolution, an icon of peace and hope the world over. The scene abruptly closes in on America's Statue of Liberty. The Lady's crown is all that is visible in the bay. Her torch is lying on its side on Staten Island and is barely recognizable.

Ava crawls on her knees nearer to the looking glass as it focuses on her hometown. The entire area surrounding her hometown appears untouched, as pristine and cozy just as she left it before she was whisked into the tower. An agonizing feeling of longing slithers in the pit of her stomach like a venomous snake ready to strike. A worrisome scowl is on her face as she focuses her undivided attention on the scene.

She compels the looking glass to zoom in on one of her favorite places. It is her hometown square. She sees the gazebo with its red, white, and blue banners, the small shops, and the telltale statues of the president she admires and his wife. The statues, like the rest of her hometown, are untouched. Then she sees her house from the vantage point high in the air. She jumps to her feet and shouts, "Nothing has been damaged around my home or even in the surrounding areas of Illinois. So, my family and friends must be okay! Thank God!" She turns to Godroh and says in a dispirited tone, "What does all of this mean? Is what I am witnessing the upcoming destruction of civilization in the Earthly World?"

Godroh does not reply but instead, he gestures with a nod of his head to the looking glass. Ava turns about and watches as the looking glass changes scenes.

Without realizing she has made it take place she had subconsciously conjured the upcoming scenes of Mégedale's downfall. Like the Earthly World cities that showed on the looking glass, the picturesque city of Mégedale, home of the Timbre and Fluescere's noble relatives, is nothing but complete desolation. The surrounding forest has evaporated. It has been replaced by vast fields of whitish ash. A few remnants of decayed, fallen trees are visible through the haze.

Wild animals are grazing on sparse patches of green in an area that once was the city's extravagant plateíazan. The treehouse neighborhoods of the katállilosly where elven and human children slept, played, and went to school, are piles of splintered, decaying wood. Little remains of the original, elegant architecture of the proud city proper as well. The king's mansion is nothing more than piles of crushed stone lying forever silent at the base of the magnificent Katarráplexouktes waterfalls. The waterfalls are nothing more than rivulets of their former, glorious self.

From what she is seeing, Ava correctly presumes the magnificent, ancient elven city was destroyed long before the capital cities of the Earthly World.

Without warning, the previous images that Ava had earlier envisioned in her mind appear on the surface of the looking glass. Columns of smoke are rising high in the air. Elves are shooting arrows, fighting dwarves with their tkalakn's, and calling out to one another urgently. Belugas seem to be running rampant in all directions like they are clueless about what they should be doing. Some are feasting on carcasses of fallen elves and dwarves. Dragons are splaying fire over the trail. Ava recognizes it as the Kuoino by the way it seems to zigzag like a snake through the forest from her vantage point in the sky. Once more she notices the strange creatures that look like a cross of a lion and an eagle.

Her subconsciousness starts to remember. Slowly yet deliberately. She abruptly cries in a forceful shout, "They are griffins, or in Fortunomy, gryphons! I should have recognized them earlier. And dwarves are mounted on them! By what I am seeing the dwarves must have declared war on the elves!" Her expression changes abruptly as the scene magnifies appreciably. "But why? Why now? And—" Her face turns pale as if she has just seen a ghost. She screams forcefully, "Steph! Oh my God, Steph! Steph look out. Behind you!"

She reaches out to touch the surface of the looking glass in a frantic act of despair to meet Steph's image, to save her Earthly World companion, her bestie from certain death.

Then she falls head over heels inside the looking glass and disappears.

2

Having fallen inside the looking glass head-on to the heat of a battle, Ava is stunned momentarily. Yet, by chance, she has enough wherewithal to realize what she must do. She intuitively recognizes that she is carrying weapons. She is wearing a sheathed sword. A longbow and quiver of arrows are slung over her shoulders. They are not the same weapons she had when she arrived in Godroh's laboratory. Yet she knows this is not the time to question how she came to possess them. She also has a sheathed, ten-inch blade on the outer portion of her left shin. She reaches down and pulls out the blade.

Words she had shrieked in Godroh's laboratory seem to echo within her mind as she screams once more.

"Steph! Oh my God, Steph! Steph look out. Behind you!"

Before Steph can even react or turn around to her shouts, Ava rushes the fifteen or so paces to where her friend is standing. She pushes her to the ground with brute force. Then she whirls around to face her friend's attacker a nanosecond later. She is surprised to see that Steph's attacker is an archer dwarf. He is aiming a crossbow in her direction. She had always thought that dwarves, at least in Earthly World movies, make use of swords. The dwarf has already let loose an arrow that was intended for Steph as she stood with her back to him. Ava positions herself between where Steph had been standing and the swiftly traveling arrow in a blink of an eye.

A typical Inner World crossbow arrow travels at the speed of approximately 220 feet per second. Since the dwarf is less than fifty feet away, the arrow is now less than inches from where Ava is standing. She looks at the arrow with a quizzical expression as it appears in her mind's eye to be moving at a turtle's pace. She quickly analyzes its trajectory and realizes it will strike her in the collarbone. She promptly crosses her arms in front of her neck. Even before the arrow reaches the manica's, it is deflected in a flicker of yellow sparks and falls harmlessly to her side.

Still clutching the blade in her right hand, Ava leaps high in the air. When she lands a split-second later, she is facing the dwarf, standing less than two feet away. The astonished archer did not even know what was happening. All he saw was a blur in the air as she soared toward him. He looks down at the blade she has pressed against the armor of his breastbone. Then he looks up into her eyes and frowns. The look on the face of the four-foot-tall, shaggy-haired, bearded dwarf is one of absolute terror.

Ava says in a growl, "Run, now! Or I will have to make you wish that you had!" The dwarf is so scared he is unable to move. He just stares at her and is trembling from head to toe. She gives him a disgusted look and shoves him in the chest with a powerful push. He stumbles backward and collapses on his rear end. Now his grey eyes appear twice their normal size as he stares up at her.

At this point, it must be told that dwarves that suit up for battle are weighed down with exceptionally heavy armor. Most components of the dwarfish armor, except for the breastplate, which is made of cast iron, consist of layer upon layer of strengthened bronze plates. Even so, armored dwarves can run almost as fast as dwarves that are not wearing armor. That is because dwarves' leg muscles, albeit stunted given their short stature, are immensely powerful. It is said that a full-grown dwarf can lift a one-ton beluga with his or her legs and toss the creature ten feet in the air effortlessly! Dwarves are also rumored to run almost as fast as elves, which is around thirty-two point six miles per hour. (In comparison, the peak running speed of an athletic, sprinting human is about twenty-seven point five miles per hour.)

On the other hand, once a fully armored dwarf is lying or sitting on the ground, getting to his or her feet is a different matter entirely. The heavily laden, armored dwarf must move onto his or her stomach and push up on all fours until it is in the kneeling position. Then the power of the dwarf's strong leg muscles propels him or her to a standing position sharply. Fast and snappy, somewhat like a tightly stretched rubber band reverts to its original shape in a snap.

"I said now!" Ava bellows with annoyance as the dwarf frantically struggles to get to his feet. That he is still trembling uncontrollably is not helping matters much. He somehow manages to turn onto his stomach despite his fright.

Ava is annoyed at the slow pace with which the dwarf is struggling to stand. She bends down and grabs him by the collar. Then she yanks him with so much force he is flung over her right shoulder. Fortunately, for him, he lands on his feet five or six yards behind her. His legs are even now churning in an all-out, frantic sprint in the direction of the forest's safety. He is anxious to get as far away from the angry elf as possible.

Ava yells after him, "You are nothing more than a short, first-rate coward! You were about to shoot my friend, Steph, while her back was turned to you. Nothing gets more cowardly than that. Now, look at you go off like a scared, pint-sized, two-legged rabbit!" She grabs the dwarf's crossbow and quiver from the ground. "Hey, wait a minute shorty! You forgot your stuff." She hurls the dwarf's weapons to the forest and mutters with a sly grin, "Shorty the coward. I like that." She watches indifferently as the weapons soar high above the trees just to settle in the treetops over fifty feet away.

Steph calls out in a cautious tone, "Ava? Ava, is that really you?" She is still lying on the ground and trying to catch her breath with what she just witnessed. Her lovely brown eyes widen with excitement. Ava turns around, sheathes her blade, and slowly walks toward her. As she draws nearer Steph shouts, "It is you! But what has happened to you? You look different somehow. And how in the world did you just do what you did? It was nothing short of a miracle. All of it!" She looks at Ava's manica's. "Whatever it is that you are wearing on your wrists, I guess they are bracers, they somehow deflected that arrow." She shakes her head a few times and then stammers in an unsteady voice, "Then – then – then you, how did you do that? You just sort of flew in the air," she points, "way over there! Then you flung the dwarf over your shoulder just to chuck his bow and arrow," she points to the treetops where the bow and quiver are visible, "way the heck over there! How in the world did you do all that?"

Ava reaches down and holds out her hand. Steph clutches it and is yanked to her feet with an effortless tug. Ava immediately pulls her close in a hug.

Steph whispers, "Whew! I am glad you did not pull me so forcefully as you did to that stupid dwarf!"

Ava releases Steph from her strong embrace and steps back a few feet. She is smiling as she looks Steph up and down. "Look at you, Steph. You look none worse for the wear." She grins. "Or however that idiom goes." She pulls Steph in close and hugs her a second time. "I have missed you so very much. I was very worried too. You cannot believe the dreadful thoughts that were running through my mind."

"I missed you as well, Ava. A whole bunch, ten cents and a nickel." She gently pushes away and looks into Ava's eyes. "But will you look at who you have become? You look many years older and even prettier."

"I do?" Ava exclaims with a shocked look. "Years older? How is that? It is not like I have a mirror or something to examine myself. I hope I do not look too old. You know, like an old lady or something. Gosh, I do not want to be older than thirteen, at least not yet. However, much has happened recently, so I may have matured somewhat. I guess it was inevitable given everything I learned in Godroh's laboratory."

Steph is nodding her head knowingly. "Godroh you say? I should have known considering how important Jordyn had said he was to you. I am relieved you were able to meet with him." She looks Ava up and down again. "But no, not overly old, nothing like, let me see how I can put it." She slowly walks in a circle around Ava. "You are about the same height, maybe a few inches taller than before, but you look more," she frowns, "how can I put it kindly? More mature? More experienced? And your attire, Ava; it is different." She touches Ava's tiara. "Are you a queen or something, maybe a goddess? The tiara is beautiful. It looks like it is made of pure gold too!"

Ava says, "Wow! I did not realize I was wearing it still." She glances down at her cloak and tugs at her sleeve. The pure white cloak is different than the one she was wearing in Godroh's laboratory. "And I did not realize until now that I am wearing this cloak either. There is no time to think about it though because more important things are happening. At least I think they are." Her expression shifts sharply. "Are you alone? Are there others? Why are you on the trail all by yourself? I thought I saw smoke in the forest. Dragons and gryphons. Did you see them? Who is with you? I must know what you know."

Steph is about to reply when Ava places a finger against her lips to silence her. She cocks her head to one side. She is listening intently to far-off sounds. She says in a whisper, "Steph, we must go further inside the forest. I just heard Galadriel's voice." By Steph's surprised reaction, she presumes that she did not hear Galadriel's anguished shouts. She thinks to herself, keen hearing – just one more of my strange, awesome powers thanks to my creator, Athena. She grabs Steph by the shoulders, so forcefully that Steph is startled by her firm grip. Her eyes are pleading as she stares into Steph's eyes. "Come with me, and whatever you do, stay well behind me! I will protect you."

Steph dutifully follows along. She is smiling as she thinks to herself, and all this time I thought I was the one who was supposed to protect *you!*

3

Ava is leaping through the forest as quickly as an Earthly World white-tailed deer. She has traveled over two hundred yards when she realizes that Steph is not behind her. She also grasps that she has sprinted through the forest more quickly and nimbly than any other elf could travel. She turns around and rapidly retraces her steps. When she comes upon Steph a few seconds later, Steph is bent over and out of breath.

"Geez, Ava!" Steph manages to say between gasps for breath. "What in the world are you now, Mighty Mouse? Maybe you ate a couple of cans of Popeye's spinach, huh? There is no way I can keep up with you even though I run much faster now than before. You know when I was a much slower human being."

"I am sorry, Steph, but there is no time to waste. We goofed around too much back there chitchatting. I should have known better." She bends at the knees and places her hands on her upper thighs. "Crawl onto my back."

"Your back?" Steph says with an astonished look. "There is no way you can carry me, Ava. I will slow you down too much. Go on ahead. I will catch up." She adds with a scowl, "Maybe eventually if I'm lucky, and you give me an hour or more."

"No arguments, Steph. Please do as I ask because there is no way I am going to leave you behind, nor will I ever be separated from you again." She gives Steph an annoyed look. "Now stop your fussing and get on!" She chuckles then says, "Before I make you."

Steph is shaking her head. She is thinking there is no way Ava can carry her. She hesitates for a few seconds. Then due to the dirty look Ava is still giving her she decides it is best to do what Ava has asked. She crawls onto Ava's back. Just as she places her arms around Ava's neck, they are sprinting through the forest at twice the speed of normal, racing elves.

Steph is being bumped and jolted brutally as Ava hops over fallen trees and zigzags around wide tree trunks. She nearly loses her grip around Ava's neck a few times, but she somehow manages to hold on. Ava is even now quickening her pace.

"Gosh, Ava! You must be running as swiftly as a wolf if not faster. Leaping over fallen branches and tearing through thickets like they are not even there! And keeping as silent as a mouse as you run." She glances at Ava's hurriedly sprinting feet. They are nothing more than a hazy blur. "No, not running. On the face of it, you look like you are floating mere inches above the forest floor! Your feet are barely touching the ground if at all. You are that fast. You are amazing! Whatever Godroh did to you is totally cool!"

Ava whispers over her shoulder, "Thanks Steph but please hush. We are getting closer. They will hear you. And Godroh did not do anything to me; however, I owe it all to him because he brought out another me." After a few moments and taking one final, towering leap high in the air over a cluster of five-foot-tall bushes, she stops running.

Steph is amazed that Ava is not even breathing hard after covering which she estimates to be more than a mile in less than two minutes. She is about to say something when Ava whispers, "Okay, jump off. Unsling your bow and get ready to fight if need be." Steph hops off her back and positions an arrow on her bowstring. Ava says, "Those look nothing like the bow and arrows Doo gave you. Where did you get them?"

Steph whispers, "They belong to Nessa."

Ava gives her a startled look. Her tone is uneasy as she says, "Nessa? Is she okay? Please tell me she is okay, Steph."

"She is okay. Well, at least she was, and I expect she still is. She should be with Galadriel and Voronwe. We got separated somehow. It was when we were shooting arrows at attacking belugas. When I realized I was alone I retraced my steps and ended up on the trail. Anyway, regarding Nessa's bow and arrows, I did not want her weapons, but she threw them on the ground and walked away. She said I needed them and that she would use her tkalakn." Ava gives her a questioning look. "All I had was a fire iron, an axe, and this knife." She pulls the knife from her hip belt. "I stole them from Haldir's cabin when I escaped. My original bow and quiver of arrows, including my sword, were left behind when Siofra and Vena kidnapped me, just before Haldir marched me off to his cabin."

Ava says, "Pretty impressive. That is a good knife. Hopefully, you will not have to use it, but if you must I am certain it will do what it is meant to do." She points to their left. "I am going to go over there where I think Galadriel is." She grabs Steph's forearm. "Stay here, and whatever you do, do not move any closer. Stay hidden, okay?"

Steph nods her head then carefully slips the knife in her hip belt. When she looks up Ava is gone.

4

Ava is hiding behind a broad tree. She is mere inches behind two dwarves that are on the peripheral of a small glade that has no trees. There are seven dwarves in all. Two are flanking either side of Nessa and Galadriel. The seventh dwarf has his back to Nessa. By the Dwarven Crossbow Patch, he has on his right shoulder, she can tell he is one of the six leaders of the Dwarven Federation, presumably from the Mountains Cross territory. Then again, he could be a representative of the Mystic Mountains territory, but she doubts it.

Nessa and Galadriel's hands are bound behind them. Galadriel is standing, while Nessa is on her knees. She is bent over a fallen warrior and sobbing. Ava cannot see who the warrior is because Nessa's frame is blocking the fallen warrior's face. She could read Nessa's mind, thereby almost certainly revealing who the warrior is, but she is selectively blocking most incoming thoughts. In this manner, she can focus on the inner thoughts of the leader as he speaks. As she expected, he is thinking a whole lot more than what he is saying. She is also relieved that there do not appear to be belugas in the vicinity. Their presence would just complicate matters. Yet their stench is lingering in the air like a bad taste in one's mouth after eating a handful of freshly sliced, raw onions.

"It appears you are leaderless," the chief dwarf says to Galadriel in a harsh, threatening manner. "Therefore, I demand you surrender your Etanpioa."

"Surrender?" Galadriel says. Her tone of voice is cold and sarcastic. "I seriously doubt there is anything left of the Etanpioa. You and your disgusting gryphons with the assistance of the traitorous dragons undoubtedly made certain of that!" She gives the dwarf a look of utter hatred. "Attacking from the air while you perched royally, and safely I must add on the back of gryphon's is heretical. It goes against the code of warfare!" She spits at his feet. "So, do with us what you must, but we shall never surrender to the likes of you cowardly, puny scum!"

Without turning about Nessa cries out in a bitter tone, "I agree. You are the worst of the most terrible cowards." She is looking down at the fallen warrior. "How could you stab her in the back? There is nothing more cowardly than slaying another while her back is to you."

The leader whirls around and asks Nessa, "What is your name?"

"I shall never give you my identity," Nessa shouts as she slides on her knees to challenge the leader face-to-face. She stares up at him angrily for a few seconds. "Never!"

"Perhaps not now. But you shall eventually. All the same, I do believe you are one of the warriors our noble friend, Haldir, had mentioned. One of you is Nessa, and one of you is Galadriel." Nessa cocks her head to one side and scowls at him with a puzzled look. "You were not with the others of your Etanpioa, so I know you are one or the other. Therefore, you are a witness of serious wrongdoings by others that are loyal to Haldir."

Nessa recognizes he is referring to Siofra and Vena. If Ava were not blocking her thoughts, she would know this important piece of information as well. Nessa gives the dwarf a disgusted look. Then she coughs up a wad of phlegm and spits it at his feet. If that insult was not enough, and to Ava's complete surprise, she sticks out her tongue. Ava supposes Nessa learned the rude gesture from her and Steph. They were often seen sticking out their tongues at uncouth and abusive warriors when their backs were turned. Sometimes they stuck their tongues out at each other in jest. However, given her predicament, Nessa is not kidding around.

In response to Nessa's insulting manners, the dwarf kicks her in the chest brutally. With her wrists bound behind her, she is off-balance. She tumbles backward and fall sideward onto the fallen warrior's legs.

Ava can now see the face of the fallen warrior. It is the Bkotn leader, Elbereth. Her heart sinks immediately. Then her anger builds little by little. Nessa had said that Elbereth was slain while her back was turned. She wants to rush out of her hiding spot and take out the leader. But she knows if she were to do so, one or both of her dear friends could be injured if not slain. There simply are too many dwarves for her to attend to at once. She must come up with a plan.

Nessa is struggling to get to her feet. The leader proclaims loudly as he glares down at her, "I will strike a deal with you. I will permit the one who is Nessa to go free. But only if the other one acknowledges she is Galadriel."

Galadriel shouts, "Why is one more important to you than the other? Neither of us is either who you say anyway. We do not know this warrior, Galadriel."

The leader's head rolls back as he laughs forcefully. "Oh, I am certain one of you is Galadriel. Your leader told me that she, Galadriel, would have her revenge for me and my comrades attacking her combined Etanpioa. When I asked her why, she said, 'Because she is my loyal warrior that is why. She will assume my command no matter what you do to me. She will carry on the finest traditions of the Bkotn Tribe. She shall have her revenge.'" He stares at Nessa with a wicked expression then declares in an ugly tone, "Or words to that effect. Then she turned her back to me, insulting me gravely. That is when I destroyed her. I ran my sword through her body. Nobody turns their back on a dwarf!" He kicks a clump of dirt onto Elbereth's corpse. "No sense having her watch herself die, do you not agree? Better to die with dignity than watch as it happens."

The leader and those guarding Galadriel and Nessa have their backs to Ava. She has had enough of the leader's insulting words. She is especially angry he had so callously kicked dirt onto Elbereth's body. She quietly steps from her hiding spot behind the tree. She moves between the two dwarves and grabs the back of their necks. She squeezes hard and knocks their helmeted heads together brutally. Their stunned eyes roll back in their sockets momentarily then their eyelids slam shut. They are unconscious before they even crumple to the ground.

She could have destroyed them easily enough. But unlike the belugas that are nothing more than vicious, predatory, soulless beasts, she would never injure a dwarf deliberately. Only in self-defense or to save one of her friends. She steps over their lifeless bodies and strolls toward the leader. He and the others do not see her approaching. She stops five paces behind the leader.

"I am Galadriel!" The leader and the other dwarves turn around, their weapons at the ready. She winks at Nessa because she can tell from Nessa's thoughts that she is about to shout out her name. "So, my dear dwarf, you have before you the new leader of the fallen leader's Etanpioa." She bows deeply. "I am at your service, my dear sir." Then she says with a sly grin, "Even if your diminutive height is not deserving of my respect nor my service." She grits her teeth. "Also, as my leader professed before you killed her in a sickening, cowardly manner, I shall have my revenge for her and the others!"

Galadriel moves forward a few steps and shouts, "No, no you must not sacrifice yourself!" One of the dwarves grabs her by her long, red hair and pulls her backward roughly. Galadriel ignores the pain shooting across the top of her head and continues to shout. "You must not forsake yourself. I forbid it!"

The leader gives Galadriel a transitory, suspicious look. Then he says to Ava, "You are not Galadriel." He is looking her up and down in a suspicious way. "You do not carry Bkotn weaponry. You also wear a crown. So, if you are not Galadriel then who are you, I wonder?" He suddenly reaches down without turning around and grabs Nessa by the hair. He yanks her to her feet and pushes her in front of him with one quick move. Then he places the blade of his sword against her throat. He calls over his shoulder as he glares at Ava, "Bring the other warrior to stand beside me." Once Galadriel is standing beside him, he says to Ava, "Tell me who you are. Because either she," he gestures to Galadriel, "or she," he moves his knife against Nessa's throat causing her to shout out in alarm, "is Galadriel. Because I am certain you are not her." His head tilts to the side as he gives Ava a curious look. "So, my pretty, young warrior, I wonder who you are because, as I said, you are not Galadriel."

Galadriel shouts in a shrill tone, "I am Galadriel! I am the one you seek." She looks at Ava and says without a sound, "I am sorry."

"Do not listen to her," Ava screams as she takes one step closer to the leader. She stares at Galadriel straight on and says in a sharp tone, "Lia, do not speak again. That is an order! Do you understand?"

Understandably, Galadriel appears confused with what Ava has said. Still, she manages to mutter a shaky, "Yes, my Lady."

Ava says in a forthright manner, "I am Galadriel. I am the one you seek, and I demand that you free my warriors. After you do, I shall go with you willingly. You have my word." She reaches down, unsheathes her blade from her thigh, and tosses it to the ground. She removes the quiver from her shoulder and tosses it along with her longbow to the ground. Then with her arms extended, she crosses her wrists feigning surrender. "I give up myself freely. Just let them go and allow them to bury our fallen leader. I implore you to do the honorable, and I shall do the same. You have my word."

A dwarf leans in close to speak to the leader. Ava reads his thoughts as he says in a whisper, "Bralead, I may be mistaken, but this could be the elf that the wizard had mentioned."

The leader, that Ava now knows as Bralead, eyes her suspiciously. She reads his thoughts as he considers what the dwarf had said.

If she is the O Poica Katharos, I must comply with her request. If I refuse to do as she asks, she will destroy all of us in the end. Therefore, I must let the others go as she has commanded of me. Perhaps we can negotiate because I believe she will honor her word and go with us willingly.

Bralead does not know that Ava has read his thoughts. Yes, she will honor her word and go with him voluntarily. Then at the right moment, she will have her revenge. She is certain the outcome will be favorable, at least for her and her friends. That is because she is conversing with Fluescere telepathically. Fluescere set off reading Ava's thoughts from the moment she called out to Steph on the trail after she tumbled out of the looking glass. Even now Fluescere is high above them circling, waiting for Ava's command to intervene if necessary.

Ava says, "Do you and I have an accord, my dear sir, Bralead?" She is pleased that he seems shocked because she knows his name. His thoughts further reveal his anxiety knowing he might be face-to-face with the all-powerful O Poica Katharos. Nevertheless, he struggles to maintain a poker face as he nods his head. Purposely emphasizing his name to irritate him further, she says in a sardonic tone, "May I ask your family name, *Bralead?*"

At first, he is hesitant to tell her his family name. But his ego quickly overtakes his prudence just as Ava had hoped. He says in a self-important, narcissistic manner, "I am Bralead Bonefursome, son of Thralotum. I am the Dwarven Federation Leader representing the distinguished Mountains Cross dwarves." He gives her a roguish look. "And may I ask your true name?" He removes his helmet and bows courteously. "Milady, who I am certain is not the one I seek, the warrior, Galadriel."

"I am Avaïnoάel, O Poica Katharos. I command you to release my fellow warriors. Do as I order or embrace death!"

Bralead steps back with an anxious look of surprise as do the others. He removes the sword from Nessa's throat and releases her. She quickly turns around and falls to her knees. She is kneeling over Elbereth's body. Galadriel pushes past the other dwarves angrily and kneels beside her.

Bralead stands motionless for a few moments and gawks at Ava with a distrustful look. He is about to say something when she shouts.

"Yes, I am she, so do as I say now!" She gives him a nasty grin. "Or you will regret it." She takes two steps toward him. She is now less than ten feet away. "Then again, would you like me to prove who I say I am?"

Never taking his eyes off Ava, Bralead shouts to the dwarf that had spoken to him earlier, "Tuzumri, seize the O Poica Katharos' weapons. Bring them to me. Then cut the prisoners' bindings. The rest of you watch the elves to ensure they do not do anything foolish."

Tuzumri approaches Ava warily, his eyes searching hers for any sign of hostility. He is trembling slightly. Just as he reaches down to gather up her weapons, she throws her arms high in the air and hollers, "Boo!" He collapses to the ground then scrambles on all fours to stand beside Bralead and his companions. When at last he manages to get to his feet and turns around, Ava giggles. That is because his bushy, burgundy beard surrounding his chubby cheeks seems to be trembling as much as the rest of his undersized, plump frame.

His comrades are also laughing. Bralead gives them a disgusted look which results in their self-disciplined bearing almost immediately. With an ugly sneer, he shakes his finger beneath Tuzumri's nose. Between tightly clenched lips he seethes, "Never show cowardice in the face of the enemy! If you ever behave in such a manner again, I will destroy you! Do you understand?"

Never taking his eyes off Ava, Tuzumri replies in a meek voice, "I understand. I am sorry."

Ava reaches down and grabs her weapons. In reaction to her sudden move, two of the dwarves point their armed crossbows at her. Bralead raises his hand. He is gesturing for them to lower their weapons. Ava is relieved they are abiding by his gesture. The guards are edgy, understandably given who she is, and she does not want to run the risk of Galadriel and Nessa being injured. She nods her head at Bralead then she tosses the weapons to his feet. She gives him a cross look and demands in a shout, "Now, cut their bindings. Return their weapons. Then allow them to attend to their fallen leader, to give her a proper burial. They will not try to harm you. I give you my word."

"Cut their bindings and return their weapons," Bralead shouts. He motions with a slight wave of his hand for Ava to draw nearer. "Please, Milady, if you will follow me."

Tuzumri says in a shaky voice, "Should we not bind her first?" Bralead gives him a disgusted look then pushes him aside.

Ava says in a cordial tone, "That will not be necessary, Tuzumri. I promised your leader I would accompany him. Therefore, I will do so without my wrists bound. It is the honorable way." She gives Bralead a nasty glance. "Your leader understands that if he were to bind me, it would be the last thing that he or the rest of you would ever do." With a nasty smirk, she adds, "I give you my word on that as well."

Nessa has been watching as Ava and the others have been talking. She jumps to her feet. "Ava, you must not allow yourself to be taken! I beg of you!" She looks down at Galadriel. "You must stop her!"

Galadriel gets to her feet and says in a gloomy but firm voice, "Nessa, she knows what she has to do. You know it as well. Trust her, okay? Besides, there is no way we can force Ava to do anything. She is going voluntarily, and she has given her word. Just like us Bkotn, she cannot go back on her word."

Nessa nods her head even as tears well up in her eyes. Then she gives Ava a strange look and taps the side of her head with her forefinger. She is gesturing for Ava to read her thoughts.

Ava gives her a slight nod. She says to Bralead, "Before I accompany you, I would like to stand here for a few moments to consider further what I am about to do. For you know I am about to put myself in peril. I would also like to pay my respects to Etanpioa's fallen leader with a moment of silence. Will you extend me that courtesy?"

Bralead pulls his sword out of its sheath. With a nod of his head he says, "Why of course, Milady. As you wish. But I must remind you that you gave me your word, and you are now my prisoner. If you go back on your word, I will slay your friends." He grins deviously. "Naturally, you will undoubtedly destroy me and my comrades in return. Hence, I shall die a hero having confronted O Poica Katharos bravely, and willingly."

Ava moves closer to Elbereth's body. "Why of course I understand, and I thank you. I gave you my word. I will accompany you." Bralead stands directly behind her. He presses the tip of the sword to the small of her back. She closes her eyes and reads Nessa's thoughts. She is saying a silent prayer at the same time.

Voronwe is safe, Ava. He is nearby and probably watching everything right now. There is something you must know. He confided in me earlier, this very day, that whilst he likes Galadriel as a friend and a fellow warrior, he adores you. And not because you are Avaïnoǽel. He loves everything about you, Ava – your mannerism, your courage, the way you talk, even the way you walk. Everything. Do you understand what I am telling you? Can you read my thoughts? Ava is blushing. She nods her head just as a timid smile appears on her face. Nessa's thoughts continue.

He told me how he felt when the two of you held hands in the plateíazan, not once but two times. How he looked in your eyes and felt lightheaded and woozy. How he cannot get you out of his mind. He said he will follow you to the ends of the Inner World if he must. Galadriel and I will link up with him as soon as we bury Elbereth. Anyway, I just wanted you to know – to give you something good to consider. May the gods give you safety. I love you my dear friend, Avaïnoǽel – my Ava. Always.

Ava opens her eyes and looks at Nessa. Nessa is crying. Ava says without a sound, "Thank you. I love you too." Nessa nods her head then kneels to attend to Elbereth's body. Galadriel kneels beside her.

"Okay, Milady," Bralead says in a respectful tone as he lightly pokes Ava in the back with his sword. "If you will move beside me." He turns to face the other dwarves. They are directly behind him and Ava.

The two dwarves that Ava had knocked out are still wobbly and not looking at all well. One of them is trying to stand up straight and not having much luck. Ava considers he, and probably the other one as well, has a concussion. She regrets that she had to hurt them. But it was much better than the alternative had she given them the means to resist.

The others have their armed crossbows pointed at the ground. Bralead says to them, "Watch her closely." Then addressing the two dwarves Ava had injured, he says, "You two keep your weapons unstrung. I do not want you shooting one of us by accident until I am certain you are feeling normal. You were unconscious for a long time. Do you understand my command?" The groggy dwarves nod their heads.

Ava gives one last glance in Nessa and Galadriel's direction as she passes them. They look up at her and nod their heads. They are replying in a non-verbal manner to what she had said without a word.

"Fluescere."

CHAPTER 6

THE EVILNESS OF BRUTALITY

*"I do not know with what weapons World War III will be fought,
but I do know that World War IV will be fought with rocks."*
—*Albert Einstein*

1

"Where are you leading me?" Ava asks.

Bralead replies in a no-nonsense manner, "First to speak to Haldir.
Then I expect he shall summon the all-powerful, Wendigorium, or take
you to him." He takes a few moments to gauge Ava's reaction. Seeing
nothing he says in a sarcastic tone, "It is my understanding you seek to
parlay with the all-powerful creature, Wendigorium. Am I correct?"

Ava replies in an impassive, carefree tone, "I look forward to
parlaying with Wendigorium." She grins. "Then I intend to destroy
him." Bralead gives her a curious look but says nothing.

Tuzumri moves closer to Bralead. Ava reads his thoughts as he
whispers. "Do you not think, my dear leader, that perhaps we are
imperiling ourselves needlessly?"

Bralead stops walking. The others stop as well. He gives Tuzumri a
cross look. "What do you imply when you say we may be imperiling
ourselves needlessly?"

Tuzumri gives Ava an anxious look. "If the prisoner is O Poica
Katharos as she says, she will destroy us in the end." His eyes seem to be
begging as he suggests, "Perhaps we should allow her to escape without
making it look intentional." He glances around. "This is the perfect spot.

No one will know. We can tell Haldir she overpowered us. As you realize, after we turn her over to him, we will be expendable. The evil wizard will find an excuse to get rid of us, to conceal the evidence of our involvement." He glances at Ava once more. "Or we could eliminate her and tell Haldir she ambushed us. That we simply were defending ourselves."

Bralead places his hand on Tuzumri's shoulder. His expression is gentle and understanding. He says in a soft tone, "Oh, Tuzumri, I have always liked you." Tuzumri gives him a questioning look then smiles cheerfully. Bralead gives him a brief, reassuring smile in return then says, "Hence, I am sorry I must do this – sniveling, shameful coward!"

Ava quickly looks away because she knows that Bralead had meant to run his sword through Tuzumri's stomach. She wanted to stop him, but with four crossbows aimed at her back, she knew she would not stand a chance.

Right now, Bralead is wiping the blade of his sword clean on his shirtsleeve as he looks down at Tuzumri's bloodied body. He grabs Tuzumri's crossbow from the ground and tosses it to one of the dwarves. "Carry this. And let this sorry excuse for a dwarf fighter be a lesson to all of you. If you show cowardly leanings like this worthless scum, you too will suffer his fate. Leave his body for the belugas. Now move!"

As they resume walking Ava is wiping away her tears. She had read Tuzumri's thoughts just before his heart stopped. She will never forget them. She says to Bralead in a threatening tone, "You do know that you will pay dearly for what you did to that innocent, young dwarf, yes? You too are a coward because you gave him no chance to defend himself!"

Bralead replies offhandedly, "Yes, I will pay. Of that I am certain. But when I do, I will hold my head up high unlike that sniveling piece of spineless trash. Now, keep moving, and I beg of you to keep your thoughts to yourself."

Ava considers wordlessly, unlike you who unknowingly cannot keep his thoughts to himself. Thoughts that reveal you are dreadfully frightened of me! She gives him a quizzical look. And what in the world do Siofra and Vena have to do with all of this?

2

Voronwe is standing next to Galadriel and Nessa. Galadriel is clutching his hand tightly. He is tempted to let go of her hand, but he is too embarrassed. He likes her, and he is certain she likes him as well. But in an entirely different way. Still, he is too much of a kind-hearted elf to let go of her hand. Besides, he considers she needs comforting right now, so he figures holding her hand cannot harm anyone. Or so he thinks. Moreover, he sort of likes the feeling in his stomach when they are holding hands.

"How long has your leader been dead?" Voronwe asks. "May I assist in burying her?"

"We found her shortly before Ava arrived," Galadriel replies. She wipes at her tears. "As you can see by the wound, she was impaled from behind by a dwarf's sword."

Nessa is kneeling over Elbereth's body and adjusting her clothes. She whispers, "Cowardly. She could not even defend herself properly!" She looks up at Galadriel and Voronwe and sees they are holding hands. She gives Voronwe a questioning look then shakes her head with an air of disgust.

Voronwe looks down at his and Galadriel's clasped hands. He gives Nessa a feeble smile and shrugs his shoulders. Nessa shakes her head once again and promptly looks away.

Galadriel says, "We do not have the necessary tools or time to bury her properly." She looks down at Nessa. Nessa is nodding her head. "We cannot leave her like this, and we cannot carry her." She lets go of Voronwe's hand and touches Nessa on the shoulder. "Do you agree that we must—"

Without replying, Nessa gets to her feet. Her head is hung low as she slowly walks from the glade inside the forest to collect branches and leaves. They will serve as kindling to cremate Elbereth's body in an open-air pyre. Voronwe follows her.

Galadriel kneels next to Elbereth's body and crosses her fallen leader's arms over her chest. She removes the arrows from Elbereth's quiver and positions them to point down in a circle around her body. Then she cuts the string of Elbereth's longbow and places the bow along the length of her torso. She removes the sheathed blade from Elbereth's thigh. She is entitled to wear the blade on her thigh as the provisional Bkotn leader. Still, she carefully wraps it in a cloth and stows it in her satchel.

Elbereth's blade is etched with an insignia that distinguishes her as the Tribe's Bkotn leader. If Galadriel is lucky enough to stay alive, she will present the sheathed blade to the Tribe as proof that Elbereth is dead. Afterward, the Tribe's elders will select a new leader. Galadriel is hopeful it will not be her, even though she is the interim leader of the Etanpioa, or what is left of it if anything at all. She appreciates she is too young and inexperienced to assume command of an Etanpioa permanently. Moreover, she is sick and tired of witnessing the senseless loss of life. Just the thought of commanding others to sacrifice their lives makes her feel sick to her stomach.

Nessa and Voronwe are carrying their second armloads of branches when Nessa stops and whispers, "Why, after everything you told me about Ava you were holding Galadriel's hand? It is not proper. You know that!"

Voronwe replies, "I could not find it in myself to release her hand, nor could I ask her to do it." He shrugs his shoulders. "I could tell she needed comforting. I did not want to hurt her feelings. So, I did nothing."

"You did nothing?" Nessa says. "You did not want to hurt her feelings? Yes, you did something – something awful to my best friend, Voronwe. You continued to lead her on which is deceitful. And all the while you were holding hands, you had a lovesick smirk on your face. And I could tell by your eyes that you were feeling rather good about yourself. What is wrong with you? Galadriel thinks that you like her as much as I know she likes you." She gives him another disgusted look and says, "No wonder our Bkotn code prohibits male elves from joining our ranks! If you hurt Galadriel further, I swear I will beat you to a bloody paste!" She turns away in a sulk and says to herself in a whisper, "Ándreste! They are nothing but trouble for us female elves!" She and Voronwe make five additional trips to gather wood for the pyre. Even though they occasionally exchange glances, they do not speak.

Once Elbereth's entire body is surrounded and covered by the kindling, Nessa removes a flintstone and piece of metal from her satchel. She sets fire to a clump of dried leaves in the center of Elbereth's body. Then she and the others watch as the pyre ignites.

"Sleep well our fearless leader," Galadriel says in a whisper. Then she takes Voronwe by the hand and leads him out of the glade in the direction Ava had gone.

Nessa walks behind them. She is teary-eyed and glaring at the back of Voronwe's head as he walks hand-in-hand with Galadriel.

3

Ava and the dwarves are much closer to the area where the main battle occurred. It had rained hard during the night, so the ground is still wet. Consequently, nearly all the fires caused by the dragons' fiery flames have died out. She considers that is a good thing for a couple of reasons. She correctly assumes the elves and dwarves that survived almost certainly are in the vicinity where the residual smoke is wafting through the trees. She expects the surviving fighters on both sides were traumatized enough from the dreadful effects of the fierce battle. They do not need to contend with raging forest fires as well, especially those who are wounded and not ambulant.

She also expects it is there, where the battle ensued, that she will meet up with Haldir. Because surely, or so she assumes, he would have been in the vicinity during the battle. Egging the dwarves in any way he could with his evil spells and intimidating threats. She also suspects, thankfully in error, that she will see many countless scores of dead or dying elven warriors. Indeed, over two dozen warriors have lost their lives. However, thankfully, the combined Etanpioa's were not wiped out completely. Many elves survived with the majority wounded, some seriously. A few are in critical condition.

The dwarves conducted a ruthless, surprise attack from the air with overwhelming numbers. Many were expert archer dwarves mounted on gryphons. Others were carried by gryphons in groups of four or five. There were over sixty gryphons in all. Most were shot down.

Approximately fifty dwarves survived the battle. They were fortunate to disembark from the gryphons before the beasts were shot from the sky. As is the dwarves' custom, they are attending to the injured of their species. The handful of elves that are not wounded must attend to their own.

Ava is continuing to communicate with Fluescere telepathically as she walks next to Bralead. The dragon is eager to come to her rescue. All the same, Ava is cautioning her to stay hidden within the clouds.

Steph is following Ava and the dwarves. She is getting closer with each passing minute. Hence, she correctly assumes that Ava can read her thoughts. She is purposely thinking a couple of things. Her most important thoughts are updating Ava where she is in relation to the small procession. "Okay, now I am behind the scorched tree with the weird hole in the tree trunk. You passed it a minute or so ago. Do you remember?

Ava nods her head.

Steph's other thoughts are purposely designed to occupy her and Ava's time. A few of her thoughts cause Ava to smile. They are her introspective recollections of fun things she and Ava shared since they arrived in the Inner World. Right now, Steph is thinking the words to her Antiquom rendition of "America the Beautiful." Just as she ends the song with the turn of phrase, *then crown thy good on Ava's hood, from grain to grain'n tree!* Ava can no longer control her emotions. Tears of glee well up in her eyes, and she bursts out laughing. Steph very nearly bursts out laughing as well as she sees Ava's reaction. Luckily, she quickly covers her mouth with her hand stifling the laugh.

Bralead is giving Ava an annoyed look. "What is so funny?"

Without looking at him she replies in a flat tone, "None of your business, butthead."

After a few minutes, the scent of scorched wood and the distinctive, unpleasant smell of death is borne by the prevailing breeze. Ava's distraught, negative reaction to the odors is unsurprising. Yet, astonishingly, she is smiling. She is smiling because of Steph's thoughts that seem to be shouting in her head.

Ava, Galadriel, Nessa, and Voronwe are here with me! I am so happy! Nessa told me that you said your dragon's name just before you left. So, unless I hear from you vocally or telepathically, I will wait until we see Fluescere. Gosh, I wish there were a way you could converse with me as well. However, I think we are too far away for me to distinguish your thoughts. Perhaps when we get closer.

Ava is also interpreting Galadriel, Voronwe, and Nessa's thoughts in turn. She can tell that they, like Steph, are anxious but awaiting whatever signal she or Fluescere will give them. Then for some odd reason, she reflexively focuses on Nessa's thoughts. She can tell that Nessa is overly disgusted about something. Then she envisions what is bothering Nessa. She is staring at Voronwe and Galadriel's hands. Their hands are clutched tightly as they dart in and out behind trees.

"Why you two-timing, double-crossing, lying trickster!"

Bralead says, "What was that you said?"

Now Ava is seething with annoyance, more so that Bralead is bugging her than envisioning what Nessa is thinking. She gives him an unpleasant look and says, "As I said a moment ago, butthead, butt out! Besides, your time is limited. I am certain you are aware of that fact! So, if I were you, I would concentrate on staying alive a little while longer and stop talking to me!"

Now she is interpreting the other dwarves' thoughts and does not like what they are thinking. Although she cannot see what they are doing – they are walking behind her – she concludes they are scheming to ambush Bralead. She also considers, correctly, that if they manage to eliminate him, she will be their next target. She may be clever and quick, but she doubts she can deflect four or five crossbow arrows coming at her at once. She stops walking and turns around. Bralead does not notice that she has stopped. She scolds, "Bralead, stop walking and turn around!"

He turns around just in time to see that one of his comrades is lowering his crossbow. The rebellious dwarf had been aiming it at him. He screams to the dwarves, "What are you doing?"

Ava is extremely upset, but she manages to say in a casual, uncaring tone, "They are conspiring to murder you while your back is turned to them."

Bralead gives her a doubtful look. Then remembering that one of the dwarves seemed to be lowering his crossbow, he says angrily, "Is she correct? Did you intend to slay me while my back was turned?"

In response to Bralead's allegation, all but one of the five dwarves raises their crossbows. The other dwarf is still too groggy from being knocked out to react. Two of the dwarves' crossbows are aimed at Bralead. Two are aimed at Ava.

One of the dwarves that Ava had knocked unconscious – he is aiming his weapon at her – says to Bralead, "You seem to have no problem murdering an Etanpioa leader while her back was turned. Or one of our comrades as he stood defenseless. You politicians from the mine cities are the same. Nothing but cowardly, well-paid do-gooders." He gives Ava a nasty look. "You are just as bad. Attacking me and my friend while our backs were turned and knocking us unconscious. That too was cowardly."

As Ava stares at the insulting dwarf with a passive expression, she is reading Steph's thoughts. Steph is telling her that she and the others are within striking distance. She looks at the dwarf straight on and pretends to reply to his insulting comments. Though she is speaking out loud for Steph's benefit. "If I were you, I would move just a bit closer, so you know what I am thinking. Just a little should do it."

Bralead and the other dwarves are giving her inquiring looks. Two of the four lower their bows. They are staring at her as she has just gone crazy.

The insulting dwarf says, "What in the gods' names are you talking about? Move closer so I will know what you are thinking? What nonsense!" He turns to his comrades and chuckles. "I always knew elves were stupider than they look. Must have something to do with their stupid-looking ears."

Ava thinks to herself, how about now, Steph?

Steph replies telepathically, I have you, Ava! Tell me what you want us to do. I will tell the others.

Ava is purposely staring at the dwarves one after another to stall for time. She says to Steph via her voice-thoughts, take out the five. I will deal with the leader myself. He is the one standing beside me. And whatever you and the others do, do not shoot to slay them! I repeat – do not slay them. Just wound them in the legs or better yet if your aim can be perfect, strike their crossbows to disarm them! There has been enough bloodshed today.

Ava gives the dwarves an endearing smile one after the other. Now all of them, except the lethargic dwarf and, of course, Bralead, are aiming their crossbows at her. She says in an innocent tone, "Can you not read my mind? I have been told that you can. You must be from another area.

The dwarves I have met can understand others' thoughts." Right away she realizes that Steph has told the others what she wants them to do. She unexpectedly shouts, "Now!"

Before the dwarves can react, Ava grabs Bralead by the forearm in the blink of an eye. She pushes him to the ground forcefully, lies next to him, and places him in a solid chokehold. She says in his ear, "You struggle, try to escape, you die."

Seconds later arrows are flying at the dwarves. Two of the five are disarmed by well-placed shots on their crossbows. Two others, which include the dwarf that is still lethargic and unarmed, are struck in the upper thigh. They collapse to their knees screaming and start to writhe on the ground with agonizing pain.

Ava is thinking to herself, four elf warriors, four well-placed arrows, four disarmed or wounded dwarves. She looks up just as the dwarf that had insulted her lets go of his arrow. He is standing less than four feet away. She hurriedly covers Bralead's body with her own to protect him. Then, as before, she watches as the speedily flying arrow races toward her. She analyzes its path and raises the manica's to her forehead. The arrow is deflected in a shower of yellow sparks. She is on her feet a nanosecond later.

The dwarf is stringing a fresh arrow on his longbow. She dashes to him and reaches out in a move as fast as a flash of lightning to snatch the crossbow from his grip. Then she punches him square in the face, purposely holding back so she will not crush his skull. He collapses on the ground next to his two wounded comrades. Ava knows his profusely bleeding nose is shattered, but she does not care. She notices that the two dwarves that were disarmed are already leaping like scared rabbits toward the safety of the forest. She turns to look at Bralead. He is getting to his feet.

"You saved my life, O Poica Katharos. How can I ever repay you?"

Ava gives him a disgusted look. "You cannot repay me, nor do I want payment. You will face a Bkotn tribunal for murdering," she points her finger at him and screams, "no, for *cowardly* murdering Elbereth, the Etanpioa leader while her back was turned." She walks up to him and yanks him upright by his collar. His feet are barely touching the ground as she screams, "I ought to do the same to you. Because you are a cowardly, presumed leader of dwarves. You even murdered one of your kind as he stood in front of you defenseless. You are nothing more to me than the dirt on the bottom of my shoes!" She yells over her shoulder, "Galadriel, Voronwe, Nessa, anybody, take this scumbag prisoner." As she glares into Bralead's frightened eyes, she hisses between her clenched jaws, "Or do whatever you must because I never want to see him again. He disgusts me." She opens her hand, thus releasing him from her powerful grip. He collapses to his knees. Then she walks over to the two injured dwarves writhing on the ground. She grabs their crossbows from the ground and tosses them to the forest. Then she turns to face Steph and the others. They are running toward her. By reading his thoughts, she can tell that Bralead is staring at her through his bloodshot, teary eyes. Before she can react, or it could be she purposely does not, he removes the dagger from his hip belt and takes his own life.

4

Dusk is settling in Artonia. Ava and the others are a mile away from where the main battle had occurred. They are warming themselves before a blazing fire. Fluescere is nearby. She and Ava are exchanging thoughts.

A dwarf is sitting next to Ava. His name is Jotog. He is the younger of the two dwarves Ava had knocked unconscious when she banged their heads together. He is young, perhaps only fifteen years old. He is a bit more alert than before, but Ava wants to keep an eye on him. She suspects he has a concussion in addition to his injured thigh. If he were to go with the other dwarves, he could die from his head injuries. She promised him that she will ask Galadriel to set him free once she is certain he has recovered sufficiently.

Earlier, Voronwe, Galadriel, and Nessa attended to Jotog and the other dwarf that was struck in the thigh. They wrapped the dwarves' wounds while Ava and Steph whittled branches for walking sticks. The elves also patched the broken nose of the insulting dwarf Ava had punched in the face. He was glaring at Ava the entire time his face was being attended to. He would not tell Ava his name, but she had asked Jotog.

"His name is Dammuth. He is ruthless. He is also notorious for holding a grudge forever. I would be careful of him if I were you. Never turn your back on him. Never challenge him."

Ava had assured Jotog that Dammuth did not frighten her in the least.

Despite Voronwe's strenuous protests, a few hours later Galadriel allowed the three injured dwarves to go free with a warning. "Just so you know," she had said gravely, "if we see each other on the battlefield we will treat you like all other hostiles. I can assure you that we will show you no mercy."

Once they were set free, the patched-up dwarves limped to the forest. After she had set the dwarves free Galadriel turned to Voronwe and snapped, "We cannot keep prisoners. You of all combatants should know that. Our priority is to attend to the injured and imprisoned warriors of the Etanpioa's." She gave him an exceptionally cross look then said in a tone that could turn one's stomach, "Both mine and Nessa's as well as yours."

The reason for Galadriel's nasty look and tone of voice was obvious to Ava and Nessa and later to Steph when Ava told her. Her look and tone were acutely obvious to Voronwe as well.

Earlier, Nessa had told Galadriel what Voronwe had said to her about his fondness for Ava. She explained that she did not want Galadriel to be deceived further. She did not want Galadriel to be hurt when and if she found out. She also said that Voronwe, just like all other male elves, was wishy-washy when it came to affection.

Galadriel's initial reaction when she learned that Voronwe had been two-timing her was utter sorrow. She cried on Nessa's shoulder for a few moments. Soon afterward, her sorrow turned to outright anger because she had been so easily misled. She was also embarrassed by what she had done. She had held Voronwe's hand quite often, hugged him more than once, and even kissed his cheek a couple of times.

Once Voronwe's asinine, fickle actions were out in the open, he immediately apologized to Galadriel and then to Ava. He also apologized to Nessa for making her feel uncomfortable. But Nessa wanted nothing to do with his apology.

"You deceived two of my closest friends. I will never forgive you. Please leave me alone."

Later, Ava and Galadriel made a pact that they would let Voronwe work out his feelings. That sooner or later he would decide which one of them, if any, he liked the most. In the meantime, they would show him no affection, but they would extend him the courtesies he deserved as a fellow warrior. Nothing more.

Ava had said to Galadriel, "Because you and I both know we like him a lot." Galadriel had nodded her head. "So, if you agree we will not compete with each other. It is unladylike. Besides, we have more important things with which we must worry."

*****

"So, what is the plan?" Nessa asks Ava.

"I will leave the logistics and planning to Galadriel. Although I am certain she will accept our input." Galadriel nods her head. "As for me, I need to hook up with Haldir. He and I must have a conversation in due course. I just hope it is more cordial than the first time we met, well, metaphorically speaking. We never met. Only that I was subjected to his cruel magic."

Steph says, "Do you think that is wise, to meet up with him?"

"I am not certain. But this much I know, and so do you. Going way back to when we first met. I am here for a purpose. To confront Wendigorium sooner or later. Considering what happened to you in Haldir's cabin and what I experienced before Flame rescued me, I am certain Haldir is our first step. Also, from what I saw in Godroh's laboratory, I, we, all of us must fight to prevent even more terrible things from happening."

"Why are you certain Haldir is our first step?" Nessa asks. "Also, can you tell us what you saw in the Great Wizard's laboratory?"

Ava places her arm around Nessa's shoulder. "I do not believe I can faceoff with Wendigorium until I first meet up with Haldir. As far as what I saw in Godroh's laboratory, I shall keep that to myself for now if it is okay." Nessa nods her head.

Ava has noticed that Voronwe has not said a single word since nightfall. It is important to her, to all of them, that he understands they value his input. She says, "What do you think, Voronwe? Do you think it is wise for me to seek out Haldir? Or do you think he will come to me?"

"Well, if I were to venture a guess, I would say he will come to you. After all, he captured you once, and he probably held Steph hostage to lure you out. But now, now that you have become stronger, he will come to you. Or at a minimum, he will make it easy for you two to come together. From what I know from the Timbre legends, Haldir is always sporting for a challenge." He adds with a sincere smile, "And you definitely will give him a challenge. Frankly, I suppose he will battle to his death if necessary."

Galadriel says, "I think Voronwe is correct, Ava." She glances in his direction but does not establish eye contact. "With one exception."

"What is that exception?" Ava asks.

"I believe Haldir knows he cannot compete with your powers, although he will try. No, I think he has no other choice but to come to you because to do otherwise will end his life or, at a minimum, ruin his reputation."

Steph suddenly blurts out, "You know, Galadriel, you may have hit the nail on the head!" Galadriel and the others, except for Ava, give her a questioning look. "Sorry, hit the nail on the head means you are one hundred percent correct. Anyway, whenever Wendigorium's name came up in Haldir and my conversations, he appeared to be scared, genuinely scared."

Ava looks at Steph with a startled expression. "Scared? Like he really was afraid of Wendigorium?"

"Exactly," Steph replies. She says to Galadriel. "Is that what you are implying?" Galadriel nods her head.

Ava says, "Well, if you are correct, then he has no other choice than to seek me out or, as Voronwe said to get close so I will know." She stretches her arms out wide and yawns loudly. "I only hope it is not tonight because I am bushed. Who wants the first watch?" She starts to giggle.

"What is so funny?" Nessa asks.

Ava says, "Flame just informed me that none of us has the first watch. She intends to stay awake all night. So, sleep tight my dear friends because you have earned it."

*****

521

Ava is gazing dreamily at the twinkling stars that are peeping beneath the trees. She has not slept a wink. She and Fluescere have been considering the previous day's events via their telepathic thoughts. Then suddenly one of the females snorts in her sleep. Ava cannot help herself as she laughs. She is not certain, but the hilarious-sounding snort seemed to come from Steph. Steph has been in REM sleep since the moment she closed her eyes.

The random snorts and occasional soft moans by the others make Ava feel homesick. Which reminds her of when her sister, Jami, produced evidence that she snores like everyone else. As the saying goes, the proof was in the pudding, and Jami was holding the pudding of proof in her hands. It was a cellphone recording of Ava's snoring episodes the previous night. The recording included some dreadfully loud, truly very funny, drawn-out snorts. The two of them could not help but laugh at the disgusting sounds. Likewise, Ava was finally obliged to admit that she snored like everyone else in the world. Jami meant to keep the recording on her cellphone because, as she had said to Ava in jest, "In case you ever want to tattletale on me for something." But Ava had erased the recording later that day. She had the passcode on Jami's phone.

Ava is glad that her female companions are sleeping through the night with the knowledge that Fluescere intends to stay awake. Yesterday was an exceptionally challenging day, especially for Galadriel and Nessa. That their legendary, courageous leader was marched away from her Etanpioa then struck down from behind by a gutless dwarf is especially traumatic for them. And Steph is still recuperating from her trek through Artonia after being held prisoner by Haldir. Although, unsurprisingly, Steph's ordeal over five days has not affected her emotionally. She is just worn out physically.

Voronwe is equally depressed. He has also lost fellow warriors. Like the others, he is anxious about those being held prisoner. Ava knows he is also feeling miserable because of what he did to Galadriel. He had harmed Nessa as well and feels she no longer trusts his judgment. In that respect he is correct. Still, as Ava and Fluescere had discussed earlier, part of the blame rests with Galadriel. As Nessa had mentioned, Galadriel was lovestruck from the beginning, so much so as she had put it, "She went way overboard with her needless fondness, thus violating her oath and risking everything. I am glad she was not caught. I am also certain she has learned her lesson."

Ava could tell that Galadriel was especially downhearted before she fell asleep. Even now she is tossing and turning restlessly. In addition to Elbereth's death, she is embarrassed because she toyed with Voronwe's emotions. Holding his hand far too often. And even going so far as hugging him and kissing his cheek. Only for him to say to Nessa that he preferred Ava's company to hers. More importantly, and rightly so, she is desperately anxious about the fate of the imprisoned Etanpioa warriors, especially the wounded. She is the leader of the combined Etanpioa, even if she is in absentia. The leadership position was passed to her when Elbereth was murdered. She understands she must do something to save the warriors. But, as she had said to Ava, what can five elves and a dragon do against heavily armed, cruel dwarves?

Even Ava does not have the answer to that question. At least not yet. Still, she is confident she ultimately will come up with a solution, a battle plan of sorts. With Fluescere's assistance, the five of them could surprise the dwarves and maybe overwhelm them. Especially now that the gryphons and dragons have disappeared. But the odds are not in their favor.

Also, having witnessed firsthand the callous brutality of the dwarves, Ava knows a surprise attack could result in many if not all the captive and wounded warriors being murdered. That Bralead slew Elbereth while her back was turned, and he had impaled Tuzumri coldheartedly, are but two examples of the dwarves' ruthlessness — and their heartless unpredictability. Therefore, she is certain the dwarves would not hesitate to destroy every warrior of the Etanpioa if for no other reason than out of spite. Besides, she knows the dwarves are keeping the ambulatory warriors alive only because they will someday serve as slaves in the dwarves' mines. She correctly assumes that the dwarves belong to the Joini clan.

As for the belugas possibly getting involved, Ava is not overly concerned about them. She has seen no sign of the smarter species, the déxypnos. As for the duds, as disgusting as it is to fathom, they probably have scattered after having their fill on fallen dwarves, warriors, and gryphons. That is, unless someone like Strum is leading them which she doubts. Then again, she considers, I cannot rule anything out at this point.

"So, you must go?" Fluescere says telepathically, interrupting Ava's contemplations. "And you want me to remain here. I must say Avaïnoåel, I find it difficult to understand why I cannot accompany you. You can benefit from my assistance. You know that."

Ava's thoughts reply, "Yes, I know, Flame. I deeply appreciate your concern. However, you must remain here to protect the others. If I need you, I shall seek your assistance." She reaches in her satchel and withdraws a quill, vial of ink, and a bit of parchment. She moves closer to the fading cinders of the firepit and scribbles a short note.

> *My dear, sweet Steph,*
>
> *Ever since we met, I have come to grasp the worth of a true friendship like ours. I am honored to be your friend, and I will always hold our friendship dear to my heart. Since the beginning, you have known I have a purpose here in the Inner World. Something in my subconscious is telling me that it is time I fulfill that purpose. I would be lying if I were to say I am not frightened. I am. Yet I am likewise resolved to meet my task head-on with dignity. If I do not see you or the others ever again, please know I will be looking down from my resting place and sending warm blessings and unending love your way. Please give my love to all our Inner World friends, especially Nessa, Galadriel, and the Mégedale queen. Give her daughter, my namesake, a loving squeeze for me, okay? Always with love & respect ~ Ava Noelle PS – Flame will not allow any of you to be in danger. I told her to whisk you away to safety if necessary. You will know it is time with three short bursts of smoke from her nostrils.*
>
> *Love always, your bestie, Ava*

"Ava, are you leaving right now?" Fluescere's voice-thoughts exclaim. "Surely you are not going to go away in the middle of the night?"

Ava reaches down and stuffs the note inside the pocket of Steph's cloak. Then she drops to her knees and kisses Steph's forehead lightly. She picks up her weapons and satchel.

"You know where I am going, Flame," she says wordlessly. "And do not attempt to follow me. You promised you would protect the others."

Fluescere replies, "Yes I did. I will keep my word, my Lady. Please be careful. If you need me, just let me know."

"I will," Ava replies telepathically. She looks down at Steph. She says in a whisper, "Goodbye, Steph. I hope to see you soon. Stay safe and God bless." She glances at Nessa and Galadriel. The two best friends are lying side by side. Galadriel has her left arm around Nessa's shoulders. Unsurprisingly, she reflexively is protecting Nessa even as she sleeps. Steph folds her hands over her heart and blows them a kiss. She looks over at Voronwe. She is not surprised that he is wide awake and staring at her. She walks over to him.

"Something tells me you must go now," Voronwe says in a whisper as he gets to his feet. "Am I right?"

"Yes, now is the time to meet Haldir face-to-face. He is out there waiting for me. I can tell by reading Siofra and Vena's thoughts." Voronwe gives her a questioning look. "Siofra and Vena are with him."

Voronwe nods his head. "I see. Do you wish for me to accompany you? Three against one are poor odds, mainly considering one is an evil wizard."

"No, but I thank you. I will be okay. He does not intend to harm me. At least I hope not. If he tries, I shall be prepared. As for Siofra and Vena, they are hardly worth a second thought." She sees that Voronwe's expression has changed markedly. She holds up her hand to stop him from saying anything further just as he blurts out, "Ava, I would like to—"

She is shaking her head from side to side vigorously. She says in a flat tone, "I already understand what you are going to say, Voronwe. Just so you know, I appreciate your considerate sentiments. My answer consists of a yes and a no. Yes, for the most part, I forgive you. I do not feel hurt or slighted in the least. Yet you hurt Galadriel and Nessa, and what you did, especially to Galadriel, was wrong. That bothers me more than anything; however, I intend to move on. This leads me to the no part of my answer. You and I have no path going forward apart from being fellow warriors. Please understand it is not personal. It is just that I fear my quest over the coming years will be long and arduous. I simply do not have time for a close relationship. I hope you understand."

Voronwe nods his head in a glum way. He opens his arms out wide and says, "May I?"

Ava hesitates a few moments. She truly does not want to hug him. However, because today may be the last day they will ever see each other, she gives in. They embrace for a few moments then she pulls back and looks him straight in the eyes. "Galadriel likes you a lot. There is no doubt in either of our minds. She will forgive you eventually. Just give her time to heal and for you to regain her trust. As for Nessa, I seriously doubt she will ever forgive you. Yes, you hurt her. She can accept that. Like me, she is ready to move on. However, you hurt her best friend, Galadriel, even more. That I fear she will never accept. But it is what it is. In the interim, please do everything in your power to keep Nessa, Galadriel, and Steph safe; that is if I do not return. Can you do that for me?"

Voronwe bows deeply and whispers, "Yes, my courageous, O Poica Katharos. You have my word."

Ava nods her head, turns, and disappears a few seconds later.

CHAPTER 7

DECENCY VERSUS WICKEDNESS

"I will place you under my spell and take you to meet Wendigorium."
—*Magnus NightMancer*

1

It is a little after daybreak when Ava strides up to Haldir. Even though his back is to her, she can tell he knows she is approaching. He turns around slowly then gives her a friendly smile. Siofra and Vena are still facing the other way. To frighten the two traitorous, former warriors, she yells in a purposely loud, exuberant voice, "Hello!"

As she had hoped, and to her delight, Siofra and Vena whirl around on their heels so quickly they just about trip over their own two feet. Ava wishes she has a smartphone, so she could capture the terrified looks on their faces for prosperity. She turns up her nose and says contemptuously, "If you do or say anything – and I mean anything at all to tick me off – you can kiss your duplicitous corpses goodbye." She moves toward them a little causing them to back away. "You are lucky I do not kick your butts here and now because of what you did to my friends, Steph, Nessa, and Galadriel."

She turns away and extends her hand to Haldir. "We meet at last, well at least in person. You and I have much to discuss." She lets go of his hand and sneers at Siofra and Vena. "Why in the world are you with these two idiots? You must know they are traitorously duplicitous. They will deceive you too if given the chance."

Haldir gives her a sly grin. "They know better than to mislead me, Ava. I owe them a debt of gratitude for providing me with the necessary information about the Etanpioa's. Otherwise, we could not have done the remarkable things that my associates, the dwarves, belugas, and gryphons, carried out."

Haldir is about to say something else when Ava shakes her head "no" to shut him up. She is incredibly angry because he was gloating when he talked about the attack on the Etanpioa's. Suddenly, weird names and details pop in her head seemingly out of nowhere. Her subconsciousness is allowing long-forgotten memories to come alive.

"First off, what do you say that you and I get something straight. You are Magnus NightMancer son of Caster NightMancer of the ancient Earthly World Greek regime known as Hellas; aka Haldir of Mountains Cross." Haldir seems genuinely surprised with what she has said. Her thoughts to scream without a sound, "Yes, yes, yes!" She has him on the defensive.

"That is your first name and surname as well as your father's name and his Earthly World title. Am I correct?" Her eyes are downturned as she says in a mocking tone, "With the name Haldir being nothing more than a creepy moniker you would prefer others of the Inner World entitle you." She grins at him deviously adding, "So, as to make you seem more frightenable. But only because the word Haldir means "tremendously evil being" in ancient Fortunomy. Whereas your rightful name, Magnus NightMancer, is no biggie. Am I correct?"

Haldir is staring at her with a dazed look of utter bewilderment. He is thinking to himself that he is dreadfully scary to others even without using his false name, Haldir. He places his hand on his chin and cocks his head like he is pondering what to say. After a few moments, he simply nods and says nothing.

"Well, good," Ava says as she gives Siofra and Vena a disgusting glance forcing them to draw back a few steps. "Therefore, Magnus NightMancer, you will address me by my rightful name, as either Avaïnoάel or O Poica Katharos. I in return shall address you as Magnus or NightMancer." She moves a few steps closer and places her hands on her hips. "Do we understand each other?"

Haldir says in an offhand tone, "Well, Avaïnoáel, it seems you know more about me than I had anticipated. It has been a least a thousand years since my rightful name was last spoken. Also, my father's name and title have not been expressed in well over two millennia." He gives her a quizzical look. "By those of the Earthly World. May I ask how you came to appreciate my proper name and that of my father?"

"You may not," Ava says candidly. "That is my business." To change the topic, she says brusquely, "Why did you hold my friend, Stephanie JoAnne Galanos, hostage?"

Haldir throws his head back laughing. He looks her straight in the eyes. "That, Avaïnoáel, is *my* business and mine alone."

Ava bites her lower lip then nods her head a few times. "Touché. I suppose I deserved that." She is getting more annoyed as the minute's tick by. To vent her frustration, she jerks her head at Siofra and Vena and gives them a nasty look. She is gratified to see they shy away. She thinks to herself, Cowards! Turning to Haldir she says, "What now may I ask?"

Haldir completely surprises her with his uncaring tone as he replies. "I will place you under my spell and take you to meet Wendigorium."

Now it is Ava's turn to laugh, which she does to a greater extent than Haldir. She squares her shoulders and says in a relaxed tone, "Under your spell, Magnus? You have got to be kidding me." She locks eyes with him. "Do you honestly think I will allow you to hex me? I have been hexed once before, and I dare say I did not like it. And that was when a friend did it." Her head tilts sideways. "But goodness, I almost forgot. You hexed me too when I was near the Solenom; did you not? Consequently, Magnus, I seriously doubt you will place me under your spell." She adds with a smirk, "Although I sincerely dare you to try."

"I am sorry, but I have no other choice," Haldir grumbles. He bends over and places his staff on the ground. Then as he straightens, he removes the wand from his robe. "Hence, shall we dispense with the pleasantries and begin?" He points the wand at Ava, or to where *Ava had been* standing two seconds before. With a perplexed expression, he turns in a wide circle, his wand at arm's length. When unexpectedly, the wand is knocked from his hand and chucked a good distance away. He quickly retrieves his staff from the ground and rushes to recover his wand.

At the same time, Siofra is shouting as she points. "I think Ava is over there, behind that tree." A split-second later she catches a brief glimpse of a blurry shadow racing toward her. Before she can even begin to figure out what it was, Ava is standing behind her.

"Siofra, do you not know it is impolite to point!" Ava yells just as she places her forearm around Siofra's neck and squeezes evenly. She does not intend to choke the vicious elf. She whispers, "Remember how you did this to Galadriel?" She squeezes a bit harder. "Only you were holding a blade against her neck making her bleed. I do not need to do the same. Just so you know, I could snap your neck with a mere flick of my wrist. Now stand still!"

Vena is standing five or six paces away. She heaves her lance with brute force. Ava promptly moves her left manica to deflect the tip of the lance as it sails toward her left side. Yellow sparks fly everywhere. It rebounds off the manica and flies out of sight.

Vena cannot believe what has happened. Ava gives her an angry look then, before Vena can react, she rushes over and pushes her in the chest forcefully. Vena sails through the air and lands hard on her backside a good distance away. She leaps to her feet, turns, and races toward the forest. She is screaming, "Oh, I pray to the gods, what just happened?"

Ava is standing behind Siofra once more. She, like Vena, is so overwhelmed she cannot move. Ava's tone is one of absolute disgust as she whispers, "You are the saddest, most revolting warrior of the Inner World. I honestly thought you had murdered Nessa. And look what you did to Vena. You corrupted her to be just like you. You are a disgrace to the Bkotn and their esteemed code." She suddenly notices that Haldir is reaching down to pick up his wand. She springs to action once more.

All at once, Siofra dashes from the clearing to what she considers is the safety of the forest. Unluckily, just like Vena, she will never be heard from again. While the duplicitous duo will meet up shortly, in due course they will disappear from the world of the living. Because the bewitched Forest of Artonia is in control of all things that enter its realm.

Ava is standing in front of Haldir a second later. She is clutching the wand he had just picked up from the ground in her left hand. He gawks at the wand for a moment, and then his gaze moves ever so slowly to focus on Ava's beguiling eyes. Right away, like the countless, innocent victims he has hexed over the millennium, he is held spellbound. Taken captive. Unable to move. Powerless to do anything but groan softly as Ava snaps his wand in two and drops the shards at his feet. He starts to shiver because he realizes that the inevitable is taking place. That he, like his shattered, magical wand passed down from his forebears, is now nothing more than a helpless, former magical wizard. A broken man. He gazes into Ava's eyes for the longest time. He is searching deep within her soul for any sign of mercy, anything to provide him amnesty. Seeing none, a tortured frown appears on his ancient face. Then his eyes close for the last time. He too will become a victim of Artonia's mystique, and the Inner World will be freed of one of the most vicious wizards of all time.

Ava is not certain if he can hear her. Even so, she says, "I am deeply sorry, Magnus. But you and I both know your time is up. The Prophecy bespoke of this day, and it has arrived at last." She places her right forefinger against Haldir's forehead.

Veritasium!

2

When Ava shouted her new, previously unknown spell, Veritasium, she had performed it without a second thought. As before, her subconsciousness brought forth the word and the ensuing outcomes to the forefront of her awareness. Outcomes which were the veracity, the truthfulness, of the complex details of Haldir's most recent thoughts. Her spell also yielded many of his greatest, top-secret memories.

Like a movie film multiplied many times to a swiftness nearly the speed of light, the cerebellum of Ava's brain is processing Haldir's thoughts and memories. Meanwhile, the brain's hippocampus is decoding and encoding Haldir's thoughts and memories equally fast. Soon, as if compelled by magic, the brain's amygdala will decide on its own which memories are to be stored and those that can be discarded as nothing more than trivial trash.

While all this is happening inside her brain, Ava is standing motionless and unemotional. She is observing Haldir's body as it decays precipitously, melting down like a square of chocolate in a saucepan. She could have walked away without any shame given his evilness. However, she wants to pay her respects. It is a decent thing to do. Because she recognizes he once was a walking, talking, intelligent creature that turned evil. Probably because of his upbringing and the teachings of his equally wicked father. Although she does not know this, she could not move right now even if she wanted to. The frontal lobe of her brain's cerebellum is swamped at present to permit any motor movement.

Her brain is also deliberately dismissing Haldir's final thoughts that had focused on his imminent, self-imposed, ill-fated death. That he too understood at the last moment of the Prophecy's forecast spoken to him by his father, Caster, long ago. That once he was defeated by O Poica Katharos, and his wand ruined, he would die naturally. Right then and there. As he is. Here and now.

Ava, understandably, is more focused on what lies ahead. *When and by what means* she can face off with Wendigorium. Still, she compels her brain to pause momentarily and focus on a few interesting aspects of Haldir's past and his mysterious, top-secret memories.

She is startled to discover that Godroh's title, Godroh of Mystic Mountains is nothing more than a catchphrase, a fictitious name. Like Haldir, he had adopted a pseudonym. Godroh's real name is Blade Gruqiohr WyrmBlood. He is the firstborn child of DragonCloud WyrmBlood. He has a twin brother, Ineuvious, and two sisters, Emal and Eitthe. Haldir's recollection of his twin brother is mysteriously blurred. Yet his recollections verify that Godroh's sisters, like his parents, are deceased.

Godroh's mother was a benevolent wizardess. Her title was Athamia Oakheart, the Enchantress. Surprisingly, she was a close advisor to Athena and Artemis. Ava is also shocked to learn that Godroh was born in 105CE, making him and his enigmatic twin brother almost two thousand years old! She suspects Haldir was just as old if not older!

She also learns that like Haldir's father, Caster, Godroh's parents dwelt during the reign of Zeus, Athena, and Ares, and other immortals, both good and evil. Godroh's father, DragonCloud, like his wife, Athamia Oakheart, the Enchantress, was a mighty sorcerer and adviser to the gods; yet because he was born of dragon blood, DragonCloud was altruistic, all-influential, and extremely powerful. According to Haldir's memories, legends state that DragonCloud's eyes were those of a serpent, and when he fought evilness, flames sprang from his mouth.

Well, that satisfies something I had envisaged some time ago, Ava considers to herself. That Godroh does have a last name; or, if truth be told, a completely different name – Blade Gruqiohr WyrmBlood, the twin son of DragonCloud and Athamia Oakheart, the Enchantress. Interesting to say the least. Especially considering that the word "wyrm" in his surname means a dragon without legs or wings. I wonder. Could Flame and Godroh, I mean Blade be related? Also, what is with Haldir's murky memory recollection of Godroh's twin brother? Is Godroh's twin still alive? Oh well, now is not the time to dwell on frivolities to satisfy my curiosity. I can always recall Haldir's memories and mull over them more thoroughly after all this is behind me.

She consciously refocuses her attention on the *when and by what means* she will confront Wendigorium.

It is then she notices that Haldir's remains have all but disappeared. She also spots something shiny lying next to what is left of his quickly rotting wooden staff. She bends over and picks it up. It is surprisingly heavy and appears to be made of pure gold. She turns it over in her hand and recognizes it as a *prostátism* as it is termed in Fortunomy. A prostátism (like its equivalent word "prostátis" in the Earthly World ancient Greek language) is a reversed pentagram, surely the evilest symbol of the dark arts. Interestingly, prostátism also means patronus. Ava guesses the charm was once attached to a woven cord that has also decayed. With a shrug of her shoulders, she stuffs the charm in her pocket and walks away from the grisly scene.

3

Ava returned to where Fluescere and the others were staying a while ago. She immediately set out to discuss a proposal to assist the Etanpioa warriors. She says to the others, "So, that is the plan. If you have doubts or suggestions, now is the time to speak up." She is pleased that the others are nodding their heads as they glance around the circle. It is apparent they agree with the basic premise of her plan.

Galadriel is the first to speak up. "I think the plan is sound, Ava. However, to make certain we are all on the same page," she glances around the circle, "I would like to go over the finer details one more time." The others nod their heads in agreement. She looks at Ava. "Is that okay?"

"Definitely," Ava says. "There is no room for error." She whispers to Fluescere, "Flame, please speak up if you have any suggestions. Because everything depends on you." Fluescere replies via telepathy that she will.

Nessa exclaims in a hushed tone, "Ava, you must know that all of us think it is remarkable that you and Fluescere can communicate telepathically. You truly are amazing. I suspect you can read anyone's thoughts, yes?"

Ava says with a grin, "Thank you, Nessa. Yes, I can read just about everyone's thoughts, the exception being Haldir's. I was unable to read his thoughts until I put him under that spell I cited. Then his recent thoughts and memories came pouring in like a torrential rainfall. I could do nothing but stand there and allow them to wash over me." She touches her finger to her forehead. "But now they are here in this ole noggin of mine. That is how I came up with our plan. Unless he was purposely deceiving me while he was vanishing, they should work." She glances around the group. "I hope our plan works because if it does not, we are going to be in a world of hurt." She notices Voronwe is giving her a curious look. She purposely does not look at him. "And just so all of you know, I intentionally block your thoughts nearly one hundred percent of the time. I do not want to invade your privacy. I could never."

*****

It takes nearly an hour for Ava and the others to re-evaluate the minuscule details of her proposal. Finally, after some back and forth, along with Fluescere's input, the group agrees to the ultimate plan.

On Ava's command, Fluescere flies to where the dwarves were last known to be holding the prisoner's captive, where the main battle occurred. Fluescere sees that the primary group has moved further along the trail than expected. She returns to hover briefly above Ava and the others to report the column's movements. "No seriously wounded elves are with the dwarves' column," she tells Ava via her voice-thoughts. "Although there are ambulatory prisoners, those able to walk. I estimate fifteen if not more slightly wounded, ambulatory prisoners. Perhaps thirty-five to forty warriors total, which includes some that do not appear to be injured. There could be more. I am not certain. The dwarves are heavily armed and number around fifty, give or take a few."

"What about the more seriously wounded warriors?" Ava says out loud. "Did you see any sign of them? Are they still alive?"

"Yes, they are alive," Fluescere replies. "Mercifully, the dwarves did not slay them probably because they wanted to leave the area as soon as possible. They remain where I last saw them, yesterday. No dwarves are guarding them or attending to their wounds. There appear to be about a dozen seriously wounded warriors that were left behind."

Ava notices the others are looking at her with anxious expressions. They want to know what Fluescere has said about the wounded. She exclaims, "They are alive! Fluescere estimates a dozen or so. No dwarves are guarding them. They seem to have been abandoned." Her thoughts quickly turn to Fluescere once more. "How far along is the column? Are there any stragglers?" She crosses her fingers because if there are no stragglers in the column the plan may not work.

"Yes, there are a few warrior stragglers," Fluescere replies. "Naturally, they are guarded by the dwarves. But most of the warriors and dwarves are in the central and forward parts of the column. Only two dwarves are guarding the stragglers as they struggle along the trail. I estimate ten or twelve warriors in all."

"Did the dwarves happen to notice you as you flew overhead?" Ava says.

"Oh, I am certain that they did. A few looked up at me as I flew above them. But they may have thought I was nothing more than a lingerer of those that had attacked the Etanpioa. Except for the extraordinary ombre color of my scales, we dragons all look the same."

Ava says, "Okay then, take one last, quick look at the column then report back as soon as you can." She quickly briefs the others on the fate of their fellow warriors. The serious and critically wounded were left behind to either die or tend to their own wounds. The main column of dwarves and their warrior prisoners are hastily moving along the trail. As she and the others had hoped, some of the slightly wounded, ambulatory warriors are straggling behind the main group. She says to Galadriel, "Have you decided which one of you is going to assist the wounded? We must get them supplies, especially things to help patch their wounds and ease their suffering."

Before Galadriel can reply Voronwe raises his hand. "I volunteered. After I attend to the more seriously injured as best as I can, I will divvy up our supplies." He gestures to the two satchels lying on the ground. They are chockfull of foodstuffs and supplies collected from all their satchels. "Then I will make haste to Mégedale, so Earendil can dispatch an Etanpioa to rescue the wounded." He shrugs his shoulders. "After that, who knows? Hopefully, I can hook up with the rest of you wherever you may be."

Ava places her hand on his shoulder. "That is brave of you, Voronwe. I cannot think of anyone other than Flame that can swiftly travel the trail to Mégedale to alert Earendil. I wish I could dispatch Flame to carry you to Mégedale, but I hope you understand. She is crucial to saving the other warriors. If the column gets south of the Unseen Valley – and I suspect it can without anything untoward happening to it – then it will be too late to save our warriors."

Voronwe replies, "I understand, and I appreciate your concern."

Ava says to the entire group, "There is no room for error. We do not have adequate supplies to sustain us more than a day or two, perhaps three if we stretch them. So, the four of us need to be extra careful and stay together. Otherwise, we could fail." She turns to Voronwe and grasps his hand. She gives it a firm squeeze. "Be careful, and God speed. We hope to see you soon."

Fluescere lands in the clearing a minute later. Voronwe quickly secures the straps of the two fully loaded satchels on her barbs. Then he pulls himself up on her back. She immediately soars in the sky in a northerly direction toward the wounded warriors. She returns ten minutes later. Ava, Steph, Galadriel, and Nessa hop on her back. Soon they are flying in a southerly direction high above the zigzagging Kuoino toward their objective.

4

A few minutes later Galadriel whispers, "There they are," she points, "down there to our right." She is sitting behind Nessa. Like before, Nessa wanted to sit at the front.

Ava says to Fluescere via telepathy, "I do not see a clearing where you can land near the rear of the column. Do you?"

"I do not," Fluescere replies. "And the trail is too narrow for me to land."

Ava says with a groan, "Okay, I guess we will have to do it the old-fashioned way." She turns her head and says to Steph who is sitting behind her, "We will have to go with plan B." Steph nods her head, but by the look on her face, Ava can tell she does not like it. Ava leans forward and says to Galadriel, "Plan B." Galadriel gives her a thumbs up and leans forward to tell Nessa what Ava has said.

Nessa whispers excitedly, "Yes! This should be sensational. Let's do it!" Without waiting for Ava's command, she quickly crawls forward onto Fluescere's neck. Ava is scared to death at how quickly and nonchalantly Nessa had crawled forward. But she does not know that Nessa has done this once before, so she is unhesitant and unafraid. Nessa reaches back with her left hand and takes hold of the coil of rope that Galadriel had looped over the leading barb of Fluescere's back. Making certain one end of the coil is securely wound around the barb, she tosses the balance of the coil over the side.

A second later she is climbing along the rope toward the treetops. All the while Fluescere is flying above the trail slowly. The dragon is also coasting as much as possible to lessen the noise of her massive wings and to reduce downwash. Once Nessa is at treetop level, Fluescere hovers momentarily allowing her to place her right foot on the highest, strong limb of a tree. Once both feet are firmly planted on the tree limb, she gives Fluescere a thumbs up and disappears.

Galadriel follows her a few seconds later.

When Galadriel lets go of the rope and disappears in the treetops, Ava slides forward on Fluescere's back. She unloops the rope from the barb and tosses it over the side. Now that Fluescere is free of the dangling rope, she says, "Okay, Flame. Let's go." Fluescere responds by flying as quietly as she can toward the front of the column.

Steph enfolds Ava's waist with her arms. "I guess this is how the Navy Scals do it back home, huh?"

Ava replies with a grin, "Yeah, I think you are right. But I bet they would give anything to have Flame as transportation rather than a noisy helicopter. Also, unlike hostiles back home, I seriously doubt the dwarves would ever consider what we just did and are about to do." She quickly goes over in her mind the elaborate details of their rescue plan.

The preliminary step called for Galadriel to dispatch one warrior to attend to the wounded. The wounded is their priority. Ava is certain that Galadriel would have picked Voronwe even if he had not volunteered. That Voronwe could travel to Mégedale much quicker than the others to alert Earendil; that is, after seeing to the wounded and giving them much needed medical and food supplies. Whereas Nessa and Steph, like Galadriel, had never been to Mégedale. Therefore, convincing Earendil to do something promptly would be tricky at best. Certainly, Ava could have done what Voronwe set out to do. However, she knows that the others would be more vulnerable and probably outmatched by the dwarves if she had. Besides, she is the only one that can communicate with Fluescere effectively. Given all that, Galadriel would have realized Voronwe was the best candidate even if he had not volunteered.

Next, their overall, ongoing strategy involved performing one of four basic, supplementary plans.

Plan A involved finding a clearing in the forest close to the stragglers then advancing on the column from the rear. There was no clearing in the vicinity, so Ava was forced to enact plan B. It consists of two parts.

So far, the first part of plan B seems to be going off without a hitch. Nessa and Galadriel are to the rear of the column where the stragglers are located. They should have the element of surprise to take out the two dwarves guarding them. Then they will arm the warriors with the dwarves' weapons. Nessa and Galadriel's being there should inspire the other warriors to regain their fighting spirit as well. Subsequently, they will advance toward the main body of the column as quickly as they can. Ava selected Nessa and Galadriel to enact this part of the plan. She knew there was no way she and Steph could climb from the treetops to the ground like their much better-trained friends. She suspects that given her new powers she could have leaped from Fluescere's back and would not be injured. However, she did not want to risk it. Besides, she had told Steph that she would never let her out of her sight going forward.

The second part of plan B is where Ava and Steph come in. Fluescere will fly them to a spot at the front of the column. In so doing, and with a bit of luck, they will place the dwarves in a quandary with armed warriors to the front and rear. Ava is hopeful that outright panic will ensue as a result. Also, considering the unswerving courage of the Bkotn and Timbre warriors, she is certain they will weigh in to crush the dwarves without hesitation. Assuredly, Fluescere's presence will help significantly as well. She might even turn the tide in their favor if things were to go south.

There was also a plan C and a plan D. In the event no stragglers were trailing behind the main group, plan C entailed Fluescere skyrocketing to the front of the column. Then the foursome would hop off her back, start shooting and hope for the best. Plan D was the simplest but less attractive of the four plans. Abort and figure out a new plan before it became too late to rescue the warriors.

Fluescere's involvement is going to be crucial. Given her large size and imperviousness, she will be a formidable adversary. That is if the dwarves do not surrender voluntarily. Ava cautioned Fluescere to be careful to not injure any warriors. She also told Fluescere to not attack recklessly. In the end, unlike unintelligent, voracious dud belugas that slay others for sport then devour their remains, dwarves are intelligent beings. True, they are nowhere as empathetic as elves. Not even close. Yet Ava does not want any dwarves to be slain or even injured seriously if possible. And she does not want a warrior hurt as well.

Now Ava and Steph can hear shouts from the rear of the column where the stragglers are located. Nessa and Galadriel have begun their attack, hopefully with the aid of some of the warriors. Ava looks down and is relieved to see that this part of the Kuoino is less dense with trees. The trail itself is wide enough for Fluescere to land safely. She says in a whisper, "Okay, Steph, Fluescere, this looks like the spot. It is time to go. Please stay safe, and I wish you both the best of luck. Oh, and one more thing. I thank you for being my wonderful friends. I could never have made it without either of you as we traveled in Antiquom. I love you both." Steph and Fluescere reply with similar words of affection.

With her sword held high above her head, Ava jumps off Fluescere's back and races to the front of the column.

EPILOGUE

"I fear not death, Avaïnoἀel, O Poica Katharos.
Although I fear you shall by and by."—Wendigorium

Ava and the others' extraordinarily bold maneuver, confronting the column from the front and rear, had achieved remarkable results. They had liberated the warrior prisoners without suffering a single casualty on either side.

Fluescere's presence had turned the tide in their favor. After she offloaded Ava and Steph, she immediately produced a nonstop torrent of red-hot flames along the entire length of the column. At first, she directed her carefully controlled flames a few inches above the warrior and dwarves' heads. Naturally, the dwarves fired a barrage of arrows at her which did no harm. Then Fluescere began to lower her stream of flames gradually until the entire column was forced to their knees. It was at that point that the elven warriors were told, presumably by Galadriel, to lie down on their stomachs. Meanwhile, the dwarves kept shooting arrows at Fluescere.

Ava saw that the dwarves' arrows were ricocheting everywhere, putting everyone at risk. She stepped from behind Fluescere and shouted, "Dwarves of the Federation of Mountains Cross, you cannot escape. I will compel my dragon to destroy you one by one if you do not surrender. Give yourselves up now!"

Suddenly, two dwarves near the center of the column released their arrows. Ava was their intended target. She could tell that Fluescere was about to destroy the arrows midflight. "No, Flame, no! Your flames will strike some of them. I have got this!" As in the past, she speedily assessed the arrows velocity and trajectory. One was about to hit her in the chest. The other was going to strike the upper thigh of her right leg. She quickly jumped to her left then reached out with her right manica and deflected them one by one in a shower of sparks. They fell harmlessly at her feet.

By now the dwarves and warriors were gawking at her. When suddenly, a dwarf at the back of the column jumped to his feet and hollered, "I command *you* to standdown!" He glanced around at the kneeling dwarves. "Are you not proud dwarves of Mountains Cross? Or are you cowards? Get to your feet now and fight!" Not a single dwarf complied.

By his bandaged broken nose, Ava knew that the shouting dwarf was Dammuth. She was not surprised by his boldness. Jotog told her that he was ruthless, that he would hold a grudge forever. She placed her hands on her hips and glared at him without emotion. Then she did the unthinkable which caused the entire column of warriors and dwarves to gasp loudly in one voice. She turned her back on him!

To this day, Ava does not know why she turned her back to Dammuth. Perhaps it was due to her utter contempt of his praised brutality. Or maybe she wanted to intimidate the dwarves further so they would not resist. It does not matter. Yet there was one thing she knew for certain at the time. She did not want Fluescere to direct a burst of flames at Dammuth. Nor did she want any of her team or trigger-happy, recently freed warriors to shoot him. She shouted over her shoulder, "Fluescere, fellow warriors, pay him no mind. He cannot harm me."

Just then a chorus of panicky gasps spread through the group anew. Dammuth had placed not one but three arrows on his crossbow. He was aiming his crossbow at Ava. She grasped his intent because she had read Steph's thoughts. "I know, Steph, I know. Please do not worry. I got this."

Dammuth shouted, "Turn your back on me you insolent elf? How dare you!" Then he pulled back hard on the crossbow string and let his arrows fly. Ava immediately turned around. She crossed her manica's over her upper chest and deflected two of the arrows in a shower of sparks. She had calculated their trajectory perfectly. Then surprising herself, she reached out and caught the third arrow by the middle of its shank a split-second before it struck her in the stomach! A second later she hurled it effortlessly in a straight line toward Dammuth. Its velocity was so swift he did not have time to dodge. It struck his helmet a split-second later at a spot that was a fraction of an inch above his forehead. She never intended to slay him, so she had aimed the arrow precisely where it struck.

Dammuth removed his helmet and studied it for a few seconds. He shook his head in amazement. Ava had hurled the arrow with so much energy, it had pierced both the front and back of his helmet. He stared at her blank faced for a few moments then dropped to his knees. Someone in the column whispered, "It is she, O Poica Katharos!" Now everyone was gawking at Ava.

She yelled in a strong voice, "Yes, it is she, the O Poica Katharos. I want the dwarves to lie on their stomachs. Now! And let me warn you," she glanced at the handful of elven warriors that were armed, "if any of you get to your feet, my comrades will destroy you." She grinned then said between clenched teeth, "Perhaps I may do it myself." Then she commanded in a shout, "Members of the combined Etanpioa, seize their weapons."

The Etanpioa warriors retrieved their confiscated weapons from the dwarves. Then they crowded the dwarves in to a large group and placed them under guard. There were fifty-three dwarves in all. None were wounded making Ava believe they had left them behind to fend for themselves.

Once everything was in order, Galadriel stated she was assuming command of the combined Etanpioa. The Bkotn warriors already knew she was their rightful leader. However, there was a bit of grumbling from the Timbre. Galadriel knew she had to boost their confidence in her as their rightful leader. She withdrew Elbereth's blade from her satchel then held it out so everyone could see it. She could tell that the warriors recognized the blade as that of an Etanpioa leader.

Later, Galadriel selected an unhurt, particularly muscular, and robust-looking Timbre warrior as her second in command. His name is Arun. The former second in command of the combined Etanpioa had fallen in battle. So had the other leaders of the individual Timbre Etanpioa's. Finally, she asked Lia to resume her position as third in command. She wanted to choose Nessa for the position, but Nessa was not having any part of being a leader.

She had explained, "Galadriel, please remember what Elbereth had said. She said Lia was to have a place in the leadership hierarchy once everything was back to normal. That Lia would eventually be third in command. Besides, I want nothing to do with a leadership role, at least not now. Otherwise, I will not be able to have any fun!"

Galadriel convened a working group that consisted of Lia, Arun, and herself. Its singular purpose was to discuss the fate of the dwarves. Ava did not want to participate. The working group quickly agreed with the recommendation that the dwarves should be freed. Their weapons should be returned to them as well. The dwarves were facing a long, arduous march through unsafe areas, including Artonia and uncharted territory well beyond. It would probably take them at least a month to reach Mountains Cross. They had to protect themselves along the way and to obtain food. Hence, the only civilized tactic was to return their weapons. Also, and more importantly, taking the dwarves with them to Mégedale would be risky. They could start trouble along the way. Then there was the question of what to do with the dwarves once they arrived in the city. They would not be assimilated within the Misty Mountain Federation of Dwarves. Hence, they would live the remainder of their lives as pariahs.

Lia had said something that cemented the working group's recommendation. "I seriously doubt any of the dwarves will take arms against us." She looked at the clustered prisoners. Like any other group of prisoners, they were a sorry lot. "See how they are staring at Ava? I bet they cannot wait to get out of here as soon as possible with or without their weapons!"

Ava approved the working group's recommendation. She also suggested that the combined Etanpioa should proceed to the Mystic Mountains. At first Galadriel politely disagreed, even though she knew that Ava could overrule her. However, Nessa convinced her to rethink her position.

She had said, "Remember what Elbereth and the Etanpioa's mission was originally. That we must escort Ava to confer with Godroh. So, considering that Ava is still being escorted by the Etanpioa, it only makes sense to continue with the original plan." She had grabbed Galadriel by the shoulders and said earnestly, "Besides, I know you want to see Mégedale as much as I!"

Galadriel countered by saying, "That does not make a lick of sense, Nessa. Ava has her dragon. She can fly anywhere she wants to with or without us. She has already consulted with Godroh. Our mission is over even though I wish it weren't." Nessa was not about to give in.

"What about our wounded Bkotn warriors, huh? Voronwe is taking them along with the wounded Timbre to Mégedale for treatment. Who is going to escort our Bkotn warriors back home after they recover sufficiently to travel? Timbre warriors?" She had laughed haughtily. "I seriously doubt it. Think about it, Galadriel. How will it look when a couple of Timbre Etanpioa march to the Unseen Valley with our wounded Bkotn heroes? All the while you and I will be trying to hide our faces in shame. Talk about awkward."

"Nessa's rationale makes perfect sense to me," Ava had offered. "Besides, I am certain that King Poldo and Prince Earendil will want to meet the new leader of the Bkotn Etanpioa. They will want to thank you and the warriors of the combined Etanpioa as well. After all, the combined Etanpioa was a unit with one purpose. To find me. However, Galadriel, I will leave the decision to you, at least as it concerns the Bkotn Etanpioa. Although, naturally, the Timbre Etanpioa must return to Mégedale either way you decide."

Galadriel said, "You know, Nessa, you definitely will make a great leader someday." Addressing Ava, she said, "I wholeheartedly agree and fully support your proposal. Especially after taking a moment to consider our code, to forsake a Bkotn is to forsake oneself."

The combined Etanpioa, along with Ava and Steph, arrived in Mégedale five days later. It took longer than usual because the ambulant that were wounded slowed their pace. Ava was extremely relieved to see that Mégedale was just the way she had left it – before she fell in the Prophecying Looking Glass. Its opulence and magnificent splendor endured, nothing like the devastation the looking glass had foretold.

The combined Etanpioa were treated as royal guests by Mégedale's citizenry. Ava was particularly pleased with the two feasts that were held in honor of the heroic warriors. The first feast was in the Great Hall. She was seated with Steph to her left and Galadriel to her right. Nessa and Voronwe were seated on the opposite side of the table. She had asked Earendil to seat her friends in that manner so Nessa and Voronwe could chat. Galadriel and Voronwe had brief conversations across the table as well. That the others of her team were carrying on with conversations made her incredibly happy. She knew right then and there that everything would be okay going forward.

Nessa and Voronwe were flanked on either side by Poldo and Estel. The royal baby, Princess Ava, was sleeping in a basinet that was perched on top of a specially configured chair next to Estel. Ava thought her namesake was the most beautiful elf child on Earth.

The second feast was held in an enormous treehouse hall that was situated in the middle of the katállilosly. Afterward, Ava, along with Steph, Galadriel, Nessa, and Voronwe, visited some of the treehouse dwellings of the Timbre elves and humans. Ava and Steph got to spend the night with a family of mixed heritage!

The next day Ava and her four companions were asked to meet with Godroh in his laboratory. When they arrived, Ava was surprised to see Poldo and Earendil were there. Godroh got straight to the point. He said, "I received this yesterday evening." He handed her a sealed envelope. The envelope was addressed to her as Avaïnoćel, O Poica Katharos. "I was going to have it delivered to you last night but thought better of it. I wanted you to enjoy your night in the katállilosly without interruption." He added with a smile, "I trust your visit with the Akáthartos family was enjoyable?" Ava nodded her head. Then his expression turned deadly serious. She noticed that Poldo and Earendil's expressions were similarly serious. It was obvious that the three of them knew something about what was inside the envelope or, at a minimum, who had sent it. She immediately blocked their thoughts.

Pointing to the letter, Godroh said, "It was delivered to me by a friend of mine that lives at the base of Mountains Cross. He arrived via his carriage. He is a trusted wizard, a good friend. I was delighted to see him after all these years." Ava could tell that he was purposely stalling, that he was about to say more about his good friend. She looked him straight in the eyes.

"Godroh, the letter is from Wendigorium. Am I correct?" Godroh nodded his head. She glanced at Poldo and Earendil. "That is why they are here, am I correct?" Godroh said that she was correct. "Because your wizarding friend gave you some insight as to what the letter said, and that you had shared it with the king and prince." Godroh nodded his head once more. "Well, I guess I should open it, hadn't I?" She looked at Steph. Steph was trembling ever so slightly. "Well, Steph, I guess the moment has arrived. Are you ready?" Steph said that she was ready no matter what the letter said. That she, along with Nessa, Galadriel, and Voronwe would be by her side no matter what.

Ava's hands were shaking slightly as she slid her fingernail beneath the wax seal on the back of the envelope. She removed the piece of parchment. The letter itself was handwritten in what appeared to be blood. She began to read.

Milady, Avaïnoáel, O Poica Katharos,

I trust this communiqué finds you well. I must declare that I concede your courage. Your heroic pursuits since we all but met in purpose in the past are laudable. You will be a formidable opponent. If we are to face each other – and I trust that you and I will since it is our destiny – you must abide by my demands. To do otherwise will result in the annihilation of everything you cherish. Mégedale, the Earthly World's grandest cities, even your own hometown in Illinois of America. Indeed, it is there I shall savor in seizing your family members and closest Earthly World friends as my retainers.

Hence Milady, you must proceed to the threshold of the enchanted Realm of Andron, the Inner World's Corridor. You and your Earthly World colleague, Stephanie, along with the Bkotn and Timbre warriors you have befriended, are welcome to join you. Others may accompany you as well, as many as you wish. Dozens of Etanpioa too. Your wizarding well-wisher, Blade Gruqiohr WyrmBlood, will tell you the swiftest way to journey.

I regret to declare you have but one calendar day after the receipt of this communiqué to abide by my demands.

With respect and admiration, I remain graciously yours,

Wendigorium (Ares)

PS - I fear not death, Avaïnoáel, O Poica Katharos. Although I fear you shall by and by.

Ava handed the letter to Godroh then she sat down on a chair in front of the hearth. Steph sat beside her. She took Ava's hand in hers. "Are you okay?" Ava nodded her head. As she smiled at Steph, she was amazed that she did not feel nervous. Instead, she felt indifferent, utterly uncaring. Because after all this time she was about to fulfill her purpose in the Inner World. Whether she liked it or not.

After reading what Wendigorium had written, Godroh handed the letter to Poldo. He handed it to Earendil then everyone passed it down the line. Nessa was the last one to read the letter. She handed it to Ava. Ava gave her a sincere smile. Then she leaned forward and tossed the letter along with the envelope in the fire. She sat motionless as it burned. The others were standing around her and Steph. She stood up and said to Godroh, "The Prophecying Looking Glass, yes?" Godroh nodded his head. She said to Steph although she already knew the answer, "Are you coming with me?"

Steph got to her feet. She said, "Unless Jordyn somehow grabs me right here and now, and I hope and pray she does not, you already know what my answer is."

Ava did not have to ask Nessa, Galadriel, and Voronwe. By their gleeful smiles she could tell they wanted to accompany her. She had also read their thoughts. She looked at them one by one and said thank you. She said to Godroh, "I would like Flame to accompany us to Andron."

Godroh replied, "I will dispatch her to the threshold of Andron as soon as possible. It will take her at least a day, perhaps less if she has favorable winds. But whatever the five of you do, do not cross the threshold until she arrives. I have been to Andron. You cannot traverse it without Fluescere's assistance."

Nessa said, "Are you not going to accompany us to Andron, Godroh?" She looked at Ava. "And who in the heck is that wizarding well-wisher, Blade Gruqiohr WyrmBlood, that Wendigorium mentioned in his letter? And what in the world is a Prophecying Looking Glass?"

Godroh was just about to reply when Ava said, "Nessa, now is not the time to tell you who Blade Gruqiohr WyrmBlood is." She winked at Godroh. "Because Godroh and I have promised to keep the wizard's identity a secret, at least for now."

Taking Ava's hint Godroh said, "Yes, we shall keep his identity a secret, at least for now. And yes, Nessa, I shall join you and the others in Andron eventually. However, before I do, I have vital tasks of great importance that demand my attention elsewhere. As far as the looking glass is concerned, well, perhaps Ava should explain." He could tell by Ava's expressions that she was reading his thoughts. Consequently, he was telling her via his thoughts the vital tasks he must attend to and when he would join her and the others. He also said he would give Fluescere additional information that Ava would have to know.

Even as she continued to read Godroh's thoughts, Ava abruptly grabbed Nessa's hand and exclaimed, "I will tell you what, Nessa! I will do much more than merely *explain* the looking glass. I will *demonstrate* its wonders to you myself!" As she pulled Nessa along by the hand – Nessa was giggling happily – she added, "Everyone, please follow me."

Once Ava saw everyone was standing in front of the looking glass, she removed the cloth. She was happy that Godroh had laundered it. In a noble tone she said, "I present the Prophecying Looking Glass. It may look like an antique, thousands of years old, polished mirror encased in lacquered wood. However, it is more magical than any of you could ever imagine. You will see for yourself in a few moments." Her eyes were welling up with tears as she said to Poldo and Earendil, "Thank you so very much for your wonderful hospitality. Please say goodbye to the Queen and our darling Princess for me, okay?" Poldo and Earendil nodded their heads. She lifted one eyebrow and tilted her head adding, "Perhaps we shall see each other once more, maybe in Andron or maybe even in Ostium?" They replied that perhaps they would, and they were looking forward to it.

Turning to face Steph, Nessa, Galadriel, and Voronwe, Ava said, "Okay, you guys, move in close, hold hands, and then close your eyes tightly." She giggled nervously. "You do not want to look because even I do not know what is going to happen!" She grabbed Steph and Nessa's hands. "One last thing, just so you know. I love each of you very much." The others answered in kind. She closed her eyes and told the looking glass via her thoughts what she wanted it to do.

Ava and the others of the closely-knit quintet of brave teenelves vanished a moment later.

THE END

APPENDIX A

GLOSSARY OF TERMS

Αθήνα is the name of the Goddess of War, Athena in the ancient Greek dialect "Attic" (the dialect of ancient Athens, Greece).

Aetós is a term referenced by the Bkotn elf, Galadriel. It denotes eagle.

Akáthartos refers to "impure" in the wizarding world of humans and among elves. Descendants of elves that have married/produced offspring with humans (ordinary or wizarding) are no longer Katharos (pure). They are Akáthartos (impure). Unlike Katharos, Akáthartos elves are not immortal. The same logic applies to descendants of wizarding humans that marry/produce offspring with ordinary humans.

Anaísthisom is a magical enchantment used by Ava Noelle as Αναΐnoάel to render another subject unconscious. The effects of the spell are temporary. The subject usually arouses within the hour.

Ándreste is a Fortunomy word that implies "(stupid) male elf." Bkotn elves commonly use the word to display their displeasure with elves of the opposite sex. The Greek word "ándres" of the Earthly World translates to "men" in English. It is a spinoff of ándreste.

Andron is the Inner World's second to oldest realm. Andron is commonly referred to as the Inner World's Corridor. Andron, or the Corridor, is a passageway from the Inner World's Yesteryear (Antiquom) to the Inner World's Future, its Tomorrow (Ostium). Andron can best be described as the Inner World's present day, the here and now.

Antiquom is the Inner World's oldest realm. Antiquom is commonly referred to as the Inner World's Yesteryear. Antiquom, or the Yesteryear, is a place of incredible prosperity, tranquility, harmony, and great optimism. Antiquom is also a land of good will and everlasting peace. Nevertheless, like all worlds, Antiquom has its share of unsavory, greedy, and evil creatures, and, sadly, conflict. Ava Noelle as Avaïnoάel begins her journey in Antiquom.

Antonia is the most enchanted forest in all Antiquom. It is known as the Forest of Artonia.

Attic Greek is the Greek dialect of the ancient city-state of Athens, Greece, of the Earthly World.

Axiui is secret duress word used by the Bkotn warriors when a warrior is in trouble. It is also used to imply that something is in the wrong.

Belugas are mutated, fur-covered elves, nearly twice as tall and much heavier than full grown elves. They are comprised of two species: déxypnos and duds. The déxypnos are the more intelligent specie of the beluga's genus, while duds, as the name implies, are the lesser intelligent specie. The duds are blind and use echolocation to navigate and stalk their prey. Déxypnos belugas are not blind. Both species are ruthless. The belugas are commanded by the evil déxypnos Strum and are cohorts of Wendigorium and the evil wizard Haldir of Mountain's Cross (See below – duds and déxypnos).

Bkotn refers to elven warriors that live one of three elven communities of the Unseen Valley adjacent to the Solenom River. The Bkotn elves protect the confines and surrounding areas of the Unseen Valley (See below – Mkleon, Smbot, and Unseen Valley).

Bkotn Code is the binding oath of Bkotn warriors: "To forsake a Bkotn is to forsake oneself."

Bltale is an Inner World butterfly that has four iridescent eyes, no antennae, and a wingspan that nearly is twelve inches in width.

Blue poison dart frog is an Earthly World reptile that Ava Noelle as Avaïnoάel thinks she is pursuing in the swamp of the Forest of Artonia.

Chicxulub impactor refers to the asteroid that crashed to Earth 66 million years ago causing a worldwide ecological disaster and the extinction of two-thirds of all organisms. The Chicxulub impactor's center is buried offshore below the Yucatán Peninsula of Mexico, a few miles from the present-day town of Chicxulub, Mexico, for which it is named. The fissure known as Thávma was created when the Chicxulub impactor crashed to Earth. Its impact launched the birth of the Inner World.

Chiton is a full-length, woolen tunic worn by the Greek Goddess of War, Athena.

Crostim Ledge provides a spectacular, scenic overlook of the Solenom River of the Forest of Artonia. It is close to the Kuoino trail that winds through the forest of Artonia.

Deep Realm is where all Inner World creatures go after death. The Deep Realm is a transitory land comparable to the Earthly World's Purgatory. If creatures were benevolent as living beings, they move on to Parádeisos (See below – Parádeisos). It is there that their innermost essence, their souls, will revel in everlasting peace. If the creatures were evil as living beings or undeserving of Parádeisos' forgiveness, they will wander endlessly in despair as ghosts and shadows. Legends also say that some benevolent creatures remain as ghosts or shadows, at least temporarily because they have unfinished affairs in the world of the living. Once they conclude their unfinished business, they enter Parádeisos to dwell in everlasting peace.

Déxypnos is the smarter species of the belugas' genus. The dumber species are duds (See above – Belugas and below – Duds).

Diádromosphere is a grand stairway of the Timbre elven city, Mégedale.

Duds refers to the dumber species of the beluga's genus. The smarter species are déxypnos (See above – Belugas and Déxypnos).

Dwarven Federation is a loosely organized group of dwarves that dwell in the mountainous parts of the Inner World. The Federation's primary purpose is to coordinate the selling and barter of mined precious metals and gems. It also serves to settle territory disputes and other conflicting issues of the diverse dwarven tribes. In times of war, the Federation's leaders coordinate battle plans. Federation leaders (of which there are six at the time of this writing) are distinguished from other dwarves by the Dwarven Crossbow Patch worn on their right shoulder.

Elven Truths Please see Appendix B for the complete description of the 9 Elven Truths.

Etanpioa refers to a company of Antiquom warrior elves.

Fortunomy is the Elvish language of the Inner World as well as the ancient world of Spardom beneath the sea (featured in novels: *Eva Roblins and the Enchanted Gate: Return of the Princess* and *Enchanted Gate Book Two: Conquest of the Hidden Valley* penned by this author using his pseudonym Eva Roblins).

Gnɑèfa is the name of a spiritual tower in the Inner World. Gnɑèfa is commonly referred to by Inner World inhabitants as the Spire of Time. A more recent adaptation of the tower is located at 667 Kensington Avenue, Buffalo, New York. The tower's magnificence is viewable on Google Maps. (For more on the tower's history go to: www.dailypublic.com/articles/02132019/looking-backward-kensington -water-tower & www.preservationready.org/ Buildings/667Kensington Avenue).

Gryphon characterizes the legendary creature of the Earthly World that is also known as the griffin. It has the body, tail, and hind legs of a lion (in Greek, "liontári"). Its head and wings are those of an eagle (in Greek, "aetós"). The gryphon, or griffin, has razor-sharp beaks and long, sharp talons. Dwarves of the Inner World employ gryphons to guard their excavated, precious metals. Highly trained gryphons are used in combat as well and are usually mounted by archer dwarves. Other gryphons carry leaders of the Dwarf Federation and ground fighters.

Hellenes (or Hellada) is the ancient and modern name of the Earthly World country Greece.

Inner World is a land of mystical beings formed when the Chicxulub impactor crashed to Earth 66 million years ago creating the Thávma (opening that connects the Earthly World with the Inner World). The Inner World consists of three realms: Antiquom, Andron, and Ostium. (Please refer to the three realms above and below for more information.)

Joini are the cruelest, most self-serving, corrupt dwarves of Antiquom. The Joini use slaves (usually elves but sometimes humans, gnomes, and trolls) to work their gold, silver, and gemstone mines. The slaves must tend to the Joini's domestic needs as well by making clothing and performing household tasks. Mercifully, the Joini do not physically abuse their slaves. The Joini are also heartless in battle and are known to slay their enemy cruelly (i.e., when their enemies backs are turned and slaying the wounded that are unfit to work the mines as slaves).

Katállilosly is the city proper of Mégedale where elves and humans live, conduct their businesses, hold official township meetings, and attend school.

Katarráplexouktes are twisted waterfalls located in the elven city of Mégedale of the Mystic Mountains.

Kensington Water Tower is where Ava's journey to the Inner World begins. The tower is located at 667 Kensington Avenue, Buffalo, New York. The tower's magnificence is viewable on Google Maps. (For more on the tower's history go to: www.dailypublic.com/articles/ 02132019/looking-backward-kensington-water-tower & www. preservationready.org/Buildings/667KensingtonAvenue). (See Tower below.)

Kéntauros is the Fortunomy word for Inner World centaurs. Unlike centaurs of Earthly World fables, Inner World centaurs are half horse (lower body) and half elf (torso). There are female centaurs in the Inner World as well. Lord Wlknoo is the ruler of the centaurs that dwell in the Mystic Mountains.

Khni is the species of Ava Noelle's feathered friend, Fedelium. Khni do not partner with other birds of their species, preferring to befriend other creatures such as elves, humans, and fairies. The exception being during the mating season when they fly off to Paravem, the mystical world of angels. Khni are also known to warn the creatures that they befriend of impending danger or dangerous ways.

Khopesh is an Egyptian sword. It is comparable to the Bkotn weapon called a tkalakn.

Knoki is a small village along the trail in the Forest of Artonia. It is a six-day march from the Unseen Valley and just beyond the fabled Crostim Ledge.

Konoanlia is a large, freshwater lake in which the Solenom River empties. It is in the center of Antiquom. The mérlin Lord Mérino rules the Konoanlia.

Kuoino is the longest trail in the Forest of Artonia. It is known for its zigzagging, up and down route. The word Kuoino stems from the Fortunomy words kuo and ino. Kuo translates to whacky, and ino means snake. Whacky snake – Kuoino.

Leípei is a charmed land of many mysteries, peculiar secrecies, and phantastic beasts. Legends say the transfigured elf Wendigorium, and the Great Wizard Godroh were born in the Leípei. It is to the south of Eastern Antiquom. It is more commonly known as the Missing Land (See below – Missing Land).

Liontári is a term referenced by the Bkotn elf, Galadriel. It is a Greek Earthly World word that translates in Greek and Fortunomy to "lion."

Manica refers to a pair a bronze wrist guards worn by Ava Noelle as Avaïnoάel. The manica's are fastened to the wrists by leather straps. Avaïnoάel's manica's first belonged to the Greek Goddess of War, Wisdom, and Handicraft, Athena.

Mégedale is a city and the home of the Timbre elves of Mystic Mountains. Humans also live in the city. Mégedale is bounded on three sides by the realms of centaurs, dragons, and unicorns, with the Mégisti Koryfí to the north.

Mégisti Koryfí is the highest peak of the Mystic Mountains. Mégisti Koryfí translates in Fortunomy to "Mightiest Peak." Legends say Mégisti Koryfí is the birthplace of Inner World dragons.

Missing Land is also known by its official title, Leípei (See above – Leípei).

Mkleon are one of three elven communities that live in the Unseen Valley of the Solenom River. Mkleon are farmers and orchardists (See below – Smbot and Unseen Valley and above – Bkotn).

Monókeros is the Fortunomy word for unicorns. Lady E-mah is the ruler of the unicorns that dwell in the Mystic Mountains.

Mons igneus means "Fire-breathing Mountain."

Mystic Mountains are the highest mountains in Antiquom, home to the Timbre elves and the elven city of Mégedale.

Nebolom is the name of the town near Mountain's Cross from where the human child Jason, was abducted. Jason's persona was transformed causing him to serve as an imposter that looked like the Great Wizard Godroh.

Netrum is a shared area to the east of the Bkotn Tribe's region where married Bkotn elves and their female offspring can visit with their husband and male offspring.

O Poica Katharos denotes The Purest of Elves. Ava Noelle, as the reawakened Avaïnoάel is recognized as the O Poica Katharos of the Inner World as well as among mystical beings of the Earthly World.

Ostium is the Inner World's future, its tomorrow. It is a world yet to come but may be starting to exist although only slightly.

Outsiders is a derogatory term used to label elves, humans, and fairies that come from the Earthly World.

Parádeisos implies "Paradise" in the Greek language of the Earthly World.

Paravem is an elven, mystical world of angels. The khni bird supposedly migrates to Paravem during the winter to mate.

Peplos is a long, outer garment worn by Ava Noelle as Avaïnoάel during the winter months.

Pinky Promise Pact is comprised of three elements: One, if either Ava Noelle as Avaïnoάel or Steph is in danger, she will send her pinky ring to the other. Two, if a situation develops that causes doubt or certainty, and to certify something as being completely true, one will send her ring to the other. Three, if Ava Noelle and Step are together and one senses danger while the other one does not, the one realizing danger will remove her ring and hide it away (see Pinky Promise Ring below).

Pinky Promise Ring is a ring that both Ava Noelle as Avaïnoάel and Steph wear on the pinky fingers of their left hands. An engraved elven emblem on the face of the ring denotes the elven creed of peace, love, and harmony. There are four rings in the entire world. One each is worn by Ava Noelle as Avaïnoάel, Steph, Godroh, and Queen Lindsial. The Pinky Promise Ring involves a secret pact known only to Ava Noelle and Stephanie (See above – Pinky Promise Pact).

Plateίazan is the piazza (city square) of the city of Mégedale.

Presto Chango is a magical enchantment used by Ava Noelle as Avaïnoάel to transform or transmute an item or creature from one thing to another (i.e., shape, color, form, genus, etc.).

Prophecy is a revelation of "What once was and what will someday be all over again." The Prophecy consists of twenty ancient scrolls and foretells the return of the O Poica Katharos – The Purest of Elves aka the Protector of the World. Ava Noelle, as Avaïnoάel, is recognized as the Earth's O Poica Katharos.

Prophecying Looking Glass is an ancient, wooden framed looking glass that dates back two and one-half thousand years. It is an accessory to the Prophecy scrolls. It too is a revelation of "What once was and what will someday be all over again," albeit in an introspective form. The glass itself is made of polished metal since silver-coated mirrors were not invented until the nineteenth century. The great wizard Godroh supposes the looking glass once belonged to Athena. However, there is no proof that it did.

Prostátism is a charm in the shape of a reversed pentagram, recognized as the evilest symbol of the dark arts. Prostátism translates to "patronus" in the ancient Greek language of the Earthly World.

Reversio is a magical enchantment used by Ava Noelle as Avaïnoάel to reverse either her or another's enchantment, depending on how she considers it in her mind.

Saganakiza is an appetizer made of vaotz. It is fried and covered with a creamy sauce (See below – vaotz).

Sanatios is a genus of flower like an Earthly World buttercup flower (Ranunculus). The word sanatios denotes "healing" in the Elvish language, Fortunomy. Sanatios are poisonous to eat and noxious to smell up close. However, sanatios are not toxic in the dry form. They are fragrant and used to make perfumes.

Smbot are one of three elven communities that live in the Unseen Valley of the Solenom River. Smbot harvest fish, mollusks, and similar creatures from the Solenom River (See above – Bkotn and Mkleon and below – Unseen Valley).

SoFEW² is Ava Noelle and Stephanie's feministic approach to the acronym SoFEW (The Society of Fairies, Elves, and Wizards), by placing the term witches before wizards and using the mathematical square root sign after the letter *W.* SoFEW (or SoFEW²) is a secret society established on October 31, 1675 by Reverend Robert Smallgood. The society was created to protect the secrecy of the Inner World and the mystical creatures that reside therein as well as on the Earthly World.

Solenom River is the lengthiest waterway in Antiquom. It covers the entire length of the Forest of Artonia.

Spardom is an ancient land of elves and other magical creatures below the sea. The ruler is Queen Lindsial. Queen Lindsial possesses one of the four Pinky Promise Rings in existence (See Pinky Promise Ring above). (Lindsial appears in novels written by this author using his pseudonym Eva Roblins: *Eva Roblins and the Enchanted Gate, Return of the Princess* and *The Enchanted Gate Book Two: Conquest of the Hidden Valley.*)

Strum is the leader of the belugas of the Inner World. Strum literally means "barbarity" in Fortunomy. The name Strum is a derivative of the Latin word "mōnstrum," which means *a thing that evokes fear and wonder.*

Tartan Ymni is the rarest of Antiquom butterflies. The Tartan Ymni has blue and gold-checkered wings. It has a 60-centimeter, or two-foot wingspan, two times lengthier than the Earthly World Queen Alexandra's Birdwing.

Thávma represents the largest fissure caused by the Chicxulub impactor 66 million years ago. Thávma is the Earthly World's entrance to the Inner World.

Thboma is an Inner World tree that is comparable to an Earthly World cacao tree.

Thkao is a tasty fruit that grows on trees. Thkao is bright orange in color and about the size of a ripe, round watermelon.

Timere refers to elven warriors that dwell in the northern mountains of Antiquom in and around the city of Mégedale (see Mégedale above). They are recognized as the most ferocious warriors of Antiquom.

Tiny Teethlings refers to baby dragons of the Inner World. Baby dragons do not have teeth, nor do they have scales. Their outer covering is of a leathery texture. Except for Fluescere, Ava Noelle's personal dragon, all Inner World dragons have skin or scales that are black in color. Fluescere's scales are ombre in color.

Tkalakn is the name of the sword used by Bkotn warriors.

Tower refers to the water tower that Ava Noelle's grandfather and great uncle "climbed" (circumnavigated) when they were youngsters. The tower is in Buffalo, New York, of the Earthly World. (See Kensington Water Tower above).

Unseen Valley is a nearly impenetrable area adjacent to the Solenom River in the Forest of Artonia. It consists of three communities of elves: Bkotn, Mkleon, and Smbot.

Vaotz is a grain like the Earthly World oryza sativa (Asian deep-water rice). Vaotz is a staple in the Inner World with many uses.

Veritasium is a magical enchantment used by Ava Noelle as Avaïnoᴕel to compel one to be truthful. Ava can also compel the victim to reveal his or her most recent thoughts and secret memories.

Yhioh is a bushytailed creature that looks like the Earthly World muskrat but with eight spidery legs instead of four. Despite its relatively small size, the yhioh is as ferocious as a ravenous Earthly World tiger and often hunts prey many times larger than its size.

Vóleïtioro is a water sport enjoyed by elves and humans of the Inner World. It is like Earthly World water volley.

Wyknonm is a rarity in the Forest of Artonia. The wyknonm resembles an Earthly World tortoise, except it has six legs instead of four.

Xylospongium is a hygienic utensil. The xylospongium consists of a wooden stick with a sea sponge fixed at one end.

Yhioh is an Inner World creature comparable to an Earthly World fattened-up muskrat. The yhioh has eight spidery legs. It has short, thick fur, which is a light blue to dark purple. As the yhioh ages, its fur changes to a murky-colored bluish black. It has a pair of razor sharp, two-inch fangs that protrude from its upper jaw. Despite its relatively small size, the yhioh is as ferocious as a ravenous tiger. It is common for the Yhioh to hunt prey many times larger than its size.

Yuki is a feathered bird that mimics whistled tunes of other birds, humans, and elves.

Zácharium is a common, natural sweetener for many confections as well as delicious beverages. Zácharium a derivative of the Earthly World Greek word "záchari."

APPENDIX B

ELVEN TRUTHS, SPELLS, AND MISC.

Elven Truth #1: Mystical Beings - elves, fairies, wizards, and witches - have coexisted with ordinary humans since the beginning of time. Their way of life constitutes the Mystical World. They blend in easily amongst the Earth's human inhabitants. For the most part, ordinary humans are unaware of their existence.

Elven Truth #2: There are other mystical beings on Earth, in addition to elves, fairies, wizards and witches. They are dragons, unicorns, centaurs, pixies, gnomes, and dwarves, to name a few. Some are good (i.e., pixies, unicorns, and gnomes); while some are evil (i.e., belugas and many dragons). Most are common in ordinary human lore (pixies, unicorns, centaurs, gnomes, dragons), while others are utterly bizarre (belugas, metamorhirío).

Elven Truth #3: To protect the well-being of elves, fairies, wizards, and witches – and to keep secret the existence of the Inner World and its strange living things - a secret Society was created on October 31, 1675 by the Reverend Robert Smallgood (9 December 1644 – 14 May 1692) of Aberfoyle, Scotland. Reverend Smallgood entitled the Society SoFEW (the "Society of Fairies, Elves, (and) Wizards.")

Elven Truth #4: Because of their genetic makeup, fairies cannot marry or produce offspring with natural humans, elves, wizards, and witches. Thus, offspring and descendants of fairies are considered Katharos (Pure). Offspring of fairies are automatically registered in SoFEW. Because they are Katharos, all fairies are eligible for positions within the SoFEW Union as well as lesser stations (See Elven Truths #7 & #8).

Elven Truth #5: The offspring and descendants of elves, wizards, and witches that do not intermarry and produce offspring with natural humans are Katharos (Pure). Their offspring are automatically registered in SoFEW. Katharos elves, wizards, and witches are eligible for positions within the SoFEW Union as well as lesser stations (See Elven Truths #7 & #8).

Elven Truth #6: Offspring and descendants of elves, wizards, and witches that intermarry with natural humans are considered Akáthartos (Impure). Nevertheless, they are automatically registered in the SoFEW for accounting purposes. The mystical powers of Akáthartos descendants gradually diminish over time and with each successive intermarriage. However, mystical powers of Akáthartos descendants can be bolstered to a limited degree when offspring are produced with a Katharos. Akáthartos are not eligible for positions within the SoFEW Union, although they may qualify for lesser stations (See Elven Truth #8 below).

Elven Truth #7: The SoFEW Union consists of the Union Secretary, his or her Undersecretaries, and the five District Secretaries. The duties of the SOFEW Union are detailed in SoFEW Addendum A.

Elven Truth #8: Per SoFEW Addendum A, only Katharos may qualify as SoFEW Union Secretary, Undersecretary, and District Secretary. Katharos and Akáthartos may qualify for lesser positions, to include those in SoFEW Union staffs if they satisfy the skill requirements.

Elven Truth #9: Avaïnoάel, O Poica Katharos. In keeping with the Inner World "Prophecy," an ordinary human female will be born on the 14th day of Dekémvrisom of the Inner World's spiritual year, 2007. Her birth will occur on a Friday. Friday is the most blessed day of the week of the Inner World. It is recognized as the most blessed day of the week of ordinary humans. In keeping with the 14th day's numerology prediction, the child will embrace independence and self-determination. She will be exceptionally curious and possess an avid interest in practical science as she matures.

The child will be given the ordinary human name Ava, surname Noelle (Ava Noelle) at birth. She will be Avaïnoάel, O Poica Katharos – the Purest of Elves, the Protector of the World. She will have supremacy over all Inner World creatures and the mystical beings living amongst ordinary humans of the Earthly World.

The SoFEW Union Secretary, and his or her Undersecretaries, as well as the five District Secretaries will support Avaïnoáel, O Poica Katharos, via their individual hierarchy's, as necessary.

~ ~ ~ ~ ~

Spells used by Avaïnoáel, O Poica Katharos

Anaísthisom renders another subject unconscious. The effects of the spell are temporary. The subject usually arouses within the hour.

Presto Chango transforms or transmutes an item or creature from one thing to another (i.e., shape, color, form, genus, etc.).

Reversio is used to reverse the spell of another magical being such as a wizard or wizardess. Avaïnoáel can also reverse her own spells using the enchantment.

Veritasium compels a subject to be truthful. It can also compel the subject to reveal his or her most recent thoughts and secret memories.

Note: Avaïnoáel may possess the power to enact other spells. However, her subconsciousness has not brought them to the attention of her awareness.

APPENDIX C

LIST OF QUOTES

""The moment you doubt whether you can fly, you cease for ever to be able to do it." – J. M. Barrie, *Peter Pan*. Dedication.

"Do not go where the path may lead, go instead where there is no path and leave a trail." – Ralph Waldo Emerson. Part I Title Page.

"Like madness is the glory of this life." – William Shakespeare, *Timon of Athens*. Part I Chapter I.

"I belong to two worlds – yours and mine." – Avaïnoάel. Part I Chapter 2.

"Ava Noelle, the world knows not of your power and of what you are capable." – the author. Part I Chapter 3.

"Give me a bag crammed with gummy bears, and I'll pay you a smile." – Ava Noelle. Part I Chapter 4.

"When we climbed the tower, we were in a new province. Like our very own innermost world." – Grandpa Jim. Part I Chapter 5.

"It is one thing to mortify curiosity, another to conquer it." – Robert Louis Stevenson. Part I Chapter 6.

"Never listen to your fears. They know nothing of your incredible power." – Stephanie JoAnne Galanos. Part I Chapter 7.

"History does not repeat itself. But it does rhyme." – Mark Twain. Part I Chapter 8.

"Knowing what must be done does away with fear." – Rosa Parks. Part I Chapter 9.

"So comes snow after fire, and even dragons have their endings." – J.R.R. Tolkien, *The Hobbit*. Part I Chapter 10.

"Never laugh at a fire-breathing dragon – unless you want to get burned." – the author. Part I Chapter 11.

"Imagination is the beginning of creation. You imagine what you desire, you will what you imagine, and at last, you create what you will." – George Bernard Shaw. Part II Title Page.

"In life the only thing that you can expect is the unexpected." – Joan Rivers. Part II Chapter I.

"In my land, the incredibly old realm of Antiquom, mystical evil creatures are everywhere." – the winged fairy Doo. Part II Chapter 2.

"To be yourself in a world that is constantly trying to make you something else is the greatest accomplishment." – Ralph Waldo Emerson. Part II Chapter 3.

"O, what a tangled web we weave, when first we practice to deceive!" – Sir Walter Scott. Part II Chapter 4.

"Not until we are lost do we begin to understand ourselves." – Henry David Thoreau. Part II Chapter 5.

"Words may sometimes utter untruths, but thoughts cannot lie." – Ava Noelle (Avaïnoάel, O Poica Katharos). Part II Chapter 6.

"One can always repay a debt of gold. But one is eternally indebted to evil." – the author. Part II. Chapter 7.

"Never confuse a single defeat with a final defeat." – F. Scott Fitzgerald. Part II Chapter 8.

"It always seems impossible until it's done." – Nelson Mandela. Part III Title Page.

"Be the change you want to see in the world." Mahatma Gandhi. Part III Chapter 1.

"Come not between the dragon and his wrath." – William Shakespeare, *King Lear*. Part III Chapter 2.

"There is magic everywhere. Akin to you. Kind-hearted, phantastic, and true." – Fluescere to Avaïnoáel. Part III Chapter 3.

"I may be a prince. But you are my queen." – Prince Earendil to Avaïnoáel. Part III Chapter 4.

"For conspiracy, I know not how it tastes, though it be dished for me to try how." – William Shakespeare, *The Winter's Tale*. Part III Chapter 5.

"Tricks and treachery are the practice of fools that don't have brains enough to be honest." – Benjamin Franklin. Part III Chapter 6.

"Injustice is achieved in two ways; either by violence or deceit." – Marcus Tullius Cicero. Part III Chapter 7.

"The future belongs to those that believe in the beauty of their dreams." – Eleanor Roosevelt. Part III Chapter 8.

"Be slow to fall into friendship; but when thou are it, continue firm and constant." – Socrates. Part III Chapter 9.

"When sorrows come, they come not single spies, but in battalions." William Shakespeare, *Hamlet*. Part III Chapter 10.

"In a gentle way you can shake the world." – Mahatma Gandhi. Part IV Title Page.

"Life is a tragedy to those who feel and a comedy to those who think." – Horace Walpole. Part IV Chapter 1.

"Victorious warriors win first and then go to war, while defeated warriors go to war first and then seek to win." – Sun Tzu. Part IV Chapter 2.

"Only the dead have seen the end of war." – Plato. Part IV Chapter 3.

"When the truth is known all doubts will perish." – Anonymous. Part V Chapter 4.

"Life and death are one, even as the river and sea are one." – Khalil Gibran. Part IV Chapter 5.

"I do not know with what weapons World War III will be fought, but I do know that World War IV will be fought with rocks." – Albert Einstein. Part IV Chapter 6.

"I will place you under my spell and take you to meet Wendigorium." – Magnus NightMancer. Part IV Chapter 7.

"I fear not death, Avaînoάel, O Poica Katharos. Although I fear you shall by and by." – Wendigorium. Part IV Epilogue.